DEATH IN
BLOODHOUND
RED

DEATH IN BLOODHOUND RED

VIRGINIA LANIER

Pineapple Press, Inc.
Sarasota, Florida

Inquiries should be addressed to:
Pineapple Press, Inc.
P.O. Box 3899
Sarasota, Florida 34230

LIBRARY OF CONGRESS CATALOGING IN PUBLICATION DATA

Lanier, Virginia
    Death in Bloodhound Red / Virginia Lanier.
        p.   cm.
    ISBN 1-56164-076-X (alk. paper)
    I. Title.
PS3562.A524D4   1995   94-43196
813'.54—dc20   CIP

First Edition
10 9 8 7 6 5 4 3

Design by Cynthia Keenan
Printed and bound by Edwards Brothers, Ann Arbor, Michigan

DEDICATION

I wish to dedicate this book to my husband, one of the good ol' boys, Robert W. Lanier, who is known in Echols, Clinch, Lowndes and Hamilton counties as "Hoss."

Without his two major sacrifices—playing golf every blessed day the wind didn't blow over seventy miles per hour or during electrical storms, and entertaining his buddies till the wee hours most nights in his private pub — this book would not have been possible.

It don't get any better than this, honey. This book's for you.

ACKNOWLEDGMENTS

I wish to thank the following people for facts, advice and encouragement: Superintendent L. R. Dugger and Sergeant Stanley W. Cribbs, Hamilton County Correctional Institute, Jasper Florida; Ed Kilby, corresponding secretary, American Bloodhound Club; Mary Michener, managing editor, *American Bloodhound Club Bulletin*; Jan Tweedie, chief of corrections, Kittitas County Seriff's Department, Ellensburg, Washington; Dr. Tim Thornhill, veterinarian, Valdosta, Georgia; Barbara Bandy, Hamilton County Library, Jasper, Florida; Von Nix, Mobile, Alabama; Karen Peek, Valdosta, Georgia; Rhonda Gaskins, Nashville, Georgia; Beth Carsh, White Springs, Florida; Sandy Griffis, Valdosta, Georgia; Cecil Ellis, computer advisor, Betty Ann Nelson, art, Fargo, Georgia; Wayne Padgett, flora, fauna and moonshine advisor, Echols County, Georgia. Many thanks to Mary Nix, a gifted savior of language and dialogue, Valdosta, Georgia.

My heartfelt gratitude to June Cussen, senior editor and publisher, for giving Jo Beth her chance. Deep appreciation to Patricia Hammond, copyeditor, for sound judgment and good advice.

The above mentioned people gave me the correct information. Any mistakes are mine and mine alone.

All the small, rural counties in southeast Georgia in this book came from my mind, not a map. All people, incidents and law enforcement personnel in this book are fictional and are not patterened after real people or situations.

DEATH IN
BLOODHOUND
RED

PROLOGUE
April 13, Tuesday

Bloodhounds can make you laugh and cuss in the same breath. They are endearing, faithful, and can sling drool ten feet in any direction. I breed them and train them and own a business. Let me rephrase that last statement: me and my friendly neighborhood bank own a business.

My name is Jo Beth Sidden. I'm always called Jo Beth, never Jo. My home and business are in southeast Georgia, and I work primarily within a three-county area bordering the Okefenokee Swamp. I love my home, and when I die — a long, long time from now, Bubba willing — I pray it will be somewhere in this area.

I am a staunch but not militant feminist. I do not hold with the theory that you have to bust every man's balls in America to achieve equality. Twist a few arms, maybe, clobber and confound them with words definitely, but no rough stuff.

April was a strange and eventful month for me. I had a few victories and many defeats. I made my share of mistakes and saved the lives of three people.

I have four paintings appraised at just under a million dollars, but the dollar amount doesn't matter, since I would not sell them if I were starving to death. I have a fifty-fifty chance of maybe inheriting a comfortable estate, if my lawyer and I can figure out the puzzling and secretive will. It is immaterial whether I inherit or not right now because I am currently under indictment for attempted murder. If the man dies, it will be murder one. It all began on April 5, a Monday. . . .

1

"MAD AS A WET HEN"
April 5, Monday, 6 A.M.

I turned left off the highway onto a narrow county dirt road. Easing the van slowly to the right across a shallow drainage ditch and up onto the grassy verge, I checked the side mirror and saw sufficient room for Wayne to park behind me, so I turned off the engine. Looking ahead in the early morning darkness, I could see seven vehicles, like good little Indians, all in a row.

It was another thirty minutes until first light. I drained the last of the coffee, closed the thermos and popped the top on a Diet Coke. Since five o'clock I had been forcing liquids and inhaling nicotine like crazy. Lighting the seventh cigarette of the day, I sat listening to the weather report on WAAC C-93 radio, a country-and-western music station.

Thirty percent chance of rain, presently sixty-five degrees, with the high predicted in the mid-eighties. The news reporter declared it a perfect April day; and weren't we lucky to be living in God's country? I had to agree with the man. Producing a very unladylike belch, I drank more Coke and puffed away. The good news was the weather. The bad news was I would be dehydrated, nicotine-deprived and five pounds lighter by sunset.

All seven vehicles before me had their overhead flashers turning and most of the driver's-side doors open. All the vans were empty. I have never understood this nonsense. No bleeding bodies, no fire or flying bullets, so why the lights and open doors? My feminine logic is puzzled by the man-child syndrome. I remembered a small wooden plaque attached to a key ring my friend Susan carried. Burned into the wood were the words, "You can tell the men from the boys by the size and cost of their toys."

I checked to see who had arrived. Two were county patrol cars, a pair of Balsa City police, two highway patrol cars and a fish and game commission car. Par for the course. The only ones missing were DEA and the Bureau of Alcohol, Tobacco and Firearms. They must be eating breakfast together; they would drop by shortly. Any happening beat napping on a back road or swilling all-night convenience store coffee.

Six of the officers were standing on the dirt road in a loose semicircle listening to the seventh man. They were illuminated briefly with each circuit of the lights. The man speaking was the bane of my life, my own Dunston County Sheriff, Samuel A. Carlson. I suspect his middle initial "A" doesn't stand for "asshole," but in my humble opinion, it would be most appropriate. He was telling his good-ol'-boy stories with plenty of hand and arm gestures. Occasional spurts of knee-slapping laughter floated across the mild and humid air.

Finishing the Coke and cigarette, I stepped out of the van and stretched until I felt joints creaking. Traffic had slowed to a crawl on the highway. Lights were attracting moths. Cars were pulling over and stopping. Small groups of people were milling around and asking each other what was going on. They were curious and hesitant but lusting for carnage. They gathered at every site I worked.

I signed to Wayne to sit awhile. Not being ready to suit up, I was savoring the early morning coolness. I admired my almost-new vans I had purchased from a local electrical contractor who was contemplating bankruptcy and/or suicide. I had turned the vans over to a former classmate who did custom bodywork, machine welding and reasonable paint jobs in an old tobacco barn at the edge of town. After he finished the work, they cost me the price of new ones but were custom-fitted for my needs.

The vans were pale green. I trailed my fingers over the deep yellow lettering on the door:

BLOODHOUNDS, INC.
JO BETH SIDDEN, OWNER AND TRAINER
SEARCH AND RESCUE UNIT ONE
DUNSTON COUNTY SHERIFF'S DEPARTMENT
BALSA CITY, GEORGIA

I hadn't wanted the county's name on the doors, and I didn't want the emergency flashers on the roof, but what the hey. The trio of county commissioners signed my yearly contract, and signed my checks for services rendered promptly, so I had the name on the door and the lights on the top; I just never turned them on. Just the dreaded silhouette above the roof, sighted in the rear-view mirror, was sufficient to slow traffic and make open lanes appear. When you're single and in your twenty-ninth year with twenty-seven years left on a humongous mortgage, two full-time employees, thirty-four dogs and more puppies due any minute, you learn to compromise. My one-year contract with Dunston County had expired three days ago and so far, not a whisper about renewal. It was nail-biting time.

There were six dog boxes built into each van, three to a side. The boxes could be opened inside or outside the van. I moved and peered into the first aluminum cage at Susie. I couldn't see her clearly, but poking two fingers through the mesh, I heard her move closer and felt her lean into my caress. Now I could see her deep hazel eyes. Her eye color was a bonus, very seldom seen in red-and-tan bloodhounds and greatly preferred when being judged in dog shows.

Her name is Sidden's Southern Lady of Sagaces Endeavors but her working handle is Susie. She is a big, gentle and affectionate animal who has already won championship status with me. She is my best scent tracker and first major success in breeding and field training. Most people assume that pedigreed bloodhounds are born with the knowledge to track. It takes at least six grueling, repetitive months of daily lessons before a bloodhound is a capable tracker, if the dog is bright.

Some dogs never learn. My failures have made excellent family pets. For the past year, in thirty-one searches as lead dog, Susie has found twenty-two and failed with nine. It should have been fourteen failures. In five of her finds, she had rotten weather and was hours past the maximum expectancy of success. In accident trauma victims there is one golden hour. The best chance of success in tracking is three hours and each additional hour lowers the odds. Dampness, humidity and brief rain showers can add hopeful time. Hot, dry heat and strong winds diminish expectations.

I moved to the next cage and smiled at Bo. A three-year old male, twenty-six inches tall, one hundred and ten pounds of muscle; stolid and faithful. He had a few flaws: his wrinkles were not deep enough, and his skull, foreface and neck wouldn't win at dog shows. Definitely not championship material, but he worked well with Susie. His flashes of brilliance were not constant, but occasionally Bo's endurance and plodding kept her going when she wanted to stop and smell the flowers. The race may go to the swiftest and brightest, but more love is saved for the slower and imperfect. He wouldn't be used for breeding, but he had a job tracking as long as he was capable. He also had my love and a home forever.

I turned and watched Lieutenant Hank Cribbs, Carlson's chief deputy, step across the ditch and approach.

"Hey Jo Beth, how they hanging?"

This was Hank's quaint way of telling me that he considered me one of the boys. He was a tad over six feet; I had to look up. He was slim and trim in his tailored gabardine and full of himself. I stared openly and pointedly at his crotch.

"They look barely average Hank, but you're so handsome and charismatic you can't expect to have everything."

He thought briefly and decided to ignore it. "Ah, the sheriff wants to know if you're ready to go, says he wants to coordinate the search."

"Come on Hank, that wasn't what he said at all, I bet." I screwed my face into a scowl, dropped my voice to a lower and slower cadence. "Tell that 'Miss Prissy Pants' to get her ass over here on the double!"

He smiled with a brief nod of agreement. "Close. Not word for word, but close. Coming?" It sounded close to a plea.

"Sure," I grinned. "Tell him I'm on the way."

I waited until I had Wayne's attention and signed I was ready. He came around his van and started unloading my gear. I picked up the bright glo-yellow jumpsuit and stepped into it, slipped it over my shoulder and zipped up the lightweight but very tough material. The bright color was for the sometime trigger-happy occupants of forest and swamp who see anything that moves as a target. Large white letters proclaimed "Rescue" on front and back. This was to reassure any bad guys I was tracking that I wasn't the law. After all, I was always out in front on any search.

The minute I zipped up I began to sweat. Wayne handed me the gun. I slipped the nylon holster over my left shoulder and fastened the strap under my right breast. Breaking open the .32, I spun the cylinder and closed it. It wasn't a cannon and wasn't capable of knocking down a determined enemy with one shot; but I was hoping six, somewhere in the body, would seriously slow him down. There were also six extra rounds slotted into the holster strap. My firing range scores were fairly accurate, and for personal reasons I felt safer wearing it.

Wayne began fastening snake leggings that were the same bright color of my suit. A normal pair is made of molded plastic with a bulge at the knee and covers only the front of the leg. Mine have a rear panel up to the bend of the knee. Snakes don't always attack from the front. If you step on one it will lash out at any surface. I was wearing Pro-Wings, athletic shoes. I can't hike all day in boots or steel-reinforced shoe tops. There is a special piece of plastic molded as a cover for the top of my shoes. Wayne knelt and locked those onto my shoe soles with a skate key. These adaptations yielded comfort for my feet and protection from snake fangs.

Gazing down at the top of Wayne's head I once again was thankful

I had found him. He was a year out of high school and had worked that year with me. He was nineteen, six feet of muscle, brown hair, brown eyes, with a large, open face, and he was totally deaf.

The sound of a rapidly approaching car caused me to turn. A news van from Channel 3 Eyewitness News in Jacksonville pulled up next to my van. Timothy Sizemore hopped out and hurried around from the passenger side.

"Ms. Sidden?"

"Yes," I replied.

"Could we do a quick stand-up interview, ask a few questions, just twenty seconds or so? I'm Tim Sizemore."

"I know; I've seen some of your reports." I needed the exposure; my advertising budget was laughable. Channel 3 could be seen in more than twelve counties in Florida and South Georgia. The kennel had four-teen puppies with huge appetites ready for market and other operating expenses overwhelming to think about. Glancing toward the sheriff and seeing his back turned while he was telling another story to his captive audience, I balanced my need against pissing off the sheriff in a big way.

"If you'll put the door panel in the frame where it's readable, ask about puppies, get a good shot of the dogs and hurry."

Sizemore didn't bother to give me an answer; he was quick to sense the need for speed. He had seen the direction of my gaze. He hustled me around to the back of the van as he was telling his cameraman the shots he wanted. Wayne had been harnessing and leashing the dogs. He walked them to me stepping out of camera range. When the cameraman switched on the lights in the pre-dawn dimness, I knew the interview was doomed. Those lights would draw the sheriff faster than a speeding bullet. I leaned close to the dogs and whispered the command to "sit." I didn't want the command overheard in case they decided they didn't want to sit, which happens sometimes. They plopped their rumps to the ground and stared toward the brightness. I relaxed and tried to appear intelligent.

"We're here at the edge of the Okefenokee Swamp, just outside Balsa City, Georgia, with Jo Beth Sidden of Bloodhounds, Inc. In just a few minutes, at first light, Ms. Sidden will undertake a search-and-res-cue mission at the request of the Dunston County Sheriff's Department. Eleven-year-old Thomas Slight is missing from his home this morning. His mother discovered his absence when she smelled smoke and went to investigate. Thomas, who is mentally impaired, had started a small fire with newspapers on the floor of his bedroom. The parents, Guy and Catherine Slight, fear that Thomas ran away when the flames frightened

him. They believe he is somewhere in the dangerous swamp behind us."
Sizemore turned toward me and held out the microphone.

"How would you assess your chances of finding Thomas?"

"We have good weather conditions at the present time and a fresh trail. We're optimistic and hopeful."

"Do you train and breed your pedigreed bloodhounds?"

(Bless you Tim.)

"That is correct, Tim. We train bloodhounds to scent trail, sniff out drugs and also to work burn sites to find suspected arson."

"Do you train all the dogs you raise? How about puppies?"

(Thank you God.)

"We have fourteen beautiful puppies ready for a good home right now and more on the way."

The sheriff stepped in front of me and grabbed Sizemore's hand, the one holding the microphone. I saw Sizemore momentarily flinch with pain, but he was a pro and quickly regained his composure.

"Sheriff Carlson will be coordinating the search efforts."

"That's right, Tim," he stated grimly. "When disaster strikes, we are here to protect and serve."

I shuffled sideways out of camera range and signed to Wayne to get my pack. Shit was going to hit the fan when the sheriff finished hogging the camera, and I wanted to be out of range. I was only half listening when I heard Tim ask what the male handler's role was in the rescue.

"Oh, that's just Wayne. He's deaf and dumb."

My rage making me reckless, I took three fast steps back into camera range. The sheriff was slack-jawed with the knowledge that he had committed a very large blunder and it had been recorded on film.

"Excuse me, Tim," I said, biting off each word. "Wayne is hearing-impaired. He's an expert tracker and dog trainer. He's my backup in today's search. If I get into trouble, it's his job to rescue me." I turned and moved to Wayne who was kneeling over my pack, adding the clip-ons. His back had been to the action, and he had no idea what was going on. I could hardly contain my glee when the lights and the camera followed me. I was going to knife the bastard, hopefully on camera.

Wayne and I had many hand signals that did not pertain to signing. I always touched his right shoulder when he needed to face me for sign language. When I touched his left shoulder, it was panic time, heads-up action or an emergency. I leaned over on camera and tapped his left shoulder. He whirled to face me and I read in his eyes that he was ready for anything. I gestured slowly and carefully so even the most novice of signers would not miss any of my message. I signed that Sheriff Carlson was to be pitied. He was uneducated in modern ways. I apologized for his insensitivity. I then stopped before I ruined the effect. Wayne nodded his head up and down and stared off-camera at the sheriff with a sad look. That boy had talent. With my back to the camera, I signed that we'd better pull a shepherd and get the flock out of here. He gave me a wink of agreement. The camera lights tracked us a few feet before going dark.

Wayne swung the thirty-pound pack onto my back, then slipped my .22 rifle into the scabbard. I held the dog leads while we both adjusted weights and straps in harmony and with dispatch. Hank strode over to meet us at the edge of the road. He was holding the lost boy's jacket, and he handed it to me without comment, and then walked away. The sheriff wasn't in sight and I was feeling a little shaky. I had made a mortal enemy and possibly lost an ally, and it wasn't even daylight. Not an exemplary beginning.

Wayne and I crossed the narrow dirt road and approached four small houses huddled in a diminutive clearing. Pushing almost to the doors and windows were entangled vines, palmettos, slash pine, water oaks, bay trees, wild magnolias and cypress trees. A riotous, cumbrous mass of both undergrowth and old-growth trees. We walked around behind the fourth house and studied the view.

A man appeared on the small rear porch. As we walked over, a worn-looking woman about forty years old joined him. She was in stretch pants and a tank top, and was hugging herself to warm her upper arms. I introduced myself and Wayne and explained I was going into the swamp to search for their son and would like to ask some questions. They were both staring at the dogs.

"Do they bite?" She asked.

"Oh, no, ma'am," I replied. "Bloodhounds are extremely gentle and very friendly. Do you have a nickname or pet name you call Thomas?"

"I sometimes call him Tom Tom, mostly just Tom."

"Who all's going?" asked the father.

"Just me and the dogs, sir." I decided to tell him why. "If I have to backtrack, the scent won't be disturbed."

I looked at the mother.

"Would Tom recognize green berries as a food source?"

"Well," she hesitated. "He's picked wild briarberries with me, but he didn't know just to pick the ripe ones. He picked them all, the red, the black and the green ones too. Had to watch him about eating the green ones."

Oh boy, I'd have one sick kid on my hands if he got hungry.

"Ma'am, how much does he weigh?"

"He's big for his age, about a hundred pounds," she said with pride. I weigh one hundred and twenty-eight most of the time but was getting lighter with each passing minute, since I was sweating buckets. I hoped I did not have to find out if I could haul 100 pounds back with me. I asked her how he was dressed.

"Just his underwear," she said. "He said it was too hot now for his jammas. He's barefoot!" She grabbed her husband's arm and shook it. "He ain't got no shoes on!"

It had just registered in her mind, this minute, that her boy had been out there over three hours with no protection for his feet. Her husband patted her back and held her awkwardly. It didn't look as if he had had much practice, but maybe I'm too much of a cynic when it comes to men. I raised my voice to get her attention.

"Mrs. Slight, I need a long-sleeved shirt, long pants, shoes and socks for Thomas. Can you get them for me?"

I took a county map from my inside jacket pocket and spread it on the porch floor.

"Mr. Slight, would you look at this map and tell me what's beyond that path over there?" It was the only break in the surrounding foliage and where I assumed the search would start.

"'Bout fifty yards in, there's a main power line through the woods. The Georgia Power people keep it mowed in the summer. It's the only place the kids have to play ball and such. It's there or in the road."

"Anything else that could be helpful?"

"Over beyond the power line, there's the train track and trestle."

Please God, let him skip the trestle or let it be twelve feet wide with a solid rail-bed and three-foot walls on each side to hide the open space below. I knew I was blowing smoke. The average rail-bed on a train trestle out in the boonies was a twelve-inch wooden beam with a rail laid in the center, supported by cross beams of huge cypress pilings, about ten or twelve feet above the creek or pond. Susie hated heights. I remembered the humiliation we all had suffered during a parade last summer. Wayne and I were resplendent in our new rescue jumpsuits, empty packs on our backs, marching about ten feet apart. We each had a pair of dogs harnessed and on long leads, ranging left and right in front of us. The crowds loved the dogs, and the dogs were having a ball. They reveled in the attention and the fast pats they received when they ran close to the curb.

All was well until we approached a three-foot-wide drainage runoff for heavy rainfall that crossed Main Street. It was covered with heavy steel mesh and you could see the sandy dry bottom about six feet below. Susie took one look and glued every muscle to the pavement, refusing to move. I couldn't budge her. She threw her head up and bayed piteously. I could have strangled her. The crowd hooted and hollered with laughter. Wayne ran over and gave me his leads, picked up Susie and lugged her across the narrow gap. We had to repeat the same embarrassing moves when we crossed Main Street. This gave another hundred or so a chance to laugh. I didn't even want to think about a train trestle.

I folded the map as Mrs. Slight returned with the clothes. Wayne took them from her, rolled them neatly into a tight bundle and secured them under my pack flap. She looked at me and I saw her chin quiver.

"Find him, Miss; please find him. He's a good boy, never meant no harm with the fire; he just forgot. I learned him never to play with matches!"

Southern pathos from the heart. I felt a lump in my throat and assured both of them I would do my very best.

I waved 'bye to Wayne, then walked a few steps and unclipped my radio. This could get interesting if Hank was still not speaking to me.

"Search One to Base. Commencing search. Radio check. One, two, three. Over."

"Base to Search One. I read you loud and clear. Good luck. Over and out." The good luck sounded warmer than just business. I must be forgiven. He must have heard by now what stupido had called Wayne. I rehooked the radio to my belt and presented Tom's jacket to Susie.

"Seek," I said firmly. "Seek," I repeated as I held the garment under her nose. "Seek," I told Bo. I held the jacket to each of their noses and repeated the command three times.

They both put their noses to the ground and Susie began to circle, Bo willing to be led. Susie started back toward the house. Wrong way. "Sit," I ordered. They both stopped and looked back at me but did not sit. They were on the command to seek and now I was asking them to sit. I was confusing them, but it couldn't be helped. They were seeking the wrong way and I used the command to "Retreat" only for emergencies. When they became too familiar with a seldom-used command they replied about sixty percent of the time.

I squatted and held out both hands, palms up, with a piece of dried deer jerky in each. "Come," I called. They gobbled their treat and watched my hands for more. Pulling out the jacket, I refreshed their scent memories and again gave each of them the "Seek" command. I stood and walked slowly backwards to the path, gently pulling the leads. They scampered around me with their noses to the ground and took the path.

Maybe I had them on the right track. Humans can't smell what bloodhounds smell, so they don't know what scent the dogs are chasing. Bloodhounds can be capricious; they can decide a fresh opossum or raccoon scent smells like fun and follow it for hours. Mine were good, but they have led me down the garden path once or twice. There's nothing to do but go on, trust and hope for the best. It was darker on the narrow path. Only half-light filtered through the branches. The footing was slippery, the muddy track was covered with pine needles, decaying oak leaves and leaves from the bay trees. It was damp and I could feel the humidity rising faster than the temperature. I sweated and suffered and lusted for nicotine.

We broke into a large open area where high power lines on heavy cement casements and huge poles bearing more than a dozen lines marched off into the distance. This was heavy voltage. I bet the voltage leaking from the lines was enough to run all the microwaves in town for a year. It was probably unsafe for children to be playing under or near them. If I found Tom, I must remember to warn his parents about the dangers of leaking voltage. The grass and briarberry bushes were still wet with dew. The big mowers had not been here to level the area under the wires, which helps to retard the spring and summer growth.

As the dogs walked steadily ahead, I was aware that my legs would be a bloody mess if it weren't for my suit. I once again blessed the manufacturers of the miracle substance used in the construction of my outfit: a more pliable version of Kevlar. The experts boast it repels thorns, cut glass, palmetto slashes, bees, horseflies, yellow flies, mosquitoes, sand flies, fire ants, spiders, all other species of creepy crawlies, fence wire, wire staples and snake fangs. I take on trust all their claims except staples and snake fangs. That's why I haven't tried to shoot a staple into my leg while I am in the suit and why I wear plastic snake leggings.

Both dogs stopped and lifted their noses to sniff the air currents above their heads. Both large heads swiveled to the right. I turned in the same direction they were gazing and saw a female deer already sporting her lighter red summer coat, standing with her twin fawns. I looked back down at Susie and Bo.

"Don't even think about it," I told them. I could almost hear them sigh as they put their heads down and started tracking again.

2

"BE THANKFUL FOR CRUMBS"
April 5, Monday, 9 A.M.

Susie stopped tracking and trotted around looking for a good place to tinkle. After she had finished, Bo had to spray his water over hers. Macho male. In a few minutes the sun would be up high enough to burn the dew from the landscape. Flying battalions of biting fame would be out in large swarms. I looked around for a bush large enough to hide behind. Silly maybe, but I can't pee while being watched by two dogs.

I tied the leads to a small pine sapling, walked a few feet to a gallberry bush and began the complicated chore of undressing. First, I slid the .22 rifle out of its scabbard on my backpack and laid it on the ground. Next, I undid the belt of the backpack and slid it off my shoulders, then unbuckled the belt holding my two canvas-covered water bottles. I also carried two plastic quart bottles of water. If I were stranded overnight, I didn't want to be forced to drink groundwater. It might not be unhealthy but it looked as unappetizing as ink. Black water, sluggish and turgid. The only free-flowing water is after flooding and it is still black from tannic acid emitted from cypress roots and ground growth. I unzipped my jumpsuit and drew my arms clear of the sleeves. I worked the top half of my suit and the cotton briefs below my knees, pulled them to the front and held them off the ground with my right hand. I squatted and fanned my bare bottom with my left hand, sweeping back and forth to keep the mosquitoes off my lily-white buns.

The only time I experience penis envy is when I have to go through this process of peeling off and suiting up again. The male widens his stance, unzips, exposes only the essential object, lets fly, shakes, returns it and zips. Voila! A simple, uncomplicated affair. It just isn't fair. Who said the sexes were equal? I resuited, reloaded the gear, collected the dogs and returned to trailing.

The dogs led off in an erratic zigzag through the knee-deep growth. Tommy must have been terrified to wade through this mess with bare feet. I felt a tightening in my gut at this thought. Insects flock to any warm body but blood draws them like heat-seeking missiles. With this humidity, briar snags and bloody scratch marks, he would be miserable by now. His wounds would start leaking body fluids, could turn septic, and fever could come quickly. Come on, Tommy, curl up and take a nap. Be under the next bush or just around the next turn. He had to be exhausted. His adrenaline rush caused by fear would have faded long ago, leaving him physically drained, tired and sleepy.

The dogs strained against their leads, forcing me to increase my effort to keep up. They could maintain a fast pace for hours, but I couldn't. I looked ahead for a place to halt for a drink and a rest break. We were now at the edge of the power line's right-of-way. Thick scrub and old-growth timber were a few yards ahead. Most of the trees in this area are planted by machines and harvested every twenty-four years. Ahead were old, natural-growth trees that had been spared the woodsman's ax for a half-century or more. They towered above the planted slash pine. It didn't look like friendly territory.

The sun dimmed for a moment, calling attention to some dirty-looking smudges sliding across the sky from the southwest. Rain would cool the dogs but wouldn't do much for me. I'd still be encased up to my neck and it would just get muggier. When the dogs started to enter a small game trail, I pulled them back and gave them the command to rest.

I pulled out some deer jerky and watched it disappear down their gullets without even a token chomp.

"Chew," I demanded. "How can you taste it if you slide it down so fast?"

Their second piece went down just as fast as the first.

"Then on the other hand, why don't you swallow it whole?"

Two sets of large liquid eyes were watching my fingers intently. I'm a soft touch when it comes to treats. Both Wayne and Rosie, Wayne's mother, also a trainer, are more disciplined with their training procedures. I follow the training manuals only as long as the instructions therein run parallel to my personal beliefs. When they differ, I march to my own drumbeat. The book says to withhold the evening meal the night before any planned exercise in fieldwork the following day. No way would I send my dogs to bed unfed and expect them to perform for several hours the next day on empty stomachs.

The theory seems to be: if the dog is half-starved, it will do somersaults and walk on water for an occasional treat. My dogs could do these tricks, if necessary, but they only have to lift a wrinkled brow and look soulful for me to start dispensing jerky with both hands.

Looking around, I spotted a small clearing under a large gallberry bush, led the dogs over and tied their leads to a branch. I scanned the immediate area and decided it was safe enough to sit. Slipping off the rifle and backpack, I turned up a canteen and drank deeply, waited a minute and drank again. I pulled off my gloves, took a face cloth from my pack and wet it. I wiped my sweating face and neck, the only part of me uncovered, and dreamed of a cigarette a foot long. I wish I had the will to quit, but I enjoy every damn puff. I've been told enough times that if I really wanted to quit, I could do it, so I guess I don't. My father died last year with Alzheimer's. He chained-smoked Camels for over forty years, so maybe I, too, can tip-toe past the "Big C."

I eyed the game trail the dogs had indicated we were going to travel. Wild animals are creatures of habit as much as we are; they take the path of least resistance. Wild hogs, turkeys, opossums, wildcats, bobcats, foxes, skunks, swamp rabbits and small black bears would use this trail. Deer, whenever possible, travel the man-plowed firebreaks.

The only serious danger to the dogs and myself when we entered the path would be an over-protective brood sow with piglets or a macho boar not paying attention and blundering right into us. They have poor eyesight, and when they feel threatened, they will charge. And, of course, the snakes. Timber rattlers, diamondbacks, coral snakes and cottonmouth moccasins are the deadliest. On the path, I would have only limited vision. Some places, where the boughs overhead would be laced and covered with vines, I would have to stoop and crawl. There would be many sharp turns and twists with very little room to maneuver.

I carry the .22 rifle for snakes, and the .32 snub-nose for Bubba, moonshiners and pot growers. I might be unfortunate enough to blunder into a pot patch or still site. You simply wouldn't believe the liquor stills and pot patches I have found during searches. I have been lucky lately, and haven't stumbled on the owners tending to these illegal enterprises, but I know it's just a matter of time until it happens.

I'm not an officer of the court; I carry no badge. I'm under contract for search and rescue only. I'm frequently asked by the officers if I've seen anything when I have been in their territory. I look them square in the eye and lie without hesitation or guilt. I will not risk my dogs or my hide for the questionable virtue of delivering a still or pot patch to the ATF or DEA. Common sense dictates that mine would be a short-lived and unhealthy career. Those guys who make their illegal products out in the woods don't get mad, they get even.

On infrequent sojourns to a local tavern or one of the juke joints out in the flatwoods, I always manage to deliver carefully worded assurances that I'm closely related to the three little monkeys. I see nothing, hear nothing and don't talk. I just hope these pearls of wisdom tossed around reach the appropriate ears. If the officers who ask me think their quarry is out where I've been, then they should slog out there and find them. It's their job, not mine.

While we were resting, the sky cleared, clouds racing away to the east. It was ten. I guessed we had covered five miles. As the crow flies, we were less than two miles from Tommy's home. The track this far had been wandering, erratic and completely senseless. How he had covered this distance was a mystery. I was worried about his feet. When the dogs found him, I hoped there would be sufficient open space so I could call for a chopper to air-lift him out. If the area was too dense, I might have a chance to use the rescue sled.

I stood and pulled on my backpack. A close path meant less air and a lot more insects. I pulled out my cloth hat, fastened the sheer lawn veil to the inside of the hat's brim and pulled the elastic under my chin, unzipping my suit far enough to tuck in the loose folds. Now the only part of me that was exposed for the insects to feed on was my face, from forehead to chin and ear to ear.

I recalled that the first time I had introduced this hat with a veil was at the end of last summer, during the six weeks of "dog days." The poison and yellow flies were at their worst because the summer had been much wetter than normal. My mind went back six months to that hot summer afternoon . . . .

3

"AS UGLY AS HOMEMADE SIN"
Six Months Earlier...
September 18, Friday, 2 P.M.

Two day-trip fishermen were forty-eight hours overdue in returning their small, rented skiff. Three days of hazy and foggy overcast skies, with no sun or compass to guide them. Their abandoned boat had been found only five miles down from their camp, its small outboard motor out of gas and an empty water jug still on board, but no clue as to the where-abouts of the men.

When I arrived and started unloading the dogs, two Herdon County deputies left the shade of the fish camp's porch and strolled over. The older of the pair handed me an unlined, nylon windbreaker jacket and a Pirate's baseball cap — items from the missing men's car. After he had pointed out a Fish and Game Commission game warden, who was to transport me to the abandoned boat site, they both tipped their hats briefly and, after half-hearted comments on good luck, they ambled back to the shade.

Even with overcast skies, it had to be ninety-five out on the parking lot. Wayne had an advanced dog training class scheduled and since the game warden was going as a guide, I had come alone. It took three trips to hump all my equipment over to the dock area under the amused scru-tiny of the game warden. I introduced myself, and, from the set of his shoulders and curt nod of acknowledgment, I sensed resentment as well as sweat leaking from every pore. I was beginning to get ticked off. I should be used to this uniform-and-gun syndrome after a year of this superior and condescending attitude from the local-yokel badge shin-ers, but I was getting fed-up fast.

We had the usual audience of a dozen or so, waiting around to see something happen. The warden was in his late forties, with a leathery tan, dark hair and dark eyes, looking competent and fit. He was silently ridiculing me and my fancy equipment with facial and eye movements.

He was dressed in his summer uniform: short-sleeved shirt, light tan pants with a dark brown stripe down the leg and black short boots. He had one haunch draped over a piling on the dock and his arms folded on his chest. I resisted the urge to push him off the dock.

I glanced down into the pontoon launch and saw a water-proof lantern, flashlight, gas can, drinking water container and rubber hip-waders. This sucker travels light. I promised myself I would keep him out after dark, even if I had to sabotage the motor. It was now about twenty after two. I unpacked my hat with veil, shook it out and placed it in a zippered pocket of my suit. As soon as the boat touched shore where we were going, the bugs would be out in force.

The warden took one look and was laughing so hard he almost fell off the dock. I continued to suit up, ignoring him. He continued to laugh. There is something about a deep belly laugh that is contagious. First I heard a snicker, then two from the audience, and soon, more than half of them were laughing right along with him. He wiped his eyes and pulled a small spray-can of insect repellent out of a back pocket. He motioned to me but before he could utter a word, he doubled up again with laughter, pure spasms of mirth.

I waited patiently for him to pull himself together. Finally I had an opening.

"Sir, the can of spray has to be left behind," I said.

"Why?" he asked belligerently.

"Citronella is the base for insect repellents. One sniff of that and the dogs couldn't smell a skunk."

"Well," he drawled, "I'll just keep out of their way." He dropped the cylinder in his pocket. I took two steps closer and stared out at the water with my back to our audience. I saw no reason to publicly humiliate him.

"Listen, Pal, lose the repellent and those cigarettes in your pocket and quit jerking my chain. If not, you can explain to Sheriff Robinson why this search attempt for two of his tax-paying citizens got scuttled at the dock."

I returned to unloading the gear, shouldered my pack and projected my voice clearly. "I'll meet you over on the south bank to load."

I walked away with the dogs and didn't look back. I knew I couldn't persuade Susie to jump the five feet down into the boat from the dock. From shallow water, she would hop aboard without any hassle.

I knew the warden would motor over to me in a few minutes. He would take his own sweet time and procrastinate, but he would be along. The warden had very good job security with civil service. It would take an act of Congress and a case of dynamite to remove him from his cushy appointment, but like all government employees, whether they were city, county, state or federal, he would adhere to the golden rule: THOU SHALT NOT ROCK THE BOAT OR MAKE WAVES.

He finally appeared and we loaded without incident. We motored slowly out the narrow, dredged channel. After we exited the channel and were in Red Wing Pond, the warden very slowly picked up speed. Green growth, lush as a rain forest, was a hundred feet away on each side of the boat. Giant cypress trees soared to heights that looked prehistoric. Water oaks, wild magnolias, light green, dark green and dank green foliage billowed out over each shoreline. The cooler air produced by the boat's movement through the water was soothing.

The dogs sat alert, front paws braced and noses up in the breeze. They had been in boats several times and were seasoned travelers. Bo was a dedicated tourist. He scanned the treeline, looked up at a buzzard riding a high thermal and seemed to be enjoying himself. Susie sat rigidly and grim-faced. She blinked occasionally but that was the only movement I spotted. She would sit this way, whether it was minutes or hours. It was something to be endured, not to enjoy. In a boat is the only time I have seen her refuse deer jerky. She apparently suffers some form of motion sickness. When we arrived she would climb out stiff-legged, but it would only be a few seconds until she was back to normal.

This pontoon boat was part of the state park's fleet. It was eight feet wide and sixteen feet long, with wooden benches running parallel on the sides, and it could accommodate up to eighteen passengers. Park employees run guided boat tours year-round, twice a day for visitors at five bucks a head. The visitors get a thirty-minute opportunity to glimpse the vastness and timelessness of this primeval place. They see a few alligators, lots of flora and some fauna, and dark waters teeming with mystery and dangerous ambiguities. They hear a rehearsed lecture on plants and local legends, and a brief history of how the swamp is protected and preserved. The guides are entertaining and pleasant, and they know the answers to most of the questions they are asked. The boat trippers get their money's worth.

I glanced forward, studying the warden as he stood relaxed in the motor well indentation centered near the front of the boat. We had traveled, so far, in mutual silence. It was entirely possible that we would be spending the night together in an aggravating and hostile environment. It was time to be professional, spread a little oil on the troubled waters. I slid forward on the seat until I was close enough for conversation over the noise of the motor.

"I'd like you to call me Jo Beth. Sheriff Robinson didn't tell me your name. What should I call you?"

"Warden Phelps," he replied dryly, without turning his head. So much for rapport. Well, I could live with that. We'll see what happens with a little honesty here. He must have a sense of humor; he sure got his jollies when he saw my hat-and-veil invention.

"Well, Warden Phelps," I said conversationally, "let's discuss this situation. You must think I'm an overbearing bitch who's had a little luck, been on television a couple of times, and it's gone straight to my head. Probably think I got my business from my father's name and money, or a husband, or a sugar-daddy maybe. You think I enjoy bossing men old enough to be my father who know more about this swamp than I'll ever learn. How am I doing so far?"

"Right on the money," he answered promptly.

"Well, on the other hand, I think you've been behind a badge long enough that you judge us civilians a mite too harshly from your lofty perch of superiority and don't even try to disguise your contempt at our pitiful attempts to measure up. Am I still on the money?"

"Obviously it's your opinion, but I doubt it's universal," he answered with a pleasant smile. I felt better. This man was at least willing to debate a little.

"Don't kid yourself, Warden Phelps, sir. You think they're gonna tell you at the time you catch them red-handed fire-hunting, or with too many bass and brim in their cooler? Wouldn't be very politic while you're standing there with your summons book and grim expression."

"Speaking of fire hunting," he said, ignoring my comment, "you any relation to Buford Sidden, lives over in Mercer?"

The lightbulb glowed above my head. My name was what he was upset about, not my outfit, personality or equipment. I should have ditched the name when I had ditched his son, but the old buzzard made me so angry by insisting that I never use the name "Sidden" again, I had hung on to it, just to spite him. Bad move, Jo Beth.

"Was, is the operative word here. Was related by marriage. Married to his only son and heir, Buford Ray Sidden, Jr., called 'Bubba.' Divorced him in eighty-five while he was serving a five-year sentence in Patton Correctional."

"I arrested Bubba and two more over in Gilsford County for fire-hunting on a federal reserve about six years ago, in eighty-seven. His daddy got the summons thrown out. Judge McAlbee said I had made an illegal search and seizure."

"Had you?" I asked.

"No way. They were so drunk I had to call for another warden to help. It was a good bust. Judge made me look like a jackass."

"Judge McAlbee was a regular at the Thursday night poker game out at Buford Senior's ranch while I was married to Bubba years ago. I bet he still sits in on most Thursday nights, smoking those little black cigars he favors." I decided to tell him a little more about local justice.

"When Bubba was convicted in eighty-five, it was for criminal assault on a waitress over in Three Forks. He was sentenced to five years but had served little more than two when they released him. He was only out for three months. That's probably when you caught him fire hunting. I hadn't heard about that arrest. If your case had been heard and he had been found guilty, they would have revoked his parole and sent him back to serve his full sentence." I stared out over the water and felt the old pain and anger churning in my gut.

He must have seen something in my expression. "What happened?"

"I put him back in Patton Correctional for the remainder of his sentence, plus three more years." I could hear the rasp in my voice. I hesitated a moment and then continued. "He was sentenced to ten years, but only served five and a half. He was released last month."

"Look, it's none of my business," he said. "You don't have to talk about it."

"I've never talked about it to anyone, but I'm all right. I was back in eighty-seven there for a minute. If your arrest had held up, none of what happened to me would have happened. I was just reflecting on it." I reached for my canteen and took several sips of water. The sun kept peeking out, then disappearing back into the haze.

"I didn't have anything to tie me to him; we were divorced, so I wasn't notified of his early release. I was working two jobs, receptionist at Sanders Insurance from eight to four, waitress at Attenburg's King Steer Steak House from five to ten. I was saving to build my kennel."

He slowed the launch, turning into a narrow channel only thirty feet wide. He reduced his speed, sat quietly and relaxed, waiting for me to continue.

"One Saturday night after the restaurant closed at ten, he caught me in the parking lot on the way to my car." I cleared my throat. "When he dropped me at the hospital at midnight he told the nurses at the emergency entrance he was just worn out from trying to reason with me and that I needed a little patching up. I was in the bed of his pickup. He didn't want me bleeding on his genuine leather 'tuck and roll' upholstery."

I had a sudden thought. "I thought the whole world, or at least southeast Georgia, was aware of my misfortune. How come you didn't hear about it, or read about it?"

He turned to face me. "Two weeks after Bubba's arrest was thrown out by Judge McAlbee, I was transferred to Savannah Wildlife Preserve. Took me two years to get transferred back here. Always wondered if the arrest was the reason for my transfer. No way to find out." I saw then that his dealings with the Sidden name had gnawed on him. No wonder he was churlish when we met.

"How bad was it?" he asked. "At the hospital."

I recited my injuries. "Both legs had fractures. Five broken ribs, right wrist and collarbone, two fingers on the right hand, three on the left. Nose and left cheekbone were crushed. Forty-seven stitches on the face, thirty more on the scalp. I was in the hospital for three months and in physical therapy for six more. I had to go back for three reconstructive surgeries on my face."

He openly scanned my face. "They sure did a good job. Can't tell that anything's happened to your face at all."

I smiled. "I had the best doctors money can buy, only because ol' Buford couldn't buy the police photos taken in emergency that night. I went to school with the photographer. He took some lulus. Good clear prints in color. He told me the desk sergeant tried to make them disappear but he had made copies. One set for me and one for him. I decided to let ol' Buford pay the bills. He's been buying Bubba out of trouble since he was in the ninth grade. Buford thought that paying the bill to make me look normal would keep me from testifying against Bubba. He actually thought I wouldn't press charges."

"So you got even," he said.

"I can't ever begin to get even. I testified and had him put away. I made the trip up to Patton every time he came up for parole, taking my pictures with me for 'show and tell.' The first three visits, they agreed with me. The fourth time they must have gotten tired of seeing the same carnage and let him go. I had a restraining order in place before his release which is about as useful as teats on a boar hog. He's coming after me. Tomorrow, next week, next month, he'll come."

"What's your plan?" he asked, eyeing the holstered gun strapped over my rescue suit. "You going to kill him?"

"God, I hope not. He enjoyed trying to destroy me. He tried it once, thinks he can do it again. It's my goal in life, to keep him from touching me. That will be my revenge, to thwart his ambitions."

He looked doubtful. "That sounds a little weird. Sorta sounds like you're setting yourself up as a target."

"Nonsense. I am the target, I was the target, and will be the target again. I'm following the rules. I've got the court order and he has been served. I'm not going after him, but by God, he'll be coming after me."

He gave me a strange look. "You're setting *him* up as the target. You're something else."

I shrugged. "Sounds like you disapprove."

He gave me a wide grin. "Hell, no. The bastard deserves anything you have planned. Just watch your back." I nodded. It was time to find out what he knew about our missing fishermen.

"Do you have any ideas on our missing guys?"

He shook his head. "First I heard was when the fish camp reported that the men hadn't returned the boat they rented. The rule is: you have to have the boat back by seven each evening; the park's gates are locked at eight. They're told if they are not back by eight, they're considered lost, and a search will be started. I didn't know they were locals until you mentioned it. It took the Coast Guard into the second day to spot the boat. Fog kept them grounded both mornings. They found the boat this morning at eleven, and guided me in by radio. When I saw the dry gas can and water cooler still aboard, I looked for their fishing equipment. It was missing. I looked around some and then called the sheriff. He said he was calling you in to search first."

I thought it over. "Give me your best guess."

"Hell, Jo Beth, I just don't know. They weren't within sight or hearing when I got there. No fishing equipment means maybe they decided to try off-shore casting, but if they were locals they would know better. They could have fallen in, but with two, you wonder. You got any ideas?"

"Why don't you try to get Sheriff Robinson on the radio? Let's double-check if they are locals, if they could swim, had a compass, knew the area well, et cetera. We need more information even to form a theory. Also, see if either has any medical conditions we need to know about. All the sheriff said to me was quote, two of his citizens, unquote. I assumed he meant locals, but you know how he talks. That could mean they are staying at the Holiday Inn. Anyway, since you were on the scene, I assumed you had all the pertinent information at hand."

"Nope," he drawled. "All I was told was the great female search expert and her dogs were coming."

"Up yours," I said laughing.

He turned into another channel running east and west. It looked exactly like the last two we were on. Christ, it was a wonder more people didn't get lost every day out here. He tried three times to raise the sheriff's department, but only got static. He shrugged and said he would try later.

Reception is iffy out here. Sometimes you're out of range; most of the time it's the dense forest and air currents. One never knows, but radios sure aren't always reliable. The Okefenokee Swamp covers more than six hundred and eighty square miles.

Its land is a contradiction of what most people expect. It's a peat quagmire in places. The build-up of vegetation on top of peat looks solid, but the very spot you're walking on can give beneath your feet and give the sensation of walking on a waterbed. The swamp has shady pine islands. Some spots are sunlit prairies, and there are several clear lakes. The sand under some vegetation is two feet, other places it can be fifteen feet or more. The swamp waters flow very slowly south. One branch flows west to the Suwannee River, another into a stream that becomes St. Marys River and exits into the Atlantic Ocean. The swamp is part water, part sand and part peat.

I looked forward and saw our destination. A small skiff was tied to the heavy growth at the water's edge. As the launch neared the shore, the warden shut down the motor, coasted to the edge, jumped out and started securing the boat to a cypress knee protruding from the water. The dogs hopped lightly to the ground and led me in circles around a small clearing, looking for the perfect place to pee.

I was holding onto their leads with my left hand and fishing in my pocket with my right to pull out my hat and veil. I fanned vigorously, then quickly got it adjusted under my collar and to the edges of my hairline. I reached over and broke off a small branch from a bay tree and stripped the leaves, crushing them with both hands. I rubbed the aromatic smell over my face, making sure I covered my eyelids. The bay tree belongs to the laurel family. Dried, the leaves are used as a spice. Green like these were, they emit a smell that, fortunately, most small-winged creatures don't like. Most people preferred eucalyptus leaves but I didn't see any and maybe the bay smell would work just as well.

Last year, after a disappointing supper date had fizzled out at nine, I decided to give two teams of our scent dogs a night hunt. Wayne arranged for the two part-time helpers to hide and we started out hunting our "victims" by moonlight. Wayne's team had found their objective right away and returned while my team was still at the starting point wandering around, noses to the ground, meandering aimlessly. I couldn't understand it. When Wayne approached to see if he could help, he started laughing and pointing and holding his nose. Because of great expectations for my night out, I had practically taken a bath in perfume, even using the matched smell in the dusting powder and lotion. My sense of smell had been deadened by proximity. Wayne said he could smell the perfume from six feet away.

A bloodhound's sense of smell is more than twenty times more powerful than a human's. I had effectively deadened their ability with my perfume. That is when I learned to use unscented cosmetics, laundry detergents and clothes softeners, and no perfumes, insect repellents or nicotine sticks around the dogs. A small price to pay for success. I only questioned this wisdom when I was being eaten alive by insects or when I could clearly kill for a cigarette.

When I looked over at the warden, he had unloaded my gear and put on his waist-high light rubber waders. I stepped into mine, pulling the suspenders over my shoulders.

"Thank you, Warden Phelps, for unloading the gear." I pulled off more bay leaves and showed him how to spread the smell on his face and arms. He looked doubtful about any help from the onslaught. I knew he was wishing for a large spray can of "Off."

As he was rubbing his arms he spoke. "I'd appreciate you calling me James." I accepted his flag of truce, gratefully.

"Sure," I beamed. "It's hi-ho, off-to-work-we-go time."

I strapped on the .32 and shouldered my pack.

"Want me to tote that thing awhile?" he asked. "Looks heavy."

"It is, but I'm so used to it, I'd be lost without it." In a pig's eye would he ever tote my gear. The helpless female will not emerge, regardless if his offer was only being polite. It implied that I was being considered less than an equal, maybe a liability.

I debated which item to present to the dogs. I chose the baseball cap. It was easier to pull in and out of a pocket. I never gave the dogs two scents to follow. If they split up later, the loss of one scent could confuse the dogs. It was my own method, not the manual's, but my percentage of finds was higher than average, so I must be doing something right. I thrust the cap under each of their noses several times and gave them the command to seek.

James watched the dogs as they put their noses to the ground and started moving slowly around the tiny clearing.

"Can they track through water?"

"Sure!" I said with a smile. "They can track through it, over it and under it. We've just started training three dogs to find submerged victims of drowning."

"How can you do that?" he asked testily.

"It ain't easy," I said deadpan. "First you have to start with a corpse under water."

He glanced at me and grimaced. "You're putting me on, right?"

"Just a little. Submerged bodies aren't found every day around here, thankfully. The dogs are progressing very well, and should be able to witness or have their evidence accepted in a court of law very soon now."

"You're doing it again," he said, curt and sharp. "Dogs can't testify."

"Regular dogs can't," I agreed. "Bloodhounds are the only breed of dog whose evidence can convict in a court of law. Their evidence is accepted in every state."

"You're serious?"

"Absolutely. In fact, one bloodhound named Nick Carter became famous years ago by having his evidence in court convict over six hundred felons."

"No shit?" he seemed surprised.

"This bloodhound, Nick Carter," I continued, "was so good that he once trailed a man with a cold trail that was one hundred and five hours old and found his man. On another case he successfully scent-trailed a murder suspect over two hundred and fifty miles and led the law to the man's front door."

"These figures are hard for dogs?" He was beginning to get interested, I could tell.

"Three hours old, the trail is probable. Six hours can be iffy, unless you have good climate conditions. After twelve hours, forget it or pray for a miracle. Nick Carter was a living legend in the thirties. He turned the people of America on to bloodhounds. Most of the roads he worked were unpaved. There weren't as many pollutants and chemicals in our air, water and ground. Still, his records are totally without equal. He was a genius."

"How do your dogs measure up, any record times and distances?" He seemed to be trying to give me an opening to brag a little. Of course, I jumped in with both feet.

"The three of us have only been working together for a year. We don't have a long history as yet, but Susie and Bo found a drifter after he had beaten two children over in Vista Pines last January. We weren't called in for twenty-seven hours. Sheriff Carlson trampled the search scene thoroughly with his mounted posse before he called me in to search. I assured the dogs they were fantastically gifted, but I suspect the fact that the homeless bum hadn't had a bath in a month had a lot to do with their success."

"She's modest," he said in fake wonderment. "I don't believe it for a minute."

"Go suck a grapefruit," I replied. "Besides, it makes a better story if you inject a little humility."

While we were talking, we were progressing in single file through some modest vegetation, nothing to catch and drag on our clothing, a fairly clean path. The dogs seemed to be on a clear scent; they weren't stopping to reconsider the smells as they often do when they are unsure of the trail. I asked James if he thought we were on a game trail.

"I've been looking for prints, but the grass is too thick," he remarked. "It could be goats or hogs."

"Goats?" I said in surprise.

"Yeah," he said with satisfaction. He liked the fact that he was giving me some information for a change. "We have some ratty-looking herds out here that are skittish and seldom seen. The natives call them ghost herds because they seem to disappear like a puff of smoke the minute you spot them."

I began to speculate out loud. "They're not indigenous to this area. Wonder where they came from?"

He laughed. "Well, the local legend has their origin in the thirties when a goatherder lost his land to a local bank. They say he drove his herd into the swamp and joined them with his dog and shotgun. It was said he took potshots at local officials, which discouraged them from pursuing him. I talked to an old Indian that lived out here about ten years ago. He was supposed to be a descendent of the Seminole tribe that once inhabited the Okefenokee. He swore he had once seen the goatherder, his dog and his goats, briefly, on a moonlit night a long time ago."

I hummed a few bars of a ghostly theme. I heard him chuckle.

"Make fun if you want, but I'm being honest. I've seen the goats only twice and believe me, I was looking hard for the old herder and his dog."

I glanced at my watch; it was just after four. We had less than four hours until first dark. We locals say first light just before dawn and first dark just before night.

"How long will it take us to motor back in the dark?" I asked.

"It's the third night before the full moon, we should have some light. I don't have a spotlight on board to pick up the channel markers. It will be much slower without lights, maybe two hours."

He surely hadn't come prepared. I was stewing inwardly. I guessed he wanted to make the trip a little more difficult for yours truly. He seemed to sense my thoughts.

"I have the equipment," he said slowly. "I just didn't see the need."

"No problem," I said with assurance while I silently seethed, resenting him and his hang-ups. I tried to be philosophical. God knows I've pulled a few dirty tricks from time to time for revenge. Who was I to judge? It was just more fun being the one who was doing it than the one it was being done to.

I trudged on in silence for a few minutes. The mosquitoes and yellow flies were increasing their attacks on my face. I was now constantly fanning my face with a gloved hand to dislodge the most persistent. The bay leaves' smell had been diluted with sweat. I should stop and smear some more on my face. From the bites I was now receiving, my face would swell tonight and itch like crazy. Only the thought that James must be suffering a lot more, with his hands, arms, neck and face exposed, kept me from stopping just yet.

I brightened when I remembered that I hadn't noticed a T-shirt under his uniform shirt. I didn't want to turn around and check, but if he wasn't wearing a cotton undershirt, these long-billed mosquitoes were homing in on his back, and his thin uniform shirt would offer little or no protection. I was sick, sick, sick to be enjoying his discomfort.

The word discomfort brought forth some memories from my hospital stays. While lying in a bed of pain, writhing in agony, a nurse would lean over the bed and say casually, "Are we feeling a little discomfort?" It made me want to show the angel of mercy what some real pain feels like.

The path suddenly became a dead end at the base of a large cypress. There was a fork to the left and one to the right. The ground was wetter and lower. Soon we would be in water.

I turned to James. I was right about the absence of an undershirt; he was getting the full treatment. He was making a repetitive motion to brush them away. Face, left arm and a sweep across his back. Switching to the left hand, it was face, right arm and back, then repeat. The dogs were deciding which path we were going to take. I pulled out the baseball cap and reinforced their scent memory. I dug out the nylon long-sleeved windbreaker and thrust it toward James.

"See if you can zip it up. It should help with the bugs." He didn't even make a token protest, so I knew he was in misery.

The jacket was useless now for scent tracking. I hoped the cap would be enough. The jacket was a tight fit but he managed to zip it. It would offer some protection for his torso and arms. I propped my rifle safely against a tree and lowered my pack, gave the dogs the command to rest and tied them to a nearby bush.

I squatted and started unpacking my pack to reach the medical kit that had two pairs of thin surgical gloves among the first-aid supplies. A pair would protect his hands. I also had an extra bug net that would protect his neck, but if he started laughing when I offered it to him, I would make him pay.

I heard a strange thump and my eyes flew to the dogs sprawled on the path to my left. They both had their heads up and were staring intently behind me. I whirled so fast in my crouch that I temporarily lost my balance. I placed both hands on the ground for stability. In the even gray of an overcast sky, I watched a nightmare unfold.

Two men stood in the path to the right of me. Both were dressed in camouflage hunting outfits and both had on waist-high waders. One was tall, over six feet, the other was shorter than me, maybe five-one or five-two. Both had on full-head masks of white stretch material which fit snugly to the contours of face and neck, with neat holes for eyes, nose and mouth. The masks disappeared into their long-billed camouflage caps and fitted nicely at the bottom into the buttoned collar of the shirts. I eyed the masks with critical approval. They would be hotter than mine but protected the face and wouldn't snag as easily as my net. I couldn't identify the material. I felt lethargic and calm. I had loads of time to ponder and speculate. They were wearing white cotton work gloves.

The tall one was behind James, holding him under the arms, and was ever so slowly lowering him to the ground. James's Smokey-the-Bear hat was still fastened by the chin strap but was twisted to the right, exposing the left side of his head. I could tell that he was unconscious, probably concussed, could be just hurt — or dead — or dying.

The short man was slightly behind and to the left of James and pointing a gun, held firmly in both hands, directly at me. The vacuum surrounding me burst. I came back to real time and noise and confusion. I reached quickly for the snap on my shoulder holster. The firing range instructor had told me, on my first lesson with the gun, never to draw or aim at a human being unless I was positive I could pull the trigger. Until this moment I had been uncertain. I now knew I was capable.

The tall man reacted explosively, dropping James and lunging for the gunman's arms. He yelled at me.

"For God's sake, Jo Beth, don't shoot! Don't shoot!"

4

"AS NAKED AS A JAY BIRD"
September 18, Friday, 5 P.M.

Gun out, I flicked off the safety, my finger on the trigger, and with arms fully extended, I assumed the two-handed firing position. There was a clear field of fire for both of them but I was going for the armed one; he had priority. The tall man's words finally penetrated my brain.

"Dear sweet Jesus," I whispered. I eased the pressure slowly from my finger. I had begun the sequence to fire. I recognized the voice. I should have, since he had been a constant companion since the third grade at Elliston Grade School — my friend, confidant, and co-conspirator in a thousand pranks, the brother I never had. We loved each other on a par with our parents and over God, without a smidgen of lust.

"Leroy?" I said in confusion, my hands trembling. My knees felt like mush and I had a sudden need to urinate. He grabbed the gun from the short man and stuck it in his belt. He pulled off his cap and stripped off the bug mask. I suddenly recognized the material. Lycra-Spandex, used in lightweight girdles. Jackie had done a neat job of sewing them. She had stitched them down the sides to be form-fitting; probably used the button-hole attachment to edge around the eyes, nose and mouth. She made all her own clothes and all the outfits for their three daughters.

There he was in all his red-haired glory. Six feet, four inches tall, two hundred forty pounds and I had almost shot him.

"Leroy!" I screamed. "Are you out of your mind? Are you insane? I almost killed you!"

He was trying to calm me. He held out a hand.

"It's over, Jo Beth. It's OK, Jo Beth. Relax, babe, it's all right now. Just put up the gun, honey. Put the gun back in the holster, Jo Beth."

I felt anger roll through me like shock waves.

"I don't need the damn gun," I yelled. "I'm gonna kill you with my bare hands!"

He reached for me and I waved the gun under his nose.

"Did you know I almost killed both of you?" I was panting with rage.

He took the gun from me gently and put it in my holster while he patted my back, trying to soothe my jangled nerves.

"What have you done?" I cried. "What are you doing out here?"

I suddenly remembered James who hadn't even crossed my mind until this moment.

"Oh my God!" I yelled. "Did you kill him? Is he dead?"

"Quit yelling," he said calmly, "or they'll be able to hear you back at the landing. He's all right, I just put him out for a while."

"You idiot!" I hollered. "He's a game warden, an officer of the law! You assaulted a badge, you dum-dum!"

"Calm down, Jo Beth. You're still in shock. Just take some deep breaths." He unhooked a canteen from my belt and held it while I tried to drink. I spilled more than I drank but it helped to ease my dry throat.

"Maybe we should tie him up," the short man suggested. "He's not gonna stay out forever."

I whirled to face him. "You shut your face. You're nothing to me. I don't know you and I don't want to know you. Just keep the mask on and shut up!"

I turned to Leroy. "Just keep it simple and brief, buddy," I said with despair. Explain what's going on and don't take all day."

"He's my sister's boy. His name is John and he's my distributor in Tampa."

"Hush, Leroy," I wailed. "I'm already aiding and abetting. Now you're making me an accessory before or after the fact, I'm not sure which. I've got to think. What is it, moonshine or marijuana?"

"'Shine," he said flatly. "Do you think I'd grow pot with June in the second grade already?"

"Why?" I asked. "You'll find another job. You and Jackie are doing OK. Why didn't you tell me you needed money?"

"You know me, Jo Beth. Eleven years at the mill and they laid me off. I don't have insurance on the girls and Jo Anne needs that surgery on her foot. She has to have the operation before she turns two; it's easier on the bones."

"Listen, Leroy, the doctors will do the surgery up in Augusta for free. I went with Jackie when she checked into it at the county building."

"I don't take charity," he said flatly. "Never have, never will."

I shook my head and sighed. A sweet redneck, the best of the breed.

He served in the National Guard, had spent almost six months in Desert Storm, lost time from his daughter's lives without a murmur, but wouldn't take free surgery from the government. I had to get him out of this; there had to be a way. I had a sudden thought. My mouth went dry and I felt like I had just swallowed cotton balls.

"Oh my Lord," I said softly.

"What's the matter?" he said, looking concerned.

I raised my eyes to my friend's face.

"What did you do with the fishermen, Leroy?" I asked, dreading the answer.

"Oh," he said with relief, "I was afraid you'd hit a snag in your thinking. They're fine. They stumbled into us yesterday; said they thought they were on solid land here, got turned around and thought they could walk back to camp after they gave out of gas for the outboard. They sure were glad to see us. We gave them water and food, took all their clothes, and put them in our little still house, back up the path a ways. We made two trips with the jugs yesterday and started moving the still today. Knew we had to get out of here after they had seen our camp and still. We got the last load on our boat now. Knew there would be a hue and cry and people would be searching. We promised we'd call and tell the authorities where they were, tonight. They spent a night out here before they found us so they know not to leave the cabin with no clothes or shoes. Had no idea it would be you searching. Think you can get me and John clear of this?"

That's my Leroy. All through school, until we graduated from high school, I was the brain and he was the brawn. He intimidated my enemies and I sweet-talked and finagled him out of jams with relatives, friends and school officials. To be honest, I was usually the reason he was in hot water, but he never complained. He knew I would bail him out. I grabbed his hand and pulled him several feet down the path, out of earshot of his cousin.

"Can you trust him, Leroy?" I whispered. "Will he keep his mouth shut forever, or will he have a few too many six months from now and brag how you two banged a badge on the head and tied him up?"

"He's family," he said with certainty. "He knows if he talks, he'll mess us both up and the family would throw him out. He knows the rules."

"Leroy, I don't want to go to prison for this. My dogs would be orphans and my business would go down the drain."

"You can depend on both of us," he promised.

"Have you got a pocket knife on you?" I asked. "I'm not talking pig-sticker here, just an ordinary pocket knife?"

"Nope, but John's got one. He uses it to clean his nails," he said rolling his eyes and smiling.

"Dumb redneck," I said fondly. "You guys think you should pick your teeth and shave with a six-inch hunting knife." He laughed.

As we took the few steps back, he asked what my plan was. I explained that he would put John's knife in a pocket of my suit and tie us both up. He should put us both together, so James could reach the knife after I suddenly remembered I had one.

"Since James hasn't seen either one of you, I'll give a different description from what the fishermen say, so they won't think highly of any of our information. The only helpful information is your difference in height, but I'll play that down. I'll tell them that you told me where the fishermen were and that you promised to call in our location as soon as you could reach a phone." He agreed that it should work.

I glanced at both of them. "If James is seriously hurt or the fishermen don't make it out without being harmed, all bets are off. Agreed?" They both nodded acceptance.

I pulled out the dog's plastic water dishes. John grabbed them and ran to the nearest standing water to fill them. I gave the dogs some pieces of deer jerky and they drank some of their water. They were under shade if the sun came back out.

John gave the dogs a critical glance. "Laziest dogs I ever seen. Didn't turn a hair when Leroy cold-cocked the man or when you were screeching and jumping up and down."

I glared at him. "My dogs are professionals. Their job is scent tracking. They are neither attack dogs nor guard dogs. You could have shot them and they would lick your hand. They are the gentlest of all breeds. Of course, if you had shot them you'd now be dead meat." I couldn't tell whether he smiled or grimaced. It was hard to read any expression behind the mask he wore.

They tied me up and I made them put the gloves and bug net on James and straighten his hat. They assured me he was breathing OK. Leroy leaned over and gave me a hug.

"Everything will work out. Thanks, Jo Beth."

I felt tears blur my eyes. Their shapes were indistinct as they moved off down the path.

I sat tied to the tree and listened to James's breathing. My hands were tied in front and I could see my watch. It was almost five, and first dark came a little before eight. I had promised Leroy one hour I really couldn't afford, but we'd just have to take the chance. I waited for my audience to wake up. I refused to think about little busted blood vessels that could be leaking inside James's head. I concentrated on thoughts of a deep, warm tub of bubble bath, a very cold beer and one cigarette after another until I was sated with nicotine.

Less than two minutes passed before James started stirring. He grunted. I waited until he opened his eyes.

"Are you all right?" I asked.

"No, I'm not all right, my head hurts," he grumbled. "Who hit me?"

"A moonshiner," I said sadly. "I was getting some rubber gloves and a net for you and didn't see them in time. I was so scared and then so worried about you." Damn, this sounded like pure corn. I hoped I sounded better to him than I sounded to me.

He peered at the net with his peripheral vision and snorted.

"I see you have me decked out in the latest fashion." He glanced at the gloves. "When do I operate?" he asked sardonically.

"I was only trying to keep you from being carted off by insects and wedged in a tree where they could eat you at their leisure," I hissed through my teeth.

"Well, time is money," he said with a not-so-pleasant smile. "Do you have a knife in your pocket?"

"Hmmm," I replied, stalling for time. This guy was not following my script.

"Knife?" he repeated, with impatience.

"I'm thinking, I'm thinking," I said. So much for the hour I had promised Leroy.

"Oh, for Christ's sake, Jo Beth," he muttered. "Sarah Bernhardt you're not. Leroy has had plenty of time for his getaway. I'm not going to chase after him, it's not necessary. I know how to find him."

"Oh shit," I said wearily. "How much did you hear?"

"All of it," he said grinning like the cat that ate the canary. "Leroy is just too nice a guy, he doesn't hit hard enough. I was bleary going down but when he dropped me the last two feet, it cleared my sinuses right quick."

"You cheater!" I yelled. "You laid there and played 'possum!"

He gave me a nasty grin. "Jo Beth, you have a nerve accusing me of being a cheater. You were lying to me ever since you thought I woke up from my nap. Anyway, you were yelling so loud, you like to have busted my eardrums. I almost put my hands over my ears, once."

"I was yelling," I yelled, "because I almost shot a total stranger and my best friend in the whole world because I thought he might have killed you!"

"Stop yelling," he commanded. "I have a headache, remember?"

I had inched over out of his reach. I had much more latitude with my bonds than Leroy had given him. I could reach into my pocket easily for the knife; I had already checked. I decided to leave the knife where it was for now. I had to think. All my plans were coming unglued. Leroy, his cousin and I were in a whole heap of trouble.

"James, Leroy is a good man. He has three small children. The youngest is not quite two. She needs surgery on her foot; it was twisted from a breach delivery. She doesn't walk well and wears a brace. I'm her godmother. Her name is Jo Anne and she was named after me — the Jo part anyway. He's a good provider and a loving husband to Jackie. He worked every day at the mill since he graduated from high school. He was laid off in July after working there eleven years. He's not going to make a vocation out of making 'shine; it's not going to be his life's work. He only needs two thousand for the surgery. He can't borrow it without a full-time job and he won't let me borrow it for him. He won't let the state do it; he calls that charity. Do you honestly think the state will miss the tax on that much whiskey? Be reasonable. Who's getting hurt? He's just a down-home redneck and that's exactly what you are. You've both got that stiff-neck pride and some damn code of honor that we females just can't comprehend."

"It's my job, Jo Beth. Having good reasons for breaking the law don't make it right."

"Bullshit," I replied. "Your job is to stop people fire-hunting for deer, catching too many of the same fish and make sure they buy a license each year. What's that got to do with making some moonshine? You gonna get a bonus for calling up old A, T and F and reporting this? Those boys and the DEA laugh at you. They call you wood clerks and ticket checkers. Report getting hit; report there was a still out here. Report you didn't see them, and I'll do the rest. The fishermen will be collaboration. Just don't stress the height. It's the only clue they'd have if you'll just keep quiet about the conversations you overheard, and the names."

"I'm curious about something," he said. "If you and this Leroy were so close, why didn't you marry him instead of that Sidden bastard?"

"Leroy and I were never sweethearts. We were good friends. He's like a brother to me."

"Well, they'll find footprints, fingerprints, or something to tie them to the site. They'll get them sooner or later."

"You want to bet?" I asked. "Let me tell you a story. I walked up on a still in the woods that the ATF boys were getting ready to blow up.

They had found it with a helicopter the day before. They came in with about thirty guys and two cases of dynamite, enough to seriously do some damage to most of Balsa City proper. It took them three hours to wire up some tanks to blow. There were enough beer cans, take-out cartons from Hardee's and empty sugar sacks lying around that it looked like a garbage dump. The moonshiners ran a sloppy operation. Don't you think that somewhere, among all that leftover debris, the moonshiners just might have left a couple of prints? I swear to God, I spotted a receipt for five hundred pounds of sugar lying on the ground in plain sight. Let me tell you the surprise ending. There were no arrests made in the case; I checked. You want me to tell you my theory?"

"I'm sure I'm going to hear it," he said impatiently.

"You betcha," I agreed. "My theory is simple. There are only a few moonshiners left. The older men who made it a living, and a way of life, are dying off in these parts. The younger ones are lazy, or on food stamps and welfare. They don't have to waste their time slogging through bug- and snake-infested areas with hundred-pound sacks of sugar on their backs, only to turn around and hump out all of those five-gallon jugs of white lightning. The cost of sugar has climbed out of sight and the hundred-gallon bottles of propane to cook off the batches aren't getting any cheaper. The profit margin is so small they really have to work to produce it, jug it and line up distribution of those customers who drink it. It costs almost as much now as shelf whisky. Now I'm willing to bet you dollars to donuts that out of every twenty stills in the county, the ATF boys know, personally, at least nineteen operators."

"Why don't they arrest them?" he asked, knowing he was saying what I wanted to hear.

"Because they're saving them for hard times — their hard times. When they need headlines or the budget is coming up in the legislature, you read about arrests. Once in a while they blow up some stills to get more publicity."

"You know, Jo Beth, you're strange," he commented. "How about digging out that knife?"

I hitched up a little straighter until I was sitting up and slipped the knife out of my pocket and kept talking while I pretended to saw away on the nylon rope.

I tried to look reflective. "Then there's the other scenario."

"Which is?" he answered with a grim expression. He was growing weary of me and my suppositions.

"I'd lie, Leroy would lie and so would his cousin. I'd get a lawyer, Leroy would get a lawyer and so would his cousin. You know three lawyers can be three times nastier than just one."

I took a deep breath and plunged right to the point.

"I guess maybe I'd get on television more than you, me being in a unique occupation and all. I guess the more weird and sensational the accusations were, the more they would put me on television. Might just become a celebrity of sorts. Shit, some people will believe almost anything, even hanky panky bedtime tales. Did you know in a poll recently, eight percent of the people interviewed believe that Elvis is still alive?"

"Did S-E-X just rear its ugly head?" he asked in amazement.

"Oh sure," I said, my voice laced with sarcasm. "Your wife would believe you, your children would believe you, all your neighbors, your supervisors, their supervisors, all the viewing public and all the people who read newspapers; they'd believe you too. Get real, James, people love to believe the worst."

"Jo Beth, you're crazy. I'm not believing this conversation. I'm old enough to be your father," he stated quietly.

"My word," I said with arched eyebrows. "You would've had to have conceived me when you were thirteen or so." Christ, this swill was making me feel sleazy but I could bat my eyelashes with the best of them if it would help Leroy.

"I'll turn fifty in December," he said. I could have sworn he sucked in his stomach.

"You don't look a day over forty-two, forty-three, maybe."

His voice was harsh. "Cut the shit. I will not be blackmailed into any deal."

I quit pretending to cut, severed the rope around my wrist and put it and the knife back in my pocket. I untied my feet leisurely, stood up and stretched.

"I bet there's enough daylight left that I could take your boat and run over to Tyler Cove and use the phone real quick to get a message to Leroy. I might even be able to find my way back before first dark, but I wouldn't count on it. There's only your word, James. There will be no clues that Leroy was ever here. Let's picture the future. Maybe you would be believed. Let's see what the results would be, say you win. Leroy goes to prison, I catch hell, lose my three county and two prison contracts, probably have to do five hundred hours of community service. I doubt I would get jail time. Jackie and the girls would have to go on food stamps and welfare. Little Jo Anne would get her operation but Daddy wouldn't be around to comfort her. Is this what you want to see happen?"

"I didn't make this mess," he reasoned. "Now dammit, untie me and let's go get the fishermen and go home. I have a headache. I'm the one who got bashed, remember? Do you go to bat like this for all your friends?"

I looked him in the eye. "I don't have many friends. I can't afford to lose one."

I cut him loose, we both drank some water and I gave him three aspirins from my first-aid kit. While I fed the dogs some deer jerky, I saw James staring at my hands.

"Is that deer jerky?" he asked.

"Yes."

"Had some luck this year?"

I gave him a smile. "Sure did. Get two every year."

"You made sure you mailed in your tags on your kills?"

"Absolutely. Always kill two the first day of hunting season. Just lucky, I guess."

"I'll bet," he answered with a grim expression. "You better never have more on hand at any given time than could be rendered from two bucks. I'll be checking on you. You go on my inspection list this instant. You know I can enter your premises and search your freezer and storage areas without a search warrant?"

I bought the jerky from two guys who hunt and trap for a living over in Mercer. When my supply ran low, they could always deliver, regardless of the season, so I had a tiny suspicion they did a little fire-hunting.

"Of course," I replied casually, "feel free to drop in any time." I would have to remember to check with my guys. Christ, something else to worry about. I now had a deer jerky checker checking on me. I wondered how many pounds of jerky could be rendered from a medium-sized deer, but I sensed that James was not the one to ask.

I thrust the cap under the dogs' noses and gave them the command to seek. They were immediately anxious and straining to go faster. We hadn't been back to trailing ten minutes when Susie and Bo began the age-old ritual, a great chorus of baying — joyous, raucous, and music to my ears.

"What's going on?" James asked with alarm. The sound can be jarring when you aren't used to it.

"Bloodhounds run mute," I explained. I had to yell for him to hear me over the baying. "They only begin baying when they are close to their object of search. Isn't the sound beautiful?"

"Not really," he yelled. When I turned back to him, he gave me a smile. "You really enjoy this, don't you?"

"You bet!" I tossed over my shoulder.

We entered a tiny clearing and the dogs went swiftly to the door of a skimpy enclosed shed and started lunging and scratching against the door. I was afraid the shack wouldn't remain standing from the onslaught and hauled the dogs back. I handed the leads to James, ran around the shed to the rear and found the clothes and shoes Leroy had placed on the ground less than ten feet from the wall.

When I returned to the door of the shack, I found James standing with the door open, blocking my view, cursing furiously and trying to restrain the dogs from entering. I peered around him into the dim interior of the tiny structure and saw the reason for his dismay. The fishermen were naked as jay birds and drunk as skunks. Leroy had failed to mention he had left the nude sportsmen a consolation prize: a gallon of pure moonshine. James put his free hand to his temple and gave me an embarrassed grin as I dumped the clothes on the dirt floor. Modesty was not an issue, so I pushed James outside to give his head a respite from the noise and let the dogs loose to reap their just deserts.

The dogs wanted to touch noses to skin, the final victory, and be petted for their efforts. Who was I to deny them? Besides, there was lots of skin exposed for nosing, some of it limp and dangling. I was hoping the dogs would sober them up a little. The drunks were bone white, but dirty from rolling around on the dirt floor. One thought he was under attack from a pride of lions; the second one screamed from nameless fears. Only the dogs were having fun.

I finally sorted them out and got them dressed. I didn't know who owned what; I just pulled on clothes and buttoned and zipped. Some articles fit and some didn't. I was only interested in getting their dirty hides under wraps. Luckily, they were near the same size and I had a fifty-fifty chance of getting it right. A thankless, dirty job, but somebody had to do it.

Finally we started the trek back to the boat; it was a miserable, aggravating journey. First in line were the dogs, then me pulling my drunk, then James with his drunk. I had finally resorted to enslavement tactics. I fished two spare leads out of my pack and fastened them around the waists of the drunken sailors. I wanted to secure them around their necks but James demurred. The leads made it much easier to get them vertical after they had fallen and couldn't, or wouldn't, get up. Controlling three leads consisting of one drunk and two dogs was not easy. We were not happy campers.

When we reached the launch, I suggested we feed them to the gators and report them lost at sea but James tied them down-wind and facing the water so they could throw up and not fall overboard. On our way back to civilization and its responsibilities, I wistfully remarked that I would sell my soul and first-born son for a cigarette.

"What would you say if I admitted that I totally disregarded your command to lose the cigarettes and had secreted them on board?" he asked.

"You wouldn't kid me, mister?" I said in a pitiful voice. "That would be cruel."

He reached inside the motor-mount housing and produced a pack of Winston Longs and a lighter. We sucked in tar and nicotine in total abandonment.

After an hour of navigating narrow channels with a five-cell flashlight, James estimated we were another hour of travel from the park landing. He tried his radio and raised the dispatcher at the sheriff's department in Herdon County. He reported we had the missing men and requested an ambulance meet us at the landing. After more than twenty-four hours of swilling moonshine, the poor wretches in the rear would be having the mother of all hangovers and possibly a case of alcohol poisoning. He also informed them that we would off-load on the south shore. He was a nice man, regardless of his decision on Leroy — and my fate. He hadn't asked about the south shoreline and I didn't volunteer any explanation.

Just a few minutes before our arrival at the dock, James motioned me closer.

"Guess we had better consult on those two moonshiners' descriptions," he remarked in an off-hand manner.

I slid closer and waited.

"Both were about five-nine or five-ten," he said.

"Average," I agreed.

"They weighed about one sixty to one seventy-five."

"Average," I murmured.

"They were white and spoke with Southern accents."

"Rednecks," I acknowledged.

"Keep it simple and don't deviate or embellish," he lectured.

"Average, average and rednecks," I recapped.

"Tell Leroy to clean up his act."

"I will, James," I told him as I gave him a hug. "Thank you. You're doing the right thing."

"No, I'm not," he said with a sad air about him, "but I'd feel like a shit if I did anything else."

We chugged up the narrow channel and I went back to untie our refugees from hell. Just as we approached the shore I gave both dogs a jerky treat. I was surprised Susie took one. It looked like she was hold-ing it in her teeth until she reached solid ground, but I couldn't be sure. I now had their attention. I knew they were staring at my hands but to onlookers they looked alert for a command.

I was sitting between the men and had each hand firmly clutching the waistband at the back of their pants. If one of these suckers fell overboard, he was on his own. I wouldn't jump into this black water at night if a dozen cameras were rolling.

Willing hands reached out to steady the boat. I clapped my hands and made a tossing motion to shore. Both dogs sailed blithely over the seats to dry land. Good dogs.

I maneuvered where I could whisper in the first ambulance attendant's ear with my back to the cameras.

"They've soaked in shine for over twenty-four hours, prepare for upheavals."

"Shit," he muttered, "I just cleaned the fuckin' floor."

James and I did fifteen minutes of stand-up interviews with the two reporters from different stations, then switched and repeated almost the same words to the other interviewers.

When we finished with the media, James left to put the boat away and I loaded the dogs. It was nice to shed the suit and feel the compara-tively cooler evening breeze on my sweat-dampened skin.

In the past eight months, James and I have met on three different occasions. We're not bosom buddies. We are wary of and hesitant about each other. It's like we're in a small leaky boat with only one bailing bucket. We cooperate because we know if one rocks the boat, we'll both sink without a trace.

5

"ANYONE CAN SING THE BLUES"
April 5, Monday, 11 A.M.

I donned my pack, pulled on my gloves and said to the dogs, "OK, this is where you earn your kibbles and my vittles. Let's do it, all right?" I put them back on Tommy's scent with his jacket and we entered the game trail. Within twenty feet, I was hunching over and then down on my hands and knees. This only lasted a few feet, then I could stand. It seemed cooler in the covered area but dimness gave that illusion, not less heat.

The path went several hundred feet before I was back on my knees again in the dim tunnel effect of thick overhead branches. The ground sloped down to my left. There was higher ground on the right side of the path. I charted it in my mind. Some years ago, a bulldozer had rumbled through here leveling everything in its path to plow a large firebreak or start a backdraft to cut off the flames of a long-ago forest fire. I must be crawling about halfway up on the left slope of the mound. The pushed-up trees had died and new growth had appeared on the slanted artificial hill.

I wondered if Tommy had found this small trail by chance in his headlong flight or whether he had been this way before and was heading to some known destination ahead. The dogs were getting impatient with me. With noses close to the ground, they only needed thirty inches or so for clearance. With my backpack I needed at least forty inches. I could slither on my belly, but only if it was absolutely necessary.

I signaled the dogs with two quick tugs on their leads, which was the command to stop momentarily. This wasn't a regular rest stop. I simply had to give my knees and elbows a short respite. The dogs didn't even sit; they stood poised to return to the pace in the next few seconds. I did a slow mental count to ten, then prepared to rise to all fours, but suddenly stopped, lying there in rigid terror. I tried not to even breathe as I listened to the most deadly sound a person can hear in thick brush.

A healthy set of rattles was sounding off somewhere to my right. The sound continued to build and intensify, a high-pitched sound of horror.

Oh, Jesus. Lying prone with my nose in the dirt, my vulnerable areas were my face and neck; all the rest were supposed to be fang-proof. As soon as my brain digested this thought, both areas felt cold and exposed. Goose bumps ran up and down my arms and legs. I felt a shiver at the base of my spine and the muscle in my right thigh sent a cramping signal that meant I would be visited very soon by Mr. Charlie Horse. The deadly buzz of rattles went on and on. Seconds seemed like hours. The dogs were quiet and still. Good dogs. Their leads were in my right hand. I didn't know what they would do. There was no predicting their reaction to a snake. Each time and each dog is different. Some want to smell and paw a snake. Some will freeze in wall-eyed terror, and others will beat a hasty retreat.

I mentally started to rehearse how I could quickly throw up both arms to protect my face and cover my neck with my gloved hands. My gut urged me to try it and my mind said don't be a fool. Snakes are lightning fast. Also, my movement to those areas might draw the attack right where I didn't want it.

The rattling stopped. Before I could speculate what this meant, I felt a light punch on my back about waist high, followed instantly by a second rap on my right leg in the thigh area. I completely lost all reason, scrambling ahead in the path, bumping into both dogs. The three of us scrabbled along the path. I was making a high-pitched, keening sound and couldn't stop. We traveled this way for several feet before the area opened up and I was able to stand. The dogs were bewildered and con-fused by the noise I was making and tried to huddle close to me, like they were trying to give comfort. I pushed them away.

I was shaking with reaction and so pumped with adrenaline I couldn't stand still. I paced back and forth. I was finally able to stop my screech-ing and commanded the dogs to rest. I tied their leads to a bush and looked for a clear spot to undress. I had to find out if there was a punc-ture in my suit, dreading what I might find. I had been so scared I wouldn't have felt two small punctures. I stripped off my gear. My hands were shaking so badly I dropped the key to my shoe covers twice before I could use it to release the covers. I unzipped and carefully pulled off the suit. Holding it up to the sunlight, I inspected the material for small holes or tears. Nothing. There were two small smears of smoke-colored viscous liquid where I thought the strikes had been made. I shuddered and pulled out my plastic bottle of isopropyl alcohol and some bandage squares and cleaned the suspected area thoroughly.

As I worked on cleaning the suit, I remembered a story my father had told me about a rattlesnake. Two men were traveling down a dirt road and had a blowout. As they knelt in the dirt to change the tire, they heard a rattlesnake in the bushes behind them. They both threw themselves sideways and scurried to safety. The snake missed the men but in striking had embedded one fang in the rubber tire and couldn't get loose. One of the men grabbed the jack handle and killed the snake. The other man changed the tire and they completed their journey. Several hours later, the tire changer suddenly became nauseated and began sweating with chills and fever. His doctor assumed it was a virus. It's hard to treat an unknown illness, so many have the same general symptoms. After several days, the other man in the story visited his friend. When he heard how soon the man had become ill after their trip, he remembered the snakebite in the tire and the man handling it. The doctor examined the man's hand and found a half-inch cut. They theorized that the venom entered the man's bloodstream through the wound in his hand. The doctor gave him antitoxin but it was too late. The man died.

Now, I don't know if this story is true. It's possible, I guess. I have heard many stories from the past that strain one's credibility. The storytellers sometimes go to great lengths to prove, authenticate and be believed. I have my own theory about these little vignettes from the past. As I grew older, and hopefully smarter, I named them "Southern Fables." They are usually told to teach morals, educate or prove a point.

My father was not the only one who told these stories. In discussions with friends, they all agreed they had heard similar stories over and over while they were growing up, from both parents. My friend Susan had another name for these fables: TTEs. She says they are told to Tease, Titillate and Entertain.

I had calmed down. The adrenaline had dissipated in my system. I felt tired and wrung out. The craving for a cigarette almost overwhelmed me. I never carry any on searches. I know I would give in and smoke if they were available, then feel a terrible guilt if the search was delayed or a failure. Depression settled around me like a fog. I needed a chocolate fix. I groped through my pack for my M & Ms. I gave the dogs some deer jerky and realized tears were about to flow. Sad, mad or glad, the end-product for me is tears. Emotional tears for women are normal. I'm a woman who cries; ergo, I'm normal. I chomped on my M & Ms, letting the tears drip off my chin and add their wetness to my sweat-drenched T-shirt.

I redressed and took the dogs into the search routine. Twice more we entered tunnels of dimness where I was on my hands and knees, but we traveled with dispatch and emerged unscathed. We pressed onward in less-matted growth and I saw we were at the apex of the mounded earth. The path appeared to have tricky footing, and it smelled rank from decayed leaves and mud. Before my mind could telegraph caution to my feet, I stepped down awkwardly on my left foot at the same instant that I felt a strong tug on the leads. Overcompensating, trying to keep my balance, my feet flew from beneath me and I went ass-over-teakettle down the short slope.

A cartwheel in my youth had been easy, but with a full pack and twenty additional years, I felt grotesque and breakable. "Oh shit!" I yelled as I came to rest in the mud. My left ankle started to throb before I could get my shoe off. It was a gentle pulsating pain that gave me hope. I worked my pack off from a sitting position and dug out my first-aid kit. I patted my sweaty foot dry with my sock. I wrapped a three-inch ace bandage comfortably snug before I started with the tape. My skin reacts to adhesive tape by raising blisters the size of quarters. Taping an ankle looks so easy when doctors in emergency rooms or pro-trainers on the sidelines of a game do it, but reality, for me, was cumbersome and difficult. I eased the tension by practicing my more colorful cuss words with different cadences and inflections. It seemed to help. I put on fresh socks and stood to test my weight. It was bearable.

I checked the time. It was eleven o'clock. I had been on the trail four hours, and Tommy had been missing a little over seven. I drank water and gathered the leads. This was not one of my best days. In less than a quarter of a mile, I could feel the tension building in my right ankle. I had been walking gingerly, keeping most of my weight off the left foot and coming down harder on my right. My right ankle was warning me that this was not acceptable behavior. The dogs' pace quickened and they strained forward, raising their heads and beginning their triumphant song of success.

My heart lightened and my ankle pain eased. We were near Tommy. I suddenly remembered that I hadn't questioned Tommy's parents on what he thought about dogs. Sometimes my deep love of animals blinds me to the fear other people might have about dogs. Bloodhounds are quite a sight giving chase and in full cry. They are large and very vocal. It could frighten him. I added my voice to the clamor, calling Tommy's name in a loud sing-song cadence, hoping he would be able to hear me and not be alarmed. I eased the pace of the excited dogs with a strong slow pull on the leads, and we navigated two sharp turns in the path and arrived. I saw a small clearing about ten feet square. Along the far edge ran a shallow creek, its water black and barely moving. I saw Tommy.

I pulled back with all my strength on the leads and heard myself yelling, "retreat, retreat," over and over in a hoarse voice loaded with tension. The disappointed dogs wanted a celebration. I tied them to a small pine sapling and studied the terrain. There wasn't any need for haste or sudden movements. There were several thick huckleberry bushes interspersed with holly, some growing over the creek, but most of the growth was very close to Tommy. I had to check the area before I took another step.

I shrugged off my pack and pulled out my snake probe. It is a slender aluminum tube about two feet long. It has three telescoping sections that slide out in graduated widths to make an eight-foot rod. I walked forward slowly with the rod extended. I stuck it between some branches near the base of the growth nearest Tommy. I moved it back and forth to agitate the branches, then reinserted it several times the length and width of the growth, watching carefully for movement. When I was sure the area was safe, I knelt next to Tommy. I hesitated. He was face down about a foot from the water's edge. He had dug several deep grooves with his hands in the soft peat, trying to get free of the horror that had found him. He was cool to the touch. In this heat, rigor mortis wouldn't be a problem yet. He was wearing only skivvies, torn and dirty. His legs had deep scratches, smeared with dried blood and mud, his feet lacerated and swollen. Insects were feeding greedily on all the exposed skin. They angered me, but it would be futile to brush them away now.

I went to my pack and pulled out the plastic body bag. I unzipped it and smoothed it out as I placed it beside his body. Come on, Jo Beth, I said silently, you know what to expect, just do it. Holding him firmly by his left shoulder and hip, I rolled him onto the bag. I sucked in a deep breath and felt my stomach churn. Oh Jesus, what a rotten break for a kid who had already suffered a loss of some mental capabilities at birth. It's moments like these when I suffer serious reservations about a Divine Being that sees even the fallen sparrow. The right side of his face had swollen to the size of a football; it had a deep purple color and there was a small amount of dried blood, caked in a downward slant.

I had no trouble identifying the species of snake that had bitten Tommy. It was a coral snake. Its venom is more powerful than any pit viper. Coral snakes don't strike cleanly with two deep punctures and then withdraw like the diamondback rattler. The coral snake's fangs are short and rigid in the upper jaw. They strike, using a chewing motion, and inflict many pairs of punctures. I could trace the track of punctures down Tommy's cheek. I counted eight different bites, but the snake's venom had not killed Tommy. I knew that when I first saw the body.

Snakes aren't instant killers. I guessed Tommy had died somewhere around nine o'clock. It would have taken him at least that long to travel to this spot. What had killed Tommy was his own fear.

I considered what must have happened. Exhausted, Tommy must have stumbled down to the creek for water and leaned over to drink. The snake was draped around the bush on a limb, taking a sunbath. They mostly feed at night, but with a warm-blooded target so near, the snake struck and hung on to chew and bite again and again. The coral snake's venom is neurotoxic and affects the nervous system. Tommy would have felt a burning pain and the swelling would have begun. Then he would have experienced paralysis, blindness and difficulty in breathing.

When these symptoms hit him, one by one, he went into severe shock and cardiac arrest. His heart stopped, and no one was around to restart it. He could have lived from the snakebite. More people died from bee stings in Texas last year than from snakebites in the entire United States. In fact, out of every two hundred snake bites, one hundred and ninety-nine survive. They may lose an arm or leg or part of a shoulder or hip due to gangrene from infection, but they survive. Tommy's hair was beautiful. Dark, lustrous and curly. I brushed a lock back from his forehead. I cleared the insects away long enough to zip up the bag. I dragged the body several feet to get it out of the sun.

I moved over and sat beside the dogs, hugging them for comfort, and started to play the old game of "if only." If only I had left sooner, but I knew it was immaterial. He had a three-hour head start before I was called. I needed the release of tension that a good two-hankie soaker could bring. I cried, not only for Tommy but for myself. After I composed myself and drank some water, I made the call.

"Rescue One to Base. Rescue One to Base, do you read me? Over." A short wait of thirty seconds or so.

"Base to Rescue One. I read you loud and clear. Over." It was Hank, sounding near enough to touch.

"Rescue One to Base. Do you have projection? Over."

"Base to Rescue One. That is affirmative. Over."

"Rescue One to Base. Call me when projection is clear."

I set the radio beside me. His answer meant the father or both parents were hovering near the radio, within hearing range. Receiving news this bad is terrible anywhere, but being at home, away from strangers, must help a little. It was twenty minutes before Hank called back.

"Base to Rescue One. Projection clear. Over."

"Rescue One to Base. Search subject was DOA. Coral snake bite and heart attack are my guesses. Have Wayne lead two deputies in with a litter. Give Wayne the following message: 'Small, tunneled game trail has disturbed snake. Take all precautions.' Over."

"Base to Rescue One. Message received and understood. Are you all right?"

"Rescue One to Base. The manufacturers are correct. The suit is totally snake-proof. Over."

"Base to Rescue One. That's great. Can you estimate their ETA? Over."

"Rescue One to Base. Approximately four hours. Over."

"Base to Rescue One. Message understood, over and out."

I untied the dogs and led them to the small creek to let them drink and cool off in the water. They waded in and sat in the six- to eight-inch-deep water and drank their fill. I let them soak in the water until I decided they were cooled off, then led them back to the shade. I fed them jerky and they sprawled in the shade to take a nap. I leaned my back against a small pine and took out my washcloth and lunch. I washed my face and hands with water from the canteen, opened a small box of raisins and cored and peeled an apple. I propped my throbbing ankle up on my backpack and relaxed. I just hoped the ankle would hold up long enough to get me out of the swamp. No way would I let two of Dunston County's deputies tote me out of here on a stretcher. I would never hear the last of the jeers and snide remarks. Most of the uniforms were waiting impatiently for me to fall on my ass and I was hoping to make them wait awhile longer. The other solution would be to let Wayne pull me out in my rescue sled, and being the first to be rescued with it didn't appeal to me either. The ankle would have to make it.

They arrived at three-thirty, trimming my estimate by a half-hour, which I allowed to their longer strides. I wasn't about to admit that Wayne was faster than I, even though his dogs, Mark Anthony and Caesar, were very good trackers. It was amazing to watch Wayne's perfect control of his dogs with hand signals and subtle management of the leads. All our trackers and drug dogs were trained to both voice and hand signals. This was to make it possible for Wayne, Rosie or me to handle any dog if necessary.

I admitted only to myself that Wayne was a slightly better tracker than I. I would remember to tell him this when I was old and gray, ready to retire. We had a silent and secretive competition going on between us. I'd tell him how good he was, much later. Wayne's dogs sounded happy to find me as they approached. We always used outsiders as victims in our exercises of scent tracking so the dogs wouldn't rely on their memory of us. I imagine the dogs thought we were playing some sort of fun game. They had never been sent for me before. I signed to Wayne about my ankle and to keep the information to himself. He raised one eyebrow in an eloquent pantomime, trying to hide a smile.

"Damn it," I signed in mock anger. "You know what I mean!" He was asking me, innocently, how a deaf boy could tell them anything, when he knew I wanted to hide my injury because of pride. His hands were so articulate that he could sell the Brooklyn Bridge to a stranger and not use sign language, just basic hand motions. I gave him a solid thump on a bicep. I was telling him not to mess with me, I'd eat him for breakfast.

We made it back in less than two hours because we could take a direct route with the easiest passage. I paid for my pride. The ankle was a hot bed of pain and every step was driving nails in it; but what is there, except for pride? Only one cameraman was on the scene. Someone in the sheriff's office tips them off for a gift now and then, but I don't know who, probably the sheriff. I sneaked past them while they were getting the standard shot of the deputies loading the body into the ambulance. I told Wayne to keep them away from me. I wanted badly to creep by Tommy's parents, but I knocked softly at the door where they were mourning their only son. I went inside and tried to ease their pain a little with some half-truths. I collected the dogs at the back porch and returned to the van and headed for home.

Wayne had beaten me home and was waiting in the courtyard. He signed he would put up the dogs and clean the van. I accepted his offer gratefully. My ankle had stiffened up on the drive home and was giving me fits. Rosie, Wayne's mother, met me at the office door. She's short, barely five feet, plump, and she loves to mother me. She's very good with the dogs, does way too much for what I pay her and bosses me around like I was her child. Her coal-black hair looks suspiciously like an expert dye job and is always elaborately coifed and curled. She's a widow and Wayne is her only child. The three of us manage to do the work of six people and, so far, we seem to thrive from the effort.

She banished me to the bathroom, telling me I stunk. This was true; I could smell myself. She said she was preparing a poultice for my ankle and ignored my groan. She said I had thirty minutes to soak before she brought my supper of beef stew, garlic rolls and peach cobbler. My mouth watered. I stopped in the small hallway to strip and drop everything I took off into the washer. I turned on the four brilliant floodlights, mounted in the four corners of the hallway, and stood between the large mirrors mounted on the east and south walls. It was tick inspection time.

I don't care how careful or bundled up you are, when you enter the woods or swamp, you can come home with ticks. Some are tiny, some the size of peas. They crawl around and find a vein, bury their heads in your hide and start sucking. Their body bladder can fill overnight with your blood and grow to the size of an ugly grape. There are many varieties of ticks in our area, but only one terrifies me: a medium-brown little monster about the size of a head on a straight pin. They have a tiny cluster of red-and-white spots on their backs almost invisible to the naked eye. If one of these little monsters should happen to tap into your bloodstream, mixing its poisonous blood thinner with your blood — so it's easier to drink — and stays at the fountain for over twenty-four hours, you can come down with Rocky Mountain spotted tick fever, and die.

Last year, a friend of mine went berry picking with his wife and son. Three days later, he was running a temperature so high he had to be hospitalized. They ran tests and on the fifth day they found a tick between his toes. On the seventh day they placed him in the operating room under micro-instruments and shaved every inch of his body, looking to see if they might have overlooked a tick. He died on the ninth day. I look very carefully for ticks and try to be very thorough. However, you can still screw up, which I discovered last fall. . . .

I have a school friend who came to see me with her five-year-old son, wanting to buy a bloodhound puppy. Her name is Jessica and she is so damn beautiful that all women hate her on sight. Ever since first grade, Jessica has been a charmer. She has beautiful blonde hair, a perfectly proportioned figure, and she has never gained an unwanted ounce. She also has perfect facial features and never knew what a zit was. She could make you feel ugly and inadequate just standing near you. She glowed with good health and perfect skin. By the sixth grade all us girls were avoiding her like the plague. For whatever the reason, Susan and I could not figure out why, Jessica decided to be our friend. Now Jessica was a nice person, and under all that glamour was a brain. She always made the honor roll. It was simply disgusting.

Susan and I did not scare small children. We had decent features, almost good shapes, a few zits, but adequate complexions, but we couldn't compete with Jessica. We decided to run her off. We played tricks on her. We ignored her. We made fun of her. We worked a campaign that would have destroyed a normal person, but unfortunately for us, Jessica was not normal. Jessica was an angel. She knew all along we were just kidding, and she finally wore us out. We were too tired to dream up new schemes, so we became her friends. We reasoned, too, that she drew boys like a magnet and we would just pick up a few of her choicest discards. Well, all her discards followed her around and tripped over us without noticing we were alive.

Susan and I heaved mutual sighs of relief after graduation when Jessica took off for college and we stayed home. I met Bubba and married him within six weeks. I was trying to get him totally committed before Jessica came home for the Christmas holidays. It took Susan until early in January to get hitched. She had almost three months to snag Harold before Jessica came home for Easter break. Susan and Harold were married one week before Jessica returned. It was a hasty wedding but quite tasteful. I had eloped. At the end of her second year in college Jessica returned for good and announced she was getting married and was having two matrons of honor, me and Susan. We had to go through the seemingly never-ending rituals of the elaborate perfect wedding, and everything was beautiful and perfect except Susan and me. Jessica was the peachiest of the peaches and we began hating her again.

Susan's marriage lasted eighteen months. Harold took off to parts unknown with a high school senior. Mine endured three miserable years. In the aftermath of our failures we both began to toy with the idea that Jessica was to blame. All our misfortunes and mistakes were laid at Jessica's feet. We had the perfect villainess.

When Jessica was pregnant with her first child, she didn't get fat and clumsy. She floated gracefully through the nine months looking radiant. She gave birth to a perfect son and enjoyed a perfect marriage. Now she was pregnant again and looking radiant and beautiful. She wanted to buy her son, Jefferson, a bloodhound puppy. She wanted the boy to have something special, so when his baby sister arrived next month, he wouldn't feel left out. He'd have a puppy to play with while she was nursing the baby. She's a perfect mother, but I guess you had already figured that out.

It was late afternoon in early September and we were having ninety-five degree temperatures with eighty percent humidity. When Jessica called to announce her visit, I raced inside and changed clothes. I put on my best white shorts, indecently short and just tight enough to make me take short breaths to keep from popping the zipper. My new uplift Eighteen-Hour bra put me on the playing field with Dolly Parton. I covered the bra with a gorgeous white thin-knit top from Barnel's that had cost way too much. Thin strapped sandals completed the outfit. I spent all the time I had left putting on my face, very carefully. Casual but chic. I couldn't compete with her beauty but maybe she would be green with envy over my crisp appearance, flat tummy and being unpregnant.

By the time she arrived, I was sweating like a pig. She drove up in her Porsche, got out and ran to hug me. She was radiantly beautiful and looked as cool as a cucumber. A smart maternity outfit flattered the slight roundness of her waistline. I clenched my teeth and smiled.

"Darling!" she cried, "you look wonderful! Isn't this heat vicious?"

"Vicious," I echoed.

We strolled out to the dog pens to inspect the puppies. Jefferson was a perfectly mannered little boy, neat, handsome and quiet. We talked of friends and events that had occurred since we last met. She admired me with her eyes and gave me another compliment.

"You look so fit!" she exclaimed.

I soaked up the flattery like a sponge. This was doing wonders for my ego. To emphasize my next remark I lifted the hem of my blouse, exposed my midriff and patted it affectionately.

"Well, I do get enough exercise."

Jessica and Jefferson were staring at me with large shocked eyes.

"What?" I said with alarm. I froze. What was wrong with me?

It seemed to me that he was staring pointedly at my belly button. I felt in it, and around it trying to make sense of what they were seeing. Jessica was shushing Jefferson and still staring at me. Her gaze seemed to be locked on the vicinity of my left breast. In haste I moved my hand to that area and encountered a grape-sized tick just below my left breast.

"Rosie!" I screamed and whirled and took off to find her. I had forgotten she was out shopping until I reached her staircase. I reversed in midstride.

"Wayne!" I shrieked. For an instant I forgot he couldn't hear. I was losing it fast. By sheer coincidence he appeared in the doorway of the kennel's grooming room. When he looked outside, he saw me and he knew instantly something was wrong. I ran to him screaming and he grabbed me by the shoulders. Thank God he could read lips, I was incapable of signing.

"I have a tick on my belly!"

He hauled me into the workroom, grabbed the tick remover and a swab and calmly signed for me to hold still and lift my blouse. I was bobbing and weaving and blubbering so violently he had to pin me to the wall with his body to remove the tick. When he had it clear, he inspected it carefully and declared it safe. I collapsed, bawling with relief. When I had pulled myself together mentally and physically, I returned to Jessica to explain. She, Jefferson and her Porsche had vanished. I nodded grimly and went inside to call Susan.

"Browse and Bargain," she answered.

"She's done it again," I began.

"Who?" she asked.

"Jessica has done it again," I repeated.

"Oh, I know," she answered quickly. "I saw her in the mall last week. I bet she hasn't gained three pounds. Wonder where she's hiding that kid? There's absolutely not enough space to tuck him under her ribs."

Susan had taken over our conversation and was wandering down her own path of thoughts. She's very good at this.

"It was a big, big tick," I confided.

"What?" she said, momentarily sidetracked.

"The only thing I can figure is that I checked under the right one twice and failed to check the left one at all."

"Are you sober?"

"Jessica found a tick under my left titty!" I yelled.

Susan exploded in laughter. It sounded like she dropped the phone. I sat and waited.

"You want to start all over again, Jo Beth?" Susan managed to say clearly before she started laughing in my ear again. I gently hung up the phone. I forgave her eventually. That's what friends are for. I shook my head. Now that the event is safely buried in the past, Susan calls it "Jessica and the tick fiasco."

I returned to my tick inspection. I brushed my hair harshly with a stiff brush, then used a rat-tailed comb to part it in thin rows so I could inspect the white scalp below. I looked under my neck, arms, back and upper thighs. On the back of my right knee I found a small tick. I shuddered. I hate the little suckers. I used the liquid tick remover my in-house vet, Ramon, mixes for me. It looks and smells like aged horse piss, but works very quickly. This beats burning them off with a cigarette, the favorite local method. If you pull them off, you risk leaving the head embedded, and infection.

I limped to the bathroom and soaked in a full steaming tub generously laced with bubble bath and sipped on a cold dark imported beer Rosie had delivered. A sybaritic ritual absolutely essential to restoring my equilibrium and beauty.

After dressing in cut-off jeans and a T-shirt, I sat at my desk and suffered the required three minutes of burning agony from Rosie's poultice. After this period the nerve endings are severely traumatized and produce only a warm, rosy glow. I inhaled nicotine and chugged beers two and three. Rosie served my supper at my desk, checked windows and doors, set the alarms and departed for home.

I always program my VCR to tape the evening news before I depart on search days. My story was used in the pre-announcements as a teaser. I ate my supper as I sat through the news, sports, weather and five station breaks before my two minutes of tape were shown. After I viewed it I clicked off the set and sat stewing in my own juices of anger and apprehension. That razor-cut, blow-dried, stiff-coifed, deal-welching little prick! He had cut the first part of our conversation down to the bare bones. No view of my door panel, no mention of training and puppies for sale. The reason was clear: he needed more time for the last part of the interview where I hung my ass out to dry by mauling the sheriff on camera.

Channel 3 always had closed captions for the hearing impaired, but this time they had reversed the sequence by having the lady signer translating my signing into voice. My signing to Wayne came across as mean and vicious. They had a shot of the sheriff showing dismay at his gaff, and another as he angrily tried to shove the camera out of his face while attempting to flee.

Oh boy. Not only was I on top of the sheriff's hit list, I knew I had drawn the antagonism of most of the local law-enforcement officials. When they see one of their own taking heat they tend to empathize. Next time it could be one of them. These reflections were made with beers four and five. I turned on the phone message machine to check for calls.

"Jo Beth, this is Jackie. I called to tell you I finished the girls' Easter outfits yesterday. The silk eyelet material you brought over really looks great over the solid colors. I'll bring them by your place before church next Sunday. Oh, Jo Anne's cast came off last week. She goes to therapy every day and the doctor says she'll walk normally soon as the muscles strengthen. Leroy says 'Hi.'"

I stopped the tape and made a notation to buy several rolls of film and three Easter baskets. I didn't know what their budget could handle right now. Leroy still hadn't landed a full-time job; he was doing every odd job he could find. I'd take the pictures and give Jackie copies. Leroy was out of the moonshine business since he had made the money for Jo Anne's surgery, and I didn't want him to even think about going back into it. I sighed. Jackie's resentment of me leaked out just a little in her voice when she mentioned Leroy's message. She knows in her heart that her jealousy is groundless and she works hard to conceal it, but we both know it's there. There is no cure, so we try to ignore it. I added chocolate bunnies to my list. As I wrote the word "bunnies," I remembered an old joke from high school.

A little boy goes into a candy store and tells the proprietor he wants a chocolate boy rabbit. The proprietor chuckles and asks him what's the difference. The little boy holds up his forefinger with his thumb a half inch down the finger to show measurement and answers, "You get this much more chocolate."

I restarted the tape.

"Ms. Sidden, this is Wade Bennett. My father was Carl Bennett, the attorney who handled your father's probated will. I'm an attorney also and have taken over my late father's law practice. In reviewing my father's cases, I find I have some questions about your father's probate. I would like to discuss this with you at your convenience. Please call me so we can set up a meeting. Thank you."

I stopped the tape again. He had questions? I had at least a hundred questions and I was eaten up with resentment and curiosity. I had run into a brick wall when I tried to get answers from his father. I had yelled and threatened; had even hired another attorney, but I was still hanging in limbo. My hired attorney said the will was legal; Carl had executed it legally, the IRS was happy and I should be also. It would be interesting to hear Wade's questions. I made a note to call him in the morning.

My next caller was my best friend, Susan.

"Hey, Jo Beth. Do you know what day this is? Call me when you get in and we'll celebrate. I saw your interview on TV and your hair was terrible! We're gonna have to do something about it and don't be stubborn. Call me and we will plan what to wear. 'Bye."

Susan has a calendar that lists most holidays and all inventors, no matter how obscure. She loves to party and uses these oddities as her excuse to celebrate. Whether it's the date of a fourth-century battle or the birthdate of a man who invented a better trace for a team of oxen, she's ready to rock and roll in their honor. I'd call her last.

I started the tape for the last call.

"Ms. Sidden, this is Caroline Nash. We purchased a puppy about two years ago for my son, Kealon. The dog was run over two weeks ago. Kealon insists he'll never have another dog but I feel his grief has lasted too long and he feels too much guilt for leaving the gate open. He's not eating or sleeping properly and I need your help. If I bring him by tomorrow after school, will you try and talk to him about another dog? If the afternoon is OK, don't bother to call back. Goodbye."

Poor Kealon, I knew exactly what he was feeling. I couldn't remember the sale. I reached over, turned on my computer and punched in the proper data. While I waited I remembered my grief and guilt when I lost Herman T. I was ten and hadn't really forgiven myself until I bought my first pedigreed breeders to start the kennel three years ago. Grief and guilt can last a lifetime. The information appeared on the screen. Kealon had been seven on the date of purchase and he was listed as the owner. He had attended all six free dog-handling classes and had taken our basic obedience course when his puppy was six months old. I remembered him now. A small towhead, quiet and well mannered. I hoped I could help him. No one had seen my need. My mother died the year I lost Herman T. and Dad was too deep in his own grief to notice mine.

The tape ended. I decided to call Susan. Before I dialed, I went to the bathroom and then to the kitchen to fetch beer number six.

"Hello," she purred.

"It's only me," I said. "That was a very sexy 'hello.' I'd rate it at least an eight."

"Practice," she replied. "Listen, let's go out. We need to celebrate your putting your head with your tatty hair right in the gator's jaws. I saw your interview. Are you out of your gourd?"

"I plead temporary insanity. He made me mad."

"Jesus, Jo Beth, your temper has caused all our troubles ever since grade school. You gotta shape up!"

"Susan," I said wearily, "I've had a lousy day. I couldn't save a kid and I twisted my ankle. I was struck by an unidentified snake while I was flat on my belly. The fangs didn't penetrate my suit; no physical damage but a hell of a lot of mental anguish. The sheriff is gunning for me as we speak and I've alienated over half the population of this county. I need sympathy and understanding."

"Where do you get the figure of over half the county?" she asked. "Only twenty-four percent voted in the election three years ago. That means seventy-six percent didn't vote. They couldn't force themselves to pull the handle next to his name and you've got to do that to get your other votes to register because he's unopposed and an incumbent. Stupid system. You should be able to mark a protest vote against him; show him how much he's disliked."

"Thank you, Susan dear, for your astute remarks on our local voting system," I said with a touch of asperity. "I'm gonna hang up now."

"You're not depressed are you?" she asked in surprise.

"Moi?" I said with irony. "Whatever gave you that idea?"

"Jo Beth, pull up your socks, stick out your chest, you're tough! Remember? Want me to come over?"

I remembered how we used to utter that phrase as our cry before going into some childhood battle. I felt a lump in my throat.

"Thanks, friend, but I'm bushed. I'm gonna take the sore ankle to bed. No more crying in my beer. OK?"

"Good night, sleep tight," she sing-songed.

"And don't let the bedbugs bite," I finished and hung up the phone. Might as well cry into one more. I finished beer number seven, hobbled around and rechecked the windows and doors Rosie had checked earlier. I made sure the alarms were activated, started the washer and went to bed.

Sometime later, when the washer had completed its cycle, in the late stillness, I heard the squeak of the cat door. Ruby, knowing the coast was clear, was coming in for a snack. I rolled silently off the bed and walked slowly to the doorway and into the hall. The small glow of the hall nightlight gave enough light to see her as she passed into the kitchen.

Last October we had become aware our rat population was diminishing and occasionally we saw a black wraith of a cat in the edge of our vision. All of us who lived here had been competing ever since to see who would be the first to bestow a pat on her head and give her a back rub, but none of us could get closer than ten or twelve feet. She was beautiful, black with huge green eyes. We put out a food dish and she responded by keeping our mice and wood rats at bay. Ramon wanted to trap her. He knew her ears were packed with mites and he wanted to protect her from all cat diseases, but I refused. Ruby having fleas would be no problem. No flea could survive for more than three days within the compound; the Orkin man made sure of that. The grounds and buildings — inside and outside — were treated, sprayed, and fogged for fleas and ticks. I had the adult dogs out in the brush for training and searches, and so I made very sure my reputation would never be sullied with fleas. I knew she was wild, but she would come around with time and lots of love. Here it was seven months later and all I had accomplished was moving her food dish a foot closer each day until it was in the kitchen. I had to prop the cat door open each night for a week before she would come inside for a bite. It seemed to take forever before she appeared in the faint glow of the nightlight on the way to the kitchen.

"Hello, pretty Ruby," I whispered lightly. Her head swiveled my way and her bright green eyes glowed eerily in the frail light. She froze and stared at me. The refrigerator's motor clicked on and she was history. I shrugged and limped back to bed. It would take her most of the night to get up the nerve to come in again. I finally drifted off to sleep.

6

"FAST AS MOODY'S GOOSE"
April 6, Tuesday, 6 A.M.

I woke up at six o'clock to a twangy beat on the radio alarm. I must have achieved a normal water balance last night because I had been up twice to drain the excess. While brushing my teeth and showering, I mentally constructed a Georgia dream country breakfast: fried smoked country ham, grits, two fresh eggs over easy, two buttermilk biscuits dripping with butter and slathered generously with homemade peach preserves. Then, with a third biscuit halved on the plate, lavishly pour a covering of thick Georgia cane syrup. A cholesterol nightmare and guaranteed to send calorie counters screaming into the bush.

This extravaganza is served in farmhouses, small diners (aptly called "greasy spoons"), and truck stops throughout Georgia. Also, you'll find it on the menus of the most exclusive restaurants in Atlanta and its rich suburbs. I have consumed more of these meals than I care to count. Now that I'm approaching thirty with the speed of a runaway train, I try to curb my appetite so I settled this morning for cornflakes, sliced banana, toast and coffee. After washing the dishes and folding the clean clothes from the dryer, I went to the office and turned on the coffeemaker. I was dressed in jeans and a long-sleeved work shirt. When I work with six-month-old puppies I keep my arms and legs covered. At this age they are very exuberant and all they want to do is play. Their nails can scratch and in this heat the scratches can easily turn septic. I neglected a scratch when I first opened the kennel and had gotten a stubborn infection that took two weeks to cure.

It was after six-thirty. Wayne came over every morning, except Sunday, at seven and we had coffee while discussing the day's work schedule. There was almost thirty minutes to spare, so I picked up my household clipboard. I absolutely loathe housework. I like to live in a clean, neat house, but hate the daily effort it takes to keep it that way. I have learned, after years of frantic cleaning sprees and then ignoring everything for two weeks, that this method doesn't cut it. I have finally developed a system that works.

You can spend a surprisingly small amount of time on the repetitive, boring jobs, as long as you do it every day without fail and pick up after yourself as you go along. Sometimes I have to change clothes several times a day. When the clothes come off they go directly into the washer. Every night, the last thing I do is start the washing machine. Half load or full, they are done each night. The next morning they go into the dryer while I bathe and dress and then I fold them after breakfast. I used to let the clothes pile up and have to spend hours washing load after load, sorting and folding. Very boring. Now it's five minutes or so and I'm up to date.

My house has an office, living room, master bedroom, guest bedroom, kitchen and bathroom. I work six days a week and plan nothing for Sunday; that's my day to do entirely what I want, when I want. Early morning searches can temporarily mess up the schedule of cleaning a room a day, but I catch up the next two days. Today was the guest bedroom's turn so I picked up the cleaning caddy from the hall closet and rolled the vacuum into the spare room.

The cleaning caddy contains window washing spray, handi-towels, an air freshener and clean ashtrays. The room has two windows which are washed on the inside whether anyone has used the room or not. Wayne does the outside windows once a month. The bed is always made since sometimes Susan stays over if we're out late. I polished the headboard, night stand and dresser, quickly cleaned the dresser, mirror and door mirror then ran the drape attachment over the drapes. Nothing was in the small trash basket. Then the room was vacuumed, working back toward the door, where I paused to inspect. Clean and dust-free. I sprayed air freshener, then looked at my watch. Twenty-five minutes, but of course this room is the easiest in the house.

I put away the cleaning caddy and vacuum. The most important thing about the schedule was I didn't stay with one chore until I was ready to scream. I used to vacuum once a week but, oh, how I dreaded that day. I only vacuumed one small room today; ten minutes is not too bad. Wayne knocked on the office door and entered as I poured coffee. He handed over his clipboard and I glanced at what his schedule would be. There were three random inspections scheduled, one being this afternoon at a large paper mill.

We furnish to firms the service of random inspections for pot and crack. What saddens me is that we have three grade schools, a middle school and the high school, which are never searched on the same day.

Sometimes we go back the next day. We have found pot on almost every search and crack several times a month. Seated at my desk with Wayne across from me in one of the customer chairs, I signed to him.

"Be careful at the mill. The men are angry and grumbling to their union. Look up and behind you at least every thirty seconds. These guys are tough and play rough."

He grinned and signed. "Sure chief. How's the ankle?"

"Great, I can hardly feel a twinge. Your mother's incendiary device burned all feeling from the nerve ends."

"Mom is taking Samson and Delilah to the warehouse over on Long Run Street where they've set up an exercise for her. I think the fire chief has his eye on her. They spent thirty minutes on the phone last night, and her side of the conversation seemed to be just giggles."

"Jealous?"

"Nah, I hope she finds someone. I've been wondering how she will make out if and when I find someone."

"Whoever she is, she'd better like bloodhounds, be willing to live in a house on the grounds here, and want at least four children." He held up four fingers and arched his eyebrows.

"Two for me and two for Rosie. After that, it's your choice."

"Thanks a lot."

"Do you think your mom's interest started in January in Atlanta when she went up there for the arson seminar? Has she said anything at all? Dropped any hints?"

He smiled. "Nothing, not a clue. The calls started soon after, but I thought it was business, not monkey business."

He cawed at his own joke. Wayne can make a few sounds. His laughter sounds like a crow call and grunt combined. I understand most of his moods now. Most people, when they first meet him, think he's surly and withdrawn, which he's not. He hates some of the reactions he receives from people. He learned early in life that people who are different are treated differently.

"Who are you taking today?"

"O'Henry."

"Do you think he's ready?"

"He hasn't had an episode in weeks. Doc thinks he is. I'm taking Chaucer along as backup just in case. Keep your fingers crossed."

I signed good luck and he waved as he left.

O'Henry is our canine patriarch in residence. He was three years old when I purchased him three years ago to start my own breeding dynasty. He cost so much I lost a lot of sleep over whether to buy him or pass. I bought and after the third successful litter of bright, healthy, well-colored and excellently boned puppies, I drew my first sigh of relief. I knew I couldn't risk such a valuable asset in swamp and bush, so we trained him on illegal drugs. He was great. I learned as he learned. I kept adding a different drug every three months. I took the risk of confusing him and weakening his abilities but he took to each new challenge like a duck to water.

About six months ago, we were working with the Balsa City Police. They had an officer working undercover in the pool halls within the city. He had made drug buys in all three establishments, and the police coordinated surprise raids to occur at ten o'clock on Friday night, the peak business hour on payday. Three poolrooms sounds excessive for our small town, but these good ol' boys sure love to play pool.

I had Chaucer, Wayne had O'Henry, and Rosie was handling Sinclair. Each of us had four officers with us and a standby unit ready to assist if needed. Wayne had just entered his poolroom and was letting O'Henry set the pace. From the crowd standing along the wall a piece of hot dog rolled across the floor within O'Henry's reach. Being a bloodhound, he snapped up the treat without hesitation. It happened so fast there was nothing Wayne could do.

Wayne reacted immediately and pulled O'Henry out of the poolroom. With hand gestures he convinced two officers to give him a high-speed siren and light trip back to Ramon, our vet. He also made them understand to have their dispatcher call ahead and alert Ramon. I found this out much later.

Entering my pool hall, I saw a man leaning over the nearest table with his back to the door. He didn't see me, Chaucer or the officers who followed us inside. The room slowly lost people-movement and all conversation except the shooter eyeing his shot, oblivious to his audience. The first inkling he had that things were not as they should be was the feeling of something moving up his leg and gently nuzzling the bulge at his crotch. He whirled and raised the cue stick as I yelled harshly: "If you touch him you die!"

The officer on my right held his hand out for the stick and the man gave it to him. The officer on my left said, "Drop your trousers, buddy." The man look horrified.

"Not in front of the lady!" he protested.

"Sorry," I said softly, "but I have to testify in court where the drugs were found. I promise I'll only inspect the drugs."

This comment drew a few ragged laughs and the tension in the room seemed to ease a bit. He unzipped hurriedly, reached in and produced a small bundle wrapped in a handkerchief.

"Thanks," I said with a smile. I turned my back when an officer moved closer to make sure there wasn't more stashed down there.

"I'd feel better if you let the little lady do the patting," he said, playing to the audience. We all laughed.

No one moved as Chaucer sniffed his way down between the tables. He stopped after passing several people and placed a big paw on a man's cowboy boot. The man was a boy really, he looked all of sixteen. Chaucer gazed up at him with his large limpid eyes and his deep facial wrinkles with a questioning look. Without thinking, the kid leaned over and gave him a pat.

"Good dog," he said. This cracked us all up and the room was filled with nervous laughter.

Chaucer twice more found drugs and both times the patrons clapped and whistled. The officers had been leading the prisoners out one by one in relays. Chaucer was enjoying the attention and would stop if someone wanted to give him a pat. When we were ready to leave, I stopped him six feet from the doorway and turned him around to face the room. Every eye in the place was watching us intently. I was going to thank them and wave but I had the urge to leave them laughing. I just hoped Chaucer would cooperate.

I gave him the command, "Retreat!" Chaucer and I backed up the six feet and out the door with perfect timing to loud applause and cat-calls.

"We're both show-offs," I told him softly while I was loading him into the van. I gave him all the deer jerky I had.

When I entered the police station to start the arrest reports, Rosie was seated at a desk already filling out her paperwork. She and Sinclair had made three finds. We exchanged stories. I glanced around.

"Heard how Wayne is doing?" I asked her.

"Not a thing. He's at that big place across from the mill," she replied. The desk sergeant walked by.

"Have you heard anything on the raid still going on?" I asked him. He glanced up, mumbled something and walked away.

"What?" I said. He kept on walking. I caught up with him and stopped in front of him, forcing him to stop.

"What?" I repeated testily.

"I need those reports right away. The sooner you finish them, the sooner you can go check," he said.

"Check what?" I asked with dread.

He hesitated. "Seems they had to take the dog to the vet, he was sick or something. How soon before you finish the reports?"

"Rosie!" I yelled. She rushed over and I grabbed her arm to tell her I would meet her at Ramon's; it was O'Henry, not Wayne, we were worrying about as we hurried to the exit.

"Aren't you going to finish these reports?" he yelled.

"Stick'em where the sun don't shine," I tossed over my shoulder as Rosie and I cleared the door.

All the way to Ramon's I was praying it wasn't serious. While I had been clowning around with my rednecks, O'Henry could be dying. Rosie and I arrived within seconds of each other. We found Ramon and Wayne having coffee in Ramon's office. He described giving O'Henry a stomach lave and taking a specimen to examine in his lab. He said O'Henry was in a cage in the treatment room and we would just have to wait to see what he had ingested, but his guess was some type of LSD.

We didn't have long to wait. Ramon had left for the lab when we heard the cage holding O'Henry rattling and bumping in the treatment room. We ran in and gawked. O'Henry was bucking in the cage like a bull at a rodeo. Each lunge was so violent that the heavy cage was being moved several inches across the floor.

Before Ramon and Wayne could subdue O'Henry, he turned and bit his flank, sinking his large teeth into his own flesh. We all scrambled to help restrain him while Ramon ran for his tranquilizer dart gun. When O'Henry finally went limp, we lifted him onto the operating table. Wayne and I wrapped padding around the leather restraining straps while Ramon held O'Henry's head and monitored his pulse.

Ramon explained he couldn't keep tranquilizing O'Henry because the shock might stop his heart, and he couldn't muzzle him because of the danger of his swallowing his tongue. Ramon rigged a padded neck brace so he couldn't reach his shoulder. Wayne sat with him the first night and I relieved him the next morning. The second night O'Henry had a very bad trip. He bayed and howled with such power and terror that none of us, humans or dogs, could sleep. After the third day the episodes passed and faded into mild twitches and nervous movements from time to time. In the past two months he had seemed healthy and free from tremors.

A week after O'Henry was drugged, I woke up to the fact that he was heavily insured. In my concern for his condition it hadn't registered that maybe I should call my insurance agent and report what had happened. He in turn notified his home office. Ramon was unable to tell if O'Henry would be able to recover his former abilities in drug searches or if he could successfully sire healthy offspring.

Several days later I received a snotty letter from the insurance company telling me I was up the creek without a paddle. I had no claim if O'Henry was permanently damaged and they were canceling his policy forthwith. It was sprinkled with whereins and therefores in heavy legalese. It was crammed with accusations of misrepresentation when I purchased the original policy. Simply stated, they told me to go suck eggs.

The company contends that I insured O'Henry as a proved breeder and he had bred successfully. In making him a drug sniffer, thus delivering him defenseless to his enemies, I had caused his possible malfunctions. I had placed him in harm's way as surely as sending him out to play in heavy traffic. Maybe they had a point, but I didn't see them returning any part of the pricey premiums I had shelled out for three years.

I dislike insurance companies even though they are a necessary evil. They float benignly along, accepting every payment and cashing your checks promptly, but raise the question about a possible claim and they lace on the gloves and come out swinging. I retaliated by removing six other policies that were currently in their care and placing them with a rival firm. I was also cynical enough to realize I could be bedding down in a den of even thicker thieves.

My problem was too much heart and not enough cold, calculating business acumen to see the dogs as assets and liabilities. I see them as warm, breathing, beautiful creatures who are part of my life; they are my extended family. I see the kennel many years in the future overrun with faulty breeders, old-age pensioners, the lame and unproductive. I envision myself old, toothless and decrepit, pushing a shopping cart from dumpster to dumpster, scavenging for food to feed them.

Rosie knocked and entered. I tried to hide my dismay at her appearance. She was wearing stretch pants in an impossible shade of purple with an orange and green blouse that not only clashed with the pants, but clanged and hissed. She was wearing jogging shoes with shocking pink socks. She could make your eyes water from twenty paces.

"Don't you look nice!" I said brightly. I'm not about to rain on her parade.

"Thanks," she beamed. "Got'em over in Ashhurst when I went to visit Aggie last week. Like the color?"

"Wow!" I said truthfully.

"How's the ankle?"

"Great," I said. I lifted my leg and flexed my foot as proof. "Hardly feel a twinge."

"I'm worried about Wayne," she said bluntly.

"Oh?" Rosie seldom confides. She wants to be seen as an authoritative figure and omniscient.

"It's that O'Henry. Wayne's been fretting and fussing about him for weeks. He don't listen to me. I tell him, he will or he won't. Worrying about it ain't gonna solve a thing, and it sure weren't his fault." I hurried to agree.

"Gotta hurry," she said. "Gotta make hay while the sun shines! I'll show those firefighters a trick or two of my own. I may not be back for dinner. May eat out!"

And may your fire chief invite you to dinner and also recommend our services to the mayor and members of the city council, amen.

Quarter till eight. Central air set at seventy-five degrees already humming away briskly. Should I catch up on yesterday's housework or obedience-train the three pups I was working with to get a short jump on the six-month age ban? I decided to clean the office first. This was yesterday's chore I had missed with the early morning call-out. I listened to the silence, then heard birds in the surrounding trees. There was no wind, so their morning calls were clear. I heard an occasional deep-throated bay. Next, a smaller voice which wasn't yet developed. A brave puppy testing his newly found ability to imitate his elders. I gazed over my favorite room in the house, a large rectangle, twenty by forty feet.

My desk sits away from the wall forming a triangle with the outside north and inside east wall. To my left the east wall is broken by a door into the kitchen and the doorway into the living room. On the south wall is the doorway to the hall leading to the bedrooms and bath. Thirty feet of built-in bookcases line the south wall. The west wall has a large sliding glass door which opens onto the back porch, courtyard, and kennel. To the right of my desk is the north outside wall with two large picture windows. From the nearest window I can see the long, curving driveway that comes from the east, and where it intersects the courtyard fence and turns left into the parking area.

Everyone comes to the rear of the house since there isn't a driveway to the front door. It is absolutely imperative that I have a fortified compound with solid protection. The fence was the most expensive single expenditure in my budget when construction was started. Fifteen acres surrounded by an eight-foot chain-link fence with the three-strand barbed wire strip at the top, slanted outward. After the alarm system was wired into the top the total bill was astronomical, but the dogs, Wayne, Rosie and I had total security. There are two gates: the main gate leading from the highway and the inside courtyard gate.

Wayne locks the gates at night and unlocks them each morning since we have customers and deliveries during the day. Anything weighing more than thirty pounds entering the front gate sets off a large bing-bong-sounding alarm in the house and kennel. Anything crossing the inside courtyard gate sets off the alarm with sounds like a huge buzzer. That means we have time to check the identity of anyone crossing the front gate and coming up the drive. There is a clear view from every room in the house except the bathroom. The carpenters solved that problem in a unique manner.

The carpenters, two brothers, cut a three-foot square above the toilet and installed a solid glass terrarium that extends into space for three feet. Most people put glass shelves in and hooks for small plants giving them exposure to the sun. This one has nothing in it. On the east side on both sides of the glass they rigged a rubber truck windshield wiper which can be moved back and forth by hand to clear condensation and frost in the winter. If I need to view the driveway from my bathroom, I step up on the toilet seat and bend out on the glass-enclosed ledge. When Susan complains about there being no plants and having increased my heating and cooling costs for nothing, I don't explain. I don't want her or anyone else to think me obsessive and living in fear. It's just a matter of living with prudence and doing whatever possible to make the house safe.

I will never, ever be assaulted by Bubba again. I will not let him force me to kill him. The murder of a human being may be the final solution to the problem, but every other option will be exercised before that happens. The legal answer, so far, is the stalking law some states now have, but it's only a small step over a wide chasm.

As it stands now, the legal system tries to guarantee everyone's rights. It can't, however, lock a man up indefinitely on a woman's word that she is worried about being killed. The man has to kill her before she can prove her case. What an option! So, doing everything possible, I stay in the cave, keep the night fire burning, huddle back in the shadows and keep a big club handy for the final solution. Shaking off the morbid thoughts, I cleaned the office very thoroughly and went to the kennel to train puppies.

When I came in a little after one, neither Wayne nor Rosie had returned. I was hot and sweaty. Having exuberant, large-boned puppies climbing, licking and drooling all over me had added a doggy aroma. I stripped and dropped the clothes in the washer. I padded, bare-assed and barefooted, into the office to check the blinking answering machine.

There was only one hang-up, but it made icy fingers drift down my spine. There hadn't been a hang-up last night, but it was the only night without one in the past two weeks. During the past three years with the kennel, I've averaged about two a week, though seldom at night. Lately I was averaging two a day, the second one usually coming around midnight.

With Bubba free less than a month, reasonable doubts were fading fast. So be it. I will not let this affect my happiness. I will take note and be extra careful, but will not get upset, amen.

The phone rang, making me jump straight up with shock. Angry at myself for being spooked so easily, I let the recorded message play without picking up the receiver. After the beep, Wade Bennett's voice announced himself, so I picked up quickly.

"Mr. Bennett, this is Jo Beth Sidden. I received your message last night and was just getting ready to call you. I've been out all morning."

"I don't mean to be persistent; it's just I'm absolutely and positively bored to distraction. I've read all of Father's files, cleaned the office and worked two crossword puzzles this morning. The local population is not exactly beating a path to my door. You're my only excuse to feel busy."

"Do you have a secretary yet? The reason I'm asking is do you have to stay there or can you leave?"

"I had a temp, but sent her home at lunchtime. Two of us sitting here waiting for the phone to ring seemed excessive."

"Then you can . . . WOW!" I had plopped down in the desk chair. The air-conditioned leather seat on my sweaty bottom felt like sitting in ice water.

"What happened?"

I laughed. "I just received a small shock."

"Electric?" he sounded concerned.

"Nope," I chuckled. "A very cold leather seat."

He thought about it. "Shorts?"

"I'm in the state my mother would have called 'the all-together.'"

"Ah," he said slowly. "What did you start to ask me before? You said, 'then you can . . .'"

"Counselor," I said with admiration, "I'm proud of you. I've just thrown out a provocative and thoughtless statement to a complete stranger, enabling anyone to conjure up a lewd mental picture, and you didn't take advantage of it. I humbly apologize."

"I fought the urge and won," he answered proudly, "but have to admit to having some prior warning."

I thought about it. "Notes your father made in mine or my father's file?"

"Right."

"Care to enlighten me on those particular notes?"

"Wild horses and water torture couldn't drag it out of me," he boasted.

"It just so happens I'm free this afternoon, so far," I hedged. "There could be a call-out, but rarely in the afternoon. Would you like to come over?"

"Yes. When?"

"Give me thirty minutes or so. Anytime after that."

"I'll be there in thirty-two minutes," he promised.

I hadn't been entirely honest with him. The chair had been a shock, but I wouldn't have made such a tasteless remark without a reason. I was running a Jo Beth test to see if he was safe enough to entertain here alone. Rosie and Wayne could be out all afternoon; the house is off the beaten path or yelling-for-help range. Safety first.

After a fast shower I dressed with care in a sundress with a full skirt thick enough I didn't have to wear a slip. It was the color of cool mint, with tiny ruffles at the breast, leaving my shoulders bare except for thin spaghetti straps. White sandals and small white earrings finished the look. My, my, I was acting like a teenager even though we had met years ago. Memory told me approximately what he would look like now, but he didn't remember me, I was sure.

In the kitchen I made a pitcher of iced tea and placed a sliced lemon, mint sprigs, sugar bowl, spoons and linen napkins on a tray. My cigarettes and lighter were in the pocket of my sundress. A hunk of Polish sausage in the fridge tempted me so I took it out and started taking big bites. I was starved, not having had lunch, and I didn't want my stomach growling while we were talking.

Taking the tray to the back porch, I turned the overhead paddle fans to low speed. Two huge sycamore trees kept the back porch protected from the sun; with the fans making a breeze it would be comfortable enough, even with eighty-one degrees displayed on the porch thermometer. Seeing the pink and red flowers on the seat cushions, I untied the strings and flipped them over to the yellow and green side, which would look better with my dress color. La de dah.

The first gate alarm sounded, so I popped the last bite of sausage into my mouth and ran through to the kitchen to watch the car approach along the driveway. When I was sure the person inside wasn't Bubba, I lit a cigarette and walked to the back porch. Wade drove slowly into the courtyard seemingly uncertain where to stop the car. I stepped down and waited at the base of the steps. As he pulled closer, got out of the car and came toward me, I took a few steps in his direction. It's not being impatient, it's Southern etiquette to greet your guests without requiring them to knock on the door or ring the bell. The edge of the porch, the top of the steps, or a few steps in his direction was proper. He held out his hand and smiled.

"Hello, I'm glad to meet you. I'm Wade Bennett."

7

"GOOD MEMORIES FADE,
BAD MEMORIES STICK IN YOUR CRAW"
April 6, Tuesday, 1:30 P.M.

"I'm Jo Beth," I replied as we shook hands.

"After reading my father's files, I feel I already know you."

"We have met before. Please call me Jo Beth."

"I'm sorry, you have to be mistaken. I'm sure I would never forget you." His clasp was firm and his voice was very pleasant.

I laughed. "How gallant. Come, let's sit on the porch and talk."

When we reached the chairs, I asked him if he would like a glass of iced tea.

"Yes, thank you," he said as he settled into the chair, making himself comfortable. He tasted the tea, spooned in sugar and stirred the contents. I compared this grown-up person with the boy I once knew. His face had matured and was much fuller. I knew he would be tall; he looked six feet or more, and he carried himself with style and had an easy graceful walk. He was tanned — not the nut brown of golf or tennis, although he looked the athletic type. Brown eyes and hair, the hair about the same shade as mine.

He relaxed in the chair. His suit was expensive and tailored, a medium gray; white shirt, dark blue tie with a small red and white stripe in an angled slash. Dull calfskin, black tasseled loafers. I imagined he had paid more for his tie than I had for my spiffy little sundress. He looked warm; the suit fabric looked too heavy for this climate, but any suit fabric looked too heavy for this climate.

"Wade, why don't you pull off your coat, shed the tie and roll up your sleeves. Get comfortable."

"Thanks," he said, then stood and removed the coat and tie. "I haven't gotten used to the humidity. Is it proper to mention perspiration in mixed company?"

"Down here," I said, "it's called sweat and it flows freely from March to November. It's discussed and cussed more than baseball and football combined."

He laughed. "My God, it's hot. The humidity almost changed my mind about staying. I don't remember it being so hot here when I was growing up."

"The young don't feel it as much as we do. Everyone swears it's getting hotter every year, but in the last fifty years, average, we're only up point two something degrees."

"Is that a daily or monthly figure?" he quipped.

I grinned. "Why did you decide to stay, Wade?" I said, "if I may be so bold as to ask."

"I went through a divorce this past year. It wasn't a bad one, but I don't think any divorce can be considered a good one."

"Hear, hear," I said, raising my glass in agreement.

"I thought: a new job, new surroundings and a new beginning. What do you think?"

"It all depends on whether you're running to or from."

He laughed. "The only person I could conceivably be running from is my mother, in Chicago, whom I love dearly, but I think the thousand miles between us is the perfect distance."

I smiled as I added tea to both our glasses, mentally noting that I would have to get more ice soon.

"Now, tell me when we met," he said.

"It was a hot summer day, July, I think. It was on the corner of Chestnut and Center streets, downtown. I was wearing cutoffs and a halter top, and my hair was a mess."

"I still would have remembered," he said stoutly. "I'm embarrassed. My mind is a complete blank. Are you sure it was me?"

"Absolutely. I can't believe you've forgotten." I tried to sound wistful, enjoying this.

He looked worried as he stared intently at me, and I could see he was frantically thumbing through his memory of semiannual visits here to see his father for the past few years. He found nothing, of course.

"Can you give me more details, a clue? I'm floored. I'm very good at remembering names and faces. I shouldn't have told you that; it makes my forgetting sound even worse."

I decided to let him off the hook, but it still disappointed me that he couldn't recall what had meant so much to me at the time.

"I was six and you were about fourteen, so this was before you moved away," I said quietly. Sensing my disappointment, he shook his head slowly.

"I'm sorry," he said. "Tell me what happened."

"Cement and gravel trucks from Concord Cement Company used to pull out on Center Street, most of them turning left on Chestnut Street. The gravel trucks always spilled some gravel in the intersection as they were making their turns. The road was paved, but it always had a coat of loose gravel; do you remember?"

"Vaguely," he said. "I mean, I remember the road but not our meeting."

"I came flying downhill on my bike. I liked to get going real fast and coast through the gravel. It made a delicious bumpy ride. I played a game of chicken with the gravel and cement trucks. I had the right-of-way; 'course I was supposed to be riding on the sidewalk, not the road, but the sidewalk was for sissies; I always used the road. The day of our meeting, I encountered a driver whose mind was elsewhere, or he didn't care if he smeared a kid into the pavement. He pulled out right in front of me as I was sailing the bike through the gravel. I stood on the brakes but lost control and the story almost ended right there. I slid on the gravel, tangled in my bike, and ended up about a foot from the truck wheels when the driver had completed his turn. He didn't stop or even slow down."

"Bastard," Wade muttered, then made a motion with his hand. "Sorry."

"No, you're right," I agreed. "Either he was a careless bastard or a sadistic bastard, but he was truly a bastard. I was scraped raw from hairline to toes. I had slid on my stomach, putting out my hands to break the fall, so my hands were a mess when I finally came to a stop. The bike was totaled, but I just knew it could be fixed. Both wheels were badly bent and it wouldn't roll at all. The only way I could get it home was to drag it, but it wouldn't slide easily. I could only drag it a short distance, then stop and whimper and sniffle a lot from the pain."

"And?" he prodded.

"And, that's when you came riding down the street on your bike. A friend was riding with you. You both rode past me, then you turned around and rode back. Your friend came back with you. You asked me what my name was and where I lived. I told you between sniffles. You asked your friend to ride his bike to my house and tow yours by the handlebars and leave it in the yard; you would join him later. You got me up, then my bike onto the sidewalk and pulled out a big white handkerchief from your pocket. I remember thinking that you were the first rich person I had ever met. None of the other boys I knew ever carried handkerchiefs. You wiped the grime, tears and blood off my face. My right knee had a deep cut; it was leaking a trail of blood down my leg, so you folded the handkerchief and tied it around my knee. Then you picked up the bike with your right hand and held my wrist in your left. My palms were bloodied, so I couldn't hold your hand. You walked me home. It was fifteen blocks and nine of them were uphill. You were my hero. I made Mother let me put your handkerchief in to soak to take out the blood stains before I would let her clean me up. Does anything ring a bell?"

"No," he groaned. "God, I feel like such a jerk, but I simply don't remember any of this." He shook his head and gave me an apologetic smile. "Did I tell you my name?"

"Oh no," I replied. "I didn't know who you were, then. I was too upset and forgot to ask you. I had to wait until September when school opened and hang around the junior high school after classes until I spotted you and could ask someone who you were. It took me over a week because I didn't know you went directly to football practice after school. I was waiting by the school bus lanes."

He held up both hands. "You'll have to stop. You make me want to cry for that little girl. It sounds as though it meant a lot to you."

"I hung around the practice field and went to all your eighth- and ninth-grade home games. I was in love with my hero. When your mother and father divorced and she took you away at the end of your ninth-grade term, I cried myself to sleep every night for weeks."

"No more," he pleaded. I continued; I was on a roll.

"You were my knight in shining armor."

"Stop!" He was excited. "You just rang a bell!" He laughed a deep coughing bray of relief. He closed his eyes in concentration, then opened them and smiled.

"You asked me if I was a boy scout. I told you no. You then asked me if I rode a white horse. I remember thinking that this kid may have a concussion. I stopped walking and felt your head for bumps and asked you if you had hit your head."

"You do remember." I was happy.

"Thank God," he murmured. "I have the feeling you would never forgive me if I hadn't."

"Excuse me a minute," I said rising from the chair.

"Certainly."

I went inside to the desk and picked up the handkerchief I had dug out of Mother's cedar chest after his call today. It was yellowed at the folds and on the top section, but inside it was fairly white. I refolded it, and carrying it concealed in my hand, I returned to the back porch.

Remembering my manners, I said, "The bathroom is through this door and the first door to the right, if you'd like to freshen up."

"Thanks," he said and went inside. When he returned, I handed him the handkerchief. He fingered it, tracing the monogrammed stitches with his finger.

"I remember when Dad gave these to me. It was the Christmas before I met you in July. When I thanked him, he lowered his voice and spoke gruffly. 'You're fourteen now, Wade, almost a man, and it's time you start learning how to act like a man. A man carries a handkerchief at all times.' For a short time in my life, I was sure that carrying a handkerchief was the mark of a man and guaranteed virility."

"And did it?" I asked.

"Not at that time," he said with a smile. He reached over to give it back to me.

"It's yours. It just took me twenty-three years to return it."

"I'd rather you hold on to it," he said. "I'd like you to hold on to it for another twenty-three years. It will help me through my old age to know I was a hero at least once."

"Consider it done."

"I remember something else," he said slowly. "Your house . . . It wasn't what one would expect."

"A shack? A hovel? A dump?" I questioned. "It was all of those. It was a miserable one-room hut right on the main drag. We had no electricity or running water. I hated it. Sometimes tourists stopped and took photographs. I felt like I was in a zoo. My mother washed clothes by hand in a five-gallon bucket using water from the service station next door, and she cooked on an old-fashioned gas range. When she died, I took over. The only difference was, I had to use a smaller bucket; couldn't handle the five-gallon size."

"But your father was famous! I read about his paintings in a Boston paper years ago. They had an exhibit of his landscapes in an art gallery there."

"Oh yes," I said softly, "but that was much later. He was discovered late in his life. When I was growing up, we were dirt poor. We didn't have two nickels to rub together. All my father painted were landscapes of Cumberland Island. He sold his pictures to tourists, five dollars for the small ones and ten dollars for the big ones. He was always able to buy canvases and oils. I never understood where he got it, but when he needed painting supplies, he always came up with the money. Sometimes a painting wouldn't sell for weeks, but he managed somehow to scrape up money. He was a very fast painter. He was also prolific, prodigious and a genius. I admired him and loved him. I think he loved me, although he never seemed to show it much. He painted almost constantly. I once saw him paint three landscapes in one day; his compulsion to put paint to canvas worked overtime. . . . You know the irony?"

He had been listening intently. "What?"

"I think of all those tourists, the ones who bought a picture for five or ten bucks — travelers from Ohio, Illinois, New York and Canada. They own an Arthur Stonley landscape and don't know it. It's hanging in a spare bedroom or stacked in the attic, or it's been sold at a garage sale or thrown out as junk. They stopped on the way to Florida and saw dozens of landscapes for sale propped on the porch of a shanty in south Georgia. They made a fantastic investment and didn't know it, still don't. The last painting that changed hands before Dad died last year was auctioned at Sotheby's for one hundred and twenty-nine thousand dollars. After he died his paintings almost doubled in value overnight. Two years ago they were selling for twenty-five to fifty thousand on the average. Go figure.

"I have four of his paintings and they're not for sale at any price. They were presents from him on my fifteenth birthday; he saw how much I loved them."

"Have you had them appraised since your father's death?"

"No. That's Sinclair's idea."

Sinclair Adams is a tax attorney with an office next door to Carl Bennett's, also now Wade's. He had handled my money decisions and taxes since I was twenty-one. I had the feeling Sinclair and Wade had discussed the paintings.

Wade was looking out toward the kennel. He changed the subject.

"You have a lovely place here. It's very quiet. I expected more noise from a thriving business in animals."

"It's siesta time, too hot for much activity. They'll get active about sundown . . . and they get very vocal at feeding time."

Wade motioned toward the office where a muted ringing could be heard.

"I think your phone is ringing."

"I have the answering machine on."

"Is the blinking light connected to the phone?"

"Yes. Wayne, my assistant, is hearing-impaired."

"How did you meet him?"

"When I opened the kennel, I had six months on my own before I hired Carson and Jane Lummings, a middle-aged couple with no children, who answered the ad in the paper. They seemed perfect; both anxious, and assuring me they could handle the job. I sensed their need and didn't check their references too closely.

"The first six months were fine, then small things started to go wrong. Carson seemed absent-minded and forgot a lot of chores. I had to start watching him more closely because special feedings were forgotten or mixed incorrectly. He had an argument with a potential customer who then decided not to buy.

"To make a long story short, I called some friends who knew the family. They came from Gilsford County and their last address was in Edna. You may not remember Edna; the population is around seven hundred, and it's about twenty miles from Collins, the county seat. I found out what was wrong. Carson was an alcoholic. When I knew what to look for, I was surprised I hadn't spotted it sooner. When I confronted him with my suspicions, he denied it. He became more surly and started sleeping later in the mornings.

"I felt sorry for Jane. She tried to do her work and his too. It all came to a screeching halt one afternoon when I came around a corner of the kennel and saw him kick a dog. I told him to pack up and get out, he was fired. It turned out that Carson had been knocking around in this world a lot longer than I had and he had been an employee-tenant before. He knew the law and I didn't. It took me four months and over five hundred dollars in legal fees to remove him. You can fire a person immediately, but the mill of eviction grinds mighty damn slow. But, your being an attorney, I don't have to explain the legal points, do I?"

"Hey," he said mildly, "I'm not the enemy. I'm the first to admit that the appropriate statutes on evictions are supposed to protect both the lessor and the lessee, but it sometimes works a hardship on the landlord."

"Ain't that the gospel truth," I said with irony.

"I saw the notation in Dad's files. I'm really sorry you had so much trouble over it, but Dad did handle the situation correctly."

"Maybe," I granted. "But I was tired, overworked and annoyed, and your father kept patting me on the back and being so condescending about the whole mess, I was almost ready to punch him out. 'My goodness, little lady,'" I mimicked, "'now don't you worry your purty little head about anything. Leave the worrying to your elders.'"

"I'm the first to admit that Dad was old-fashioned and a bit of a sexist bigot. Will that admission appease your indignation or are we having our first fight?"

"Sorry," I said, shaking my head, "it's not your fault."

"It seems I've inherited some resentment in regard to my father's treatment of you, so even though it's not my fault, it is my business, so let's get everything out in the open and discuss our options. You, as the injured party, have the choice of weapons. What will it be? Sabers at sunrise?" He gave me a quirky, lopsided grin.

"Oh, Christ," I said with a grimace. "You'll have me reluctant to bring up the subject that we both know we're avoiding, the will."

"Yes," he said simply, "the will. I have my father's notes and all the pertinent legal documents, and to be perfectly honest, I don't understand it, so I can certainly appreciate the fact that you were in the dark and demanded answers. Did my father ever explain?"

"Not on your chinny, chin, chin," I said with a hoarse cackle. "Would you care for some more iced tea?" I saw his incomprehension of my answer and gave him a translation.

"It means absolutely, unequivocally no, nada, not even a hint. It's an old Southern expression lifted from an ancient bedtime story for the kiddies."

"Sometimes of late" — he was amused — "I feel like I crossed a border without a tourist guidebook. Do they print one for the Southern language?"

You did cross a border, sir, the Mason-Dixon. You can't learn Southern from books, you have to be tutored by a true Son of the South or a Daughter of the Confederacy."

"My," he said. "You sound like a true patriot."

"My country, right or wrong," I agreed, "but if you had called me that in 1981, you would have gotten a different answer."

"What happened in 1981?" he asked.

"My God, and to think you were born in Georgia! In 1977, we sent one of our best sons up to Washington. The most humane, honest and truly dedicated man who ever took the oath of office. The thirty-ninth President of the United States, James Earl Carter."

"And . . . ," he prompted.

"They humiliated him in a thousand ways. The money changers, the carpetbaggers, all those lily-livered Republican crooks, insiders and permanent Washington parasites. But most of all, I blame the media. It was the rawest, most flagrant and most inexcusable abuse of media power I've ever seen. They spent ninety-eight percent of their coverage jeering at his honest and truthful answers about his Christianity and lifestyle, his desire to make a difference, his dedication to strive for world peace. He talked funny, had a big-toothed smile and some wacky family members, so they gleefully dedicated themselves to seeing how cruel and mocking they could be, at his expense. Most of the nation's sheep who

jumped on the media's bandwagon and laughed at all their brutal casti-
gation wanted a two-bit actor who memorized what was put in front of
him and practiced in front of a mirror. It's my opinion they got what
they deserved. I'm just ashamed that Georgia stood still for it. If we
didn't have the guts to declare war over his mistreatment, we could
have at least seceded from the Union!"

"Wow," he exclaimed. "The lady does have strong views."

"I'll climb down from my soapbox now; it's ancient history, but an
old wound that will never heal. Enough said. Let's change the subject to
you. Where did you move when your mother took you away at fifteen?"

"Boston. She missed her relatives and family connections; she was
never happy here. I'm surprised she stuck it out for fifteen years. She
always thought Georgia was like the Australian Outback — too far from
civilization, no theaters or art museums."

"She thought we didn't have museums?" I asked with amazement.
"Didn't she know about 'Rigby's Alligator and Crocodile Museum and
Souvenirs' out on Highway 301? And theaters? How about 'Pittman's
Theatre in the Round: Twelve Gorgeous Nudes in the Flesh Nightly,'
on Old Rountree Road?"

He laughed. "I doubt she ever heard of them."

"Good," I said with a smile. "Local sleaze, but the gators aren't bad.
Where did you go to school?"

"Groton, then Harvard Law School."

"I'm impressed. Even down here in the outback we've heard of
Groton and Harvard Law."

"My mother is a Wainwright," he said with mock disdain. "All sons
of Wainwrights go to Groton and Harvard Law. It's one of the 'Boston
Commandments.'"

"I just might retain you as my legal eagle," I said. "I'm a sucker for
name droppers. What happened next?"

"I passed the bar exam and joined the staff of the district attorney's
office. I've always wanted to be a trial lawyer, not shuffle bonds and
corporate debentures."

"Oh my goodness," I said with a wry smile, "I bet your mother was
very unhappy."

"Practically catatonic at first, but she finally came around when her
friends suggested that it was good experience for going into politics.
She was agreeable, for a while, with my decision."

He looked at me and I motioned for him to continue.

"Next, I met the girl I soon married. She wanted prestige and money,
so I resigned from the district attorney's office and joined a law firm

employing about two hundred associates and occupying six floors of a downtown high-rise. I hated it; I felt like I was working in a huge beehive. I haven't been in a courtroom since I resigned as ADA, over two years ago."

"How many years did you spend in the DA's office?"

"Seven."

"Have you considered going back into prosecution instead of defense? I'm sure Bobby Don Robbins could use some experienced help, even with his excellent new assistant from New Jersey. When Bobby Don tries cases, he loses more than he wins."

"Not really. It's time I moved on. I want to try to defend cases for a change."

"Well, give the locals a little time. They knew your father, so you have half the battle won; you'll just have to act like a real Southerner. Make them forget you've been living up north."

"How should I act . . . to be considered a real Southerner?"

"First, don't forget 'You all.' It's slurred together and comes out sounding like 'Yawl,' the word for a small sailboat. Next, always say 'Yes ma'am' and 'No sir' to everyone, regardless of their age. Walk out to meet your clients, never sit behind a desk and make them come to you. It makes them think they are important to you. Also, walk them out and prolong the goodbyes, even if you're very busy. We rednecks have a lot of pride; we like to think we're special and want to be treated special."

He nodded and motioned for me to continue.

"If they want to talk, let them talk. Don't sound curt and business-like; act interested and even be nosy about their affairs. The dullest subject in the world is someone else's aches and pains; any woman who's had one thinks her gall bladder surgery was unique and a medical miracle. She may go on and on until your eyes glaze over, but it pays off. This same woman will gush to all her friends and relations what a good lawyer you are, even if all you did was show her where to pay her fine for a parking violation. Considering this lady has about twenty-five blood relations living within a stone's throw and knows everyone in town on a first-name basis, it's very good advertising. Word-of-mouth will make or break you."

"Do you mind if I take notes?" he asked with a smile.

I laughed and stood. I reached for the tea pitcher. I needed more tea and ice.

"I'll be right —" the harsh bing-bong on the first driveway alarm reverberated through the outdoor amplifiers, causing my heart to drop into my gut and me to lose all coordination. I dropped the pitcher and it shattered as it hit the twelve-inch floorboards of the porch.

"Shit," I gasped, as I whirled to run inside.

"What is it?" asked Wade in alarm.

"Stay here and stay put. Don't move around!" I ordered shortly as I took off through the office doorway heading for the kitchen window. As soon as I reached it, I could see the light green shape of my van. When I could tell it was Wayne driving, I sagged against the counter with relief. I hadn't been paying attention and the alarm had scared the hell out of me.

Remembering Wade, I grabbed a dish towel, dampened it under the faucet and grabbed the broom and dustpan from the pantry. The strident buzzer of the courtyard gate sounded as I reached the porch. Wade was standing stiffly where I had left him. Good man. Now I had to snow him and calm him down.

"I'm so clumsy," I said in an aggravated tone. "Did any tea get on your pants? Here's a damp towel, just pat any spots. You didn't move and step in any glass, did you? Stand still while I sweep up the glass. Wouldn't you know the pitcher is the next-to-last piece of Mama's family crystal. All I have left now is a goblet." I stooped to sweep the glass into the dustpan. Wayne drove into the courtyard and continued down the drive to the kennel, giving a brief wave as he passed.

"That's Wayne," I said as I stood. "As soon as he finishes unloading, he'll come over and I'll introduce you."

Wade waited until I returned from putting the glass into the trash. "What's going on, Jo Beth?" he questioned.

"What do you mean?" I said, as though I didn't have any idea what he was talking about.

"Don't give me that wide-eyed look!" he said harshly. "I saw your face. You were terrified."

"Nonsense," I said brightly. "I was aggravated about breaking Mama's pitcher."

"Bullshit," he said with a snort. "You were so scared, it scared me. Why didn't you want me to move around? Were you afraid I'd get caught in a crossfire?"

"Crossfire?" I was wondering how much his father had written about me in his damn files.

"Dammit, Jo Beth! I've read Dad's files and I've pumped Sinclair about you. Our offices are right next door to each other, you know."

"Sinclair has a big mouth," I said.

"He cares about you. Here, not ten minutes ago, you told me to be nosy about my clients' affairs. You are going to be a client, aren't you?"

"I haven't decided as yet," I answered primly. I glanced at him and saw his jaw tighten.

"Look, Wade," I said in a reasonable tone, "you seem to be a very nice man and I appreciate your taking the time to drop by and chat with me. I'm sure you're a very competent attorney, but I don't know you well enough to make you a confidant of all my girlish secrets."

He gave me a tight smile. Leaning back in his chair, he raised his right leg, placed it on his left and relaxed.

"I've just realized why my father, on more than one occasion, had to resist the urge to put you across his knee and deliver a few whacks on your derriere. Not only am I a capable attorney, my father was a capable attorney, regardless of the inexplicable will he executed for your father. I'm sure if we pool our information we can find a reasonable explanation and a solution."

He saw I was going to interrupt and held up a hand.

"My father had the transcript of your ex-husband's trial in your file, which I have read from cover to cover. Your ex-husband's sentence was duly noted. It doesn't take a Clarence Darrow to ascertain you're living with a siege mentality; ergo, your ex-husband must have been granted early release. One minute you're friendly and the next you're barely civil and shutting me out. I'm trying to help. Why won't you let me?"

"Help?" I choked out in anger. "You want to help? Just who in the hell do you think you are? I don't have a phone booth and I doubt if you own tights and a cape. Judas Priest and Christ on a crutch," I yelled. "Bubba would eat you for breakfast, tailored pants and all! Don't you think if I wanted a male standing out in front to fend off his first few blows, I couldn't have found one in the past eight years? I'm not exactly dog meat, you know!" I made an effort to calm down and speak more softly. He started to answer and I held up both hands to silence him.

"Wade, you think like a man. Anyone I could have stood having near me would think like a man. Bubba thinks like a wild animal, and acts like one. It was hard for me to believe the happy-go-lucky, slightly dumb, young redneck I married eleven years ago has turned into such a monster. He has assaulted several local males who are meaner than average. All of them refused to bring charges; they are terrified of him. I have enough to worry about keeping my own hide intact without having to worry about anyone else getting hurt because of me. Thanks for the offer, but no thanks."

"Are you finished?" he asked politely.

"For now," I said.

"Good. Now listen for a change. You're an intelligent woman who's had to face a challenge for several years, and from what I can see and understand, you have done a very good job of it, alone. In doing so, I believe you have systematically fended off all friends and associates who might have been in a position to offer advice, encouragement or active assistance. I believe you needed this incentive to make you feel more in control, for your ego and self-esteem. I understand you might have needed that feeling in the past, but enough is enough. Eight years have proved your worth, encouraged your ego and built your self-esteem. It's time to share with others what you have been carrying alone. You need close friends and advisors. I'm applying for the position. I accept the possible dangers as well as the possible rewards."

"Rewards?" I questioned with a knowing look.

"You surely are suspicious." He said with a grin. "I meant that I might find someone who would defend, advise and befriend me."

"You can have that, free from obligations," I offered.

"So can you," he replied firmly.

"I doubt if I can give up any control of my life," I mused. "I've been in charge too long."

"Who's asking for control?" he countered. "Just advice and the comfort of a new friend."

"I haven't made any new friends in a while. It may take some time," I cautioned.

"I'll grow on you," he said with smugness.

I saw Wayne approaching. I was anxious to learn how O'Henry performed. Wade stood. I spoke to Wade and signed to Wayne.

"Wade, I'd like to introduce my friend and associate, Wayne Frazier. Wayne, this is my new friend and attorney, Wade Bennett." Where had that come from? I surprised myself accepting his offer so easily. Could it be that I was mellowing in my old age? Nah. . . .

Wade spoke and signed simultaneously. "Very nice to meet you, Wayne. Jo Beth's been telling me how valuable you are to her. I hope we can be friends." He stuck out his hand.

Wayne and I stared at him in amazement. We couldn't have been more surprised if Wade had stuck out his tongue and tapped out a dance routine with live music coming from the wings. Wade looked as if he'd just swallowed a canary. The show-off was pleased with our reactions. I pulled a chair close for Wayne and he sat down. I signed to Wayne and ignored Wade. Let him follow the signing if he could, and he obviously could. His signing had been fast and accurate. I asked Wayne with my hands how O'Henry had done. Wayne signed that O'Henry had acted like he had never been trained to scent drugs and had never been on a sweep. He had wandered around aimlessly with his head up and hadn't searched for anything. He asked me if I thought he could be retrained. I shrugged and signed, "Who knows? There's nothing in the training manual to go by." Wayne wanted to know if he could try to retrain him on his own time. I told him he could try anytime, but promise not to be disappointed if O'Henry couldn't regain his old skills. He was a little long in the tooth to train again from scratch, and it would be a long, drawn-out process, but if he wanted to try, have at it.

Wayne signed to Wade that he enjoyed meeting him and went inside the office to fill out the invoices for the sweeps and check on messages. At that moment, the first gate's alarm sounded. I forced myself to sit still. Wayne was inside and just as diligent as I was. I would have plenty of warning.

"When and why did you learn signing?" I asked.

"Two years ago, when I joined the beehive. A lady lawyer in the cubicle next to mine was hearing-impaired. We were both dissatisfied with the firm and became friends. We had lunch together every day for six months. She taught me how to sign and I taught her how to gain ten pounds from eating lunch every day instead of attending her aerobics class on her lunch hour. It was worth keeping the surprise. You should have seen your faces."

"Show-off."

"Guilty as charged."

I changed the subject as Rosie drove the van into the courtyard. She stared at the unfamiliar car and at us, forgetting to wave.

"That's Rosie, Wayne's mother. She'll be over shortly when she unloads the dogs."

"You were going to tell me how you found Wayne. We got away from your story."

"Wayne was due to graduate from the school for the deaf over in Davis, in Herdon County, in May of last year. One of his instructors knew he was interested in animals; he was thinking about becoming a vet. She saw my ad in the paper and called me. I had been limping along for over six months with day help, after finally evicting the Lummings. I was going to make sure when someone else moved in, I would be making the right choice.

"I drove down there the next day and met with Wayne and an interpreter. He talked to his mother and she was willing to move in and give it a try. She was working as a waitress. She is a widow and Wayne is her only chick. I arranged for temporary help to stay here while I took a crash course in signing. The rest is history. I was very, very lucky; they are both worth their weight in gold."

"He's a handsome dude," Wade remarked.

"He will make someone a good husband one of these days. I only hope she will be good enough for him."

"Do you give him enough time off for dating?"

"Christ," I said laughing. "He comes and goes as he pleases. You sound like you think I chain him to the bedpost every night."

"No such notion at all," he assured me. "What if she drags him away from here?"

"Over my dead body."

"Ah ha," he said with a nod. He had gotten the reaction he was striving for; he now knew I was possessive of Wayne.

"Go fly a kite," I told him. He laughed.

"Tell me about your father," he suggested.

"What do you want to know?" I asked.

"Anything and everything," he said. "We've got to figure out why the unusual will and why my father permitted it."

"Well, for starters, my father didn't see me, speak to me, or communicate with me in any way, for seven years before his death."

8

"SHARP AS A TACK"
April 6, Tuesday, 4 P.M.

"You're kidding!" he said with surprise.

"Nope. I graduated from high school, started dating Bubba and wanted to get married right away. My father absolutely forbade it and tried to break us up. Naturally I was stubborn, so we eloped to Alabama. Three days later I returned home to Daddy, expecting him to forgive and forget his anger and dislike of Bubba. It didn't happen. He was beside himself with rage."

"I guess we've found the reason for the unusual will already," he said. "He was using the will to punish you for going against his wishes."

"I don't think so," I said slowly. "I believe it went back to my childhood somehow, even before Mother died. I can't explain it. I haven't a clue why, but at times there was a faint sense of unease in my family. I pride myself in reading people's faces and figuring out what they are thinking. Your father never said a word, but when I came up with the thought that Dad's reason for the unusual will lay in the very distant past, it seemed to me your father was mentally nodding his head in agreement."

The front gate alarm sounded again, loud and harsh in our ears. I jumped, but forced myself to sit still. Wayne was still inside. He would look and be as efficient as always. Wade watched me try to act unconcerned.

"Why don't you go check?" he suggested. I jumped up and almost thanked him before I caught myself. I'd have to watch this guy; he was slick. He had me following orders before the ink was dry on our friendship pact. I met Wayne in the office and he signed that it was a blue station wagon with a woman and small child. Damn, twice today I had let my blood pressure soar for nothing. I wasn't paying attention to business. It was obviously Caroline Nash and her son Kealon. I glanced at my watch. School had been out for thirty minutes.

I quickly outlined the strategy for handling Kealon and told Wayne to loosen the catch on the small gate at the east side of the drive, telling him I would try to delay them. He hurried out and rejoined Wade as the station wagon pulled slowly into the courtyard.

"Wade, would you help me pull off a small con? Turn your charm on for the lady; I need five minutes at the car before we enter the kennel area."

He gestured for me to go first. "Lead on, Macduff."

We strolled slowly out to the station wagon. Caroline Nash was out of her front seat, holding her door open, and saying something to Kealon. She straightened when we walked up. She looked frustrated. I introduced Wade to her. He went right to work.

"Howdy, ma'am," he said pumping her hand and hanging on far too long. "I'm sure glad to make your acquaintance, I surely am. You're just as purty as a speckled pup."

God, he was confusing Western with Southern, the big ham, but it seemed to be working. She was gazing up at him like a mongoose at a cobra. He was charming the pants off her. When there was a brief pause in the conversation, I jumped in quickly.

"You two chat for a minute while I talk to Kealon," I told them. She looked startled, as if she had forgotten I was there. I went around the wagon to Kealon's window.

"Hi, Kealon. Do you remember me?" He looked at me and slowly nodded yes.

"I was sorry to hear about Buster. You must really miss him." He looked at me and blinked about three times but didn't speak.

"Do you really miss him very much?" I asked again. I needed a response to see which way the wind was blowing. He waited awhile and he nodded yes again. He looked small for his age, mostly arms, legs and big eyes. God, was I ever this young? I felt like I was trudging uphill.

"Kealon, your mom brought you here because I need to ask you for a big favor."

His eyes met mine. "I don't want another dog," he said clearly.

"I know, Kealon." I said in agreement. "I can understand how you feel. I was ten years old when I lost my dog. His name was Herman T. I knew I would never want another dog as long as I lived."

Kealon focused his gaze on my face. He had been staring out through the windshield.

"You have dogs now," he said. It was close to an accusation. I was not only trudging up the hill, I was wearing snowshoes.

"There's a very good reason why I have dogs now Kealon; would you like to hear it?" (What are you gonna do if he says no?)

"Why?" he finally asked. He seemed a teeny bit interested.

"Because they need me," I told him. "I train them, feed them, give them medicine when they're sick, but most of all, Kealon, I give them love. They need love very much."

"I'll never have another dog," he said firmly.

"I understand, Kealon," I said patiently. "I want to show you something in the kennel. Would you come with me and listen to what I have to say? It won't take but a minute and you can say no if you can't help me. Please?"

"Okay," he said. It came out sounding small and lost. My heart went out to him. I opened the door while he unbuckled his seatbelt, then climbed out of the car. I took his hand and looked across the hood at his mother and Wade. They were silent now and stood watching us.

"Care to come with us?" I asked.

We entered the kennel area through the east walk gate. I fingered the latch as Kealon, his mom and Wade passed through. I sure hoped it was loosened enough. Closing the gate softly with my hand, I held it closed for a second. The catch held and I breathed a small sigh of relief.

I led my party of three around the east corner of the kennel to nursery row and stopped them in front of Gloria Steinem's lodgings. She was spread out in the shade and her twelve hyper puppies were suckling at her engorged and tender nipples. She was four days away from freedom. The puppies would be removed from her sight and she would get her hard-earned rest on Saturday. Gloria lifted her head and stared wearily in our direction. She was thoroughly fed up with being a mother and damn tired of having them pulling on the teats. A rambunctious pup had stuck a fat paw in her right eye yesterday and it was red and leaking fluid. We had put drops in, but it would probably take another twenty-four hours to clear up.

She stared at us just long enough to see that everything was under control, then wearily dropped her head. With only eight active nipples and twelve mouths to feed, her feedings took twice as long as usual. The four who were unattached to a spigot were always nudging another one away before they'd had their fill. The squirming mass of bodies looked to be weaving an intricate pattern by rooting over and under their litter-mates searching for an empty teat. Gloria was dreaming about sleeping twenty hours out of twenty-four.

Wayne had placed the puppy in the far corner of the pen not five minutes before. The age of the puppy was six days less than Gloria's dozen and the difference was striking. He had been pulled from his mother's warm body and placed on the rough cement of the pen. The puppy looked scared and frightened. He whimpered and raised his little face and we could see the white, milky appearance of his eyes. He had been born with a thin membrane growth over both eyes. Rare, but easily treatable. Ramon had performed the light surgery three days ago.

Ramon had assured me that all was well and the eyes would clear up completely in the next two to four days. The puppy looked pathetic, neglected and blind. Perfect. Gloria wasn't exhibiting any maternal instincts for a perfectly good reason — it wasn't her puppy. The mother of this puppy resided around the corner in the west side of nursery row. I knelt in front of the puppy. Kealon stared down at him. Then he looked at me.

"What's wrong with him?"

"Kealon, do you know what rejection means?"

"No," he said.

"His mother doesn't want him. She won't feed him. He's lonely, afraid and he has sick eyes." I breathed a silent apology to both canine mothers for my outrageous lies about their character. This puppy was a fat butterball. I hoped that Kealon wouldn't realize he was being scammed. When compared to the other puppies, this one did look smaller, but he was far from being hungry. Caroline and Wade were standing quietly a few feet away, but could hear us.

"Kealon, can I ask you for a favor?"

"What?" he asked.

"Would you take care of this sick puppy for a few days? He needs special care and I'm just too busy to nurse him back to good health." I saw he was going to say no; he was starting a negative motion with his head. I held up both hands.

"Listen Kealon, you don't have to keep him forever; just take care of him for a few days. I'll take him back as soon as he's well."

"I can't," he said. He looked miserable.

"Why?" I asked.

"I killed Buster," he mumbled. He stared over the puppy's head to the treeline in back of the kennel.

"Of course you didn't!" I said harshly. "Whatever gave you that idea? It was an accident. Your mother explained to me what happened. The gate latch was loose. Mine does the same thing. Two of my dogs got loose last week, but it wasn't my fault, it was the stupid gate latch."

"I forgot to close the gate." Poor little guy. Honest and hurting.

"Kealon, you're wrong. Come with me." I took him past his mother and Wade, over to the east walk gate.

"Watch," I said.

Please God, be good. I crossed my fingers for protection. I pulled the gate open and slammed it hard. It held for one long second while my stomach churned, then, ever so slowly it swung back free from the loosened latch. Kealon's eyes widened. He stared at the slow moving gate as it continued gaining momentum, equal to the product of its mass and its velocity.

"You should get it fixed," he said in a voice that I had not heard before.

"I know," I said and gave a deep sigh. "I'm just so busy with the dogs and feedings and a sick puppy and giving them medicine and giving them the affection they need, I just don't have the time."

We walked back to Gloria Steinem and the lonely puppy in the corner of her enclosure. Wayne came around the corner and handed me the small bottle of eye drops. Very good timing, my friend. Wayne walked away and I stood staring at the medicine bottle and ignored Kealon. He was watching the puppy.

"Will his eyes get better?" He didn't move his eyes from the puppy as he asked the question.

"Sure," I said. "The drops go in his eyes twice a day, morning and night. He can eat some puppy food softened with milk, but he'll need a bottle too, for the next seven days."

The pup needed a bottle like he needed another pound of puppy fat; the bottle was Kealon's therapy.

"Maybe I could take care of him for a few days," he said carefully. We were coming down the home stretch, me and Sea Hope, with no one in front between us and the finish line. We had it made!

"Great," I said casually, going for the puppy quickly, before Kealon had second thoughts. When I placed the puppy in his arms, I told him, "Kealon, we grown-ups want to chat for a minute. Why don't you wait in the car? Can you manage the gate?"

"Yes, ma'am," he said firmly. I stood and watched him carefully open the gate, close it and wait to see if it latched. He turned toward the car and I joined Caroline Nash and Wade.

"The pup's eyes are fine, Mrs. Nash. The drops are just a precaution. They should completely clear in the next couple of days. I'll mail you his health certificate, breeding stats and the form to fill out for AKC registry. Be sure the milk is cut half-and-half with water. I have a feeling the pup is going to get all the milk he can hold for a while and he's fat enough already."

"I don't know how to thank you," she began. "We've been so worried about him. He hasn't been eating. He has nightmares and has lost a lot of sleep."

"Will your husband object?" I asked, mainly to stiffen her backbone a little. She had mentioned her husband felt Kealon shouldn't have another dog.

"I can handle my husband," she said with authority. Good for you, lady. Stick to your guns. Make him eat those negative remarks about Kealon.

"How much should I make the check for?" she inquired as she reached in her purse for her checkbook.

"The puppy is a gift to Kealon. There's no charge. The first checkup at the clinic out front is free like before; the six standard obedience lessons are free at six months. I'm happy I was able to help Kealon."

"Oh, but I couldn't," she protested. "The dog is much too expensive a gift!"

"I insist," I said in my firm, don't-give-me-any-grief voice. "I'm paying an old personal debt."

She looked uncertain. "Are you sure?"

"If you feel any reluctance in accepting a gift, Mrs. Nash, and if you can afford the gesture, a donation to the local SPCA would be nice. Mail them a check. They do fine work for many animals." My little needle about if she could afford it was to secure more money for our local volunteer pound. I knew damn well she could afford it. Her address was Sylvan Glades, the best yuppie address money could buy; the smallest house started at a quarter of a million. The little running-around-town number on her back would retail for three big ones. I hear that up north their big ones are a thousand. Here, we operate on a much smaller scale; our big one is a hundred-dollar bill.

Walking back to the family wagon, I thought Wade was overdoing his gallant Lothario routine; there wasn't a need for his attentions any longer. I tried sending him a dirty look, but apparently he had forgotten I was tagging along; he had eyes only for Mrs. Gotrocks.

As she was backing up her vehicle to turn around, I heard Kealon ask her, "Mom, can we stop at McDonald's?" When she passed us, returning to the driveway to leave, she slowed and I saw her mouth a silent thank-you to me, unshed tears in her eyes. Good luck, Mom. Kealon is lucky to have you.

As soon as she disappeared from view, I fumbled cigarettes from the pocket of my sundress and lit up. I inhaled with pleasure and turned to Wade.

"I need a drink. Let's go inside. It's too hot out here."

He studied his watch a second before he nodded. I jumped right in.

"Excuse me. The sun is not quite over the yardarm in this time zone, but in over half the world it is, or do you have an early supper engagement? A pill to take? A train to catch?"

He looked at me with a startled expression. "I was wondering if I had overstayed my welcome. I've been here the better part of three hours. I hate visitors who don't have the good sense to leave when it's time. If you want me to leave, just tell me, I can take it. If I'm in the way, just heave me out. It's the only way you can get rid of me. I have absolutely no place to go and nothing to do when I get there."

"Very good, Counselor," I said in admiration. "You're fast on your feet. You covered your faux pas with the watch with both aplomb and dispatch. I salute you!" I waited.

"You're waiting for the truth, right?"

"It would be the right thing to do," I said solemnly.

"I ate a very small bowl of cereal this morning. I've been trying to drop ten pounds and I can't jog or even walk in this humidity until I get acclimated. I almost had a heat stroke the first day I tried to jog. I was delaying lunch as long as possible so I wouldn't be starving and eat too much at the evening meal. I called you and got so excited about meeting you, I forgot to eat on the way over. I absolutely cannot drink on an empty stomach. Three beers or two shots of booze, I would be a disgusting drunk, singing Harvard songs and reciting reams of poetry."

"How hungry are you?" I said in a loud sing-song chant, giving him the lead-in for a joke.

"I'm so hungry, I could eat the north end of a southbound skunk!" he replied.

"My favorite involves the ass end of a rag doll and a screen door," I told him. "Let's eat!"

We crossed the courtyard and entered the sliding glass door to the office. As I crossed the threshold, I flipped on the switch that controls the tiny floods which illuminate the four landscapes on the wall. I stood in silence in front of the paintings. Wade joined me. "Are these your father's?" I didn't answer him, just stood there gazing at the paintings. After a couple of minutes, I turned to him.

"What do you think of them?"

His gaze remained on the paintings and he spoke slowly and with frequent pauses.

"I don't really know, Jo Beth. Truthfully, I'm a peasant about art. I never see in paintings what other people see. For example: I could never get excited about the *Mona Lisa* or *Whistler's Mother*. I'm just hopelessly ignorant about great art. I'm sorry if that offends you."

"Congratulations, Counselor," I said laughing, "You have just passed Jo Beth's 'Bull Shitters and Phonies Elimination Test' with flying colors!"

"These aren't his paintings?"

"I painted them in the tenth grade when I decided to compete with my father. I read an article that suggested most talent was inherited from either parent, more than people realized. It urged young people to attempt to excel in their parents' field of expertise. When my father saw my pathetic attempts he laughed so hard he nearly busted a gut. When I explained about the article I'd read, he became very angry, yelling that it was all garbage and greatly exaggerated." Something flickered way back there in my mind where I store the bits and pieces and debris of past events. I tried to bring it out to the light, but it was gone.

"You didn't keep trying?"

"God no. I hate to be humiliated. One of my many flaws — I can't stand to be ridiculed." I switched off the floods and walked almost the length of the office and crossed the room to the south wall. The entire wall was solid built-in bookcases with one exception. There was a recessed, paneled square at eye level which contained four landscapes measuring twenty-four by thirty-six inches. They were all the same view of Cumberland Island, painted at four different times of the year: spring, summer, fall and winter. Our seasonal changes are subtle; no great leaps from bleakness to snow, or thaw to lush foliage. The changes were mostly light and the way the shadows shifted with the sun's seasonal positions. Observant natives could name each correctly; tourists had to study each canvas much longer.

"I'll be in the kitchen," I told him.

Opening the refrigerator, I started piling food on the table. The baggie of Polish sausage, mayonnaise, sweet pickles, dill pickles, green tomato pickles, olives, mustard and ketchup. I popped a small casserole of macaroni and cheese into the microwave. Rosie had made it when she cooked my weekly small baked ham, so I could slice from it for lunch every day. She cooked a ham every Monday morning, and since this was Tuesday, it was mostly intact. I also took out a package of sharp cheddar cheese, a head of lettuce and three tomatoes. I rinsed the lettuce and sliced the tomatoes, then went back to the refrigerator for a cucumber. I peeled and sliced it and added two partial loaves of bread (wheat and rye) to the crowded table. Grabbing plates and silverware, two sharp knives, cheese slicer and several salad forks for the different pickle jars, I then took the casserole from the microwave and stuck in a spoon. I'm not expert in the kitchen, but I'm damn fast. I checked my hair, using as a mirror a picture hanging on the kitchen wall. It would have to do; I was starved. I heard the toilet flush and called out, "It's ready!"

Wade eyed the table with a grin. "God, that looks wonderful." I opened two bottles of beer and we both took our seats.

"Would you like to say the blessing?" I offered.

He looked blank. "I haven't done that in years." He looked embarrassed. "I've forgotten."

"I'll say it this time, but from now on we take turns, agreed?"

"Sure."

I bowed my head and closed my eyes. "Heavenly Father, we thank you for this food and all your blessings, amen." When I raised my head he was just straightening his.

"I'm not religious at all, Wade; I seldom attend church. But all properly brought-up Southerners say grace before eating, from the high chair to the grave. Dig in and wait on yourself. If it has to be sliced, you're the slicer, also the dicer, dipper, and so on. If I've forgotten anything, ask for it."

"Thank you," he said with enthusiasm. We started the construction of giant sandwiches. I talked while I worked.

"I'm surprised you haven't run into the problem of saying grace before now. Dining invitations are strewn about like confetti here. Haven't you received any? You've been here three weeks?"

I had to wait until he swallowed. "Yes, to both. I've been here and have received dozens of invitations, some from complete strangers, but I've been ducking and making excuses. You're my first friend."

"Why on earth would you do that?" I asked.

"Because I wasn't going to stay down here. I was just here for Dad's funeral and to close out his practice. I didn't want to accumulate social obligations I couldn't repay."

"But you told me on the phone a few hours ago that you were taking over your father's practice. Wasn't that what you said?"

"Jo Beth, I have a confession to make. I want you to keep in mind, however, that I prevaricated to you over the phone before I met you, so those lies shouldn't count now that we are friends. Agreed?"

"Sure," I said. "I'm a fair-minded person."

"It was that weird will your father had my father write. I closed out every file that was open and rechecked all the closed ones. The only one I wasn't satisfied with was yours. It gave me an itch I couldn't scratch. Mysteries intrigue me."

"Are you telling me that my father's will is causing you to move here permanently?" I was skeptical.

"Oh no," he assured me, "I would have talked to you, maybe spent a day or so on it, but I was planning on going back."

"So you're not staying," I said flatly. I felt disappointed, but it was for the best. I had enough distractions in my life just now without adding another one.

He started making his second sandwich. "You misunderstood me," he said. "I'm staying. I'm definitely moving here to stay."

"When did you make up your mind?" I took a big bite of my sandwich. He looked at his watch.

"About thirty minutes ago, while I was staring at those god-awful pictures you painted in the tenth grade."

I stared at him with my mouth full. I was so surprised I forgot to chew. He laughed and with his right hand made his fingers and thumb meet and part several times to remind me. When I was capable of speech, I knew I sounded a little sarcastic, but I really didn't give a flip.

"Would you care to elaborate on your reasoning process while making this decision?"

"Okay, here's how it went: I stood there debating whether to lie through my teeth and praise those pictures, thus flattering you, or find some diplomatic way to avoid the truthful answer. So I negated my ability to understand and appreciate art. A little birdie whispered in my right ear that you were not the type to appreciate fawning flattery. I always listen to the birdies that whisper in my right ear. They are usually correct. Now the birdies that whisper in my left ear, they lead me astray. They convince me to do terrible things; I should never listen to the little birdies that sit on my left shoulder and whisper into . . ."

I interrupted. "I'm gonna strangle you if you don't get on with it!"

He chuckled. "Okay, okay, I said to myself. Wade, I said, you know you like this woman a lot already. Be sure and think carefully about how you answer her. You don't want to blow your chances with her just by saying the wrong thing, because you want her to like you and because . . ."

"Stop!" I cried. "No more. Do you actually expect me to believe you have decided to move down here permanently, just to take a shot at — and I'll try to phrase it delicately — 'trying to get into my panties'?"

"Absolutely," he said with a satisfied grin. "How I admire a lady who can capsulize and elucidate so concisely."

I rolled my eyes with exasperation. "Gee, how romantic."

"No, I'm serious. I woke up one morning last week and discovered I'm thirty-five and all alone, without an heir in sight. I said to myself it's time I settled down and started a family."

"God, Wade, you don't sound like a very good sport to me. Down here we do a lot of hunting. Good sportsmanship requires you plug your gun for certain game and use the appropriate-sized shell. If you'll visit the Country Club for the Saturday night dinner-dance, and shoot off a couple of zingers like 'settle down' and 'raise a family' to a room half-filled with thirty-year-old divorcees, you'll be engaged to three different women before you can reach the door."

"Unsportsmanship?" he said with surprise. "I thought the correct thing was to declare your intentions right away, be open and honest. Not so?"

"It sounds like you're cheating a little, 'baiting the field' or 'shooting a grounded bird.'"

He shook his head slowly. "I don't understand women."

I smiled. "Want another beer?"

"Yes, thank you," he said politely.

I opened two and handed one across the table. We chewed in comfortable silence.

"The macaroni and cheese is delicious and the ham is excellent," he said between bites.

"Rosie is the cooker and I'm the cookee she cooks for. She's constantly bringing over care packages for the freezer, and hot food. I know she's spending her hard-earned money on food for me, so I go out shopping, buy a couple of hams, a roast, steaks and chops and take them to her. During the next week she cooks them and carts them back down the stairs to me."

"You need to be firm," he suggested. "Don't accept the next offering."

"Are you crazy? I feel guilty, not stupid. She's a wonderful cook. You should taste her pot roast."

He laughed. "I'll buy two tomorrow and tell her that you're dying for pot roast, but it's one for her and one for us."

"Us? As in you and me?"

"Quick study, that's what you are. Yes, you and me. Okay?" He cocked his head and waited.

I didn't answer right away. I could hear the kitchen clock ticking. The refrigerator was purring away. The air conditioner rumbled to a temporary stop. My stomach was content and tight against the dress fabric. The beer was cold and tart on my tongue. Languor settled softly on my shoulders. I blinked. Christ, a few soft words and I was acting like one of my bitches in heat — all caution forgotten and limp with anticipation. I sat up straighter. I was saved by the bell. The phone issued a summons.

"Excuse me." I rose and hurried out to stand by the desk but didn't touch the phone. The answering machine began its spiel and I stood and thought about nothing. After an eternal ten seconds or so I heard the circuit disconnect. Pushing the rewind button and running it back to the beginning, I listened to the call that came in right after Wade's arrival and heard a silence and another disconnect. Two hang-ups in a little more than five hours. A new record.

I lit a cigarette and returned to the kitchen. Wade's plate was empty with his silverware neatly aligned in the center.

"You wash the dishes," I told him, "while I put the food away."

He seemed a little uncertain with my brusqueness but he immediately stood and began to clear the table. I concentrated on getting the proper lids on everything and resealing the bread and leftover meats.

"Was your phone call bad news?" he asked.

My head was in the refrigerator, where I was pushing back items to make room for the jars in my hand. "Hang-up," I said, and it sounded louder than usual. It seemed to echo inside the white expanse.

"You get many of those on your machine?"

"I have lately," I said with a wry twist of my head and hand as I cleared the freezer's edge and faced him.

"Think it's your ex-husband?"

"Look, Wade, do me a favor, will you? Call him Bubba or bastard or whatever, but try not to call him my ex-husband again. The term offends me and reminds me of intimacies I'd rather forget."

"Sure," he said, sounding subdued. I regretted taking out my anger on him, but I'll be damned if I was going to apologize. The table was cleared. Wade was wiping the dishcloth with sure strokes over the surface using his right hand and drying the dampness with the dish towel in his left.

"Very efficient," I praised. A small token for my rudeness. He glanced up at me and winked.

"I've been batchin' for three weeks now. I let Dad's housekeeper go; I couldn't stand her."

"Who was she?" I was curious.

"A Mrs. Atkins. She was totally incompetent and acted like she couldn't hear anything I said. I know she could hear well; I whispered from fifteen feet the second day with her back turned."

"Mrs. Cora Atkins. She likes a little nip now and then," I said with a grin. "Like on the quarter-hour, half-hour and, of course, on the hour.

She's partial to moonshine. She was probably soused most of the times you saw her."

"Did she need the money? I felt guilty about firing her."

"Don't worry, she's amply fixed. She has more than enough to keep her in moonshine for the rest of her life."

"You sound like you approve of her drinking."

"She's certainly old enough to indulge. She raised four children and buried two husbands. If the world looks better to her through a daily quart of moonshine, who are we to judge?"

"Live and let live?"

"Exactly. You living out at Tara all by yourself?"

"What did you call the house . . . Tara?" He spurted surprised laughter. "You mean the mansion in *Gone With The Wind*?"

"Sure, that's what the locals have called it for years."

He defended his birthright. "It's half the size of Tara. It only has six bedrooms and fourteen rooms, total."

"Did you forget to count the ballroom?" I asked with a grin. He saw I was kidding.

"It's a small ballroom. I'd completely forgotten it." He shrugged eloquently and pretended to hand me an object. Sweeping low in a theatrical bow, he mimicked, "If you'll be so kind as to hold my mint julep, I'll go dance with Scarlett now."

"Boy," I said in admiration, "you paraphrased that racist quote quite nicely."

Becoming serious, he said quietly, "I don't know what's going to happen to the place. I don't have enough money to keep the fifty acres mowed as often as needed."

"You're putting me on," I scoffed. "Your father was rich. Don't you inherit?"

"My father disliked the word 'rich'; he liked to think his position was 'well off' or 'comfortably fixed.' I've seen his office files; he sure didn't add to his fortune in the last twenty years from his law practice. First Federal is handling the estate's probate. Their trust department says it will be at least three months before I know where I stand. Anyway, I always had the impression, gleaned from little clues my mother dropped, that most of the money was hers. I'm sure my mother didn't leave any down here when she left. She's so tight she squeaks."

"The taxes on that place must be horrendous." I was thinking of my own heavy tax burden.

"The county may end up with my 'white elephant' by default. I may end up in the poorhouse," he said calmly.

"Do you need a loan for walking-around money till probate clears?" I was being nosy about his finances but was afraid he had nothing coming in.

"Thanks for asking. I'm okay now, but ask again after the probate clears. I may need some get-out-of-town money," he said with a smile. "I guess I've got an honest face. You're the second person to offer me a loan since I came down. Dad's gardener seemed very worried about me when I was trying to see how little I could spend on the place while I'm waiting for probate. He offered to work on credit while I waited and even offered me a personal loan."

"Sounds like a nice man," I remarked idly. "I wonder if I know him?"

"His first name is Hector. He told me his last name but he speaks such broken English, I didn't catch it and I didn't want to keep asking."

I felt a faint tremor of alarm. I sure hoped to hell he wasn't who I thought he was.

"Little guy? Wears black pants and ruffle-fronted white shirts? Looks like a matador?"

"That's him. I've only seem him three times and that's what he had on each time. Is he a local character or something?"

I mumbled a positive response while I pondered how to find out what I needed to know without alarming him.

"Wade, you mentioned fifty acres of mowing for the estate. I thought there was a lot more land than that."

"Oh sure," he replied. "A little better than six hundred acres, but only fifty has to be mowed, thank God. The rest is not cleared. The property line runs down to and parallel with Tyler's Creek."

"Have you been exploring in the uncleared area since you've been down here? Seen any deer?"

"I did that number in my youth. Since I've been back it's been too muggy to be tramping around in the bush."

Thank God for small favors — at least he hadn't inadvertently stepped into the frying pan, yet. One more question to confirm my suspicions.

"Your father was an avid hunter, wasn't he?"

"He used to be. About eight or nine years ago he became a conservationist. Of course," he said with a smile of irony, "this was after he had four trophy heads mounted on the wall of his den. He said something like, 'I'm tired of shootin' those purty little creatures; seems a shame to keep killing 'em off.' He wouldn't even let his old pals hunt on his land anymore."

Christ. Worst case scenario. Suspicions confirmed. And to think that Carl, Wade's father, had acted so goody-goody with me in his law office, the hypocrite! I had a feeling Wade was going to go into shock when his father's estate was settled. Hector's cousin had been caught in one of my random sweeps of Pine Industries last fall. I had been in the station when Hector arrived to bail him out. A deputy had seen the look of hate Hector had sent my way. The deputy told me who Hector was and said he bet if he hand-vacuumed Hector, where he stood, he would find enough marijuana to roll a cigarette. I sighed. More problems.

"Earth to Jo Beth," he said softly.

"I'm sorry," I said with a smile. I started laying the groundwork. "Wade, I've never seen your family estate. I'd like to be with you when you take a tour of the old stomping grounds you had as a kid. Will you wait until I can go with you?"

He looked happy. "It's a date." I guess he thought I was coming on to him, but it couldn't be helped. I wanted him to remember this conversation.

"Promise?"

He gave me a searching glance. "Of course."

"Call it a girlish whim," I said lightly.

"Somehow," he said, sounding rueful, "I can't picture you having girlish whims."

"I'll bet I surprise you." In fact, he could count on it.

9

"SO MAD I COULD CHEW NAILS"
April 6, Tuesday, 6 P.M.

The phone rang. I gave a sudden lurch and muttered "Oh shit" as I listened, waiting through the interminable delay of my message and the beep. The voice startled me. I was sure it was going to be another hang-up.

I turned my head and saw Wade standing in the kitchen doorway looking uncertain about whether he should join me in the office. I beckoned him closer, snapped on the speaker phone and shut off the answering tape. I should have been recording the message, but the speaker amplifier wouldn't work with the recording device on, a nasty little quirk it had recently developed. Sooner or later, my electrical gadgets turn on me. I didn't want Wade left in the dark in the coming conversation.

"Say again, Deputy," I asked for Wade's benefit. He was now close enough he could hear both sides of the conversation.

"Deputy Talbot, dispatcher for Gilsford County Sheriff's Department," he repeated.

"I'm on the line, Roger."

"Hi, Jo Beth. How you doing?"

"Fine, Roger. What's up?" I pulled a pad and pen closer.

"It's six-oh-five, Jo Beth. I logged it."

"Six-oh-five is correct, Roger, thanks." My local nightmare, Sheriff Carlson, had screwed me up on the time element more than once. For protection I had warned the dispatchers in the tri-county area to vocalize the time, record and log it — or I wouldn't show up.

"We have a WMC, age seventy-three, Ancel Tew. That's T-E-W, one hundred and ninety Seegars Road, Constine. Subject has advanced Alzheimer's; departure route known, time known, no double "H" required. Search authorized by Sheriff Scroggins at six p.m. Deputy Mason on duty at scene."

"What was the departure time?"

"Oh, sorry, Jo Beth. Approximately four-thirty p.m."

"Why the delay?" I was annoyed. An hour and a half wasted.

"Subject's son-in-law tried to find him first." Shit. It would take another hour to get there.

"Call Deputy Mason and tell him my tentative ETA is seven p.m. I'll confirm en route. Anything else?"

"That's it. Good luck."

"Thanks, Roger." I reset the answering machine and turned to Wade. "Gotta go. Want to see what I do?"

"I'd love to go. Do you think they'll mind?"

"Who?"

"The deputies. Think they'll say anything?"

"Wade, I don't think you understand what I do. I'm an independent contractor, not an officer of the law. I don't take orders from them, I give them. If they don't like what I do, I can pick up my marbles and come home."

I was dialing Rosie's number and mentally making lists.

"Hello."

"Rosie. Jo Beth. Has Wayne eaten?"

"Not yet."

"Feed him quick. Have you got a pen?"

"Yes."

"Tell him to load both vans. I want Susie and Bo. His choice for his van. Tell him to load extra waders, gloves and a hat for Wade. Here's the address. One hundred and ninety Seegars Road, Constine. Tell him my ETA is seven p.m. I have to make a stop on the way, so load my van first. Got it?" She read it back to me.

"One hundred and ninety Seegars Road, Constine, is correct. Hold on a second." I turned to Wade. "Got a jacket or coat at your place, lined or heavy, that you don't mind getting scratched?"

"I have a bomber jacket."

"Perfect, but I warn you, it will get scratched."

"It's much too hot to wear," he protested.

"Better hot than snake bit," I said lightly.

"Absolutely, no question," he quickly agreed.

"That's it, Rosie. Thanks."

I turned to Wade. "It will take me about ten minutes to dress. Make sure Wayne has those three items for you. Remember what they are?"

"Hat, waders and gloves."

"Good man." He beamed. How like children we are at times. Give us praise and we'll bust our butts for more. I know I sure will. I'll do more for praise than I will for money any day.

"Tell Wayne I want your car garaged. He'll show you where."

"It's okay outside."

"There is a spot about five hundred yards down the road. With a decent set of binoculars you can get a clear view of the entire courtyard."

"I see," he said, as though he really didn't.

"I don't want to advertise your presence here, Wade. Why forewarn the enemy when you have a secret weapon?"

Wade looked hopeful. "Am I your secret weapon?"

"You bet!" I said with gusto. "Let's get cracking."

I went to the bedroom and removed the sundress and fancy underwear. I put on plain white cotton briefs and an all-cotton bra. Jeans and a cotton T-shirt. Heavy cotton socks and Pro-Wing walkers. I grabbed a lightweight, denim jacket in case of rain or the night air turning cool on the way home.

I headed for the office while lifting my T-shirt and tying a bandanna around my waist. Wade rushed back in. He stared curiously at the bandanna.

"I wear it to get my scent on it. I leave it with Wayne when I start the search, just in case he has to scent-track me with the dogs."

"You mean you sometimes get lost?" He thought that was funny, the tracker tracking a tracker.

"No, it would mean I was down for some reason and couldn't make it back."

"Oh," he said, sounding subdued.

I grabbed my wallet and slid it into my jeans. "Let's roll," I said happily. I always enjoy the beginning of a hunt. Wayne had the van packed, ready, and parked in the drive for quick departure. I took a quick peek at Susie and Bo and gave them some sweet talk. I drove through both gates, turned onto Highway 301 and put the pedal to the metal.

The van rolls along sweetly at seventy but it seems to take forever to get to your destination. This highway was two lanes but was busy with back road loafers as well as working commuters trying to set new records for the trip home.

"Shouldn't you turn on your lights and siren?"

I glanced at Wade. He sounded a tad nervous. Payback time, guy. "Never use them!"

"Why?"

"Against my principles!" We were having to yell; with the windows open, hearing over the wind noise was difficult.

How many girls in the past had to hold on and try to suppress their fears when you drove too fast, showing off? Let's see how you react, Wade, to some white-knuckle time. This was for my sisters everywhere.

My heart pumped faster to elevate the adrenaline flowing through my system. You need it for fast, safe driving; it increases your alertness. Even after we reached the four-lane section of the road I couldn't attain the smooth road rhythm that is the mark of a very good driver because of the speeders ahead. The smart ones drove with quick glances to the rearview mirrors; they would see the overhead silhouette of the emergency light, take their foot off the gas pedal and remain in the same lane. The dumb ones would let me get too close, discover the van bearing down on them and panic. They would hit the brakes, weave and rapidly change lanes. The only direction you could be sure they weren't going was straight up. You had to guard against all the alternatives. I was having a ball.

Wade toughed it out. I was proud of him. He didn't whimper or pound the dashboard. When I slowed for his driveway, I reached across and patted his shoulder.

"Relax, Counselor. I've taken all the driving tests that deputies, highway patrolmen and policemen have to take. You're in safe hands. All you have to worry about are all the drivers who haven't taken these tests."

"That's very reassuring," he said with heavy irony. I laughed.

"Got any boots with you?"

"No."

"Heavy climbing shoes or such?"

"Nope."

"Joggers?"

"Yep."

"Good. You have five minutes. Heavy pants, long-sleeved shirt, thick socks, joggers and bomber jacket. Okay?"

"I'll be right back."

I lit a cigarette and waited. I gazed up at the mansion. Six tall columns, everything gleaming white with black shutters and trim. Twelve black high-back rocking chairs were spaced evenly across the front. The wide, covered expanse on the building couldn't be called a front porch. It must have a fancier name; it was huge.

What would it have been like to be an only child like me, growing up in this house? Obviously they must have had servants. I wondered if he had been given chores. If he had, I somehow knew it hadn't been lugging a bucket of water to wash the wide front steps. Had he been lonely? I couldn't picture him knocking a tin can around the front lawn with a stick, one of my many games of childhood.

He tested the lock after closing the front door of the house and ran down the steps toward the van. His jeans and fancy shirt made him look taller and slimmer. He threw the bomber jacket onto the seat and slid in beside me. I took off around the curving drive.

"Are we on schedule?" he asked.

"Did you ever play stickball as a kid?" I questioned.

"Beg your pardon?"

I shook my head as I accelerated, bobbing and weaving through the residential streets.

"I was back in the past, wool-gathering. There's a map case on the floorboard by your left foot. Pull out the one for Gilsford County. We'll be entering from the south on County Road One Twenty-seven. We've got about thirty minutes to make thirty-seven-plus miles. In Constine, find one ninety Seegars Road and figure out the best way to get there."

"We're surely going to be late?" He made it a question.

"Not if I can help it."

He groaned. "I was afraid of that."

It was twelve after seven p.m. when we stopped in front of the modest brick house that was our destination. The two-lane traffic on Highway 127 didn't allow me to pass many cars, but the wide four-lane, leading into the small town of Constine, did. There were three traffic lights; I crossed two on yellow, and one turned red while I was a hundred yards away. Wade had braced both hands on the dashboard anticipating a screeching stop, but I sailed on through it. I had seen from way back that both approaches were clear, but he hadn't. He had sucked in a lot of air and let it explode from his lungs.

"My God!" he yelled. It was a thoroughly satisfying experience.

There were two cruisers blocking the drive, one city and one county. I pulled out on the lawn, passed them and pulled around to the rear of the house near a double garage with a second floor above it. The officers, bless their pea-picking little brains, often pulled up, left their doors open and lights rotating, effectively blocking the very ambulance they had just previously summoned. Go figure.

Wade had called out street names and which way to turn from the map but had said nothing after the well-run red light.

"We have arrived," I said.

"So it seems." His manner was cool.

"Upset?"

"I'll get over it," he answered. "You scared the pants off me back there."

"First opportunity, I'll give you a chance to get even," I told him.

"I'm looking forward to it," he answered grimly and bared his teeth in a snarl. I laughed. We got out and met in front of the van.

We watched a Gilsford County deputy and a Constine police officer approach from the rear of the house.

"Miz Sidden." He briefly touched the brim of his brown Stetson. "You can begin the search now. A witness saw the old man enter the woods in that direction about four-thirty this afternoon." He was pointing behind the house toward a thick expanse of woods and a swampy area.

"Really?" I said politely. I put my arms over my head and stretched to relieve the tension from the high-speed drive. I turned to Wade. "Let's go inside and speak to the family," I told him.

"Hold it!" The deputy's speech was terse and clipped. "That's not necessary. I've told you where to search and when he left. Anything else is wasting time. You'd better get started." He hooked his thumbs in his wide holster belt and posed for us. I knew he was showing off for his city police cohort and I could have handled the situation tactfully, but what the hell. I was gonna show off because of Wade and also because I'm just naturally abrasive when I'm the target of petty authority.

"Listen, asshole," I said in a casual manner. "Quit strutting like a peacock and get out of my face. The minute I step out of that van, I'm in charge of this action." I was happy to note that his thick neck above his uniform collar had turned an alarming red.

"I don't want to hear any opinion you may have," I continued. "I want you to speak to me only if I ask you a question. Is that clear?"

"Who the hell you think you are?" he snarled. "You can't talk to me this way . . . I'll . . ." his face was so red I was afraid he was nearing a stroke. He was in his thirties, but about 30 pounds overweight. That had to be a seventeen-inch neck bulging above his collar.

"I'm your superior, Buddy, in more ways than one. Be sure and tell Sheriff Scroggins I arrived at seven-twelve and left at seven-fourteen and the reason for the departure. Let's go, Wade. We can still watch most of the Braves' game." Wade obediently walked around the van and got in. I was fastening my seat belt when the deputy took a couple of strides closer.

"You're leaving?" He looked thunderstruck.

"The man is observant," I told Wade. "See how quick he caught on?" I shoved the gearshift into reverse and started to back up. The deputy was taking fast strides, trying to stay alongside my window. I ignored him.

"I'm sorry," he spat at me. It was so painful to say, he had rushed to get through it.

"That's a start," I commented with my foot on the brake.

"I didn't realize you were in charge of the scene. This is the first dog search I've had," he admitted with reluctance. I shifted into park and turned the key.

I hopped out and stuck out my hand. I can be gracious with total capitulation from the offender.

"Deputy Mason," I said glancing at his name tag, "I'm Jo Beth Sidden. Me and my associate are going inside to talk to the family. We'll be out shortly."

"Sure," he mumbled. When we passed the city officer, he was trying to act invisible and was not looking our way.

When we were out of hearing of the officers, Wade leaned near me. "That was brutal."

I started paraphrasing an old Churchill speech, "We'll fight from the rooftops . . . we'll fight on the beaches . . ."

"It's a battle? Is that what you're saying? A battle of the sexes?"

"You betcha," I vowed. "Until every woman on earth is treated as an equal and not like a second-class citizen. Amen."

He rolled his eyes in dismay, stepped in front of me, knocked on the door, then stepped back.

The man who came to the door was only slightly smaller than Paul Bunyan. Wade and I had to tilt our heads far back since we were standing at the bottom of the steps and the man, at floor level, would go six feet, six inches at least; if he could weigh on regular scales that went only to three hundred pounds, I would be very surprised. A large, thick, curly beard and a full head of black hair, also curly, added to his bulky appearance. Wade and I gawked up at him. I surely wouldn't want to meet this dude in a dark alley.

"Mr. Tew?" I asked.

"Fender. Albert Fender. My wife's name is May Belle Fender. Her father is the man that's missing."

I walked up the steps and opened the screen door, went inside and held the door for Wade. Fender reluctantly backed up, but not enough. I stuck out my hand and saw it disappear in a dinner-plate-sized hand. It was a gentle shake, thank God. His grip reminded me of the play-dough we had squeezed in kindergarten, cold and clammy. I wanted to look at his palm to see if my hand had left an indention. His touch made me want to wipe my hand down the side of my jeans.

"My name is Jo Beth Sidden. My dogs will do the tracking. This is an associate, Wade Bennett." Wade shook hands and, since monster-man only took one step backwards as we entered the door, we had to sidle to clear his bulk. I felt a reluctance to brush against him and sucked in every part of me possible in order to get around him. I had the feeling we were about as welcome as the seven-year itch. Why the dislike?

"Could I speak to your wife?"

He frowned. "I'm the one who saw him leave. She was asleep. I'll show you where to look." He reached for the back screen door.

"I need to talk to her," I explained. "She's the closest next-of-kin. Just routine." This wasn't my reason at all, but he seemed determined not to invite me any further in than the door.

"I don't want her upset; she's worn out."

"I'm afraid I have to insist. Is this the way?" I asked and started walking to the opposite door of the kitchen. I didn't look back and was in the hallway heading for the living room before he realized what was happening.

"Hey," I heard him rumble, but I had arrived. Two women were sitting close together on the sofa to the left of the door.

A young woman was half-supporting an older woman who looked fifty but was probably much younger. She seemed to be in shock. She raised her head and tried to focus her gaze on me, but was unsuccessful. I stepped closer and directed a question to the younger woman.

"Have you given her any sedatives?"

"I've been here since five o'clock. She hasn't had anything since then. I think that's the problem. Her husband gave her a sleeping pill at two and she's having trouble staying awake." The younger woman stared at me.

I was aware of Wade and Albert Fender somewhere behind me. I had a feeling this woman was trying to tell me something but couldn't with the older woman's husband present. I looked steadily at her and nodded my head just a fraction.

I turned and faced the men who were standing just inside the door-way to the hall. Wade looked poised and alert. He must have been re-ceiving the same vibes as I was. Big Al was glowering at me and looked like a volcano about to erupt.

I gave them a small smile and tried to look and sound like a medical whiz. I directed my focus on Big Al.

"Your wife needs a small dose of Dexedrine to relieve her lassitude from the effect of the sleeping pill. In about an hour she'll be fine. It works slowly, so it doesn't do any harm or pose a threat to her nervous system."

I thought it sounded pretty good for an off-the-cuff diagnosis. The only medical expertise I could claim was a ninety-minute Red Cross Home Safety course held in the high school gym each year. I had attended the course last May. Having read somewhere that Dexedrine was a close cousin to speed, it sounded logical you'd need speed, an upper, to fight a sleeping pill, a downer. I had dangled the hour's wait for bait. I had a gut feeling he was all for keeping her exactly as she was, which was completely out of the picture. I wasn't about to give the woman any kind of drug. My plan was to get Wade outside to alert the deputy to lure Fender out of hearing, so I could pump the unidentified lady about what was going on.

"You're not going to give her nothing. Leave her alone! I won't have you messing with her," he yelled.

"Well. It's your decision, of course," I said casually, "but I thought it would be best to treat her here and let her sleep it off in her own bed. If not, I have no choice but to call an ambulance. Her condition requires it." I glanced toward the phone. "May I use this phone?"

"Stay away from the phone!" he bellowed. Wade eased a foot closer to Fender. I placed most of my weight on the balls of my feet, ready to run like hell if he took a step toward me. I took a deep breath.

"Either I use this phone, Mr. Fender, or have the deputy request an ambulance on the police radio, or I give her a small pill and put her to bed. It's your decision."

We waited. "She don't need no pill or no ambulance. My wife is just tired and sleepy. Now you leave her alone and go find her daddy out there in them woods. She ain't your worry. I want you out of my house, now!"

Shit, Godzilla had called my bluff. Now what? I didn't think his wife needed a doctor either; I was just trying to get some information about the old man and was certain I wouldn't believe anything the mountain-man said under oath. I would have to try the unidentified lady. Maybe she knew something helpful.

"It's your decision to make, Mr. Fender." I tried to sound harmless and humble. "Just let me ask the lady here some questions. It would only take a minute or so."

"You can ask them outside. I want all of you out of here!" I had no choice. Wade and I left by the back door. The woman with May Belle Fender didn't come out. I had seen the look she sent across the room as I was leaving. She knew if she came outside to answer questions, the hulk wouldn't let her back in. I didn't know whether she was a relative or a friend.

Outside, Wade and I stood a few feet from the back door.

"Nice guy," Wade said.

"What's your impression of what you've seen?" I wanted someone else's opinion. Maybe I was off the wall with mine.

"Very strange. He looks capable of snapping a backbone as easily as a chicken wishbone. Christ, he made me sweat just looking at him."

"My sentiments exactly, but why? Usually in these situations the relatives are eager to help. They volunteer more information than needed. They're grateful for anyone's help, and they're anxious about the missing subject's welfare. Another thing, did you notice the house?"

"Not really. I was too busy keeping an eye on Mighty Joe Young."

I chuckled. "I got a glimpse inside the old man's bedroom from the hallway. It was clean and smelled normal. The whole house was spotless. There isn't any money being spent there, but everything is clean and fresh. It takes a lot of hard work to keep a house clean and smelling good with a seventy-three-year-old patient with advanced Alzheimer's."

That was it! That's what was bugging me. Roger, the dispatcher, had used that expression: advanced Alzheimer's. So, what was any old, advanced Alzheimer's victim doing flitting through the woods? At that stage, patients are bedridden. It didn't make sense, and the time factor was stranger still. Supposedly, the old man disappeared at four-thirty p.m.; the young woman had arrived at five to find the wife zonked on some sleeping drug. What happened between four-thirty and six p.m., when the authorities were called?

"No," I said quickly, "back to four-thirty. If the son-in-law, of unusual proportions, saw the old man headed for the woods —" I turned and estimated the distance "— less than a hundred yards away, why didn't he nip out and retrieve him, which would have been a piece of cake, and bring him back?"

"Stranger and stranger," Wade said slowly. "Maybe he didn't want to bring him back."

"Good guess," I said. "I've been thinking along those lines. Also, the old guy could be twenty yards out in the woods, tired and confused. Damn, I wish I had more information." I fumed. "Where's the deputy?" We walked where we could look down the drive. The two officers were standing by the first patrol car.

"Wade, go smooth some feathers. Agree with the deputy about what a bitch I am. Try and find out what he knows, if anything. Check on Wayne. He should be parked out front somewhere. Bring him up to date on what we know so far, which is next to nothing. Tell him to stand by. I'm gonna take the dogs to the edge of the clearing and try to pick up a scent. If I do, then I'll suit up. Right now I can't picture him out there, and that worries me. I've never felt this strange before."

"Yes, ma'am," he said with a mock salute.

"Too bossy?"

"Not just yet. I'll let you know."

I had to watch this guy; he was making all the right moves. On the way to the van I tried to put my pessimism aside. I was not used to feeling down; normally my feelings are between a Pollyanna mood and cheerfully optimistic. I didn't precipitate disaster. I unloaded Susie and Bo, connecting them to their leads, then let them find their choice of ground to take a pee. I hated to go back and confront Godzilla, but had no choice. I had to have an article of clothing worn by Ancel Tew for the dogs. I saw Wade standing with the officers. I walked to the back door and knocked loudly. I didn't have long to wait.

He opened the door and scowled. "What do you want?"

"Mr. Fender, I need something Ancel Tew has worn that hasn't been washed. It's for the dogs to smell his scent."

"Wait here," he commanded and closed the door. I didn't say thank you. Being pleasant to this hulk set my teeth on edge. I glanced at my watch. It was almost eight o'clock. I checked the sunset behind me. I had less than thirty minutes of adequate light. He opened the door and thrust a gray sweater in my direction. I took it and he slammed the door. I shot him with a mental gun and examined the sweater.

It buttoned down the front and had a shawl collar. It seemed to be cotton and some type of synthetic blend. I checked the front for food stains but found no spills. The buttonholes were not sprung as though they had been opened, released and reclosed a few times. I buried my face in the material, took a deep breath and caught a faint smell of bleach and what I call dryer breath. No musty odor of illness or perspiration. I felt anger and frustration. I guessed I had a fifty-fifty chance that Tew had worn this garment after it had been washed. This was when Mrs. May Belle Fender was needed, awake and alert.

A dog's sense of smell is twenty times more powerful than a human's. One of them might be able to pick up a scent, but I was doubtful. I took them to the edge of the clearing, presented the sweater and gave them the command to "Seek." I started them in a large, shallow figure-eight pattern, which would overlap and possibly give a viable scent trail.

After thirty-five minutes of fruitless searching, I stopped to take a breather. The dogs had not picked up any scent trail and we had run out of daylight. Wade walked toward me through the early darkness with the light spilling out of the house behind him in pale yellow rectangles. In the last half hour the dew had saturated the grass and this should have made the scent easier to find; but not so, they were simply circling in confusion.

"How's it going?" he asked.

"Well, either Ancel Tew has never set foot this far from the house, or King Kong gave me a clean sweater from Ancel's chest of drawers, or the dogs are on a hunger strike because I forgot their deer jerky. Take your pick."

Wade was waving his arms around and using his hands like windshield wiper blades in front of his face.

"What are these things?" he gasped. In opening his mouth and inhaling, he probably had sucked a few into his mouth.

"You've forgotten these pesky creatures after spending your childhood here?" I chided him. "You should have remembered that all of Georgia below the gnat line is abounding with zillions of gnats, which are really tiny flies. They love warm, moist places."

"They can't be good for you. Are they dangerous?" He gagged and made a spitting motion. He felt them on the back of his throat.

"Well, they can blind cows, but they only give humans the pinkeye, an inflammation caused by the transmission of bacteria, which is painful, but not deadly."

He was wildly flapping his arms, which was completely ineffectual.

"No, no," I said. "Watch me." I pursed the right side of my mouth and aimed a puff of air toward the right eye, then reversed the process and repeated it on the left eye.

"The theory is that gnats can't stand a wind gust of ten miles per hour, so blow hard. A native also wears 'Skin-So-Soft.'"

"Skin what?"

"It's a lotion made by Avon Cosmetics. The locals even rub down their horses with it. It will make you smell so nice even men will like you," I told him.

"No, thanks," he said with a grimace.

"It's either that or you pin strips of fabric softener sheets to your hair, but you'll still smell good."

"Nothing else works?" he asked.

"Sure, insect repellent works fine, but we natives don't take the easy way out. When it gets dark, they won't bother you anymore, but you'll beg to have them back instead of the mosquitoes gnawing any exposed part of your body. Did you learn anything about Ancel Tew?"

"Not much," he admitted. "First, Deputy Mason thinks you are a snotty bitch who wishes she had balls instead of ovaries. I agreed with him loud and often, as per your instructions."

"It's a popular opinion among the local lawmen," I told him. "Go on."

"Deputy Mason said he received the call and arrived here about a quarter to six. Mr. Fender informed him about his father-in-law's disappearance around four-thirty and said he had seen him entering the edge of the woods."

"Did he ask Fender why he let over an hour go by before reporting it?"

"Deputy Mason said Mr. Fender stated he tried to wake his wife to tell her he was going after her father, but she was incoherent from the sleeping pill and he couldn't leave her in that condition. He called a neighbor, asked her to come over and stay with his wife while he searched for Mr. Tew."

"Did Fender say he actually went into the woods looking for Mr. Tew?"

"Yes. He said Mr. Fender told him he searched for several minutes in the area where he saw Mr. Tew enter the woods. He realized it was impossible to search alone, came back and dialed nine-one-one."

"A logical explanation, but I don't buy it. If he really saw him out there, he could have nipped out and easily caught the old man and brought him back in five minutes. He knew his wife was sedated. Why waste time trying to wake her?"

"Maybe he panicked. It happens."

"I think it's hogwash," I said. "I'm going to take the dogs to the van and load them; they couldn't find a thing. Maybe Wayne will have better luck with his dogs. If you don't mind, Wade, would you ask Wayne to bring his dogs for a try?"

"Sure," he answered.

I stood in the darkness and watched him stride toward the house. I stooped and petted the dogs, telling them it wasn't their fault. They nuzzled my hands, wanting their treats. I apologized. "Sorry guys, I forgot your jerky, but I'll make it up to you." I gave them the command to "Load up" and they obediently started trotting toward the van. I had to give them a tug to slow their gait.

As we came around the back of the garage there was enough light from the house and an outside nightlight above the stair landing to see the dogs clearly. They were casting from side to side and both had their noses pointed straight up in the air. My pulse quickened. Bloodhounds track two ways: with their noses to the ground when they have a ground scent, and up in the air where they can actually smell the scent of the person they are seeking. They both stopped and tested the breeze. I took a deep breath and raised my eyes upward.

The outside staircase leading to the second story above the garage was on this side. The double garage was brick, but the room above and the staircase were wood. It must have been added after the house was built. I gazed at the doorway at the top of the stairs. The door was closed and shades were drawn over the two windows facing me. I couldn't hear a motor from an air conditioner nor see lights. In this heat the inside temperature would probably be over one hundred degrees.

Obviously no one was home. I didn't know if anyone lived there; it could be used for storage. The dogs strained forward and began that wonderful strange baying, their joyous announcement that they had found their target.

10

"BATTY AS A BEDBUG"
April 6, Tuesday 8 P.M.

Caught off guard, I let the dogs pull me to the foot of the staircase before my mind took over. I dragged them back and started yelling the command to "Retreat." It was hard to do; they were celebrating. Manhandling them around, I got them headed for the van. A confrontation was possible shortly, and I wanted the dogs safe and out of the way before it happened.

I was loading Susie when I saw the deputy and his city pal come running up the drive with Wayne and Wade right on their heels. I ignored the deputy and started to load Bo. Wayne rushed up and took over the task. I shot him a grateful look.

"What's going on here?" Deputy Mason yelled. He had to yell to be heard over the dogs' howls, as they were in full voice and would not be denied their moment.

"Follow me," I said loudly and started to walk toward the deputy's patrol car. They had no choice but to follow. I had to sell Mason on my plan, but couldn't think with dogs baying in my ear. When we reached the car, I stopped and turned. I had their attention.

"Deputy, we need to plan on how to handle this before we do something rash. I think I know where Ancel Tew is, but we need to get Fender out of the house before you confront him or I can get back in. The first thing we need to do is call for plenty of backup and an ambulance. There's a possibility he's still alive."

"Where is he?" Mason demanded.

"He's upstairs in the building over the garage."

All four heads turned to stare upwards at the building.

"Look at me!" I said harshly and four heads swiveled back toward me. "Fender is in there right now keeping track of what's going on out here. Doesn't it seem strange to you that he hasn't come out to see what all the noise is about? The only way he's coming out of that house is for us to trick him. I think I have the best chance of doing that."

"I can get him out," Mason said grimly as he walked away.

"Deputy!" I yelled. He stopped and turned. "If you go to the door looking like that with your hand on your gun, you're going to spook him. Then you'll get the door slammed in your face. There are two women inside the house. He could take them hostage. Let me try first. What can you lose? If it doesn't work, you can still confront him."

"You say you've found Tew. You've done your job. Now I'm going to do mine without any interference from you — or do you think you're in charge?"

"You need backup," I said, trying to reason with him. "That gorilla in there is operating under stress and fear. I wouldn't want to say 'hello' without at least four more warm bodies with me."

He gave me a small sneer. "Well, Miz Sidden, that's what separates the gals from the men."

"It's your call, Deputy, and may the good Lord have mercy!" I uttered with sarcasm.

He gave a satisfied nod to his city buddy. Then they swaggered off like they were heading for the O.K. Corral. It was my own damn fault. My quick temper and faster mouth had done it again. I had tap-danced on his balls about an hour ago and now he was proving they were alive, well, and full of testosterone.

I turned to Wade and Wayne. I signed because it would save time. I told them we had to get into the building upstairs, which I was sure would be locked. I asked Wayne to search the garage for a crowbar or ax and bring it upstairs.

Wade and I headed for the stairs. "How sure are you that he's upstairs?" he asked.

"Positive," I said. "But just in case this is the first time the dogs are wrong, will we be breaking a law by forcing the door open and entering?"

"Nope. If you have reason to believe someone needs help behind a locked door, you can force it open and enter to give aid. In Boston we called it the 'smelling smoke excuse.' You would be surprised to find how many men with arrest warrants in their pockets smelled smoke, gas, or heard a moan from inside a place they believed their suspect to be hiding and not answering their knock."

When Wade and I reached the top of the landing, I opened the screen door and tried the doorknob. The door was locked. The top half of the door was glass and covered with a tightly gathered lace panel. I put my nose to the glass, using my hands to shut out the outside light, but still couldn't see anything. It was pitch black inside. I hadn't grabbed the flashlight. Great! What if the electricity was off or there were no light bulbs?

"What do you think, Counselor? Want to try a shoulder?"

"I'd rather try a shoe on the glass," he replied. "I think a shoulder would hurt. It can't be as easy as it looks on TV."

"Chicken," I said, smiling at him. Wade was standing awkwardly on one leg, the other bent to remove his left shoe. He had just slipped the shoe from his foot and was holding it in his right hand. His mouth was open and he was staring past me to the bottom of the stairs. I whirled to face disaster. The tableau seemed to unfold in slow motion. Wayne had his back to me with a crowbar resting on his left shoulder like a baseball bat. He was facing a lumbering Fender, who seemed as big and unstoppable as a Mack truck. I wanted time out. I wanted the action to stop so I could caution Wayne not to pull his swing — to tell him to aim a foot behind the monster and knock a home run.

Wayne swung, but didn't put his heart into it. He had time enough to think of all that gray matter in Fender's skull and the amount of damage a strong swing of the crowbar could accomplish. Wayne had opted for Fender's shoulder. The pain brought Fender to a halt, but only momentarily. He brought the very same shoulder Wayne had popped forward in a roundhouse swing, catching Wayne below his right ear with a hamlike fist. I saw Wayne falling to the right too close to the brick wall. When he was down, I could only see his feet, and they weren't moving.

I gawked at Fender. He was staring down at Wayne to see if he was going to get up. I wasted several seconds acting stupid. I yelled "Come on," to Wade, then charged down the stairs. I came down as far as I could until Fender started up toward me. When he was committed to the stairs, I grabbed the hand-rail with both hands, stooped and swung my body out into space, then dropped to the grass below. I had jumped without checking the height from ground level, guessing it to be not more than ten feet.

I landed on my heels and tailbone. It felt like I had driven my coccyx a foot up my spine. The pain was intense. I looked around wildly for Wade. The damn fool was still on the stairs, waiting for Fender to climb up to him. Wade had both arms above his head, holding his shoe. I felt hysterical laughter trying to surface. It looked like David waiting for Goliath, except David had had at least a slingshot and rock, while Wade had only a jogging shoe. It didn't occur to me until much later that Wade had remained on the stairs to ensure Fender's coming for him first, thus giving me time to get free.

I stood. When that worked, I tried running. My plan was to run around and grab the crowbar Wayne had dropped, then run up the stairs behind Fender and attack his legs. A couple of good swings should slow him down a little. It was a good plan; there just wasn't enough time. Wade threw the shoe, then planted his foot in Fender's midsection. I grabbed the crowbar and had my foot on the bottom step when Fender grabbed Wade's foot in flight, using Wade's own momentum to jerk him off-balance and down the stairs to his right. It looked like Wade had landed face down, but I couldn't be sure, since I had troubles of my own.

Fender had started down the stairs toward me, stepping clear of Wade, quick as a cat. I whirled and took off for the van. I was sure I could outrun the big ape. It was time to get a lot of reinforcements on the scene; bodies were lying around like bowling pins. Both Wade and Wayne were down and I assumed that the two officers had suffered the same fate.

As I ran, I fished in my pocket for the keys. I hadn't locked the van, but I always take the keys. I was still holding the crowbar. I didn't think it would be a good idea to throw it down with Fender breathing down my neck. I made it to the van, jumped in, threw the crowbar on the right floorboard, pressed the master lock and started the automatic windows upward. God, they wouldn't operate without the ignition turned on! I finally got the key inserted, turned, and the master lock engaged with the windows starting slowly upward. God, they moved slow! I started composing the scathing letter I would write the Chevy people if I lost this race and was still able to write.

The windows finally closed, just as Fender aimed a blow at the window's glass about twelve inches from my left ear. I couldn't believe the glass could remain intact after such an assault! I shoved the gear lever into reverse, spun the wheel and quickly backed up twelve feet or so. I hadn't looked behind me — I couldn't spare the time — but I was clear of Fender.

He stood and looked at me. The car was partially turned in the drive. I risked a fast glance in the rearview mirror. There was only a foot or two before the thick hedge of hibiscus cut off my view. If I went toward Fender, I didn't have enough turning space to clear him on the first attempt. I would have to go forward a few feet, back up some, then cut the wheel sharply to clear the side of his house. I remembered leaving the driveway to the right as I negotiated around the police cars to get into this cul-de-sac. Now, I would have to negotiate back around them to get out.

As I was planning my getaway, Fender came toward me in a shuffling lope. Seeing red, I stomped down on the gas and headed straight toward him. This was war; I'd figure out how to avoid him later. I did the one thing he was not expecting. It froze him into position a few seconds, which was a few too many for him. When I saw he wasn't moving, I stomped the brakes and prayed. He finally started moving backward, too late, and threw up his hands. He was slammed backward against the house and pinned to the wall by the grill of the van like a butterfly in a scrapbook. The engine of the van was running and my foot was still pressing down as hard as possible on the brakes, with the car still in gear. Fender was conscious and squirming, trying to get free, so at least I hadn't killed him yet.

I started to review my options. I could put the van in park, then turn off the ignition key and release the brakes. Wait! Some memory kept nudging me, not letting me touch the gear lever. Sometimes, when I started to park the van and moved the gear lever into park, I remembered the van would move forward at least four or five inches. If it moved forward four or five inches now, Fender would be crushed and I would be guilty of vehicular homicide. Justifiable maybe, but not my wish. I kept my foot pressed hard on the brake pedal, the van's motor running, the engine in gear, while I thought some more. I'm the average woman when it comes to car engines. I don't know what makes them go. As long as there's gas in the tank, oil up to the "Full" mark, and I have regular service on the vehicle, I expect it to go. I know as much about engines as the average car mechanic knows about coddling eggs. There were four unconscious men on the premises and here I was dreading the laughs and raw jokes I knew I would get from the rescuing officers. I was ashamed of myself. The men could be badly hurt and two of them were friends.

I grabbed the mike and put in the call to the dispatcher for the Gilsford County Sheriff's Department.

"Roger, this is Jo Beth Siddon in Rescue Unit One. I'm at one ninety Seegars Road. There are two officers and two civilians down. We need ambulances and assistance right away. Do you read?"

The mike exploded with sound.

"Say again, Jo Beth. Did you say four down? Over."

"Roger, I have four down; injured, not shot. Just get us some help, okay?"

"You got backup and ambulances on the way, Jo Beth. Hang on, they'll be there before you know it! What happened?"

Ignoring his last question, I replaced the microphone on the dash.

The whole story would be all over town in an hour. I'd bet I had help on the way! Any patrol car within radio range would be high-tailing it here as fast as possible. I prayed that the first one here would be an understanding soul and keep his mouth shut, but I knew this was way too much to ask. I would have to put up with their horse-laughs. Ah well, I just hoped no one was badly hurt, and that poor old Ancel Tew upstairs was still breathing, but I wouldn't bet on it. I reached over and dug a cigarette from the pack on the seat beside me, lit it and took a deep drag. The lull before the storm.

I heard the faint sound of a siren in the distance, getting closer and louder. I looked again at Fender who was glowering at me; at least he had stopped trying to pull free; it probably hurt too much. I wondered if he was busted up inside, but I didn't really care much. I heard a siren die, brakes squeal, a door slam and footsteps running up the drive. I released the window beside me and waited.

The young patrolman who appeared at my window had a City of Constine patch on his uniform sleeve.

"What happened?" he asked, breathless. "Who's he?" He was indicating Fender.

"First, let's get him cuffed. Do you happen to have some leg irons with you?" I inquired.

"Yes, ma'am," he said in a short manner. He didn't like the way this conversation was going; he was supposed to give the orders.

"Cuff him and put him in the legs irons, and be careful; he's dangerous," I said. He went for the leg irons. When he returned, he stopped at my window. "Back up some."

"No way. I'm not moving an inch until he's under full restraint," I said.

He looked as if he wanted to argue, but he was in his early twenties, with very little experience in police work. He decided to do as I said until someone else arrived. I sat there watching his mind work out his decision. He walked around the front of the van and eyed Fender. I heard another car approach and saw Deputy Sergeant Tom Lyons of Gilsford County Sheriff's Department walking up the drive.

"What's up, Jo Beth?" he asked.

"Help Junior up there get our maniac in shackles," I said, "and I'll fill you in."

"You think they're necessary?" he asked with a twinkle in his eyes.

"We have four down; care to make it six?"

"Not tonight," he said with good humor. "I've got plans for later." He went to help the raw recruit.

I looked down the drive as Deputy Mavis Johns of Gilsford County Sheriff's Department approached and saw possible salvation. She hurried up with her gun drawn.

"Put the cannon away, Mavis," I told her. "Christ, it looks like a biggy. What is it?"

"Nine millimeter Glock," she answered proudly. "What's up? Who's down?"

"Later," I said in haste. "What do you know about transmissions?"

She was quick to sense a weakness. "Have a problem, do we?"

"You bet," I said, then briefly explained, ending with, "It's not going to take them long to get that monster in chains. How do I get the van off him without smearing him against the wall? And Mavis, this is just between you and me, right?"

"Sisters, unite?" She smiled.

"You got it," I said with relief. "Now give."

She leaned lazily on the window with her elbows. "You know that deputy over in Dunston County, the loot? The tall one who has the hots for you — what's his name?"

"You know his name, Mavis," I said, gritting my teeth. "It's Hank Cribbs. What do you want?"

"Dinner with him at the King Steer. Maybe dancing later at Porky's. At least four hours of his undivided attention."

"Christ, Mavis, give me a break here; my leg is numb. I don't know Hank that well. I've never even been out with him. Call him up and invite him out. This is the nineties!"

"Nice chatting with you, Jo Beth. I'd better go hold Deputy Mason's hand. He's a fellow officer, you know? He's one of the guys who's injured, isn't he? Do I go around back?"

"I've got a long memory," I told her quietly, but she wasn't listening; she was already on her way.

I looked up and saw Deputy Lyons making a twisting motion with his right hand. I reached for the key and turned the motor off. Nothing happened. I drew a deep breath and eased my foot off the brake pedal. So far, so good. Tom was making a motion with both hands, telling me to back up. I moved the gear shift from drive to park, turned the key, and heard the engine start. I looked at Tom again, and he again made the back-up gesture, so I gingerly moved the gear lever into reverse and when the van didn't move, I quickly gave it gas and backed several feet before stopping. I believed Tom's instructions would be carefully thought out, mainly because he was standing between the van and the wall when he gave them.

An ambulance and more patrol cars were arriving. I got out, stretched creaking joints and walked to where Tom and the young city officer were standing. Fender had slumped down in a sitting position with his back against the wall of the house.

"Let's check on my guys," I said to Tom. I turned to the city officer, just to needle a bit. "Don't forget to read him his rights."

As we walked away, I told Tom what had happened. I told him it was my fault that Mason had acted so macho, then told him why.

He glanced at me. "You do have a talent for rubbing people the wrong way, Jo Beth," he said mildly.

"I know," I said. "I'm working on it. Thanks for being so nice about it."

He laughed. "Don't get the wrong idea, Jo Beth. I have the same opinion about you as the rest of the guys. I'm a political animal. I'm next in line when Sheriff Scroggins retires next year. Sheriff Scroggins likes you, so I'm nice to you. I need his endorsement to run for his office successfully. I try to be nice to everybody right now."

"Thanks for being honest," I said. "Sorry I can't vote for you. I live over in Dunston County."

"I know." he said. "That's why I was honest."

I gave him a grin. "I think we're gonna get along just fine. We're both gonna be around here awhile. Maybe I can keep you honest in your treatment of women and maybe you can keep me honest in my dealings with your officers. Who knows? We might find some common ground."

"Anything is possible," he agreed.

We found Wayne sitting on the stairs next to a dazed Wade. The entire right side of Wayne's face was swelling, his right eye already swollen shut. I signed and asked him if he was hurt anywhere else. He reluctantly pointed to the back of his head. I leaned over to see better in the glaring headlights of cars parked all over the lawn below and sucked in a quick breath. The nasty cut on the back of his head had stopped bleeding, but there was a lot of dried blood crusted around the wound. His shirt collar was soaked as well as the back of his shirt.

I signed to him that the head would require stitches, so he should go to the hospital in the ambulance when they got around to loading him and not to give me any argument. He started shaking his head, so I hurriedly held up both hands to stop him. I told him I would meet him at the hospital and wouldn't call Rosie if it wasn't necessary. I knew that was his main concern; he didn't want her to worry.

He signed acceptance, so I turned to Wade. He was conscious but not alert when I knelt in front of him.

"How's it going, Counselor?" I asked him. He tried to focus on my face.

"I see two of you. That's one too many . . . and I have a headache," he said slowly. "What happened?"

He probably had a concussion. It was my fault for bringing him and wanting to show off. Way to go, Jo Beth. You've really screwed up now. I patted him on the shoulder and told him everything would be all right. I sure as hell hoped so.

Deputy Lyons had turned and was yelling at two ambulance attendants. They came up the stairs and took over. They led Wayne and Wade down the stairs after I told both of them again that I would see them at the hospital.

The deputy and I watched as they climbed into the ambulance. I turned to him.

"The old man is upstairs here," I said. "Do we break the door down or go ask Fender's wife for a key?" I suddenly felt tired and just wanted to sit down for a few minutes.

"I'll get some muscle up here," he said. "I've still got plans for tonight, although it looks like it's going to take awhile."

He left to get some help. I wasn't even mildly curious about his plans. He was in his late thirties and looked attractive enough, but I couldn't feel any sympathy for his delayed plans. Too many people were hurting tonight. I leaned against the stair railing, and after a short wait, watched while two husky officers demolished the door lock and splintered the door facing.

I followed them inside. The small apartment was so hot and airless that we immediately broke out in a sweat and stared taking deeper breaths. The electricity was on and the apartment had light bulbs. All three men were stomping around the small apartment on the hardwood floors looking for Ancel Tew.

I waited in the small living room. It was sparsely furnished with used furniture. They surely had "used up all the good" in it. My heart warmed when I remembered that old expression. I had first heard it as a small child listening to my mother and a neighbor named Janna Sue, who was mother's best and only friend for the last ten years of her life. That had been Janna Sue's favorite saying. My mother was very frugal, from necessity rather than inclination. When Mother finally tossed some object that was completely worn out, Janna Sue would nod her head and wisely agree that Mother had used up all the good in it.

No one was currently living here, but it wasn't as dusty or musty as expected, which was a tribute to Mrs. May Belle Fender's dedication to cleanliness. She must have dusted and aired the place on a regular basis.

Deputy Lyons stuck his head around the corner of the small living room.

"What made you think the missing man was up here?" he asked.

"The dogs told me," I answered.

The three officers moved back into the small room. With the four of us, the room seemed crowded and much hotter.

"Well, I'm afraid the dogs told you wrong this time," Lyons said. "He's not here." The other two officers were standing at ease and enjoying the conversation about dogs talking. I could see a small twitch every so often in their expressions, as though it was hard to keep from laughing.

"The dogs said he's here, so he's here," I said with a lot more assurance than I felt. This caused all three of them to smile.

"Well, Jo Beth, we'll wait out on the stairs while you look for him. It's a lot cooler out there."

I stood in silence while the trio tromped out to the small landing outside. I made a grim promise to Susie and Bo that their muzzles would be white with age before they got another jerky treat if they were wrong.

I looked around the living room. The sofa was covered with a fitted cover printed in faded cabbage roses. I knelt on the floor and lifted the front dust ruffle. Although there was about an eight-inch clearance from the floor to the bottom of the seat, Ancel Tew wasn't under there.

I began to try and reconstruct what I thought might have happened early this afternoon downstairs in the Fender house. The wife had been sedated. I didn't know if this was premeditated or coincidental, but I felt that Fender had done something to Ancel Tew. He had struck him in anger or deliberately choked him, or something. Fearing the wife's reaction to her father's injury, and not wanting to be accused of a crime and its consequences, he panicked and decided to concoct a story about Ancel wandering off. Not wanting, either, to be seen carrying a body, his only option was to hide the body in the house somewhere. Then he would wait until everyone had cleared out, the search called off, then take the body down the path from the house and kick a few leaves over it for cover. With any luck, the body wouldn't be found until hunting season by a hunter. By that time, the cause of death would be harder to prove, which would improve his chances of getting away with murder. It was doubtful, under those circumstances, that they would even perform an autopsy on an old man who had Alzheimer's and had probably wandered off and died in the woods. I liked my theory, but the only way to prove it was to find the body.

I'd bet Fender had almost flipped when he learned that bloodhounds had been called in. He hadn't counted on that in his hurried plan. By the time he had heard about the dogs coming, he was committed to it. No wonder he was so hostile toward me; he could see his plan unraveling.

I went into the tiny bedroom and glanced around. The bed had no linen on it and it was such an obvious hiding place, I almost didn't look under it, and when I did, sure enough, there was nothing there. The bathroom could be searched with a glance. No built-in cabinets, just tub, wash basin and commode. I entered the kitchen and saw only two cabinets below the sink hiding only plumbing, and two more tiny ones above the sink. Along the opposite wall a wide shelf had been built to be used as a table, a cheap solution for a breakfast nook. Placed in front of the shelf were two tall wooden barstools. Tew wasn't in the kitchen. That had to be the end of the search as there were no more rooms.

I stood in the sweltering heat trying to think where I would hide a body, knowing there could be a room-to-room search. Standing there in contemplation I glanced toward the ceiling. Most inexpensive homes in Georgia don't have attics, but have a crawl space four to five feet in height, depending on the pitch of the roof. They also have open rafters above the ceiling.

A lot of men in Georgia have discovered how awkward these spaces can be in the last twenty years or so of interest in energy conservation. They've had to crawl around on their hands and knees trying to install rolls of fiberglass to hold in heat in winter and cool air in summer. Some have punched holes in their sheet-rock ceilings when their feet slipped on the rafters, and others have fallen completely through to the room below — but the space is most often large enough to conceal a body.

The kitchen didn't have an opening in the ceiling. They are usually placed in closets or hallways. Walking back into the miniature hall, I looked up and saw an opening about two and a half feet square. My heart started pumping faster and I felt adrenaline begin to flow. I went back to the kitchen for one of the tall stools and placed it under the opening to estimate its height. Using it, my five-foot, seven-inch height should make it possible for me to look around above the ceiling without having to crawl up there among the spiders, which I hate. Although I didn't have a flashlight and would probably need one to see any distance, maybe there would be enough light from the hall to take a quick peek. Who was I kidding? I was grasping at straws because I didn't want to meet the trio on the stairs until I had a body for them.

Bracing myself with my palm flat against the wall, I got up on the stool and slowly straightened. While I couldn't stand straight, being almost a foot too tall, hunched over I could place both hands on the square and push it upward. It lifted easily and I tried sliding it to the right, but something was blocking the panel's movement, so I tried moving it to the left, and felt it yield in that direction. Putting both hands in the opening for balance, I slowly straightened until my head was through it.

I was gazing directly at Ancel Tew, lying on his back not six inches from the edge of the hole, about nine inches from my face. It took a second before my mind registered comprehension of the sight. My lungs filled with air in an instinctive scream. I realized that I mustn't be so predictably feminine. I let the air out with a whoosh and started taking little panting breaths. To adjust to the sight more quickly I clung to the edge of the opening with both hands and took quick little peeks at Ancel.

When I felt able to maintain my balance with one hand, I reached gently for his wrist. The skin was warm. I couldn't believe it! The heat was stifling in the crawl space, but when the blood stops flowing through the veins, the flesh feels cool very quickly. Little Tommy had felt cool even in bright sunlight and heat, and so had the fisherman with the heart attack last fall.

He had to be alive; there was no other explanation. He had been up here almost five hours and he was still alive! I fumbled for a pulse under his jaw, but didn't know if my hand was in the right spot or not. I took a deep breath and stood up as tall as possible, using the tips of my toes, then put my ear to his chest, straining to hear the thin, thready beat. It was music to my ears.

I lowered my body just far enough to clear my head from the crawl space and sucked in oxygen.

"Hey, Deputy!" I yelled as loud as possible and with intense satisfaction. "Get your ass in here!"

11

I heard what sounded like a muffled curse and the frantic pounding of feet on the hardwood floor. A startled Deputy Tom Lyons appeared in the small hallway.

"He's alive," I said quickly. "Is an ambulance still downstairs?"

"I'll see," he said and turned, but one of the officers behind him yelled, "I'll check," and took off running.

"So your dogs were right," he said with a grin.

"Yep," I replied. We grinned at each other. There is nothing so satisfying as knowing you've snatched another one from the jaws of the grim reaper.

"You want some help down from there?" he offered and stepped closer.

"I think I'll stay with him till the EMTs arrive," I told him.

"That's good," he agreed.

It was twenty minutes or more before they came to get him down. They had to recall an ambulance that had left empty and was already back at the hospital. When two EMTs crowded into the hall, I eased myself down with both of them steadying me as I backed down from the stool. They promised they would take care of him, so I went outside. I didn't want to watch while they were getting him down from the crawl space; it was going to be tough.

When I walked out on the stairs drenched in sweat, the night air chilled me. I asked Tom if he would have one of his men drive Wayne's van to the hospital and wait there until I could leave and then drive it to Dunston County for me. I explained why he couldn't take it directly to the kennel. It would upset Rosie and we didn't want her to worry.

He detailed two men, one to drive the van and the other to follow in a patrol car to drive them both back. I thanked him and promised to be at his office tomorrow morning to fill out the report.

"Sure you don't want to do the reports tonight after you leave the hospital?" he asked with a grin. We just couldn't stop grinning at each other.

"You've got plans and I've got plans, so be good." I told him.

Upon reaching the van, I opened each dog box and gave Susie and Bo a few quick words of love and praise. They had done so much and hadn't been allowed to celebrate or been praised in all the confusion. They'd just been tossed into the box. I promised them a big hamburger from the first fast-food restaurant we came to.

It turned out to be a McDonald's about three blocks from the hospital. When I pulled into the lane leading to the take-out window, the small parade behind pulled in also. At the ordering speaker, I jumped out, ran back, and told the officers I was getting a burger for the dogs; did they want anything? They both laughed and gave me their orders, trying to give me money, too, but I waved their offer aside. I felt so good, I would have treated the whole world if I could have afforded it.

I ordered four Big Macs with cheese, plain for the dogs, two Big Macs, dressed, for the officers, and coffee, then ordered French fries and a large Diet Coke for myself. We were drawing a crowd. People entering and leaving the restaurant were stopping to see what was going on with two vans and a patrol car. I decided to give a small performance to the onlookers in the interest of public relations. (Who was I trying to kid? I was gonna show off again.) When the order arrived, I paid for it and flipped open each dog box as I passed it, then gave the officers their food and placed mine on the seat of the van. Even the officers got out to watch the feeding take place.

The dogs had all been to drive-up windows before. They knew what the wonderful odors on the air meant so they sat up very straight and tried to contain their anticipation. I stopped in front of Susie's box, unwrapped her burger, waved it under her nose and gave the command "Hold!" I placed it gently in her jaws. She held it, trying not to quiver. I repeated the maneuver until all four dogs were holding their burgers. I decided I'd better not push the wait too long; someone might break training.

I gave the command "Eat!" and half of the four burgers disappeared instantly, then four jaws snatched the second halves out of the air before they could fall. Two bites were all it took. I closed the cages to enthusiastic applause, waved to the crowd, and pulled out of the drive. I really couldn't decide who was the biggest ham, the dogs or me. Ah, no contest . . . I was.

I gobbled as many fries as possible in the three blocks to the hospital and took the Coke in with me. I stopped in the emergency room and set it down before going up to the counter. I know hospitals; they have strict rules about everything. I was sure they wouldn't allow cold drinks inside the waiting room. I was right. I had been spotted with the Coke by a passing nurse.

"You'll have to get rid of the drink," she said sourly. "No drinks in the waiting room."

"Of course," I said. I hurried back around the corner and placed the cup out of sight, behind a sofa. I could come back and rescue it later, but, being dehydrated, I really needed it now, so took a large swig before deserting it. I went over to the counter. The lady behind it looked up.

"I'm here to check on Wade Bennett, Wayne Frazier, and the two officers who were brought in a few minutes ago, from one ninety Seegars Road."

"Are you a relative?" she asked. She hadn't consulted any list on her desk. I reached for my wallet.

"Official on the scene," I said in a bored tone, as I waved the Gilsford County gun permit under her nose. It was light blue, with my thumbprint, vital statistics, signature of Sheriff Scroggins, and Gilsford County in large lettering — it looked official as hell. If you run a bluff, you have to do it quickly and not stand still for a lot of questions. People in authority don't patiently answer questions. She reached out and steadied my hand so she could read the card.

"That's a gun permit," she said with sarcasm.

"Which means I carry a gun," I told her in my meanest voice.

"Where?" she said with irony, as her eyes flicked over my tight jeans and T-shirt. I was trying to think up a caustic remark when she looked behind me and I felt a hand on my shoulder. I turned and was caught in a bear hug by Sheriff Scroggins. He is three inches shorter than I, outweighs me by eighty pounds or so and has a deep booming voice. As a child, I felt that if he commanded the dead to rise, they would have to do something. He and my dad had been fishing buddies and I had known him forever.

"Jo Beth, honey!" he thundered. He was holding me clear off the floor and my ribs were aching.

"Put me down!" I gasped. "I think you broke a rib!"

"Sorry, honey," he boomed. His voice hit the wall and echoed down the hall. I enjoyed seeing the flinch I spotted on Stone Face behind the counter. He set me back on my feet and continued to pat my back and shoulders with both hands. Sheriff Scroggins is a toucher, but not a groper or lecher. Some men and women read him wrong. He's a warm, caring, big-hearted man who gives and receives comfort from touching. I don't know about men, but I feel that a woman who can't distinguish between a grope and a loving touch has emotional problems and misses a lot of good in life.

"The boys told me how great you were. My, my, simply amazing, those dogs of yours. Come on back with me, while I get the scoop from the doc on their condition."

"Just a sec," I replied and ran back to retrieve the Coke from behind the sofa. If I had a free card, I might as well use it. When I returned, Stone Face was telling me, with her glare, that someday I might be admitted on a stretcher and she would make me wait and wait and wait. Out of sight of the sheriff, I shot her a bird and stuck out my tongue simultaneously. Now we both knew how we felt about each other.

As we walked down the hall, the sheriff was heaping praise on me like a proud parent. I sipped the Coke and was thankful he was a bene-factor and long-time friend. He had been a great help to me in my busi-ness. He approached a nurse and asked her to fetch the doc. She glared at me and the Coke, but I ignored her. When the doctor arrived, he was young, wearing bloody greens and was impatient.

"I've got an assault victim and a suspicious stomach waiting, so make it quick." He was carrying a clipboard. I had been trying lately to learn to read upside down. The view was a clear shot, but a doctor's handwriting? Hopeless. The sheriff explained the five people we were interested in. The doctor consulted his clipboard.

"Your deputy has a broken jaw and some facial lacerations. He's getting wired up in surgery now. Should be fine. If there's no concus-sion, he should be released in the morning." He glanced at his notes. "The man with impaired hearing has nine stitches in his scalp, facial trauma and a dislocated shoulder. The other man has a slight concus-sion and three broken ribs. I'm holding both of the last two mentioned, overnight. With no complications, they should both be released tomor-row. The elderly man," he stopped to search his notes for his name. I guess his news required the name. "Ancel Tew? He didn't make it. Car-diac arrest during transit. They couldn't restart and neither could we. He was pronounced at ten-oh-five p.m."

The tears started to flow. I remembered the thready beat in the frail chest under my fingers. No more, all gone. Probably happened while I was showing off at the drive-up window. The doctor left after saying we could see the patients briefly in the emergency rooms where they were waiting to be transferred to rooms. The sheriff saw my tears.

"Now, honey, you gave him a chance. Without you, he wouldn't had no chance at all. You did good, so don't feel bad." He held and patted and consoled me. I felt miserable, but I had to visit the guys.

We walked down the hall. "You gonna be all right?" he asked. I assured him I was fine. Then we split up to visit our men. I stuck my head in two cubicles before finding Wayne.

"Hey, Slugger," I signed.

He signed that he hadn't hit him hard enough. I agreed and asked how his dislocated shoulder felt. He looked at me and gave a sheepish grin.

"You're a sneaky Pete," I signed. "Didn't want to tell me. Knew I wouldn't let you handle the dogs with a bum shoulder. No classes and no searches until it heals, understood?"

He pleaded with me for the classes, said we'd get too far behind, swore he could work without the dogs pulling on his shoulder. "No, no and no," I signed. He looked sulky. Sometimes I forgot that he was only nineteen, still a teenager. I spent the next fifteen minutes joking him out of his moody spell until they came to take him upstairs.

It was an orderly with a wheelchair and a young college girl from the office staff. She was carrying a clipboard. I told her I would follow them upstairs and give her the information needed for her forms. She smiled and told me that she and Wayne could manage. She signed to Wayne that she was enrolled at Southern Methodist and was going for a BA in social services. I told Wayne that Rosie or I, or both, would be up next morning to take him home. I left them happily signing away, knowing he wouldn't miss me.

I went down the hallway looking for Wade until an annoyed nurse told me he had already been taken upstairs. When I asked her very sweetly to find out the room number, she left and came back with the number and a put-upon air.

I don't understand nurses. As a waitress, I ran my tail off for a lot less money than she was making, was just as skilled in my profession as she is in hers, and was a lot nicer to my customers than she was with visitors.

I rode the elevator to the third floor and hiked down the corridor to find Wade. A nurse was taking his blood pressure and temperature. She ordered me out as though I was seeing secret procedures requiring dedicated and total security. I told her that Sheriff Scroggins had obtained permission for me to visit for fifteen minutes. She told me, in a very tart voice, that Sheriff Scroggins didn't run this hospital.

"Lady, I know that, and you know that, but I doubt if Sheriff

Scroggins knows that. He's down in the emergency room right now, so you want to go tell him?" She took her machine and her haughty expression with her.

"You should have asked for your readings; it's your body and your right to know," I told him. He was propped up in almost a sitting position and looked and acted more alert than when I had last seen him. "Hit anyone with a shoe lately?"

"I'm only seeing one of you now, which is a vast improvement, but I still have the headache. I don't want to throw any more shoes; what I needed was a guided missile. How's Wayne?"

"Nine stitches in his scalp, dislocated shoulder, and a very sore face." I told him about the officers' injuries, showing off at McDonald's, and about finding and losing Ancel Tew.

"You can't save everyone, Jo Beth. Be thankful for the ones you save and learn not to feel guilty about the ones you lose," he said with a very sweet smile. "I wish I could have seen the dogs with their hamburgers. In fact, I wish I had a hamburger."

"They won't feed you tonight," I told him. You were injured after the kitchen closed. You have to be in your hospital room at least three hours prior to their mealtime before you can get a tray."

"You wouldn't have a couple of aspirins on you, by any chance?" He looked hopeful.

"Sorry, they won't give you anything for your discomfort." I told him. "They don't have any pain in hospitals, only a little discomfort. Ask me anything. I'm an expert on hospitals."

"Why won't they give me something for my headache?" He was honestly puzzled.

"You are slightly concussed. You can't have any medication. They also won't let you get any sleep tonight. They'll be in here every fifteen minutes taking your pulse and blood pressure and sticking you for blood samples for the lab. If you happen to doze off, they'll rush in and wake you up."

"I've asked four different people for a couple of aspirin. Why didn't one of them tell me I couldn't have any, and I would have quit asking. Every one of them said, 'I'll check,' 'I'll see,' or 'I'll ask for you.'"

"Wade," I told him kindly, "all nurses are trained in a special school to keep every scrap of pertinent information about your condition out of your sight, out of your hearing, and to keep you totally in the dark."

"I take it that you've had some bad experiences with nurses?" He moved to push up straighter in bed. The pain pulled his mouth closed and widened his eyes.

"I've had a few bad ones; the resentment lingers," I said. "My heart tells me there are many, many good and dedicated professionals out there, but my mind says, 'Oh, yeah?' Maybe you'll have better luck. How are the ribs?"

"From neck to knees, I feel like I've been beaten with a baseball bat," he stated. "Must have been my pratfall down the stairs."

"You have three broken ribs," I told him. "I'd suggest you move around as little as possible."

My news shocked him. "I have three broken ribs and they didn't even tell me?" His voice had risen; he was indignant.

"To be fair, the doctor is quite busy tonight; he doesn't have time for bedside chats and you couldn't pull it out of the nurses with torture. I was with the sheriff when I heard about your condition. If I had been alone, I probably wouldn't have been told."

"And when do you think they'll get around to telling me?"

"If your concussion hasn't gotten any worse by morning, he'll probably release you. Don't forget to ask for a prescription for pain medication. They sometimes forget in their mad rush from room to room on their morning rounds. 'Course they never forget to bill each patient a good pop for each visit."

"Which reminds me," he said. "Will they take a credit card for the bill?"

"You won't need one," I said. "As of six-oh-five p.m. yesterday, you are employed by Bloodhounds, Inc., as a legal consultant and on-the-scene advisor. You're completely covered on my insurance. I'll stop at the office downstairs on the way home."

"Won't that raise your premiums?" he asked.

"Absolutely not," I said with mock indignation, lying through my teeth. "The premiums are so high already, that if they try to raise them, they're automatically indicted for fraud. I'm gonna have to run, Wade. There're two deputies downstairs twiddling their thumbs waiting for me so they can help get Wayne's van home. If you'll give me your keys, I'll stop by your house in the morning and bring some fresh clothes for you."

"I have no idea where they are," he said blankly.

I pulled open his nightstand drawer, finding only a telephone directory and Gideon Bible. Over in the clothes closet I found the pants and shirt he had been wearing and one shoe on the floor under them.

"They're probably downstairs locked up with your other valuables," I said, "which means I'll need a note from you to be able to pick them up. I'll be right back."

I went down the hallway to the nurses' station and borrowed pen and paper. I returned them to Wade, waiting as he wrote the note for the desk. I asked if there was anything else he needed before I left.

"A dozen aspirin," he said wistfully.

I patted him on his back. "Sorry."

"I'll settle for a goodnight kiss," he told me. "I'm having trouble getting this romance started."

"It's early days, Counselor," I told him on the way to the door. "It's early days."

Downstairs, it only took twenty minutes to give the admissions clerk insurance information on Wayne and Wade and get possession of Wade's keys. That had to have set a record. Outside, the deputies were patiently waiting. I guess it's the first thing they learn to do, hurry up and wait. I explained about Wayne's shoe being thrown downstairs, asking if they would try to locate it and leave it with Deputy Lyons at the County Building, as I had to go by there in the morning and fill out the report. They said they would check. I asked them if they knew where we were going, nodding as they confirmed knowledge of the kennel's location. I put on the denim jacket before going out since it had turned cooler and I like to ride with the windows open.

The forty-mile ride took an hour. I stayed on fifty-five, enjoying the country oldies on the radio. At night they play old ballads and softer melodies than during the daytime. The air felt damp and smelled cleaner, which meant a good chance of rain by morning. The forecast was only forty percent, but I had learned long ago to temper the expert's opinions with my own. I was right about half the time and so were they, so we were about even on accurate predictions at any given time.

I got out and unlocked both gates, and when the three vehicles were in the courtyard, Rosie hurried down the stairs to greet us. When she saw the deputy emerge from Wayne's van, she lost color and stood, frozen. I hurried over to reassure her. I had to tell her several times that Wayne was okay, and then detail his injuries before she drew a deep breath. When I saw she was feeling normal again, I walked over to the two deputies, shook hands and thanked them. As they drove out, I walked behind them to lock both gates.

When I returned, Rosie was unloading Wayne's dogs. I fed Susie and Bo, leaving them happily devouring their very late evening meal, then did a fast job of straightening and cleaning both vans. Rosie had left to fix a late meal for me, even after my protests. With Rosie around, I never went to bed hungry.

After walking into the house, I stripped, dumped the clothes in and started the washer. Rosie yelled from the kitchen for me to take my time in the shower; she was making biscuits. I spent twenty minutes scrubbing the bathroom fixtures, wiping down walls and damp mopping the floor before showering. It was my chore for tomorrow morning and I knew how rushed I'd be then. I was blow-drying my hair when she called. I left it damp, put on shorty pajamas, stopped in the office to unhook the answering machine, then got a pad and went to eat.

Rosie had spooned her homemade beef hash, with slivers of new potatoes, baby carrots, sweet peas and chipped Vidalia onions, lavishly over two halved biscuits. It filled the plate. She had also made a plate for herself, saying she had been waiting to eat with Wayne. We shared a plate of sliced tomatoes.

"Rosie," I told her between bites, "when I weigh two hundred pounds, you'll be sorry you fed me so well." She was impatient to hear the whole story about the earlier events. I told it all in chronological order, not pausing when Wayne had failed to take Fender out. After I reached the conclusion of the story and she had made her comments, I went back to the part about Wayne pulling his swing. She smiled and shook her head.

"That boy doesn't have a mean bone in his body," she said proudly.

"Rosie," I said softly, "Wayne is a warm, gentle human being, but he's going to have to learn how to defend himself. Why do you think he carries a twenty-two rifle and a thirty-eight-caliber revolver? Why do you think we go to the police firing range once a month to practice? Tell me, do you honestly think he's capable of firing a gun at another human being?"

She looked uncertain. "If they know he's armed, they wouldn't dare mess with him." I just looked at her.

We both had our heads in the sand, I told her. I wanted to ease the tension, so I told her how the dogs had reacted to their new command to "Hold" their food at the restaurant earlier.

"We put that command into our training a week after O'Henry was poisoned," I told her. "It was to protect them, but remember, one dog had to get poisoned before we knew there was a possibility of their getting hurt."

"What are you trying to tell me?" she said, a sad look on her face.

"We can't continue to send Wayne out where there's a possibility of his getting hurt, now that we both know he's emotionally incapable of defending himself." I had stressed the "we" because, without her help, I couldn't help Wayne.

"So, what are we gonna do?" she asked. I breathed a little easier;

she had accepted half the responsibility.

"I don't know," I told her truthfully, "but until we find a solution, I won't send him in harm's way. No searches, rescues or sweeps. There's more than enough for him to do around here. Training, holding classes, and keeping this place in business. He has to train an assistant; now's a good time to find one. It will keep him busy here."

She stood, starting to clear the table. I put my arms around her, holding her close. I knew she was worried.

"Go home," I told her. "You cooked, I wash dishes." I walked her to the back porch and said good night. She said she would be over at seven in the morning. I watched until she was inside her door and the light on the steps went out.

I washed the dishes and sat at the table with a cigarette before playing back the messages on the machine.

I felt sad about Wayne. For a year we had gone on searches together. A year of no problems for him. I had made sure he was trained in weapons use and in self-defense. Personally, I hadn't let myself have doubts. For myself, I had constantly had doubts until that day last fall on the island, when I had come within a hair's breadth of shooting Leroy and his cousin. Wayne might remain lucky for another year, maybe forever, but I know what I would feel if he were any more seriously injured than now. I couldn't send him out to play with the bad boys if he couldn't play by their rules.

The phone rang. The answering machine was unplugged and sitting in front of me on the table. I had to answer as it could be a call-out. Picking up the cigarette and taking it with me, I waited four rings before answering.

"Jo Beth Sidden," I said. In the comparative silence, I could hear the thump of a jukebox, in spite of the hand obviously cupped over the receiver. Bubba was getting sloppy. It was the first time he had let any background noise be heard.

"Listen, Bubba, your phone calls are not working out like you planned while you were up there in Patton Correctional," I told him in a calm, controlled voice. "I'm not quaking in my boots, or even annoyed. You're wasting your daddy's quarters when you could be trying to impress someone with your muscles. You didn't learn anything or get any smarter in the past eight years. Go home to Daddy if he can still stand to have you lying around drunk all the time."

I clapped a hand over the receiver so he couldn't hear my breathing, holding the phone in a death grip.

In a whisky-soaked voice, I heard one word. "Bitch."

The phone was hung up. I heard the click through a white-hot haze of hatred. What a stupid, stupid thing for me to do. I sank down at the desk because suddenly my legs were made of Jell-O. I had not only pulled the tiger's tail, but had also grabbed him by his nuts. I glanced at my watch. 1:30 a.m. The bars would close in thirty minutes. After that, who knew what the bastard might do. I brought the answering machine back to the office to take the messages.

The first call was from a female who sounded like she was between eight and ten years old. She started talking before the beep, so I missed the first part of the conversation, which contained her name, but I could understand her message.

". . . and Mommy said I could spend it on a dog. Do your puppies cost more than fifty dollars? If they don't, call me real soon. Do you have a white poodle? I think they're cute. My daddy says white poodles are for sissies, but that's what I want. Would you call me back if you have a white puppy? His hair has to be curly, too. Do your poodles have curly hair? My brother says it costs a lot of money to have poodles get a haircut, but I can give it a haircut myself."

She was still talking when her time ran out and she hadn't gotten around to leaving a telephone number, so I couldn't return her call tomorrow. She was probably working from the Yellow Pages, where this kennel was listed first. Not realizing that the tape had cut her message short, she would think that because she was a kid, the grown-up at the other end didn't take her seriously. I hated that. I had been ten myself once long ago and knew what it was like to be ignored by adults. I hoped she called back so I could explain.

The next call was from the barracuda.

"ADA Stevens. McAlbee moved seven cases up from next week because his calendar got screwed up. State vs. J. J. Johnson is set for two p.m. tomorrow. Be there. He's had two continuances already and if he tries again tomorrow, I'm going to nail his ass. And Sidden, for God's sake, wear a dress. You know how McAlbee hates pants on a quote, lady, unquote, and don't forget your notebook. See ya."

The barracuda is a hard-nosed blonde transplanted from somewhere in New Jersey to our bucolic setting. She is an assistant district attorney working under our easy-going District Attorney Bobby Don Robbins. Her name is Charlene Stevens, accurately called "the barracuda" by everyone connected with law enforcement, except in her presence. The swath she is cutting in our local judicial system is reminiscent of Sherman's March through Georgia. They say Bobby Don developed ulcers a month after hiring her and can't get rid of her because she wins all her cases, except where the local fix is set in concrete. She makes them sweat and long for more peaceful times. She is such a militant feminist, she makes me sound like Melanie in *Gone with the Wind*.

The case she was referring to was one of those weird arrests that makes lawmen believe there really is a God helping them make arrests of big-time drug dealers. I was working with O'Henry one day; it was the second week in May of last year. A warm day, ninety degrees at noon, but the humidity was very low, so it was fairly pleasant. We had gathered at an abandoned warehouse near the center of some small businesses, a middle-class neighborhood, and a small downtown park. The mothers in the neighborhood brought their small children there to play. Teenagers shot baskets on two cement courts. Enough shade and picnic tables drew quite a few downtown workers to eat their lunches there. The sheriff's department had received numerous complaints from the mothers that drugs were being sold right out in the open. The GBI (Georgia Bureau of Investigation) and DEA were running an undercover operation throughout the city, but were stalling on arresting anyone. They like to make large splashy cases, arrest fifty to seventy-five at once and grab the headlines.

These agencies sometimes keep men undercover for two years or more, making scores of buys before they make their big spectacular raids. Sheriff Sammy Carlson was an ass-kissing toady when it came to the big agencies, but he had received too many complaints from people who voted in this county to keep ignoring the problem.

The sheriff had authorized the sweep, but had gotten cold feet at the last minute. Afraid of upsetting the big boys, he had sent only six men. Lt. Hank Cribbs was leading the raid. He was furious about having only five men available, in addition to himself.

"We'll get about six crooks," he complained. "Time we grab the first ones, every dealer in the park will split, fast."

"True," I agreed, "but that's six off the streets for a couple of hours."

He smiled at the irony. Usually the guys caught with drugs were out on bond before the men who had caught them were finished with the paperwork. We were standing out in the open, in bright May sunshine: six men, three county patrol cars, my van, O'Henry and me. We were talking in normal tones and had even slammed car doors and called greetings to each other. O'Henry had been standing quietly by my side, waiting to go to work. He lifted his nose, sniffed the air and began to strain against the long lead. He was trying to reach the steps of the abandoned warehouse.

"Ah so . . . ," I said with surprise. "Hank, I think we have a nibble.

Our cork is bobbing up and down."

Hank saw O'Henry straining against his lead. He turned, signaling to his men, who came closer, not knowing what was happening. He quickly whispered instructions.

"Sirmans, Rigdon, cover the back. I'll give you two minutes, go." Hank looked at me. "Jo Beth?"

I let O'Henry pull me up the concrete steps to the dock. It was twenty feet wide and at least a hundred feet long. The building was red brick, with large metal roll-up doors, spaced about twenty feet apart; all were closed. O'Henry led us to where the door handle was, near the floor.

All the men had their guns drawn, and two stepped forward to lift the large door. Hank nodded and the door flew up easily. The sight that greeted us left us all momentarily motionless, except for O'Henry. He moved forward quickly until he was standing in front of J. J. Johnson.

J. J. was sitting comfortably in a folding lawn chair, resplendent in his drug-dealing finery, sipping an imported beer from the cooler next to the chair. On a card table to his left there was a boom box playing jazz at a reasonable level of sound and four newspaper-wrapped bundles.

He sat staring at O'Henry, his hand frozen, holding the beer which had been on its way to his mouth extended in the air.

"Whatthefuck!" he yelled. He had unfrozen. "You ain't supposed to be here. You ain't got no business being here!"

Hank gave him a wide grin and winked at me behind J. J.'s back. O'Henry was delighted. He nosed the newspaper packages, then, sensing the excitement in the room, he almost crawled in J. J.'s lap, crowding closer for a hug. As Hank was snapping the cuffs on J. J.'s arm, J. J. was pushing at O'Henry. I left O'Henry alone, letting him crowd J. J. I saw it was distracting him.

"How's tricks, J. J.?" Hank asked as he flipped off the radio and hefted one of the bundles.

"What do you think, Jo Beth . . . a whole pound?"

"Absolutely," I replied. "J. J. is a big man around these parts." I didn't know J. J. or his name from Adam; I was just following Hank's lead. I dug cigarettes out and lit up.

"Damn straight," J. J bragged. "Get this dog off me! I know my rights. You ain't suppose to be here!" He stared at the smoke billowing from my cigarette. "Get that smoke out of my face! Call off the damn dog!" O'Henry thought he had found a playmate. When J. J. pushed him away with his handcuffed hands, O'Henry just bounced back closer.

"A little birdie whispered to me that you had an ear into the state attorney's office, J. J., but I couldn't believe it." Hank said with a satisfied smile. "Damned if he didn't give you up, J. J. We caught him with a wiretap. He was happy to roll over for a suspended sentence and being fired."

Hank was staring at me, willing me to help him, but I was afraid of saying the wrong thing and blowing it. The only black I knew in the state attorney's office was a sweet guy who had two beautiful children to whom I had given a tour of the kennel several months before starting searches and sweeps. Twin boys, bright and eager to learn more about the search dogs. Their father had come with the grade-school class on a tour in the interest of drug prevention. I thought his name was James, but wasn't sure. He couldn't possibly be the one. I took a chance.

Moving closer, I perched my denim-clad rump on the edge of the card table and blew smoke in J. J.'s breathing space.

"How come you put your trust in a white man, J. J.?" I asked him. "It done in the Indians, and now you. You ought to have known better."

"He's a dead man, that Curly is a walking dead man!" he yelled. "Get away. Shoo. Shoo!" This was directed at O'Henry.

I pulled O'Henry clear, at least ten feet to the side, and gave him praise and hugged him. I didn't want to look or talk to Hank right this minute, and I'm sure the feeling was mutual. We all knew Curly. He was our hometown boy who had made good. He had worked a year, then gone to law school a year, putting himself through the hard way. He had lived at home with his mother and hadn't even owned a car until he was thirty-four years old. His hair had disappeared after he turned thirty. When he finally passed his bar exams he went to work in the district attorney's office for several years before becoming an assistant state's attorney. He was in his early forties now, well-liked, respected, and was called Curly with affection by all who knew him. He had just purchased a Porsche. Now we knew who had paid for it.

I took O'Henry out to load up, and Hank joined me. He looked sick.

"Hank," I began tentatively.

"Don't even ask," he said harshly. "There were five deputies standing there when that asshole dropped his bombshell. Do you think the seven of us can keep a secret like that in this town? Get real. What was the poor bastard thinking of?"

"He was probably trying to buy back his youth," I said sadly. I was thinking of my five lost years when I had worked two jobs, merely existing rather than living, in order to attain my dream.

"What will they do to him?" I asked.

"Disgrace, disbarment and de prison." He tried to joke but the misery was thick in his voice.

Curly admitted his involvement when confronted, pleaded guilty and received a ten-year sentence. He also received his disgrace and disbarment. J. J. would finally be tried, starting tomorrow.

The last call on the tape was a hang-up — an earlier call from Bubba. I checked all the doors and windows, drank most of a glass of water and went to bed. I didn't expect to sleep, being so wired from my verbal joust with Bubba. I closed my eyes, relaxed, and slept like the dead.

12

"ONE FOOT IN THE GRAVE,
THE OTHER ON A BANANA PEEL"
April 7, Wednesday, 6 A.M.

I woke at 6:07, having slept through the five-minute news broadcast. Rain was pounding against the windows in solid waves. We were getting what is known locally as a "toad strangler." I looked through the glass observation cube in the bathroom, but couldn't see the large trunk of a magnolia tree twelve feet away.

After plugging in the coffee, I took a fast shower, then dressed in jeans, sweatshirt and joggers. Everyone would look like a drowned rat this morning. The three cups of coffee and four cigarettes for breakfast offset the heavy after-midnight meal which had left me bloated and feeling logy. The rain would be a hindrance to me, but the farmers needed it so badly. I could visualize them outside in their long johns and Skivvies, shouting and jumping for joy at the heavy water coming down.

Today, I needed to make a list because it was going to be very full. At a quarter of seven, I grabbed an umbrella and ran splashing through puddles and heavy downpour to the kennel for a fast walk around to check the dogs. Stopping briefly to check Gloria Steinem's eye, which was clear. I told her to buck up — only two more days — but she didn't look like she believed me. I saw every dog for a second; none appeared to have problems.

I had to call Ramon and ask if he could handle the night feeding for a few days. It would be too much for Rosie, and I might get stuck at the trial for a few days. Every time some county commissioner complained about my fees for search, rescue, and sweeps being too high, I would show them a normal month in my journals. Wayne, Rosie, and I often sat for hours on end, just to be told to come back the next day or that the trial had a continuance to some future date. We all three joked about tush rash from sitting in pools of sweat on hardwood benches in courtrooms without air conditioning.

I ran back through the rain just as Rosie arrived. We went over the day's schedule. I told Rosie I was thinking of bringing Wade to stay for a few days. Both men had to recuperate, and they could be company for each other. She thought it was a wonderful idea. 'Course, she's a natural-born matchmaker, and I knew what she was thinking.

I left at seven-fifteen and stopped by the friendly neighborhood bank, used my cash card and asked for one hundred dollars. The machine was friendly and dispensed five crisp twenties. My generosity at McDonald's last night had cleaned me out of cash, so walking-around money was necessary. When I got to Wade's long driveway turning off the highway, the rain was still heavy. The windshield wipers were swatting away on high, but the view still was not great. I slowed and looked carefully for any sign of Wade's yardman's truck, hoping he didn't have a key for the main house. I wouldn't want to meet Hector in the hallway on this dark and dank morning. I'm not one of his favorite people.

I took the curving driveway to the left of the house, drove slowly around to the back and stopped to look at the large garage. It could hold four cars easily and had a workshop or equipment storage room. It was two-storied with wooden stairs on the outside at each end of the building. Two units for servants — my, my. I continued on the curving drive around the house until I was back at the front door. I didn't know why I was dreading the trip inside to pack a few clothes for Wade. I decided I had read too many Gothic novels. Pushing open the van door, I opened the umbrella, sloshed up to the porch and tried the most likely looking key, which opened the door. My plan was to blaze a trail of lights upstairs, turning them off as I returned.

A white flash of lightning briefly lit up the interior to an operating-room brightness. I flicked on a light switch and stood transfixed by the magnificent chandelier centered high above the foyer. Hundreds of candle-shaped bulbs glowed from various heights in an intricate pattern. The ceiling was two stories high, with a highly polished wooden balcony edged with a three-foot-high railing, running the width of the room between two stately staircases.

As I climbed the stairs on the left, I remembered the two glass lamps we had used in our squalid little shack. It had been my job to keep the glass base full of kerosene, the cotton wick trimmed and the glass shades washed free of smoke. This was after Mama died, when I was ten, until Daddy and I moved into an apartment with electricity when I was fourteen. I smiled at the difference in lifestyles Wade and I had experienced. My beginnings had taught me to want more and had given me the desire to work hard to attain goals. Wade seemed to want less. He didn't seem concerned about losing all this opulence.

I saw a hallway going to the left at the top of the stairs. I wish I had asked how to find his room; I hated peeking into each room trying to discover his. I was lucky. The second room from the stairs was his. Spotting his suitcase sitting out in the open, I was glad he wasn't neat and hadn't tucked it out of sight. I picked several shirts and slacks from the closet, leaving his suits hanging, then found two pairs of loafers and his slippers. His bathrobe and toilet articles were in the bathroom. He had drawn a circle for a face with a downward curve for a frown in shaving cream on the mirror. He must have felt lousy while shaving yesterday. I grabbed the can of shaving cream, squirted a glob in my hand and added a straight line of dots going downward from each dot representing eyes. Now his frowning face was dripping tears. It seemed appropriate on this wet dreary morning.

I picked up the smaller suitcase, placed it on the bed and neatly folded his clothes. He wore white jockey briefs. I added T-shirts, socks, and handkerchiefs. I put his travel clock and a bookmarked law book which were on his nightstand in with the clothes. Studying the room he had left at fifteen years of age, I saw junior varsity pictures on the wall. He hadn't packed them when he left; he must have taken the upheaval hard. Living in a mansion doesn't mean a happy life. I closed the case and went downstairs, turning off lights as I cleared each area, then splashed back to the van and pulled out for Collins, the county seat of Gilsford County.

Since the rain had eased off somewhat, I left the window open and turned the heater on to help dry me out. I've never seen any poll taken on the question of raincoats, but my guestimate would be that less than ten percent of South Georgians even own raincoats. They are useless in the heat here. We run from building to building, car to shelter and stay damp on high-humidity days.

The drive to Collins took thirty minutes, but I still had to drive another twelve miles to Constine to pick Wade up from the hospital. I parked a block from the county building, running with a umbrella like everyone else having to venture out into the open today. I entered the sheriff's office and asked the clerk where I could find Deputy Lyons. The desk deputy directed me down the hall and to the third door on the right. Lyons was seated behind a metal desk near a window. Of the nine desks in the room, only two had men sitting behind them. I was glad Mavis wasn't around this morning. I didn't feel mean enough to give her a hard time.

"Morning, Tom," I greeted him.

"Hey, Jo Beth," he answered. He sounded cheerful. I also noticed that he had spoken louder than necessary to draw the attention of the other two in the room. Tom must have some trick up his sleeve. I pulled up a metal chair and propped the umbrella at my feet.

"How's the uniformed wounded?" I asked.

"I hear Mason is blaming you for his busted jaw. Hear he's real unhappy."

"Why me?" I questioned, admitting nothing. I had explained last night all I was going to.

"He said you got him so mad and riled up, he plumb forgot procedure. 'Course he had to write this; his jaw's wired shut and he can't talk."

"He'll get over it. Listen, Tom. I need to get the report filled out and be on the way. I have to check on my wounded, see if they can be released, then get back for court this afternoon in Balsa City."

"Sure thing." He pulled out a report form and slid it across the desk. I looked around.

"Can I use that desk?" I pointed to the one directly behind his.

"Of course." He stood and cleared two half-filled paper cups of coffee from the surface, pulling the chair out for me with a flourish.

"Thanks," I muttered. He remained standing near the desk. I rolled the form into the machine and started typing. I knew he still had something to say, but pretended to be engrossed in the report, ignoring him.

He remained silent for less than a minute. He was in a hurry. I braced myself for whatever it was.

"It isn't often we get a visit from a real live heroine, is it, men? I think we should feel honored. Hear about the medal?"

I raised my eyes from the report, looking at him.

"What medal?" I fed him the lines he wanted to hear. Let him have his fun.

"You haven't heard about the medal yet?" He molded his face into great astonishment.

"Just get to the punch line, Tom. I know you're dying to tell me," I said quietly.

"Sheriff Scroggins' been on the horn all morning, talking to the county commissioners, trying to get them to give you a medal or proclamation for your 'bravery in action' last night. Aren't you pleased?"

He was darting quick glances back and forth between us and the two listening deputies. He wanted to make sure they were following every word. I forced warmth into my voice and a pleased smile to my face.

"I sure am, Tom. I want to thank you all for your help. I appreciate it." I stood to shake his hand.

He stuck out his hand with reluctance and a bewildered expression.

"You ain't mad? Last year you threw a fit when the sheriff even suggested the idea on the Landers search!"

"That was just false modesty," I said with a chuckle. "I've got two medals now on my ego wall at home. It's great publicity for the business — the kind you can't buy."

He was unhappy that his bomb had been a dud. He glanced at the deputies, who had started looking very busy and wouldn't meet his eyes. After all, he could be sheriff next year. I should have let it drop right there, but couldn't resist doing a little tweaking of my own.

"Oh, Tom," I said softly, so I wouldn't alert the other two, "I need another form."

I pulled the one I had been typing out of the machine, folded it, and put it in my pocket, eyes never leaving his.

He pulled another form out of the drawer, starting to hand it to me, when his eyes widened with recognition of what my actions implied.

"Let me see the one in your pocket," he said harshly. "You can't go and change your report just 'cause I was riding you a little!"

"Don't be an ass," I said deadpan, still holding my eyes on his. "We're buddies, remember?"

He thought it over, realizing there wasn't much he could do about it. He glared and strode out of the room.

The snotty bitch strikes again. Asinine and childish, but hot damn, it felt good. I unfolded the report from my pocket, rolled it into the machine and finished it, saying what they always said: exactly what had happened. When you're faced with one of these beauties sometimes over a year from now, there's enough trouble remembering each little detail without trying to be cute. During the cross-examination, the defense tries to pick apart each line, so that's the reason most law enforcement personnel are constantly writing in little pocket-sized notebooks. You note the color of the shirt, the weather, car makes and colors; everything you can think of to jog your memory later.

After leaving the report with the deputy at the front desk, I left quickly. I didn't want to run into the sheriff right now; I might do something rash. He knew how I felt about these awards he was trying to get for me, if what Tom had said was true. The presentations are murder. I hate having to stand there, trying to look demure, aw-shucking and acting humble. I detest the politicians who flock to these "award ceremonies" and "photo opportunities." Give them a platform and a microphone, their eyes glaze over and they spout such saccharine and insufferable platitudes, it makes me want to throw up.

It was almost ten when I walked into the hospital room. Wade was staring at the door showing great impatience.

"Good morning," I said brightly.

"Hi. You didn't spot the doctor in the hall on your way here, did you? They have been promising me that he was on his way since before eight. He must have stopped off in Detroit."

"Sorry, didn't see him. It's a little early. I'd guess maybe thirty more minutes."

"You're kidding!"

"Trust me; I know about these things. He's seeing all the ones who are going to be here all day. The ones who are a possibility for release are seen last."

"But, for God's sake, why?"

"It's their way of doing things, Wade. After all, those are the r-u-l-e-s." I was only teasing him; I had no idea how they chose to see patients. For all I knew, they drew straws.

"Did you get a good night's sleep?"

"Now I know you're kidding. They kept the damn blood pressure cuff on all night. They came in and pumped it up about every ten minutes. Turned on all the lights, talked real loud, and half the time would forget to switch the lights off. One nurse came in, turned on all the overhead lights, looked around and left the lights on when she left, not doing a thing while she was in here. I bet I got out of bed twenty times to turn off the lights only to have them pop in again before I could close my eyes. I feel like I've been on a treadmill all night."

"I know who the nurse was, the one who didn't do anything? She was the morals monitor."

"The what?" he asked, bewildered.

"Your hospital bed is wired to pick up voice, you know. Well, her job is to listen for heavy breathing, rush in, and try and catch you playing with yourself under the covers."

"Having fun?" he asked in a level tone.

"I'm sorry, Counselor, truly I am. I thought a little humor might perk you up."

"You're forgiven," he said with a smile, "But I won't forget. I'll pay you back. Just wait."

He tried to chuckle in an evil manner, but winced with the effort.

"How are the ribs?"

"Hurt," he admitted. "I never had a broken bone until I met you."

"Take a guy to a party and all I get is complaints. I was all set to ask you to another one, but now I don't know."

"I love to go to parties. Just tell the big guy 'no more dances'; I don't like the way he leads."

"No more dances," I promised. "I took the chance that you might say yes to spending a few days at my place while you recharge your batteries. I packed a few things for you this morning. Want to stay with me?"

Wade glanced behind me. I had one hip propped on his bed, with my back to the door.

"I love these Georgia Peaches, Doc. Meet them one day, and they invite you to move in the next."

It was the same rumpled and hurried doctor from last night, minus the bloody greens. He was wearing a white lab coat over street clothes. He walked around the bed, leaned over Wade, and started checking his eyes using a flashlight.

"With your ribs," he said wryly, "you're safe for at least seven days. After that, you'll be at her mercy."

Wade and I laughed politely, then I offered to leave. He waved a "don't bother" and had Wade sit up as he listened to his chest. He moved the stethoscope around to Wade's back, listening to whatever they listen for.

"Seven days with bed rest, another week with only light lifting, preferably none. I'm going to write you a prescription for codeine. Have you ever used it before?"

Wade told him that he had.

"Take one every four hours. No drinking or driving when you take them. This is for the discomfort you might experience. I'll sign your chart out and you can go home with the lady."

Wade thanked him. I told him goodbye and he left.

"I'm going to get dressed," Wade said happily. I told him to take his time. The doctor would need a few minutes to write up his chart. A nurse who wasn't busy would have to be found, then she would have to hunt up a wheelchair — all before he could leave.

"I certainly don't need a wheelchair," he told me.

I sighed, glancing down at my watch. I told him I would wait in the hall while he dressed, then closed the door to the room behind me.

Ten minutes later, an ashen-faced Wade opened the door and walked slowly and gingerly back to the bed, where he sat down very carefully.

"You look a little green around the gills," I told him. He rolled his eyes and tried to wink, but his heart wasn't in it. I excused myself, telling him I would be back in a jiffy, then hurried down the hall to find a nurse sitting behind a desk in the nurses' station, paging through a fashion magazine. I explained that Wade needed something for pain now; that it would be a few minutes before we could get the prescription filled. She didn't look at me while I was speaking and didn't glance my way when she answered.

"It's shift change," she said in a bored tone. "You'll have to wait until the charge nurse is back on the floor."

I sorted through the options on my voice range and decided on a bellowing contralto.

"It's just a crying shame, how you treat patients in PAIN," I thundered. I took a deep breath to add volume. "HE'S HURTING BAD! WHY CAN'T YOU DO SOMETHING FOR HIS PAIN? HE'S IN AGONY! DO SOMETHING! FOR THE LOVE OF GOD, EASE HIS SUFFERING! DO YOU HEAR ME?"

I know I ruined her whole day. She was so startled, she almost fell out of her chair. Heads were popping out of rooms down both hallways. A shocked doctor — Wade's doctor — ran from behind a partition directly behind the nurse's desk, where he had been writing up charts. He didn't ask about the problem; he had heard me clearly. In fact, the whole damn third floor had heard me clearly.

He said a few brief words to her in a low voice. She scurried down the hall as the doctor eyed me with a sour expression.

"That wasn't necessary," he said.

"I'm afraid it was, Doctor," I said angrily. "I had just told the nurse that one of the patients under her care was in a great deal of pain. She just didn't give a damn. She couldn't even be bothered to raise her eyes from her fashion magazine. That's a disgrace, Doctor."

"You don't understand our procedures," he snapped.

"I'm afraid I do, Doctor, and they stink. More and more of us lowly mortals who come here for treatment are getting the message daily — of how inefficient, uncaring, and conceited you people are."

Two nurses came quickly down the hall. The first nurse had fetched her charge nurse, who was fiftyish, fat, and frowning.

"What's the trouble here?" she asked in a demanding voice. Several people were still watching from doorways.

The doctor glared at her. "It isn't your concern, Nurse. Medicate the patient in three-oh-seven and release him immediately."

"Thanks, Doc," I sang out with gusto. He didn't slow down; in fact, he put on speed to escape.

The charge nurse grabbed Wade's chart, consulted it, then quickly unlocked a cabinet and snatched what was needed. I kept pace with her as she picked them up and put them down on her way down the corridor.

"You've got your nerve," she spat out viciously.

"No, no, sweetie," I told her in a cheerful voice. "You've got your pecking order mixed up. I'm not in your chain of command. He jumped on you. Now, you're supposed to chew out tootsie back there; she started it all."

She snorted, but kept her mouth shut. I guess little tootsie had given me a good review, or perhaps she was afraid of Doctor Snide.

We entered Wade's room and the nurse poured Wade some water to drink with the pill she presented in a little paper cup. His eyes darted between the nurse and me. In spite of his pain, he seemed interested in the difference in our expressions. I was smiling, but the nurse looked as though she had just swallowed a frog. She left quickly.

I sat in the visitor's chair. "Someone will be along in a trice to wheel you out of here."

"What did I miss?" he asked.

"Could you hear me, way down here?" I was pleased. Smoking three packs a day on slow days had not taken away my volume.

"I'm sure they could hear you in the parking lot," he replied with a wry grin. "Did they give you a hard time?"

"I was doing the giving; they were receiving, I'm afraid. Did it embarrass you?"

"Absolutely not," he replied, looking happy. "You went to bat for me. I like that."

"Good," I said with relief. If he had been embarrassed, the romance would have been over before ever getting started. I was trying to curb my aggressive behavior, but, knowing myself, it wouldn't be wise to count on any great success.

A nurse arrived with a wheelchair, looking nervous. She had probably been warned about me. The only words spoken during the journey were on the first floor when I informed her that we'd rather go out through the emergency entrance. She obediently headed the correct way and seemed relieved when we reached the curb. Wade stood and thanked her politely. He then walked carefully to the van and got in slowly. I knew he was suffering. I'd had five broken ribs once, along with other broken bones. I imagine three hurt just as much as five. When he was settled and had his seat belt fastened, I turned to him.

"Wade, I want you to promise me something. If I am ever injured and unconscious anywhere around here, up to and including this parking lot, take me anywhere but here. I'd never make it out of this place alive."

He tried to hold his side to stop his laughter.

"Don't, Jo Beth. I can't laugh. Please don't make me laugh," he begged weakly.

"Sorry." I backed out of the parking space and turned the van toward home.

The skies had almost cleared, leaving only small smudges of dark clouds floating in the weak sunshine. A lot of moist wind was blowing hot, humid air from east to west.

Wade broke the silence.

"Can we stop and get something to eat on the way? I'm starving."

"Didn't they give you any breakfast?"

"It was grits and toast," he said with distaste.

"You grew up on grits, at least until you were fifteen. Don't you like them?" I was surprised.

"Let's just say that, after doing without them for the last twenty years, I now wonder how I ate them in the first fifteen."

"That's blasphemous!" I said in awe. "All true Sons of the South have grits every morning and with all seafood dinners. I know — we'll invent some rare intestinal disease that won't allow you to eat them. How about Hategritsanosis?"

"Ah, come on. They wouldn't even notice."

"Not notice? Don't you believe it. The South was built on grits and red-eye gravy, hog jowls and blackeye peas, and chitlins, good stuff like that."

"I don't remember chitlins," he said. "Chitlins?"

"I don't think we should discuss what chitlins are made of, right this minute. We are approaching food. How does a big roast beef sound?"

"Great, with lots of horseradish."

I slowed and turned into Hardees, ordered, then drove up to the take-out window. Wade handed me a ten-dollar bill which I handed to Lilly Summers, a girl I had gone to high school with.

"Hi, Lilly, how's everything?"

"Hey, Jo Beth. Everything is fine with me. Still trying to catch a man. Looks like you've done caught one for yourself."

"Nah," I said, smiling. "He's my lawyer."

"Well, introduce me, you silly goose. Never can tell when I might need a lawyer."

I introduced them while they smiled and nodded at each other. She disappeared for a minute, then returned with our food. She handed the change to me, which I handed to Wade, then took the food bag.

"Saw you on television a couple of nights back. Bet old Carlson is mad with you. You sure fixed his wagon."

"I guess," I answered vaguely. I glanced in the rearview mirror and was glad to see a car pull up behind us.

"There's someone behind us, Lilly. Gotta go."

"Call me sometime," she urged.

"Sure thing," I promised. I wouldn't call and she wouldn't expect me to. Why people keep making useless requests and promises is a mystery to me. We had never been close. We now lived over forty miles apart and didn't travel in the same circles. I guess we do it because it's easier to pretend there's a friendship going on and to practice our Southern social graces.

We were back on Highway 301 when Wade spoke.

"Want to eat as we ride?"

"I'm gonna have to. I have to be in court at Balsa City at two. Would you fix my sandwich for me? Smear horseradish on both sides." I told him about the knife and salt and pepper in the glove compartment. I eat in the van a lot.

Wade passed the sandwich and I ate with my left hand while driving with my right.

"This Carlson person Lilly mentioned. Would that be Sheriff Carlson?"

I nodded because my mouth was full.

"Why is the sheriff angry with you?"

It had only been forty-eight hours ago, but it seemed like a month. I told him a brief version of what had taken place. He was surprised I hadn't mentioned the incident. I asked him when I should have told him — before or after he threw the shoe. He brightened when I told him there was a tape of it at home. He confessed he wanted to see me in my working outfit. I told him I looked like an overloaded Easter Bunny.

The skies had now completely cleared, leaving a bright blue expanse with thin ribbons of white, floating slowly in an easterly direction. The pavements were almost dry; only scattered potholes full of water were left to mark the passage of the thunderstorm. The air was heating up and becoming much too humid, but it was clean and dust-free.

I glanced over at Wade as I drove. He looked a little better. The pain pill had taken away most of the pain, and his color had improved. He was gazing out the window at the passing landscape. I wondered if he could be content down here. I wondered what had really made him decide to stay here and keep his father's office open. I knew it wasn't my lily-white bod or charming personality. Maybe he was having his mid-life crisis a few years early. I wondered how he was going to react to the news that his father was very likely a pot producer for the past ten years or so. I wondered what was going through his mind as he looked out the window. When people I am with become silent and withdrawn, I always wish I could peek into their skulls and see their thoughts. I wondered about a lot of things.

13

"AS BOLD AS BRASS"
April 7, Wednesday, NOON

When I pulled off the highway, I stopped to check the mailbox. There was a double handful, mostly circulars, advertisements and people who wanted money for feed, water, gas, electricity, taxes, supplies and donations. As I pulled into the courtyard, Ramon and his wife, Carol, were coming downstairs from Rosie's. They came over as we were getting out of the van. I introduced them to Wade.

Ramon turned to me. "I've checked the yard. The dogs are fine. I'll handle Wayne's chores, including the nightly feedings."

"If you get rushed, holler and I'll call in some part-time help," I told him. He waved a list Wayne had given him.

"What I can't handle, Carol can pitch in." Carol nodded agreement, her face turning a bright red. She was so easily embarrassed. She was twenty-two, but sometimes seemed to be about sixteen emotionally. I thanked them both and mentioned I was about to put the patient to bed. Carol giggled and again turned crimson. She was a good kid. Her social skills were a little weak, but I had seen her hold a huge German Shepherd, made wild with pain, as steady and as competently as a seasoned vet.

They left, and Wade and I had started into the house when I heard the driveway alarm. I hustled him inside and stood at the door until I recognized the UPS delivery van. Going out to meet the driver, I signed for a package slightly larger than a bread box. I saw the leather-goods firm's logo on the label. Wayne must have ordered more collars.

Inside the house, I placed the box on the desk, then carried Wade's suitcase to the spare bedroom, pleased he hadn't made a big deal about carrying it himself. Ninety percent or more of the men I know would have put up a fight to carry it, even with three broken ribs, knowing it wasn't heavy and that I was perfectly capable of handling it easily. They would view the matter as a male/female thing. Not just good manners, but a chance once again to show the little lady that men were the stronger species and always in control.

I gave him a tour of the house, showing him the bathroom he had already seen and used yesterday, explained my clothes-washing practices and pointed out the washing machine. He went to the bathroom while I quickly unpacked and put his clothes on hangers in the closet. It felt strange, handling men's clothing again. It had been eight years since I had put a man's shirt on a hanger. When Wade came out of the bathroom, he eased down on a side chair, watching me. I asked him if he wanted to lie down for a while. He said the pill was working and he wasn't hurting anywhere. I cautioned him about being too active this afternoon while I was in court, then I shut up. I was sounding too domestic.

After going to the kitchen and making iced tea, I took the pitcher and glasses to the office and sat at the desk. Wade was standing in front of the bookcases staring at the four blank wooden panels where yesterday he had seen my father's paintings.

"What happened to the paintings?"

"Oh," I said, then leaned over and hit the wall switch that was hidden by the window drape beside my desk. The four heavy lead-lined wooden panels slowly rose up and out of sight, revealing the paintings behind them.

"That's neat!" he said with admiration. "What made you think of that?"

"Necessity," I said in a wry tone. "Bubba hated my father and his paintings, even before he began to hate me. I've always figured if he ever made it inside here, it would be a toss-up which he would go for first, me or the paintings. I knew if I kept them near me, they had to be protected. The carpenters thought up the panels. The insurance company lowered my premiums twenty percent when they saw the security, which helped, as they were very, very high."

"Why do you insure them? You told me you would never sell them. Why not save the premium money, which mounts up over an extended period? If they were destroyed, they would be gone, but if the premium were put into a good interest-bearing account each year, it wouldn't be a total loss."

"If they were destroyed, I would take the insurance money and try to buy some of his work from collectors. That would take a great deal of money, so I scrape up the premiums."

"You must have loved your father very much."

"Yes . . . I did."

I stood. "I'm going to run upstairs for a minute to check on Wayne."

"Tell him to visit me if he feels like it. We can compare bruises."

I went across the courtyard and upstairs. Wayne was on the couch in his pajamas with his appointment book, pad and pen. I sucked in air when I saw his face. The whole right side was terribly bruised, his right eye hidden in swollen flesh. The skin was the color of eggplant and stretched to the point of bursting. He saw my expression and smiled.

He signed that it only hurt when he tried to wink with his right eye. I signed that was typical male bullshit, why didn't he admit that it hurt like hell. He laughed and signed, okay, it hurt like hell. I told him that was more like it and punched him lightly on his right shoulder. I hoped I hadn't hit a sore spot. He signed that his mother was in the kitchen cooking enough to make us gain five pounds in the week of his convalescing. I signed two weeks, dammit, and left him with a stubborn look on his face.

I went into the kitchen to Rosie who was chopping vegetables.

"Hi, Rosie. How is your patient really doing?"

"He keeps telling me he'll be well in a couple of days," she fumed. "And he says not to bother filling the pain prescription, that he doesn't hurt, when I know full well that he does."

"You make sure he takes them. Give me his prescription and I'll drop his and Wade's off at Lowell's Drugs on the way to court. Can you pick them up? I don't know how long I'll be stuck in court and Wade will need a pill at three."

"Sure. I'm cooking that big rump roast you bought last week. I cut it in half, and, along with two casseroles, there'll be plenty for four."

"Sounds good. I'm going to pick up some wine after court. Wade drinks it. I'll bring you a bottle. Any preference?"

She laughed. "The only wine I'm familiar with is Ripple. Surprise me." She had been searching her purse and handed me Wayne's prescription.

"Rosie, I don't have but a minute. I've got to get dressed for court, but I want you to start thinking about something. I'm thinking seriously about hiring Jarel full-time when he graduates from high school in June. Do you think he and Wayne will work well together?"

She looked stricken. "You're replacing Wayne already?"

"Of course not," I said. "You know better than that. We have enough work for another handler, and Jarel is good with the dogs. I just wanted your opinion if they can work together closely. I don't know how they feel about each other."

She looked worried. "Jarel has some views that Wayne doesn't hold with and neither do I," she said, trying to be diplomatic.

"Rosie, Jarel is black and we're white. Is that the basis of the different views, or is there more?"

"Did you know, he told Wayne awhile back that the establishment was so rotten and riddled with fraud and corruption, it should be pulled down and we should start all over?"

"Rosie, there are times when I think that's a very good idea myself. Did you hear what I just said? I'm just stating an opinion, not planning to do anything about it — neither is Jarel. He's trying to formulate his beliefs and stretching his wings a little, trying to mature."

"You think he can chase those niggers down over at Colton Correctional?"

I sighed. "Rosie, you're way behind the times. The word 'nigger' was replaced years ago with 'black.' Now they wish to be called 'African-American.'"

"When they're in prison for robbing and killing whites and their own kind, they're still niggers to me," she said with conviction.

She made a good point, just as Bubba was white trash sleaze because of his actions, even though his father has money and his family has lived here for six generations. You are what you do and how you react to the rules of your tribe. Simple but true justice. This idea to hire Jarel full-time was going to be trickier than I had realized.

"Think on it," I told her and left.

I went downstairs and found Wade on the back porch reading a magazine. I told him I had to get dressed for court and went inside. After a shower, I dried my hair and laid out a powder-blue two-piece linen dress that would have been as stylish in the fifties as it is today. It was the Chanel style with self-covered buttons and a close-fitting skirt. I knew I would have to wear a control panty. No way would the skirt hang straight without it. I rolled on nude-colored pantyhose. I stood and took a deep breath. Upon discovery that the breath was possible, I also realized I would suffer this afternoon trying to look the image Judge McAlbee liked.

It was useless for me to try impressing the judge; he hated my guts. He belonged to the "good ol' boy" network that Buford Sidden, Senior, had founded. I was dressing for Charlene Stevens, the ADA. They didn't call her the barracuda for nothing. I didn't want her pissed with me. The white pumps with three-inch heels made my legs look better. After filling a clutch bag with my gun, wallet, cigarettes, keys, prescriptions, comb, and lipstick, the purse looked like a pregnant rabbit, but it couldn't be helped. I had to have the gun. Just like American Express, I never left home without it. A dusting of powder, eyebrow pencil and lipstick, and white pearl earrings finished the look. Done!

On the way out to the back porch, I practiced swiveling my hips in the tight skirt, hoping I didn't twist an ankle wearing these ridiculous heels. The long, low whistle Wade produced when he saw me was worth the constricted gut and possible turned ankle. I thrust one hip forward, placing one hand on it, just as I'd seen the slinky models stand. I was far from slinky, but maybe this pose would made me look a little slinky.

"You look fantastic!" Wade said with a huge smile.

"Thanks. Rosie will bring you pain pills before one is due. I don't know when I'll be back. Judge McAlbee is not predictable. God knows when he'll decide to go home."

"Don't worry about me. I'm planning on taking a nap."

"Good idea. See you later."

As I was walking away, I concentrated on placing one foot directly in front of the other. I'd read somewhere it was the best way to get good movement out of your buns. When I slowed the van for the turn onto the driveway, a glance to the porch showed Wade holding his right hand aloft, his thumb and forefinger forming a perfect circle, waving his left. The swivel must have been a success.

I dropped the prescriptions and Wade's blood-stained trousers from last night at their respective destinations. Having to park three blocks from the courthouse told me there must be a heavy docket this afternoon. I might be stuck till dark. Noticing the clouds forming again led me to think we might also get some more rain. On the second floor I click-clacked along the marble floor making more noise than anyone and watching for cracks in the floor. Get a heel caught in one of those suckers, it could do great damage.

Damn, they had the machine out checking for weapons. Harvey, one of the bailiffs, was monitoring the traffic going in. Harvey dearly loved dirty jokes. He was about fifty-five, four times a grandfather and a nice guy. He knew how to listen, laugh, and make no personal comments. I hate a creep who, after the punch line, has to ruin it by making some personal, slimy insinuations. Maybe I could con Harvey by telling a joke.

"Hi, Harvey," I said with warmth.

"Howdy do, Miz Sidden," he replied. "You sure look spiffy today."

"Thanks. I've got a good one for you."

He glanced behind me and saw the waiting couple.

"Just a mo," he told me. I moved around to his left while he was checking out the couple. When he turned back to me, I had put a palm on either side of me and hoisted myself up on the table, legs dangling, patiently waiting to tell him my joke.

"Well, these two guys had gone fishing down by the creek, and..."

He held up one finger. "Just a mo." He turned to check out another prospective juror. They were easy to spot. Most of them were carrying their summonses in their hands so they could check and make sure they were at the right courtroom. When Harvey turned back to me the second time, I had slid around the end of the table, my legs hanging in the space where he was standing.

"Shoot."

"While they were fishing, one had to tinkle, so he pulled out his tally-whacker . . ." I looked at the line forming in front of his machine. He turned quickly and began to rush them through. He turned back to me.

"A big snake bit him, right on the end of his tally-whacker and the guy hollered and fell to the ground." More people had arrived and I pointed. He began checking them through and I checked my watch. I had three minutes till two.

When Harvey turned back, I took up my tale.

"His friend rushed over and cried, 'What should I do?'"

Harvey had to leave again. This time it took him two minutes. I saw it was one minute till two. I sure hoped Judge McAlbee was on time today. Harvey was ready again.

"The snake-bit guy told his friend to run and call the doctor, using a phone about a quarter of a mile down the road, and find out what to do. The friend ran all the way to the phone and called the doctor. The doctor told him to cut an 'x' with his knife over the snakebite and suck the poison out. The friend ran back to the snakebite victim. 'What did the doctor say?' he cried."

I stood and picked up my purse.

"The friend leaned over his snakebitten buddy and said, 'The doctor says you're gonna die!'"

Harvey let out a deep belly laugh and grabbed his stomach.

"See you, Harvey," I told him, walking into the courtroom just as the clerk was calling for everyone to rise.

I looked over the courtroom to see who I knew and spotted Lt. Hank Cribbs sitting on the first row talking to Charlene Stevens, the ADA.

Judge McAlbee strode in and took his seat. He had always reminded me of a buzzard, with his coal-black hair (had to be a dye job) and the way he flapped his arms in his long black robe. When he walked fast, he seemed ready to take flight. He told the clerk to call the first case.

"State versus J. J. Johnson!"

Charlene walked up to take her place at the prosecutor's table while Philip Mansfield walked over to the defense table. J. J. obviously was still solvent, even after the county had confiscated his cars and home. Philip Mansfield didn't come cheap. He practiced in Collins, forty miles away. This meant he was being paid big bucks to commute.

J. J. was escorted in between two county jail guards. He was handcuffed and shackled. J. J. had four priors. If he was convicted on this offense, as a repeat offender he would get mandatory life. He was staring around the courtroom looking for someone. I sure hoped it wasn't me. The guards forced him to sit before he spotted his target. I saw him turn and stare back over his shoulder. Surely it wasn't me. He sure looked the type to carry a grudge. I remembered what he had said about Curly being a walking dead man and began to feel uneasy. My skirt was too tight and the girdle was cutting off circulation. Hell, I just got here. At this rate I'd be a nervous wreck by five.

Judge McAlbee rapped his gavel several times for silence. When he had everyone's attention, he began his speech.

"Thank you, ladies and gentlemen, for answering your call to jury duty. Will everyone who received a summons for this court raise your hands, please?"

About fifty hands went in the air, most of them around me. He went on to identify Charlene by name, having her stand facing the spectators. He did the same for Philip Mansfield. He also had J. J. stand and turn around. J. J.'s eyes were roaming back and forth over the crowd. I had to resist the urge to peek at him through my fingers. The judge asked several questions inquiring if anyone was related to any of those standing, including himself, through business, marriage or by blood, to please raise their hands. No one responded. He told the principals up front to sit down.

I breathed a little easier with J. J. facing forward. I had never felt this way before or during a trial. It was unnerving. I tuned back into what the judge was saying. He was asking if it would create undue hardship on any prospective jurors to serve during this trial. Three hands went up. The judge started with the woman on his left and nearest the front, asking her to stand and state her name. When she had done this, he asked what the problem would be. She said she had three small children in school. He asked if she worked outside the home. After she answered "no," he told her that he had ladies with small children at home who worked full-time serving on his juries; she was not excused. She sat down. The second one to stand was a man about sixty who explained that his wife was in the hospital, scheduled for major surgery the following morning; he was excused. The third person was a woman so obviously pregnant you wanted to suggest a fast trip to the nearest hospital, instead of struggling to stand so she could waste time talking to a judge. It seemed the judge could also hear the clock ticking. He said he only needed her name so that she could be excused. We all breathed easier when she waddled out of the courtroom.

The judge then told us that twelve names would be called and those people were to come up and fill the juror seats so that they could be questioned by the prosecuting and defense attorneys. Everyone else was to remain seated until the court could determine if they would be needed.

In the confusion of twelve people leaving their seats, I slid over more than halfway down the bench and checked the angle of sight. I was blocked from J. J.'s view by a big, wide farmer. Now, if my farmer wasn't called to serve, I was set.

The next thirty minutes were very boring, with the same questions being put to the twelve after they had been sworn in. I sat, hot and sleepy, lulled by the droning voices at the front of the courtroom.

A startled yell, cut off almost immediately by a deadly clickety-clack, brought me up and out of my stupor in a heartbeat. When you've heard that sound before, you remember it well. On the shooting range, I had stood listening to the men practice-firing their riot guns, pumping their twelve-gauge shotguns and blowing their paper targets apart. On the range, the sound had been ominous. Here in the warm courtroom, it was bone-chilling. The pumping sound was followed immediately by the shotgun's booming voice — an explosion of sound that rolled through the cavernous room in shock waves of tremendous intonations.

14

"SOBER AS A JUDGE"
April 7, Wednesday, 2:45 P.M.

I hit the floor and rolled under the bench in front of me. It wasn't planned; it just happened. I was still clutching my purse. I couldn't hear anything, but understood the absence of sound was because the noise from the explosion had temporarily deafened me. People would be screaming, panicking, moving around. From my low view I could see legs jerking and moving, some standing, others still seated. Slowly, sounds started penetrating my vacuum. I dug in the purse for my gun, then clutched it in both hands. For the first time, I looked at it in disgust. What a puny little weapon. I wanted the magnum from my nightstand, a pearl-handled .45, a cannon, anything but this pea shooter.

I focused my eyes on the portion of the center aisle I could see and discovered jeans-covered legs with high-top athletic shoes standing clear of other legs. That must be the shooter. I wondered if he was alone or if there were more. The damn fool (or fools) must be crazy. The sheriff's department was downstairs about thirty feet to the left, if the layout was correct in my mind. I wondered who was going to get killed here this afternoon. Wondering temporarily what the hasty scramble under the bench had done to my dress, I quickly reasoned that bullet holes would have been much worse and pulled my mind back to the scene. The panic sounds were diminishing slowly. I could hear two, no, three different voices yelling "shut up," "get down," and variations on that theme. I thought I heard J. J.'s voice up front, but couldn't make out what he was saying, it was so fast and panicky. I thought about moving where I could see better, but I didn't want to move. I liked it here and didn't want to trade the known for the unknown. I watched the jeans and high-tops turn in a circle. There must be another one of them up front near J. J. I wondered if one was also at the door. Christ, I was doing it again — wool-gathering when I should be alert and listening for every scrap of

163

sound and movement. I strained to concentrate, lying on my stomach, propped on elbows, hands braced in front of my face, my fingers around the gun, holding my head up and sideways in an uncomfortable position. If this lasted a long time, my neck would be stiff from the tension. I hoped a stiff neck was all that came from this.

I heard running footsteps and saw two pairs of legs pass, those closest standing still. One pair was wearing blue work pants: J. J. had been wearing blue work pants and blue short-sleeved chambray shirt, along with athletic shoes. I had absently wondered earlier why Phillip Mansfield had allowed his client to come to court dressed in that manner. Usually, defendants, in order to make a good impression, are advised to dress in business or church attire. Now I realized that the work clothes were meant to blend in on the street after the break, and of course, the running shoes were for running. My pair of legs backed out behind them. While I couldn't see when they cleared the door and departed, it was very evident. The noise in the room increased suddenly — screaming, loud talking and a lot of movement.

At least they had gotten the leg-irons off J. J.; none had passed me. I idly wondered if he still was wearing handcuffs. Now I began to see some local legs head for the door. Not me, I liked it right here. I thought about the fact that they might have barricaded the doors to the building, forcing them to retreat back into this room. I can be cautious and have been cowardly at times. Today I was both.

Less than five minutes after the defendant escaped with his two buddies, I heard several sharp cracking sounds and the loud cough of more than one shotgun. It sounded like it came from downstairs or outside, so I decided I could move a little. Crawling out slowly, I raised up on my knees, feeling a run in a stocking travel quickly from thigh to heel. An hour of wear and four bucks down the drain. Well, it could have been worse. After taking two steps forward, I realized I listed to port and discovered the heel broken off the left shoe. Shit. I didn't remember how much they had cost. Since the hose were shot, I reached down to pull off both shoes and realized I was still clutching the gun, but the purse was somewhere under the bench. Retrieving the purse, I put the gun away, and in afterthought, picked up the heel and tucked it in awkwardly as well. Maybe it could be repaired.

Looking back to the door, I didn't see Harvey. He had probably gone downstairs to check on the gun battle. I spotted the large chunk of ceiling which had fallen from the shotgun blast. At least no one appeared wounded in the room. Hank was putting away his gun and looking down behind Judge McAlbee's bench. Hank pulled the judge to his feet and the judge took off for his chambers. Probably has to go, I thought, realizing I did, too.

I walked up and sat down at the table beside Charlene while she eyed my creased and dirty clothes.

"Jesus Christ, Jo Beth. I'll bet you looked great until you started wallowing around on the floor."

I saw her gun still lying on the table. She hadn't found the energy to put it away. It didn't seem fair that she could bring hers in here freely, while I had to sneak mine in. She had a smear of grease or something on her chest.

"That stain on your boob doesn't help your outfit, either," I told her. She glanced down and both of us started laughing. We let out great whoops of sound, releasing the tension.

Hank walked over and stood watching us laugh.

"It's a toss-up who I should slap first," he said.

Charlene and I both glared at him. He glanced first at me and then Charlene. We kept looking without speaking.

"It was a joke, girls. Just a joke."

"Typical male reaction," Charlene commented. I agreed.

"Christ," he muttered and left, shaking his head. Charlene and I smiled at each other.

"I think he's coming along nicely," she said thoughtfully.

"He's learning, but I sure have been having trouble with everyone else. . . ."

Charlene glanced around the courtroom. It had emptied quickly. She picked up her gun and put it back in her purse. I needed some nicotine.

"See ya," I told her. She nodded and began to stack her papers.

I was stopped three times on the way downstairs by eager people wanting to know what happened. I told them I didn't have a clue. They would stare at the shoes in my hand, the filthy clothes, and give me a dirty look. A cigarette was a priority when I reached the fresh air outside and stood looking around. To the left was a mob standing in a semicircle, growing larger by the minute. They must have gotten one of them, at least. I wasn't interested enough to elbow my way through the mob to find out; I also didn't want to view any dead bodies which might be lying around, but it was necessary to get to the van which was in the same direction, so I walked gingerly down the steep steps. The rain-cooled sidewalk felt good on my stockinged feet.

The sun was behind the clouds. A glance up showed more rain coming. It wasn't three yet. It felt as though I had been in that courtroom for hours. Clark Baker walked up to me. He's the assistant chief of police for Balsa City and a friend. He is forty-six years old, with dishwater-colored hair, graying at the sides. A small and compact man, he was the best player on the city police softball team. His son, Jeff, a senior in high school, worked part-time training dogs as part of a research project.

"Are you all right?" He looked concerned.

"Sure. I rolled under a bench. Broke my heel. Do you know what happened out here?"

"I didn't see any of it. Heard the dispatcher calling everybody to the courthouse. I was only a mile away, but the shooting was all over by the time I got here. I've heard four different versions so far, but they are generally the same. Three came out and seven deputies were behind those patrol cars waiting for them out here. There're three bodies over there, so I guess they got them all. They took the court bailiff, Harvey Coleman, off in an ambulance a few minutes ago. I haven't heard how bad it is."

"Shit," I said. "Anybody else?"

"Not that I know about."

"Thanks, Clark. I gotta get home."

"Anytime." He stood a moment. "Jo Beth, has Bubba been causing you any trouble since he's been released?"

"Just some phone calls, so far."

"Anytime he does, call me. Day or night. The station always knows where I am."

"Thanks, Clark," I said with warmth. When people really care, it makes you feel better.

My step was lighter as I crossed the street. A few cars were sitting in the street with no people in them. I hoped I was far enough from the action so I could get the van out of its parking space and miss the snarl of traffic. Listening to the six o'clock news would tell me what happened. Getting out of traffic, I drove home slowly, avoiding main streets. The traffic was like Flatlanders Week; everyone was driving to see the excitement. A small-town fender-bender was news. This large happening would be hashed and rehashed for months to come. Also, no details of the story would be told the same way twice.

As the van pulled into the courtyard I saw Wade and Wayne sitting on the back porch. They both came out to meet me. Rosie came running down the stairs. She had heard a news flash on the radio and had told the others. She had been on the phone calling the hospital. All they had heard was that there had been an attempted escape from one of the courtrooms. We stood next to the van while I related what I knew. Rosie was loud and fussy because she had been worried. I hugged her and swore I was okay. She eyed my clothes, shook her head, and went back to the kitchen.

Wade and Wayne followed me to the porch. Wayne took the shoes I carried and held his hand out for the broken heel. He was good at mending our kennel leather, so maybe he could fix the heel. I stated I was was going to take a bath and lie down for a while. Wade recommended a long nap.

Remembering to strip in my room, since there was a guest in the house, I trudged to the bathroom for a brief shower. I felt like I had spent the day stringing tobacco and picking peas. I had done both in the summers from ages eleven to fifteen. At fifteen, Daddy had started making good money on his paintings and had given me a generous allowance, which brought about retirement from the produce and tobacco fields where I had worked for twelve dollars a day, two Pepsis and a home-cooked meal. I remembered the days of heat and sweat. That was exactly how I felt now. The air conditioner was chugging away as I put on underwear and sprawled across the bed.

My mind's tape of the afternoon's events began rolling. I lay there and viewed the scenes step-by-step in my mind. I decided I just might have done everything right by rolling out of sight under the bench. J. J. might not have been looking for his buddies when he had been scanning the spectators; he could have been looking for me. I would never know that for sure, but I did know for a fact that J. J. was in the morgue, and if he had ever been a threat, he wasn't now. I drifted off to sleep.

15

When I woke up, I stared at the clock. It took a few seconds to realize it was evening instead of morning and to remember what had happened. I felt refreshed. I stretched, then put on a pair of cool culottes with a green and white sleeveless blouse, brushed my hair and slipped into sandals. I was starved, no breakfast and just the roast beef sandwich at lunch. I went to find Wade.

Wade and Wayne were in the office playing the board game Clue.

"Hi, guys," I said and signed, "When do we eat?"

"Now," they both responded. Wade asked how I felt. Wayne signed that Rosie would fix a tray if I didn't feel like going upstairs. I told them both that I felt fine. Upstairs, I helped Rosie put the meal on the table, over her objections.

We had a wonderful meal: pot roast you could cut with a fork, potatoes and carrots in a thick natural gravy, fresh string beans from Rosie's garden (the first of the year's crop), a tossed salad with light vinaigrette dressing, and hot buttermilk biscuits.

They told me the news about the shooting before we started eating. Two men had gone in to take J. J. out of the courtroom, and all three had been shot on the street, trying to escape. Harvey, my joke-loving bailiff, had caught several shotgun pellets in his right thigh while trying to stop the escapees on the steps. He didn't know his country cousins were waiting outside to cut them down. His wounds were superficial and he was expected to be walking again in a few days.

I groaned when Wayne set the electric ice-cream churn on the kitchen counter and started dishing out ice cream.

"Why didn't you tell me," I complained. "I wouldn't have eaten so much of everything. What kind is it?"

"Peach," he signed with a grin, knowing it to be my favorite.

"Just a little bit," I said with doubt. "I don't have room."

Wayne knew me, so he filled the dish. He didn't want to make a second trip to the churn.

I washed dishes while Wade, Wayne and Rosie played two games of cut-throat cribbage. I had begged off, being lousy at the game and not wanting Wade to know I consistently lost. Wayne and Rosie knew why I wasn't playing, so kept making sly remarks about how I played. I didn't let them goad me into playing, priding myself on my good judgment. Wade beat both of them, twice. This could cause problems later, as I am a lousy loser and Wade professed he loved the game. I decided to adopt Scarlett's attitude and think about it tomorrow.

Wade and I came downstairs at nine. We walked through the kennel with Wade asking questions. He noticed the name boards hanging to the right of each pen, calling them out as we passed the cages: O'Henry, Chaucer, Sinclair, Tolstoy, Frost, and Dickens. He chuckled.

"We do have fun naming the dogs," I admitted, then explained a strange thing we had noticed, which had been consistent.

"We name the dogs before starting any serious obedience training," I told him. "It started out as a joke, or maybe a contest. We try to guess, judging by their temperament and reflexes, what they will be best suited for, what kind of training we'll start them on. Those six you mentioned are drug dogs."

"You name all your drug dogs for writers and poets?" he guessed.

"Right, and these six are the best."

"You just made good guesses on their abilities," he stated, some doubt in his expression.

"I guess. It's a little unnerving, but we haven't been wrong yet."

Still strolling, we had reached the nursery section. He stopped in front of Gloria Steinem's pen.

"Looks like you made a mistake here," he said with a grin.

"We really didn't," I laughed. "That's what's so damn strange. Gloria was never meant to be bred. Carson Lemmings, the helper before Wayne, got drunk one night and put Gloria in the pen with O'Henry when she was in season. She had the first litter and the puppies were so perfect and healthy, we've bred her twice more. She's a good mother, but she hates having babies. This is her last batch. I've promised her, 'No more puppies.' Tomorrow she gets her freedom. We'll train her to be a drug dog," I said with a laugh. "After all, Gloria Steinem qualifies as a writer."

"In some circles," he said reluctantly. I laughed. He wasn't going to pull me into controversy tonight; I felt too good.

We strolled back to the house. Upon my inquiry as to how he felt, he answered that the pills were working fine. When we entered the office, I went to the desk to check for messages. A hang-up, my dry clean-ing was ready, and another hang-up. I made no comment. Noticing that Wayne had opened the leather-goods box UPS had delivered earlier, I picked up one of the collars lying on the desk to inspect it, then showed it to Wade.

"Look at this," I said. "It has the name of the kennel, the address and phone number burned into the leather on the inside of the collar. I like it. Wonder how much it costs?"

"Wayne said there was a letter inside explaining," he said. "Said it was something the company was doing for its good customers and left them there for you to see. He liked them, too."

I read the cover letter, saying they would be personalizing all the leather goods ordered in the future at no extra charge. If we didn't like the service, we should let them know. I was pleased with it. Good ad-vertising. We always send each dog or puppy purchased to their new home with their own collar and leash. Each dog has one for training. We don't recycle them. On the scent-trained and fire-trained dogs, we also send their own harnesses and leads. The dogs are so expensive we try to go first class, including some extras.

Going to the stereo, I started a CD with Patsy Cline singing her songs to a slower beat, some old favorites. Wade relaxed his sore ribs onto the couch slowly, then patted the soft leather beside him.

"Feel like talking?" he asked.

"Sure. Let me make some iced tea, or would you prefer something else?"

"Iced tea is fine."

Upon returning with a tray holding tea and glasses, I set it on the coffee table in front of the couch, then placed a lighter and cigarettes beside them.

"What would you like to talk about?" I asked while pouring tea.

"You. We have to figure out this will. I want to hear everything, so start at the beginning."

"Well, here goes. My father was a painter whose special interest was landscapes of Cumberland Island. He went fishing occasionally if he felt his painting wasn't going well. I used to believe my father loved my mother, painting, fishing, and me, in that order. I decided early on that I came fourth in his affections."

"Did he ever leave the state to paint?"

"No, he only painted Cumberland Island, never, to my knowledge, anything else. I remember Mother crying once on my birthday, maybe the sixth or seventh, because we didn't have money for film or a camera. She begged Father to paint my picture; said I was growing so fast, she didn't want to forget what I looked like as a child. I guess the reason I remember it at all is because it was the only time I can remember her really being angry at him. He refused and she was furious. She died when I was ten. I have no baby pictures," I said with a smile.

"Listen, Jo Beth, if this is too painful . . . ," he began.

I waved a hand to stop him. "It's painful, but I've never told anyone. I've never had anyone who wanted to hear it."

"I want to hear every word." He briefly laid his hand over mine resting on the couch.

"When Mother died, I didn't even have a picture of her. I missed her terribly. I asked Father to paint a picture of her for me. You see, I thought the reason he wouldn't paint me was because he didn't love me. I knew he loved my mother; he adored her. When he refused to paint her picture, I began to feel better for some reason. I never found out why he painted nothing but Cumberland Island."

"Could it have been that he wasn't as good with the human form as with landscapes?"

"He had enormous talent," I said quietly. "On canvas, he made the sun shine, moss move with the wind and rain-dampened bark smell moldy. How can you doubt his competence when you've seen the four oils I own?"

Wade made no comment, only patted my hand again. With reluctance, I downgraded his 'nine' rating on my Jo Beth scale to a seven. This guy was chintzy with compliments about my father's work. I remembered yesterday afternoon and realized he had not made any comment at all on Father's work. I hadn't picked up on it until just now. I decided to adopt a wait-and-see attitude.

"Please continue," he urged.

Why not? It might help dredge up some memory to help solve the puzzle. "After Mother died, I was terribly lonely. I'd never had any classmates or friends visit my house. It looked so terrible, I was ashamed of it, but it never seemed to bother Father. I was all right during school, but at home the loneliness hit. He seemed to sense this, finally, and started taking me with him to Cumberland during the summer. He would work feverishly sketching and making color samples on several paintings, then bring them home to finish."

"One day he took me fishing and we stopped off to see a man who had a litter of bloodhound puppies. I was thrilled, thinking they were the most beautiful puppies I had ever seen. The man gave me one, which I named Herman T., and I wasn't lonely for a while. The name was out of respect for our esteemed Senator Herman Talmadge. Daddy and Sheriff Scroggins were always discussing politics, and Herman Talmadge's name was mentioned often. We didn't have a fenced-in area, so I had to tie him in the backyard while I was at school, since he wanted to follow me everywhere. One day the knot in the rope came loose, and he was run over trying to follow me. I found him on the way home from school. I felt so responsible for his death that I punished myself by not having another dog for years. The next one I owned was O'Henry, who was the first breeder for the kennel."

The talking made me thirsty. As I raised my glass to sip the tea, Wade excused himself to go to the bathroom. I walked to the window and saw the stars were out. I guessed our rain was over for the night. It had stopped during my nap this afternoon. When Wade returned, I continued.

"I just remembered something that happened before Mother died. I must have been in third grade and about nine years old. The teacher asked us to bring a photostat of our birth certificates to school. We were studying Civics and she wanted to see how many of us were from different states. When I asked for mine, both Mother and Daddy seemed upset. About three days later, they handed me a photostat of a "Live Birth Certificate" from Balsa City Memorial. When I gave it to the teacher, she looked at it and said, "quite impossible." The minute she said it, she was sorry, I could tell. She explained, as though she'd caught herself, that she didn't know what she had been thinking about to utter such nonsense. She then said the certificate was just fine. I didn't know what she meant by 'quite impossible' until I turned twenty-one."

"Why was it impossible?" he questioned.

"I was born in October of nineteen sixty-four. Balsa City Hospital was built and opened its doors to the first patients in nineteen sixty-six. Before that, the hospital was in Vista Pines and was called Dunston County Memorial."

"I see," he said thoughtfully. "What do you think happened?"

"My first theory, when I was about twenty-one, was that my parents had been guilty of some hanky-panky. I thought they hadn't been married the respectable period of time and didn't want me to know about it."

"What changed your mind?" He was curious.

"A couple of days later, I was going through Mother's cedar chest and found their marriage license. They were married in nineteen fifty-four, ten full years before I was born."

"So what's your theory now?"

"Let's go back to when I was ten. We're getting ahead of the story. From the time Mother died when I was ten, my father would answer none of my questions, even casual ones, about my birth or their parents or other relatives. It really hurt, but I excused him, making myself believe it was too painful for him to remember and we could talk after he had time to heal, but no discussions ever materialized. When I was fifteen, things got a lot easier for us. Dad's paintings started to bring in a lot more money. We moved to a nice apartment and I finally had a lot of nice things. I didn't work in the summers, had fun and money to spend for the first time in my life. Daddy and I seemed to get along better. He even gave me a generous allowance. When I graduated from high school, he bought me a 1982 Ford convertible. During my senior year, I met Bubba. After I met him, I never dated anyone else."

"I'm curious," he said. "What attracted you to Bubba?"

I was ashamed and didn't want to tell him. I had discussed the question with several of my friends in the past several years and been surprised at the answers I had received. They also made me feel better, knowing that I wasn't the only idiot who graduated that year.

"I'll tell you, if you promise not to laugh."

"I promise," he said, holding his fingers folded like a Boy Scout.

"I thought he had the best-looking truck in the whole county." I saw his eyes twinkle and warned him, "You promised." He nodded his head, afraid to speak.

"You think you're so cool at that age and you know it all," I said. "One of my girlfriends had a stranger reason, I think. She said that when she went out with her husband-to-be the first night, he was amazed at how short she was, because he was quite tall. He stuck his arm straight out and she could walk under it without bending her head. Since she was plump (and they had made this observation in front of a display glass window which served as their mirror) she decided right then to marry him. She told me that she thought his height made her look slimmer."

"Women aren't the only ones who marry for silly reasons," he admitted. "I married my wife because of the way she smelled."

I laughed.

"No fair," he said. "I couldn't laugh at you. It was her perfume. I thought it was the best smell I had ever been fortunate enough to smell. I found out later that an ex-boyfriend had bought it and that she didn't like the fragrance, but used it because it was very expensive. Back to your story," he said.

"Daddy hated Bubba from the very first date. The more Daddy found fault with him, the more determined I became to marry him. We eloped, drove over into Alabama and were married by a justice of the peace. I sent Daddy a telegram. I was too chicken to call him. We came back three days later. Daddy and I had a housekeeper by then. He'd had the housekeeper pack all my things and put them in the living room floor; they were waiting there when I got back home. Daddy was gone and the housekeeper handed me a letter from him. It said that I was no longer his daughter and for me to leave and never come back. I left with Bubba. Within a month, Bubba and I were fussing and fighting; the honeymoon was over.

"I got a job at an insurance agency as a receptionist. Bubba quit working and drank all the time. His daddy had spoiled him rotten, bought him a new truck every year, gave him drinking and running-around money. I paid the rent and bought groceries. He didn't waste any of his daddy's money on things like food and lodging. A month after I had finally had enough and moved out, he was arrested for sexual battery on a waitress. He was tried and sent to prison. You've read the rest of the story in your father's files."

"But not about you and your father. Please finish the story," he said.

"Well, the three years I was married to Bubba, I didn't know where my father was. I didn't try to find him. After I left Bubba, I went to your father because I knew he was Daddy's lawyer. He promised to see what he could do and promised to make sure my father got any correspondence I sent. I wrote letter after letter begging him to forgive me, but never received a reply. Finally, I just mailed a card on Christmas, Easter, his birthday and Father's Day. He never answered any of them.

"On my twenty-first birthday, I received a shipment from my father. He'd sent mother's trunk with all my childhood mementos and the few pieces of good furniture she had been left by her mother. You see, Mother had gone through the very same thing I had. Her father gave up on her because of her marriage to my father. I had lived in the very same town with my grandfather and never knew about it — or him — until I was twenty-one."

"How did you find out?" Wade asked. He was only asking questions to keep me going. He had probably read most of this in his father's files. His father had known the whole story.

"At the time of my twenty-first birthday, when I received all my possessions from Father, I was in the pits of hell. I was divorcing Bubba, didn't know where my father was; then out of the blue, here comes all those pitiful childhood memories. I was a basket case. I had no one. Then I did what a lot of people do when they can't stand their life and don't see any future. My friend Susan and I went out and got roaring drunk."

I stopped to light a cigarette while Wade went to get more ice for our glasses. When he returned, he made a circular motion with his right forefinger for me to continue, then eased down slowly into his seat, taking out the vial of codeine.

"Hurting?"

"A little," he admitted.

"Why don't you go lie down, give the pill a chance to work?"

"I wouldn't feel any better in bed than here. Finish telling what happened. You had just gotten roaring drunk . . ."

"When I woke up the next morning, I felt too sick to die. I started drinking coffee, smoking cigarettes, and telling myself I was a big fool. I decided I was going to start living my life a lot differently. I made a lot of resolutions that morning. I mentally drew up a game plan for the rest of my life, got out pad and pen, and started sketching the kennel I would build someday, if I could ever save enough to even begin. A receptionist in this town is not paid big bucks. I didn't have two nickels to rub together left over from my weekly paycheck. For the past eight years, I have been so thankful about my firm resolve to change my life that morning. When the mail came that afternoon, I might have done things a lot differently if it hadn't been for the commitment that morning. In the mail was a letter from a local bank. Grandfather had died when I was ten years old, two weeks after Mother, and before he'd had a chance to change his will. In fact, when he died, he was not aware of Mother's death. He'd left everything to her, with the stipulation that if she predeceased him, her children were to inherit."

"You didn't have any idea of this inheritance?" He sounded like he was hearing this for the first time. Maybe his father's files weren't as complete as I had thought.

"Absolutely no idea. Here I had money, building up interest nicely from the time I was ten, plus the farmhouse and land. The bank was instructed not to inform me of this inheritance until my twenty-first birthday. I was stunned. Here I was making plans with no money in sight that morning, then discovering I had money coming to me in the afternoon. I decided it was a sign from above that I had the right game plan. The bank explained that the funds and property would not be transferred to me until my twenty-fifth birthday. That suited me fine. These twenty acres the kennel is on and about fifty-eight thousand dollars were in the estate at the time of probate when I was ten. The original farmhouse was on the property, along with several outbuildings. The house was built in the early nineteen hundreds. The bank paid the taxes each year, along with minimum upkeep. I decided to work as hard as possible between twenty-one and twenty-five, putting every penny possible in the bank. I lived in the kitchen and dining room of the house. From eight-thirty to four-thirty, I worked as the receptionist at Sanders Insurance Agency for Dudley Sanders. From five till ten for six nights a week, I waited tables at Attenburg's King Steer Steak House out on Old Mill Road."

"How did you manage to keep going with a schedule like that?"

"Every time I banked a couple of hundred dollars, I felt closer to my goal. In addition, I thought that working so hard and saving so diligently would make the bank see how serious I was. I knew it would take a lot more money than was in the savings account for my dream to become reality.

"I saw my father on the morning Bubba and I eloped when I was eighteen. He never spoke to me again before his death, but I saw him again and went to visit him often. Let me explain. I was twenty-one in nineteen eighty-five when I divorced Bubba. I worked the two jobs until nineteen eighty-seven, when Bubba got out of prison and put me in the hospital. I was in and out of surgery for six months, then back to two jobs for the next three years, until nineteen ninety. I found out later, from your father, that Father had been in Europe, living with a lady in France for three years or more.

"It seems the lady had been stripping him of his assets while he was sick over there. He was worried she might have had him sign something he didn't remember."

Wade smiled. "That clears up part of the will, why he was so careful to refute any will which might have been signed in France. He wanted to make sure that his last will couldn't be successfully contested. Is that why he moved back here from France — to leave her?"

"That was part of it. The main reason was because he was ill and wanted to find out what was wrong. He checked into Mayo Clinic where they diagnosed Alzheimer's disease. He had one year of fair health before he was placed in the nursing home."

"My father didn't tell you any of this until after your father died last year in the nursing home?"

"Not a peep. He said my father made him promise never to tell me until after his death. You remember I told you I sent cards four times a year on special occasions?"

Wade looked up and gave me an affirmative nod; he was still getting dates set in his mind.

"Two years ago, I received a phone call from a very nervous man in Gainesville, Florida. He said he had some information about my father and begged me to promise I wouldn't tell anyone he had called. I promised and met him in a coffee shop in Gainesville the next day. He was an attendant at the nursing home where your father had placed my father. Father was comatose, having suffered a stroke six months before, and never regained consciousness before his death last year. . . ."

Wade stopped me. "I just want to be sure I understand you; you mentioned you had talked to him."

"That's correct. I talked to him for hours every time I went down there. I don't know if he could hear me, but he never spoke."

"Do you think he heard you?" Always the lawyer — restate and clarify.

"I like to think so, but even John, the attendant, thought it highly unlikely."

"Tell me about the attendant."

"John had opened all the mail for Father and decorated the room with my cards. I'm glad Father got to see them and to know that everything was going well with me before he had his stroke. Your father was furious when he found me down there visiting one Sunday. He wanted to know how I found out. I told him I had hired a private detective from Waycross. I visited Dad every Sunday until he died."

"My father was wrong." Wade passed solemn judgment.

"I don't know, Wade. I used to think so, but came to the conclusion he was only carrying out his old friend's wishes. If I had a secret I wanted kept, your father would have been the one I would have trusted."

"Your father loved you, Jo Beth. He didn't want you to see him suffer."

"Nice try, Wade, but he had five years of good health after I divorced Bubba, before he became ill. I think he loved me too, but it's getting harder lately to convince myself of that. I was hoping the will would clear up the mystery, but it's only created more questions."

"We'll find the answers, Jo Beth. I promise you," he said.

He had more belief than I did, but he hadn't been trying to find answers long enough to become discouraged. Wait until he'd spent a year on it, like I had.

"Let's go back to when you were twenty-one and going through your mother's trunk. Was the 'impossible' certificate of birth from the hospital among your things?"

"Nope. I never saw it after I was nine."

"Do you believe it was a fake?"

"Of course. Dad probably had a friend who worked in the hospital or had some pull there. They just took a blank and filled in the statistics, then photocopied it. It wasn't supposed to fool anyone but a nine-year-old, and it did; at least for a while."

"You never found your birth certificate?"

"Never. I tried all the usual places. Wrote the Bureau of Vital Statistics in Atlanta. No record of a birth for Jo Beth Stonley in the state of Georgia. I went three years either way. You can only fudge so much on age, you know. Jo Beth Stonley wasn't born in Georgia."

"Have you tried other states?"

"I once toyed with the idea of trying the other forty-seven continental states for three years either way, but it never got beyond thought. I didn't follow through because I believed it would be a waste of time. You see, I don't believe Stonley is my real name or my birth name."

"That's a logical conclusion," he remarked. "I was thinking along the same lines. If not, why would they produce a fake certificate of birth? So, are we agreed that you must be adopted?"

"Not necessarily. There're other possibilities. I could have been stolen as a baby. You read about it, every so often, where children are taken. When they aren't found, they're presumed dead, but it's a possibility."

"You've had longer to study about this. What is your best guess?"

"I honestly don't have a theory except that the will is connected in some way. My father wasn't a devious man. I know everything sounds confused now, but I think there is a complete explanation, somewhere."

"*Where* is the key," he said thoughtfully. He looked down at his notes. "I'll be changing the subject, but I'm curious. Is the vet a partner in your business?"

"No, not really. The building he's in and the land belong to me. I hold a note on all his equipment. He pays me in services for my animals. I knew I would need a vet close by and one I could count on not to close up shop and leave if business was slow for a while. The solution was Ramon. I snagged him right after he graduated. He had no money to open a practice, so I was able to lure him here with this set-up. He's been here for over two years and is keeping his head above water. He's been able to pay off some of his note to me and all his government loans for his education. He's happy, so I'm happy."

"You're quite the businesswoman, Jo Beth," he said in admiration. "You've thought of everything."

I had to laugh. "If that's true, will you please explain why I don't know who I am, why I'm living under siege — as you so aptly put it —

and can't go to the corner grocery for a loaf of bread without being armed? Christ, my life is a mess!"

He changed the subject again. "Tell me about building the kennel," he queried. "You mentioned two brothers."

"The Jensen brothers. They retired from forty years of carpentry six months before I was old enough to draw from the trust fund. They are bachelors and live together. They fished one summer and hunted one fall season, then were bored to tears. I looked them up when I heard they were doing odd jobs around town. They didn't need the money, they needed a project."

"I wanted to use the lumber from the old farmhouse to build this house, kennel and the vet office complex. They tore down the old house, with the help of day laborers. Every scrap of lumber in this place came from my grandfather's homestead. It saved a great deal of money, and there's still enough lumber left to add on to the kennel, build Wayne a house somewhere on the land, and much more. It's stored in the shed the brothers built, near the back of the property."

"You are such a good organizer that your success is understandable," Wade said warmly. "We need a solution to the will."

"I know. I know," I said wearily, "but nothing comes to mind. You asked for my best guess, now let me have yours."

"I was afraid you were going to ask that. It seems we have nothing tangible to work with. I just wish I could talk to my father's retired law partner. He might shed some light on our riddle. I've been trying to reach him ever since I came down South. He must be on a long vacation. He wasn't at Father's funeral, so he must be out of the country. I'll start trying to track him down tomorrow."

"Counselor, I hate to spoil your plans for tomorrow, but I have some bad news."

"Tell me," he said.

"Tomorrow is going to be a bad rib day for you. My doctor tried to tell me and I didn't believe him, but it turned out he was painfully right."

"Ouch. I'll try to be brave," he said manfully.

"The best solution is to double up on the painkillers and try not to move around much for the first few days."

"How many broken bones did you have?"

"A few more than your three ribs, but they've healed very nicely."

"Why do you try to act so brave?" He sounded a little testy. "Why not discuss it with me?"

"Pain and the rehash of pain can become addictive, Wade. I've heard men and women recount every grunt and groan of their operations and afflictions. I find it boring and try to put the whole incident in perspective and put it behind me."

"You also clam up when someone tries to get close or share some of your bad times. You've been a loner too long."

"You're absolutely right," I said briskly. "I'm going to bed."

I closed the panels to the paintings, checked the security switches, outside doors and windows, then stopped by the couch where he was still sitting.

"I've checked everything, so don't touch any of the openings. Just turn out the lights. Good night. Sleep well."

"Thank you," he answered shortly. "I appreciate your concern."

I stripped, put on shorty pajamas, and started the washer. Wade was miffed because I kept most of my feelings to myself, but I hadn't had anyone who cared for such a long time that I'd forgotten how to share. What little understanding I had received from Bubba early on in our marriage had faded into the past. My reticence was ingrained. I was beginning to wonder if I was capable of change. With this unsettling thought, I prepared myself for sleep.

16

"SLICK AS A PEELED ONION"
April 8, Thursday, 7 A.M.

I was folding clothes when Wade came out of his room on the way to the bathroom.

"Good morning," I said with a smile. "Did you sleep well?"

"So-so," he answered vaguely and kept on walking. He was in his robe.

"Coffee's ready," I called after him as I put away the clothes and vacuumed the living room — wasted floor space seldom used, except when it's cold enough for a fire in the winter. When Susan or other friends stop by, we visit in the office or kitchen.

When the household chores for the day were done, I joined Wade in the kitchen, poured a cup of coffee and lit a cigarette. Wade, who had taken great pains with his appearance today, was dressed in soft gray slacks, a casual pullover sweater and black loafers. His face seemed drawn and he looked uncomfortable. He moved a little in his chair under my frank appraisal.

"I can see you're hurting," I said quietly. "Have you taken a pill?"

"Two," he admitted. "They haven't had time to take effect," he said with a weak smile.

"They'll work better in bed. Why don't you put on your pajamas and lie back down."

"Maybe later. What are your plans for today?"

"Just to keep things running smoothly since Wayne's out of service — maybe a couple of random sweeps, if any are planned, make a few phone calls, go grocery shopping, pick up dry cleaning and some pictures left to be developed, mostly just running around. Do you need anything from town?"

"Not a thing. Did you get any hang-ups in the middle of the night?"

"Not a one," I said with false cheer. "That's an improvement."

"I find that ominous," he said.

"So do I," I confessed. "It breaks his pattern. I failed to mention my short conversation with him night before last."

"You sure did," he stated with a grim expression. "What did you discuss?"

"I just mentioned that his phone calls didn't have me shaking in my boots and he could make better use of his time."

"What did he say?"

"'Bitch' was the only response I heard. I hung up on him."

"Did he call back?"

"Nope."

"Not too smart, Sidden."

"Sidden?" I cocked my head and looked quizzical.

"Well, you call me Counselor and I decided we might do better on a buddy level for a while. I can't carry on a courtship with three broken ribs and have doors slammed in my face at the same time. This will ease the tension and keep you from tightening up on me."

"Sure thing," I said in agreement. Boy, was he upset! Oh well, you can't win 'em all. It seemed I had managed to cut romance off at its roots before it had had time to bloom.

"What sounds good for breakfast?" I made myself sound perky and bright.

"Nothing for me," he said. "Food doesn't sound good right now, maybe later. I'll have another cup of coffee with my pain."

I left him to it, went upstairs and had another cup of coffee with Rosie. Wayne was still in bed. She had two random sweeps and was taking over Wayne's advanced obedience class at ten. She planned to do the sweeps this afternoon, if I didn't need her. I didn't.

I went to the kennel and stopped in front of Gloria Steinem's pen. It was a day early, but I felt generous.

"Deliverance day, my beauty. Freedom awaits," I told her. I pulled the greedy puppies from her teats and snapped on a leash. She didn't believe me until I closed the gate on the nursery. She looked up in gratitude and I stooped and hugged her neck. "You just retired from the baby factory, sweetheart." I took her to spinster's row and put her in an empty pen. I placed the wooden sign with her name on the hooks. "Enjoy."

I went back with a deep plastic basket and removed six of the twelve puppies to a pen in the puppy section. I had to make two trips. They were fat as piglets and surprisingly heavy. I filled the feed containers with our puppy supplement and turned on the automatic watering containers. They weren't unhappy about losing their mother; they began exploring every inch of their new home. I returned to the nursery and scrubbed and disinfected the empty pen. I can't use a jet-stream attachment on the hose without getting wet from the knees down.

Going back to the house, I found Wade had gone to his room. His door was closed; I assumed he was lying down. I changed into dry clothes and shoes. After paying some bills and catching up with the computer additions, I made a grocery list and took off for town.

I picked up the developed prints and stocked up on film. Down the street, I walked through the Dollar General and picked out three Easter baskets, chocolate bunnies and lots of hair ribbons. When passing a display of irresistibly soft white Easter bunnies with large pastel ribboned bows, I bought three, matching them with the color of the girls' dresses. Leroy would be indulgent and enjoy the girls' happiness. Jackie would make tart remarks about spoiling them and overdoing things. It wouldn't spoil my happiness. She let me hang around and visit June, Jannette, Jo Anne and their father, my best friend. I could absorb her snips and snipes in order to visit freely; it was a small price to pay.

While picking up the dry cleaning, I learned Harvey was doing great. I stopped at the florist and had two balloons delivered to his hospital room. One was printed with tiny red kisses on a white background and spelled "My Hero" in red hearts. The second was yellow with blue letters spelling "You Jerk, You Should Have Known Better!" I signed both cards: "The Jokester."

After finishing everything but the grocery shopping, I stopped at the Browse and Bargain Books to see if Susan was free for lunch. If Wade got hungry, there was plenty of food in the refrigerator. Susan was delighted to see me and said yes to lunch. I waited while she ran back to her office to make a quick phone call. We went to a small greasy spoon only two blocks away. We were addicted to the big, lush hamburgers, large servings of fries — all glistening with grease hot from the grill — thick, ripe tomatoes and generous slices of Vidalia onions. We sipped our iced tea while waiting for the food. The air conditioner was trying to keep up with the grill's heat, but we still sweated while we ate.

Susan told me about a hassle she'd had earlier that morning with a soft-porn salesman and a new wrinkle his company had for convincing reluctant bookstore owners they should display their magazines openly. The salesman said they were completely wrapped in cellophane to keep teenagers from peeking, with shading in the cellophane in discreet places to ensure no one would see total nudity. Susan said she had politely declined, but the salesman was adamant. She said she'd had to be embarrassingly direct with him.

Susan had said to him, "Listen, sleazeball, I wouldn't sell your dirty books advocating and condoning violence against women if they were perfumed and yielded a three hundred percent profit."

"That's when he threatened me," muttered Susan.

"Threatened?" I said with raised eyebrows. "How could he threaten you?"

She sighed. "Seems my two best-selling lines of books are owned by the company that puts out the 'adult' material. If I don't buy the smut, I don't get to buy the others."

"Is that legal?"

"I don't know. I called my lawyer, but he was in court. He'll call back when he's free. They'll probably get away with it. They could simply say they had decided to place their books in the supermarkets and convenience stores, which they don't do now. My sales would drop without them and they know it."

"Are you going to sell their trash?"

"Probably," she said with a glum expression. "Then the Southern Ladies Guild and my church congregation will picket, maybe even organize a boycott of the store."

Our burgers and fries arrived. We shook ketchup bottles and used the salt and pepper. We chewed and I gave Susan's problem more thought.

"The salesman might be doing this on his own. Why don't you call the home office and check?" I suggested.

"I hadn't thought of that," she said. "If it was their idea, do you think they would tell me?"

"Probably not, but you could get an idea from the way they react to your news. Make sure you go higher than the switchboard, just say you have a complaint and try to reach some brass."

"Good idea. I'll try it unless my lawyer tells me not to."

"He'll probably tell you to sue," I said with a smile. She laughed.

"Speaking of lawyers . . . ," I said.

"I'm all ears," she murmured.

"I have one as a house guest."

"You're putting me on!" Susan said in a shocked voice. "Are you kidding?"

"Nope. I brought him to the house straight from the hospital yesterday morning. We're good buddies, period."

"Now I know you're joshing me," she uttered with feeling. "You don't bring good buddies home to visit. What gives?"

I told her about the events of night-before-last. She hadn't read the paper.

"Miss reading the paper for two nights and I'm a week behind in local news. I've had a date two nights running."

"Who?" I was skeptical. Susan was as much a loner as I.

"Brian's back in town, didn't I tell you?" Susan was trying for the innocent look.

I groaned. "No, you didn't tell me, Susan," I said, raising my voice a notch. "You knew what I would say. Have you lost your mind?"

"Now, Jo Beth, I know you don't like him, but he's really changed. I can tell. He's left his wife for good. He's filing for divorce as soon as he finds a job. He's staying with his sister until he gets settled in."

"Of course you've checked this out?" Asking, but already knowing the answer.

"Jo Beth, honey, you are so suspicious! I tell you he's a different man than he was last year. I can see the changes. He's admitted to telling me all those lies last year. He's apologized and just wants a chance to prove that he's changed."

What could I say? I know Brian is a leech and a con artist and that he lives off women. I'd had Hank check him out last year and I knew his history. He had been in questionable scrapes with women for years. They would file a complaint and then withdraw it. He had been arrested once for bunco and twice for fraud. Hank and I paid him a visit last year. He then decided to leave town suddenly and I had held Susan's hand while she suffered from his sudden departure. She didn't know about Hank and me having a hand in his leaving. Now he was back. Did he think we would stand by and let her be victimized? I was afraid to say too much. I'd check with Hank. He'd know what to do.

"Susan, you know how I feel about him. Don't trust him, please."

"Don't you believe that people can change?" She propped her elbows on the table and stared at me.

"Not him," I said.

"You're wrong, Jo Beth, and I'll prove it to you. I called Brian before I left the store and asked him to join us. He has something to say to you."

I looked into her eyes and saw her anger. I knew I was in deep shit.

"Susan," I began.

"Hello, darling," Susan said with warmth. She was looking over my left shoulder. Brian Colby came into view. He gave me a smarmy smile and held out his hand.

"I want us to be friends, forgive and forget." He was grinning at me. I ignored the outstretched hand and stood while reaching in my wallet. I pulled out a ten-dollar bill and laid it next to my plate. I looked at Susan. She was staring at me with a stony expression.

"When you want to talk," I said to her, "Give me a call. I'll explain what I did and why."

"I guess this means that you don't want to be friends with Susan and me?" He wanted to gloat.

"Not with you or the horse you rode in on," I told him with crisp diction. "Susan has always been my friend and always will be."

I heard his nervous laughter as I walked out. Outside and out of sight, I leaned weakly against the hot cement-block wall. Damn him for turning Susan against me. I had lost a friendship that couldn't be replaced. Bitter tears stung my eyelids. I straightened up and went to buy groceries to try and get my mind off it.

When I arrived back at the house, Wayne and Wade were eating sandwiches. I told them I had eaten downtown. I brought in the groceries and started putting them away. Wayne signed that Rosie had left for two sweeps and we discussed my two. He offered to load the van and I just stared at him. He looked sheepish and signed that he was just kidding. I gave him a pretend-right-cross to the chin and waved goodbye to Wade. I couldn't get out of there fast enough. I felt weepy. I worked the combination on the wall safe in the grooming room, removed a baggie of marijuana and two more with just small amounts of crack and cocaine. The drugs were furnished by the DEA. At the start of the searches I had signed an affidavit that they could come on my property and check the controlled substances inventory at any time without a search warrant. They never had as yet, but the three of us signed out each batch to travel and signed it back in.

I loaded up Tolstoy and Frost, filled my pockets with deer jerky, and pulled out of the courtyard a little after two. I was headed for Cannon Trucking Company, a large freight terminal out in the county's industrial complex. It was two hundred acres and zoned for commercial use. Cannon had donated the land to the county for zero taxes for thirty years. He had gotten a deal. He had been here forever, but the county had yet to score on attracting more industry with free land to build on and low, low taxes.

I pulled the van behind an empty warehouse a half-block from the freight terminal and dialed the plant's security office from a pay phone on the corner. We don't use the county radios while working on private sweeps. When security answered, I explained I was coming in on a drug sweep. The guard said he was familiar with the routine and would place the guards. He said he had four men available and to give him five minutes. I watched through binoculars until I saw a plant guard stroll out to the guard shack at the gate. He covered the gate man so he couldn't warn the incoming truckers or use his phone to call anyone inside.

I waited until the double doors opened on the west side of the building, where the executives parked their cars under cover. When the road was clear, no semis departing or arriving, I cranked up and quickly covered the distance to the gate and through the open west doors. After I pulled inside, a guard behind me closed the doors. I unloaded Tolstoy and Frost and gave them both a good sniff of the drugs.

We walked quickly through the office corridor and startled several secretaries and two executive types. Two guards were waiting by the door leading to the warehouse. One explained the fourth man was on the metal catwalk high above the loading platform with a radio, so he could watch both phones and both doors. One guard turned right to cover the only entrance to the warehouse.

I entered the warehouse with one guard. The first man to see us was on a forklift. He stopped his machine and sat quietly as we approached. He had been through a sweep before. He stepped down from the machine and smiled at the dogs as they sniffed their way around him and his machine. The second forklift operator was shocked. No one had told him about the sweeps. He stopped his machine and just sat there in a stupor. I had to repeat my request for him to step down from the machine. He climbed down shakily and asked what he was being arrested for. The guard explained we were checking for drugs and the man looked relieved. He was clear of drugs. I didn't say anything but felt the company would be wise to run a complete background check on the man. He had looked terrified for a while, in my opinion. He wasn't concealing drugs, but he sure had something to hide. But then, if it wasn't drugs, it wasn't my business. We continued on through the warehouse aisles doing a snake dance, weaving around corners and doubling back and didn't find a thing.

On the loading platform, I counted the semi-trucks with trailers backed in that were being loaded. There were twelve. I made a bet with myself that we would find two stashes. I went down the concrete steps between the backed-in semis and started on the one to my left. The driver was standing by the driver's side with his hand on the door handle. I could tell from his expression he thought we were bad news. He let go of the door, letting it close, and stood defiantly with his arms folded over his chest.

Tolstoy got to the door a second before Frost. He raised up on hind legs and clawed at the door panel. The guard opened it for him. He sailed into the truck without effort and ducked behind the curtain of the sleeping compartment. I was holding both long leads and the guard crawled into the truck. He backed out of the truck cab holding a small vial of pills. He opened it and showed me the contents. Speed. An orange, lopsided, almost triangular pill with a groove running down the center. There were twenty-six in the bottle. Good for probation and a drug rehabilitation program with no priors. With priors, six months on the county farm, which, in reality, would be closer to two months if they were crowded. The worst punishment would be the loss of his chauffeur's license. Georgia had put a new, tougher policy in force this year with a more thorough test of the driver's ability. To lose his license was to lose this job and the ability to make a living driving any truck. Still, they carry and take drugs — drugs which allow truckers to drive from eighteen to twenty-four straight hours without sleep. The guard asked for his company identification card and chauffeur's license. The man handed them over and the guard called on his radio for the hallway door guard to come and hold the man while they waited for the police. My guard and I went through the next four trucks without finding anything.

At the sixth truck, we approached the driver and the guard spoke to him.

"Hey, John, how you doing?"

"Fine, Tim, and you?" the man had a nice smile. I gave Tolstoy and Frost a piece of jerky, which disappeared so fast, I gave them another. The guard, Tim, punched John on the shoulder and turned to me.

"John is a newlywed. Got married last month and became a daddy at the same time. How are the boys?"

John's pleasant smile dimmed and he looked troubled.

"We've all got some adjusting to do, Tim, but we'll work it out." John had sounded positive, but I sensed trouble in paradise. The kids probably resented the new "daddy" in their lives.

Tolstoy turned on his lead, raised his head and tugged me toward the truck door. He whined and Frost joined him, pawing at the door. Tim and I stared at John. There was nothing on his face but faint surprise. I handed both leads to Tim.

"Hold them," I said, then opened the truck door, and Tolstoy jumped lightly into the cab. I blocked Frost from joining him with my knee and climbed up on the step, looking back at John again. He was gazing at Tolstoy with a puzzled expression, but no fear. He wasn't tense or nervous. I hoisted myself up and joined Tolstoy in the cab. His tail was swishing back and forth in an excited rhythm while pawing at the backside of the narrow bunk mattress. I ran a hand down beside the mattress and inched my fingers along the small opening between the mattress and the wall. Feeling the smooth softness of a plastic baggie made me blink with surprise. I would have bet a million bucks the guy was clean. I pulled out the baggie and looked at it in the dim light, my body still behind the dividing curtain.

For God's sake, the man had shake. I couldn't believe it. "Shake" in our neck of the woods refers to the large shade leaves that are cropped periodically from the marijuana plants. Most growers didn't even fool with them; there's very little profit. The shake smells potent, but you'd have to roll several cigarettes from this pitiful stash to get even a little high. The teenagers call it "poor-boy pot." It sells for five bucks an ounce. The growers who sell it chop up stems and leaves, dry it, and hope they can push it to teenagers. I didn't believe this settled family man was using this shit. It didn't make sense. Georgia law, however, has zero tolerance and doesn't make any distinction about quality or quantity. I knew of a quarter-of-a-million-dollar airplane that had been successfully confiscated because of two marijuana seeds.

On an impulse I didn't want to examine too closely, I folded the small baggie and tucked it between my breasts. I felt around my bra to make sure nothing could be seen. I gave Tolstoy another piece of deer jerky and hoped he wouldn't give me away. It would be quite embarrassing if he reached up and began to paw my chest. I grabbed a box that still held two donuts and crawled out of the cab with a grin.

"I have to apologize; the dogs sometimes forget their manners. They smelled your jelly donuts."

Both men laughed, Tim with relief and John, who acted unconcerned, said, "If they're allowed, they are welcome to the donuts." I promptly opened the box, gave the dogs the command to "hold" and placed them gently in their mouths. Wayne must never hear of this; he would skin me alive for feeding his dogs a jelly donut. At the command to "eat" the donuts disappeared. I needed to speak with John alone before making a complete ass of myself. I could still go back inside the sleeper and "find" the shake if I didn't like his answers. I turned to Tim.

"I hate to ask you, but could you find me a Diet Coke? I'm dying of thirst."

"Sure," he said, and handed over the leads he had been holding. "Be right back." He took off toward the steps. I hoped there was enough time. I looked at John.

"I found the shake." I said it as an accusation.

"What?" he said politely.

"I found the shake," I repeated with impatience, not knowing how long it would take Tim to fetch a Coke. "Don't you know the penalty is the same for shake or the finest sensemilla?"

"I'm afraid I don't understand what you're implying," he answered convincingly. I was sure he was in the dark about the discovery.

"How old are the boys?" He was startled by my question. "Hurry up," I said. "We don't have a lot of time. I'm trying to help you."

"My stepsons? They're twelve and fourteen. Why do you ask?"

"Been having trouble with the boys? My guess, they didn't want Mama getting married, don't like the fact that a man is in the house and giving orders. Help me here John, nod yes or no."

"Yes," he said reluctantly. "How did you know?"

"Your stepsons planted an ounce of shake in your sleeper. I'm risking my reputation by not reporting it. I think you didn't have anything to do with it. Don't mention it to them; talk gets around. Be warned and check your rig each time before you hit the road. You've got your work cut out for you, trying to win them over. For god's sake don't breathe a word to anyone, even your wife. It would have been your job and reputation if I had reported the find. It's my job and reputation if you spill the beans. Do I make myself clear?"

"Yes," he said quietly. "Thank you." He acted like he understood. I sure hoped so.

Tim hurried up with three Cokes. They were the real thing, not diet, but I pretended eagerness, and we stood and chatted while we drank. The sugar would help my nervous flutters. Why did I do these things? I should know better. There was too much riding on continued good will and future business to take these chances. Just because I thought the man was innocent and had liked his smile wasn't enough reason to stick my neck out and risk getting it chopped. Ah, who was I kidding? I enjoyed taking risks. I was on a high from knowing I had done the right thing. You make your choices, then live with them.

Tim and I finished searching the six semis being loaded and found no more drugs. I'd won the mental bet about finding two stashes of drugs. We worked the back parking lot in the afternoon heat. There were more than a dozen trucks parked, waiting for drivers and to be loaded. They were clean, also. I loaded the dogs while Tim waited and we both went back to the air-conditioned offices and settled in the small security office suite.

Security had two rooms in the establishment. A front breakroom with cheap couches, a few girlie magazines, coffee and Coke machines and a small adjoining office with three large filing cabinets, one desk and two chairs. Tim took the desk chair, leaving me the other one. I unfolded the sweep report that I had picked up from the van, and Tim pulled out his notebook. I borrowed a pen.

"What was the driver's name who had the speed?"

Tim furnished the man's name and employment number as we sat and wrote up our reports. I finished first and slid it over for his signature. He finished his, then slid it across to me. I signed, and leaned back.

"Isn't air-conditioning wonderful?" I stretched, feeling the perspiration drying on my arms and legs. The heat had been brutal on the black-topped parking lot, and in circling more than a dozen semi-trucks with trailers, we must have trudged over two miles on its sticky tar surface.

He offered Coke or coffee, but I declined. He leaned back in the swivel chair and placed his feet on the small metal desk.

He smiled. "What did you find in John's cab?"

I slowly straightened in the chair and turned my eyes in his direction.

"What?" I looked at him with a puzzled expression.

"Very good," he complimented me. "You'd do well in Little Theatre, but I feel you're doing what you like, and you're very good at it. We never did introduce ourselves. My name is Tim Fergerson and I'm in charge of this shift's security. Two years from now, when Walt, my superior, retires, I become chief of security here at Cannon Trucking. I earned a BA degree in Business Administration at Drexler College before joining the police force in Waycross. After five years on duty, a damn speeder I was chasing lost it and slid under a semi-truck and I couldn't dodge the truck. It crushed my left hip and I was retired on a half-pension. I can walk all day, but I can't run well enough to be a cop, so I went into security. I go to Southern Baptist College three nights a week to study criminal law. So you see, Miz Sidden, I didn't just fall off a turnip truck out on Highway 301."

"Call me Jo Beth," I said. I was hoarse and had to clear my throat.

"Great, Jo Beth." He smiled kindly. "Now, what did you find in John's truck?"

I looked at him. He was in his early thirties and looked very good in his uniform. It was tailored and fit his lean build and muscular shoulders. He was slightly under six feet, maybe five feet ten inches, with brown curly hair and brown eyes. The hair was styled expertly, his eyes were clear and his face glowed with intelligence. Boy, Jo Beth, what a keen observer you are. You didn't even see him. Talk about a chameleon, he was an expert.

"That's quite a trick, blending into the woodwork. Did you cultivate it, or does it come naturally?" I was curious.

"I work at it; it comes in useful sometimes. Fooled you, I see."

"Oh yes," I said. "You fooled me. You disappeared into the rent-a-cop uniform, someone to send for a Coke." I winced at my lack of attention.

"You haven't answered the question," he reminded me. I glanced suggestively around the room, as though looking for bugs.

"The office isn't bugged," he said. "I check it personally three times a week."

"Is John a friend of yours?" I was stalling for time.

"He's related by marriage, a cousin of my wife, a fact that isn't well known around here for obvious reasons. I'd like to keep it that way."

"It was an ounce of shake. Some people I can read very easily," I said with irony. "I knew he wasn't a user. I decided that his stepsons were trying to set him up. I do sweeps at the grade schools and high schools around here; I've found these 'poor-boy' baggies in too many lockers. It wasn't adult and it wasn't my read on John, so I made a fast decision."

"I appreciate what you did for him. I want you to know I owe you a big one; so does John. You can collect anytime. Count on it."

"You almost gave me a coronary," I uttered waspishly.

"Sorry, but I had to find out if you were withholding for other reasons."

"What other reasons?" I was surprised.

"Blackmail," he said simply. "For money or for an informant in the company."

I thought about it. He was right, that could have been possible.

"Okay, you're forgiven, and you and John owe me one. I gotta run. I have another sweep, and they close at five."

He walked me to the van.

"John is lucky to have you for a relative," I told him.

He shrugged. "It's partly my fault. My wife and I went to John's house last Sunday for dinner. Uncle Tim spent over an hour with the boys, telling them what he did at the office. The drug sweeps were mentioned. They were interested and asked questions. I gave the little bastards the idea."

I chuckled and we shook hands.

"See you," he said. I drove away smiling. I had lost my best friend today for interfering in her life and here I was, tempting fate by poking my nose into other people's business. I just never learn.

17

"TOO DRUNK TO HIT THE GROUND WITH A HAT"
April 8, Thursday, 4:30 P.M.

The next sweep was a small paper mill, a branch doing specialty orders. It was thirty miles from its huge home office and these guys were hot dogs. Their work was dangerous, yet some of them lived like there was no tomorrow. I stopped and called the foreman. He was waiting at the back door, ready to open it at my approach.

The van was parked behind a thick stand of pine trees and the dogs and I were in the building before the machine operators knew we were on the premises. The home office and mill owners were concerned, since in the past year there had been two injuries, one fairly bad and one disastrous. Both had been blamed on drug use by machine operators. The company's insurance premiums had shot out of sight. Using the dogs was one solution; the other was unscheduled drug testing; we suspected some of the workers still smoked, sniffed or injected.

It's a policy never to come up behind men who are operating machinery, since startling them could cause a move which could cost fingers or a hand, so I made sure we were facing them and they could see the dogs and me. To tell the truth, I was nervous in the open like this. Only two large machines were in use. I walked the dogs slowly into the line of sight of the first operator, who gave me a wave. The dogs walked around him and the machinery, not finding a thing.

The second operator saw us too late to get away with his toss. When he spotted us, he reached above his head and threw something into the machinery. Those large flashing blades made the object disappear; they would have made a five-foot log disappear. I glanced at the foreman and he looked away quickly. He was probably a friend. Some friend, to let this guy operate dangerous machinery while using drugs.

The noise level in the mill was so high that speech was impossible. I motioned to the foreman to follow me to the sound-proofed office at the end of the building. He walked next to me, looking upset and nervous. When we entered the hallway, I motioned him over to the water cooler. The corner was crowded with the two of us and two dogs, but I didn't want anyone hearing our conversation.

"What's his name?" I said quietly.

He told me because he had to, not because he wanted to. I wrote the operator's name in a memo book.

"You saw him toss the drugs?" I said.

"I didn't see no such thing," he declared, red-faced and belligerent.

"Okay, sport," I told him angrily. "We'll play it your way. I'll write into the report what I saw and that you told me you didn't see the incident. We'll both sign it, but we both know you're lying. Your friend in there will keep on operating and keep on using. If anything happens to him, like losing an arm or his life, we'll both know who is partially responsible, won't we?"

"Fuck you," he said tonelessly, walking away. I took that to mean he agreed with my reasoning, so I went in and wrote the strongest-worded report possible. If whoever made the decision decided he wasn't guilty, then so be it. You do what you can and try not to worry about the outcome too much. Loading the dogs, I split the remaining deer jerky between them.

On the way home, I decided to drive by Wade's house. He had no idea of my suspicions about his father, and I couldn't begin to think how to break the news. The information Wade had innocently handed me added up to his father growing marijuana, but I couldn't be absolutely certain; it was purely conjecture.

Several hundred yards before reaching Wade's driveway, I turned right onto a narrow county dirt road, following its gentle curve for almost a quarter of a mile, then pulled over to a driveway entrance created by concrete pipe and several loads of dirt and sat in the stillness, listening. After my hearing adjusted, I could hear several wrens and a persistent bluejay. I felt the van move when one of the dogs flopped down in a different position.

I really shouldn't be doing this, but reasoned that Wade was physically in no condition to take on the action and worry. I would simply check to see if anything was going on and then go home. Having convinced myself that my actions were justified, I opened the van door, picked up the binoculars from the seat, and started walking due south into the planted pines. After a couple of hundred feet, I could see the back of Wade's house through the saplings, and even had a clear view of the driveway.

Raising the glasses, I scanned the driveway and saw Hector's old truck parked near the back door of the house. Another car was further down the drive. Thankfully, its rear end was to me. All new cars look so much alike to me and there are so many models that I find it hard to identify as many as when I was a teenager, but I could see that it was light tan or beige, four-door, and had some kind of decal on the rear window. Since I had nothing with me to write down the license number, I committed it to memory. I could ask Hank to run it for me.

I searched the grounds with the glasses but didn't see Hector or lawnmowers at work. I scanned the windows of the house first, and detected no movement, then moved the glasses to the building above the garage area and got a shock. The door opening onto the stairs nearest me was open and a man was standing in the doorway, holding the screen door open. He seemed to be talking with someone inside the building. I squinted to get a better view of the man's face, but could only see about half his profile. I had never seen the man before. He was fairly short, had dark curly hair and looked to be somewhere around forty. Estimating his height compared to the doorway, I came up with about five feet, seven inches. He was white, not Hispanic, so it wasn't Hector's cousin, whom I had caught before in a drug sweep.

He finished his conversation with whoever was inside and turned so that I got a full frontal view. I tried to memorize his features. Hank had told me the secret of identifying people — their ears. I just couldn't get the hang of it. To tell the truth, most ears look alike to me, but I focused on the man's ears as he descended the stairs. He moved casually and with confidence, not as though doing anything illegal or underhanded. I felt a small worm of doubt move inside me. According to Wade, no one had the right to be upstairs, downstairs, or even on the property except Hector when he was mowing the lawn.

I stood as quietly as possible, being bitten by several species of flying insects. I knew I was safely out of sight, but the sun was getting lower and I didn't want any light flashes reflecting off the lens of the binoculars. When another man appeared on the stairs, I braced the glasses against the trunk of a pine to my right, focusing on his face. It was Hector. He locked the door with a key, then tested it to be sure it was locked. I'd bet a dollar against a donut that a key for that door wouldn't be on Wade's keyring. The first man had left, so I waited until Hector climbed into his beat-up truck and moved down the drive before I left the woods. There was no need to follow them, because I had no idea which way either of them would turn when they reached the highway.

I arrived home a little after six and had the dogs unloaded, fed and the van cleaned out by six-thirty. I spoke briefly with Ramon, who had just finished the feedings, before he left. He told me he had ordered more vitamin supplements yesterday, and for me to tell Wayne so he wouldn't over-order. The vitamins have a shelf life of only ninety to one hundred twenty days. He said that Wayne sometimes over-ordered. I promised to pass the message on to Wayne. Ramon was a fusspot, constantly checking our supplies, looking for expiration dates and issuing instructions about over-ordering. Wayne and I knew his ways and overlooked them.

When I entered the office, Wayne, Wade, and Rosie were watching Dan Rather on the national news. When I told them I'd be back shortly, Rosie assumed correctly I was going to take a bath. She followed me to the bedroom and chatted while I stripped and put on a cotton robe and slippers. She told me Wade had made spaghetti sauce that had been simmering for about six hours; she said it smelled like he knew what he was doing. I agreed. I'd caught a whiff passing through the hall.

Rosie said we were eating downstairs tonight. The salad was ready and so were the rolls. She said to give her twenty minutes and we could eat, since the water was already simmering for the pasta and the oven preheated for the rolls. I walked over and gave her a hug. She was momentarily startled, but hugged me back with gusto.

"What's wrong, chicken? You look down."

"Susan doesn't want to be my friend anymore. All I have are you and Wayne," I told her.

"You're not counting Wade?" Her shrewd eyes questioned mine.

"It's too early to count Wade," I said.

"No, it's not," she answered. "You seemed to be counting him yesterday. What happened?"

"I'm not sure of anything except I've been on my own too long to fall into the arms of the first man who makes a move on me. It just doesn't feel right."

"Having doubts is perfectly natural," she said. She patted my shoulder and ran a hand over my curls.

"You feel down about Susan. What you need is a good, hot meal. Take your shower and get dressed. Hurry up; you have twenty minutes." She gave me a swat on the fanny.

After the bath, I put on a loose shift of melon-colored cotton and sandals. My hair was damp and kinky, but I just combed it and left it alone since I didn't have time to dry it.

The meal was delicious! Rosie had made apple tarts and I ate two of them. Her cure for the blues is a full stomach. After Rosie and I did dishes, we joined the men in the office. Rosie and Wayne stayed only long enough to be polite. I saw a signal pass between them, then they both jumped up together, saying their goodnights. Wade and I were alone a few minutes after eight.

"They sure picked up on the chill around here, didn't they?" he said with a humorous grin.

"It's a gift of mine," I said truthfully. "Sooner or later I chill everyone out."

"Boy, that was a pithy observation," he said quietly. "Did you have a bad day at the office, dear?"

"I managed to sprinkle a little dissent around. I shoved you away last night and tore it with my best friend, Susan, today. She doesn't want to have anything further to do with me . . . and I can't really blame her. I meddle in everyone's life every day. The good news is that two guys owe me a big one."

"So tell me all about your day, dear. I really am interested."

"Cut it out," I said. "I don't feel like laughing."

"You want to get drunk? On top of the pills I took today, I'll bet two glasses of wine would put me under."

"I'm out of wine," I told him.

"I had the liquor store deliver some," he said. "I replenished your nonexistent wine cellar."

"Wine is fine," I said. "I'll get it. Is it in the fridge?"

"Sit still," he insisted. "I will serve no wine before its time."

I groaned. While Wade went to fetch the wine, I moved to the couch and put my feet on the coffee table. Maybe Wade would loosen up a little after a couple of drinks. I didn't think mixing wine with codeine was such a good idea, but two glasses shouldn't cause problems. Wade returned with a bottle of red wine, and two crystal goblets. I only possessed two. Susan and I use them when we want to add class to a meal of pizza eaten straight from the box.

"Here we are," he said as he filled the glasses.

"I propose a toast," he said as he handed me the glass. "To days without pain."

"Forever and ever, amen."

"So tell me about Susan," he said as he settled on the other half of the couch.

"A suitor from last year turned up this week and told Susan how a friend of mine on the county sheriff's payroll and I ran him out of town last year."

"You must have had a good reason," he replied.

"Bless you, I did, but Susan doesn't see it that way. I don't know what the creep told her, but she doesn't want to hear my side of it. I went behind her back and meddled in her love life. Case closed."

"She'll get over it; give her time. A creep, you said?"

"A con man who fleeces gullible women. Has some priors."

"Tell me, Sidden, did you have your friendly county employee run a check on me? I could have priors and such."

I recounted drinks at supper. We had two bottles at the table. I think Wayne had only one glass . . . Rosie at least two. I couldn't be sure, because I hadn't been seriously counting, but I think I had three. That left ample wine for Wade. His tone sounded half-serious/half-jest, but I was a tad weary from running into fishhooks hidden in vanilla pudding. So much for the loosening process — he sounded loose enough to me.

"Funny you should ask that question. Actually, that thought did cross my mind less than three hours ago. Oh, say about a quarter of six, to be exact."

The answer rocked him. He set his glass down slowly on the coffee table and visibly straightened his shoulders.

"What happened at a quarter to six?" He looked totally confused.

"I was staked out in the woods a couple of hundred yards from the rear of your house and was monitoring the traffic on your driveway with binoculars." I took a sip of wine, looking at him.

"Mother of God," he uttered fervently. "I don't believe this. Are you serious?"

"Oh, yes," I said casually. "Believe it, Counselor."

"Why?" He sounded totally bewildered.

"Just trying to help a friend," I said in a pleasant voice. "That's usually how I get into these predicaments."

"Would you please elaborate?" His voice was husky. I didn't know if the wine was getting to him or it came from suppressing the desire to pound me over the head with something.

"You don't mind if I do a little pontificating, do you? Just a trifle?" I was being sweet and polite.

"Take your time," he said slowly, trying to relax.

Much better. "Counselor, I'll have to give you some facts first. Some of these problems we have here in South Georgia aren't indigenous to downtown Boston and your affluent suburbs, where you've lived for the past several years. First, did you know that some sixty million Americans have smoked pot? Over ten million smoke pot on a regular basis, right here in the U.S. of A. Now, I don't know money-wise just where Georgia is on the national income scale, but I would hazard a guess we're in the lowest ten percent bracket. With all the marijuana that's grown worldwide, to take care of those ten million who puff away every day, quite a bit of it is home-grown, even here in the state of Georgia. We have lots of trees and very few people and most of those people need money."

I sipped more wine, then continued.

"We have a term here that we use often. It's called 'land management economics.' It means that any landowner who has fifty acres or more of land is usually suspected of growing marijuana. It's a fast way of getting rich or staying rich. It yields high earnings with a low percentage chance of getting caught. Of every one hundred growers, twenty have their crop found and destroyed without any criminal penalties. Seven are caught, of which five are tried, leaving only two who actually serve more than three years in prison. The downside is, when they do catch you, they confiscate land, guns, bank accounts, cars, house furnishings, jewelry; in fact, any and everything they can get their hands on — and they have mighty sticky fingers."

I paused to sip the wine. I don't usually drink wine, but it's a fine throat lubricant.

"Will you stop this lecture and get to whatever point you're trying to make?" His voice was raw. I saw then that he was extremely angry, but trying to hang onto his temper.

"You want the shorter version? No problem. Your father has been growing marijuana on his property for the last eight to ten years of his life. His property, soon to be yours, is still being used for that purpose. You'd better get your act together fast and do something about it, or you'll be sitting on your can in a federal prison not even owning the shirt on your back, much less anything else. Is that condensed enough for you?"

"Bull," he stammered. He was so shocked he couldn't manage to string words together into a sentence. I sipped more wine and waited.

"Do you have any proof?" he finally asked.

"Sure don't."

"Then what gives you the right to make these ridiculous charges?" He was visibly upset.

"I'll tell you what, Counselor, I'm a gambler and purely love to bet on a sure thing. I'll bet you my entire future inheritance, if I have one, and if I ever find out how much it is, against what you have in your personal checking account today. We'll get a lawyer and call it a promissory note or something to make it legal since gambling debts can't be collected legally in Georgia. Does that convince you?"

"You're crazy," he said, sounding weary but no less upset. "You don't know what you're talking about."

"On some things that's true," I admitted. "But not this, Counselor. You can take it to the bank."

"You have obviously put together several erroneous conclusions about my father and are using them to build this fantasy of yours. Would you please outline them for me? Sorry I rushed you a little while ago. Tell me what you suspect. I want to hear it."

He was a lawyer, all right. Sweet reason had just kicked in. My anger had cooled and I was feeling rotten for throwing it at him like a bomb, instead of using my brains.

"I'll be glad to do so. First, your feeling that your mother had the greater amount of money and that she took it with her twenty years ago. Second, your own conclusions that your father didn't make a bundle with his practice in the last twenty years. Third, your huge house has been excellently maintained. Those old houses simply drink money. Paint, roof, manicured yards, upkeep, plus God knows how much in taxes every year. The house hasn't suffered; it isn't rundown or neglected; ergo, money has been poured into it over the years. Example: Across the back of the house those beautiful green-and-white, custom-made window awnings to block afternoon sun couldn't be replaced for less than ten grand, and they have to be replaced about every five years. We're talking forty thousand just for window awnings. Think he could afford such a luxury out of his earnings? I think not."

My glass was empty so Wade filled it, then I took a couple of swallows and continued.

"Fourth, the bank estate people have had three weeks and you expect several more weeks before you find out where you stand. Say your father left you the house and furnishings and forty thousand in the bank with no other property. How long do you think it would take to add up those figures? Three days? A week? Get real; the bank is stalling because the estate is large and bulky. By bulk, I mean other real estate. He couldn't get away with leaving cash; he had to spend the money on something so he could leave it to you legitimately. Your father was a very smart man. He probably set up so many enterprises, your poor trustees are swamped in paperwork and complex deals. Let's hope he kept it reasonable and didn't go overboard, because there is absolutely no way you could prove this money was earned in his practice or on the stock market or in real estate; there aren't any records."

I excused myself and went to the bathroom. I splashed my face with water and dried it roughly with a towel, trying to get some color in my cheeks, then brushed the frizzy hair into a softer style, washed my hands and returned to "the education of Wade."

"Fifth, your father quit hunting his wooded area, and used conservation as an excuse to keep all his hunting buddies off his land.

"Sixth, the willingness of your Hispanic gardener to lend you money to tide you over until the estate is settled. He knows the estate will be big. He probably has plans to continue working the same deal with you. If that doesn't pan out, he probably has plans to blackmail you out of a big chunk of your money. Also, he was afraid you were going to discontinue mowing for a while and he would lose the legitimate reason for being on your property often.

"Seventh, this afternoon I observed two men on your property having a meeting in the upstairs quarters, on the right as you face that garage building. When the stranger came down the stairs, he ambled, casual and unhurried, as though he belonged there. Hector, who was the second man there, locked the door and was very careful to make sure the lock engaged. I bet you don't have a key to that door anywhere. And, last but not least, when I saw Hector in the police station last fall, I heard an officer remark that if his clothes were vacuumed for marijuana, you could roll a cigarette from what you found on him. That means it's common police knowledge that he's in the business. I rest my case."

As I sipped wine, I had smoked one cigarette after another. I always chain smoke when drinking. Wade was quiet for a long time.

"I don't like what I'm thinking," he said softly.

"And what is that?"

"What you said made sense and you may be right."

"Wade, don't judge your father too harshly. Had I been in his position, I would have done the same thing."

"You've got to be kidding!" He was surprised at the statement.

"Wade, everything your father was and wanted to have was wrapped up in that house. When his money ran out, he must have tried to borrow on it and been turned down because he couldn't show enough income to repay the loan. Every man or woman has their price. He didn't want to lose the house, then scrimp and just get by in his old age. His pride, his creature comforts, his chance to leave you an inheritance were all being threatened."

"And you would do the same?" I detected a faint sneer.

"In a New York minute! If the kennel were threatened and everything I've worked hard for these past eight years was going down the drain, you'd see small patches of pot spring up like mushrooms on the back fifteen acres. Not having much room, I'd plant on Federal Game

Reserve lands; the guys who do are cleaning up. It also eliminates having your property confiscated."

"You sound as if you mean it," he murmured.

"I've broken the law for a friend. Do you think I'd do less for myself? Anyway, if I needed a rationalization to salve my conscience, a nationally known coalition is battling to have marijuana legalized by nineteen ninety-seven. I'd just be rushing the date a little."

He shook his head. "You simply amaze me."

I think Wade was seeing me in a different light; he had spotted my feet of clay and was disappointed. Mr. Straight-Arrow was disillusioned. I really was sorry. God, we need every straight arrow we can find in America and more. We also need hosts of angels in filmy white gowns and delicate wings, but the wings would become loaded with acid rain and pollution so they couldn't fly anymore, and the pristine gowns would get coated by mud-clinging dirty politicians and ruthless big business practices. Compound these with the nation's sheep who run from truth and justice and don't want to get involved. What can you do? Pull off the useless and tattered symbols, put on jeans and sweatshirt and fight your own battles with a different set of rules, geared to fit the occasion. It's called survival.

Wayde stood. He tried a smile that didn't quite reach his heart.

"I think I'll just go try a few of my keys on the upstairs lock. I'm curious."

"Sit down, Wade," I said flatly. "You're sitting on a powder keg and you mustn't do anything to explode it prematurely. Every move has to be planned. We're going to need more help and a lot of luck to get you out of this with your fortune intact."

"We?" He was not smiling.

"We." I said firmly. "You were willing to help me and I'm willing to help you."

"I just don't think we could work together," he replied.

"Would you explain that remark?" I was getting ticked.

"Sure," he said in a mild tone. "You want to produce, direct, and star in everything. You don't leave enough for this poor helpless male to do."

"Oh, crap," I said mockingly. "Did the macho male get his ego bruised?"

"I have three broken ribs, not brain damage," he shot back, then stood and scanned the room.

"What are you looking for?"

"I was just checking to see if I had left anything in here," he replied.

"Where are you going?" He looked like he was preparing to leave the house.

"To pack," he said quietly.

"You're leaving?" This was getting serious. I didn't want him to try and confront Hector alone. The man was dangerous and Wade was in no condition for any kind of confrontation.

He gave me a level look. "I want to thank you for your hospitality. I appreciate your efforts on my behalf. I think I can manage my own affairs from here on. Thanks again for having me here."

He was back in five minutes. It sure didn't take him long to pack. He stopped and set his suitcase on the floor at his feet.

"I'm sorry, Wade, if I seemed bossy and gave too many orders. I've been alone and on my own for eight years. That means taking charge has become a habit."

"You needn't apologize," he said with a smile. "I guess I'm just old-fashioned. I like helpless and soft women who can't balance a checkbook or change a truck tire."

"I imagine that type of woman would become a bore and a nuisance after a while," I said in a cool tone. "If you're trying to get even, it was a poor effort."

I saw him compress his lips in the effort to bite back a retort.

"You forgot to return the house keys after you picked up my things for me; could you get them?"

"Will you sit down, and let's discuss this calmly, like adults?" I was going to remain calm with him.

"No thanks, just get the keys, will you?" He was impatient to leave.

"Are you afraid to discuss this? Think I might be right?" I taunted. Christ, now *I* was losing it.

"The keys?"

"You bet! Hold your horses!" I crossed swiftly to the desk, scrabbled for the keys, turned and tossed them in his general direction. He plucked them out of the air with his right hand, and I saw him wince. Good. He deserved a little pain right now, for being so stubborn.

"Thanks again. Goodnight." He picked up his suitcase and departed.

I went to the kitchen and turned off the gate alarms. I walked back to the office, feeling defeated and sad. I needed to talk to someone, and Hank came to mind. I couldn't tell him about Wade's problem; he would be out in the woods at daybreak searching to see if my theory was correct. I just needed to be around someone who liked me. I was feeling lower than a snake crawling in a ditch.

Hank was working days this week. I went to the phone and called him, hoping he would be at home. He answered on the third ring.

"Are you busy or something?"

"Hi, Jo Beth. What's up?"

"I need you, Hank. Can you meet me somewhere?"

"Andy's in twenty minutes?"

"Thanks, Hank. See ya." I hung up and ran into the bedroom, changed my shift for jeans and a dark blue long-sleeved shirt, and sandals for navy sneakers and socks.

By the time I had unlocked and relocked the gates and driven the three miles to Andy's, I was five minutes late.

Hank had already arrived. I spotted his blue Thunderbird in the parking lot. He was sitting in a rear booth near the back door. I slid into the booth opposite him. He was in dark slacks, wearing a brown pullover. His hair was damp. He looked fresh out of a shower.

"I hope I didn't interrupt anything," I said.

"Nothing important — supper with a friend."

"Anyone I know?" I questioned idly, just making chitchat.

He hesitated briefly. "Charlene Stevens." That brought my wandering thoughts to a screeching halt. I stared at him. At my shocked expression, he reddened beneath his tan.

"Oh my God," I said with a moan. "The barracuda?"

"We're just casual friends," he said lamely. "Nothing serious."

I thought back to our phone conversation, hoping against hope that he hadn't mentioned my name, then remembered . . . he had.

"You called me by name on the phone!" I wailed. "Please, Hank, say it isn't so; say you're putting me on."

"I told you, it's casual-like . . ." He was getting concerned with my reaction. "It's only now and then . . . when we . . ." He stopped to clear his throat, afraid he'd said too much. I closed my eyes, silently chanting my calming mantra, "I will not get upset, I will not get upset." I crossed my fingers for good luck.

"Before or after?" I demanded.

He looked uncomfortable, not wanting to answer.

"Hank?"

"Before." He looked to see if that was the answer I wanted. It sure as hell wasn't!

"I'm dead meat!" I said in misery. I was too upset to be discreet with the information I had received in confidence from Charlene last month.

"In case you think I'm overreacting and you don't understand the danger," I told him in a deadly voice, "Listen up. Dear Charlene cornered me in the little girl's room of the courthouse last month and took me into her confidence. Seems there's this 'hunk' she's crazy about and she wanted information. She has to work closely with this 'God's gift to women,' as she put it, and wanted to know if there was any gossip floating around about her. She was hesitant to name her lover. She said I would understand, because of all the rumors she had heard about you and me. I assured her that any rumors about us were completely false; there was absolutely nothing going on, past or current. I told her to enjoy herself and not worry about rumors, but that I hadn't heard any about her and her friend. She went away happy."

That conniving, devious, prosecuting bitch had been pumping me to see if she had any competition, and I hadn't caught on. I'd thought she was offering friendship by sharing a personal concern in her life.

"She really means nothing to me," he explained. "I just get lonely sometimes. I keep asking, but you won't go out with me. It's over as far as I'm concerned."

The man hadn't been listening to what I was trying to tell him. He thought I was jealous. My word, he was an innocent.

"Hank, ol' buddy, listen to me carefully 'cause I'm going to ask questions later. Charlene now thinks I lied to her and that you've been boffing both of us. She's not a woman who shares anything. She thinks you've been toying with her affections and that I know about it and am making her the butt of jokes. They don't call her the barracuda for nothing. We are both tied for first place on her 'shit list!' Need I say more?"

"I think you're just upset," he said, sounding smug. "I don't think she'll cause any problems."

I nodded numbly. I tried, but he's a man. He couldn't comprehend the situation of any woman scorned, and especially this woman's great capacity for hatred and revenge. He should be packing and begging for a transfer to Alaska. I should already be on my way to Mexico, listening to a language tape to learn Spanish in three easy lessons.

"I need a drink," I said, looking around.

"I'll get it," he offered quickly and stood.

"C. C. and water. Make it a double."

When Hank returned with the drinks, I downed half of mine in two swallows.

"Why did you want to see me?"

I looked at him. He seemed happy as a clam. Little did he know.

"This wasn't one of my better days, Hank. I just want to sit here and drink for a while. I'm still in shock about Charlene. I need to regroup or gestate or something."

"What can she do?" he said with a smile, "Shoot us?"

"No . . ." I said slowly in contemplation. "That's too quick; she'll be more subtle. Starting tomorrow, lover boy, she'll make sure that cases you thought were all tied up neatly have to have more exhaustive investigations. You'll be running down needless witnesses and worthless facts. A lot of technicalities that were previously overlooked are gonna be discovered and placed in the spotlight. You're gonna get chewed by both Sheriff Carlson and DA Robbins, many, many times. Your reports are gonna get lost and you'll always be turning them in late. Nothing you do is going to be enough, correct, or pleasing to her. She is smart enough and sharp enough to think up ways to bitch us both up; ways we can't even begin to imagine."

I jumped up, grabbed both glasses and went for refills. When I returned, Hank had begun to grasp the problem.

"What can we do?" He finally sounded concerned.

"I'm gonna tell you what to do. I'm good at solving other people's problems," I said dryly. "You've got to promise not to bitch and moan. Agreed?"

"Maybe," he said with caution. "It all depends."

"No ifs, ands, or maybes," I said harshly. "Without your promise to do exactly as I tell you, I'll walk out of here and lie through my teeth to Charlene tomorrow. I'll tell her you forced me to call you last night exactly when I did, because you wanted an excuse to go see another woman. I'll say you threatened to harass my boyfriend if I didn't make the call. She'll forgive me; she'll only hear the part about my boyfriend and she'll be sure I didn't receive any boffing, that it was the other woman. She'll murder you. I'm getting very tired of trying to help people and getting kicked in the teeth for my efforts. Take it or leave it; I'm just too tired to care."

He took a long pull on his drink and shrugged his shoulders. "I surrender," he said with a pained grin. "I agree, but that doesn't mean I like it. What do I have to do?"

"When we leave here, we're going by Alice's Flower Pot and you're gonna wrap a note around two twenties for Alice, telling her to deliver flowers to Charlene at the courthouse first thing in the morning. Tell her to include the note you're gonna write this minute. We'll slip it under the door. You'll apologize for leaving her last night, but your good buddy, Stan, is currently boffing me and asked you to help me with Bubba's abusive phone calls. You met with me and tried to convince me that you can't help on telephone calls from him. Tell her you are tired of hearing me whine. Tell her you're crazy about her and don't want to lose her.

Use the word 'love' at least three times, 'need' at least twice. Put in something about her nice skin; she does have beautiful skin. You're gonna have to wine and dine her every night for the next couple of weeks. After that, you can taper off to twice a week, then once a week. Get the picture?"

He looked unhappy. "I really don't want to do that. It would be lies, all lies."

"Why not," I snapped. "You've had her in the sack lately. She must mean something to you."

"Pure and simple lust and sexual frustration. I dated her because you won't date me."

"Well, just be thankful you have something to work with. A lot of people don't even have that."

"You are jealous," he said, sounding happy.

"Ah, get stuffed," I said. He was hopeless.

We had two more drinks before I decided I was feeling better. He wrote the note on paper from his pocket notebook. I read it and he didn't put in everything I mentioned, but he had enough to sound contrite.

"She still might get angry with you," Hank said at one point. "How are you going to keep her from taking it out on you?"

I smiled and changed the subject. I told him about Susan, and Brian's return. My plan to handle Charlene was simple: I didn't have one. There was no way to get both of us off the hook. In being vindictive, she could do Hank a great deal of damage. Being a deputy in a small town wasn't an easy job. She had fewer chances of hurting me, but I knew she could make my life miserable if she really tried. I didn't think she would buy any innocence on my part. I was just going to hunker down and ride out the storm somehow.

Hank had said something and I had missed it.

"I didn't hear you," I excused.

"I said I'll run that Brian out of town in the next couple of days."

"No, don't do a thing about him, Hank. That's the whole point of Susan's being angry with me. We can't interfere. It's her life. Just leave him alone."

"He'll clean her out," he predicted with disgust.

"Maybe so, but we have to let her make her own mistakes. We'll just have to pick up the pieces and put her back together if he cons her."

Hank made another trip to the bar and brought back fresh drinks. On weeknights, Andy's doesn't have a cocktail waitress for the tables and booths, just on the weekends. We both drank.

"Who's your new boyfriend?" Hank was acting coy.

Christ, living in a small town was like living in a fishbowl. We hadn't even been in the van together except the day I brought him home from the hospital. No townspeople had visited during his stay and I was sure that Rosie and Wayne hadn't blabbed it all over town.

"How did you hear about it?" I was irritated. "Was it on TV, or radio . . . or do you use the grapevine and jungle drums?"

Hank laughed. "You took a pair of expensive men's slacks to the dry cleaners. The inseam was too long and the waist too small for them to be Wayne's. My Aunt Minnie works there in the mornings, part-time. She told her daughter Penelope at lunchtime and Penelope is a friend of my sister, Faye Ann. Faye Ann called me tonight when I got home. That's your grapevine."

"And a very efficient one," I said, slurring my words. I had forgotten about the pants. They were Wade's, the pair he was wearing when he fell down the stairs. Some of Wayne's blood had soaked into the trousers. I was afraid I would set the stains if I tried to wash them. Hank's Aunt Minnie had measured the waist and inseam? Boy, she belonged in the CIA. If everybody in town were half as attentive to details as she, we could wipe out local crime overnight.

"What did the lab report say about the bloodstains?" I stressed my sarcasm.

Hank chuckled. "I called Sheriff Scroggins. I had heard about the ruckus over there and he was the one who told me about the Boston lawyer and you picking him up and all. I figured you and Rosie were taking care of him. How long is he going to stay with you?"

"He's already left," I said with glum resignation. All of a sudden, I didn't feel so good. The room tilted and, feeling cold sweat on my forehead, I mentally tried to count the drinks. Wine during and after supper. Three here, no, four, and all were doubles. I shuddered. No wonder I was soused. I stood up to make my announcement, pronouncing each word clearly and distinctly.

"I'm going to be sick."

Hank grabbed me and hustled out the back door, positioning me over a trash can, one hand on my forehead, the other around my waist. The smell rising from the trash can did the trick. I lost half of my stomach's contents. The other half stayed down there arguing with my stomach. He gave me his handkerchief and walked me back inside to the ladies room. I washed my face and rinsed my mouth several times, trying to focus on the mirror. I felt terrible and looked worse.

"I'll drive you home in a minute," he told me. "Give me the keys to your van. I've called a patrol car."

"Am I under arrest?" I felt grumpy. It would be a fitting end to a miserable day. I glanced up at the two blurred Hanks who were standing in front of me.

"No, silly. He's going to drive your van home and I'll drive him back here to his unit."

"Give me your keys," he repeated patiently.

I laboriously ran my hands in both pockets. "Nothing there," I said. Suddenly the whole mess became funny. I started giggling.

Hank backed me gently against the wall.

"Stand up straight," he ordered. I slowly straightened and stood at attention. I tried to salute, but couldn't find my forehead with my hand. Hank held me upright with his left hand on my shoulder and gently patted my pockets. He extracted the keys, dangling them in front of my blurred eyes. Suddenly, I was euphoric! The keys were found! The keys to the kingdom! All's well. Midnight crows and all's well! I was being propelled through a dark and mystic cave. I could hear scraps of tantalizing speech, just out of reach.

". . . load on, never thought I'd see . . ."

". . . keys . . . don't spread it around . . ."

". . . your ice princess . . . yeah . . . yeah . . ."

Who was the ice princess? She wasn't in my cave. The dragon rescued the princess. No, that wasn't right. The prince slew the dragon. Why did he do that? The poor little dragon. Poor, poor little dragon. Why did he have to be slewed?

I was flying. I looked out the cockpit. No, the car lights showed a tall man standing at a fence. That meant I was on the ground.

"Jo Beth! Jo Beth! What's the combination?"

"Nine-nine-nine," I mumbled. "No, you're supposed to dial nine-one-one. That was it. You dialed nine-one-one and they told you the time. If you dialed nine-nine-nine, that was when you were worried."

I was flying again. Objects were sailing past my head. Nope, I couldn't fly; everyone knew I couldn't fly. I was in bed, having a bad dream; it made me feel swimmy-headed. I turned on my side and went to sleep.

18

"HAPPY AS A DEAD PIG IN THE SUNSHINE"
April 9, Friday, 7 A.M.

I heard music, rolled over and sat up. Oh, my Lord, the pain was intense. With vicious suddenness, I felt nauseous, stumbled to the bathroom and unloaded, then sat on the commode and emptied my aching bladder. Oh, my God, I was dying! I stepped into the shower and howled at the cold water. Eventually though, the water heated and melted the chill. Standing on shaky legs, I leaned against the wall, letting the water pound on my face for a long, long time.

Turning off the taps, I pondered the next move. Robe. I struggled into the terrycloth robe, incapable of leaning over to dry myself. What the robe didn't absorb would have to depend on evaporation. With toothpaste on the brush, I stared straight ahead, eyes unfocused, avoiding the view in the mirror. When it was time to rinse and gargle, I realized there was a problem. For all the tea in China, I couldn't tilt to lean over the bowl. Standing very straight, I bent at the knees until my face was almost level with the sink, then let the rinse water run down my chin. Messy, but it worked. I wiped my mouth but wasn't up to mouthwash just yet. I started into the kitchen when clothes strewn on the floor caught my eye. How could there be such a mess? Bending at the knees only, I picked up bra, sweatshirt, jeans and panties in a line from the bathroom to the bed, then remembered pulling them off this morning on the way to the bathroom, after having slept in my clothes. Oh my God! Last night's events began flooding my senses in random scenes.

Eyes closed, I leaned weakly against the wall. I didn't want to remember, but it all came back in quick starts and stops. I padded barefoot to the kitchen, opened the refrigerator, and, moving only my eyes until they located the orange juice, bent at the knees to pick it up, and drank directly from the carton. It was delicious! I drank too much, felt bloated, then ran back to the bathroom and was sick all over again.

Deciding against trying coffee, I went to the medicine cabinet, picked up the pink stuff, drank a slug straight from the bottle and stood waiting to see if it was going to argue about staying down. When some of the queasiness had left, I decided the only place to be was in bed. My hair was still wet, but that was the least of the problems. The room was spinning so wildly when I lay down that as my eyes closed I prayed for oblivion.

On awaking, I found the sun much brighter, could hear the air conditioner running. It must be late. I rolled over and stared at the clock, surprised to find it nearly eleven. I sighed and sat up slowly, to be sure the room didn't spin. I decided I was going to live. Another trip to the bathroom, and this time, only emptied my bladder. This left me well enough for more juice, and even coffee sounded good. Back in the bedroom, the sudden urge to clean hit, so I removed the bed linen and stuffed it in the washer, then went to the guest bedroom and stripped the bed. It was the only evidence of its recent occupancy. I took that linen back to the washer and started the load.

Dressed in jeans, sweatshirt and walking shoes, I poured a cup of coffee and sat down at the desk, glared at the wine and glasses on the coffee table, then got up, cleaned them up, too, and put glasses away. I poured the small amount remaining in the bottle down the drain and tossed the bottle without rechecking the label. It was very doubtful I would be drinking much wine in the future. Beer and pretzels would be preferred. Wanting to be alone, it seemed a good idea to watch rental movies on the VCR and eat popcorn.

The house-cleaning schedule was out of whack, but to hell with it. Enough cleaning had been done for the day. I sat at the desk drinking coffee, then decided on toast, too. In the kitchen, I dropped two slices into the toaster, assembled plate, butter and homemade peach jam, and stood waiting for the toast. Why does it take so long when you stand there waiting? Normally, you push down the slices, rush to the toilet for a quick break and after you hurry back, the toast is up and cold. When you stand and wait, it takes five minutes.

I drank coffee, chewed the toast and eyed the answering machine, but didn't reach over and turn it on. Looking out the window, I sighed, contemplating the bright sunshine and the grass that grew so fast you could almost see it. I should hire Jarel to mow the grass. Wayne wouldn't be up to it for a few more days and it was already too high. Memory took me back three years when I first met Jarel. . . .

I had been in my new home three weeks. I'd seen the kid on several occasions and had asked the carpenters who he was. They didn't know, but he'd been standing there regularly for the past few months. They said at first they had been leery of him, thinking he was looking for something to steal. They watched him, but he never came closer, even before the fence was installed. They said they had grown so used to him that he was just part of the scenery.

The morning I first spoke to him, I had been to the kennel to check the dogs. There were four of them, newly purchased: O'Henry, the prized male, and three breeding bitches, all with pedigrees and very expensive. It was before Ramon's arrival, so I worried constantly about their health and checked them several times a day. I also worried about being in over my head. I had read and studied and visited other kennels, but had never raised or trained dogs before.

The boy was in his usual place. For the first six months, I had been alone, no one upstairs, no vet up front on the highway. Since we were the only two humans in several thousand square yards of space, I decided to walk over and talk to him. He was a skinny kid about five feet, five inches tall with hair so short it looked shaven. He stood his ground as I approached. I was thinking he might be frightened and run. Not Jarel.

"Hi," I said. "How you doing?"

"Ain't doing nuddin."

"I can see that," I said patiently. "What I asked was, how are you?"

"Why you care?" Boy, this kid was a prickly pear.

"Just trying to be friendly."

"Wid a nigger?"

"You're a young man I'm trying to engage in conversation. You're a black boy or an African-American, but you're not a nigger, understood?"

"Dat's what dey calls me alla time."

"Well, they're wrong."

"Wat's you doing here?"

"I'm trying to talk to you," I said. He gave me a wide sneer and pointed to the kennel.

"Oh," I said. "Didn't you see the sign out there?" I pointed back to the highway where the brand new sign had just been installed. He didn't bother to turn his head in the sign's direction.

"Wad's it say?" he asked casually.

"Can't you read?"

"Nope."

"How old are you?"

"Foateen."

"Don't you go to school?"

"Alla time."

"And you can't read?"

"Nope."

That was the beginning of a very difficult friendship. I went to a reading instructor and got the materials to teach him how to read. He was aggressive, intolerant, impatient and stubborn, but he learned as fast as I could teach him. I tutored him each afternoon for two hours that summer. When he could read well enough, we made a trip to the local library where I encouraged him to apply for a card. I searched the shelves for books on famous black people in sports, politics, and the sciences. Maybe you could say I had created a monster.

After three years of top academic honors, he would graduate from high school in the upper five percent of his class. He is still aggressive, intolerant, impatient and stubborn, and, with guidance, he has developed one more trait; he's a militant racist. He rubs everybody the wrong way. He advocates violence for change, instant and violent uprisings, burning down all government buildings.

Having him work part-time here for the past three years, I've learned that he is good with animals, but lousy with people.

I'd call him tomorrow and see if he could cut the grass and do a few chores. It would also be a good time to sound him out and see if he had decided what he was going to do with his life. He might like a job here, and he might not. You never knew with Jarel.

Finally feeling better, I decided to check the answering machine. I played the tape and, surprise, surprise! There wasn't one message from nine last night until almost noon today. There also were no hang-ups.

"Whoopee," I said softly, thinking "no news is good news."

The phone rang. I listened until Hank started to identify himself, then picked up the receiver.

"It's me, Hank," I said.

"Hey, Jo Beth. How you feeling?"

"I'll live," I answered in a subdued voice. "Thanks for getting me home last night. I didn't throw up on you or swing from any chandeliers, did I?"

"Nope, you're a very classy drunk."

"Gee, thanks," I said grumpily. He laughed.

"I've got a search for you."

"I don't know," I said doubtfully. "Hank, you know Wayne has a dislocated shoulder and I doubt if I could control a Pekinese today, much less two healthy bloodhounds. I'm just out of bed and not up to running a marathon. What is it?"

"A three-year-old girl in Three Forks, been missing from Azalea Park for over an hour. The Flatlanders Races and Picnic are being held there today and tomorrow. In the past hour a lot of people have tramped over the ground you'd have to cover. Sheriff Carlson just authorized the search. He had a call from the governor's office. Seems the kid's daddy was in the National Guard and was killed during Desert Storm. The American Legion brass runs the picnic and contacted the governor. The little girl's daddy being killed isn't the toughest part. The mother is in a wheelchair with MS and little Tessie is her only child."

Oh boy! I couldn't turn this one down with two broken legs.

"What's the weather forecast? I haven't been up long."

"It's eighty degrees right now; they're predicting eighty-nine, sixty-seven percent humidity, and sixty percent chance of afternoon and evening thundershowers," he said, sounding just like the local weatherman.

"Which end of the park should I enter, north or south?"

"The south end, right up against the swamp."

"Somehow, I knew you'd say that. Give me thirty minutes. No, make it forty-five. I forgot Wayne can't help load."

"ETA forty-five minutes. Hurry, Jo Beth. The mother is frantic."

"Understandable. See ya."

I hung up and went to load the dogs and gear. I didn't want Wayne to know until I was ready. He would want to help. I grabbed my pack from the kennel grooming room, checked the medications, deciding to add more calamine lotion. If I was lucky, I could load her up with bug spray on the way back. Thinking that the child was three, scared and alone, I added a large Huggie to my pack. Baby oil. Anything else? Yes, the child's sling. I had purchased one of those indoor child's swings made of white canvas and discarded the frame. Leroy's wife, Jackie, had sewn straps of white canvas for the neck and chest straps, so I could buckle it around my torso. That way I had both hands free for the dogs, could ride the child in front and still manage the backpack. I rolled it up and added it to the pack, then put fresh water in the canteens.

I loaded Susie and Bo, who were like kids being let out of school early; they were raring to go, dancing and prancing and hard to load. Putting jerky treats in both side pockets as I reached the truck, I ran down a mental checklist. I had loaded pack, suit, shoe covers, canteen, rifle, and the thirty-two, holster and bullets. I ran back to the grooming room and pulled out a handful of individual hand wipes in sealed packets and arranged them to be flat in two front zip-pockets, then went to the refrigerator and got three large sticks of Tootsie Rolls. They were about six inches long. When kids are lost, nothing will stop the howling quicker than a gooey piece of chocolate they can eat and drip all over themselves. They love it. I packed them, inside a Ziploc bag, between the folded towels in the pack. They would get gooey quickly in the heat and humidity.

I went upstairs to tell Rosie and Wayne where I was going. I was thankful, when I told Rosie to be sure and not let Wayne talk her into driving over there, that he was taking a nap. He would be worried because I would be going into the Okefenokee without a backup set of dogs and a search partner in case I had need of one. I'd just have to make sure I wouldn't need rescuing.

I saw the questions in her eyes about Wade and decided to get the explanation over with.

"We'll be three for supper; I no longer have a house guest."

"Wayne mentioned what happened last night. Do you think he'll be visiting?" This was very tactful of Rosie. I knew she was dying for details.

"I'll give you a blow-by-blow rundown tonight," I told her with a smile. "I've got to hurry." She wished me good luck.

I felt sick and puny and was numb from worrying about the problems with Wade and Charlene and Susan. I climbed into the van and waved to Rosie. She stood on the steps and watched me pull out. I had to put aside my lousy state of health and focus on the search. You can't daydream while strolling through the Okefenokee. I sped down Highway 301 to Three Forks, twelve miles away, passed the northern entrance to the park and continued on the highway for another four miles. I slowed for the southern entrance and was waved through the gate by a forest ranger; today I got in free.

I took the small, paved, curving drive for another mile, passing campers, tents, campsites and picnic tables with their own individual shelters. Each shelter on both sides of the road had concrete tables with benches and barbecue grills and were packed with people. This was a yearly event, with rubber inner-tube races for all ages at the northern dock in the afternoon.

I knew this park well. As a child I had taken swimming lessons here which were sponsored by the Red Cross. They picked us up in our neighborhoods in stake-bodied trucks that could hold twenty or more kids and drove us in here three days a week in the summer. They fed us Kool-Aid and cookies about eleven o'clock, but when we reached home about one-thirty or so, we would be so hungry from the morning of swimming we would eat until our stomachs ached. As a teenager, different school classes had held outings here often. I had explored all the nature trails and a little beyond, to the edge of the swamp area. I hoped Tessie was not the exploring type. Just the fact that she had wandered off made me sweat. I kept seeing Tom Tom's face in my dreams. I sure didn't want to add another one.

I drove up and parked where I saw the county sheriff's department vehicles and a milling crowd of gawkers or concerned citizens, whichever category fit them. I saw the Channel Three TV truck and knew I would be getting a visit from Timothy Sizemore, their slick reporter who had done me out of air time the last time he interviewed me. I started unloading equipment, knowing Hank would be along shortly. A crowd began gathering around the dogs in the truck, and me. People hurried over to see what was going on. Something new to watch. I always felt self-conscious when people watched me gear up. I wanted to hurry and get out of their sight. I could hear some of their comments. Parents would try to answer their children's endless questions, and show-offs would talk loud and crack jokes to draw the crowd's laughter and attention. I had seen and heard it all before, but it still embarrassed me. I tried to ignore them, never making eye contact, but it's harder to do than most people realize.

I pulled on the suit and zipped up. I was strapping on the gun when Hank arrived.

"Hey, Jo Beth, how's the head?" He spoke in a low voice.

"Fairly clear." I opened the gun's cylinder and checked the load, with it pointed at the ground and toward the truck. I slipped the extra six bullets into the slots on the holster, then indicated to Hank to hold the pack for me. He held it up while I slipped the straps over my shoulders and adjusted the waist belt. He hooked on the two water canteens and expertly checked the rifle.

"Rifle's loaded," he said, and slid it into the scabbard on my pack.

"Thanks."

He stooped and fitted my shoe covers and tightened them with the key I handed him.

"Daddy, what are those things for?" a little voice piped.

"Officer?" said an uncertain voice. "My son would like to know what those plastic things on the shoes are for?"

"Snake protection," Hank answered shortly. Hank knew as well as I did that when you answer one question from the crowd, several will follow. They all have questions and most are hesitant about asking. Let one speak and they all feel more confident about getting an answer. Hank had been addressed and since the man was so close and it was fairly quiet, it would have been rude to ignore him.

Another male voice asked Hank why it was necessary for me to carry two guns. What would the handgun be used for? Good question. I left Hank to answer it and walked around to the other side of the van, away from the crowd, and unloaded the dogs. I hooked them to their leads and walked a few feet from the truck to let them pee. They were watched intently by the large crowd, but it didn't bother them a bit. Susie squatted and Bo lifted his leg, then he had to smell Susie's rear end. I heard several titters. Did they really see humor or were they simply embarrassed about watching a perfectly predictable response of animals in mixed company? Americans pride themselves on being worldly and knowledgeable, but we're really quite gauche and backward about the way we deal with bodily functions and sexual routines in comparison with European responses. I had picked up these facts from reading, since we don't have many Europeans in Balsa City, Georgia.

Hank had broken free of the questioners and joined me.

"Where's the mother?" I asked.

"She's over there under that blue-and-white awning," he said, pointing to the spot. She was about a hundred yards to my right.

"Let's get it over with." I was dreading the interview. People in pain always seem to pass some of it on to me. I can't steel myself to feel nothing.

"You never did tell me why you needed me last night," he reminded me. He was keeping pace with me. I had to stop and choke up more on the leads; the dogs were frisky and wanted to explore in different directions.

"Later. I can't think about anything else right now," I told him. "Oh, oh," I said under my breath. I'd spotted Timothy and his cameraman angling across the grass to intercept us before we reached the tent. I stopped and waited. I'd have it out with him here where we couldn't be overheard. He hurried up and gave me a dazzling smile.

"Jo Beth, glad I caught you. We'll just do a quick stand-up, before you start." He motioned to his cameraman to start filming.

"Shut off that camera, or your name is mud, do you hear me?"

"What's wrong?" he asked in vast surprise, giving the "stop" signal to his cameraman.

"You sawed-off, conniving, welshing little twerp," I told him. "You conned me once, but never again. You stick that camera in my face and I'll make you eat it!"

"It wasn't my fault, believe me. They cut what you wanted because of the good material on the sheriff. They only give me so much time."

He was pleading. It felt good to make him sweat a little. I pretended to think it over.

"Well, I may have something . . ."

"Anything you want, you just name it," His voice throbbed with sincerity. He would promise anything for a story. I turned to Hank and winked, out of Timothy's sight.

"Hank, you go on ahead. I'll catch up with you in a minute." Hank turned on his heel and strode off. He knew I was angling to make some kind of deal and didn't want a witness.

"Listen up, Tim, I don't have much time and you have to get it right the first time; there are no retakes on this one. I don't have to point out to you, do I, that this story has everything?"

"You're right. Talk to me!" He was almost drooling. A dead hero father, an invalid mother in a wheelchair, a lost child. He was a reporter; he knew.

"With your help, I can get you an exclusive —" I had spotted the Channel 32 truck, but for the moment, they hadn't seen me "— but there's a price."

"Name it, it's yours!" He would sell his sister to the devil for a good story.

"I've got a strong feeling on this one. I want you close enough to hear all transmissions between Lt. Cribbs and me. Don't leave for anything, because you can't run off and take a leak and come back and ask if I called in. Cribbs would be able to put two and two together later and we'd both be in a jam. Do you understand?"

"I'm with you, Jo Beth," he replied with relish. This had started to sound sneaky. He loved it.

"I call in sometimes to check and see if the subject has been found. I want you listening to that transmission. When it comes, exactly fifteen minutes later, I'll be coming out of the woods, carrying Tessie, alive and well, we all hope. Now before I tell you where I'm coming out, I want a promise of an in-depth interview. Either you or a female reporter. I want a stroll through the kennel, lots of shots of cute little puppies and their parents. A special feature. You know what I mean."

"You got it, I swear."

"You see the dark brown building behind you?" He turned to look. "Yeah, got it."

"I want you to have the mother over there behind the building, waiting. There's a plowed firebreak behind the building and out of sight into the woods."

"Look, I really appreciate this, but how do I accomplish that? She may not listen to a reporter," he said, plaintively.

"The brown building is the park bathrooms. After the call, whisper in her ear that you are a reporter from Channel Three and where you want her to go. I'll pave the way, where she'll do what you say. After you get her behind the building and out of sight of everyone, you tell her immediately that Tessie is safe and coming out in fifteen minutes. I don't want her worrying a minute longer than necessary. If you wait to tell her, to get a surprised reaction, it will mean the end of cooperation from me, got it? Just don't alert anyone to your actions. You know it's going to be one hell of a scene, so don't screw it up. I'll only come out once; there's no replay."

"Fifteen minutes after your call, you'll be coming out at the fire-break. I'll have her there."

"Screw it up," I warned, "and you'll have Sheriff Carlson holding Tessie and giving a campaign speech."

"It'll be done right," he promised.

My trick wouldn't hurt Tessie or her mother. They were going to be on camera; no way to avoid it. I was just making sure I got the coverage rather than that pompous sheriff. Channel 32 would be pissed, but they hadn't done much for me lately. Maybe it would wake them up and they would do a feature, too. Every little bit helps. I joined Hank in the tent. He introduced me to the mother. She looked fragile and wan. She was trying to hold on and not go to pieces. She had a small yellow sunsuit with a ketchup stain on its bib in her lap. She held it out to me.

"Is it all right? She was wearing it earlier; I had to change her."

I took it. "It's perfect. What color is she wearing now?"

"Blue," she said, and her mouth quivered. She was barely hanging on.

"You call her Tessie?"

"Yes. Her name is Teresa, but we've always called her Tessie."

"Is Tessie afraid of large dogs?"

She looked at the dogs. "She'll love them," she whispered. "She isn't afraid of any animal."

I took her hand, leaned close, looking into her eyes, then reached down and gave her a hug while whispering in her ear. "A Channel Three reporter may come to you later and ask you to do something. Please do it and act naturally. Tell no one, as a favor to me. I'll find Tessie and bring her back, I promise."

I stood and shook her hand. She smiled and thanked me for helping.

Hank and I started over to where they suspected Tessie had entered the swamp.

"What are you cooking up, Jo Beth?"

"You don't want to know. Just act natural and everything will be fine, I hope. Is Sheriff Carlson here?"

"With all these constituents gathered to spend the day? You bet he is. To hear him tell it, he's purely tuckered out from shaking hands, patting backs and kissing babies."

"Is it his ego? No one ever opposes him. He doesn't have an opponent in sight, even though it's election year. You stand the best chance of defeating him, but I can't talk you into even thinking about running."

"I put the question to him about two months ago. He was complaining how his arthritis was hurting from him shaking hands so much. You know what he said? 'Boy, I have to cram myself down their throats all the time to keep anybody from running against me,' then he looked at me with those pig eyes and said, 'Don't you even think about it.'"

"He scare you off?"

"Hell no. I just don't think I have enough support to beat him this year. Maybe in four years."

"I don't know if I can stand him for four more years," I said. I rubbed my right temple where I had a splitting headache.

"You okay?"

"I've got a hangover headache 'this big,'" I said, holding my hands with the leads as far apart as possible.

Hank chuckled. "The things I could tell you . . ."

"Don't," I groaned. "Don't torture me."

"I won't," he replied, "if you'll have supper with me soon."

"Not until you finish your sentence with Charlene," I said crisply.

"Fine," he agreed happily. He thought he had finally gotten a "maybe" out of me about going out with him. It even sounded that way to me. Now I might be stuck with a supper date.

"Listen, Hank, if I happen to call in this afternoon, find Sheriff Carlson and stick to him like glue and play nice-nice. That way, you'll be clear."

He looked at me while we were walking. "Oh Lord, you're gonna give him a stroke, Jo Beth."

"Then you'll be sheriff a lot sooner than you planned," I said with a grin.

"If you don't get me fired first," he complained.

"Did you send flowers?"

"Yeah, she called to thank me and didn't sound mad. We're having a late supper tonight." He sounded a little embarrassed.

"Great," I told him. "Our plan is working. Keep up the good work."

He gave me a look I couldn't read.

We had reached the edge of the woods where Tessie had last been seen. It was a nature trail leading back to the park in a random pattern after about a mile of running partially along the lake and swamp.

"Hank, I forgot to ask. Has Tessie had any experience in the water?"

"Her mother told me she liked wading at the beach and shallow kiddie pools. Not afraid of the water. Not too concerned when she lost her balance and got ducked at the beach, but can't swim or float yet."

"Okay," I said with a dry mouth. I unhooked the canteen and took a couple of swallows. I noticed quite a few people had followed us across the grass from where we had left Tessie's mother.

"Hank, I guess you'll have to tell them to stay back. I'm going to start the search pattern."

"Good luck," he said as he turned to leave. "Radio check?"

"As soon as they pick up a scent." He went to keep the crowd from coming closer. I could see two teenagers pointing toward the path. I knelt by the dogs and rubbed their ears and told them what fine animals they were and that we were going to find Tessie, then they would get to celebrate. I knew they hadn't understood a word of what I said, but they knew from my actions what was expected of them.

I pulled out the sunsuit and gave them a good smell.

"Seek," I told them. "Seek!" They put their noses to the ground and started their random ambling, covering the ground with a fast gait and total concentration. I had seen this reaction many, many times, but it never failed to amaze me, how they could become so totally committed to finding one small smell out of hundreds, possibly thousands.

I knew the training had helped focus their search and discipline had seasoned them, but their gift of scent trailing had been deeply embedded in their genes from thousands of ancestors. A picture of a bloodhound today looks exactly like the first known pictures of bloodhounds in the middle eighteen hundreds. Keeping the breeding lineage so pure also had preserved their hereditary characteristics of smell.

I was no expert. I was still a novice in breeding and training but felt that Susie could hold her own with all the great legends, the famous bloodhounds of the past. I was extremely proud of both of them, Bo for his stamina and courage, Susie for her great trailing ability and perfect bone configuration and stance. They were an awesome combination.

They moved with quick disjointed stops and starts. I was sweating out the wine and liquor of the night before and could feel the sweat damping my clothing under the suit, traveling down my arms and legs, my crotch and between my breasts. I felt itchy and my nerve ends felt raw. I'd probably have a dandy case of heat rash by sunset. I could almost smell the alcohol evaporating through my pores.

On our first pass, about twenty yards from where Tessie was suppose to have traveled, the dogs sailed right past the trail and kept on going. My spirits suffered a small decline. Too many tramping the path may have obliterated the trail. I knew it was too early to tell, but I hadn't been kidding Tim about having a good feeling about this rescue. Being very superstitious, I take little signs as omens. My mind tells me this is a lot of hogwash, but my heart doesn't listen for some reason. On the fast trip here, I hadn't caught one red light. This was a good sign. My mind scoffed and said, "Well, Ninny, you only had four or five between there and here," but my heart said, "Oh, yeah. Well, you could have been stopped four or five times, so there!" Another sign was my suit. Almost all the time lately, the leg zippers would stick on one side or the other. I would have to do some awkward bending and jiggling to unstick them. Today, they had slid the six inches down my legs like they were greased. "Real scientific," scoffed my logical mind. "A good omen," chanted my hopeful heart.

The dogs were ranging out closer to the edge of the wooded area. They turned and headed toward the path I hoped was the correct one. They stopped often, moving their noses over the ground in a rough circular motion. Susie stopped. I had reached for one of my gloves and was holding both leads in my left hand, working the tight right glove on. Her sudden lunge caught me unprepared and she pulled free. She ran several yards before obeying my command to stop. Bo and I joined her and she was quivering with impatience to move. I hastily put on the left glove and checked the time before I covered my watch. It was twelve forty-five.

Tessie had been missing about three hours. I stuck the sundress under both their noses, but Susie was in a hurry. She strained forward. I began to hope that she had locked onto Tessie's scent trail. At the command to "Seek," both dogs surged forward. I sensed that Bo had caught Susie's excitement, not the scent. He was agreeable to following her lead, which was not as rare in canines as it was with humans. I had to increase my pace to keep up with them, practically running behind. Susie hesitated at the trail opening briefly, then plunged ahead. I was elated. She was definitely on a scent — Tessie's, I hoped. I put my mind to this particular trail. I had been over it many times in the past, but not for several years. I knew it returned to the park after a mile, maybe a mile and a half of winding trails; all the nature trails were planned that way.

My heart lurched. Oh, shit! I had completely forgotten that this trail had a couple of small wooden bridges — heightened walkways, really. I tried to remember how high they were above the water below them. We'd had plenty of rainfall since the first of the year. What with the "No-Name" storm of the century in February and two fairly extensive thunderstorms in March, some rivers and creeks would flood and crest about the middle of April. We were above average in rainfall, so the small run-off creeks below the walkways should be full.

God, I prayed the black water was only a foot or so under the bridges. Susie wasn't afraid of heights — just empty space below her, which was practically the same thing, but I was grasping at straws.

I commanded the dogs to "Hold." They stopped, but Susie wasn't happy about the delay. I unhooked the radio and called Hank.

"Radio check from Rescue One to Base, over."

Hank answered me. "Base, I read you, loud and clear."

"Hank, were you on this trail earlier?"

"That is affirmative," he replied.

"What's the distance between the bridge and the water?"

"What's the depth of the water?" He was perplexed. He didn't understand my concern.

"No," I said with patience, "what is the distance from the bottom of the walkway boards to the surface of the water? If you knew Susie, like I know Susie . . ." I had no idea how many people were listening on this open channel and didn't want to speak in the open about Susie's fear of heights. I just hoped he would catch the clue.

"Oh, yes, I understand," he replied. He caught on quickly. He should have; he had ragged me about my embarrassment at Susie's infamous parade episode.

"It's three to four feet, I'm afraid," he answered, knowing it wasn't what I wanted to hear.

My heart did another nose-dive. I doubted Susie would walk on a six-foot-wide walkway with about two inches between each of the two-by-six-inch boards which formed the surface, especially if they had four feet of space between them and the water.

"Hank, call Rosie and tell her to load Caesar and Anthony. Just the dogs, no gear, and get them here fast. I might need them. And, Hank, . . . silence is golden," I said pointedly and slowly. I planned to show Susie on the circuit, starting in Jacksonville, Florida, in the early fall. I didn't want Tim or the newspapers talking or writing about her in a cutesy way, exposing her fear. Dog trainers and handlers who follow the dog show circuits are notorious gossips. I didn't want her labeled with a defect before she was ever shown.

"Message and meaning acknowledged," he said smoothly. "Over and out."

I relaxed somewhat. If Susie refused the walkways, it wouldn't take long to get back and start over with Caesar and Anthony. The clock was ticking for Tessie. Each minute of exposure in the swamp added to her plight.

I gave both dogs a piece of jerky and some pats, then refreshed their scent and gave the command to "Seek." Susie was eager, Bo close on her heels. The vegetation on each side of the path was kept under control and was cleared for ten feet on either side. Wildflowers and several species of lilies and ferns grew in profusion in the rich damp soil. Some of the water plants were beautiful. Pale blues and yellows and snow-white lotuslike blossoms. Some were wilted in the heat, but their relatives looked bright in the shade. Tall trees were thick with moss that had proliferated in the winter. A lot of moss had been blown down by thunderstorms, and many trees were down from the violent storm in February. This part of the swamp had a lot of fallen trees to testify to the storm's intensity.

I noticed it was getting cloudy. Too early in the day for the expected thunderstorms. I hoped we were out of here before they arrived. It could get hairy. Under a lot of tall trees during thunder and lightning is not where you want to be. The more trees, the more danger of lightning strikes near you. This was thick, old growth, not planted in rows for harvest. A natural forest — dangerous during electrical storms.

I was already panting from the fast pace and was thankful for having eaten two pieces of toast, but some jerky or M&M's might be needed soon. I felt weak and shaky. My blood sugar was out of kilter from the drinking last night. I couldn't remember if it raised or lowered your blood-sugar level. Heavy drinking wasn't a habit, and the way I was feeling now, I was ready to take the pledge.

We came to a boarded walkway resting on the ground. It was about thirty feet long and curved right in four or five sections. Susie sailed over the surface without any hesitation but, of course, it was on the ground. I hoped the feel of the wood beneath her paws and its solidness would prepare her for the small bridges, knowing that was wishful thinking. We were on a straight path and I could see the first bridge ahead about fifty yards. There was a slight elevation in the wood and I could see handrails.

I tried to steel myself against disappointment. I wanted so badly for Susie to make this rescue. It would look great on her resumé when entering her in dog shows. We neared the small, wooden bridge and I crossed my fingers. Susie was going at the fastest pace allowable. I can't maintain a fast pace for long periods with full gear, having to pace myself for the long haul, so I had been putting on the brakes for a few yards. Susie started up the boards. With her nose to the ground, it was easy for her to spot the open space beneath her. I estimated the distance from the boards to the water at about three feet. She stopped, staring at the space below her, and planted her fanny firmly on the boards, gazing straight ahead. With a disappointed sigh I walked around her and led Bo on about six feet in front of Susie, then gave him the command to "Rest." He flopped on the boards, panting furiously, and looked at Susie. He knew something was wrong, but didn't know what.

We had traveled approximately half a mile. It wasn't time for a rest break here, but we were taking one. I unstrapped the pack, eased it from my shoulders, then sat down beside it. I dug out the bag of M&M's and tossed a few into my mouth, then unzipped a side pocket and dug out several pieces of deer jerky. I gave one to Bo, which he swallowed whole, and offered the rest in Susie's direction, my palm open. She looked at the jerky; she looked at me, and she looked below her. She hadn't forgotten why she'd sat down, and didn't budge.

There were two choices: I could tie Susie's lead to the hand rail and continue with Bo — we were on the scent, hopefully, but he could lose it later and I would be that much further behind in regard to time spent — or I could go back and start again with Caesar and Anthony. They were good scent trackers — not in Susie's class, but above average. I looked at Bo. He looked so damn solid and dependable, I wondered why I hesitated.

I had never used him alone on a major rescue. I thought about how a wrong decision could harm Tessie. She was the most important consideration, and time was passing. I had to make a decision. I threw another handful of M & M's in my mouth and propped the bag, one strap on my shoulder, up against the handrail, then slipped my arm through the other shoulder strap. I gulped down a lot of water, almost half the canteen, put on the gloves and walked back to Susie.

"Susie Pie," I said, "Bo and I are going to find Tessie. Want to come with us?" I untied her lead and tugged gently, but her butt was cemented to the boards. When a strong one-hundred-and-ten-pound dog braces her muscles against moving, you'll need a four-wheel-drive truck to do it. I retied her lead to the handrail and told her, "Don't leave till we come back." Thinking I heard a small whimper as we walked away, I didn't turn to listen; neither did Bo.

Susie sat and watched stoically as I fed Bo the deer jerky, gave him several pats, let him smell the sundress again, and gave him the command to "Seek." We moved across the short bridge, and in a few yards we rounded a curve and were out of Susie's sight. In the next ten seconds, Bo and I were subjected to the most horrible cry of anguish I have ever heard. It stopped us both in our tracks. Even when poor O'Henry was in the throes of LSD, his demented screams didn't compare to this torturous howl. Bo whirled and started back toward Susie and I was right on his tail. If it had been twenty yards further, I couldn't have lasted. Hanging on to the lead, I ran with him. We all collapsed in a heap, Susie and Bo with joyous howls, and me fast approaching heatstroke.

When I finally got my breath back, I assured Susie I would never leave her again, gathered the leads and prepared to back-track as fast as possible to exchange dog teams. I glanced at Susie and was stunned. She was crawling away from me toward the bridge expanse with grim determination. Her haunches were trembling and she was jerking like she had apoplexy, but by God, she was moving onto the bridge!

19

"PRETTY AS A SPECKLED PUP"
April 9, Friday, 1 P.M.

I turned around and just stared. Bo walked to her side and glanced back at me as if to say, "What's wrong? Do something!" He tentatively tried to nuzzle her head, a gentle nudge, trying to get her to stand. She ignored him. She concentrated on the herculean task of extending a shoulder and foreleg and dragging the weight of her body forward with her hind legs scrubbing on the wooden surface, trying to find purchase to assist her thrust. It wasn't a pretty sight. Tears formed in my eyes and my throat closed. I had never viewed such a display of raw courage and guts from a dog before and knew what I was seeing was a champion.

She battled for every inch. It seemed like hours. Just watching her made me tired. I had to keep glancing at my watch to be sure that only a minute had passed, then another. Bo resigned himself to pacing slowly beside her, the only way he knew how to help. At last she made her painful way onto terra firma. Her head was hanging loosely, and saliva was trickling out the corners of her mouth. She was on shaky legs and walked slowly to the shallow water about ten feet away. I held her lead while she waded out until her belly and flanks were covered. Bo splashed happily around her in circles, but she stood quietly regaining her strength. When she left the water voluntarily, I presented the sundress and gave the command to "Seek." She was back in business. She hadn't conquered her fear; she had crossed the bridge in spite of it, using the only solution she was capable of. I was so proud of her!

For the next hundred yards or so, they maintained a brisk pace. I was feeling a little shaky, but managed to keep up with them and didn't have to slow their pace. The path took a gentle turn to the right, but Susie and Bo went straight ahead. It was a small game trail. I stopped them momentarily and stooped the approximate height of a three-year-old. I saw that Tessie had probably entered this path standing up, but I would have to duck-waddle through it. It led straight down to the water and I saw ahead what I believed had lured her off the nature trail. Bright lilies in a beautiful shade of buttercup yellow were growing in small bunches as though they had been carefully arranged by a florist. These bouquets were divided and surrounded by dark green ferns, lush and thick. She must have wandered down here to pick some — probably wanted them for her mother. The dogs confirmed my theory by stopping and running in small zigzag patterns back and forth between several bunches. I saw two different spots where the ferns were crushed and lily stems broken. I could almost see her in the slightly cooler shade, bending over to reach for the flowers. I shook my head and turned to the dogs. Susie was ready to go; she had found the scent where Tessie had waded back to the game trail.

There were roots exposed, cypress knees — knobby and difficult to walk around on the narrow path — but the dirt was damper near the water. Did she walk this way because the ground felt good on her bare feet? She had been barefooted when she disappeared. I had noticed the hot boards back at the bridge while bracing myself to stand. Here, under the tree's shade, the ground was cooler and wet and would feel good oozing between her toes.

I noticed the creek on our left as we walked. It was running swiftly enough that it was free of green scum caused by the pine trees shedding pollen. There was no problem with the water. If she drank any, it shouldn't do her any harm. The sky suddenly grew darker with deep purple clouds covering the sun. It was early in the day yet for thunderstorms to start, but they didn't always follow the schedule. This one could be a loner — could unload and be on its way in five minutes, or could hang around for hours. The one thing you can't accurately predict in South Georgia is the weather.

If there were large boomers, Tessie would be terrified. If there were large, close boomers, I would be terrified, too. The dogs never flinched or jerked with the noise from thunder and lightning.

When puppies turned three months old, they all got frequent trips to the police firing range. We would load a litter of puppies into the van and drive to the range on practice days for the policemen and county deputies. The best way to not have gun-shy dogs is to make them familiar with firearms noise when very young, letting them hear the sound periodically for the first year. We made careful notes of the puppies who were frightened — those went to good homes as pets. Who's to say that they didn't get the better bargain? They were pampered, petted and secure. We misfits, Susie, Bo and I, just hang around and work at rescuing people. It was a dirty job, but somebody had to do it.

We continued to wind around the game trail as the ground rose slightly. It was a quarter till two. I estimated we had traveled a little over two miles. More deep purple clouds could be seen through the trees. Any minute now, the bottom was going to drop out of the sky and we would be awash with rain. On this slight rise we were coming up to, a heavy pouring rain would completely wash away Tessie's lingering scent. Ten feet of running water can purify a stream where cows had filled up and emptied. With the slight drop behind us, the water would run swiftly to the lowest point.

Susie raised her head and breathed the cooler air that was blowing gently in our faces. The sound that broke from her throat brought chillbumps to my arms inside the suit. That wonderful, loud, joyous celebration. Bo was only a second or so behind her. He was singing alto to her soprano. I joined them in thankful laughter, wanting to skip forward. So did Susie and Bo; they were moving faster than I could run.

We climbed a little higher, where some logging crew had dredged and drained this area so they could reach the more inaccessible giant cypress trees. The soil under our feet now looked like white beach sand that had never been walked on. It was packed firmly by the last rain. We were traveling too fast to check for small footprints. The dogs told me she was just ahead and I believed them. I just hoped that she was not hurt. Several big, cold drops of rain hit my face and head. It felt good on the mosquito bites. The wind had started coming in small gusts, a sure sign we were directly in the path of the storm. Please, not now. Hold off just a few more minutes.

An open expanse appeared on the right. It looked to be about half an acre. I wondered what this level area was for and why no trees grew on it. The sand looked gritty and had turned a dark beige color. This must be the dredged area. Something in the sand must have retarded growth. No, I finally spotted some blackened stumps. That solved the puzzle. This area had burned recently and new growth was limited to wild grass and a few light-green gallberry bushes.

The dogs turned right onto the grass and hurried to the shade of several wild magnolia trees at the edge of the clearing. I saw the blue of her sunsuit before seeing the child. Pulling back on the leash, I gave the "Retreat" command several times before the dogs drew back. She was lying on the brown sand with her back toward me. I saw a small handful of wilted leaves near her side. My heart was heavy. No one could sleep through the noise the dogs were making. I dragged them to the closest tree and slipped their leads around a bole.

Pulling off the gloves, I walked toward her. The wind was increasing and so were the raindrops. I walked around her so that I could see her face. The dogs were howling their heads off. I could see no obvious injuries, but she was filthy from head to toe. The mud had dried and looked crusty and streaked. I knelt next to her and touched her upper arm.

"Tessie? Tessie, can you hear me?"

She opened her eyes and focused on me. Her eyes widened and she looked startled.

"Its okay, Tessie. You're safe, honey. It's all right, Tessie. I'm a friend. I've come to take you to your mother."

"Mama?" she asked.

"Yes, Tessie, your mama," I told her. I was wiping away the tears and sweat stinging my face.

"I was asleep," she said, and yawned.

"You were in a coma," I teased her, laughing. "Are you hurt? Do you hurt anywhere, honey?"

"I'm hungry," she said. "I ate a banana for breakfast but that was a long time ago. Did I sleep all night?"

"No, honey, you just had a nap. Tessie, we're gonna have to cover up; it's starting to rain." The wind was much stronger. I saw a jagged flash of lightning and heard the thunder follow immediately, which indicated the storm was near.

"I hear dogs a-woo-wooing," she said.

"Yes, honey, the dogs are mine and they are woo-wooing because they're happy they found you. Can I pick you up?"

"I can walk."

"Okay, but we have to hurry. The dogs love you. Do you like dogs?"

"Yes'm. Can I pet them?"

"You bet. Grab my hand; we have to run." I clutched her hand and we started moving toward the dogs. It started pouring. We reached the dogs and they were ecstatic. Tessie was trying to hug both of them, letting them lick her face. The rain was a solid wall, and lightning was ripping the darkness apart with more frequent thrusts, and claps of thunder rolled through the trees. I quickly untied the dogs and grabbed Tessie in my arms without asking, heading for the open field.

I couldn't run, just shamble and shuffle. I didn't want to risk falling while holding her. I couldn't see the ground, so it was a matter of looking slightly ahead of the dogs for stumps and holes. I finally reached the center of the open space, set Tessie down, unhooked the pack, and yanked out a towel, a body bag, and a plastic ground sheet. It was awkward working with the leads in my left hand and Tessie clinging to my right leg. I unzipped the body bag far enough to slide Tessie inside. She wouldn't turn loose my leg, so I had to pry her arms away. There wasn't enough time to explain what I was doing and get her cooperation. She would have had a difficult time hearing me. She was like a stubborn cat being stuffed into a wet paper bag, and she didn't appreciate it. I added the towel. The rain was now solid stinging waves being tossed about in the wind. Lightning was cracking all around us and thunder was a numbing roar. I flapped the ground sheet to open it, bunched one side, and anchored it with my pack, pulling it over us with the pack inside the plastic tarp. I had to fight the loose side; it was being snapped like a sail in the wind. I gathered the loose folds and shoved them under me, lying flat, head to head with Tessie. I had the dog leads under me along with both sides of the plastic sheet, and we were now under shelter. The only parts of my body covered were my head and shoulders.

I looked at Tessie and laughed. We looked like drowned rats, our hair soaked flat to our skulls, water running down our faces. I reached out carefully to touch her skin. It was cold from the rain, but now that we were out of the wind, it would heat up fast under the plastic. I tried to rub her with the towel, but every time I moved, the plastic sheet tried to pull free. The condensation from our breathing and body warmth was clinging to the underside of the plastic. We were as wet inside as we were outside, but at least we were out of the stinging downpour and chilling wind. I worked my fingers in the plastic until I could grasp an edge and lift it a little to let fresh air in; it had already grown stuffy under the tarp.

"I wanna go home," she stated plaintively. She'd had all she could take. She was soaked and hungry and wanted her mother. The sound of the storm outside was scaring her. She was resting on her elbows facing me and our faces were only about a foot apart so I could hear her easily.

"Hold this edge of the plastic for me, honey, and I'll try to dig out some candy." She brightened with the thought of candy, and grasped it eagerly. I moved cautiously and lifted the flap of the pack. I groped around thinking I would never be able to reach the Tootsie Rolls. I felt them at the tips of my fingers, but eventually worked them free and out of the pack. I opened the wrapper for her and took one myself. We chewed and smiled at each other.

"It's good," she announced between bites.

"Best I ever had," I agreed.

"Can we go home now?"

"Soon, Tessie. As soon as it stops raining."

"The dogs are getting wet," she informed me.

"The dogs love the rain; it won't hurt them a bit. They'll curl up and take a nap while we wait." They were both lying close to my right thigh and foot. When I had moved for the candy, I had touched the solid softness and felt one of them shift position.

"Can they see in the dark?" She was worried about finding her way back. She knew she had walked a long way trying to find her way back earlier.

"It will be lighter soon, after the clouds go away, and the sun will come back. We can find our way back just fine."

The storm lasted twenty-five minutes, but it seemed much longer to me. Tessie asked a lot of questions. I didn't know if she was normally this gregarious or just needed assurance, but I answered, explained, and tried to entertain her. My head was splitting and my stomach needed solid food instead of chocolate. I didn't attempt to reach the aspirins; it wouldn't be worth the effort. I just lay there and chatted brightly, smiling a lot to reassure her, but I suffered.

The lightning and thunder left first, slowly rumbling away to the east, the sound diminishing through the trees. The rain slowed and faded to a light drizzle. A drizzle we could handle. I raised the plastic sheet and looked out. There were scudding dark clouds, but they didn't produce lightning; the storm had moved away from us. I released the plastic and started folding it the best I could. Both the ground sheet and the wet body bag were hard to handle. I wadded both of them into as tight a ball as possible and fastened them outside the backpack — after I helped myself to two aspirins. I shared the canteen with Tessie, gave her another Tootsie Roll and unrolled the canvas sling.

The dogs were happy to see us emerge from our cocoon, and Tessie hugged and patted them. I put the sling on first, fastening it around my waist, but had a bitch of a time working the backpack on and getting it settled properly. I picked up the dog leads, then knelt on the ground.

"Hop in, Tessie. A seat just for you."

"I can walk," she said.

I took her hand, pulled her close, and gave her a hug. I told her we had to hurry and go see her mother. I lifted her into the seat facing away from me and strapped her in. She wasn't as heavy as expected, but it was going to be hard to stand from the kneeling position with this load. I put Bo on my right side, positioned Susie on the left and ordered them to "Stay." Placing my hands on their backs, I quickly pushed down, managed to get one foot under me, then regained my footing. So far, so good. I shrugged and adjusted the load as best I could. Tessie's head was slightly below my chin, so vision was okay, but her legs thumped my thighs at every step. It couldn't be helped. Annoying, but not painful to either of us.

The air was cool after the rain. I left the towel out to put around her shoulders, being afraid she would get chilled, but she shrugged it off. With her back next to me and my breath on the top of her head, she would probably stay warm enough. I couldn't feel the chill. I was encased in armour and soon sweat was pouring down my face. I glanced at my watch. It was two-thirty. Vain and cynical thoughts now combined with relief to make me feel less than noble. I realized if I hurried, we would be back in time for Tim to make a mad dash for Jacksonville and the six o'clock news. I was as crass and brash as the media people. There was just more sweat in making my deadline.

I grinned and started hoofing it faster. When we reached the small fork that went to the left and up to the original nature trail, I continued around the small game trail beside the water. It was agreeable to the dogs. They were rain-cooled, rested, and had drunk their fill from the river. I let Tessie feed them some jerky treats. She trustingly held the meat out in her chubby little fingers and these two prize chompers removed the treats as delicately as light-fingered pickpockets, then scarfed them down.

We were going back a different route, one that would cut off more than a mile of the return trip, I estimated, and should bring us out quite close to the firebreak where I wanted to make the grand entrance. We made good time.

There was one small wash to wade through, but I could see it only came to my knees. I picked my way through the water carefully. If I fell here, it would be a devil of a time getting back on my feet. We made it fine and Tessie giggled when the dogs shook off the excess water, sprinkling us liberally.

I unhooked the radio, hoping the moisture hadn't gotten into it, and sent my message.

"Rescue One to Base. Do you read me? Over."

"Base to Rescue One, we read you loud and clear." Hank stressed the we. Bless his heart, he was helping out. He had deduced the signal was the call. He was letting me know that Timothy was listening. It wouldn't surprise me to find that Tim had tried to sit in Hank's lap. I'd bet he had hovered close to Hank to get this call.

"Has the subject been found?" I asked.

"That's a negative," replied Hank. The irony came through clearly.

"Just checking. Will keep in touch," I said, feeling like a sneak. "Over and out."

I found the firebreak with no problem and followed it until I was near enough to hear shouts and laughter from the kids playing and the distant drone of the loudspeaker, over near the water sports. I checked my watch and let the exact fifteen minutes pass, then waited for two more long minutes to give Tim plenty of time to set up. At last it was time.

I took a deep breath. "Okay, Tessie, Susie, Bo; it's showtime!"

I popped the leads twice and, I swear to God, the dogs seemed to understand. They picked up the pace and seemed to straighten even higher, almost prancing. Maybe I was giving them too much credit; they could also hear and smell the people who were near.

Maybe it only happens once in a lifetime, but everything clicked and fell into place. Suddenly the sun came out and bathed us in its golden light. I was carrying a photogenic, curly-haired towhead who had been lost in the dreaded swamp for five hours and she was smiling. She was smeared, childlike, with chocolate on her face and stomach. Two beautiful and greatly talented dogs led the way, looking alert and catching every eye. I was in a bright orange rescue suit with pack and rifle showing.

I left the firebreak and strode with confidence into full view of Timothy, the cameraman, and the mother. Tessie started calling "Mama!" and Mama was calling "Tessie!" and Tim was pushing the wheelchair, the ham! 'Course that was like the pot calling the kettle black, because I was hamming it up pretty good, myself.

The cameraman was shooting from just behind and slightly to the right of the wheelchair, to get us all in the frame. The mother was reaching up and outward toward her child; Tessie, with her chubby little arms, was reaching yearningly down toward her mother. The dogs were reddish-colored, blue sunsuit, bright yellow-orange rescue suit, green grass, blue skies — all wet and glistening. God was in His heaven and all was right with the world. What more could you ask for in a picture?

I was told later by Fred, our local newspaper editor, that there may have been a newspaper in Outer Mongolia that didn't run the picture, but every other newspaper snatched it off the wire and started setting type for the caption that would run underneath it on the first page of the next edition.

After the emotional reunion and Timothy had left for the fast run to Jacksonville, I walked back to the van and greeted a worried Rosie. She had parked next to the van. I told her what had occurred and she was thrilled with Tessie's rescue and that Susie had found a way to function, in spite of her fear. I was hoping to avoid the sheriff, but knew that was asking too much. I saw him hurrying across the picnic grounds and hastily sent Rosie on her way. She was just as outspoken as the sheriff, and I didn't want her involved in the coming fray. She cranked up and pulled out just as Sheriff Carlson stomped up, accompanied by a very reluctant Hank.

"You bitch," he hissed. "I'll get you for this!"

"Why hello, sheriff!" I yelled in a loud voice. I was hoping to draw a crowd. At least he wouldn't shoot me in front of a lot of people.

He cast a hasty look around to see if anyone was paying attention.

"Lower your voice," he rasped furiously. "That was a stupid stunt and it's damn sure going to cost you plenty. I'll make sure the county doesn't renew your contract for this, you grandstanding bitch!"

"Wow," I yelled. "Thank you, sir, for those kind words!"

I had spotted four onlookers moving closer and waved them on. "The sheriff is the one responsible for the fast rescue of little Tessie today. He deserves a round of applause. Let's give him a hand for being a good sheriff and selling the county commissioners, so they would hire me!" There was a smattering of applause and six more onlookers came forward. Thank God, there were several more hurrying up, so they wouldn't miss anything.

"The sheriff is running for reelection this November and I want everyone who resides in Dunston County to come forward and shake his hand. He's just been telling me what a good rescue we had today and how both of us made it possible, weren't you, Sheriff?"

"Well . . . I . . . it sure was," he stammered lamely. He smiled weakly and shook the first hand offered. The damn sheep actually were starting to form an informal line to shake his hand. I couldn't believe it. Well, I've always said you could sell shit, if you advertised it effectively and wrapped it in an attractive package. People buy empty, sealed tin cans every day in Georgia at tourist traps because the label promises, "Pure Georgia Air." They could be sealed in Hoboken, as far as we know.

By the third handshake, the sheriff had shifted into high gear and was spouting campaign rhetoric. I eased gently back out of his line of sight and walked around the front of the van. Hank broke away and followed me.

"Got a little upset, did he?" I asked.

"God, Jo Beth, you sure do like to live dangerously," he whispered. "He almost shit in his pants. You should have seen him. He did every-thing but jump up and down and pull his hair. Some teenager came running up and said Teresa had been found and told him where. When he started around the corner of the bathroom, he spotted the Channel

Three news team and asked them if they wanted some pictures of him. They told him politely they had plenty and to watch the six o'clock news."

"Thanks for helping me, pal. I've gotta run before he runs out of potential voters around there. When you go back around, see if you can recognize a few of them. I may need a couple of witnesses to his remarks today, if he tries to scuttle me with the county commissioners. That's all I was trying to do, to spike his guns, if he begins attacking me."

"Will do, but don't call me to testify," he said with a smile.

"I promise," I said and gave him a swift hug. He looked at me with his dark eyes. "Just felt like hugging somebody," I explained. "I'm still on a high from delivering Tessie to her mama. See ya."

"Sure," he said with a mysterious smile. I wondered what he was smiling about. I had hugged him before, I think. I was trying to remember.

I pulled out and took the park roads toward the highway. When we were out of sight, I stopped and quickly stripped off the suit. God, it felt good to feel the rain-cooled air against my skin. I lit the first cigarette since before noon and pulled the smoke deep into my lungs. I smoked three in a row before stopping at the crossroads about eight miles from home to order a hamburger and a large Coke for me and two plain double cheeseburgers for Susie and Bo. The girl in the drive-through window said she had heard about Tessie's rescue on the radio. The man in the car behind us jumped out and gave the girl a ten-dollar bill saying he was paying for the order. I smiled and thanked him. He watched me feed the dogs and seemed to think he got his money's worth, just watching them hold the burgers and wait for permission to eat. He asked how I trained them to do that. The answer was "lots of practice," which was absolutely correct. You have to repeat an exercise so many times, you find yourself repeating it in your sleep. Repetition is the key to training — and bright dogs to work with.

When I arrived at home, it was after four o'clock. I drank two glasses of iced tea while soaking in a warm bath. Rosie had met me when I arrived and took over putting the van and dogs away. She told me that Wayne had a female visitor and she was looking for something to do to delay going back upstairs so that they could have some privacy. She mentioned that she had four pups out for basic obedience training and had found one was very bright and quick to pick up commands. She was sure he was a winner. I told her to push him, move him up to the next step of training; dogs who were quick and bright became bored with having to repeat the same exercise over and over after they had mastered it.

In my bath, I savoured the memory tape of Tessie and her mother's reunion. This bright memory would help on long lonely nights when I couldn't sleep. I wondered if Wade had done anything stupid about his problem and if Susan might someday forgive me, and if Brian Colby was going to give her grief. I sat in the bubble bath and soaked and sipped on iced tea, smoking cigarettes. I had a blister the size of a dime on the ball of my right foot and a smaller one on the left. Wet socks had rubbed them raw in only a mile or so. I was glad the hike hadn't been longer.

Rosie had told me she had put supper in the fridge. When I got out of the bath, dressed in shorts and a brief halter top, I went into the kitchen and peeked inside the refrigerator to see what it was. A small tuna and pasta casserole and a container of cole slaw. Looked delicious, but I'd have to wait awhile until the hamburger had settled.

There were no messages waiting and, better still, no hang-ups. I tried calling Wade at home, but didn't get an answer. I worked on the mail for a while and then got comfortable in a recliner with a book I was a little more than halfway through. I kept eyeing the clock on the wall and when it was five minutes till six, I turned on the TV to Channel Three and the news. They used a fast still shot of the rescue scene, then moved to a standing female reporter. She told everyone that a dramatic rescue of a three-year-old girl from the Okeefenokee Swamp would be shown at eleven tonight. I had either been bumped by the president or the Russian situation, or they hadn't had time to edit the film before air time. They mentioned it was an exclusive coverage by their feature reporter, Timothy Sizemore. They also might be trying to lure more watchers for their eleven o'clock news, but this was one watcher they wouldn't have because I'd never last until eleven p.m., but would record it for viewing later. I got interested in the book and finished it with no interruptions. I had heard the dogs when Ramon came to feed them but didn't go out. The lamp had to be turned on for the last thirty pages. It was clouding up for more rain, and the room was growing dim.

I wandered into the kitchen and decided to eat. It was after seven and food sounded good. I started a new book and read while eating. By nine-thirty I was pleasantly relaxed and sleepy. I made the rounds locking up and flipped the switches to charge the fence. I filled Ruby's food dish, freshened her water dish, then went to bed.

20

I swam up out of the darkness of sleep with the harsh bing-bong of the alarm at the first gate reverberating in my ears. I rolled off the bed, grabbed the magnum from the nightstand drawer with my right hand, picked up the cellular phone with the left and flopped belly-down on the carpet before being fully awake. Shaking my head to clear it, I blinked to clear my vision and crawled to the bedroom window on my elbows, keeping as low as possible. The blinds and drapes in the house are seldom closed, since no one can see into the house unless they circumvent the security gates, which was obviously what had happened now.

I looked out but could see nothing. There are five security lights on the property, three arranged in back and two in front, illuminating almost all of the front drive. I was picking out Rosie's telephone number from the faint light through the window. She answered on the second ring, her voice hoarse with sleep.

"Hello?"

"Rosie, it's Jo Beth. Wake up. Keep Wayne inside and keep out of sight. Don't turn on the lights, and get Wayne's thirty-eight, just in case. Don't let Wayne come out, even if you have to lock him in. Someone penetrated the first security gate about two minutes ago. Don't come out, even if you hear gunshots. Is that clear?"

"Should I call the police?"

"No, I'll do it."

"I'm praying," she said.

"Good. Hang up."

I disconnected. Not seeing anything meant one of two things. Either they were still at the first gate, which is out of sight, or they were already past the viewing space and at the second gate.

The strident buzzer sounded the alarm on the second gate. I froze with surprise. I should have been prepared to hear it. I had been telling myself that this whole affair was simply a malfunction, that I would soon be cussing the electric gremlins that plague all machines with electrical cords and moving parts.

If whoever it was had cleared the second gate, they were now in the courtyard. They could surely handle the sliding glass doors to the office if they had gotten through the gates. I didn't know how long I had spent dithering but it was time to head for the hidey hole. When the carpenters had discussed the security possibilities, they had pushed for a secret shallow closet, with a glass mirror on a hidden door for camouflage. I had explained that Bubba's weapon of choice was a lead-filled baseball bat and that a full-length mirror would be too tempting a target.

They finally settled on a square trap door in the floor right beside the bed, where I could step down to the sandy ground below the house. The clearance between the bedroom floor and the ground below is only two and a half feet, but it's sufficient for my size. I'm not fond of shag carpet, but had chosen a short thick shag for the bedroom so that its fullness would effectively hide the cut square. I felt over the bed's headboard leg, then moved my fingers back a foot in a straight line. I dug my fingers into the lush pile and felt for the edge of the trap door. I found it easily. I hadn't tried it in over a year, complacent about some of the ground's security, but it worked fine.

I lifted it up and back, stepped down into the darkness, and groped for the small loop of canvas nailed to the inside of the door for a handle just as I heard the glass door of the office shatter. I pulled the trapdoor closed as I scooted backwards on my stomach on the dirt. I was in darkness so dense that I stretched my eyes wider to be sure I had them open rather than squeezed shut.

I heard glass breaking again and it sounded less destructive, but I knew it was only because the floor and the carpet overhead were cushioning the sound. Running a close second to my fear of snakes is a fear of spiders. I told myself I would not think about spiders. In the darkness as I felt for the antenna on the phone and picked out the numbers nine-one-one by touch, I thought about spiders. Large brown house spiders with a body the size of a quarter. Six or eight legs more than two inches long. They can scurry so quickly across the ceiling that you can lose sight of them. Then there are smaller, black, fuzzy spiders that could jump two feet in your direction if you startle them. Both species prefer dark dry isolated places for their habitat, which was exactly the description of my current habitat.

"Nine-one-one, may I help you?" It sounded like Bennie Tatum, one of the dispatchers for the Dunston County Sheriff's Department. I had heard the 911 system operated out of the sheriff's office. Someone had told me recently that they were having trouble getting the bugs out of the system. Our area had only had the emergency system for about ten months. Rural Georgia operates about twenty years behind its more progressive cities and most states.

"This is Jo Beth Sidden, three miles north on Highway Three-oh-one. I have an armed intruder breaking down the door to my house as we speak."

"Didn't you lock your gates, Jo Beth?" he asked. Yep, it was Bennie; I recognized his voice.

"Yes, Bennie, but someone breached the security gates," I replied, trying to be patient.

"What's your address, Jo Beth?"

"Bennie, you know damn well where I live."

"The computer's down, Jo Beth, and when that happens, we have to fill out a route slip. Just bear with me, gal, and we'll have somebody out there real soon. Now, what's your address?"

"Bennie, have you radioed to send help, yet?"

"I have to write the address on the route slip, Jo Beth. This dang machine eats the paper when you feed it in, 'cause it won't give it back to you. I got chewed out last week for . . ."

"BENNIE, GET THE LEAD OUT AND GET ME SOME HELP OUT HERE. MY HOUSE IS BEING DESTROYED AND I'M IN PHYSICAL DANGER. DO YOU UNDERSTAND?"

"Now, girlie, just keep your britches on. I tole you true. As soon as you give me your address, I can send help, not before. What's your address?"

"Woodpecker Route One, Box 98-A," I said through gritted teeth.

I had yelled fairly loudly, but didn't think there was a chance of whoever was up there hearing. The crashes, bumps, and odd noises I was hearing from the office area were fairly muted. I was sure Bubba couldn't have . . . well, I had finally faced the truth. I'd used 'they' in my thoughts, but had known from the get-go that it was Bubba. Even after the savage pounding he had inflicted on me five years ago, I still had trouble believing the happy, carefree, good-ol'-boy I had married eleven years ago was the destructive monster upstairs now. A monster who seriously wanted to inflict fatal damage on me.

"You just stay on the line, Jo Beth. I'm sending some city boys; they can get there quicker. They'll be there before you know it."

"It was nice chatting with you, Bennie," I said.

I closed my eyes for a moment, concentrating on the noise upstairs.

It sounded like he was still in the office. He had probably run through the place, room by room, searching for me. Since I was not present, he had methodically started destroying everything, beginning in the office. Since he had broken the glass door, he had no way of securing it against my escaping that way.

I tried to envision the damage. He had probably broken the computer screen before sweeping it off the desk to crash on the floor. The typewriter, the answering machine, and phone would be next. My genuine imitation Tiffany lamp was on the desk with the other things. . . . and the porcelain vase with the Chinese dragons. He couldn't miss the mirror behind the sofa. Oh . . . my . . . God! Dad's pictures! In the three years of living here I had only forgotten twice to close the security panels for the night. I jerked my mind back to last night, replaying my actions. I had gotten sleepy. I'd locked the office door, checked the two east windows, flipped the switch behind the drapes — I breathed a little easier. I was sure I'd closed the panels.

Let's see. He'd probably destroy the non-famous canvases, but that was no great loss to the art world. The only reason I kept them was to remind myself of my failure to be like my father and to see the look on some people's faces when they thought they were viewing my father's masterpieces. They had been good for a few laughs, but I wouldn't miss them.

The sounds above me were getting louder. He was in the bedroom above me. I gently placed the phone in the dirt by my side, careful not to disconnect, so that Bennie wouldn't try to call back. Wiping the sweat from my left hand on my shorty pajamas, I transferred the heavy magnum there so I could wipe it dry. The air was nasty and stale. I heard the mirror on the closet door break. The floor squeaked from the pressure of a step. I tried to guess what was going on. The sounds had a rhythm and they were evenly spaced. Dear God, how infantile! He was jumping up and down on the bed! It was the only conclusion I could draw. I heard a loud thump, then a sharp whack. Maybe the night stand or the lamp breaking, or both. I heard glass shatter and the same sound again. It must be the bedroom windows.

I hoped he didn't have the large hunting knife he usually wore on his belt. He kept it razor sharp. If he started on my clothes . . . I'd lie here in misery and do nothing. I wasn't physically his equal, and my life was worth more than the clothes. My only options were to lie here and listen to the damage, or open the trapdoor, stand, and aim carefully to blow him away. That certainly wasn't the ideal solution. I might be forced to shoot him, but it wouldn't be for destroying a few articles of clothing.

The boys in blue were taking their own sweet time getting here. There had been time enough to get here from Jacksonville! I had forgotten the eleven o'clock news tape stored in the VCR upstairs. I'd bet the tape, VCR, and television were ready for the dump. I'd also bet the insurance company would cancel my policy after tonight. It would be tough to find other coverage. At least the worry about what was going on upstairs had taken my mind off spiders. The only time I had practiced using the hidey hole was in the daytime. If I'd tried it at night, I'd have known it was dark as Hades down here and could have bought one of those magnetic wall flashlights. Then I could have seen what was crawling around me. My face felt flush, my heart started flopping around like a gaffed fish and I felt a tightness in my throat. I must be getting a touch of claustrophobia from the solidness looming above me. The stale air and my vivid imagination weren't helping, either. Maybe it was best I didn't have a flashlight — if I saw a cornered coon, a coiled rattler or a woods rat over in one of the corners, I'd probably fire the gun in panic and the whole world would know where I was hiding.

I could see a faint section in front of me that was lighter than the darkness. My eyes had adjusted and I was seeing a faint spill of light from the nightlight outside coming through the small slits of the air vent about six feet in front of me. That was where I would make my exit if the Keystone Cops ever arrived. The noise was more faint now, but still with lots of crashes and tinkling. He must be in the kitchen breaking everything breakable. I hoped he missed the tea set my father had given me for my sixteenth birthday. It was blown glass from Holland, pale blue, six glasses and pitcher and tray, all bearing my initials. They were wrapped in plastic to keep them free of dust and in plain sight on top of the refrigerator.

Listening to more thuds, I speculated on the microwave, toaster and other small appliances. Wondered who was having a small appliance sale. I'd also probably need to find a large appliance sale, too. I was getting giddy; first I'd been scared, now I was getting mad!

At last! The cavalry! I could hear the faint sound of sirens, even down here. Two different sirens. One officer alone wouldn't answer an "armed intruder" call. They always need backup. The sounds above continued. I guess Bubba wasn't paying attention. I picked up the phone, dug my elbows in the dirt and pulled and scuffled to the air vent.

The underpinning of the house was white brick with an aluminum air vent every twelve feet. The carpenters had straightened the vent grooves slightly so that there was some visibility to the outside but not noticeable from the outside. The sirens were louder now; they were approaching the turn to the drive. I watched the two police cruisers squeal up the drive and heard them when they reached the courtyard. They turned the sirens off and I heard two tiny thuds, but couldn't tell if they were from Bubba or the car doors slamming, then I heard another crash from the kitchen area. He'd get caught in the act. That should keep his daddy from pulling any strings. He'd go back to prison and I'd sleep a lot easier at night. What a waste of humanity! He'd spent all of eight years, except for two months, in prison, and now he was going to be sentenced to at least two or three more years. Violation of parole, breaking and entering, and criminal damage to property — all while under a restraining order. That should produce about eighteen months of peace for me, more wasted years for him.

I heard some muted yelling from upstairs, then a few more thumps. It seemed that Bubba was not going quietly. There could be an additional charge of resisting arrest and assaulting police officers. I pushed the vent out, suddenly anxious to breathe fresh air and to stand up and stretch. The vent moved freely for a few inches, then was stopped by the cypress mulch in front of it. There was a three-foot strip around the entire house for a flower bed and shrubbery. Nothing was planted in front of any vents, but the mulch was down to keep weeds from growing. I pushed harder, moving the vent further out with each push, finally working it open.

The vent was in the center and wire mesh was plastered with simulated brick. I used my hands to pull myself through after placing the phone and gun to the left outside the opening. I slithered out and stood up. God, the fresh air was wonderful! I closed the vent, then carefully shoved and patted the mulch back into place. I'd never mentioned the hidey hole to anyone, not even Susan, Rosie or Wayne. I felt a secret was best kept when no one was told. Starting with the top of my head, I dusted and brushed off while letting my vision adjust.

I went up the front steps on tip-toe and peered into the living room through the window. I didn't see anything but a totally trashed room. I crept over to the shutter next to the front door, inched my fingers into a crack and slid out a spare front door key. After unlocking the door I replaced the key in its crack. As I straightened, a tiny jolt of delayed information popped into my mind. My costly burglar alarm, activated carefully each night for the past three years, was as silent as the grave. It should have gone off with tremendous noise long ago and kept going until it was disarmed. What was really annoying was that there had been several glitches and false alarms in the past that had almost turned my hair gray. I made a mental note to call the company and threaten everything in the book if they didn't refund the purchase price and cost of installation.

I eased the screen door open, then the front door, and picked up the gun and phone, pushing the door closed with my shoulder. I walked, dodging broken glass, a lamp, bookends, and anything else that could be tossed. I was barefoot and didn't need a nasty gash in my foot.

I found Patrolmen Andy Carpenter and Floyd Graham, Balsa City police officers, eyeing the wreck that was once my favorite room in the house. I hoped someday it would be again.

"Hi, guys," I said. They both were startled at my silent approach.

"Where you been hiding, girl?" Andy said harshly. He didn't like me and he didn't like the fact that I had seen him jump when I spoke.

"Outside," I said shortly. "Girls under ten are called girls, Andy. Try Jo Beth or Miz Sidden or 'hey, you' if you want to address me."

"Whooeee, you still got that smart mouth," said Floyd with a raspy chuckle.

These good-ol'-boys were Bubba's age, both in their early thirties and both had added at least ten inches to their waists since high school. Andy's younger sister had graduated with my class and I knew Floyd's wife when I saw her. I felt sorry for her; she always looked pinch-mouthed and nervous when I spotted her around town. I guess her main problem was Floyd.

I saw both of them smirking at my thin pajamas barely covering my crotch, so I went to find a robe and shoes. I stepped gingerly through the mess and finally found both. After I was properly covered and shod, I returned to find them still standing and scanning with relish the destruction Bubba had inflicted.

"You and Bubba must have had some fight," Andy said with admiration.

"Jo Beth, you should quit agitating Bubba," Floyd said. "You know this violates his parole. You still mad at him for messing you up a little years ago?"

"Have you got Bubba cuffed and locked in a back seat?" I asked quietly.

"Yeah. You gonna press charges?" Andy questioned.

I wasn't going to waste my time on these two. I kept my temper under control.

"I'm filing charges," I said clearly. "I'll be down in the morning." I gave both of them a cold smile. "This office is wired and sound activated. I'll bring the tape with me to play for Chief Ballard. He'll probably use it for show-and-tell in his next seminar on how to handle a violent domestic dispute. In the meantime, please take your prisoner and get the hell off my property."

They didn't want to believe me about the tape. Both of them glanced around uneasily and seemed at a loss for words. Andy finally cleared his throat.

"The bail hearing will be at ten o'clock. You have to be there before that to press charges."

"I'll be there with bells on," I replied firmly.

They both tried to act like leaving was their idea, to strut a little, adjust some leather, but they couldn't quite pull it off. They beat a hasty retreat. Even if the office was wired and I had taped their asinine comments, I wouldn't have gone running to Chief Ballard. We got along well, but I fight my own battles. I just wanted them out of here, now, and wanted Bubba behind bars. I was losing steam fast.

I looked around for a place to sit down, but there was nowhere without litter. I put the magnum down, realizing I was still holding it even after putting on the robe and shoes and dialing Rosie's number.

"Everything is under control. They arrested Bubba and he's on his way to jail. Go back to sleep. Everything's a mess here, but it can wait until daylight."

"You've got to be kidding! We're on our way," she said and hung up.

I sighed. All I wanted was to find the bed, change the linens and pull the covers over my head. I hadn't looked closely at the damage and didn't want to look until I'd had time to adjust to the shock. I picked my way to the kitchen and had to kick some blue glass aside and right two chairs before being able to reach the refrigerator. My throat was dry. I drank straight from the milk carton, then gazed at the empty expanse on top of the refrigerator and concentrated on keeping the milk down.

I heard Rosie's shocked and distressed reaction to the damage and went in to join them in the office. They were both fully dressed and gazing around with stunned expressions.

"It's not as bad as it looks," I remarked dryly. "It's worse." I signed to Wayne as I spoke, then smiled at both of them. Rosie came over, hugged me, and patted my shoulder. Wayne shook his head and went to look at the other rooms.

"Where did you hide?" she asked quietly. "You did play it smart and hide, didn't you?"

"I played it smart. I hid outside the bedroom." This was technically correct; I surely wasn't in it.

"I was so scared," she admitted. "We watched when they brought him out. He was struggling and trying to fight. The short officer had to hit him with his nightstick before they could get him in the back seat, even handcuffed." The short one was Floyd, who had counseled to kiss and make up.

"Well," I said to reassure her, "now we have at least a year or more of breathing room."

She looked around in sadness. "It doesn't seem possible that one man could do this much damage in just twenty minutes or so."

"He used a baseball bat. It will be around here somewhere. As soon as I find it, I'm gonna burn it."

"Come upstairs with us tonight," she offered. "Sleep on the couch. We'll clean this up in the morning."

"I need my own bed, Rosie. I'll be fine. Let's go make coffee and have some Danish. I have one that's gonna turn stale if it isn't eaten in the next fifteen minutes."

We made our way into the kitchen and Wayne joined us. Rosie found a dishcloth and Wayne and I picked up the tablecloth by its corners and carried it over to the trash can to dump cloth and contents. We crunched over broken glass, sugar, flour, cornmeal and all other dry ingredients that had been stored in glass containers on the counter. Rosie located the coffee pot, made coffee, and I located a roll of paper towels to serve as plates for our Danish. Bubba had also opened all the cabinets and dumped all breakables on the floor. Liquids stored in glass had been thrown at the walls, appliances and cabinets. He'd achieved a lot in twenty minutes.

Wayne and Rosie added milk from the carton to their coffee and I felt a twinge of guilt for having drunk from the carton earlier. I had chastised Susan once or twice for the practice and she had told me, "We all do it, honey, but we pretend fastidiousness when we see other people do it." I guess she was right.

We drank coffee, nibbled Danish, and got a little silly. I was smoking and cracking jokes; they were laughing with the release of nervous tension when I started losing it. My hysterical laughter turned into racking sobs as I put my head down on the table and bawled like a baby.

Rosie held me and murmured comforting words as she motioned Wayne off to bed. She put her arms around me and led me to the bathroom when my sobbing slowed down to just sniffles. She told me to shower. I was smeared with dirt. I stepped under the shower, but didn't have the energy to shampoo and scrub with soap. I just stood there while the water pounded my head and body, thinking about nothing.

After a while, Rosie reached in, turned the taps off, and held a terrycloth robe while I slid it over my arms. She had to point out the shower clogs to protect my feet. I leaned over at her command and she toweled my head until it was just damp. I was incapable of coordinated actions.

She guided me to the bedroom and I saw she had placed the mattress back on the bed and had put on fresh linens. I collapsed bonelessly onto the bed and remembered to tell her that I had to be at the courthouse at nine-thirty a.m. I heard her turn off the air conditioner which had been chugging away because of the broken windows and sliding door. She turned on the ceiling fan above the bed and pulled the sheet over me. The bedroom light went out and it was the last thing I remembered as I fell off the cliff's edge into sleep.

21

I awoke suddenly to music. Not remembering the events of last night till I sat up in bed, I gasped at the chaos all around. Then I sat there blinking, idly wondering where the clock radio was. Obviously it was still working somewhere. Using my eyes, I followed the cord from the outlet until it disappeared under the bed.

I slipped on shower clogs, then realized I was wearing a terrycloth robe — and sweating. With the windows open, the humidity in the room was high. Dropping the robe on the bed, I shuffled cautiously to the closet. This situation called for some real shoes. Most of the contents of the closet were strewn on the floor in heaps, but a casual inspection didn't turn up too many items slashed with a knife. Bubba hadn't spent a lot of time in here after he'd broken out the windows and smashed the two mirrors. Eyeing the mattress stuffing that had leaked onto the floor, I guessed, upon giving it some thought, that Rosie had flipped it to the un-slashed side last night, since the surface I'd slept on had been smooth. I found socks where they belonged, in the sock drawer. Thank God for small favors. I had just straightened that drawer this week, a dreaded chore. The drawers, with their contents intact, were still in the dresser. That was a good omen, which started the day well.

After dressing in jeans and a T-shirt, a quick toothbrushing and face washing, I went to the kitchen to start coffee. Crunching over to the fridge for juice, I drank straight from the carton. My manners were deteriorating.

I carried a dishtowel into the office, my next destination. I wiped the desk clear of broken glass and lamp fragments, located and plugged the phone in, and took heart at hearing a dial tone. Things were looking up. The answering machine was in several pieces. My hand automatically righted the desk chair and I saw that one arm was severed from the frame. The casters still worked, so I cleared glass off the plastic chair mat with my foot and was back in business. Sitting down, I saw with relief that Bubba hadn't given any thought to what a paper blizzard would do to the office. It was good to know I wouldn't have to sort through the many piles of paper in the desk, unless the data couldn't be salvaged from the ravaged computer lying on its side a few feet away. I'd worry about it later.

The smell of coffee sent me back into the kitchen. After pouring the steaming cup, it was back to the office to start the "to do" list, its first notation to call the insurance agent. A glance at the clock, which wasn't broken, told me I needed to call him at his home in twenty minutes. The glance also reminded me that I didn't even know the time of last night's invasion. Not once had I checked the time. Maybe Rosie would know.

The next entry on the list was to call Tim Fergerson at Cannon Trucking. I would invite him and his relative, John, the trucker whose step-sons had planted shake in this cab, to lunch. I was going to call in some markers with swift dispatch. It would probably drive them nuts all morning, wondering what I wanted. Boy, would they be surprised! The phone rang.

"Jo Beth Sidden."

"Miz Sidden, this is Maynard Anderson, one of your county commissioners? I didn't get you out of bed, did I?"

Maynard, the fox. He was a small banty rooster who also slightly resembled a fox.

"Not at all. What can I do for you, Commissioner?"

"Saw the pictures of your rescue on TV last night. Just wanted to congratulate you on your fine work. We're very pleased with your services, Miz Sidden. I believe I can speak for my fellow commissioners, Mr. Easton and Mr. Porter. I'm sure we'll be able to sign your contract for next year."

"Well, it's nice of you to say so, Commissioner, but there has to be a fee adjustment on this next contract, which is a week overdue," I said casually. "You know how prices just keep on going up."

He'd wanted to call first, before the others thought of it. As for the price adjustment remark, I had to strike while the iron was hot, or kick 'em when they're down or something in that vein.

"I'm sure we'll be able to work something out," he said, a trifle cooler. "We'll be getting in touch with you."

"Thanks for the call, Commissioner," I said and hung up.

The phone rang again. Rosie, this time.

"I just wanted to check and see if you're up," she said.

"Up and feeling good. Rosie, what time last night did this mess start?"

"When you called, it was 1:30 a.m.," she said. "I wrote down the time and we got back to bed at two-forty a.m."

"You mean it only took an hour?" I was surprised. "It sure seemed to last longer to me."

"That's what I told Wayne this morning. We'll see you after breakfast. Want to come up and eat?"

"I've already eaten," I lied. "See ya."

I called the insurance agent. He agreed to come by on the way to his office so repairs could begin earlier. He was one of the good guys. I looked up Tim Fergerson's home phone number. He answered on the third ring.

"Tim, this is Jo Beth Sidden from Bloodhounds, Inc. I wondered if you're free for lunch today — and I hope you'll bring John along with you."

"I can be," he said slowly, feeling his way. "I believe John can join us."

"I hate to be calling so early, but something's come up," I said pointedly. I wanted him to know this wasn't social.

"I see. When and where?"

"How about Chester's at one?"

"Fine."

"See ya."

He was wary and curious; I couldn't fault him for that. He'd know soon enough.

Realizing I was hungry, I made a bacon and banana sandwich. It's a great breakfast combination. I was just finishing when Rosie and Wayne arrived. Wayne came in with two galvanized trash cans, a long-handled poop scoop and a broom. He saw my look, held up a hand for silence, and started signing.

"This is the fourth day and I feel fine. My stitches are healing clean and the shoulder doesn't hurt. I'll be careful not to place any stress on the injury. Most jockeys ride race horses with dislocated shoulders, according to Dick Francis. You're just being too protective. Agreed?"

I glanced at Rosie for help, but she just shrugged her shoulders. Wayne grinned from ear to ear when I shrugged mine, too. I rolled my eyes at Rosie and we all laughed. Wayne started signing again.

"I went out at dawn and checked the fences. He used a pair of bolt cutters with very long handles. He must have tremendous strength. I found them in his truck and took them and stored them in the lumber shed. They towed his truck away over an hour ago. No one mentioned bolt cutters."

"Thanks, Wayne. Frankly, it never entered my mind to wonder how he got in here. When you come across his baseball bat somewhere in here, put it in the same place."

I started working in the bedroom, since I had to dress before long and go into town to sign the warrant against Bubba and do some emergency shopping. I got the kitchen broom and a dustpan and started on the floor. Most of it was cleared by eight when it was time to call the glass people. The insurance agent had arrived and was talking with Rosie as I walked in.

"I trust your ex-husband is not going to make a habit of this, because if he does, we may have to cancel your coverage," he said, with a twinkle in his eye as he winked at Rosie.

"It should be fairly safe to cover me for the next couple of years," I told him with a smile. "He should be in jail that long."

"Good, good," he answered. "Always hate to lose a good customer!"

He walked around, punching numbers into a hand-held calculator and speaking into a pocket recorder.

Dressing in a cool, two-piece cotton outfit, I put on low-heeled pumps and found a small shoulder bag to match, foregoing hose; it was simply too hot. I looked around for a mirror to check my hemline and discovered the only mirror I now possessed was a hand-held oval belonging to the dresser set. The hemline felt okay. I decided on no makeup.

I asked Wayne if he would pick up the two severed locks and put them in the van and told Rosie I'd be gone most of the day, since there was a lot of shopping to do, and relayed that the glass people had promised to be here right after lunch. Saturday was time-and-a-half, but what the hey; I wasn't waiting till Monday for air conditioning if I could help it. She said to take my time; she'd be there all day. Wayne had backed our old pickup as close to the back porch as possible and was loading broken, useless items in the back. I sighed as I saw he had almost a full load already. Bubba had made kindling of the end tables, coffee table, and a glass-front knick-knack storage piece which I'd prized. The couches, love seat and occasional chairs all had their cushions slashed, but Wayne explained he was loading for the dump now; the slashed furniture would be carried to the Salvation Army reupholstery store in the next load.

I stopped at the locksmith, since there was plenty of time to get to the courthouse. All city prisoners were held in the county jail. They had saved money by consolidating the jails, doing away with city lock-ups.

My friend was shocked when I showed him the sheared locks, saying it must have taken a hell of a pair of bolt cutters. He shook his head and went to find replacements with a four-digit code. He gave full credit on the old locks, saying the company would reimburse him.

I stopped at the film shop and picked up some prints that had required special handling. They were glamour shots of Susie which I'd had enlarged. When she won her first blue ribbon, I was going to get her portrait painted to display in the office.

I arrived at the courthouse at ten after nine and had to drive around to hunt a parking place, as usual. I went up the wide steep steps into the vast central hall and headed to the sheriff's department booking section. They could tell me where to file charges.

I was in the corridor twenty feet from the sheriff's office when I saw Wade hurrying out with a worried expression on his face. I slowed my progress and prepared a smile of greeting. He spotted me and strode toward me, reaching for my arm. I thought he wanted to shake hands, so I dutifully stuck mine out. He ignored it and grabbed my elbow, glancing around.

"Have you heard?" He was trying to turn me in my tracks. I resisted and stared at him, forcing him to stop.

"Heard what?"

"Come on," he said grimly. "I'll tell you on the way."

"I'm sorry, Wade. I have to go file charges before a bond hearing. I can't be late. Heard what?"

"You have plenty of time," he uttered ominously. I went numb. I didn't like the sound of that at all. I let him hustle me out of the courthouse and across the street to the "Annex," a bar and grill where the booths are high-backed and the back room almost too dark to see your food. A lot of deals had been cut back here. You ordered up front and served yourself. Wade placed me in the last booth on the right with my back turned to the front while he went to get coffee.

I knew it was bad news and I sat quietly trying not to think. I wasn't in the mood for bad news. The day had been bearable, so far, but I had the feeling it was going to change. I needed time to prepare myself.

Wade returned with the coffee. He sat opposite me, facing the room. There was no crowd since the courthouse was only open half a day on Saturday. The court calendar was so jammed, they'd started the practice about six months ago. Of course, you couldn't buy driver's licenses, pay taxes or fines, or do any of the chores you do on weekdays.

"Jo Beth, I'm sorry," he began.

"Go ahead, Wade. I'm ready. Tell me."

"I came to the courthouse this morning to look up some old, can-
celed loan deeds I found in Dad's strongbox at home. Someone told me
the clerk's office was open today, but only for trials and arraignments,
not the normal workday business. I went to the restroom and heard two
officers discussing you and what had happened last night and this morning."

"I know what happened last night; tell me what happened this morning."

"These men were county deputies. One told the other he had just
attended the shortest preliminary hearing on record, and an hour earlier
than usual. He said they were told to bring the prisoner, Buford Sidden,
Jr., into the courtroom at ten minutes to eight. Judge McAlbee had called
the hearing one hour earlier than usual. He said they brought him up and
the judge, Sidden's lawyer, and the prosecutor were waiting."

"Charlene Stevens?" I asked. He nodded his head. It figured.

"Go on," I said softly. I guess I knew what was coming, but it just
didn't seem possible.

"The deputy told his friend they sat Buford Sidden, Jr., down and
read the charges against him. The judge called for the arresting officers,
but they weren't in the courtroom. The judge remarked they would wait
only five minutes for them. The deputy said five minutes went by without anyone saying a word. The judge called for the arresting officers
again; and again no one appeared. The judge asked if a warrant had
been issued and the prosecutor said no, because a complaint hadn't been
filed, either by the victim or the officers. The judge said he had no other
choice but to release the prisoner; if a warrant was issued, he would be
expected to appear. Buford Sidden, Jr., walked out about ten minutes
after eight with his lawyer by his side. I'm sorry, Jo Beth."

I slid over in the booth, turned my body around to sit sideways, and
lowered my head between my knees. I had felt the swirling blackness
approaching and was taking precautions. I heard Wade asking from a
great distance if I was all right. After a couple of minutes there was
sufficient blood flow to my numbed brain and I straightened.

"It was cut and dried," I said softly. "Ol' Buford Senior must have
gotten Judge McAlbee out of bed by five in the morning to have this all
set up by eight. The judge will swear he notified the bailiff of the eight
o'clock hearing, and didn't the prosecutor arrive on time? The bailiff
will swear he notified the desk sergeant, and he will swear he called the
police officers and on, and on, but they are lying."

"Why would they conspire to delay the inevitable?"

"This is Buford Senior's way of sending me a message about how powerful he is. This will allow Bubba to have a few more days of vacation before he has to go back to the joint. You know, I felt so safe I almost didn't bring my gun with me this morning. I thought I could relax for a few months. Isn't that strange?" I tried to hide a huge yawn. Suddenly, I was very sleepy. All I wanted was to curl up and take a nap. I realized what was happening. My brain was getting tired of trying to cope and was shutting down my nervous system — or vice-versa; I couldn't remember which was correct. I picked up the cup of coffee and drank steadily until it was finished. The caffeine would help.

"I need a Coke, Wade."

He slid from the booth and went to get one for me as I lit a cigarette. The nicotine would help. I'd bet a big shot of morphine would really help. When Wade set the Coke down, I managed to dredge up a smile for him. It wasn't easy since we were discussing an issue that could have dire consequences.

"You haven't gone and done something silly after I used my imagination too freely about your father, have you?"

"Are you now saying it was just your imagination?"

"Stranger things have happened." I was trying to sound enigmatic, but ended up sounding like a dork. I decided to stay with bluntness.

"Have you tried to get in upstairs?" That sounded blunt enough for me.

He looked upset. "No," he said shortly. "I'm waiting until Hector gets back on the property, then I'll confront him and see what he knows. Would you like to be present when I question him?"

"Not particularly," I offered casually. I'd try one more time. "How're the ribs, Counselor?"

"Healing nicely," he replied. "I should be able to go at least six rounds with Hector by Tuesday or Wednesday."

"Sorry, did it sound like I was prying?"

"A little. Listen, Jo Beth, would you like some company today and tonight?"

"I don't think so, Counselor," I answered. "We all like to solve our own problems, don't we?"

I saw pain and anger flash across his face.

"You don't give up, do you?"

"Thanks, Wade, for telling me about Bubba being released; I appreciate your concern. Today hasn't been a winner, so far. You're absolutely right. I've just begun to fight," I said, sliding out of the booth. It was a very good exit line; there was no use diluting it by saying goodbye — I just walked out.

Across the street I entered the sheriff's department and proceeded to the booking desk.

"Good morning, Sergeant Pennington."

"Morning Miz Sidden. What can I do for you?" He spoke much louder than normal. He wanted as many observers as possible to witness the coming rout he had planned. I could almost feel ears turning in our direction.

"I wanted to know where to go to sign a complaint against my ex-husband. City officers arrested him last night after he forced entry and criminally damaged my property."

"Is he in the lock-up here?" He put on his glasses and pretended to check a list. Well, okay, two can play this game. When I was changing purses this morning, I'd dropped in the portable tape recorder when I realized I'd be going to Sears in the mall. Gremlins had infected it about a month ago and I kept forgetting to take it back. I thought I saw a way to speed up this action. I slipped the non-working recorder out of my purse and placed it on the counter.

"I assume he was brought here, since the city hasn't had holding cells for over a year." I answered clearly and politely, aiming my voice toward the recorder. The sergeant stared at the recorder with the same intensity, as if I'd just placed a live snake in front of him.

"What's that for?" He sounded surly.

"Are you indicating the pocket recorder?"

"Yeah. What's it for?"

"Sergeant, I find it's a great help to me in my line of work. Sometimes, even months later when I have to testify against someone, it helps keep the records straight."

"Your ex-husband was released this morning," he stated, glancing at the recorder. "No charges had been filed and the judge turned him loose."

"Which judge was that?" I asked politely.

"Judge McAlbee, tenth district, same as always."

"Did Judge McAlbee's clerk call you this morning and inform you that the court appearance time had been moved up to eight?"

He looked at me with consternation, acting uneasy.

"I don't have to answer that," he said.

"Why ever not?" I asked innocently.

"Well, look who's here!" I heard a familiar female voice say, then turned to see Charlene Stevens standing behind me.

"Hello, Charlene," I replied calmly. "I was trying to find out where to go to press charges against my ex-husband."

"You'll have to come to my office," she said with satisfaction. "You were late and we had to turn him loose. Sorry."

The sergeant had cleared his throat twice trying to get Charlene's attention, but she was focused on me.

"She has a tape recorder, Miz Stevens," he blurted.

"That's illegal," she snapped at me. "You didn't ask my permission."

"But I didn't need to ask, Charlene. I was taping a conversation between Sergeant Pennington and myself. You weren't part of it until you interrupted."

"What did you tell her?" she hissed at him, then instantly regretted saying so on the tape. She stared at me.

"Come with me to my office," she ordered. "I'll take your complaint."

"Fine," I told her.

"Thanks, Sergeant," I said with warmth. "Thanks for being so candid."

Charlene glared at him. He was shaking his head from side to side in denial.

"I didn't tell her anything!" he assured her. She gave a snort of disgust and walked away. I followed her.

We went upstairs, turning two corners before entering the district attorney's office. Charlene had a small cubicle just to the left as we entered the reception room. Several desks were scattered around the room and all were occupied. Wade's father, Carl, had told me once that he could remember when the district attorney for the county had no assistant. Trials were held once a year. One DA could easily handle four or five counties. This hectic, noisy office was so far behind they were plea-bargaining left and right to ease some of the caseloads. Anyway, they didn't have room in jail for the felons when they did convict. This is progress?

There were three metal straight chairs lined up in front of her desk. I sat in one and Charlene busied herself with her papers for a while to show me she had bigger and better fish to fry. Finally, she pulled out a legal pad and looked at me. I reminded myself to hold on to my temper. This was a barracuda, swimming in her own little bay, and she would love to have me for lunch.

"Can you prove you didn't invite him out there and let him in?" She snapped the question, then reminded me I didn't have her permission to tape this conversation.

"Oh I couldn't tape you if I wanted to, Charlene. The darn recorder came down with gremlins about a month ago. I'm taking it in for repair today, and I only set it on the counter while I searched for cigarettes in my purse. Sergeant Pennington started sweating and drew the wrong conclusion. I was just joshing him a little; no offense intended."

Her eyes glittered brightly. "Can you prove you didn't invite him out there and let him in?" she repeated the question. She was interrogating me, not taking a statement.

"Yes, I can. He left the bolt cutters he used to shear the locks on the property. His fingerprints are all over them and they are brand new. I believe he purchased them locally within the last few days. It shouldn't be hard to prove."

"Can you prove he did the actual damage and you didn't do it — trying to frame him?" She gave me a nasty smile.

"Oh, yes. He also left his lead-filled baseball bat. It too is covered with his prints and there are enough fragments of glass and paint embedded in its wooden surface to prove he used it there."

She didn't like the answers she was getting. She wanted me on the defensive, confused and uncertain. She decided to switch tactics.

"You know he won't get much time for this. Why bother?"

"He'll get his remaining time not served because he violated his parole. Also, remember he violated a restraining order. He should get at least four years and serve at least a year and a half. I'll settle for that."

"I seriously doubt Judge McAlbee will give him a sentence like that," she stated with confidence.

"Well, there's always the 'Friend of the Court' brief and appeal," I said musingly. "I've always believed that manipulating judges gets reversed on appeal much more often than those who follow guidelines."

"You surely are a vengeful bitch!" she snarled.

"Dear God, Charlene, you know zip about what's been going on around here for years. I'm just trying to survive. When did you join the elite circle of movers, shakers and fixers?"

"Only when we have the same goals and want the same results." She looked smug.

"You sound like the sweet young thing from the church choir who was surprised when someone called her a whore. She explained that she didn't work at the whorehouse, she just helped out when they were rushed on Saturday nights."

She tossed her head and changed the subject again. Now we were getting down to the nitty-gritty.

"I want you to leave Hank alone. We're dating now; you'll just have to stop throwing yourself at him. Understood?"

"Christ, Charlene; listen up. Read my lips. I don't want Hank. I haven't dated Hank. I haven't been boffed by Hank. Do I have to draw you a picture?"

"If you'll come in tomorrow, the affidavit will be ready for your signature," she said with resentment oozing from every pore.

"On Easter Sunday?" I looked doubtful.

"Make it Monday." She was unconcerned. I knew when I came in Monday, it wouldn't be ready. I made a mental bet it would be at least Thursday before the papers could be signed. Then they would take their own sweet time to serve the warrant, if he could be found. Buying extra time for Bubba and buying favors for all who helped were the trademarks of "Mr. Fixit" himself, Bubba's daddy. In most small towns, the system stinks about fifty percent of the time. Well, you ninny, it's the price you pay for living in paradise.

I left the courthouse and visited the office supply section of Stern's. I found a chair exactly like the one-armed one at home and it only cost seventy dollars more than it had three years ago. I looked around and found the same brand of answering machine as the old one. I knew how to operate it and didn't want to enter new territory; besides, it was on sale. The person writing up the sales slip told me I was getting a bargain. She also took my name and number, promising she would call the computer technician so he could retrieve my data, set me up with a new machine and get things going again. She said they would deliver the chair this afternoon.

By the time I had finished shopping at Stern's, I realized I would only be about thirty minutes early for my lunch date if I went directly to Chester's. I decided to go now and have a drink before Tim and John arrived. Maybe it would oil my tongue so I could sell them the plan.

On the way to the parking lot I met a woman with a little boy about four years old holding her hand. She was waiting to cross the street. She saw me and smiled. Though she didn't look familiar, I returned her smile and started to walk past her.

"Excuse me," she said. "Aren't you the lady who handles bloodhounds? I saw you on TV last night."

"Yes, I am," I replied.

"I want to tell you that we are so grateful that you work to find lost children. I have the tiger here and I'm always so afraid he'll wander off." She glanced down at her son.

"Thank you. If he ever disappears, just call," I said.

"I will," she promised. I felt a small lift of spirits. At least in some places I was appreciated.

I reached the restaurant only twenty minutes early. Telling the waiter I needed a table for three, I waited at the bar. They serve great food here — large fish platters, huge steaks, roast beef above and beyond perfection — all with lots of cholesterol, fat and heartburn.

I decided on a beer. If I was gonna pay four bucks for a drink, I didn't want four ounces of white house wine. The waiter came to lead me and transfer the beer to a table next to a window. The view was of the parking lot, but that was no problem. I'd rather watch people walk from and to their cars than stare at a wall.

Tim and John stopped at the arched entryway of the dining room and John spotted me. He pointed me out to Tim and a waiter escorted them over to the table. I stood to shake their hands and thanked them for coming. I asked them if they would like a drink before lunch. Seeing the tall dark bottle of imported brew, they told the waiter they'd have the same.

We discussed general topics — the weather, the rescue of Tessie and the resulting TV coverage. Tim asked a question about the voice-over commentator and I had to confess I hadn't seen the broadcast or the tape. They both gave me looks that were hard to read. It wasn't a definite "Oh, yeah?" or "You've got to be putting me on," but it was close enough that both faces were registering doubts. I hadn't wanted to mention last night. I'd wanted to use this time explaining in very general terms why I needed them, but I understood that I'd have to clear up that statement to their satisfaction or I might lose their cooperation before stating my case. Anyway, Fred, the local newspaper editor, might have gotten wind of the visit. If so, I could count on it being in tomorrow's paper. In a town this size, there are very few secrets that aren't known sooner or later.

I explained as briefly as possible the events of last night and saw the puzzlement leave their faces and concern take over. They both spoke up, wanting to know how they could help.

"Look fellows, I appreciate your concern, but everything about last night is under control. I wasn't going to mention it until I saw my credibility fading at the admission of missing the TV story. Forget last night. That isn't what this meeting is about. Here comes the waiter for the order. Have you decided what you're having?"

Tim ordered fish, John was having pot roast, and I decided on their "Man-Sized Ground Round Deluxe Burger" with cottage fries. I knew the meal would be too heavy, but hunger makes me order too much food every time.

After the waiter finished taking the orders and had returned with the second beers, I told them I was going to tell them a story about a hypothetical friend with a hypothetical problem.

"I'm going to tell this in general terms so you won't be able to guess the friend's identity, and I want to ask for your help. Solving the problem will take all of Monday, from about four in the morning until possibly dark. It'll be hot, dirty work and there is some danger. If you decide to say no, please feel free to say so anytime during this discussion. You are under no obligation for what I did last Thursday. I'm asking the two of you because I need some strong men I can trust to keep quiet about what we do from now to infinity, not because you said you owe me. I've lived here all my life, but I'm a loner. I can't put together enough people to do it without you."

When I stopped to lubricate my throat, both men remained silent.

"This chore has to be done all at once; it can't be spread over several days, or I would do it alone. Have I lost you or can I continue?"

"I have a question. Is it legal?" Tim smiled at me. "John and I have professions and family. Needless to say, we don't want to tarnish either one."

I pondered the question. "Technically, we would be unlawfully trespassing on private property. The property owner would be mad as hell with me if he knew this was going on without his knowledge and consent, but he would never press charges against any of us. The problem is male ego. He is not physically capable of handling this and it can't wait until he's well enough to tackle it."

"Then I have a question," said John. "What's the danger?"

"Let me tell you the story and you can decide. I want you both to give me your word that if I give away the identity of the friend while telling the story, so you can make an informed decision, you'll never reveal your knowledge to anyone." They nodded. "My friend's father died recently and the friend inherited a house with a few acres of grass around it and six hundred acres of woods at the back of the property. He knew his father only by reputation and from occasional visits with him. His parents were divorced and he hadn't lived here for a long time. From various clues which he unknowingly dropped, I've come to believe that his father has been in business with his gardener for the past ten years or so growing marijuana in large quantities on the property. The friend was aghast at my reasoning and wanted to wait until there was proof positive so he could march down to the DEA and confess all. The friend is an honest man, but not very practical. John, you may not know the score with the DEA, but I don't have to tell you, Tim, just how clean they will pick him. They'll confiscate his property down to his socks while praising him for his honesty and cracking jokes behind his back about his stupidity.

"The friend's father built up trust here for nearly fifty years. The friend can live and work down here and trade on his father's trust if the family name isn't tarnished with drugs. If this isn't handled just right, the friend will be labeled for life. You both know how these people are in this town. They give trust slowly and withdraw it quickly and with finality."

I stopped talking when the food arrived. The hamburger was huge, as was the serving of potatoes, which were deep-fried with their skins. There were eight quarters sliced lengthwise, which meant there were two potatoes. Paul Bunyan would have been sated with this repast. I took a bite of the hamburger and almost swooned. It was juicy, delicious and had been basted with some type of wine sauce. Christ, I'd weigh a ton if I ate like this on a regular basis. I resumed the story between bites.

"I want to accomplish two things. Using my dogs trained to find pot, on Monday I want to go to his property and find every stinking marijuana plant on that acreage, pull it up, and clear the area so thoroughly that even if they catch the gardener, they can never prove pot was grown on the land. Also, there's an upstairs area I believe they use to store seedlings, or maybe last year's crop, or maybe just supplies. I want to clean it so thoroughly they won't be able to find one marijuana seed or fingerprint. There'll be one person watching the friend so we'll know where he is before we start on the storage area. The other person will be watching the gardener so he won't come in and surprise us. I have the manpower for these two chores. I have one man to go with me, and I'll need two more — hopefully you two — so I can go in with two dogs and two two-man teams. Any questions?" I took a big bite.

"I have one," said John. "Where's the danger you mentioned?"

Tim answered for me, my mouth being full. "If the operation is as big as Jo Beth thinks it is, the gardener may have field hands or partners we could run into out there."

John now understood the problem. "Would we carry weapons?"

"Of course. You'd go with my helper and carry a twenty-two for snakes. Tim would go with me, carrying a twenty-two for snakes. My helper and I would handle the dogs and carry handguns for the snakes-in-the-grass." I took another bite and moaned inwardly with pleasure.

Tim stood. "Would you excuse us a minute, Jo Beth? John and I need to wash our hands." John pushed away from the table and they both took off for the little boys' room. I smiled. I thought women were the only ones who huddled in the facilities and made decisions.

They returned shortly and sat down to their food. Tim looked at me and grinned.

"You have two volunteers."

"Great!" I said, taking a relieved breath. "Do you both own hip waders?" They nodded yes. I told them what to wear and bring with them: thick gloves, heavy boots, hip waders, wide-brimmed hats, and extra socks. I said they couldn't carry cigarettes or wear bug spray, cologne, or scented deodorant. Also, if they used hair oil or spray, to shampoo and not use any on Monday; it helped with the bugs to have clean, oil- and scent-free hair.

We agreed to meet at the Winn Dixie parking lot, eight miles out on Highway 301, at four in the morning on Monday. I told them to come in the same vehicle and to time the trip so they wouldn't get there too early and have to sit in the car and wait. I didn't want to attract the attention of law enforcement people on their routine patrols. If they were questioned by a curious cop checking out the parking lot before I arrived, their story was a frog-gigging expedition and they were waiting for friends to join them. We finished the meal and I caught the tab. I thought for a moment and made a notation on the back of the receipt that the lunch was for two breeders from Ohio on a buying trip. I hoped Sinclair, my accountant, wouldn't want their names and addresses. He didn't appreciate my creative attempts to lighten the tax burden.

I went shopping at the mall for the next two hours. The first stop was at Sears, where I bought a new mattress, a Tiffany lamp for the desk and a twenty-five-inch-screen TV and a VCR. Both departments promised delivery later in the afternoon. I bought two hand-held vacuum cleaners. Rosie and I both had one, so that was the four required for the job. Maybe after this expedition, I could use the two extra ones in the grooming room. I wondered if the dogs might like to be vacuumed instead of brushed. I bought glasses, two tea pitchers, plates, bowls, and six salad bowls in an attractive wine color. That should hold me until I could list the extent of damage in the kitchen. I'm a fast shopper, not particularly enjoying shopping. I don't go from store to store comparing prices. I grab the first thing that appeals to me and suits my needs.

Hiking to the parking lot and back four different times with armloads of packages helped to digest the large lunch. After two pairs of jeans and three tops, I decided I'd spent enough money for one day; the checking account had taken a beating. Future purchases would have to be charged until the insurance money materialized.

I arrived home just after four. Two cars were parked in the courtyard. Rosie came running from the office, bubbling with excitement.

"You won't believe what's been happening!" she said in a rush. "The phone has been ringing off the hook; it's been driving me crazy! I hope you bought an answering machine."

I grinned and motioned to the pile of loot in the van.

"Among other things," I said.

"We've sold two puppies!" she cried. "And two more women are bringing their husbands by later. They really sounded like they'll be back."

"Wow! You sold two? That's wonderful!" I told her. She was brimming with pride.

"Well, Wayne helped," she admitted, sharing the credit.

"The two little women couldn't make a major purchase without their hubbies' permission?"

"Something like that, but I think they'll be back," she said, laughing.

"It just bugs me that they have to ask. They'll be doing all the feeding, watering, cleaning up puddles and piddles, running to the vet, attending training lessons, and they have to ask the boss." I shook my head. "We have a long way to go, Virginia!"

I looked at the two cars.

"Do you think Wayne needs me? Showing two groups can get tricky."

"They're sisters. They met here and want to see the dogs together," Rosie answered. "They want to get their kids a puppy for Easter presents."

"Well, it sure beats dyed baby chicks and baby bunnies," I said with laughter.

The phone rang and Rosie took off to answer it, carrying a package. It took four trips to unload. The glass installers had come, finished, and left. The air conditioner was on and the air felt wonderful. I made a pitcher of iced tea and poured a glass before starting to unwrap glassware and dishes. I ran a sinkful of hot suds and started soaking the purchases. There should be a special place in hell, especially hot, for the person responsible for the glue on glass and dish labels. The glue is a thousand times stronger than needed. If everyone in America refused to buy an item that had the damn hard-to-remove labels, we could have them replaced with easy pull-offs in a week. The only problem with this theory: we're so self-centered and indifferent we can't even band together and stop war, hunger or drugs, so my label banning wasn't in the cards.

The first gate alarm sounded and I watched from the kitchen window until I saw Stern's delivery van with the desk chair. I went out to show them where to take it. They both were gaping at the old pickup loaded high with broken items and trash cans loaded with debris. They thought the sight was knee-slapping funny for some strange reason.

"What happened?" one gasped.

"Termites," I replied shortly and went back to the kitchen. Let them figure out where to put the chair. They unpacked it outside, cleaned up the packing material and brought the chair inside to set it behind the desk. They placed the unsigned delivery slip on the desk and silently departed. This action was to demonstrate their disapproval of my snotty answer. Their efficient unpacking, fast departure, and silence was appreciated and silently applauded.

Wayne brought the two sisters to the office for me to do their paperwork while he went back to pack the puppies. We have sturdy cardboard carry-home cartons, printed with our name and address. We instruct the new owners to use the carton for a few days until the puppy gets used to being alone. We place a canvas-covered toy that vaguely resembles a bloodhound inside each box. We rub the toy on the puppy's littermates to get their scent on the fabric. This gives it the smell of home and they don't whine so much their first night in a new environment. It also allows visitors who admire the puppies and think about getting one to see our name and address in large letters on the box. I'm always in there pitching the product.

The sisters wrote checks and I filled out some of the papers and explained about the free obedience lessons and the free visit to the vet. I told them I would mail their completed forms and apologized for the computer being down. It was sitting on the floor behind the desk waiting for the technician to try and retrieve the data stored in its damaged and broken frame. The sisters eyed the mangled machine and probably thought it was not only down, but dead, dead, dead. Their manners were too good to say so.

After they left, I took all four checks we had received today out of the desk drawer to admire and to fill out a deposit slip. I'd run it to the night deposit later. It would give the checking account a healthy boost. I began singing my own version of "Balling the Jack": "First, you put it in, and then you take it out, that's what checking is all about."

I went back and loaded the sink full of suds with more labeled items, and scrubbed the ones that had soaked. Wayne came in, unpacked the answering machine and plugged it in. I took a shower and put on jeans and sweatshirt. Rosie and Wayne came to the kitchen and we discussed our day. I told them how much I appreciated their cleaning and bragged on the sales. The two minutes or so of rescue pictures, beamed into approximately thirteen counties in Florida and Georgia, had produced the bonanza of four sales today. They had all mentioned the broadcast, asked to see Susie and Bo and mentioned they just had to have a blood-hound after seeing the film. It had also brought the avalanche of phone calls that Rosie had been stuck with all day. There were still ten puppies out there that could use a good home as much as my checking account could use the infusion of their sale prices.

After they had savored the day's victories, I told them about Bubba being free without charges as yet. They were outraged at the partisan handling I had endured and expressed their concern that he was still running around loose. I convinced them that he would be picked up soon. I didn't believe it — but maybe they did.

I told them what was planned for Monday and what roles they would play, if they wanted to participate. They both said that it was a given, no need to ask. I said I needed Rosie to tail Wade all day with a portable radio, and Wayne would follow Hector. I explained about my newly found buddies, saying they owed me a favor. I didn't elaborate. Wayne wanted to handle one of the dogs, but I convinced him I needed him more to shadow Hector and that Leroy had worked with the dogs enough to handle a pot search.

I called Leroy and told him I was on the way over to get the girls out of the house for a few minutes. Wayne helped me load the Easter bas-kets, candy and stuffed bunnies. I drove over and helped Jackie get them into the back of her closet before the girls returned. I took the camera and four rolls of film and showed her how to use it. I explained what had happened last night, that I didn't want the girls to see the destruction, and also not to mention that I had bought the gifts, to let the girls as-sume they were from them. She balked at that suggestion, but I kept talking and explaining until I wore her down. I said that the county had my phone monitored and I didn't want any personal calls coming through and several other good-sounding lies to make her agree. Most of us rednecks have too much pride. Jackie and Leroy needed the hugs and kisses and thank-yous for the gifts. They hadn't been able to give their girls many treats in the past few months. We Southerners are poor re-ceivers of gifts and charity. Even the act of receiving the best-intended charity wounds our pride. One wrong word or glance and we'll tell you to stuff it.

Jackie finally agreed after much debate, but I had to cover the same ground with Leroy, telling the same lies and making them sound believable. Before I left, I asked Jackie if she still had the head covers she had made for Leroy and his cousin. I asked to borrow them. She had four that were perfect for our needs, if I could get the men to wear them. Leroy agreed to go along on Monday, as I had known he would. He unloaded the four hand vacuums I'd brought over and said he had just the items to pack them in, not to worry. He would load them and the cleaning supplies and cloths I had brought. He was going to carry them into the woods near where I had observed, through binoculars, the men on the stairs. He would leave them sometime Sunday afternoon, and he wouldn't forget to bring the camera on Monday morning. I played with the girls for a few minutes and left.

I went by the bank and deposited the checks in the night depository drawer. On the way to the grocery store, I pondered the power of television, which I decided is awesome. It had created the sales of puppies just from the rescue tape. It controls mostly what we buy, what we eat, what we drink, what we think about any given subject and our view of the world.

I went into the store and rushed around with the basket, since it closed at seven; I had almost left my visit too late. I purchased deli-baked rolls, ham, pastrami, Monterey Jack cheese, kosher dills, and olives. These items were for the lunch I'd pack for Monday. The stores would be closed for the holiday tomorrow. Annette, the check-out girl, laughed at my apology for the late purchases, telling me she was used to my being late.

"I was thinking about you all week. My daughter Lacey was a very colorful dyed Easter egg in her fifth-grade school pageant yesterday. Does that ring any bells?"

"How time flies," I said with a smile. "It seems only yesterday that you stabbed me with that stiletto and I bled all over my white bunny tail. I was the only bunny in the hutch scene with a red and white polka-dot tail. Miz Carter had to hunt for a Band-Aid and apply pressure to the wound. I was bleeding like a stuck pig."

"You're kidding, aren't you?" she said, not knowing whether to believe me or not.

"Cross my heart," I said, winking at her while putting my check-book away. "Are we gaining a little weight?"

"Three months' worth," she said, beaming. "We decided to try one more time for a boy. Our three girls need a brother."

"And if it's a girl?"

"Then our four girls will not need a brother," she said with conviction.

I wished her a happy Easter and left. Leaving the parking lot, I turned right and drove six blocks to Alice's Flower Pot. The front was dark but the lights were on in the rear of her store. I pulled up to the curb in front of the back door. When I knocked on the door, she opened it almost immediately.

"Come in, Jo Beth. Who did you forget for tomorrow?"

"No one. Just hand me a card and an order form and I'll do the rest. Get back to your arrangements. I know you're running late; you have a strong history of running late. Why don't you hire some extra help for the holiday rushes?"

"And pay out all the profits? No way. I have a new system. I don't sleep the night before a flower holiday."

She handed me a card and order form. I found her phone book, looked up Annette's address, and wrote "Congratulations on eighteen more years of PTA" and signed it.

Alice glanced at the order form and card and laughed.

"Again? I don't know how they manage. It's all Phil and I can do to feed and clothe our two."

"If you hadn't stole Phil away from me in the tenth grade, you'd still be flying the 'friendly skies' and vacationing in Hawaii and I'd be trying to cope with a handsome son and beautiful daughter."

"You didn't stand a chance after I sneaked a kiss under the mistletoe at the Christmas Ball. He is the best kisser in the Western Hemisphere."

"I'll have to take your word on that," I said with a sigh. "We hadn't progressed that far."

"Do you have a ceramic bunny planter? One that has the flowers for the tail?"

She reached above her head and pulled one from the shelf.

"Perfect. Fill it with red and white baby mums, if you've got any."

"Sure."

"No ribbons or ferns or baby's breath. Just the mums. It's supposed to remind her of a past event. Monday or Tuesday will be fine; whenever you get caught up." I wrote the check and we wished each other a happy Easter.

I stopped and picked up a large pizza and salads for the three of us. On the way home, my thoughts turned back to the rescue tape. Wayne and Rosie had watched the rescue tape last night but hadn't taped it because I usually did. I regretted not seeing it, but I also felt that Bubba had seen it and that had been the catalyst making him attack. Maybe it was for the best. I'd been thinking about asking Timothy to make a copy for me, but decided to forget it. I might view it in a different light now.

Wayne, Rosie and I ate upstairs and I came downstairs at eight-thirty. We all had to get up at five in the morning. I spent almost an hour in the kitchen making a list of things that needed to be replaced. As the list grew, I became more discouraged. Some things can't be put on a list and replaced. When a memento is destroyed, the little memory-jog it produces by its presence is gone. I'd still remember all the events, just not as often, and some memories would completely fade away.

I went to bed a little after ten. Wayne had put the new, stronger, four-digit coded locks on the gates, but I still didn't feel as safe as in the past. Lying there in the darkness, I remembered how easily and quickly Bubba had crumbled the defenses. It took a long time to go to sleep.

22

"SLY AS A FOX IN THE HENHOUSE"
April 11, Easter Sunday, 12:15 P.M.

Wayne, Rosie, and I had spent the entire morning on the serving line at the Salvation Army's kitchen. This was our second year, so we knew what to expect. We stood behind steaming pans of food, ladling out grits, scrambled eggs, spearing ham or bacon, and using tongs for the biscuits.

This service to the community makes us feel virtuous. We arrive in the dark before dawn and perform any chore that needs doing. My arms were tired, but my heart felt lighter.

We arrived home at 12:15. The first thing I did was take a shower. I'd just dressed when the phone rang with someone inquiring about the price of a bloodhound. I heard a shocked gasp at my quote on the cost of a six-month-old pedigreed bloodhound. That old saying, "If you have to ask the price, you can't afford it," usually is true in today's market.

I called Hank at work, hoping to catch him before he went to lunch.

"Hank, Jo Beth. Happy Easter."

"Hey," he said, lowering his voice to a more intimate level. Someone must have been standing near him.

"Happy Easter to you, too. How you doing?"

"Fine," I said briskly. "I need a favor. I have a tag number I'd like you to run for me. Here it is . . ." and read the number to him.

After a short silence he answered in a harsher voice. Someone must have been bugging him while he was trying to talk to me.

"Sure," he said shortly. "Glad to be of service. I'll get back to you," and he hung up.

When he called back, he was all business, giving me the name of Terrance Webber and a Rose Hill address which didn't ring any bells. I sensed his displeasure with someone and wanted to commiserate.

"Someone giving you a bad time at work?" I inquired with sympathy.

"No, not at work," he said softly. "Just a personal problem. I can't get through to her. I'm wasting my time."

"Keep your chin up; it'll be over soon," I consoled. He had to mean Charlene. I guessed he was bored with wining and dining her.

"I doubt it," he said as he hung up.

He really sounded down. If it weren't so darn dangerous with Charlene on the warpath, I would have asked him to supper. Maybe in a week or two.

Wayne came in about two and asked for the garbage since he was going to the dump with the pickup. I gave him what I had and followed him out. He pulled off slowly, the old scrap-heap truck loaded.

Out in the grooming room, I started loading the van for tomorrow. I rinsed eight canteens and filled them with water, repacked two back-packs, added large plastic bags and twist ties, put two machetes on the outside of each pack and tightened them firmly. Wade's land was old growth, which meant it would have thick underbrush and vines. I tested one blade with a finger, finding it razor sharp. Wayne manages his time with remarkable efficiency, keeping equipment maintenance up to date. He never gets behind in his chores the way I do; I'm usually a couple of days behind.

I carried both backpacks out to the van, adding two more boxes of plastic bags on the second trip. According to the plants I had stumbled across last spring, the marijuana plants should be from a foot to two feet high. The stems would be pliant and easy to cram into the lawn bags for the trip back here to burn them.

When you live on the outskirts of town, you're responsible for your own trash disposal, since there's no garbage pickup. The county fur-nishes large dumpsters in various locations around the county cross-roads. Yard and other debris has to be hauled to the county dump. I'd hired a backhoe operator to dig a hole on the back of my property where we dump all burnable items, cover it with wire mesh and burn it. Using a few of the stored logs for winter would get a fire going which would consume the plants.

Back at the office, I found that no calls had come in, and made a note to call the House of Mirrors in Waycross to get the destroyed mir-rors replaced. Knowing I wouldn't get back tomorrow in time to make the call, I also made a note to Rosie, asking if she would call. Suddenly I was restless, wanting to be out doing something. Going to the empty space on the wall where my poor efforts at painting had hung, I realized I missed them more than I'd thought I would.

Bubba's bat had broken through the drywall in several places, meaning that, after the wall was repaired, the rooms would need to be painted, too.

I sat at the desk and made a few more notes of the repairs needed. The first gate alarm sounded and I could see a beige sedan with one male occupant. The man had dark hair and wore sunglasses, but I could see clearly that it wasn't Bubba.

I went to the back porch and stood until the man had gotten out of the car. As he stood looking around, I saw that he was tall, dark and handsome with his hair in a longer style and slicked back. I personally didn't like the wet, sleek look, but it didn't detract much from this man's general appearance. He certainly had a large bright smile and beautiful teeth.

I walked toward him smiling in welcome.

"Hi. May I help you?"

"Are you Miz Siddens, the owner?" He gave me another of his high-wattage smiles.

"Yes, I'm Jo Beth Sidden," and stuck out my hand. He gave me a crisp handshake, noting my correction of the name.

"Miss Sidden, I'm very glad you're here today. I know that Sunday is a difficult day to do business in the South, but I have to catch a plane in the morning."

"I'm usually here on Sundays, even Easter Sunday." I stood and waited for him to state his business. The first guess was that he was a salesman of some sort, but after a closer look at his clothing, I knew that wasn't correct. He was wearing expensively cut clothing and European shoes. His look was "money."

"I saw the pictures of your rescue on television Friday night in Jacksonville. I finished my business there yesterday and came up here today. I'm interested in breeding bloodhounds and wondered if you have any breeding animals for sale."

My mind rapidly flipped through the available breeders. Every owner tries to change their bloodlines every year or so. We buy, trade or sell to each other, always hoping to get more champions. My mind stopped at O'Henry. I'd make full disclosure of the drug episode. If he wanted to give him a try, I would guarantee his buy-back if he didn't produce excellent puppies.

"What are you looking for and how many?" I wasn't going to commit to an answer just yet.

"I thought I would start with one male and female, since I'm a novice. Starting out slowly, I can build a good kennel and learn along the way." I was treated to another of his dazzling smiles.

Judy, Peg, Nancy, and Sally. All possible. No, not Judy. She was my favorite mama dog. I bit my lip in concentration, feeling a nagging reluctance growing in the pit of my stomach. Was it because I didn't want to part with two of the dogs, or was it because there was some doubt about this man and his character? Was I getting cynical, getting to trust no man? Whatever, this dude was giving me iffy vibes.

We strolled out to the kennels and he looked, asked questions and admired the animals. He finally introduced himself. His name was Jackson Hanaiker and he said he was from Lansing, Michigan. His last name rang a bell. I asked if he had any local relatives. He laughed and said no; that he was a business consultant for a firm with a branch office in Lansing and headquarters in New York. He mostly commuted back and forth between the two cities, also occasionally made trips to other cities, such as Jacksonville. He said he'd wanted to raise some animals as a hobby and for his own enjoyment. He hadn't decided on which breed until he'd seen the news tape Friday, and decided that it would be bloodhounds. He was very personable and earnest, knocking himself out to win my approval. I reluctantly began telling myself that he seemed sincere and aboveboard.

I told him the complete history of O'Henry and his acid trip experience. He seemed interested. I walked him back to Sally's pen and told him her breeding history and showed him three of the puppies from her last litter. I decided to test his intentions by naming the price for O'Henry alone and the price for both. He didn't gasp, faint or swoon, so I decided he had already checked on prices, or had enough money to indulge in the hobby of his choice.

I walked him back to O'Henry's quarters with him still doing his selling job, which I put down to male ego. He sensed my hesitancy and was determined to make me like him.

"When can I pick them up?" He smiled at me.

"You don't want them shipped?" I said with suspicion.

"No," he said, laughing. "Don't look so suspicious. I have some free time and have been thinking that if I did buy any dogs down here, I might lease the appropriate vehicle and drive back with them. Get to know them. It sounds like a restful change from my usual hectic pace."

Driving a thousand miles with two bloodhounds wasn't my idea of restful. He would have his hands full and would definitely need earplugs. I started trying to discourage him from driving back with them, but he countered each objection I raised with sensible-sounding solutions. I finally grew quiet.

"When can I pick them up?" He sounded eager.

I made up my mind. It was a good business move. I needed to buy new blood for the kennel. This kind of buyer didn't show up every week. I decided I was acting like a reluctant mother, sending her kids off to school for the first time. I knew I had to do it. I just hated to send them out in the real world where I couldn't watch over them.

"As soon as the papers are filled out and your check has cleared, about three days."

"Good," he said with a handshake. "Lets start filling them out."

I didn't look at either dog that I had just promised to sell as we walked back through the kennel. I felt that I had just sold them into slavery or was being unfaithful or something. It just didn't feel right. Probably just missing them already.

I took him to the office and went to get a dinette chair from the kitchen so that he could sit down. The couch was impossible and both the side chairs had been destroyed. I'd have to do something about furniture soon. The two sister buyers from yesterday had stood with good grace, but it had only taken five minutes or so. This guy was going to get a grilling. I saw him looking around the office and was glad I hadn't opened the panel on my father's landscapes. This thought snapped my emotions back to reality. I was being ridiculous. Did I trust him, or not? I sighed. He didn't make a comment on the obvious condition of the office, and I didn't volunteer an explanation.

I filled out the papers and he used the desk edge to write out his check. It was over an hour before he left. I kept thinking of different things I'd failed to mention about each dog and had given him a long list of instructions. He had patiently taken out a small notebook and dutifully noted all of my comments. During the time he was in the office, I'd heard and seen Wayne come back from the dump, but he hadn't come in, seeing the car outside.

When Jackson Hanaiker drove away, I watched until he was out of sight, driving slowly and carefully out of the drive. I went outside to find Wayne and showed him what was packed for tomorrow, asking if there was anything I had forgotten. I told him I'd just sold O'Henry and Sally. He was shocked and dismayed. After a moment, he signed, asking me if it was because I needed the money. I told him no, we were doing great. We just needed to inject some new blood into our lineage. He looked sad at my decision, and I knew damn well I was sad about it.

Wayne checked the van again and signed that I'd forgotten my gloves. I remembered that I was going to rotate the pair. I tried to rotate each of the three pairs after each use. I looked on the workbench where I knew I'd placed them after Tessie's rescue, then went and checked the pocket of the rescue suit. They just weren't there. Wayne helped me search. We looked everywhere. It galls me to misplace anything. I get irritated, then get angry at myself.

Wayne signed, "They'll show up."

I agreed, but didn't like these little mysteries. If I couldn't find them, I'd probably end up blaming the wood rats.

I went back into the office. On an impulse, I called Fred Stoker, editor, manager, and owner of the *Dunston County Daily Times.* He was my number-one fan, always giving glowing reports about all my rescues. He has lived here all his sixty years and knows everything about everyone in the county, including where all the bodies are buried, who buried them and why.

"Times," he answered with a lilt. He lives, eats, sleeps and breathes the newspaper. He's always there.

"Hi, Fred. This is Jo Beth." I had been calling him Fred for three years. He insisted on it, since the day I placed my first ad in his newspaper. He told me we were contemporaries and should use first names. I still don't feel right about it.

"Hey, Jo Beth. You did it again, kid! I bet you're selling dogs like hotcakes out there! That photog who shot your rescue sure got lucky. He's going to win himself a prize or two with that film."

"Business is good, Fred. Does the name Hanaiker ring any bells?"

"Hanaiker?" The line was silent for a second or two. "There was a Hanaiker who lived here thirty, maybe thirty-two years ago, over on Cumberland Island. Used to come down for the winter. Benson was his first name. Very rich. Didn't mix with the common folk. He was in investments or investment banking. Wrote an article on him one year when he arrived. His lawyer called up fuming and fussing; said Mr. Hanaiker valued his privacy. I apologized. Didn't ever mention him in print after that. He'd be about ten to fifteen years older than I am. May be dead for all I know. Haven't heard that name in years. Is that the one?"

"You apologized?" I couldn't believe my ears. Fred was a character. He tweaked every nose in town, whether they needed tweaking or not.

"Well, back then I was trying to ingratiate myself with high society in these parts. Now, I'd tell him to go suck an egg."

"I don't know if it means anything or not, but a man came to the kennel today, about thirty, thirty-five, named Jackson Hanaiker, and wrote a very large check on a New York bank for two breeders. I asked him if he had relatives in the area, but didn't ask if he used to have any.

The name rang a bell, but it was a very weak signal. I was curious."

"Make sure the check is good before he gets the dogs."

"I will. Thanks, Fred."

"You bet. Ah, Jo Beth, you had your picture on the front page today and I ran a good story. Have you seen it?"

"Sorry, Fred, I haven't. Wayne, Rosie and I cooked at the Salvation Army's breakfast this morning. I just haven't had the time. I know it's great. Thanks again."

"I have the story about Bubba set to run tomorrow," he said slowly. "Is it going to cause you problems?"

My heart sank. No one wants to be known as a loser or a victim.

"Fred, it's news; it happened. Don't worry, I can handle it."

"Good girl. I'm glad you understand. I couldn't kill it."

"It's okay."

"We'll be talking soon, Jo Beth."

Fred was amazing. He had pulled the name Hanaiker out of his mind without consulting any files. What a memory. If a Hanaiker had lived here thirty or thirty-five years ago, I sure wouldn't have known him, or even have heard about him. It's maddening to have a memory just out of reach. Finally, I just let it go. Maybe it would come to me later. I made a list of the furniture needing to be replaced. After the deposit of the fat check from Hanaiker, the checking account would be very healthy indeed. Maybe in a week or so we could get back to normal.

Wayne came over and I helped him load the couch and chair onto the pickup. He planned to take them to the Salvation Army's pickup site. They would repair and recover the pieces for sale. I drove over and deposited Hanaiker's check in the night deposit, Rosie, Wayne and I ate shepherd's pie topped with biscuits, and a salad. I was proud of myself. I only had one helping and only ate two of Rosie's fried peach turnovers. We all had to go to bed early since we would be getting up before dawn. I read until nine-thirty, then laid clothes out for quick dressing and climbed into bed.

I heard the squeak of the cat door and gave Ruby time to get to the kitchen. I slipped out of bed, walked barefoot down the hall, and, without turning on a light, stood in the kitchen doorway and spoke to the cat. I couldn't see her, just the glint from her green eyes when she turned her head. I told her what a beautiful creature she was, bragging on her shamelessly. I wanted her to get used to my voice so that in the future, I might even get to pet the damn cat I'd been cajoling and sweet-talking for months.

Going back to bed, I composed myself for sleep and was drifting into a foggy, drowsy state when my mind stumbled over the name Hanaiker. I opened my eyes in the near darkness and remembered. My father had come home one night when I was very small, maybe four or five. I remembered him pacing back and forth in our small front room where I slept on the sofa. I was terrified because he was shouting and my mother was yelling at him and I didn't know what was going to happen next.

I pretended to sleep, keeping my eyes closed, trying to make sense of his tirade. I only remember three words that stuck in my mind. Dad had been shouting, "That devil Hanaiker!" They both finally realized they were screaming at each other and that I might be awake. It was in the winter and I was snuggled down in the dark folds of the quilts. I kept my eyes closed and didn't move a muscle when they came over to check on me.

They continued their discussion in the bedroom and lowered their voices. I remember thinking that the devil's name was Hanaiker. I had always thought the devil's name was just devil, but now I'd heard his full name, Devil Hanaiker.

I smiled to myself. The memory had been buried back in the recesses of my mind as a child and tonight it had worked its way to the surface. Daddy must have known the man Fred had described to me today. They must have had some sort of argument or confrontation for Daddy to be so angry. I drifted off to sleep feeling better about the sale of the dogs. What had happened years ago could have no connection with the here and now. That Hanaiker and my dog-purchasing Hanaiker were different people entirely. I was pleased that I had an explanation for my unease and glad the irritating worry of not being able to remember was solved. I drifted off to sleep.

23

"SO DRY, YOU COULD SPIT COTTON"
April 12, Monday, 3 A.M.

When the alarm went off at three, I felt alive and tingly instantly upon waking. I was facing the unknown today, taking a risk. It was what made life have meaning. I loved the excitement, the adrenalin rushes, and not knowing what was going to happen next. I dressed and checked out the glass cubicle in the bathrooon to make sure the lights were on upstairs indicating that Rosie and Wayne were awake. I didn't see how Bubba could have missed this expanse of glass, but I guessed the deputies came before he could finish. It was odd that he broke the medicine cabinet mirror while missing a larger and more obvious target, but I was glad. It would have taken days to get this glass ordered and rebuilt.

Wayne and I had discussed which dogs to use today and we had decided on Tolstoy and Frost. Tolstoy loved the leash and would be glad to be working. Leroy should be able to handle him with ease.

In fifteen minutes I was heading upstairs for coffee. Wayne had just finished loading the dogs and signed that he had put a bag of deer jerky on the front seat. I gave him a sheepish grin. He knew I gave the dogs too many treats; this was his way of teasing me about it.

We had coffee and went over the plans one last time. I was smoking one cigarette after another and Wayne began to wave the smoke from his area. I apologized and stubbed it out. I knew Wayne was leaving before Rosie. The small barrio where most of our Spanish and Mexicans lived stirred early in the morning. Many of them worked menial jobs that started at first light. We had told Rosie that she didn't have to stake out Wade's place till at least seven, but we both knew she would be there at daybreak, afraid she would miss him. He probably got up between seven and eight, leaving for his office just before nine, unless he ate breakfast out. She was bright-eyed with excitement, using cop terms and having a ball. God, I hoped she didn't lose him; she would be hell to live with for a month.

I left at fifteen minutes to four, trying to time the trip exactly. I remembered the lunches at the last second and ran back to grab them from the refrigerator. I put them in the ice chest, which Wayne had loaded with Diet Cokes and Gatorade.

I drove at a steady forty miles an hour in order to keep some bored, suspicious officer on patrol from spotting the van and following just for something to do.

When I pulled into the Winn Dixie parking lot at two minutes to four, I was happy to see a red Toyota parked there under the large lights. I'd told them to park directly under a light because it would create the appearance of average citizens worried about security and their car. The local guys cruising for suspicious cars would run the plate to see if it was stolen and wouldn't do anything else.

The minute they saw me turn into the lot, they got out and Tim locked his car. They climbed into the van with subdued good mornings. Everyone is usually nervous and on edge at the start of an unknown enterprise. I hoped we didn't have anything to be edgy about. John sat in the front seat and Tim leaned against the passage wall. I offered Cokes or Gatorade, but they both declined. I turned the radio off after hearing the weather forecast.

"If we get stopped for any reason, let me do the talking. If they ask you your name and where we're going, tell them we're going frog hunting down by Tyler's Creek on a friend's land. The friend is Wade Bennett, a local lawyer who's just moved down here from Boston. His late father, Carl Bennett, is the suspected pot grower. Wade is not along because of three broken ribs he got while on a rescue with me last week. If the person who stops us mentions the rescue, don't laugh about it, even if he does. The local guys in the area are very sensitive about the fact that a very large maniac took two officers down along with two civilians, leaving me the only one standing before he was stopped. They resent me. If they can find any reason to hassle me, they will hassle. We will be shooting only the larger bullfrogs with the twenty-twos. They'll laugh about that. If you were macho rednecks you would be gigging them, so they'll think you're amateurs. Got it?"

"What if they check with Wade?" Tim asked.

"I doubt they'd go that far, but if they do, we'll be blown out of the water. They won't be suspicious, just bored and curious. All we should have a big chance of meeting are county and city guys from Three Forks and possibly a state patrol car on Highway Three-oh-one. If we're stopped, and if they're really obnoxious, they may search the van just to delay and aggravate me. If that happens, I have two small bags of marijuana in the van. It belongs to DEA and I'll tell them a different story, but all you know about are the frogs, nothing about marijuana. Agreed?"

"What's the different story?" John was curious.

"I have no idea," I said truthfully. "I'll have to make one up." They both laughed a little nervously. I knew Tim could handle this with his background, but I didn't know about John. Hell, he ought to have nerves of steel; he drove an eighteen-wheeler for a living. Truckers terrify me on a highway.

Leroy was waiting patiently next to a street lamp on his corner. He hopped in and I introduced him as I backed the van, turning to return to Highway 301. We had an uneventful drive and arrived at the creek bed on a small, curving, three-path road at four twenty-five. We were now across the creek and approximately at the back and center of Wade's property.

I explained the need to move quickly and get the van out of sight. I sent Leroy to scout for an opening in the trees where we could park the van. I pointed out the equipment for Tim and John to unload and carry the twenty yards into the trees, handed out three flashlights and grabbed one for myself. We found a suitable spot to place the loads and ran back to check the van for anything that might have been forgotten.

Unloading the dogs, I tied their leashes to a tree about thirty feet from where we would be sitting. I told Tim and Leroy to take a machete while I carried Leroy's and mine. The three of us walked in front of the van as Leroy backed it about fifty feet down the road till he reached the spot he'd found. I handed Leroy his machete and the four of us started chopping gallberry and titi limbs to place around the van. Both shrubs are thick and would effectively hide it. Even in bright sunlight, it wouldn't be spotted unless someone walked up on it.

Back where our supplies were stacked, I pulled out four trash bags and passed them around, since the ground was wet with dew. We sat in a tight circle, knees almost touching in order for them to see the map using their flashlights and hear instructions. I ran a line down the acreage, dividing it in half. I explained how Leroy and I would work the dogs about five hundred yards apart. When we found a field we would stop and clear it. I explained that the plants would probably be planted around heavy brush and trees in random patterns rather than neat rows. Farmers used to plant large squares of pot in the middle of their cornfields with a planter, but Georgia received federal funding in the eighties and the helicopter pot patrols put an end to neat rows. Sometimes there will be four or five plants near each other. The helicopter patrols spot the plants from the air by their color. If the plants are scattered and dispersed with other colors, they aren't easily found. I told them about my walking into a scattered field of plants, twelve feet high, with brown trashbags cut into thin strips and tied to their branches.

A lot of growers are now using kiddie wading pools and five-gallon plastic buckets. These are painted in camouflage colors, making them harder to spot. They'll also cut brush and let it dry to help break up the colors. I warned them not to speak loudly since a human voice can be magnified in some places among trees and deadened in others.

Leroy and I had our portable radios to keep in touch and I had two small tin toys on chains for Tim and John to hang around their necks. I explained that they made a noise similar to crickets and cicadas. These were for signaling me or Leroy in the event they wanted to get our attention or became lost. Their signal was to click the toys for five seconds at a time. It was an easy signal to hear and the sound carried quite a distance.

I warned them to watch where they stepped and to avoid brushing against the gallberry bushes in the early morning hours. Some snakes like to drape over a limb in the cool morning air. Drag your feet slowly in the water and don't splash. This alerts small game and snakes in the water so that they'll move out of the way.

I expected us to be alone in the woods, but the unexpected does happen. If they spotted anyone, they were to stand very still and judiciously sound off using the clicker. This would alert the other partner. I explained that the dogs would run mute and were trained not to bay when they found plants, but that sometimes they would be startled into loud bays. We would quiet them as soon as possible, but don't be startled at the noise. I unloaded four Gatorades and passed them around. I explained to drink every drop if possible since they would need all the liquid they could manage. Tim and I had been smoking, but the dogs were far enough away that the smoke shouldn't bother them.

I explained that if they ran out of water in their canteens, the creek water was okay as long as it was flowing freely but they shouldn't drink pond or standing water. It could be okay, but why take chances?

I glanced at my watch, seeing that it was five-thirty. Time to suit up. We all started getting dressed. I discovered that John had brought a cream-colored straw hat. I whispered to him that I'd buy him a new one as I walked down to the creek and smeared mud over it until it was mottled. Leroy helped me shoulder my backpack. Tim offered to carry it.

"I'm used to it by now and know the woods, but thanks for asking."

Leroy knelt to get acquainted with Tolstoy. He fondled his ears while

I softly went over several commands to refresh his memory. Leroy had worked occasionally with the dogs in the past, so I felt he knew enough to handle Tolstoy. I checked them over one more time and passed out the head covers against bugs. I said it was up to them whether or not they wore them. They were hot but effective. They would also serve to hide identity if we met up with any of Hector's helpers in the woods. I had soaked them in green food coloring and dried them. When we started to sweat, our faces would be green until we scrubbed them in the bath.

I noticed that John put his cover on immediately, as did Leroy and I, but Tim rolled his up and stuck it inside his hip-waders. Tim and John shouldered the .22 rifles.

It was too dark to start work, but I wanted to get out on Wade's land before daylight. There would be no plants near the edge of any road. Hunters always encroached a short way into the posted woods, calling up their dogs during hunting season. That was when the plants were large, blooming and smelled the strongest. Plants would be at least a couple of hundred feet back from the road. I directed them with my flashlight to smooth over our footprints on the sandy road. We scuffed and brushed with our shoes until the road didn't show prints leading into the woods.

"It's time, guys," I said. "Let's do it."

Leroy and John walked down the edge of the road on the grass and weeds to keep from leaving prints and were soon out of sight. I stooped at the creek's edge and grabbed a handful of mud and began to rub it into my bright orange, almost glow-in-the-dark suit. Today I certainly didn't want to stand out and be easily seen. Tim picked up some mud and helped with the backs of my legs.

I took the lead with Frost. He was feeling especially good this dark moonless morning, electric with excitement. As I put the open bag of marijuana to his nose, he had sniffed loudly three times. This was a regular routine with him, as was walking in a tight circle twice before lying down. Some dogs pick up the weirdest habits and they're very consistent with them.

Tim was behind me. We were going to penetrate at least a hundred feet before splitting up. We'd gone less than half that distance when I stopped so suddenly that Tim almost ran into me. Holding my hand up to signal a stop, I then wiggled it back and forth in a rapid motion which was a danger signal. We snapped the flashlights off and listened intently. I'd picked up the sound of rattlers much faster than Tim because I'd been listening for them. I slowly moved my feet backwards, tugging gently on Frost's lead. He'd heard or smelled the snake. I could tell by the way he tilted his head and held his ears, his wrinkles moving about three inches higher on his head. He was a good dog. He remained calm and was slowly scanning the brush around us.

I determined that the sound was coming from the trail in front of us, held up my hand to catch Tim's eye, and handed the lead back to him. He took it from my hand and I inched around Frost till I was in front. Knowing my suit was snake-proof, I crept forward for about eight feet before using the flashlight.

The flashlight lit up a strange battle. Two large snakes were locked in a deadly duel. One was a rattlesnake about thirty inches long, but wide around the middle. His rattles were a continuous blur of noise and movement as they rolled and thrashed. The other snake was a king snake, longer than the rattler, but less than half the size around the middle. I walked back to Tim and told him I wanted him to see something. Using two flashlights, we could see the snakes clearly.

The king snake was in the process of swallowing the rattlesnake's head. It was a grotesque sight. Looking at the size of the two, it didn't seem possible that one snake could eat another one its own size. It was slowly happening before our eyes. The king snake worked the rattler further into its mouth as the rattles weakened, then stopped. Every so often the rattlesnake would jerk and the rattles would sing briefly, but this was from death contractions. It might take the king snake an hour or longer, but eventually the whole rattlesnake would be inside the king snake. This is a rare sight for humans to see. Leroy had returned my camera this morning loaded with film and ready. I slipped it out of my suit and shot four different angles, hoping to get a clear picture showing the details. King snakes are nonpoisonous and immune to rattlesnake venom. The two snakes are deadly enemies.

I walked casually around the king snake, since he was no threat to anyone. He wouldn't have given up the rattlesnake for a tiny pink piglet, much less for these strange-looking people with tough hides. Tim wasn't so sure and made a wide detour on the path. Frost didn't show any concern as he walked around the pair. I guess nature has some way to let dogs know if they are in danger. There's so much we'll never know about dogs. If only they could talk with us.

When we'd penetrated about a hundred yards into Wade's acreage, I motioned for a stop, took a drink of water and noticed that Tim had his face mask on now. Insects were so thick you had to blow out little puffs of air to clear them from the front of your nose and mouth in order to breathe. I'd had so much practice in the past that I did it unconsciously and had shown Tim, but he would forget and was taking in insects every third or fourth breath. He looked miserable. He muffled several sneezes that breathing in gnats produces. I pulled out a blue bandanna I always carry in a pocket and motioned for Tim to stop. I put several pleated folds in the material, unpinned two safety pins from my collar lining and pinned the mask over his nose and mouth, just loose enough so he could breathe. It didn't keep every gnat out, just nine out of ten. He whispered his thanks and we went back to hacking our way through.

I presented the marijuana to Frost again and he took his usual three sniffs. I whispered "seek" several times into his ear. He'd only gone a short distance when he stopped suddenly, raised his head and looked back at me. His tail was wagging slowly. This was old hat to him. Whether it was packed in bales and sealed in a drum inside hollowed clay objects from Mexico or growing green in the woods, he knew when he smelled the product. I glanced around and spotted several plants. Tim hadn't spotted them. The sky was lightening so that the flashlight was more of a hindrance than a help. I snapped mine off and on to signal and Tim glanced in my direction. He was about ten feet behind and to the right of me. I made a circlular motion with my right arm and pointed to the ground. He gave a perplexed shrug. I walked over and pointed at the plants between us. He was standing five feet from two marijuana plants and hadn't seen them. We both grinned.

My heart soared. I had been right! I made a fist and shoved it straight up in victory. By God, here was marijuana growing exactly where I'd told Wade it would be! Until this moment there had been a fifty-fifty chance that the unrelated clues were wrong. I moved close to Tim and whispered for him not to overlook a single plant. I told him I was moving to my right to pull plants, and when he was finished to join me.

He nodded in understanding as Frost and I went to the right. The ground was damper here, which meant there would be fewer plants, but they would grow larger. In wet soil, the plants have to be mounded so they won't drown or get root rot. The first plants Frost found had been about eighteen inches high. The seventeen he pointed out to me were on scattered mounds, blending perfectly with the shrubs and almost three feet high. We were sending a lot of profits down the drain on every plant we yanked. There would be some angry Mexicans when they returned to tend their gardens. As I pulled, bent, and crammed the willowy plants into a plastic bag, I scattered the dirt mound with my shoes, then kicked loose straw and leaves over the area. There was a forty percent chance of rain tonight, which wasn't as high as I'd have liked since showers would hide more evidence of our visit. One good shower of a quarter inch would make this spot look as if man had never set foot here. That was the object of this endeavour, leaving no trace of recent or past plantings.

Tim joined me as I finished strewing the straw to cover the rawness of the exposed dirt and my scuff marks. He whispered he had found twenty-three plants and I told him I had found seventeen. We were trying to keep a running total in our heads so we could come up with a reasonable estimate of the profits Carl and Hector had wrested from this plot of ground in the probable eight years of harvesting.

The "street value" quotes made by DEA spokesmen in their press releases and on-the-scene interviews are cotton candy dreams separated entirely from reality. The huge quotes sound impressive and look good on paper, justifying their jobs. The locals who know and the locals who grow collapse with laughter when hearing the much-inflated values.

When we had a total count, we would immediately halve it. With marijuana, at least half the plants turn out to be males and have to be pulled up and destroyed so they can't pollinate the female plants. In late summer and early fall, a plant can produce male nodules or "balls" overnight. If a male is not pulled quickly and taken out of the female's area, on the first windy day it can pollinate fifty or more females. The ideal marjuana is seedless. Heavily seeded marijuana sells, but it is not as potent and therefore sells for much less. In today's market, a pound of perfectly manicured seedless buds of sensimilla will sell for five grand per pound, easily. Locally grown marijuana, heavy with seeds, will bring only two to three grand. If the buyer will take ten pounds or more, they are given huge discounts. The main object, which is second only to the money, is to move the product — get it out of house or barn and off the property quickly to prevent arrest or confiscation.

We went from small patch to small patch, bending, pulling, and packing the bright green slender plants in plastic bags. When the bags were full, we twist-tied the tops and left them under a covering bush. We would collect them on our way back.

As I straightened to shift my backpack to a more comfortable position, I caught a movement off to my right and slightly downward. I dropped as silently as possible to my belly and looked wildly around for Tim. He walked into view from my left and when he saw me prone, he dropped like a stone. Good reflexes. I turned my head in the direction I had seen movement and widened my eyes, then relaxed them, and slowly scanned the area. I couldn't see well. My view was restricted by my closeness to the ground and a bush about five feet from my face.

I gave Tim a signal to stay put and eased out of my pack. I then inched forward about a yard to my right where the view was unobstructed.

What I saw started my heart hammering and dried my mouth. I was looking at a magnificent animal that has never been an inhabitant of these forest lands. It was a sleek, tawny-colored adult cougar. She was lying on her side with her eyes closed and unaware of us lying less than twenty yards away from her.

24

"AS TIDY AS A CAT"
April 12, Monday, 7:30 A.M.

When I had first been alerted, I had gathered Frost close with the lead in my left hand and gripped his harness with my right. He had crawled with me on my yard-long journey. I was afraid to take my eyes off the cougar, but I had to give Frost a command. Wayne handled Frost the most and he was well versed in hand signals. I pulled his head around and gave him the hand signal to "Stay!" I repeated it twice.

I feared when I returned my sight to the cougar she would be gone, that she had been a figment of my imagination, but there she was, and there were two kits playing and tumbling around her. The kits had produced the movement that had caught my eye. The magnificent mama was relaxed, dozing with her head upright but ever vigilant, even in repose.

I had read the newspapers in February that reported the Florida Game and Fresh Water Fish Commission had released ten adult Texas Cougars to roam in the wild. They had tried the experiment five years ago and all the cats died or were killed except three, which they captured and returned to captivity. These newly released cougars would make their home in North Florida and South Georgia, mostly in the area between Lake City, Florida, and Fargo, Georgia. The cougars wore electronic collars and were tracked by plane, by the commission, at least three times a week.

What was so exciting about this cougar was it could not be one of the ten that were released two months ago. The kits playing around her were at least two months old and none of the females in the group of ten released were pregnant. The cougar in front of me had to be a survivor of the first experiment that was tried five years ago, and a male had survived along with her. The kits were living proof. I removed my glove and wiped my sweaty palm on Frost's left flank. I worked my hand down to the zippered side pocket where I carried my camera. Please

God, let me get one good picture, that's all I ask, just one. Without a picture, no one would ever believe what I was witnessing. My slight movement to reach the camera had shifted my angle of vision and a palmetto frond blocked the cougar's head. I silently prayed for time as I set the adjustments and raised the camera as I slowly inched to my left. Time seemed to stand still. I pressed the shutter and started clicking away. Through the viewfinder I saw her raise her head and look directly at me. I couldn't stop pressing the button. I had taken four shots of the snakes and I had twenty exposures left. I was going to use every one. The cougar whirled and gained her balance in one fluid motion. Her muscles rippled along her flank as she trotted off to my right with her young scampering after her. I blinked and they were gone.

I came back to real time. Birds and insects were making sounds all around me. I began to worry about the light. It wasn't full-blown daylight as yet. Had it been sufficient for good clear pictures? Now I had another problem to sweat. I replaced the camera and stood. Tim came over to see what the danger was, a drawn, intent look on his face. He looked pointedly at me for an explanation. I was bubbling with joy.

"Sorry," I whispered. "For a short time there I forgot all about you being with me. I saw a Texas cougar with two kits. She has to be a survivor of the original experiment five years ago and a male had to survive also." He stared at me blankly. Obviously he hadn't read about it. I told him about the cougars from Texas being released in North Florida, how it was hoped they would adapt to the woods here and multiply. The cougar is a close relative of the Florida panther that had vanished from these woods. Only a small number of panthers remained in South Florida. If the three-year experiment worked, they were going to release more.

"Aren't they dangerous?" he asked.

"I imagine she would have protected her young if she viewed us as a threat, but she would try to flee with her offspring first."

He shrugged with indifference. He didn't share my enthusiasm. In all fairness, he hadn't seen the beautiful creature, but I could tell the news of the cougar didn't stir him. To each his own. Some people didn't appreciate beautiful creatures of the wild. He might be interested in whales and, frankly, whales didn't push my buttons. When it comes to animals in and around Okefenokee, my home, that's where my heart and soul abound with interest. I hugged the memory of the cougar in my mind and knew the vision of her, and her progeny, surviving free and enjoying these flatwoods, would remain with me forever.

By nine my back was aching. I wasn't used to stooping and bending so much with a thirty-pound load on my shoulders. I had sweated a gallon of water and was starving; it was time to call a halt. Tim looked as bad as I felt. The hordes of gnats had disappeared with the advancing sun and heat. We still had yellow flies, horse flies and mosquitoes, but we could breathe much easier. We found shade and Tim helped me remove my pack. We slumped with our backs against adjoining trees. I started digging in my pack for the sandwiches.

"Ham or salami?"

He brightened a little. "Ham."

We unwrapped and chewed in silence. After we had eaten our sandwiches and drunk from our canteens, we just rested.

"I think we can talk, if we keep it down. Have you noticed, we are getting into much wetter ground?"

"Yeah, what does that mean?"

"We're going to be wading soon, I imagine. We can't go around because the swamp area might have an island in the center, which is an ideal place to plant. We can't miss anything. How are you holding up?"

"My male ego is saying 'you can make it if she can make it,' but I'm beginning to think it's lying. How much does that pack weigh?"

"Thirty pounds or so," I said with a smile.

"Jesus," he said with disgust. "I didn't know just how badly out of shape I am and how far I am over the hill. I'm joining a health club tomorrow."

"Not tomorrow." I gave him a grin. "Tomorrow you'll feel like you've been run over by a dump truck. Maybe Thursday."

"This rifle is driving me nuts," he complained. "Every time I bend over, the strap slides off my shoulder."

"Sorry, but if you need it, you'll need it in a hurry. If you fasten it firmly, it could take too long to get it free."

"How long you been doing this kind of work?"

"Three years with the kennel, just the past year on search and rescue."

"You must be in great shape," he said with envy.

"Don't you believe it. I eat too much, I love greasy foods, and smoke three packs a day. I'm approaching the big three-oh. When that happens, I'm going to start eating less grease, eat the right food and stop smoking. I've put if off way too long."

"Oh, to be thirty again," he said sadly.

He couldn't be a day over thirty-four, thirty-five at the most. I got to my feet, suppressing my giggles, and he held the pack while I adjusted my burden.

It took us until twelve-thirty to get within sight of the house. I had been watching for several minutes. I knew we were getting close. I could hear sounds now and then from the highway traffic. We had heard nothing but one excited bay from Tolstoy at eleven. Leroy had been able to control him, and only one sound-off could be mistaken for a lost dog in a bog or caught in an animal trap, if the sound had been overheard. Some people still trap for animal pelts around here. I hate the traps; I'm afraid my dogs might step in one. I destroy all I find.

Tim and I advanced slowly to where we could watch the house and the back driveway. Nothing moved. The house seemed deserted and no cars were parked in the driveway. We started working our way to the left to intersect with Leroy and John. We found them in less than ten minutes. Leroy said they had arrived there twenty minutes ago. Poor John looked like he was about to have a stroke. I couldn't believe he had rested for twenty minutes and was still that red in the face.

"Are you all right?" I had no idea what you did for a stroke. This moment made up my mind; if I were going to be in the woods with people who might have a stroke on me, I was going to have to learn more about medicine than I knew now. A starting place would be EMT classes.

"Sure," he answered, trying for humor, "point me in the right direction, I can still crawl."

I switched plans for the return sweep right then. When we finished the apartment, John would work back to the van with Tim and me. I would let Leroy start working back alone, and when we finished we could go back to meet him and help him finish. I wanted John where I could keep an eye on him. Tim and I had our second sandwich for lunch.

We all rested another fifteen minutes, then Leroy said he and John would bring back the equipment. John swore to me that he was okay and left with Leroy. Tim and I finished our lunch. We compared the count we kept in our heads, and among the four of us, we believed we had pulled up and destroyed at least two thousand small plants.

"How many do you think are still out there?" Tim asked, cutting his eyes to the acreage we had covered this morning.

"About the same amount we found this morning, give or take a few hundred."

"Jesus," he mumbled. I didn't think that required an answer.

"How much do you think they cleared last year?"

"Well, if we find about the same amount this afternoon as we did this morning, we'll start with the figure of four thousand plants. Cut that figure in half because, of the male plants that have to be destroyed, that leaves two thousand. Last fall we were short on rainfall. That should have meant a good crop for them because they didn't lose plants in the low areas, but they had to work their tails off to irrigate the ones on high ground. Those left would be susceptible to termites, deer, wood rats and swamp rabbits."

"Deer?"

"Yeah," I said with a smile. "This guy I know tends bar out in redneck territory. He hears all the sad tales of woe from some growers out there. He can do a thirty-minute routine, keeping you in stitches from laughing so hard. One grower said when he first started growing the weed he was living in a small aluminum trailer, far back in the swamp. He said the only high ground around was the small island his trailer was on. He planted all around his trailer, just leaving a small trail wide enough to get in and out the door. He said that fall, about three weeks from harvest, when the buds on the plants were almost at their peak of potency, he was awakened by a knocking and banging sound on the aluminum skin of the trailer. He rushed out to find a deer actually leaning against the trailer wall for balance and more than a dozen of his valuable plants with their branches stripped bare. He said the deer was so high on pot he didn't have the stomach to kill it. He reversed his shotgun and whacked the deer on his flank to send him on his way. He said the deer just looked at him and started making pitiful sounds of anguish, like he had been gut-shot, and slid slowly to the ground. When the deer started snoring the man became so disgusted he left him there and went back to bed. He said that was just the beginning. He started trying to sit up all night using Coleman lanterns, playing his portable radio and walking patrol. While he was on the north side the deer would be munching on the south side. He was finally forced to crop about two weeks too early and still lost half his crop. He estimated the deer devoured more than fifteen thousand dollars worth of pot in just one week. The deer had patiently waited while he watered, fertilized, fought termites, root rot and strung tin cans to scare the rabbits. When the pot smelled ripe, the deer came in and helped him harvest."

"What do they do about the deer now?"

"I've been told the newest treatment is a mothball and water solution, or a chemical spray that has the same ingredients in it. They use a garden sprayer and spray about every two weeks or just after a rain, but nothing I have heard of is entirely deer-proof. You can still hear some hilarious tales from bow hunters when they walk up on a deer high on pot."

Leroy and John returned carrying our cleaning equipment in two sturdy-looking canvas bags with straps for the shoulders and drawstrings for closures.

"What are those?" I had never seen bags just like those.

"Seabags," Leroy explained. "I bought them in an Army/Navy surplus store, years ago. They come in handy for hauling supplies."

Now I remembered them. I had seen them in old movies about World War II. I unhooked my radio. Time to find out if we knew where Wade and Hector were. I tried Rosie first. After three times and receiving no answer, I began to get antsy.

"Let me try," suggested Leroy.

"Tonto to Annie Oakley," Leroy said clearly. "Do you read me?"

We sometimes get carried away, Rosie, Wayne and I. We have a lot of fun naming dogs, events and selecting radio call "handles." For today, I was the Lone Ranger and Wayne was Wild Bill Hickock. Tim and John were exchanging amused glances. They probably thought we were kooks.

"Tonto to Annie Oakley," Leroy repeated.

"Annie Oakley to Tonto, I read you loud and clear," answered Rosie. She sounded breathless, as if she had been running.

"Annie has an appointment with the man for four. Explained I might be a little late, but was told not to worry, the man would be in his office all afternoon. Over."

"Tonto to Annie Oakley, we read you loud and clear. Over and out."

Leroy looked at me and winked.

"Hand it over. You can't call Wayne unless you've taught yourself Morse lately," I told him as I reached for the radio. I had my pad and pen out.

"I've never fully understood your system of talking back and forth with buttons and lights. How does he know you're calling him?"

"In a situation similar to this, he keeps his radio within his sight at all times. All our equipment is modified with these red and green lights and a sending switch, see right here?" I was pointing at two small round glass circles, just below the plastic mesh for the speaker. "This toggle switch activates the lights. Green is for dots and red is for dashes. Watch." I moved the toggle switch rapidly back and forth, and the small viewing windows flashed red and green lights, alternating with my rhythm. I waited for Wayne to start sending. Suddenly the tiny lights started flashing with an almost impossible speed. I groaned and held down the normal button to transmit; this jammed Wayne's flashing light show. I shook my head and gritted my teeth.

Leroy looked at me with surprise. "What's wrong?"

"I sometimes forget that Wayne is only nineteen," I said with aggravation. "He's showing off; he's much faster than I am in Morse code, in sending and receiving."

Leroy chuckled and I rolled my eyes. When I released the button, the lights remained dark. I started sending.

"What did you say?" Leroy had waited until I had stopped my message.

"I told him to shape up, or I'd pound him later."

"I know that worried him," Leroy said with a smile.

"He got the message," I murmured as I started writing Wayne's signals down on the pad. He sent, "Sorry. H on mower, three hours tops." I signaled "message received" and turned to the guys.

"If the rooster don't crow and the creek don't rise, we should have three hours for our housecleaning. Let's do it."

We stashed all our gear behind a thick outcropping of titi. It wasn't blooming yet. Next month the bee population would start gathering nectar from these plants and gallberry bushes to make the best-tasting honey in the whole wide world. Another bountiful crop Georgia produces.

I left my backpack, tied the dogs to sturdy titi limbs and, with Leroy's help, started hacking a hole in the ground with a machete. When it was deep enough I rolled up a trash bag to the depth of the hole and lined it. I emptied the water from my canteen and motioned for the others to do the same. There was enough water to fill the basin, and the dogs started lapping it up. All I picked up were my empty canteen, several pairs of disposable rubber gloves, lock picks, and cigarettes.

It felt so good to be released from the sweltering suit. I didn't have a dry thread in my clothing, but the small breezes felt so good on my flushed skin. John mentioned, only half in jest, that he wanted to pull his boots off; his feet were hurting. I cautioned him that his feet would swell and he might not be able to get his boots back on. He shrugged with resignation.

The men removed their hip waders and long-sleeved shirts. Leroy was wearing Wayne's holster with the thirty-eight and I was wearing mine with the thirty-two. With Leroy and John humping the seabags and Tim and I carrying four canteens apiece, we looked like armed, daytime burglars who were going to steal water and go to sea. We walked boldly across the wide expanse of grass, up the driveway and single file up the stairs. The guys collapsed on the stairs. There wasn't room to sit on the small landing with the screen door open and for me to work on the lock.

I fished out the little kit of nutcracker picks and probes and went to work. After five minutes I was frustrated, sweating and worried. We couldn't bust the damn lock and I wasn't accomplishing diddly squat.

"You want me to try?" Tim sounded very casual.

I glared at him. "You mean you know how to do this shit and you let me stoop here sweating bullets for five minutes? Get your ass up here and get busy!"

He calmly took the picks from my hand and had the door open in less than three minutes.

"My, my," I said, rolling my eyes as I brushed past him into the room. I should have thanked him, but sometimes I'm a sore loser. I pulled out four pairs of the thin gloves from my pocket. Our hands were sweaty and they were difficult to get on. Leroy began to unload the vacuums. I glanced over at Tim. He was the only one I suspected would recognize the stale odor of marijuana in the apartment. He nodded his head; he had caught the scent also.

"Shall we open the windows?" he inquired.

"We shall," I agreed. We went through the apartment and opened every window, plus I propped the front door open. I asked Tim if he would take the picks, go to the other apartment at the opposite end of the building, check and see if it had anything in it and if it had a pot smell. Leroy and John had already picked a room and started vacuuming.

I decided when Tim returned I would post John in a window that overlooked the drive where he could see each side of the driveway that curved around the house. With all the vacuums going, we wouldn't be able to hear a squad of troops marching up the stairs. He could use the rest. I was smoking my head off, dragging furiously to inhale and get my nicotine blood gasses back to their normal dangerous level. I made a fast inspection of the premises. The apartment was adequately furnished with expensive furniture. It certainly wasn't cast-offs from the main house. Carl had used some of the money here. The furniture was pushed against one wall in every room. I found about twenty large plastic paint drop-cloths folded in one closet in the first bedroom. Something else we would have to carry out of here. They had been used to protect the carpet from water and potting soil damage. This apartment is where they soaked the seeds so they would sprout and come up faster. They then planted them in portable seed beds and grew them under grow-bulbs for indoor plants.

I looked with dismay at the track lighting installed across the dining room ceiling. Every damn socket was filled with the obvious spotlight-shaped blue bulbs. We'd have to get all those out. The kitchen was fully stocked with dishes and cookware. The beds were dismantled and stacked against the bedroom walls. We could never finish this task in three hours. I found a six-foot aluminum ladder in the kitchen broom closet, also an upright modern vacuum cleaner. I rolled it out and pushed it to John. I decided against the lookout. The upright vacuum would make his work easier for him and we had tons of work here.

I put the stepladder under the strip lighting and started harvesting the blue bulbs and placing them in a plastic bag. Tim pulled on my pants leg. I climbed down from the ladder to be able to hear him.

"The other apartment is clear. Dusty, with all the furniture placed correctly. It hasn't been used in months, or more."

"Thank God for small favors," I uttered with relief. "Tim, will you gather all those plastic sheets out of the closet in the first bedroom and cram them in a plastic bag? We've got loads of stuff we have to haul out of here." I had found two stacks of black plastic potting trays in the hall closet; also, two fifty-pound bags of potting soil and nineteen fifty-pound sacks of pulverized Peruvian bird guano. The bastards had over-ordered on the fertilizer. I went to find Leroy. He was the strongest, so I asked him to start carrying all the fertilizer and potting soil downstairs.

I stepped out onto the landing to call Rosie. Wayne should stay with Hector; he was the biggest threat. We would just have to assume that Wade would stay in his office until late afternoon.

"Lone Ranger to Annie Oakley. Do you read me?" I only tried twice, then ran back in and grabbed Leroy's radio. Back outside, she answered on the first call.

"Annie Oakley to the Lone Ranger, I read you loud and clear, over."

"Annie, we need you at the man's house, ASAP. Over."

"Trouble? Over."

"When you arrive. Don't pick wildflowers, but don't get a ticket. Over."

"Understood. Over and out."

Leroy came by me on the stairs with a fifty-pound sack of fertilizer on his left shoulder, carrying a plastic sack full of potting trays in his right hand.

"We're gonna have to stop meeting like this," he quipped.

"You tell me your sign and I'll tell you mine," I told him over my shoulder.

At least Hector was smart enough with his money. He still lived in the barrio, drove the beat-up truck and cut enough lawns to look legitimate. I bet he was doubling his actual income when he filled out his taxes, and more. That way, he could feed money into his bank account and branch out with more machinery and workers. I surely hoped so, because his pot-growing days on this land were over.

I started hand-vacuuming the furniture in the living room, going under the couch and then the chair cushions. Tim had finished with the floor and I started dragging furniture around until it was arranged in a tasteful way. Using a cloth sprayed with cleaner, I started on the walls, reaching as high as I could to remove all fingerprints. When I came to a window, I grabbed a bottle of Windex and paper towels. I didn't care if they had a few smears; we weren't trying for perfection. We were sweating like joggers. The windows had been open for almost thirty minutes. I ran around closing them and turned on the air conditioner.

All the fingerprint wiping was in case Hector was caught either with pot or too much money. This way, in case he tried to cut a deal by implicating his dead partner, Carl, he would have no proof that he had ever been in these rooms. His story would not pan out, and hopefully, he would not be believed.

Finally, I finished the living room just as Rosie arrived. I filled her in while she donned the gloves I gave her. I told her to start in the kitchen. I suggested she start with one cabinet, wash the dishes, wipe the inside and outside of the cabinet doors and put the dishes back wet. This way, we could save some time.

I moved to the first bedroom. Tim had finished vacuuming and was putting the bed back together. I started on the walls. After he arranged the furniture, he dusted. Rosie called from the doorway and said I had to see something in the kitchen. We hurried back there and I stared with dismay at the canned goods stored in the pantry. There was enough food on those shelves to feed dozens of hungry folks for a month. I spotted two plastic clothes hampers by the washer and dryer. I told her to call the guys; we were going to take a break. I opened the refrigerator and found a shelf had been taken out near the bottom and a full case of canned Cokes were stored in their six-pack cartons. I glanced at my watch and saw it was now two-thirty. We still had to take a break. We had a long way to go.

The five of us sat at the table and drank Cokes while Tim and I lit up cigarettes.

"There's a ton of food in the kitchen pantry and they handled every damn can putting it in there. There are two plastic baskets for clothes; we'll take turns. Load up all you can easily carry in a basket and haul it downstairs to Rosie's van. Dump it in the dog boxes. We'll donate it to the Salvation Army. We don't have time to wipe all the cans. After two trips, hand a basket to someone else and go back to what you were doing before. That way, one person doesn't have to make thirty or more trips up and down those stairs."

We rested for twenty minutes and I managed to smoke two cigarettes in that period. I always smoke faster when I'm nervous.

Tim and I finished the bedroom and he started on the hall while I took the bathroom. I sprayed and wiped and sprayed and wiped. All the walls, fixtures and medicine cabinet. Shit, it was loaded with disposable razors, shaving cream, aftershave lotions, toothbrushes, toothpaste, aspirin, antacid tablets, and on and on. I swept the shelves clean into a plastic bag, tied it with a twist and set it by the front door. I went to the kitchen for a mop. Rosie handed me a plastic basket and grinned.

"It's your turn."

"Thanks a heap," I said with a grimace.

She laughed and I left to fill my quota. I filled the first basket too full of cans. I thought I would never get it down the stairs. It's very hard to step out into space when you can't see your feet and where you are stepping — at least it is for me. I put my left elbow on the stair railing and eased down one step at a time. It felt safer. I thought I would be able to catch myself if I stepped wrong. I met Leroy on the stairs as he was coming back from a fertilizer haul.

"Need some help?" He smiled sweetly, knowing I would take exception to his offer.

"I bet you've put on ten pounds since you're only working part-time," I retorted.

"Have not."

"Have too."

"Have not!"

"Have too!"

His voice faded as he went inside the apartment and I stopped my taunting as I rounded the van and started tossing the canned goods into the dog box. This method was inefficient; we were handling the cans twice. If we had enough plastic trash bags upstairs, I would line my next basket and twist-tie it; that way I could pull it out and put the whole bag directly inside.

Going back upstairs I had the thought that I would be happy never to grow up. I still acted like a child and I wanted this childhood to go directly into my second childhood. I didn't want thirty years of acting like an adult between them.

My second trip was shorter by at least four minutes. I explained how to line the baskets to Tim as I handed mine over. We had three unopened boxes of plastic bags on the pantry shelf. Whoever the pot grower was who stocked the shelves believed in plenty of backup supplies. When Tim had filled his first basket and left, I grabbed the other basket and started tumbling in cans. I filled the basket about three-quarters full, tied it with a twist and set it right outside the pantry door.

"Wrap the excess bag around your hands and I bet we can carry two at a time," I said to Tim. "The weight will be more balanced."

He hefted two sacks and could handle them easily.

"Where did you receive your EE training," he said as he left.

"I'm no efficiency expert," I yelled, so he could hear me. "Just highly intelligent!" I don't know if he heard me. He was out of sight.

Leroy came in to report he was now stacking stuff in the van's middle walkway. All the dog boxes were full. We tried to estimate how many bags of canned goods we would have while I was filling baskets. I said we'd just have to pray we had enough room. If not, we would have to lug them into the woods where we left our seabags and vacuums and come back for them later. I had four more plastic bags ready to go. He grabbed two in each hand and headed out.

"Show off! You're gonna get a hernia doing that!"

"Just working off those ten pounds you mentioned," he yelled back. I shook my head. Men. I bet he hadn't noticed the extra weight. The only time he weighed was in the doctor's office during a check-up; he had no problem with his weight. I also bet he found some scales and weighed tomorrow. He had taken me seriously.

I kept loading bags and Rosie joined me. She had finished the kitchen and it was now three-thirty. I asked her if she would mop the bathroom floor. I didn't have time to do it. She left and John reported he had finished the dining room. I explained I hadn't finished taking down the blue bulbs and handed him three cartons of four sixty-watt bulbs in the soft white I had saved from the supplies in the plastic bags.

"Put these in every fifth or sixth socket. We don't have enough to fill them all; spread them out evenly."

Tim stepped into the doorway and said he thought everything was done. I told him I had forgotten the outside of the front door and to be sure to get the outside casings as well. I finished filling the bags, finally. They were carrying them downstairs almost as fast as I could fill them because all three men were making the trips back and forth now.

Rosie came back with 409 cleaner and started on the pantry shelving. I asked her about the refrigerator, inside and outside. She said she had thrown the opened food away, wiped the inside and outside of the refrigerator and the stove, but were we going to leave the upright freezer full? I groaned and lit a cigarette. Would this nightmare ever end? I followed her out to the freezer I had completely overlooked, and opened the door.

Inside was crammed with every kind of frozen delicacy you can buy. Lobster tails, shrimp, scallops cooked and uncooked, pies, cakes and assorted rolls and goodies from Sara Lee. Boxes of hamburger patties, sausage patties, chickens cooked and uncooked. Frozen vegetables of every kind. My mind flashed to Leroy.

"Rosie, we'll load all this food in plastic bags and put it on the front floorboard and seat. You have been to Leroy and Jackie's house, haven't you?"

"Once, but I can find it again."

"Sure?"

"Positive."

"Okay, when you leave here, go directly there." I consulted my watch. Jackie would be home from work. "Tell her I need a place to store the food. Don't give any explanation. Pretend you don't know anything. I know Leroy has two freezers and I'm betting there's plenty of room in them. I'll have to sell both of them on the idea of keeping the food, but I'll worry about that tomorrow. Okay?"

"I think it's great," she said with a huge smile. "What about some of the canned goods?"

"Wouldn't take them. The only thing I have going for me on the frozen stuff is that it's perishable. I'm going to have a hard time with the frozen foods; the canned goods would look too much like charity."

She went back to the pantry shelves and I wearily opened a plastic bag and started packing the frozen goodies. When the men finished the canned goods, they came over for the bags with the frozen food. I cautioned them to put them in the front seat, that they had to have a fast trip home to the freezer. I didn't mention to Leroy that I had his freezer in mind.

As soon as the frozen food was loaded, I sent Rosie on her way. I told her to help Jackie store the frozen food and then go straight home and be sure she didn't let Wayne start on those fifty-pound fertilizer sacks; his shoulder wasn't well enough.

When I got back upstairs, the guys had filled the water canteens and Leroy had the seabags packed and by the door. We started in the kitchen and wiped the freezer on the inside and outside, to be sure. We stopped in every room and tried to spot something we might have missed. We were tossing questions at each other. John was waiting for someone to mention light fixtures, but no one thought of them. He had to mention them himself.

"I took off all the shades on the ones on the ceiling, wiped them and wiped the light bulbs."

We were all lavish with our praise. I never would have thought of those lights. We started to look closer. Tim spotted the floor air conditioning vents. Leroy went downstairs for a tool to take the covers off. John fetched the upright vacuum and set up the small round brush attachment. Leroy undid the screws on the vents and removed the lid. We all whistled or said something. The vent had dirt and dust, marijuana leaves that had been crushed underfoot, seeds and some small twiglike branches that had dried. We had to open, vacuum and close twelve floor vents. We put the vacuum away and were at the front door when I yelled we hadn't emptied the vacuum bag. Leroy and I ran back and he handed the disposable bag to me. We had already emptied and wiped down all the plastic trash cans. I carried the disposable bag in one hand and draped the four full canteens, two to each arm. Tim had four canteens and Leroy and John each had a seabag. Tim snapped his fingers, remembering to turn off the air conditioner.

We stood on the small landing and hated to lock the door. We knew the minute we pulled the door closed and locked it, we would think of something we had overlooked.

I took a deep breath. "Lock it," I said harshly to Tim who was the last one out. "If we think of anything else, it's too damn bad. To hell with it." He pulled the door closed and we tramped down the stairs, across the large lawn and back into the trees where the dogs were waiting and our equipment was stored.

It was four-thirty. I dressed quickly in my suit and Leroy fastened my snake covers. The men donned their waders and long- sleeved shirts. I fed the dogs some jerky and saw they still had water in the plastic-lined water hole. I kicked dirt on the plastic bag and Leroy scrubbed dirt into the hole with the side of his shoe and we smoothed out our footprints.

We had a smaller corridor to work going back than coming in, but it still took us until almost seven o'clock to work back to the creek. As we worked and pulled marijuana plants, I explained to Tim that everything had taken much longer than I had planned. I hadn't counted on all the fertilizer, canned goods, and a ton of frozen food — all that stuff took time we couldn't afford.

I explained that the best time for pot growers to visit their plants to work, or just inspect them, was right after dawn and just before dark. It was cooler and there was less chance of running into any DEA personnel. The DEA gathered its task force from surrounding cities and counties. Since they always wanted plenty of men in on the raid, some had to drive over seventy-five miles to get to the designated site. Everyone knew they couldn't get a task force into the field before nine and sometimes ten in the morning. Same thing with afternoons. The men had miles to drive before reaching home, so they always finished about five. The locals here called them the nine-to-five raiders.

Tim laughed. He told me he had worked a lot of overtime with the DEA during pot-harvesting time when he had been on the police force. He said they only paid thirty cents a mile if you had to drive your car, five bucks for a meal and it took about six weeks to receive an overtime check from the DEA's regional office. He said the money came in handy, however, because police work hadn't paid enough to support his wife and two daughters.

We found more plants than we expected and they were harder to pull. We filled more bags, which took us longer, but just before seven we walked to the creek. It was still light enough to see, but we were running out of daylight and we still had to haul all the bags out. Leroy and I removed our packs and pulled out the body bags and rescue sleds. I opened a large bag of M&M's and gave everyone a handful, telling them it would give them instant energy. Tim and John admitted they needed some because they were weary to the bone. Leroy and I were in much better shape; we lead a more physical existence than they.

I was very proud of them. They had hung in there when it didn't mean much to them about the pot, just that they had made a promise to me. After a ten-minute rest, we started back in to get five bags in the body bag and six bags in the rescue sled. I hooked Tim up to the body bag and he could handle it easily. The rescue sled was also easy to pull. As we pulled, they got hung up on vines and roots a couple of times, but we made very good time going back with the first load. Leroy and John had reached our staging area before us, left twelve bags and gone back for more. We drank water and I let Frost stand in the creek for a few minutes before we headed back. I had mentally estimated nineteen bags, but we hauled back twenty-one. John and Leroy had a total of twenty-five bags. We estimated a total count of four thousand plants destroyed.

Leroy backed the van until he was level with us. I sent Tim to the left, down the dirt road. He had his flashlight to use if he spotted car lights; he would wave it around until he got our attention, then hide in the greenery. John headed to the right. We couldn't be spotted with large stuffed trash bags on this road at night. So far, I hadn't heard any gossip about Wade's land and I wanted to keep it that way. These ol' boys who live out here drive the back roads, watch for car tracks, look at people, tags and vehicles with the same intensity.

Leroy and I loaded the van and the dogs. I gave them the last of the jerky. There wouldn't be cheeseburgers tonight; we still had too much to do. I had called Wayne at six-thirty and told him to leave Hector. He reported that Hector had finished at five and seemed to be home and settled in for the night. I pulled off the hot suit while Leroy backed up for John. We picked Tim up and started home. I handed everyone some wet wipes and told them to scrub their faces and hands to get rid of the green dye. There wasn't much green on our faces; most of it had washed away with sweat. I passed drinks to everyone from the cooler and lit a cigarette. There wasn't much conversation; we were just too tired to talk. Leroy drove to his corner and left the van idling in the street. I gave him a hug.

"Thanks, big guy," I said.

"Anytime, chicken," he replied. He shook hands with Tim and John. Sliding over on the seat, I waved as I pulled away, but he had already turned toward home. I hoped Jackie didn't take out her frustration and jealousy on him because he helped me. He was a good man.

When we pulled into the Winn Dixie parking lot, I was at a loss for words.

"What can I say, guys, except thanks. If you ever need me, just whistle. You do know how to whistle, don't you?"

My impersonation of Bacall's voice wasn't the best, but they seemed to know who I was aping and gave me some tired chuckles. Tim stuck out his hand, but I gave them both a hug. They climbed out of the van and I waved as I was pulling away.

I never did finish calculating how much potential drug money Hector and his cohorts had garnered each year. I took the four thousand plants and halved it, then took twenty-five percent for termites, root rot, deer and swamp bunnies, and revised the total to fifteen hundred plants. You average a pound a plant; some had more, some had less, but a pound a plant would do for a round figure. The selling price would be five grand per pound. These people had a class operation going. There would be no seeds; it would be sensimilla.

If I wasn't too tired to multiply correctly, that came to about seven hundred and fifty thousand bucks. I didn't know how many belonged to this grower's association, but even with ten to share, it would be seventy-five grand apiece, if they divvied up equally, which I seriously doubted. The field hands who did the scut work would get a lot less; that was the standing Golden Rule of agriculture.

When I arrived home, Wayne and Rosie were waiting. Wayne unloaded the dogs and handed them to Rosie. She offered to go to our burning dump with Wayne, but I told her to go to bed; Wayne and I could manage. Wayne had been out earlier and started a roaring fire. I sat with him in the darkness as he slowly dumped one bag at a time into the fire so it would burn quickly and not pack and smolder. It took us over two hours. I had repellent for the bugs; Wayne supplied a lift-out seat and cushion from the van. I had a Coke and many cigarettes.

The moonless night with roaring and flickering flames from the fire made the night seem eternal, and problems — and problem people — seemed unimportant and in the far distant past. Wayne woke me at midnight and I sleepwalked to the van and rode home. After taking a long, hot shower and letting the water pound my shoulders and back, I made the rounds, checking doors and windows, checking the panel for the landscapes, which hadn't been opened. I went into the kitchen and activated the fence. Rosie had left a note on the table.

"Casserole in the oven, potato salad in the fridge." I took the small casserole out and opened it. Baked beans, wiener slices, bacon strips, and pineapple. It looked delicious. I replaced the lid and returned it to the fridge. It would be just as delicious for breakfast. I checked Ruby's bowl and saw that Rosie had remembered to fill it. I was just too damn tired to eat. I went to bed without checking the answering machine. It could wait till morning. I was asleep before my head hit the pillow and I could get my eyes closed.

25

"THAT SHOULD JAR YOUR MOTHER'S PRESERVES"
April 13, Tuesday, 7:15 A.M.

Awaking from a dream about the cougars, I stretched my legs under the sheet and, with my eyes closed, relived the look of the cougar, her healthy offspring, and the peaceful tableau they had created. The pot growers didn't have daily chores this time of year, just occasional spraying, some fertilizing and checking for insect damage, but it still surprised me to see the cougar so relaxed on ground that had been walked on so recently by man. Maybe being in captivity for a while had made her not fear the smell of man. I hoped not, because man was the cougar's deadliest threat. I wished her and her kits a long and happy life. I would take the film in this morning and I would be able to view it this afternoon.

I stood, but wasn't prepared for the sharp stab of pain in my lower back. Christ, it felt like a muscle spasm. I hobbled around the room trying to loosen the sore muscles from yesterday's marathon exertions. In the bathroom, I let the hot water pound on my back. God, we had been lucky yesterday. Wade's land was free of pot and I had been privileged to witness a miracle in the wild. My mind felt freer and worries seemed less troublesome. Who knew, maybe today I would be able to sign the complaint against Bubba, but I didn't count on it. Let them play their delaying game, but I would prevail, amen. A little morning prayer and promise combined.

I dressed in a white linen skirt and a loden-green tailored blouse and added white sandals and a white shoulder bag. I checked the .32 before I put it in the bag. The coffee was ready, the casserole hot, and I pushed down the toast. I ate last night's dinner for breakfast with keen enjoyment. After the dishes, I checked the answering machine while enjoying a third cup of coffee. There were no messages. Either Rosie had checked yesterday afternoon, or I hadn't received any. I glanced across the desk, but there were no messages or notes.

Pulling the calendar over, I saw that Rosie had cleared the messages and we had received an order. Habar's Kennel in Johnston, Ohio, had ordered another puppy from us. I believe we have sold them three in the past. Forgetting I was without the services of a computer, I made a move toward the missing machine to verify my memory. If that computer technician didn't come and save the day, my files would be in one confused mess. I didn't want to think about going through this year's paperwork to find out where I stood.

Wayne came in at eight. After getting him a cup of coffee, I told him to leave Rosie's van until I got back from town and I would help him unload. He signed that he had taken care of everything and had just finished vacuuming the van and repacking the backpacks.

"But you couldn't have!" I said with sharp surprise. "All that food and fertilizer . . ."

He motioned for my attention and signed: "Mom told me what you planned for the food. I went at seven when I knew there would be men there just finishing their evening meal. I had eight helpers who unloaded the bags. I gave them everything except the two bags of trash and the bag with the razors, cologne, and aftershave and everything; I kept that for me. I spread all the plastic sheets and potting trays in four different locations, in the dumpsters. You know how the poor unemployed and old-age pensioners scavenge through those dumpsters. Every useable thing will disappear before the trash trucks come. I left the fertilizer till this morning. I drove the van up alongside Mom's compost heap, cut the sacks and poured them in the pile. She's so pleased; we'll put it around her plants and shrubbery. It was no sweat."

"I appreciate your efforts, but I swear to God, Wayne, you are more stubborn and bull-headed than I am!"

"No way!" He cawed with laughter.

My advice to take it easy for a few more days fell on deaf ears, and this pun was intended. Wayne would have appreciated the humor, but I didn't share it with him. Instead, I told him about the cougar. He was as delighted with the news as I was.

"Are you going to call the commission and tell them?" he signed. "I bet they flip!"

"Only if I have good, clear shots of her and her young. They wouldn't believe me otherwise," I signed. "And then, maybe they won't believe the pictures either."

After he left for the kennel, I gazed out the office window at the morning. It was a beautiful day. The dew glistened on the grass and shrubs, and two small birds had a mock fight near the window. A hummingbird was loading up on the sugared water from the feeder. I bent closer to the pane to see his miniature features more clearly, a tiny miracle in this great expanse of sun and air and sky that we enjoy. I had a friend tell me once that seeing a deer on her drive to work in the morning made her whole day. However fleeting the glimpse, she said she knew nothing could really go wrong on a day when you have seen such a graceful and beautiful creature. I felt the same way about a tiny hummingbird. If this minuscule creature could survive and thrive, how could we do less?

I heard a squeak from the cat door, some cautious silence and another squeak. Moving only my eyes, I saw a black shape scurry toward a dented metal wastebasket. It was her only hiding place on that side of the room. The couch, chairs, and coffee table were missing.

"Good morning, Ruby," I said in a normal tone of voice. I had graduated from whispering sweet nothings in a babyish voice. Nothing was working. I was willing to change my approach. I heard her faint, dutiful answering "meow." It was strange to hear the small, inadequate timbre of sound from such a large and robust-looking cat. I didn't know if it was just fear and insecurity, or some kind of throat problem. I sat quietly while she made her slow painful journey from hiding place to hiding place to reach her food dish. It was clearly evident she wasn't ready to be pals, as yet.

I left the house at nine. I had called the House of Mirrors and they were sending an installer with the materials this afternoon. The lady had explained that I would be charged an additional fee for any distance over their fifty-mile installation limit, of which I was well aware. People who have to secure services from a distance always pay through the nose for the privilege of having them accept our money.

I should have called Hank to see how he was doing; he sure had been moody and strange the last few days. I decided to wait a couple of days; maybe he would feel better about Charlene and his forced courtship. I called Jackie. She didn't have to go to work until noon and she agreed to see me after I told her I must talk to her.

When I arrived, she led me to the kitchen, poured me a cup of coffee and waited patiently for me to tell her why I was there. I decided to tell her everything we had done yesterday. Maybe if I was open with her, she would feel different about me. After telling her the story, I asked for her silence. She gave the assurance freely.

"You see," she explained evenly, "my friends think I'm insane for letting you come into my home, so I really have no one I could tell if I wanted to."

Oh, Jackie, don't cut me out of your life, your husband and girls mean too much to me for me to lose them. I gave her a bright smile.

"Jackie, I want to be your friend, please believe that. Please take the frozen food, it would be a sin to waste it."

"I understand why. It now has no legal owner. I will accept it because I, too, think it would be a shame to waste it when we could use it. As I said, I agree to use it. I just don't agree to like the idea one little bit."

I stood, managed a cheery smile and gave her a hug that my heart didn't believe was sincere. She accepted it with as much grace as she could muster, which wasn't nearly enough.

My second stop was the photo shop. I left the film and asked for the two-hour service. The clerk said I could pick it up after eleven o'clock. Arriving at the bank, and finding a parking space next to a reserved handicapped slot, I observed an obviously healthy woman pull into it. Locking the van, I watched her jump out of her car and actually run across the sidewalk toward the small shopping mall adjoining the bank building. This really bugs me. Granted, she may have a disability sticker on her vehicle. Granted, she may drive a disabled person around. But today, right now, she was alone, so she shouldn't use the space.

Entering the bank, I headed straight to Charles Seymore's desk which was located in the open lobby like most of the other junior executives. He had only a desk-high wooden railing to outline his working area. Two customer chairs faced his desk; I sat down in one and greeted him.

"Hi Charlie," I said with gusto. "How're they hanging?" I love to tease him; he was such a self-righteous prig in high school.

"Good morning," he uttered without a smile. "Jo Beth, you really shouldn't be so vulgar. It's most unbecoming." He gave me a fish-eyed stare.

"Charlie, I need an out-of-state check verified, one I placed in the night deposit after hours on Sunday. Here's the check number and name." I fished out my scrap of paper with the information and laid it on his desk. He picked it up as if it were a smelly diaper and disappeared. I sat down, lit a cigarette and contemplated how neither of us — Charlie nor me — had really changed in essential ways since high school. He was still a prig and I was as stubborn as ever. He was gone ten minutes.

"The check has been certified by phone. New York is drafting the amount by wire within three hours, but I have instructed the computer to show your account deposited and you can draw on the funds immediately, if you so desire." He tried to smile and failed miserably.

"Thank you, Charlie. That was nice of you," I told him with great warmth and got up and left.

In the van, six blocks from the courthouse, I turned left on Seedly

Drive and headed for the mall. I'd buy some furniture first before going to the courthouse and trying to file charges. I was feeling a little hyper from my encounter with Charlie; the wasted trip to Charlene's office would only depress me. When I pulled into the mall's parking lot and started the hike across the tarmac, I spotted a little boy wearing a very large bandage, being conned by his mother. She was telling him it wouldn't hurt a bit when the stitches were removed.

Damn, I had completely forgotten to remind Wayne to get his stitches out today. He hadn't mentioned them, so he had forgotten also. I found a phone booth just inside the mall. I looked up Dr. Sellers' number and dialed his office. Faye, his receptionist, office clerk, nurse, and wife, answered.

"Faye, this is Jo Beth Sidden. Wayne needs some stitches taken out of a cut he received over in Constine last week. Do you think the doctor could see him sometime today?"

"Sure, Jo Beth. Just tell him to come in anytime. I'll work him in between appointments so he shouldn't have to wait too long. How's your leg doing?"

Boy, she had a phenomenal memory. Over six months ago, sand fly bites on my right ankle had turned septic. I had to take antibiotics and Faye had found I needed a booster shot for tetanus. I had suffered the shot in silence and she had rewarded me with a lollipop.

"It's great, Faye. I'll call Wayne. Thanks." I dialed the house and got a busy signal. I wandered over to Wadsworth Candy Shop and admired all the different kinds of chocolate on display. After five minutes, I redialed my number and got a busy signal again. I would try again later.

I entered Standell's and walked among the many, many couches until an off-white, over-stuffed sofa and matching love seat caught my eye. I sank down in comfort. It didn't scratch, didn't have loose cushions that constantly needed straightening and it would look great in the office. I selected two side chairs in a nubby rust-colored fabric. They promised delivery this afternoon. I looked at lamps, side and coffee tables, but couldn't make up my mind which ones I like best. I went out into the mall and found a phone booth occupied by a woman who looked as if the receiver was permanently attached to her ear. I decided to find a restroom while she finished her conversation.

When I returned, the lady shopper was still going strong. I decided to try again later. I went into J.C. Penney's and found a gorgeous set of dishes. They were too expensive and too elaborate to hold my culinary efforts, but I splurged and bought them. They gave me a claim check for their dock area pick-up site. I returned to the mall area and phoned Rosie. She picked up on the first ring.

"Hi Rosie, I just remembered Wayne's stitches come out today. Doctor Sellers can see —" I stopped speaking. Rosie was yelling in a panicky voice.

"Jo Beth listen, listen to me! Call Hank. Hang up and call Hank and if anyone answers other than Hank, don't use your name. Do you hear me? Call Hank now!" She hung up on me.

Oh my God. Something bad was happening, and I didn't have a clue. I sat down slowly on the small swing-out stool and took a deep breath. I will not panic, I will not panic, I silently chanted my calming mantra. What had happened? Oh God, oh God, Rosie sounded hysterical. I carefully dialed Hank's number at the sheriff's department.

"Lieutenant Cribbs," he answered crisply.

"Hi, it's me. What's up?" My voice sounded weak and hesitant. I didn't really want any bad news today. I didn't need any more grief.

"Well, Joseph," he said casually, "it's about time you got in touch. Been looking all over town for you. Don't you know you're supposed to keep in touch? You haven't done any snitching lately. You ready to meet?"

"Where?" I said in a slightly firmer timbre. It was obvious he wasn't supposed to be talking to me, so that meant I was the one in trouble and nobody close had died, or been run over, or anything fatal. Maybe I could handle this bad news.

"Listen, buddy boy," he said harshly. "Walk, don't run to your buggy and haul ass to meet me. Remember the overpass where you found the shoe? Jasmine wouldn't forget it. Check with her. You got it?"

"Nope." I said, but he didn't hear me; he had hung up.

I held the dead phone to my ear and thought. The overpass he mentioned was where a black man had lost a shoe as he was trying to outrun the dogs. The man had been fourth in a line of stopped cars when he suspected it was a drug search. We had set up our roadblock on the low overpass, which was the only entrance and exit to shanty town, a small black conclave that was a maze of small shanties, lots of overgrown shrubbery, abandoned shacks and weeds. He had bailed out of the car and sailed over the fourteen-foot clearance into the heavy growth below.

We had to go around by the road and by the time we entered shanty town, they had embraced him into the maze and warrens. All we ever found were articles of clothing he had hastily discarded and lots of black pepper. It was a trick as old as the hills, but sometimes it still worked. I had been working Chaucer and Frost. The second time they went into a sneezing frenzy, I pulled them off the scent and gave up the chase. Each household the fleeing man had passed through had emptied their black pepper cans in the path he had traveled. The man had lost a shoe on his fourteen-foot plunge, so I knew the overpass Hank meant — but who or what was Jasmine?

I didn't really want to move, but I forced myself out of the phone booth and walked out of the mall to the van. He had said walk, not run, which I assumed he meant not to hurry and call attention to the van. I was being sought, but for what? If I was blown for the laws I bent yesterday, it would prove embarrassing to all concerned, but I doubted an alert to apprehend me would be issued for that reason. What was going on?

I pulled out of the parking lot and turned toward the direction of the overpass. The van seemed to get bigger and greener as I navigated the three miles across town. I started planning my route. It sounded wise to stay off the main drags, even if it took a little longer to reach the spot where I was headed. Jasmine? I wished I was invisible. I saw a light bar across the top of a vehicle in the distance and turned right. I couldn't get lost in this town if I tried. I knew every street, alley and traffic light.

I slowed down and caught the first green light, found the perfect pace and made the next four, but was caught on the fifth. I sat there sweating until the light turned. I took my much bigger and much greener van down three more side streets until the overpass was in sight. I slowed my speed and scanned both sides of the road. Jasmine wasn't blooming yet and I doubted if I could recognize the green bushes if I passed any. If he was referring to a specific patch of shrubbery, I was in trouble.

I passed two small businesses, one a vacant filling station and the other a rickety vegetable stand, now strangled with vines and dog fennel, six feet high. On my right was a small white building, with "Jasmine's B-B-Q" on a small wooden sign standing on the handkerchief-sized lawn.

Ah so . . . the mystery was solved. I parked in front of the door and tried to stroll casually the ten-foot walk to the building. The door opened before I reached it.

"Can you back into a tight place?" she asked.

"Yes," I replied. She was a beautiful black girl who looked to be in her twenties. Her hair was as short as mine and almost as curly. She had beautiful white teeth that flashed as she spoke, but she hadn't smiled and didn't look happy to see me.

"Pull around the corner and back into the shed at the rear of the building," she instructed. "Drop the tarp and tie each side to the post and come in through the back door." She disappeared back inside.

I drove around the building on a small rutted road to the shed and backed in carefully. I had about a six-inch clearance on each side. I backed closer to the right side so I would be able to squeeze out of the van's door. I dropped the dark green tarp and tied the frayed rope to both posts. I glanced around. I hadn't seen anyone while I was backing into the shed; maybe no one had seen me.

The rear door led into her bedroom. It was small, immaculate and painted an off-white, which made the room seem larger. The bedspread and drapes were a medium-rose color and the carpet was apple green. The wood furniture was cheap veneer but gleaming with polish. She hadn't loaded the walls with a lot of junk. There were only three pictures: one was a pastel of a rainy Paris street scene, one was two white kittens against a blue background, and the third was a framed charcoal silhouette of her head and shoulders. Whoever had sketched it was very good. The artist had caught her haughty carriage and aristocratic neck. I checked the tiny bathroom from the doorway. Stark white enamel paint, white fixtures, fluffy towels, shower curtain, and throw rug in a matching pink. I'm a hopeless snoop. I dropped to my knees to check under the bed. Not a dust bunny in sight. The door opened before I could regain my feet.

"Looking for dust bunnies," I said with a weak smile.

"Find any?" Her eyes flashed. I didn't know if she was pissed or found it humorous that she had caught me on my knees.

"Nope, even my mother would approve," I declared. A little white lie. My mother died when I was ten, but I felt I needed a compliment for her right about now.

"Good. Come into the living room. You can check behind the sofa."

I followed her into the room, feeling like a peeping Tom. This room was also off-white. Colorful multicolored drapes on the two windows, which had closed white venetian blinds. She had turned on a reading lamp by her easy chair and the room glowed with color. A couch in deep rose, two side chairs in dark green and the same apple-green carpet of the bedroom. This gal had created a restful room, with minimal furnishings and smart color choices.

"I apologize for snooping. It's a habit I was born with and one I can't seem to curb."

"I even look in medicine cabinets when I visit," she said with a grin.

"Tell me about you and Hank," I said laughing.

She glared at me and quickly narrowed her eyes. "You mean how this here black chick and this white po-leece-man is gettin it on, every chance they gets?" She had spoken in the exaggerated mush-mouth drawl of the Southern black.

"Of course not," I said briskly. "Look, we've started off on the wrong foot, you catching me peeking under your bed and misunderstanding my nosy question. I warned you I was a snoop."

"It's my turn to apologize," she said in a soft and articulate voice. "I'm a retired whore and overly sensitive to any hint of sexual innuendoes."

I blinked. It is very seldom I am caught so off-guard. "I'm Jo Beth Sidden," I said, reaching out to offer my hand and speaking in my best glad-to-meet-you voice. "How long have you been retired?"

It cracked her up. She started that deep belly laughter that is so hard to control and just as hard to ignore. I joined her. My nerves were raw wires from my tense trip across town and the fear of what was going down. Hank had me terrified. We collapsed on the sofa and finally gained control of our near hysterical mirth. I fished for a tissue in my purse. She offered her Kleenex box on the lamp table. We both dried our eyes.

"I'm Jasmine Jones," she said as we finally shook hands. "I've been retired six years. Hank said he would call as soon as he could get away to a pay phone and when you had plenty of time to get here. He didn't tell me your problem; he didn't have time. I met Hank ten years ago, when he joined the sheriff's department. He arrested me for soliciting his first week on the job. He was shocked at my age and long arrest record. I had been on the street since I was twelve. He ran off my current pimp and kept away anyone else trying to run me. Working on my own, I was able to save my money.

"It took him four years, but he finally talked me into going straight. He arrested me fourteen times, then would come down to the jail to harp and cajole, trying to straighten me out. With the money I had saved, and Hank co-signing at the bank for a loan, I was able to buy this place. And Jo Beth, in answer to your next question, we were never lovers. I was willing, I even offered, but he politely turned me down. Said he would rather be my friend. So you can see why I would do this favor for him. It's the first one he's ever asked. I'd wade through a swamp, hip-deep in alligators, for him; and I think you're some kind of fool."

"Me?" I asked, to the bolt from the blue. "Why am I a fool?"

"Now, girlfriend, Hank's been in love with you for almost a year. Don't tell me you didn't know."

"All the uniforms want is a little nookie and bragging rights to use during their beer and bull sessions," I answered with heat. "He's just one of a dozen or more who're always in there pitching their product. I'd lose any chance of acceptance as an almost equal if I went out with just one of them. I say, almost equal, because none of them will ever consider us equal, regardless of our performance or worth."

"My God," she said in wonder. "I scratched a person and found a rabid feminist. Are you a racist, as well?"

"Only if they are of the masculine gender," I answered with a snap in my voice.

"You're wrong about Hank; he's nuts about you."

"He's just frustrated because I keep turning him down. Besides, I've currently matched him up with an assistant district attorney."

"I've heard about Charlene," she said dryly. "Listen Jo Beth, she's really doing a number on him. Just don't waffle around too long, you might regret it."

The phone rang and we both jumped. Jasmine answered. "Hello. Just a second." She handed me the phone.

"Yes, Hank."

"They found Bubba last night. The grand jury has been in session for three weeks now. They whipped up a quick charge sheet and Charlene presented it to them this morning at ten. They bypassed everyone else and put this case first. They returned an indictment less than thirty minutes ago. I'm sorry, Jo Beth."

I closed my eyes with relief. I could sleep at night again. No more cringing when the front-gate alarm sounded. I opened my eyes. What was that skulking cross-town trip all about? Why was he sorry? Facts weren't adding up correctly.

"Hank, you scared the crap out of me. What was that coded call from your desk all about? Don't you know I'm happy they picked up the bastard? I'm glad they handed down the indictment. What's wrong with you?"

"I'm your friend, Jo Beth, but my ten years on the force made me run a check. As your friend, I knew you were innocent. It just wasn't your style."

"What wasn't my style?" I asked alarmed. The fear was returning.

"They found Bubba about midnight, out near the county dump site. His head was bashed in and most all of his bones are broken. It's a lot worse than what he did to you. The indictment is for attempted murder, and it has your name on it. They think you did it."

26

"AS QUICK AS GREASED LIGHTNING"
April 13, Tuesday, 11 A.M.

I took a ragged breath and gripped the receiver. I was trying to think.

"Why do they think I did it?" I questioned.

"Come on, Jo Beth, you're the perfect suspect. It was even done with his own baseball bat."

"No. Not his bat," I said slowly, "unless he bought one Saturday while he was on the run, which I doubt. His bat is at my place. It was left there when he was arrested."

"The police didn't take it as evidence?"

"Those good ol' boys are friends of Bubba. You could say they ran a pretty sloppy investigation. They told me I should kiss and make up."

"I hope to hell that bat is still at your place and not down in the property room as evidence," he said quickly.

"You can have Wayne check. I'm pretty sure it's still there. Wayne put it way back in the lumber shed. It wasn't where anyone could see it and lift it. I may be the prime suspect, but Bubba had more enemies than friends. There are plenty of people who would like to see him hurt or dying. Is he dying, by the way?"

I was trying very hard not to wish for his death. It made me feel guilty when the thought crept into my mind.

"It can go either way. The doctor said he has less than a fifty-fifty chance of making it. He's been in a coma since they found him."

"They've got something else as evidence, Hank. Charlene isn't stupid. She had to have more to base her case on than just motive."

"I think she does, too," he said with anger. "Charlene won't tell me what it is." I don't know how I managed a laugh.

"Charlene is a crack prosecutor, Hank. Her pillow talk would not involve discussing evidence. You've got a lot to learn about women."

"We'll discuss that later," he said. "Right now, I want to know where you were yesterday, between noon and two p.m. The doctor said his injuries were about twelve hours old when he was found at midnight. Tell me where you were and I'll start establishing your alibi now, while people's minds are fresh. By the way, I got in touch with Wade and Sinclair. They are both working hard for you. Wade is busy on legal work and Sinclair is running around digging up bail money. You won't be able to post a property bond on this one. Sheriff Carlson is after blood. He wants you behind bars, unable to make bail. I haven't told Wade or Sinclair where you are. That way, they won't be concealing evidence of your whereabouts until they can arrange for you to come in. Now, where were you yesterday, between noon and two? Remember everyone who saw you and talked to you. I have a pen, go ahead."

Oh boy. Between noon and two p.m. yesterday, I was busily engaged in removing fingerprints and evidence of marijuana from Wade's apartment, with three men who would probably lose their jobs and reputations if they had to back up my alibi. Then there was Wade. He would know for sure his father was a big-time drug dealer, and I knew that was knowledge he didn't want to possess. Plus, he would lose everything.

"Ah, I'll have to get back to you on that," I said lamely.

"For God's sake, Jo Beth," he thundered, "it's not a difficult question. Everybody knows where they were yesterday. Don't be coy with me. If you were doing something with someone you don't want me to know about, forget it. You're in big trouble. If you had a date, it isn't important. Where were you?"

For Christ's sake, why does every man, when he senses a woman is holding something back, automatically assume it's another man. Is it ego-blindness or sexual tunnel vision?

"I went for a drive." It sounded stupid, but it couldn't be disproved.

He groaned. "Is that what you want me to check out, a drive? Did you stop for gas? Get something to eat? See anyone who knows you? Did you have any proof of a drive at all?"

"No," I admitted.

"I see. Sit tight and try to think about the fact that this isn't a game. Let me speak to Jasmine. I'll call you when I have more news."

I gladly surrendered the phone to Jasmine and left to use her bathroom. I splashed water on my face and patted it dry. I looked at my reflection and silently mouthed the words, "Wanted felon." I was a wanted felon. I made a childish mistake eleven years ago by marrying a new pickup truck that came with a man. Eleven years seemed a long enough penance for one mistake. How much longer? It wasn't beyond the realm of possibility that I could be convicted of this crime. I had enemies in all the wrong places: the sheriff's department with a sheriff who would love to see me in the slammer, and an assistant district attorney who would rejoice in sending me there. I stuck my tongue out at my reflection and tried to wiggle my ears.

In the living room, Jasmine had finished her conversation with Hank and was sitting on the sofa. She patted the seat beside her and told me to sit.

"Hank wants me to educate you a little. First, we have to do something right away you're not going to like. Your lawyer, Wade, wants some clear close-up Polaroid shots of you, undressed, showing front, back, and side views to prove you didn't have any bruises or injuries before you surrendered to the authorities."

I thought about my scars. My clothes covered them by day and darkness covered them during my rare sexual encounters. I shook my head back and forth.

"Don't start shaking your head," she snapped. "You haven't even heard the worst part. These pictures have to be signed and attested to by someone who is above reproach, with an impeccable reputation. As you can imagine, I don't qualify, with my past record and occupation. We have to have a third party present when I take the photos. The only person I could think of, in my limited circle of acquaintances, is the Reverend Euttis B. Johnson of the Pentecostal Holiness Fundamental Gospel Church, which is about five blocks from here. He's well known and his word is accepted in both white and black communities. Hank agreed with my choice. How about you?"

"No, no, no!" I shook my head from side to side for added emphasis.

"Hank told me you would be stubborn about this, but I credited you with having more good sense. He was right, I'll just have to educate you on our local incarceration procedures. I want you to listen carefully. I won't exaggerate. Everybody who owns a TV has seen the fingerprinting and picture procedures with the number hung around your neck. Now I'll tell you the part you don't see on TV. If your lawyer can't convince a judge who sits outside this district to come in with you when you surrender, they will have you inside, under lockup, until your lawyer can find a judge to set bail. They are planning on Judge McAlbee taking a powder the minute they haul you in, or you surrender. There will be no judge to set your bail."

Jasmine put her finger to her lips for silence and eased through the partially opened door into her business. She returned shortly carrying a tray with two glasses of iced tea. She locked the door and gave me one of the glasses. She explained she didn't want the woman who was working today to know I was here because she was a notorious gossip. I had been aware of a low murmur of voices, but hadn't equated it with business being conducted a few feet away. Jasmine must have sensed that my throat was dry. The tea was delicious. I knew I wasn't going to like what I was going to hear next. She continued with my education.

"After the fingerprinting and photo sessions, they take you back to the women's section, down a long corridor and stop out in the open. There are two head 'keys.' They are the women in charge. One is named Annie but she is called Tiny. She weighs about two hundred and fifty pounds. She is in her thirties and strong as an ox. The other one is Grace Freedman and she is always called 'Miz Grace.' She's the most dangerous of the two. Tiny looks like someone's grandmother. She always operates with two huge white women inmates who are strong and brutal. They get special privileges for being her helpers.

"Regardless of who's on duty, the routine is the same. They stop you in the corridor, in full view of the long row of cells, and make you strip. The door that is directly behind you, while you strip, leads to the men's section. It has a viewing slot about six inches wide running from head level to about knee level. Usually, only a couple of white male guards peek through the slot, but you'd be a celebrity. I bet you would draw a crowd. They don't get that many attractive, straight white women to drool over. Our lady guards don their rubber gloves; Miz Grace always lets one of her helpers do the inspection. She knows the helpers are stronger than she, and can inflict more pain. Seems Miz Grace suffers from arthritis in her fingers.

"They grope your anus, they probe and they hurt. Then they move to the front and make sure your clitoris is pinched sharply and your vagina is clear of all drugs. They also probe and try to hurt you. Both Annie and Miz Grace own a Polaroid camera. They take lots of pictures while this humiliation is going on. With young, attractive, black females, the top price they get from the deputies is five bucks a snap. I bet your pictures would sell like hotcakes. They'll be taking lots of pictures of you. Some of those deputies have quite a collection of Polaroids."

She stopped and eyed me with compassion. "It's what you'll have to face if your friends can't succeed in their efforts to keep you from being locked up."

I looked at her through a glaze of tears. I knew in my heart that every word she had uttered was the gospel truth. Where was my indignation, my shock and anger that these things were happening right under our noses and we were letting them happen? I knew, but I didn't want to face the knowledge.

We are complacent; these things would never happen to us. We didn't commit crimes. The people to whom these things were happening, well, they committed crimes. They deserved punishment, didn't they? It was only when your own personal goose was about to be cooked that you screamed "Brutality" and "Abuse." All this occurs with our implied consent because we sit back, let it happen and do nothing. I made a promise at that moment I would do something about this abuse, somehow, some way. I didn't brag to Jasmine that I was going to stop it; I never bragged about what I was going to do. I just did it, and then crowed.

I moistened my throat with the last drops of iced tea before I tried to speak. I was surprised that my voice sounded so steady. "Do you think Reverend Johnson will be available?"

"Good girl," she said with a smile, "I'll call him."

I wandered into the bedroom and stood in front of the picture of Paris, but I didn't see it. I didn't want to hear the conversation with the Reverend, and I didn't want to meet the Reverend. I cringed at the thought of him looking at my scarred body. The doctors had said in five years the scars will fade. It had been six years, and they still loomed red and ugly in my mind. Susan swears you would need a magnifying glass to spot them in broad daylight. Maybe she is right, but I can see them: bright and shiny, red and puckered, a patchwork quilt of hurts.

Jasmine entered the bedroom and removed a Japanese style, multi-colored silk robe from a hanger and placed it on the bed.

"He'll be here in ten minutes," she said crisply. "Leave your bra and panties on. Do you want me to introduce you to him, or just keep quiet?"

"Introduce me. I'll want to thank him . . . afterwards. Introduce me afterwards," I said with a faint utterance.

"It isn't necessary," she said softly.

"It is to me," I said.

I undressed in the tiny bathroom, folding my clothes neatly and placing them on the closed toilet seat. I wrapped the silk robe around me. I could smell a faint hint of perfume on the robe. Jasmine wore Jasmine perfume.

I entered the bedroom and stood near the wall not thinking about anything, just staring into space. I heard a muted conversation and Jasmine and Reverend Johnson entered the room. I recognized him from several pictures I had seen in Fred's *Dunston County Daily Times*.

Jasmine was all business. She looked through the camera viewfinder and said she was ready. I slipped off the robe, held my chin up and turned when she said turn. After four flashes, she said she was finished and they left the room. Back in the bathroom, I dressed again and joined them in the living room.

Reverend Johnson was short and slim; he appeared to be in his late sixties. His hair was black with silver sprinkled liberally in all his tight, sausagelike curls.

"I'm Jo Beth Sidden," I said, as I held out my hand. "Thank you for helping me."

His hand was thin and bony, his grip weak and fleeting. The Reverend was more embarrassed than I was.

"You're welcome," he said in a soft voice. He nodded briefly in my direction, nodded again at Jasmine and departed.

"Isn't he sweet? He signed the back of each photo, dated them and wrote the time. He will testify if it's necessary. He's been trying to convert me to his religion, but I can't leave my faith."

"What's your affiliation?" I was curious.

"Hard Shell Baptist," she enunciated with dulcet tones. "The only road to salvation."

I had seen the sparkle in her eyes and knew she was putting me on, trying to cheer me up.

"I always thought the Holiness religion had eternal salvation pretty well sewed up," I told her. "My mother was Holiness." I said this, as if it proved my point. She laughed.

"We could debate our respective religions, but I'd much rather hear about your dogs and what you do." So, I told her.

God, did I ever! It was like my fear and humiliation had opened the dam and my life history flowed out from my lips. I told her things even Susan didn't know. Jasmine had a special knack for listening. It's a gift and hard to fake. She really, truly wanted to hear what I was telling her. Her expression of understanding and the need to know more seemed to draw the stories out and, as I talked, my confidence in her grew. I finally ran down, like a clock unwinding. I leaned back against the couch, limp and exhausted, and closed my eyes. She had brought in a pitcher of tea after the Reverend departed.

"What did you put in the tea, truth serum?" Over an hour had passed. It was now twelve-thirty. Where was everyone? Why didn't someone call?

I suddenly remembered Hanaiker.

"May I use your phone?"

"Sure." She placed it in front of me.

I called Rosie. I had to listen to five minutes of how worried and scared she and Wayne were. I told her to call Hanaiker at his hotel; she would find his number on my desk calendar. I told her his check had cleared and he could pick up the dogs. I asked her to put the new collars, with our name and address on the inside, on the dogs because they would be traveling by car through several states. I asked her to hug O'Henry and Sally for me. I reminded her of Wayne's stitches and to ask him to pick up the cougar prints from the photo shop. I was still on the phone with her when Sinclair arrived. I told her we'd talk later and hung up.

Sinclair had knocked on the diner door, and Jasmine released the lock and invited him inside. Sinclair is three inches shorter than I; he fights the calorie battle daily and almost always loses. He is redheaded with a pale white complexion that was constantly peeling from sunburn. He should avoid the sun entirely, but he waterskis, swims and stays out in it every weekend. He was dressed like a very conservative banker. The material in his suit was dark, very lightweight, with a pinstripe that was almost undetectable. He also wore a snowy white shirt, staid tie and black, lace-up, wing-tip shoes. He was an unorthodox Jew, my tax attorney who saved me money daily, and a very good friend.

"Sinclair, I'd like you to meet my friend, Jasmine Jones. Jasmine. This is Sinclair Adams, my tax attorney." Sinclair was stunned by her beauty. He held her hand much longer than necessary.

"My dear Jasmine," he stated eloquently, "if I didn't have a wife who spends all my money, and three children who eat me out of house and home, would you fly to Tahiti with me next weekend?"

"Maybe next year," she said cheerfully.

"I'll enter that in my appointment book," he breathed. He was still holding her hand.

"Ah, Sinclair," I said to break the spell, "did you have something to discuss with me?" He reluctantly freed her hand and reached for his briefcase. Now he was all business.

"I have some papers for you to sign for the bank. I promised them back, signed, by two this afternoon under penalty of death," he stated.

Jasmine rose gracefully from the couch. "I'll just wait in the bedroom," she murmured.

"Sit down," I commanded. "You're a big part of this and it's your home we've invaded. We're only going to discuss money."

Sinclair opened the lid of his briefcase and picked up the bank papers. Underneath there was nothing but money. Bundle after bundle, row after row, all tightly packed. The whole briefcase was loaded with money. Jasmine and I stared openly at all the bills. It was the most money I had ever seen in one place.

"There's one hundred thousand dollars here," Sinclair explained. "Twenty-seven thousand is yours. I cashed in two of your bonds and it only cost you three hundred dollars and change in penalties; it was the cheapest way to go. Thirty-three thousand is mine and fifteen thousand belongs to Wade. The bank kicked in twenty-five on a thirty-day promissory note. If this isn't settled in thirty days, we'll cash in more securities, or arrange a more advantageous long-term loan from the bank. Hank and Wade seem to think that one hundred thousand will be sufficient. Hank was tipped earlier by a friend that they aren't going to allow a property bond. It's a new weapon for the prosecution in their drug war. It's questionable in your case, but we didn't want to sit around arguing points of law while you were incarcerated."

"Thanks, Sinclair," I said. I was awed by the money. I couldn't take my eyes off the bundles. He closed the lid and the spell was broken.

"I'll leave it here while I run back to the bank and do some other errands. You have your gun?"

"Always," I replied.

Jasmine spoke. "It will be absolutely safe here. I belong to the Association."

"The Association?" Sinclair and I both asked almost in unison.

"It's a protection racket," she said. "It's the cost of doing business in this part of town. No one would dare cause a disturbance, vandalize, or rob this place. Did you happen to notice the daisy painted over the front door?" We both shook our heads, no. "It's the symbol that means I'm a member in good standing. If anyone causes any damage, they will be caught, skinned alive, and hung up in the village square."

"You're kidding!" I exclaimed in horror.

"Just a little," she said with a smile. "They just cut both heel strings and dump them for the gators in the Okefenokee."

"That's better," I said with heavy irony. "I believe we have reasonable expectations of tight security here," I said to Sinclair.

"I wonder if they have a downtown branch?" Sinclair was in deep thought and talking to himself. "You could drop your liability, cut out the debugging sweeps, drop the security patrol's monthly fee. Just pay for coverage on natural disasters. Do they cover residences and vehicles? I bet you could save a bundle by consolidating."

"Sinclair!" I said, sounding shocked. Sounded good to me, too. That shows how far we've come in this modern world; the old protection racket, brought here from the old countries over a hundred years ago, was now sounding like a viable alternative to what we now pay for peace of mind.

"Just a fleeting thought," he assured me. "Back to business. Rosie said tell you she sent," he closed his eyes to concentrate and remember, "the navy voile suit, white blouse, pearls and spectator pumps. If you need a different outfit, Wayne can run it over to you."

"That's fine," I assured him.

"Good," he beamed. "I'll just fetch it out of the car."

Jasmine had seen my expression.

"Maybe something of mine would fit," she offered.

"It's not that." I shrugged. "It's the outfit I wear to funerals." She made no comment. We both were aware of how appropriate it could turn out to be.

The phone rang. Jasmine answered and handed it to me. "Your lawyer," she said softly.

"Hi Sidden," Wade said. "Are you doing all right?"

"Just peachy," I said brightly. "When do we get this show on the road?"

"As soon as the lady judge arrives. She's coming from Savannah. I was lucky. I caught her still at home this morning. She had to sign some papers at her office, then she was going to hit the road. She said to expect her about two o'clock. Knowing Constance, I'm planning on three. Don't expect anything to happen until three."

"Why is she doing this, Wade?"

"She was a near and dear friend of my father, if you get my drift." He tried to sound casual and almost succeeded. "Another thing, she's Judge McAlbee's boss. She's head judge of this district and didn't like the aspersions I was casting on one of her own. She wants to see for herself what's going on down here. I hope to Christ we can convince her the allegations are untrue. If not, we're both dead meat."

"Thanks for sticking your neck out for me," I told him.

"Anytime. We're friends, remember?" I almost said, "Oh yeah?" but I decided I shouldn't push my luck. If I pissed him off and he dropped me, I could end up "Polaroid of the Month" down at the local jail.

"Get some rest," he advised. "I want you composed, dignified and, most important, mute, when I pick you up."

"Composed, dignified and mute," I repeated quickly. "Any other instructions?"

"Yes," he spoke softly. "Lose the wise-ass attitude." He hung up.

I just sat there. What was wrong with me? He was trying to help and I was being bitchy. I felt lousy. I wasn't in control. My fate was being decided by an elderly female judge, a gung-ho deputy who supposedly had the hots for me, a tax attorney, a retired whore, not to mention Wade, whom I had known a total of one week. They were mine and in my corner. Who did I think I rated, Marvin Belli and Mean Joe Green? Jasmine came back through the business door carrying a tray loaded with delicious-smelling food, and Sinclair entered with my court garb in a plastic garment bag, along with my blue duffel bag. As he left he gave me a hug and Jasmine a pat on her back. I was sure he would have been happier if he could have reversed the gestures. He turned down Jasmine's offer of food and said he had to run.

On the tray there were two barbecue sandwiches loaded with a rich, thick sauce; creamy cole slaw; and delicious-looking baked beans. It was one o'clock in the afternoon. Jasmine placed the tray on the coffee table and fixed me a plate. I sat on the sofa and enjoyed every bite.

"The condemned ate a hearty meal," I stated, sated.

"The food at the jail is atrocious," she said casually, then looked stricken. I managed a laugh.

"Oh ye of little faith," I quipped.

I told her we couldn't expect any action until three o'clock at the earliest. After we had stuffed ourselves she led me to the bedroom, insisted I undress and take a nap. I said I couldn't possibly sleep. She said to try. I did, and I did.

27

"AS SMOOTH AS SILK"
April 13, Tuesday, 3 P.M.

Jasmine shook my shoulder to wake me. She said Wade had called to say he was on his way. I washed my face and dressed in the clothes Sinclair had brought earlier. The high-necked blouse felt all right in this air conditioning, but I would swelter in the courtroom. If I was going to spend a lot of my future time in the courthouse I would have to arouse the citizenry to find some way to afford air conditioning. But first, I had to stay out of jail.

I brushed my hair vigorously and when no flakes landed on my jacket, I took it to be a good omen. I was also having a good hair day. Since I didn't give a tinker's dam whether my hair looked good or not, every strand lay curled in the proper order. I decided to stay with pale makeup, but then remembered the TV lights. If they were on the scene, my pale complexion would make me look embalmed. I applied bright red lipstick, a little blush and a smidgen of pressed powder. If I had to face a trial by jury, I would wear my war paint. I went out to seek Jasmine's approval.

She inspected me thoroughly, having me turn slowly while she checked my hemline. She ran for her manicure scissors; I had a dark blue thread peeking below the hem. She snipped it and checked the balance of the hem for flaws. She dropped a couple of drops of Murine into each eye because she said they were a tiny bit red, which probably meant they looked like two cherries floating in buttermilk. She cautioned me to sit carefully; voile creased so easily, especially lined voile. I told her I would stand the entire journey. She smiled nervously.

My hand had picked up a slight flutter from somewhere, and I was blinking too often for comfort. At last, Wade arrived. I took in his apparel. He looked ready to argue a case before the Supreme Court. He was very handsome, suave, urbane, a typical Back Bay Boston aristocrat to his fingertips. He smiled at Jasmine as I stepped forward to intro-

323

duce them. Remembering the fifteen grand he had donated to the bail pot, I reached up and gave him a hug. He seemed embarrassed by my display of affection.

I was having trouble reading his reactions. He must be a little uptight about his first appearance in court down here. Nah, that couldn't be the reason. He had been a prosecutor with a busy calendar in Boston. He wouldn't let my case throw him. I'd worry about what was bugging him later. I hugged Jasmine and she wished me luck.

We walked through the small dining area of Jasmine's business, observed by four surprised patrons and one astonished waitress. I knew she was trying to figure out how I got past her and inside Jasmine's apartment. Wade held the rear door of his sedan open and I slid in to sit beside Sinclair. Wade handed the briefcase, with the cash, to Sinclair and closed the door. Sinclair placed the case on the carpet between his knees. I glanced in front of me and saw a small woman who looked to be in her sixties with short, curled gray hair. Her hair was so thin and the curls so evenly spaced, they looked glued to her scalp. The face was wrinkled, the lips thin and drawn together, but her smile was pleasant. Wade climbed in and started the introductions. She was half turned in her seat and didn't offer to shake hands. She stated she suffered from arthritis and fluttered her fingers. I thanked her for coming.

"Don't thank me yet," she answered with tartness. "If the hearing is conducted correctly, I won't interfere." She turned back to face forward.

I decided silence was the best policy.

Sinclair asked me, "Are you nervous?" He placed a hand over mine.

"Terrified," I answered.

Wade glanced back at me as we waited at a red light.

"Don't answer any questions unless I'm present. If there are reporters, as we are going in, don't make any statements. Let me do the talking."

"Yes, sir," I said humbly. He started to comment, glanced at the judge and changed his mind. Only the muted sounds of traffic could be heard. The air conditioner hummed away and kept us cool. I would have been cool without it. I had a chunk of ice in my chest. I thought about the highly seasoned baked beans I had eaten for lunch. I certainly hoped they wouldn't cause flatulence here in this quiet, enclosed space with three silent witnesses. I practiced tightening the ol' puckering strings.

We arrived at the courthouse and Wade pulled into a perfect parking space, directly in front of, and fifteen feet from, the courthouse steps. That figured. If it had been me, I would have circled the block twenty times and still not found this perfect spot. Either you have it, or you don't.

I opened my door and climbed out. Judge Constance Dalby waited for Wade to open her door. She exited the car with slow dignity and started up the steps. She was wearing a gray silk dress that didn't possess a wrinkle and she had driven over a hundred miles to get here. Under the same conditions, my silk would have looked as if I had slept in it. At a gesture from Wade, Sinclair switched his briefcase to his left hand, hurried up the steps and offered his right arm to the judge to escort her in.

Wade fell into step with me.

"Behave yourself in there, Sidden," he cautioned.

I stopped dead on the steps and faced him. "I'm house-broken, toilet-trained, and know how to act in polite society," I hissed through clenched teeth. "You're treating me like a simpleton who has to be locked in the back bedroom when company comes. Cut it out."

"It's only because I don't know what damn foolish thing you're going to do next," he whispered hotly. I started to really zing him and caught myself. I clamped my lips together and forced a calm, dignified expression to appear.

"Shall we go in?" I presented my left elbow. He took my arm in silence and we mounted the steps. The chunk of ice in my chest seemed to grow with each step. We passed the corridor that led to the sheriff's department without being spotted.

I felt like I was wading through water with the tide against me. I began to put a little push into each step. Wade pressed his fingers into my flesh above my elbow to slow me down. We entered the corridor that led to the courtroom. With my peripheral vision, I spotted a deputy whose name I couldn't recall. He suddenly stopped, gawked, reversed his direction and hit the back stairs, going down almost in a gallop. Sheriff Carlson was about to be alerted.

As the four of us entered the courtroom, a bailiff was sitting on the edge of the recording clerk's desk, and Charlene, seated at the prosecutor's table, was reading papers. No defense attorney was present and Judge McAlbee wasn't on the bench. We had arrived during a recess. The bailiff quickly slid off the desk and headed for the judge's chambers to warn him; he had recognized Judge Dalby. The recording clerk looked flustered. She didn't know if she should acknowledge our presence or not. She decided to ignore us.

Charlene was so intent with the papers before her, she didn't realize anything was amiss until Judge McAlbee entered the courtroom like he had been shot from a cannon. He was flapping his arms so hard, trying to half run and fasten his robe at the same time. I couldn't help but think he was going to levitate to the bench.

Charlene raised her head and turned it in our direction. Wade opened the wooden gate and escorted me in front of the judge. I could feel her eyes on my back and I heard her chair scrape on the floor as she pushed it back to rise. Judge McAlbee still had his gaze directed toward Judge Dalby and I guessed he was trying to formulate a greeting. Charlene wasn't aware that Judge Dalby was being seated by Sinclair in the second row behind her. There were approximately twenty spectators scattered about the room. A few had stood when they saw the judge enter, but were now settling back in their seats. I had spotted no media members in the room as I was walking down the center aisle.

Since Judge McAlbee was still silent, Charlene took the initiative.

"Your Honor," she stated in a loud voice," this woman is under indictment for attempted murder. The sheriff should be summoned to arrest her."

"Your Honor," Wade also used a loud voice, which at last captured Judge McAlbee's attention, "my client, Jo Beth Sidden, has just been made aware of the charges against her and is here to surrender to the court. I respectfully request an emergency bail hearing so my client can go about her daily business of saving lives."

"The state is opposed to bail in this case, Your Honor," Charlene called out. She glared at the bailiff. "What's wrong with you? Go inform Sheriff Carlson this minute!" The bailiff stood. He didn't know whether to go or not. He looked up at Judge McAlbee.

"I think bail is appropriate in this case," mumbled Judge McAlbee. He had finally decided his course of action. The missing sheriff and Buford Sidden, Senior, were future bad news. The slight figure in the second row was his boss and was in the immediate here and now.

"What?" screeched Charlene. "There's no bail in this case. That was understood!"

"Young woman, I will not be spoken to in that tone of voice in my courtroom," he thundered. "You're an officer of the court and I demand an apology, or I'll find you in contempt of court!" I saw now how Judge McAlbee was going to play this scene. He was going to throw Charlene to the wolves, maybe even the sheriff. I didn't give a damn about the sheriff, but Charlene was playing without a scorecard. Granted, she was a bitch, but she was also a sister. I slumped and started mumbling that I had to sit down. Wade was so intent in watching the judge he didn't realize I had defected and was taking backward steps, getting closer to

Charlene and the prosecutor's table. Charlene, in seeing my distress, had instinctively reached out to support me. I let most of my weight sag against her and she was forced to lower me into the chair; she couldn't support my full weight. I whispered quickly into her ear.

"Cool it. Judge Dalby is in the second row. You're being set up."

I felt her stiffen, her only acknowledgment of hearing me.

"Are you all right?" she questioned in a neutral voice. She started pounding me on my back. That isn't what you do to a person who feels faint, but it wasn't a bad move. I started coughing, and she kept pounding away. Wade had reached me and was anxiously hovering and patting my right shoulder. I straightened, accepted Wade's handkerchief and held it to my sweaty brow.

"Enough," I said to Charlene and coughed into the handkerchief one last time. I told Wade I was fine and stood up.

"Are you able to continue?" asked Judge McAlbee.

"Yes, Your Honor, I feel much better," I replied.

"Your Honor," said Charlene in her nicest voice, "I sincerely apologize for my precipitous speech a few minutes ago. I meant no disrespect to the court. In my zeal to see justice done, I forgot myself and I ask the court's forgiveness. The state will agree to a fifty-thousand-dollar bail, in cash, no property deeds as security."

"I think twenty-five thousand dollars is quite sufficient, due to the nature of this case," Judge McAlbee snapped back. He didn't like the way Charlene was landing on her feet.

"The state agrees," she responded swiftly and sat down.

"My client agrees," Wade answered smoothly.

"The defendant will be remanded into custody until bail has been posted," answered the judge.

"I have the money right here, Your Honor," said Sinclair, as he entered the arena with his briefcase. He had it on the clerk's desk and opened before the judge could blink. He started stacking banded bundles of bills in front of the astonished clerk. She picked up a packet and started to count it.

"You may sit down until the clerk can issue a receipt," the judge told us. We turned, Wade took my arm and guided me through the gate to the first bench. We sat down in front of Judge Dalby.

"Court is adjourned for ten minutes. Bailiff?" Judge McAlbee flapped his way out of court. The bailiff hurried after him.

In less than two minutes the bailiff was back and he walked over to where Judge Dalby was seated. "Judge McAlbee wants to know if you'll join him in his chambers, Judge Dalby."

"Thank you," she answered him. She walked steadily out of the courtroom with the bailiff leading the way and never glanced in our direction.

Charlene sat quietly, shuffled her papers, and pretended to read them. She didn't fidget or turn around. She was waiting for the same thing I was waiting for, the appearance of the sheriff. The clerk was still counting money, and Sinclair was watching her count. There was a low hum of disjointed conversations in the cavernous room. More people had filtered in, probably on the case that had been in recess when we arrived.

The sheriff must have been out of his office. He had had plenty of time to show up by now. I sat and tried to imagine what would be happening to me now — if Wade hadn't known an influential judge, if Sinclair hadn't been able to put his hands on sufficient money, if Jasmine's place hadn't been a safe harbor until a safety net was in place for me.

So far, it had gone like clockwork, but I was still on shaky ground. I had to find out what kind of evidence Charlene thought it would take to prove my guilt. I needed to know who had busted up Bubba and also who had tried to frame me. The only conclusion I could reach was that if Charlene had some type of evidence, someone had to have planted it. Whoever planted the evidence wanted me found guilty. It had to be someone who wanted Bubba dead and didn't want to pay the price for making him that way. I would have to find out who hated him enough to kill him. It seemed that whoever it was should have made sure he was dead before dumping him. An idle thought crossed my mind; maybe the person hadn't wanted him dead; that might be why he was still alive. That didn't make sense. Mentally I was going in circles. The puzzle was missing a lot of pieces.

I heard heels clicking against the marble, and more than one set of footsteps rapidly approaching. Neither Wade nor I turned to see who was coming, but I saw Wade's muscles tense through the fabric of his coat. Charlene didn't turn around even when Sheriff Carlson and Hank stopped in front of us.

"Jo Beth Sidden," Sheriff Carlson boomed, "you're under arrest for attempted murder. Stand up." He motioned to Hank. "Cuff her and read her her rights."

Wade started to rise. Sheriff Carlson pushed him back in his seat. "Don't interfere in an arrest, boy," he snarled. Charlene turned in her seat and sat watching. I glanced at Hank. I didn't want him doing anything foolish.

"Get on your feet," the sheriff said to me in a controlled monotone. I put a hand on Wade's shoulder to warn him not to interfere and started to my feet. This man was dangerous. He had worn the mantle of authority so long, he thought of himself as the epitome of law and order. He wouldn't take a lawyer's word, or mine. I thought I knew what Charlene was hanging back for, but I wasn't sure. I thought she was waiting until he had stepped into it good before she gave him the word. She wanted some revenge for almost getting clobbered by Judge McAlbee. However, I didn't know if I could count on Charlene; she might not be feeling sisterly, after all.

As I gained my feet, Sheriff Carlson put a hand on my shoulder and shoved me toward Hank. He caught me. Wade came to his feet and Sinclair came through the wooden gate. Everything was happening at once.

"Sheriff Carlson!" Her voice wasn't raised above a normal tone, but it rang with authority. We all turned toward the woman who spoke. Sheriff Carlson was staring into the steely eyes and grim countenance of Judge Constance Dalby. He removed his hat and smiled at her.

"Howdy, Judge Dalby," he said with genuine pleasure. "I'll be with you in just a few minutes. I'm arresting this woman for attempted murder."

"Sheriff, she has posted bail and is free to go," she said clearly.

"Bail?" he said with a puzzled expression. "This woman here?" He pointed at me. "She's not allowed bail, unless she can come up with one hundred thousand dollars," he said. "Judge McAlbee is denying her bail."

"Judge McAlbee granted twenty-five thousand dollars, cash bail, at least twenty minutes ago," she informed him. "You're mistaken."

"Twenty-five thousand?" He still hadn't caught on. "No way, we decided on one hundred thousand, cash money, and no property or deed security," he corrected her.

"Since when do a judge and sheriff collude on bail, discuss it, and decide on an amount?" she questioned. He stared at her. The message was penetrating his brain that things were no longer going as planned. It finally dawned on him just whom he was discussing bail with.

"Ah, twenty-five thousand, you said?" He was stalling for time.

"It has been posted. Ms. Sidden is free to go," she told him.

"Well, if bail's been posted, I better be getting back downstairs," he stated. He looked around like he was searching for something or someone.

"Sheriff Carlson," she said.

"Yes, ma'am," he said, still gazing everywhere except toward her.

"There have been some disturbing allegations made to my office. I don't think an investigation is needed at this time, but since this is an unusual case, I feel I should make what I'm saying to you very clear. If Ms. Sidden is to be arrested or to be picked up for questioning, I want to be informed personally before it happens. Do I make myself perfectly clear?"

"Yes, ma'am," he replied.

"Thank you, Sheriff," she told him. She started down the middle aisle of the courtroom in the slow deliberate walk I had seen earlier.

Wade, Sinclair and I followed her out, walking a discreet distance behind her. We walked in together and I didn't see the need or reason to separate going out, but Wade kept slowing me down and letting her walk alone. I finally asked him why.

"She didn't like what she had to do in there today," he explained. "I don't want you talking to her until she has a chance to calm down. You don't know it, but she's very angry. She had to side with you today and publicly chastise two officers of the court. She knows it's not entirely your fault, but it still galls her."

"Entirely? She knows it's not entirely my fault?" I glared at him in disbelief.

"Don't start, Sidden," he warned.

I closed my mouth, but I was boiling inside. Who the hell did he think he was talking to. Entirely? I was flabbergasted.

Judge Dalby was waiting in the car. We had another silent trip across town.

When we pulled in front of Jasmine's establishment, I was prepared to say my thanks and depart. Judge Dalby spoke.

"Wade, will you and Mr. Adams allow me a few words with Ms. Sidden?"

They bailed out of the car like they had been goosed. It appeared I was going to converse with the judge alone. She turned in her seat, trying to face me. I slid over just enough so she wouldn't get a crick in her neck and her angle of sight wouldn't be so sharp.

"Why did you warn the prosecutor that she was being monitored by me, Ms. Sidden?" She sounded calm and I didn't hear any anger in her voice.

"I didn't want to see her sandbagged. She's a dedicated prosecutor, and we all make mistakes from time to time. She is angry with me about a personal matter and just chose the wrong cohorts in seeking revenge," I said with truth. I decided not to try and con this lady. She had the power to blow me out of the water.

"I thought you considered her your enemy," she remarked.

"We share a common struggle, Judge Dalby. The bond of sister-hood overrides the lesser personal squabble."

"Very commendable. I could have used some of the 'sisterhood' you mentioned while I was fighting my way up in my career choice. My generation didn't help each other as much as we should have. I hope Wade's assessment of your innocence is correct. I wish you well and hope you have a successful conclusion with your case, Ms. Sidden. You may tell Wade I am ready to leave."

I thanked her and left to find the men. A very nice lady. I felt much better. Things were looking up again. I joined Wade, Sinclair and Jasmine in her living room. I spoke to Wade first.

"She's ready to leave, Wade. Thanks again for your help. Sinclair will return your money. Send me a bill."

"You can expect one," he snapped. He said goodbye to Jasmine and left hurriedly. Sinclair walked to me, put his hands on my shoulders and raised an eyebrow.

"A little abrupt?"

"It hasn't been one of my better days, Sinclair. I'll think about it tomorrow," I said wearily. I reached and gave him a hug.

"Thanks again. Get Wade's and your money back to work earning interest. Put the two thousand of mine in my checking account. I have a lot of things to buy and the insurance will take weeks."

"Yes, ma'am, and I'm sending you a bill, too."

"Of course you are," I said with a grin. He blew a kiss to Jasmine and left.

"I'm so glad everything worked out okay," Jasmine told me. "You look beat. Want to talk about it?" She seemed concerned.

"Thanks, but I'll take a rain check, if I may. I'm so glad to have met you and I appreciate all your help. Will you have lunch with me soon? Can I call you?"

"You're welcome, and please call, I'd love to see you again."

I changed into my skirt and blouse. I hate to drive wearing heels and hose. I gathered all my belongings and climbed into the van. I couldn't believe it was only a little after four o'clock. It seemed this day had already lasted a week. I headed for home and for once decided not to plan ahead on anything. I just rested and drove, thinking about taking a shower and having a few cold beers. That sounded like a winner to me.

When I drove into the courtyard, I saw two vehicles, one with a "Computer Center, Inc." logo and the other a Standell's delivery truck. Well, the shower would have to wait, but I could still have the beers.

Rosie came out on the back porch and wanted to know what happened. Rosie has a very infectious giggle. I giggled back.

The furniture men were just leaving. Rosie had arranged the pieces, not to my liking, but I would change them in a few days instead of doing it now. I told her the arrangement looked fine.

The computer expert used a lot of strange words I didn't understand, but I didn't care as long as the computer worked. He had been able to retrieve all the collective knowledge that was in the machine. That was good news. The bad news was the bill. He had tactfully left it on my desk. I winced when I saw the total cost. I decided he hadn't been tactful, just prudent. He wanted a head start out of here before I saw the cost of a new machine and his efforts to save my data. Thank God for insurance.

Over my first beer, I told Rosie what had happened in court today and about Jasmine. She said she would like to meet her. I suspected she wanted to pump Jasmine about her past life and her knowledge of men. She might be able to clarify a few fuzzy facts for me, too.

She informed me that O'Henry and Sally were no longer with us. Mr. Hanaiker had picked them up soon after she called him. I felt a twitch of remorse about selling them, but that was a foolish reaction. Wayne was minus his stitches and the wound had almost healed. She told me Wayne had seen Jason Colby's youngest daughter, who was sixteen, and she was expecting. We both tut-tutted. Here was a teenager whose biggest worry in the past had been what she was going to wear on Saturday night. Now she was facing motherhood.

While we were sitting at the kitchen table, Rosie remembered the cougar pictures. She left to get them. The pictures were great. Two or three were a little too dark for perfect clarity, but most had enough light and were excellent. I'd call the Florida Game and Fish Commission tomorrow. They should be very excited about this surprising news. Rosie said she had cleaned my suit with the dried mud from yesterday, and Wayne had already repacked the backpacks. I thanked her and asked if she or Wayne had found my missing gloves. She said they hadn't.

Rosie left for the kennel and I opened my second beer. I suddenly jumped up, determined to find those gloves. Taking the beer with me, I went to the grooming room. I started a "Jo Beth hunt" which required searching in a scientific manner. I started at the top of every room and surface and searched carefully to the bottom. Everything was moved, looked under and put back in place. I was pleasantly exhausted when I finished. About halfway through, Wayne and Rosie joined me.

After our unsuccessful search, the three of us shook our heads. The gloves were not on the premises. I had a clear memory of placing them on the workbench when I returned from Tessie's rescue on Friday afternoon. I took care of my equipment. Maintenance was one area I never let fall too far behind. I knew I had placed the gloves on the bench to clean them and rotate them with another pair. They were gone, and suddenly I knew with certainty they had been stolen and who had taken them. Another piece of the puzzle fell into place.

I returned to the office and called Jackson Hanaiker's motel. He had checked out about two hours ago, leaving no forwarding address. I called freight dispatch and found no record of the dogs being shipped anywhere this afternoon. I thought he might have been lying about traveling with them. For what reason would he steal a pair of gloves that were too small for him. I was almost certain he had stolen them, but why? The gloves weren't valuable. I ordered three pairs at a time. If I rotated them, they wore well for six months or so; then I replaced them. I questioned Rosie and Wayne again. There was a faint possibility that one of the two women who had viewed the dogs had taken them. Rosie and Wayne were both certain they hadn't left their customers alone for a minute; they hadn't had an opportunity to lift them. Hanaiker had. I had left him alone when he asked to use a bathroom. I had wandered to the kennel to wait for him. He had plenty of time to pick them up and put them in his car, but why?

Just as I opened beer number three, a little after six, Hank called. We discussed Jasmine and what had happened at the courthouse.

"Who has the Polaroids? I want a peek," he kidded. At least I assumed he was kidding.

"Wade does, in a sealed envelope," I replied. "You have a large collection?"

"I see Jasmine filled you in," he said. "I don't collect them, but I've been buying back Jasmine's over the years. I think I have most of them. I'd appreciate you not mentioning this to Jasmine."

"My lips are sealed. It's a nice gesture, Hank."

"I've told you all along I'm a nice guy, you just don't listen."

"I'm finally sold. Thanks again for what you did for me today. Without you, it would have been a disaster."

"Do you think Charlene will thank you?"

"Who cares? She would have done the same for me, I think."

"I wonder," Hank replied in a thoughtful manner.

I soaked in the tub for a half hour with beer number four. While drying off, I looked at myself in the new mirrors. Rosie said the installers had been fast and efficient. She said they had been eaten up with curiosity about all the broken mirrors and she finally took pity on them and told them what had happened. She said she hoped I didn't mind. I did, but I knew it had to be all over town and a sanitized report had been in Fred's paper, so why not tell Waycross too? I told her, of course not.

Every mirror had been replaced except the dresser mirror. It had to be ordered and it would take two or three weeks. It had to be ground or something because of the shape. I would have to call a drywall man to repair the holes before I could call a painter. I was just thankful I felt the same about my house, and still loved it, even with its present blemishes. At least Bubba hadn't destroyed this part of my life.

Rosie brought in a platter of goodies, saying she knew I needed to relax. Veal cutlet, macaroni and cheese, spinach salad, and two blueberry tarts. I saved three bites of the cutlet for Ruby's dish and devoured the rest. I ate at the desk while going through my address book trying to pick out someone who worked at the hospital and whom I knew well enough to pump for information about Bubba. In the P's I finally found a friend — Glydia Powell would do nicely. I hadn't seen her in over a year. I hoped she was still working there.

I called her at home. A young voice explained that her mother was in the bathroom, but she could take a message. I left my name and number. I was finishing the last of the tarts when she called.

"Glydia, do you know anyone in the intensive care unit?"

"You're in luck. It's on my rotation. I have the seven-to-three shift, starting Thursday morning. Worried about Bubba?"

"Only to the extent I was indicted this morning for attempting to murder him. I'm out on bail."

"What were they thinking about?" she said with laughter. "Don't they know if you had done it, it wouldn't have been botched? You would have finished the job. He sure deserves killing. I know the girl he assaulted in eighty-five. She is a friend of my sister, Kate. Did you know her?"

"No, but after I filed for divorce, I went to see her when she got out of the hospital. Is she any better?"

"She's almost a basket case. She's seeing a psychiatrist, but I don't think he's doing her any good."

"Have you heard anything about Bubba?"

"The word is, he probably won't make it. Extensive internal damage and he had a few wallops on his head, which caused the coma. I'll know more when I go on shift Thursday, or do you need to know sooner?"

"Thursday will be fine, Glydia, and thanks so much."

"You're welcome. I'll call Thursday night."

"Thanks."

In the kitchen, I washed the plate from supper and replenished the iced tea glass. Back in the office, I sat and smoked and cogitated. I searched through the desk and found the Waycross phone book. It always feels odd, using a regular-sized phone directory. Balsa City's is the size of a large greeting card, about forty pages, with the first twenty-five explaining how to use the phone. We call eight-hundred numbers for repairs and the business office. Our repair number is ninety miles away and our business office is one hundred and eighty miles away. Our payments go to Florida. Another inconvenience of living in paradise with large uninhabited areas.

I looked under Private Investigators and found three listed. Two sounded like business security. Only one was listed with a person's name. I decided I would try George Harris. He sounded more my speed — a lone wolf, not affiliated with a larger agency. Probably starving to death in Waycross, which would be considered a very small town to the rest of the world. To us, however, it was a metropolis.

I reached his answering machine and left my name and number. I was dressing for bed when he returned the call at nine-fifteen. I reached the phone before it started the message.

"Mr. Harris, my name is Jo Beth Sidden. Would your schedule allow you to do an investigation for me in Balsa City? It might take several days."

"What would I be investigating, Miz Sidden?"

"I was indicted by the grand jury this morning on an attempted murder charge."

"I was aware of that fact, Miz Sidden. You were on the six o'clock news. Doesn't your lawyer have his own investigator?"

"I believe the answers I need are entwined with my personal life. It wouldn't be unsavory or illegal. Are you free to help me?"

"I can be there tomorrow afternoon, after lunch. Is that satisfactory?"

"Yes, that will be fine. I live at my kennel's location. Do you need directions?"

"I've seen your sign on Highway Three-oh-one, going to Balsa City. I'll see you around one."

"Thank you," I said and hung up. I could have kicked myself the minute I hung up; I had forgotten to ask what he charged per day. Not very businesslike. Now he would think I was an airhead with money to burn.

I puttered around, doing nothing remarkable, just a few chores. My cleaning schedule was in shambles. I had to get my life organized and back on track. I went to bed and dreamed of huge, white women with no clothes on. They had large, pendulous breasts and distended stomachs and encircled me, threatening and menacing, each of them brandishing a plumber's helper. Go figure.

28

"EVEN A BLIND HOG FINDS
AN ACORN NOW AND THEN"
April 14, Wednesday, 6 A.M.

I awoke feeling bright-eyed and bushy-tailed. I was finally starting to help myself instead of just letting things happen to me. I had known for years I had inconsistencies in my life, beginning, I felt, with my birth. My head had been in the sand too long. It was time to deal with what I didn't know about myself.

I put my cleaning schedule back on track and met with Wayne at seven. We discussed his sweeps and then I decided to do some dog training. I was falling behind because of everything that had happened in the past few days. I spent the morning with six puppies that seemed to have forgotten everything I had taught them. Patiently, I started working on basic obedience, working one-on-one for fifteen minutes. That's about the limit of their attention span at six months. Just before ten, I went inside and called the operator for the number of the Florida Game and Fish Commission. A man answered.

"I would like to speak to someone who works with the cougar release program, if I may," I replied to his greeting.

"I'm sure I can help you," he replied smoothly. "You need information, or want to report a sighting?" He sounded like he went through this procedure many times a day.

"Well . . ." I said doubtfully, "I really need to talk with someone who works closely with the program. It will keep me from explaining my information twice."

"If you have sighted a cougar, I can check your sighting information with our known locations. We fly almost daily for a radio check. We'll know immediately if your information is correct. Is that it?" He seemed slightly bored. He sure didn't have a known location for these cougars; they didn't even know these three existed. This information would blow his socks off — if he believed me. I wondered how many erroneous sightings were called in each day by people who had seen house cats, bobcats and other animals. That was why I was so thankful for the pictures. My time would have been wasted without them.

"I saw a mother cougar with two healthy kits day before yesterday just out of Balsa City, Georgia, in a heavy old growth of timber near the edge of the Okefenokee," I told him.

There was a ten-second silence. I imagined him rolling his eyes and shaking his head in resignation. Another mistaken amateur nature buff who loves to make strange phone calls.

"Well, thank you for calling," he said, dismissing my message. "I'll be sure to give them your information."

"Did I forget to mention I have clear pictures of the three of them?"

Another short silence. This time he was thinking I was running some type of scam, possibly for publicity to get my name in the papers. Little did he know. My name was already in the news. Publicity I didn't need or want.

"Would you like to leave your name and number?" Others would know how to deal with this.

"Yes, please." I gave him my name and number.

"I would also like you to write down this name," I told him. "Tell the people in charge of the cougar program to check with James Phelps. He is a game warden in the Okefenokee Swamp at the Fargo Landing. He can tell them I'm not a kook and I have more publicity than I can handle right now. Will you do that?"

"Yes, ma'am, I surely will," he promised. I thanked him and hung up.

I knew they needed the information and I hoped he passed it on. They had high hopes the cougars could adapt to their new environment and multiply and I had proof their program was working. I hoped they would respond. If they didn't, I wouldn't try again.

The answering machine informed me that Wade wanted me to call and Sinclair wanted me to call. I decided to call Sinclair first. I am a procrastinator and when I have a choice, I always take care of the easiest job first. Wade wanted an alibi and I couldn't produce one. Office personnel connected me to Sinclair.

"Hello, Sinclair. This is Jo Beth. You rang?"

"Get yourself down here, kiddo, sometime today. You have to sign your income tax forms, plus the very small check to pay them, since I'm such a great finagler and reducer of taxes. Today's the fourteenth. Tomorrow at midnight the eagle squeals, you know."

"Oh God, Sinclair, I had completely forgotten the tax deadline. You spent most of the thirteenth running around gathering money for my bail, when this is the busiest and most hectic time of the year for you, and you didn't even mention the fact. I'm so glad you did. I have no desire to be locked up, but it cost you valuable time. Can you ever forgive me?"

"No forgiveness needed, just part of my service. I'm so organized, I only had to work until four in the morning to get caught up. This, of course, will be reflected in the enormous bill I send you for my services."

"Thanks, good friend. I'll make it up to you. How about I give you my first-born son and sing your praises to everyone I meet?"

"Forget the first-born, I already have three who are bankrupting me physically and mentally, as we speak."

"I'll be down sometime today."

"See ya," he said and hung up. Boy, I didn't deserve his loyalty, but I was thankful to have it. I grimaced and dialed Wade. His temp connected us.

"Wade, this is Jo Beth. Did you have a question?"

"Just where were you from noon until two on Monday. A simple request, any lawyer would agree. Why the secrecy?"

"Sorry, Wade, truly I am. I was out riding, saw no one, ate nothing, didn't buy gas and can't prove where I was. Sorry."

"So am I. Do you wish to hire another attorney?"

"Only if you're bailing out on me. Is that what you want?"

"I can't defend you properly, Jo Beth, if you tie my hands. I can see me now, facing a jury. 'Ladies and gentlemen, my client has no alibi. She is a busy businesswoman who took an aimless drive in a town she has lived in all her life. She can't cross a street without meeting a dozen people who know her, but strangely, on this day when she desperately needs to have an alibi, she wasn't seen and can't produce one witness to her whereabouts for over two hours. Keep in mind, this was while her ex-husband, whom she hated, was being beaten within an inch of dying.' It wouldn't fly in Peoria and it won't work here."

"Sorry. Riding around still stands."

"Very well. I'm drawing up some necessary motions this morning to start the case, but I suggest you look for another attorney in the near future. The trial won't be for several weeks, but the new man will need all the time he can get with that defense."

"I see," I said evenly. "Thank you for your services, Wade. I'll let you know when I find another lawyer. So long."

I hung up and sat there thinking. He sure didn't protest too much.

Well, so be it. I had a lot of other things to worry about — I'd worry about him later.

At noon, I put the puppy I was working with back in his pen and told Rosie and Wayne I was expecting an investigator I had hired to be here about one o'clock. I said he would take up the rest of the day and not to count on me. I might have to leave with him sometime in the afternoon. We were standing in the grooming room when we heard the first gate alarm. Oh hell, I thought, he's early and has caught me looking bedraggled and slobbered on. Bloodhounds drool, especially bloodhound puppies. I needed a shower before meeting anyone. I started toward the house, but Alice's flower delivery van came whizzing around the corner of the courtyard before I could get to the back porch.

I slowed when I saw the writing on the van. Someone was getting flowers and I bet it wasn't me. It wasn't. Wayne met the van and took delivery of a long slim white box. He walked past me with a wink and continued on to where his mother was standing in the doorway of the kennel, watching. She seemed nervous when she realized the flowers were for her. I walked slowly back to see them and ask who sent them. The florist's van didn't arrive here with flowers very often. This was a happening. The flowers were long-stemmed, deep wine-colored roses. Wayne and I stood impatiently waiting while she read the enclosed card. Her face flushed and she told us they were from the fire chief.

"Simon Clemments." I drawled out his name and was asking questions with my eyes. She could only nod, looking first at me and then Wayne. She knew we were going to tease her and she wanted to get it over with.

"They are beautiful, aren't they, Wayne?"

"Beautiful," he signed. "Can we read the card?"

"No," she said in a firm voice. Wayne and I laughed.

"Can you give us a hint?" I asked.

"He asked me to supper on Sunday," she said reluctantly.

"Let me smell them." She held the long box under my nose and I drew in the heavy fragrance.

"I'm going to put them in water," she said hastily and fled. I looked at Wayne and he put both hands under the left side of his chin and batted his lashes at me. I laughed and left to take a shower.

I donned white culottes and a teal-green sweatshirt. I refuse to wear sweatshirts that have business logos, cutesy sayings or pictures on them; I would feel like a walking billboard. I stopped the practice altogether when I noticed people's eyes automatically drop to your chest to read the message you're wearing before they reach your face.

I loaded a ham sandwich with too many olives, knowing the calories would be astronomical. I was going to start eating more sensibly — tomorrow. Tonight was pizza night.

George Harris drove up at ten minutes past one. Punctual and not at all like I had pictured him. He climbed out of a dark blue economy car that looked like a Ford, but I couldn't be sure. Most small cars look alike to me. He stretched and I strolled out on the porch to greet him. He was about five feet, nine inches and thick through the chest. Must do weights, I thought; he had the enlarged neck that went with weight lifting. Brown hair and eyes. A pleasant smile. A little on the stocky side, but good-looking. We shook hands and introduced ourselves.

I led him to the office and we sat in the conversation area, which as yet had no tables or lamps. I mentioned the destruction that had occurred four days ago and the fact that I hadn't finished refurbishing yet, which was why there were spots and smears on some of the walls and some furniture pieces were missing. He said he really hadn't noticed. In a pig's eye he hadn't noticed. I had seen the quick flickered glances upon entering. He had the damn room memorized in a second. I jumped right in.

"What are your rates?" I inquired.

"One fifty per day and one hundred in expenses. Two fifty total."

"Jesus," I said in surprise. " Isn't that a little steep?"

"I'm glad I didn't come here this afternoon to buy a bloodhound," he answered with a smile. "I bet I'd choke on the price of say, a pedigreed one-year-old that's been housebroken and has good manners?"

"Touché," I said with a grin. I decided to try and whittle him down on the expense charges, the only place there was a possibility of economizing.

"I have a perfectly good guest bedroom that won't set me back fifty bucks a night and there's plenty of food around. Not exactly gourmet dining, but neither is Balsa City's. I think I can safely say that Rosie and I could measure up to anything the town has to offer in the way of food, but you might have to cook some of it if I get busy. An apron and the kitchen is not exactly my forte."

"Well," he said with a serious expression, "I don't do windows, if that's part of the deal, but the rest sounds fine with me. I'll keep track of the mileage and out-of-pocket expenses. I have to warn you, however, a detective, in order to gain information, has to occasionally booze it up in a local bar. That's added to your tab."

"Speaking of booze," I offered, "would you like a beer?"

"Sounds good," he agreed. I went to the kitchen, brought back two cold cans and sat down. "Would you like a glass?" I propped my feet on the dented trash can.

"If I do, I'll trot out to the kitchen and fetch it myself. That is the message, isn't it?" His tone was amused.

"You got it," I said with a smile. "Where should I start?"

"With what you want me to find out for you. Then *I* can ask questions," he commented. He pulled out a small black book like mine, and a pen.

"First," I said, "do you have a contract you want me to sign and do you want an advance before we start?"

"I don't have too much difficulty in collecting my fees from people smaller than I am, so I should be able to handle you easily. As for the advance, if I have to buy any information, I might need one. I didn't bring too much cash with me, just two hundred. If I need more, I'll let you know."

"One more question. In telling you what you need to know, I'll have to reveal some confidential information that can't be repeated. In that sense, are you like a lawyer or priest?"

"The only way I resemble a lawyer or priest is I keep my mouth shut or I would be out of business, fast. You have my word, I won't blab your secrets all over town. Now I need a promise. Sometimes the lines get a little blurred when you're trying to secure information people are reluctant to part with. The fine line between legality and morality can sometimes be questionable. I also don't want my methods blabbed around town. What I do, I'll be doing for your benefit. I just need to know my deeds won't come back to haunt me."

"Just as long as you don't kill or seriously maim anyone, you have my word," I assured him.

"Jesus, lady," he said laughing. "You misunderstood me."

"The hell I did," I said quietly. "Listen, I think we're two unorthodox, kindred spirits, you might say, and we like to succeed. I cut a few corners now and then. I've even taken a chance and broken the law a little when I was fairly certain I wouldn't get caught. Just don't go overboard and do anything stupid. The information I need isn't worth it. Agreed?"

"Well, I'm glad we understand each other; it makes things easier," he said with a lazy smile.

"Another thing. I want you to know I didn't attack my ex-husband and leave him for dead on the side of the road."

"Fred has convinced me of that," he said.

"Fred?" I said with a start. "*Dunston County Daily Times* Fred?"

"Yep, I got to his place at eight this morning. We had breakfast together while I read the file he has on you. I have to tell you, lady, you live a colorful life. He has a lot of newsprint on you in his morgue."

"Why don't you call me Jo Beth," I offered. "Lady" was getting to me.

"Jo Beth it is. And you can call me George; you are never called 'Jo,' right?"

"Fred again, I see. That is correct. My ex-husband called me Jo against my wishes. No one has ever shortened it before or since."

"I'll remember."

"George," I said slowly. "Usually detectives are called 'Buck' or 'Jock' or 'Butch' or something; 'George' sounds a little tame."

"George is a famous name," he retorted. "There's 'Peppard,' 'Washington,' 'Bush,' 'Kings I through VIII' from England, and so on."

"There's also 'Gorgeous' and the 'Chicken Man,' Cheap! Cheap! Cheap!" The Chicken Man was a Waycross car lot owner who appeared in his own television commercials dressed in a ridiculous chicken-feathered outfit yelling his cars were "Cheap! Cheap! Cheap!" while flapping his wings.

"You wound me, Jo Beth, just cut me to the quick," he said with a chuckle.

"Sorry, I couldn't resist. I guess I'd better get started."

I told him all my suspicions about my birth, the firm belief I now held that the name "Hanaiker" had something to do with my past, the late-night argument I overheard as a child and the suspicion that my dog-purchasing Hanaiker had stolen a pair of gloves from my workbench.

"Have you ever had a hunch you can't tell where it came from, like a bolt from the blue? Well, I also think the gloves must be the evidence Charlene thinks will convict me of attacking Bubba. Does that make sense?"

"None at all," he said reasonably, "but I've had the same kind of hunch before. We'll just have to find out what makes you jump from A to C, bypassing B. Maybe it's something you know unconsciously and can't bring to the surface of your mind. Stranger things have happened."

"Thank you for not sneering and saying 'woman's intuition' in that manly tone of voice."

"Hey, Fred warned me you were a flaming feminist," he confided.

"Flaming?" I raised my voice. "Flaming feminist?"

"Bad choice," he amended hastily. "How does energetic feminist sound?"

"Much better," I said, mollified.

"I have to meet a guy," he said, glancing at his watch, "thirty minutes from now in a bar I'm not familiar with. Why don't you tag along? You can direct me around your city, unless you have something planned?"

"I haven't a thing planned," I said promptly. "I won't be in the way?"

"Nah. He gets me the scoop I need on local people. We'll huddle in a corner out of earshot for him to pass on the info. Then I'll come back and tell you what I've learned. My guy likes to think of himself as a secret agent. He's missing a couple of bricks from a full load, but his information is always reliable. I won't introduce you. It would spoil his fun."

"Do I need to dress?" I indicated my culottes.

"I have a feeling you'll be overdressed just as you are," he assured me. "He usually meets me in the lowest knock-down dive available."

"I'll just get my purse," I said feeling happy.

In the bedroom, I added small pearl earrings, two white bracelets, a little blush, eyeliner and lipstick. No sense in looking pale and wan. I was in motion, I was doing something. Hot damn, it sure felt good!

While turning into the drive out of the courtyard, I mentioned I needed to stop at my accountant's office to sign my tax returns, if it wouldn't make him late for his appointment. He groaned.

"Oh God, I keep forgetting!" He slapped the steering wheel. "What's today?"

"Wednesday, April 14," I replied wide-eyed. "You haven't finished your taxes yet?"

"Finished? I haven't even started!" He saw my expression.

"I have all the bits and pieces together," he explained, "I've just been putting it off. I hate to sit down and sort it out."

"Maybe I can help," I said thinking fast. "Do you have anyone who could fax your information over here? I could ask Sinclair, my accountant, to work on it tomorrow. There's still a few hours left."

"Relax, Jo Beth, I'm here to help you with your problems, not vice versa. So I'll be a few days late. What can they do, hang me?"

"The word is 'penalize.' They'll penalize you right out of your socks. Why won't you let me try?"

"Not your worry. Case closed. Let's discuss something else." He sounded a little put-off about me wanting to help.

"One of my failings in life is trying to help my friends. I go around trying to neaten up and patch up their lives when I hear they have a problem."

"Why do you think you do this?"

I told him to turn left at the next intersection; we were nearing Sinclair's office.

"I know why I do it. Psychiatrists are wrong. You can understand why you do things, but that doesn't always stop you. My life is such a mess, with no viable solution in sight so I vent my frustrations by trying to put other people's lives together."

"And they don't always appreciate your efforts? Poor baby," he said lightly.

"A few even go so far as to accuse me of being nosy," I said with humor. "The ingrates!"

I told him to park anywhere along the street; we had arrived at Sinclair's office. He parked, I hopped out and ran lightly up the sidewalk into the office building. Sinclair's office was on the second floor and could best be described as controlled bedlam. His three employees were elbow deep in stacks of files and paper-clipped bundles. Cardboard accordion files and large manila envelopes spilled off the desks and were scattered around the room leaving only a narrow trail for passage. I picked my way to one of the desks and gave the girl my name. She frowned and tapped her pencil against her teeth. Without a word, she got up and scooted into Sinclair's office.

She returned quickly with the forms and handed me a pen, making a clear space on her desk so I could sign them. I didn't flinch when I saw the tax amount. He was right; it was lower than last year. I signed the prepared check clipped to the return. He kept a maintenance bank account for me and kept track of my insurance premiums, quarterly social security deductions and withholding worries on my employees. He also calculated their bimonthly checks, a hassle I detested after having muddled through it my first year in business.

By the time I got downstairs it was raining so hard it was streaming down the building's front door and I couldn't see George's car. I stood there for a minute hoping it would slack off and then I saw him easing to the curb about fifteen feet away. I dashed to the car and fell in the open door. He said there should be paper towels on the back seat.

I turned in the seat, leaned over, and looked at what he carried in the back. He sure was prepared. There were all sorts of goodies: a pillow, blanket, sleeping bag, canned snacks, crackers, thermos, ice chest, flashlight, tarp, camera case, binoculars, and several items I couldn't identify because they were neatly wrapped in plastic, but I didn't see an umbrella.

"You don't believe in umbrellas?" I asked as I straightened in the seat and unrolled several sheets of paper towels, patting myself dry.

"Lost mine. Left it somewhere last week and just hadn't got around to replacing it."

"Well, replace it at the bar. You left one somewhere, so you just pick up one somewhere else. It all equals out. It's called supply and demand."

"It's called stealing," he said, giving me a wink.

I was wet. The air conditioner was blowing cold air on my wet skin. This is how you catch pneumonia on a sunny day in April. I sneezed. He turned off the air and lowered his window a little.

"It will be like a steam bath in here in three minutes," I said.

"Better than a rotten cold," he replied. "Which way?"

I hadn't been paying attention. I hate it when other people do that to me. You're driving someone somewhere and you don't know the way. Your guide is yapping away and lets you drive by your turn and doesn't catch it until you're three blocks past. I paid attention and called out the next three turns at the proper time.

When we reached the bar the rain had slowed to a heavy drizzle. I got wet all over again walking from the car. We sat on bar stools with several other patrons who were all talking about the weather, an inexhaustible topic in our area. There was a row of vinyl-covered booths behind us. The back bar was glass, and rows of open bottles stood on the narrow shelves. The roof over the service area was lowered from the room's ceiling, and formed with egg cartons spray-painted black. Typical hole-in-the-wall sleaze.

The bartender was loud, hearty, overweight and about forty. Everyone called him Jack. He came over and asked us about the weather and what would we have. We ordered Budweisers. It's what the rednecks drink, almost to a man. If I owned a bar here I would stock ninety-nine cases of Budweiser and one assorted case of other brands. If you wanted imported beer, they laughed. If you mentioned white wine, they looked at you as if you had just admitted you were gay.

We sat and drank and talked about what everybody else was talking about: the weather, what was on TV, and how the Braves would do this year.

The bartender came back with a folded piece of paper in his hand. I could see the numbers, one through four, spaced evenly on the front fold and circled. I also knew what was inside the fold: "You will pick number three!" I had first seen this trick about fourteen years ago when I was still in high school. He beamed at me.

"Want to make a wager, missy?"

I raised an eyebrow.

"You see this here piece of paper?"

I acknowledged I did.

"It's got four numbers on it. I bet you a dollar I can pick out, in advance, the number you will pick. Want to try it?"

"Sure," I said, placing a dollar bill on the bar. "I bet you can't guess."

He suddenly became serious. He laid the folded piece of paper in front of me. "Pick a number," he said. "You have four choices." He lifted his hands. "Now, I won't touch the paper again. I already wrote down inside the number you will pick; I bet you a buck."

"Nope, not a chance," I said, "I'm very unpredictable."

A flicker of doubt crossed his features. Though eighty-seven percent would pick three, I just might be one of the thirteen percent of the population who would go with one, two or four. If that happened, he would be standing there with egg on his face. I hesitated and drew out the suspense by moving my pencil and hovering over the numbers. I finally took pity on him and dutifully put a large "X" under three. The bartender laughed with relief and gloated. The rest of the patrons relaxed. I decided Jack must be a sore loser.

"Look inside," he insisted, "I knew you'd pick three!" I shook my head and handed him the buck when I had read what he had written inside. Everyone laughed and got back to the business of drinking.

"That was nice of you," George said softly. "I'm surprised you let him win. I had you marked as being too competitive."

"I must not look like a redneck," I said. "We cut our teeth on small scams like that one and the saltshaker and the fly, the five matches and the crumpled five-dollar bill. I took a lot of lunch money away from tenth graders with those tricks. I just couldn't disappoint him. It's not the money; I bet he buys us a drink before we leave. It's the satisfaction, for just a moment, of being the center of attention and feeling superior."

George spotted his contact in a back booth. He said he should be back shortly. I sat and contemplated my image in the bar mirror. The rain had removed most of my makeup and I had finished off the rest by patting myself dry. I looked washed out in the dim light. It was my natural look; I decided to leave it alone.

The annoying drunken Romeo who seems to haunt every bar shambled toward me, breathed heavy beer-laden fumes in my face and leaning a body that smelled like dead catfish against my shoulder.

"Can I buy you a drink, you purdy little thang," he slobbered in my right ear. You can't be pleasant, polite, or ladylike-firm with this type of drunk. I now have ten years experience dealing with this type of aberration. You send them away quickly or they become a pain in the ass. I sent him away quickly.

I gave him a small smile and whispered into his left ear. He straightened quickly, looked at me boozily, and then slowly shook his head. He walked back to his seat, putting one foot directly in front of the other in mock sobriety. I went back to contemplating my image in the mirror.

George slid back on the stool. I glanced behind him to see if I could catch a glimpse of his informant, but he had already left.

"What did you say to the drunk?" he questioned.

"I told him to go back to his seat," I answered.

"Or . . . ," he prodded.

"Or I would use the straight razor taped to my thigh to carve him up a little," I admitted.

"Pretty drastic solution for a helpless and ineffectual drunk," he judged.

"Ineffectual?" I gave him a cool glance. "You weren't downwind from him. He had rotten breath and body odor and was physically leaning on me. I'm not supposed to be offended and get rid of him in an expeditious fashion? Get real," I said in irritation.

"You may have a point," he reluctantly admitted.

"You bet your ass," I said sweetly. I was really tired of men judging my every move and action, making allowances for other men and assuming I went for the throat far too often. I should have left it alone and not pursued justice.

"What you wanted and expected me to do was what we females have done in the past for generations when we receive unwanted attentions. I should have smiled in embarrassment and tried to ignore him, which would only have encouraged him. I should have shied away and tried to make the best of it, pretending to be a good sport until my hero, in this case you, returned. You would have benignly patted him on the back and suggested he leave the little lady alone and return to his seat. You would have even patiently argued with him, at least let him salvage a little of his dignity, and he would have finally shambled away, with you possibly buying him a drink. What crap! The man may have had a lot to drink, but he could walk and he could talk and he could think. He knew he was being offensive. It's a form of harassment they can get away with when they are in their cups. He knew exactly what he was doing. I solved the problem quietly, quickly and efficiently and I get criticized — Jesus."

"Look. I think I owe you an apology. I had never seen the feminine viewpoint before. We men try to look mature and good-natured and understanding in that situation. I guess we don't want people to think we're acting unreasonably. Am I forgiven?"

"Sure," I said.

The bartender arrived with a beer on the house. We looked at each other and grinned. I sensed George was ready to leave, but we sat there, drank the free beer and bought another one before we left.

It was four o'clock when we left the bar. George asked where we could go to talk. I directed him to Big Creek Park about two miles out of town at the edge of the swamp. We sat on a picnic table made of concrete and placed our feet on the seat. He had stopped on the way and bought a six-pack and a bag of ice. He handed me a Bud from the cooler.

The rain had cleared and the park was almost deserted this afternoon. We sat and watched the dark water flowing down the creek bed headed for the Suwannee River and points south. The sun was just behind the huge cypress, bay and oak trees. There was a beautiful rainbow in the east. The rain-cooled air was a bearable and pleasant eighty degrees.

George pulled out his notebook. "I got my informant started this morning at ten, before we talked, on some information I received from Fred. This informant has complete access to several computers; he's considered a computer genius. If you happened to have recognized him, don't ever let on that you know he works for me; I'd never get any information from him again."

"I didn't see him — the bar was too dark," I said. This was true, but George had just told me who his amateur "spy" was. He was "Little Bemis" to the people who knew him. Big Bemis, his older brother, was the town's traitor. He had made All-State for three years in a row in high school and had marched off to play football for South Carolina instead of Georgia because, he insisted, they offered a better deal: a black Trans Am. After four years of glory as a college fullback, he had had only three years in the pros before a hip injury ended his football career, and he faded into obscurity.

During Big Bemis's three years of good money, he had sent his baby brother, then fourteen, a computer for Christmas. Little Bemis was the "Great White Hope" for our high school's chances of, again, having an All-State candidate and any success on the football team. Within a month, Little Bemis quit the football team and spent all his time playing with his computer. The high school coaches and alumni gnashed their teeth, begged, pleaded and threatened to no avail. I heard the rumor that they had even offered him a Trans Am, which was ridiculous, because he was two years shy of being old enough to drive it.

Little Bemis was an outcast and oddball his four years of high school. Upon graduation, he went to work for Apex-Semex, Inc., a timber and strip-mining conglomerate, whose home office was located here, but had state-wide interests. Little Bemis drove a black Trans Am and traded for the latest model every year. He attended all high school football games and wore his older brother's sweater with the football letter. I had assumed he had undying loyalty to his conglomerate. George's access to him gave me hope. I just might be able to use him in the future.

George had been staring at his notebook. He looked up and frowned at me.

"My informant knew the man whose name you gave me, the one you had your deputy run the license check on. He says he has his own dossier on all the players in town. Did your deputy tell you he didn't know the man you asked him to run the plates on?"

I reached into my memory of the phone call from Hank, which had been short and sweet, and ran the conversation through my mind.

"No," I said, "and like an idiot, I forgot to ask him. He was upset about someone or something at work. I think. He was very curt. All he said was the address and hung up."

"I was wondering because the man, John H. Pearson, is Sheriff Samuel A. Carlson's brother-in-law, his wife's brother. My man says that Pearson is rumored to have struck it rich in something in the past several years. He personally suspects drug money but doesn't have anything to back it up, no facts. He says Pearson has been in many business ventures with a man by the name of Andrew J. Carpenter. This Carpenter is a retired lawyer. Know him?"

"Ah, yes indeed. Mr. Carpenter's great granddaddy was a founding father in this town. Andrew Carpenter is local royalty. He's also Carl Bennett's old law partner and Carl Bennett is Wade Bennett's late father, and Wade is my lawyer. Get the picture? So Pearson, our mystery man who was talking with Hector on the stairs, is none other than Sheriff Carlson's brother-in-law. Well, well, the plot thickens."

"You see a connection?"

"Well, don't you? No wonder the pot growers on Wade's property had such a large operation and felt so secure. Sheriff Carlson knows everything the DEA knows about what goes on in this area, including every undercover man they plant and every planned raid."

This also gave me a big break I wouldn't mention to George. This gave me a handle on the sheriff and I already knew how I was going to use the knowledge.

"Fred informed me of your father's will this morning. When your father died last year and you didn't inherit any of his paintings, Fred started digging. The local rumor was your father was holding back a cache of paintings, hoping the price would keep rising as fast as they had in the past few years. Everyone expected to see you selling some of them and start some lavish spending. When you didn't, he got curious and started digging."

"Did he find anything?" I had to ask. I didn't know if George would say if Fred had confided in him.

"Not a blessed thing," George said with a grin. "It really bugged him. Fred likes to know who's doing what to who."

"Whom."

"What?"

"No, whom. I think it's who's doing what to whom."

"Whatever."

"Who's on third?" I asked George. "Do we sound a little like Abbott and Costello?"

"Cut it out," he cautioned. "I'm trying to be serious here."

"You know, Fred should have come to me when he had questions. We could have worked together. We might have saved each other some time."

"You said you knew Fred. He is nosy, he just doesn't want to appear nosy, and you didn't ask for his help."

"My mistake. I should have asked, but I closed my eyes and hoped the mystery would go away."

"Fred read from his notes and gave me the gist of the will, but he must be in error about one fact: there had to be someone named to inherit. That's what wills are for. Have you got a copy at home?"

"Better yet, I have it memorized. I carry it around in my head so I can refer to it often," I told him, using a light, bantering tone of voice.

"Give."

I recited:

"'I, Arthur Henry Stonley, being of sound mind, declare this will, as my final will and testament. This will supersedes any and all prior wills, signed before this date, whether here in the United States of America, or abroad on foreign soil.

After payment of my just debts and all medical expenses, the balance of my estate including all assets of paintings, real estate and cash on deposit, shall be held in trust, with special instructions as to who benefits and date of distribution, with my attorney and lifelong friend, Carl Jackson Bennett.

If Carl Jackson Bennett precedes me in death, the trust will be executed by First State Bank, its Estate Trust Division located at 187 Main Street, Balsa City, Georgia.

Executed this day, the twentieth of January, in the year of our Lord, nineteen hundred and ninety.

Signed, Arthur Henry Stonley'"

"This will was probated last year, just after his death?"

"Yes."

"And you've heard nothing since?"

"Not a whisper."

"What does your lawyer say? How long do you wait?"

"It all depends on who you talk to. Wade, my present attorney, says we have to wait indefinitely, until we hear something from someone. The lawyer I hired last year, after Carl's death and nothing happened, says we'd have a good chance of legally challenging the will seven years after Carl's death, but we would open a can of worms if the will was set aside."

"What is the can of worms?"

"If the will was invalidated, all living relatives would share equally. There are my father's three first cousins; their children, totaling nine; their children's children, totaling thirty-six; and their children's children's children, totaling ninety-two at last count, which was last year. They are so prolific, there's probably a dozen more by now — I don't keep track. And of course last, but not least, you add me to the count. That was the total that the lawyer mentioned, on my last meeting with him."

"Wow," he said softly, "that's quite a can of worms."

"I am hoping for paintings. If there are paintings, they would be dumped on the marketplace at once and sold to the highest bidder. It would effectively drive down the price of my father's paintings forever. This can't happen. I couldn't stand it. Can you understand?"

"I can now."

"What do we do now?" I wanted some action.

"We go back to the house and I start phoning. I'm going to call investigators in several cities and try to track down this Hanaiker who purchased your dogs. That will mean additional fees for the operators. Are you willing to spend the dough?"

"Willing and able," I responded. "Ready to go?"

"Might as well."

We drove home through the fresh air while the shadows lengthened across the road and the sun dipped lower behind the huge forest. I gave him a tour of the house and opened the panels to allow him to view my father's paintings. He made a couple of banal comments and didn't seem impressed. I didn't fault him for his lack of interest. If my father hadn't painted them, I might not have appreciated their worth, or seen their beauty.

He brought in his duffel bag and ice chest. He placed the duffel bag in the guest room and the ice chest by my desk. He pulled out his black notebook and address book and started dialing. I wandered around nervously, going out to check on the dogs, then going upstairs to Rosie's. I told her I was going for pizza. She said she had a deep-dish cobbler and would make a salad. I went downstairs and told George what the two gate alarms sounded like, that I was going for pizza, and Rosie and Wayne were coming down to eat with us.

We ate pizza, salad and wild blackberry cobbler. George switched to iced tea with the meal and I breathed a little easier. Bubba, and others in these environs, once started on beer seemed to crave total oblivion or the benchmark of one full case, whichever came first. We all carried our tea glasses back to the office where we had to set them on the floor beside the chairs and couch. I had to buy some more furniture — tomorrow.

George had little difficulty in conversing with Wayne. Rosie and I were so used to signing and talking for other people's benefit, we never gave it a thought. She translated for George when Wayne was facing her way, and I did the same when he was facing in my direction. Wayne and Rosie left at nine-thirty. George tried some numbers he wasn't able to reach earlier. Shortly after ten, I started locking up and explained my security and my washing machine routine. George asked for a book; he said he sometimes had difficulty falling asleep in strange surroundings. I said good night and left him standing in front of a bookshelf, browsing. I had no difficulty in falling asleep and I didn't dream of large naked women with plungers, thank God.

29

"AS CROOKED AS A COILED SNAKE"
April 15, Thursday, 6 A.M.

The clock radio woke me and I listened to the news. Nothing earth-shattering was happening, except in faraway places. Bosnia and China didn't receive my full attention this morning. I was keyed up thinking about what I would say to the sheriff when I decided to approach him, and hoping we found out something today. I knew it was too soon to expect answers, but I was aching to do something positive, to act, to know. Hell, I'd let the answers drift for years, not really making the effort, and now I wanted to know a million things all at once.

I dressed in jeans and a long-sleeved shirt. If I didn't get to tag along somewhere with George, I needed to do more dog training. I brushed, flossed, and then started the coffee. I turned on the oven and opened canned biscuits, placed six strips of bacon in the countertop broiler, put four eggs in a small bowl and placed it next to the frying pan. I poured a cup of coffee and lit my first cigarette. I was glad George smoked. I was always aware of my friends leaning back away from my smoke, and felt guilty when I read the secondhand smoke studies, but not guilty enough to quit.

I was on my second cup of coffee and third cigarette when I heard George in the bathroom. He came into the kitchen with damp hair neatly combed, and casually dressed in jeans and a short-sleeved shirt. He didn't look a day over thirty. We both said good morning and he poured coffee, adding creamer and one sugar, and then lit up. We sat with smoke curling around our faces.

"How old are you?" I asked.

"Forty-two," he grunted. "Ancient by your standards."

"True, true," I mocked. "Were you in service?"

"One tour of 'Nam with the marines. That was enough for me."

We sat in companionable silence. After he finished his first cigarette, I stood.

"How do you like your eggs?"

"Over easy. Can I help?"

"You can set the table," I replied. "The dishes and silverware are here and there," I said, indicating their locations. I put the biscuits in the oven, turned on the tabletop broiler and sat back down with my coffee. He opened the refrigerator and placed butter, jelly and jam on the table without me having to tell him. I turned the bacon and broke the eggs into the frying pan. When the food was cooked I slid the eggs from pan to plate without breaking the yolks, which was a good omen. He said the blessing. I ate three biscuits and George ate six. We were almost finished when I heard the squeak of the cat door.

"We are about to have company," I told him. "Try not to make any sudden movements, or her breakfast will be delayed about three hours. It's a cat that hasn't yet decided if this is going to be her home."

We sat quietly, and presently Ruby walked trembling to her dish, keeping her eye on us while she hunched over her food.

"Good morning, Ruby," I said in a normal voice. She scooted behind the refrigerator.

"Damn. I got away with speaking to her last time."

"But I wasn't here," he said. "I'm a distraction. How long have you been working to tame her?"

"Since last October," I said in defeat.

"I hate to tell you this, but some cats never learn to trust. Have you tried peeing in her dish?"

"I beg your pardon?" I was shocked. "Surely you jest."

"Some animal behavioral scientists hold with the theory that animals mark the boundaries of their territories with their piss. If you mark her dish, maybe she will understand you're the boss and behave accordingly."

"That's one weird theory, George."

He shrugged. "Worth a try. Couldn't hurt."

"Maybe I'll just threaten her with it," I compromised.

"She's your cat. You'll have to learn to bell her."

He gathered the dirty dishes and started a sink of dishwater. I saved the remaining two bites of bacon for Ruby's dish. When I finished clearing the table, it was time for Wayne to come down. I checked the answering machine and had no messages. George passed by, popping the dishcloth on the way to the washer. A very well-house-broken male. I wondered who had trained him; he could be married for all I knew. I hadn't asked.

He finished in the kitchen and walked into the office.

"Are you married?"

"Not anymore. I was for four years — in my twenties. Single ever since." He shook his head.

"I know what you're thinking; she isn't the one who taught me how to keep house. I taught myself after I got tired of living in a pigsty. I do my own shopping, pay my bills, and keep a neat house. I'm thoroughly domesticated. I even do my own cooking."

"You put off paying your income taxes," I teased.

"Doesn't everybody? I hate paying money to those blood-suckers to waste."

Wayne walked in just as Ruby had gathered her nerve to make a dash for freedom. She skidded to a stop and hid behind the wastebasket. Most of her tail showed, but she thought she was hidden. I asked George if he wanted to sit at the desk to make calls. He chose the couch, saying it was too early. Wayne signed his plans for the day. I told him I didn't have plans, but signed I might train puppies if George didn't need me. I sent word to Rosie I might go shopping for furniture later and if she needed anything to send down a list.

George was telling me a funny story about one of his missing husband cases in answer to my query if he could discuss any of his work. The phone rang and I glanced at my watch. It was an elated Hank.

"Good news, Jo Beth, you're off the hook! I'm at the hospital, been here since three-damn-thirty when they called and said Bubba was gaining consciousness. He's been trying to wake up since two this morning. The good news is: We have a dying declarative statement and he can't back out of it later, when his daddy chews him out for letting you off the hook. He was correctly warned he could be nearing death, and I questioned him with Sergeant P. C. Sirmans and in the doctor's presence. He can't claim confusion. We kept asking for details and he kept supplying them. He's madder at his unknown assailant than he is at you — if that's possible. He says his attacker was a man and he can recognize him if he ever sees him again. They'll have to drop the charges. The doctor is giving us his statement and P. C. and I are heading to the station right now to write up our report. I called you before I tried calling the sheriff. He probably hasn't arrived as yet. Say something!"

"That's wonderful, just wonderful," I blubbered. I wanted to laugh and cry at the same time, and it was coming out garbled. George came over and I handed him the phone and headed for the bedroom. As I was leaving I could hear him explaining who he was to Hank. I lay on the bed and cried with relief. I tried to convince myself that a few tears were for Bubba, but I knew better. I was sure some were tears of disappointment that my problem didn't have a permanent solution, but that made me want to cry more. I thought I was a better person than to wish for a man's death, a man I had even loved — I think — rather briefly more than ten years ago, but I was human. I knew in brief dark moments I had wished for his death.

I finally finished weeping and went to the bathroom to repair the damage. My eyes were red and puffy and I tried using eyedrops. Saying to hell with it, I joined George just as the phone rang. He was sitting at the desk; I waved for him to answer and continued on to the couch.

The call was for him. I could hear him asking questions and could see that he was writing. Since he was using the phone, I wandered out and went upstairs to tell Wayne and Rosie the good news. When I returned, George was just hanging up the phone. He drummed his pencil on the desk and stared off into space.

"What?" I said, suddenly feeling fluttery again.

"The first call was from Fred. He found an interesting item on the AP wire this morning. Remember when he was talking to you last week, and he mentioned a Hanaiker who used to spend winters on Cumberland Island? The man who gave him trouble about a newspaper article?"

"Yes," I said, hardly daring to breathe. I knew this was important and had something to do with me, but I didn't know what to expect.

"Well, it was on the AP that Benson T. Hanaiker, seventy-two years old, from Andrel, New York, and Cumberland Island, Georgia, died at his home last night with complications from heart bypass surgery performed two weeks ago. Seems he had been in a coma for days, but was moved to his home yesterday."

"Did Fred say if any relatives were mentioned?"

"He read me the article. It only had four lines, no mention of any survivors."

"What was the name of that city again?" I reached up on the bookshelf for the atlas.

"Andrel," he answered, spelling it for me. I found it in the extreme southeastern part of the state, population 1,540. Small town? No — tiny town. My mind was racing. I looked back to find the name of the county seat. It was Fontain, population 9,700. Another small town. That should make it easier to find information about someone. I wondered who this man was and why I felt it was important for me to find out more about him. A glimmer of light was being beamed on my puzzle. I felt I now had a working handle on its solution.

"Would you call Fred back and find out if Andrel has a newspaper? I bet it doesn't, not even a weekly, but I bet Fontain has — it's the county seat."

"Gee, we think alike," he noted with a straight face. "I asked Fred to check it, and he's doing just that, probably right about now."

I paced the room. My mind was in high gear. I stopped suddenly.

"George, we have to have someone at that funeral with a camera. We need to know if my Jackson Hanaiker shows up, and we need pictures. Do you think you can find someone to be there?"

"I'll give it a shot as soon as Fred calls back with the information. I told him to be sure and find out where and when the funeral will be held."

"I know you're the investigator," I said with a grin, "but I'm used to working alone. If I step on your toes, just tell me."

"Hey," he said with a shrug, "two heads are better than one. I still get paid whether you or I think of what we need to do next. I've been slightly ahead of you so far, but you might come up with something I missed. It's possible." He sounded like he meant it. Maybe he didn't resent me tossing suggestions around.

"The second call I answered a few minutes ago was the operative I had checking in New York City. He's checked the phone books, utilities, the usual sources for someone well established, and came up with zilch on Jackson Hanaiker, except for his bank account, which, by the way, has less than three hundred dollars as a present balance. Another transfer yesterday of four thousand almost emptied the account. Right now he's working on where the money was transferred."

"I think we're wasting his time. I think I know where the money was transferred. I bet you a hundred bucks it was sent to Jackson Hanaiker's account in Andrel or Fontain, New York. Want to bet?"

"No bet. My mama didn't raise no foolish children," he replied.

"You know, George, the way you found out his bank balance and the transfer of funds yesterday, by just two phone calls, makes me feel uneasy about my bank account being vulnerable. Whatever happened to bank confidentiality?"

"Jo Beth, you're living in a dream world. There never has been bank confidentiality," he said, and I could almost hear the patient sigh as he explained the facts to me.

"Before computers, people kept the books and people will always talk for the right reasons or the right amount of money. Since computers, hundreds of thousands of people scan any information they need by dipping into any computer they want to use, at anytime, day, night, weekend or holiday."

"If you wanted to know my checking account balance right now, how long would it take you?" To me, this didn't seem possible. Even I have to know a secret code to get information if I should need it.

"After I reached my party, about twenty minutes."

Jesus. "How about my savings account, loan transactions, bonds at the bank?"

"Same amount of time. It's all one neatly listed package that scrolls up on the computer, with a touch of a few keys and the right passwords."

"How about my stock purchases, investments?"

"Might take a few minutes longer if my hacker had to go into the exchange computers. There are no secrets in this new electronic age."

It was frightening how much you could find out about anyone so quickly, but it sounded useful. I decided I would get to know Little Bemis as soon as possible. He was the man with the answers.

"George, Hanaiker had to get out here to meet me and he had to have a good reason — so he bought some dogs. God, I should be kicked for selling him O'Henry and Sally. I have no idea what's happening to them. They were his excuse to visit twice, enabling him to pick up something of mine to leave at the scene when he attacked Bubba — but the 'why' is driving me bananas."

"That was a pretty expensive way to meet you, and setting up that bank account cost him time and money. You're making some speculative leaps we can't fill in with facts — yet. Just take it easy, and wait till we get facts, not conjecture."

"You see, he didn't know what I would charge for the dogs. He had asked around and knew the ballpark figure, but he put the extra four grand in his account so he would have enough if I decided to gouge him. And George, he's not rich. He needs that money, or he wouldn't have withdrawn the balance down to three hundred so soon. Why didn't he clear out the account and close it? He had completed his plan. Why leave the account open?"

George shrugged and resumed his phone work. I wasn't very patient. I paced the floor and was getting on George's nerves with my questions. I forced myself to wander outside to see what Wayne was doing. He had called in one of the part-time people we used during school hours, a retired man who lived about two miles away. He loved animals and needed the extra money. I remembered his name was Mr. Dixon. Wayne was training two eighteen-month-old dogs for scent trailing. I walked to the workbench at the edge of the courtyard near where Mr. Dixon was parked. They were working in the field, to the right and slightly to the rear of the kennel. I couldn't see either of them. Rosie was gone with a van. She probably had her arson dogs practicing in one of the abandoned buildings we used downtown. I couldn't keep my mind

on anything for long, so I didn't even take out a puppy to work with —
I was too nervous.

I forced myself to stay outside for thirty minutes, then strolled back
in. George was talking to someone on the phone. I sat quietly and tried
not to fidget. George hung up and picked up his notebook.

"The funeral is Saturday morning at eleven at the First Congrega-
tional Church in Andrel, New York. I'm trying to find someone close by
to cover it. Fred is still trying to reach someone at the paper in Andrel.
It's a weekly, he thinks, and no one is answering the phone."

"We're still in the same time zone up there, aren't we?"

"Yep. Let me continue to run up your phone bill," he told me.

I headed to the kitchen to make iced tea. Time crawled. A little after
ten, I called Wade from upstairs on Rosie's phone. He said Hank had
called him earlier. He said he was glad I was free of the charge. It was a
brief conversation. I mentioned the private investigator I had hired, but
he didn't seem very interested when I started explaining the Hanaikers;
I told him I'd talk to him soon. He acted like a stranger. I wouldn't call
him again unless it was absolutely necessary. I tried to call Charlene but
she was out of her office. I'd try again later. I still had to sign the charges
against Bubba, but there was no pressure. He would be in the hospital at
least a few more days.

I returned downstairs and received more information from George.
He had spoken to Fred again, and Fred had found an old clipping on
Muriel Hanaiker that had slipped between the Hanaiker file and the di-
vider. She was the wife of Benson T. Hanaiker and had committed sui-
cide in 1966 at the age of twenty-seven, leaving a husband and a child.
I wondered if she was Jackson's mother, and why she took her own life.
We would know soon.

George had reached an investigator in Lansing who was trying to
find some trace of Jackson Hanaiker in that city. Hanaiker had stated
that he lived there and commuted to New York. If we found anything
there I would be greatly surprised. George said it was best to make sure
of the negative facts; they could be just as important as the positive
ones.

I went back upstairs and tried Charlene again. She was available
this time.

"Charlene, this is Jo Beth. Do you have the papers ready for me to
sign on Bubba's charges?" I kept my voice neutral.

"Congratulations," she said. That was all. I waited. When I didn't
respond, she spoke.

"Be here at one. Your papers will be ready." She hung up without saying anything else. I could understand that. A lot of ambitious women were sore losers. I was one myself. I didn't fault her for being disappointed that I had wiggled free. She had seen her case go out the window with Bubba's statement. Hank had told George that Bubba had gotten a good look at his attacker and could identify him . . . if he ever sees him again. I hadn't asked, just lifted my brow quizzically. Yes, George had told me, the description could possibly fit Jackson Hanaiker.

I went back downstairs to see what was going on. George patiently told me nothing had happened in the twenty minutes I had been gone. I went back to the grooming room and started polishing Susie and Bo's harnesses. I used saddle soap and worked it in with my hands. I then rubbed the harnesses back and forth on the nubby weave towel we kept tacked to the grooming table. I lost myself for a few minutes in the mindless task. Wayne and Mr. Dixon came in to get a Coke. It's hot work hiding from animals and trying to get them to search for only one smell. Wayne signed that both dogs were coming along nicely. He never expected too much from them and never pushed them.

I told Wayne I was going to the supermarket for something for lunch. I went to Winn Dixie's deli and bought a bucket of fried chicken, potato salad, rolls, and some fresh pastries, tomatoes, lettuce and cucumbers. I was back in the courtyard in thirty minutes. I spread lunch on the table, adding paper plates, and called in the troops.

At one-fifteen, I entered Charlene's office, where a secretary was eating lunch. I signed the papers so Bubba's charges and subsequent warrant could be issued.

The afternoon was completely boring, unproductive and restless. George was outside with Wayne saying he needed to stretch his legs. He had spent most of the day on the phone. A little after six, the phone rang. It was Glydia.

"Hey," she said, "I know you've been told Bubba is awake. They were taking his statement when I came on duty this morning. I thought I'd call and give you an up-date on his condition."

"I'm glad you did. How's he doing?"

"Oh hell, Jo Beth, I won't pussyfoot around. He's going to make it, I'd guess. He seems to have all his marbles. The doctors can't get over the fact that his lungs are clear, since they really took a bashing. If he doesn't develop pneumonia, or a blood clot, or infection, or an aneurysm, or God knows what else, it looks like he'll be able to walk out of here, eventually."

"Thanks, Glydia, I really appreciate your help. If you ever need me, give me a ring — I owe you."

"You bet. See ya."

After supper, while George and I were in the office discussing the information we had uncovered, he looked at his watch and announced he had to go out for a while. I resisted the temptation to ask if I was allowed to tag along. When no invitation was offered, I wrapped myself in my dignity and told him I had loads of computer work to do.

It took almost an hour to enter my sales, bank deposits and other data that had accumulated since Bubba's destruction of my old computer. I returned to the kitchen and made a pot of coffee and sat quietly, drinking coffee and smoking. I let all the accumulated data, all the bits and pieces I had learned thus far just circulate in my brain without pressure for a solution. Within the drifting mass in my brain, I began to see a viable scenario that would fit the facts I had discovered so far. If my cogitation was correct, within the next few days, I could expect a visit or a phone call; no, it would be a phone call from one more lawyer that would confirm my theory. I sighed. I could live with it. I really had no choice. I might not like the solution, but I could live with it.

At 7:30 I took a fresh cup of coffee and my cigarettes to the office and sat staring at the silent telephone. I was trying to ignore the swirling tempest inside me. My mind was trying to use sweet reason, my heart was pumping and jumping — cheering me on — and my gut was whining from the pressure. I reached for the phone book, looked up the number and dialed quickly, before my mind prevailed. The call lasted almost an hour and my hand was unsteady as I cradled the receiver. My mind mentally shrugged and said the deed is done — now you'll have to live with the consequences. My heart was humming a cheerful little ditty. My gut demanded an Alka-Seltzer.

Back in the kitchen drinking the fizzy brew, I watched Ruby nervously make her way to her bowl. When she started eating, I talked in a soft voice and explained to her what I had done. She would lift her head and stop chewing at intervals, giving me a soft, weak "meow" of what I chose to believe was agreement.

I wasn't sleepy, but went to bed a little after ten so I would appear indifferent to George's comings and goings. I was still awake when he returned at eleven. I had flopped back and forth enough to rumple the sheets. I straightened them and lay stiff as a board on a neat bed and prepared for sleep. It took forever.

30

"AS DUMB AS A STUMP"

April 16, Friday, 6 A.M.

I woke at my usual hour and made a huge breakfast for George using country ham, grits and eggs. I even made red-eye gravy, but I still used canned biscuits. I wasn't in the mood to make them from scratch. After breakfast, George did the dishes while I met with Wayne in the office. When he left, George went with him to the kennel for morning rounds.

I had dressed for comfort in jeans and a sweatshirt. I hadn't tried to talk myself into training dogs today because I knew I couldn't train unless I could focus all my attention on the animal. Having only missed a week, I knew a few more days wouldn't mean disaster. I was not going to waste another day like yesterday, moping around and acting silly. I had my answers, and I was going to be productive today, if it killed me. The kitchen was my cleaning chore. So be it, I would give it a thorough cleaning and when the stores opened, I would go shopping for a lot of things I needed.

I was on a kitchen ladder lining a top cabinet with shelf paper when I heard the phone. I jumped down and went into the office to listen to the message in case it was for George, since he was still outside at the kennel. I was just in time to hear James Phelps, game warden extraordinaire, identifying himself on the tape. I picked up the receiver.

"Hi James, this is Jo Beth. How you doing?"

"Just fine. Jo Beth, I need to see you. How busy are you this morning? Can you work me in for a few minutes? I can be there in an hour."

"I'm free at the present time, but there's always the possibility of a call-out. Do you have a car phone?" I didn't want him to drive all this way and be left hanging.

"Yeah, but it's on the fritz again. I'll take my chances. Maybe I'll see you in an hour or so?"

"Sure, come on over." I guessed that wiser heads at the Florida Game and Fish Commission had decided to call James and have him check out what I was making noises about.

Back on the ladder, I heard the phone ring again. I hopped down and dashed back to listen. I had very carefully concealed my irritation from George about being left alone last night, and I was on my best behavior. This call was for me also. It was Wade.

"What can I do for you, Counselor?"

"I have Andrew J. Carpenter sitting in my office and I have some answers. How soon can you get here?" he asked in a crisp voice.

"I'm on my way," I replied and hung up. I raced out to the kennel and found George standing in a corner of the grooming room watching Wayne putting his two scent-tracker trainees through some simple commands. I arrived breathless. My heart was battering my ribs and I was full of hope. I told George about Wade's call and asked if he wanted to come with me.

"It's legal stuff, Jo Beth. They wouldn't want me included. I'll stay near the phone. I'm expecting some call-backs." He noticed my breathing and apparent excitement.

"Slow down, girl. Take a deep breath. Are you okay to drive?" He sounded concerned. I was huffing and puffing like a locomotive.

"Sure," I said casually. "It just threw me for a minute. I'm fine. Be back as soon as I can."

"I hope it's good news," he said.

"Thanks."

I forced myself to walk back instead of running but as soon as I was out of sight I turned on the speed. I dressed in a white shift, white sandals, grabbed a white shoulder bag and threw in the necessary items. No makeup. I ran a comb through my curls on the way to the van. I drove sedately out of the driveway and gave George a casual wave. When I turned onto the highway I developed a heavy foot.

I tried keeping my mind a blank, refusing to speculate. I would know something soon. This was not the expected call I knew would come in a few days. This was icing on the cake, a break I hadn't expected after waiting so long.

Wade's temporary help took my name and departed to tell him I was there. I stood in the reception area and took steadying breaths. She returned and told me to go right in. Wade came to the door and took my arm. He smiled briefly and silently walked me over to introduce me to a man I had seen many times but had never met. I had seen Carpenter around town with Carl Bennett, but I could not remember ever having had a conversation with the man. Wherever he had been, he had acquired a beautiful tan.

He was thin, very well dressed, had white hair and a white Vandyke beard. He was about my height, looked to be in his sixties and was very well preserved. He was wearing a tad too much jewelry for a small-town lawyer. I spotted a large wafer-thin wrist watch, gold cuff links, pinkie diamond and I caught a glint of gold at his throat. This was definitely a no-no, for a seemingly conservative lawyer his age. He was grinning like a Cheshire cat as he accepted my hand and cuddled it within his own. My recent knowledge of him, gleaned from George's informant, made me view his actions with distrust. I managed to hold a polite smile though I felt like asking him how much he had cleared on pot last year.

"My dear Jo Beth," he said with charm. "I'm so sorry I was out of the country when Carl died. It would have been so much easier if I had been here for you and Wade."

"And why is that?" I asked politely.

"I'm the alternate executor of your father's will and also for Wade's father's will." He beamed at me.

"I understand you have some answers," I said quietly. I was ready to get this show on the road and stop pussyfooting around. He had tenderly deposited me in a chair and I scooted it to the right so I could see both of their faces clearly. Carpenter didn't miss my move. He sat a tiny bit straighter and cleared his throat.

"I gave Wade the legal papers and I have a personal letter I am to hand you at this time."

I waited. When I didn't respond verbally, he reached for his brief-case, which was propped against his chair, and pulled out a business-sized envelope. As I accepted it, I glanced down and saw my name — Jo Beth Stonley Sidden — written across the envelope in a wavy scrawl. I recognized my father's handwriting. I opened the flap of my shoulder bag and placed the envelope inside. I thanked him politely and turned my eyes on Wade. I could see that Carpenter was disconcerted that I hadn't immediately ripped the envelope open and devoured its contents. I had waited this long. I could wait a little longer. I was waiting for Wade — the ball was in his court.

"This is a codicil to your father's will dated January twentieth, nineteen ninety," Wade said, holding up a blue-backed document. "It's fourteen pages of instructions and legal niceties. Would you like me to read the contents in its entirety, or simply tell you what it means?"

"Just explain it, Wade," I said. My voice felt rusty and unused.

"You are your father's sole heir and beneficiary. There is no explanation why this will could not have been probated upon your father's death." He looked at me. "I'm sorry, Jo Beth, truly I am. You shouldn't have been kept waiting this long. It's legal, in Andrew's and my judgment. It will be filed at the courthouse Monday. Then you will find out just how much you have coming in cash and resources."

I remained silent and shifted my gaze to Carpenter. He was shaking his head slowly and shrugged when he saw he had my attention.

"Neither your father nor Carl ever mentioned anything about this in their instructions to me. I, too, am sorry that I can't explain the mystery." He stood. "If the letter I gave you raises any questions, please feel free to call me, but I can't see how I could be of any help — I'm completely in the dark."

We made polite noises and he shook Wade's hand and then held mine much too long. I thought he would never leave. He hesitated and nodded his head toward my purse.

"If the contents of your father's letter clears up your questions, and you are free to do so, I'd greatly appreciate hearing anything you can tell me." He was reluctant to leave. I gave him a brief smile with no assurances. I think he knew it would be a cold day in hell before he heard anything from me. Wade walked him to the door, then came back and sat down at his desk. He sighed heavily.

"I, too, got a letter from my father. He was quite sentimental. He went on and on about my childhood here with him. I didn't realize he missed me so much when I left at fifteen. You were completely wrong about him, Jo Beth. He went to great lengths to apologize for his failure to leave me a substantial estate. He was sorry that his years of practice, here in this small town he dearly loved, had netted him so little. In his letter he begged me repeatedly not to sell the place. He referred to my not selling the estate a dozen times or more."

"Wade," I began. How could I phrase this question without him snapping at me, or being suspicious? "I know you and I have had some differences of opinion on several issues," I said slowly, feeling my way. "After I read my letter, if possible, without violating any confidences of my father, I will let you read it. Would you let me read your father's letter?" I kept my fingers crossed hidden in the folds of my shift.

"Of course," he said quickly. He probably thought I wanted to verify his claim that his father wasn't guilty of making a fortune on marijuana. But I knew damn well he had grown it and made heavy money doing so. If he hadn't put the money in real estate, bonds, or something, there was a hell of a lot of cash floating around somewhere. The thousands he had poured into the house and grounds in maintenance and taxes didn't make a dent in the bundle he had made over the years. I knew Carpenter must be sweating peach seeds, worrying that the letter confessed all to Wade and might implicate him. Carpenter must have some redeeming graces — he had passed the letter on to Wade. I doubted I would have been so honorable. I would have held off about twenty-four hours, steamed the letter open and read it. Maybe he did. Then again, Wade had been quick to say I could read his letter. Maybe Carpenter had requested a peek and Wade obliged. I had formed a galloping-horseback theory the minute Wade had explained his letter's contents. If Wade's estate was modest, it was the next logical conclusion. My theory had bounced around like a ball in a pinball machine and the current bounce had me convinced this letter was a blueprint for a treasure hunt.

Wade opened a desk drawer, removed the letter and handed it to me. He walked to his only window and stood with his back to me, staring down at the parking lot below.

The letter was handwritten, and from its bulk, I estimated at least twenty pages or so. On the first page, about halfway down, a phrase brought a grin to my face. I was glad Wade wasn't facing my way. The letter explained to Wade that his father regretted the current laws kept him from leaving him a large and fluid estate. You bet, too much cash in the bank arouses the interest of both the IRS and the DEA.

I read on. The first childhood memory Carl mentioned was the time Wade had broken his arm when he fell off his sack swing at nine years old. He described the tree, in case Wade had forgotten which one. But the last line of the paragraph was the key. He said he had sat many times on the concrete bench in front of the tree and knew that under his feet was the ground Wade had played on.

Eureka! My theory was right; in fact, I was right on the money — literally. It was as clear as if he had drawn a treasure map and placed an "X" on the spot. Dig here, he was telling his son, dig here for the first cache. I'm too much of a moral coward to confess all, but if you're as bright as I think you are, you will read between the lines, use the money to keep the house, and not judge me too harshly. If you don't figure it out, you can show this letter to your children and keep it in the family because it's perfectly innocent.

I wondered what he had used. In the old days it had been glass fruit jars buried to thwart robbers and revenue agents. However, technology had produced metal detectors and all fruit jars have metal lids or glass lids with metal fasteners. But science had produced plastic. That would have been my choice. An all-plastic, wide-mouthed thermos jug. The gallon size, so you could toss in lots of those little packets that absorb dampness, like the ones you put in your salt shaker. I could visualize rolls of hundred-dollar bills, packed tightly with the moisture-proof packets. A couple of dabs of Super Glue and screw on the lid. Guaranteed to last several lifetimes; protected from water, fire, insects, and all government agencies.

In his letter, Wade's father reminisced about several other childhood mishaps and pranks, and each had the same careful explanations to their exact locations. I quickly scanned the rest of the letter. The last paragraph brought tears to my eyes. It was one last plea to find the money, to forgive him and just how much he had loved his son, all vague and couched in careful terms. He died still sitting on the fence.

I knew now I owed Carpenter a mental apology. He didn't sweat this letter; he must have helped Carl compose it. Carpenter had made enough money to last his lifetime and he had no heirs. He, too, would probably leave his estate to Wade — in case he never discovered his father's money. Carpenter would also be around awhile longer in case Wade needed help.

I stood and joined Wade at the window.

"He loved you very much," I told him. "You should preserve this letter for your children and try in every way possible to keep your house."

"I've been thinking along the same lines," he admitted. "Knowing I didn't have enough money to handle it, I tried to tell myself I didn't want or need it, but I guess I love the place more than I knew. I know I will inherit mother's money someday; maybe I can hold on until then. Who knows?"

"Well, where there's a will, there's a way," I said to give comfort. God, what a banal pun.

"Listen," he said. "I'll have some news for you tomorrow."

"About what?"

"About me. I'll tell you tomorrow. I won't have all the facts until then, okay?"

"Sure."

I was walking down the staircase from his office when I remembered James had called. His visit had completely slipped my mind. I glanced at my watch. If he had arrived an hour after he had called, he would have been waiting almost thirty minutes before I could make it back. I'd have to come back and shop later.

When I drove into the courtyard, I saw James standing by his truck talking to George. I apologized for having gone on an errand. I told them to come inside and I would make iced tea. They followed me into the office. I excused myself and went to the bedroom, slipped the letter out of my purse, fingered it, and placed it back inside. I would read it later. Now that I had the answers, I was in no hurry.

I made the iced tea and took it to the office. James and George seemed to getting along well; they were discussing the Braves.

"It's been awhile, James," I said, when comments ceased.

"Well, thankfully, not too many fishermen get lost in Okefenokee," he replied. I explained to George that James and I had once worked together in rescuing two lost fishermen.

"Were you successful?" George asked. James and I laughed and then took turns telling him about bringing the two drunks back to the landing — first on dog leads, then tied to the boat to keep them from falling overboard. We didn't mention Leroy and his cousin.

"Tell me, James, what did the Florida Fish and Game Commission tell you when they got in touch?"

"That you had called in some preposterous tale about an adult cougar and two kits — alive and well and living in the swamp." He gave me a slow smile to let me know he was enjoying this exchange.

"What did you tell them?" I returned his smile.

"I told them if that little gal said she had pictures of cougars, they better damn well believe her and take her seriously."

He knew that referring to me as "that little gal" would frost me, but it was a gentle jab and I chose to ignore it.

"That earned you the privilege of seeing some snaps," I told him. I walked over and handed him the envelope with the photographs and returned to my seat. "The first four exposures show a king snake eating a timber rattler. It was taken before first light and in heavy bush. There wasn't enough light for the pictures to be excellent — but they ain't bad."

James looked up again from the second picture.

"You know, I've been walking these woods and swamps for over twenty years and I have never seen this happen. I've heard tales of them swallowing rattlers whole, but never saw it personally, or saw pictures."

"I was lucky," I said, being modest and demure. He went back to the photographs. I explained to George about the Florida Cougar Release Program. He said he had read several articles about it in the Waycross paper. James finally lifted his head from the pictures.

"Very clear pictures. Did you want me to pass them on to the FFGC?" His voice had been subdued and he seemed unhappy.

"That's it? That's your response?" I said in amazement. "No whoopees or wows? What gives?"

"I just don't believe in the program. I don't share your enthusiasm for the project. Frankly, I was hoping it would fail," he admitted.

"You-have-got-to-be-kidding!" I pronounced each word slowly and distinctly.

"Nope, it's the way I feel personally about the project. It's not my department's feeling. They are quite enthusiastic about the experiment. I would get drummed out of the corps if they thought I was going around knocking it. It's a pity you didn't have a crowd with you when you took these pictures: a couple of Supreme Court judges, a Catholic bishop, someone like a Walter Cronkite. Was anyone with you?"

I was deep in thought. I let his last question just lie there.

"It's not good for our wildlife?" I knew he loved the swamp and all its denizens. That could be the only reason he would be against the program. James hesitated and glanced at George.

"I don't have any feelings, pro or con, and I never gossip," George answered him with a grin. "It's bad for business."

"It's not good for our wildlife," James stated.

"You don't think they will accept the pictures as proof?" I asked him.

"Jo Beth, they claim they recovered all the bodies of the seven that died or were killed and picked up the remaining three. They say it just isn't possible."

"Oh sure, this adult female Texas cougar got tired of the Lone Star State, packed her bag, swam the Gulf of Mexico, hitchhiked through the Florida Peninsula — getting laid by God knows what — pitched her little tent on the edge of Okefenokee, produced two kits that looked just like cougars, and she just happened to decide to homestead only a few miles from the release of the original ten cougars?"

"They swear it isn't possible," James asserted.

I walked over and retrieved the prints.

"The pictures I showed you," I said thoughtfully, "were of a rather large wildcat. They were badly focused and overexposed. I was so embarrassed when you identified the animal, I wouldn't allow you to have the pictures and tore them up — in your presence. You can be sure they will hear nothing more from me." James studied my features.

"It will be hard to sit on those pictures; they're beauties. You sure?"

"Absolutely," I told him. "I'm good at keeping secrets."

"Yes you are," he replied with a smile as he stood.

"Stay for lunch. We're having sandwiches," I offered.

"Sorry, I have to be in Waycross at two. Some other time?"

"Anytime," I told him with warmth, and after he and George shook hands, I walked him to his truck.

"I was sorry to hear about your troubles," he said.

"Thanks. He's in the hospital with troubles of his own now."

"Did it feel good to get even?"

I looked at him and laughed. "You haven't heard the latest. He woke up from a coma yesterday and named a male assailant. I'm off the hook."

"I was hoping you did it. It would have been good therapy for you — evening the score."

"Thanks for the thought — I think," I said with doubt.

He laughed. "Take care."

"You too." I gave him a hug and waved when he turned to enter the drive.

Over sandwiches at lunch, George informed me he had found an insurance adjuster in a town about fifty miles from Andrel who would take pictures at the funeral tomorrow.

"He's a photographer?"

"He's an adjuster, Jo Beth. He takes pictures all the time."

"You told him to take pictures of all the males?"

"From teenagers to octogenarians."

"He's going to fax all the pictures to Sinclair's office?"

"Yep," he said patiently. "He promised he wouldn't let his shirt touch his back from the time he took the pictures until he arrived home, developed them, and went to his office to fax them. Barring accidents and acts of God, he estimates you will have them in your hot little hands by five tomorrow afternoon."

"He didn't say 'hot little hands,'" I teased.

"Nope, those are my descriptive adjectives," he admitted, between bites.

I shook a kosher dill spear in his face.

"You're getting testy because I'm double-checking your instructions. You don't like your clients looking over your shoulder."

"Am not."

"Are too."

"Am not."

"Are too." He stared at me.

"Are you ticklish?"

"No way," I said with confidence, as I took a big bite of my sandwich. He picked up his napkin, wiped his mouth and pushed away from the table. My mouth was full; it was chew or choke. I saw he was coming around the table after me. I jumped up and ran into the living room, chewing fiercely, and assumed a dead serious expression as I backed away from him.

"Don't you dare touch me," I told him darkly. "I'm extremely ticklish and I have this leaky heart valve condition — I'd croak on you. Stay. I mean it!"

I realized now I should have kept running and not stopped to reason with him. I turned to sprint and he caught me, tossed me on the sofa and held me there. I was screaming "No!" in a continuous litany as he started fingering under my arms like he was strumming a banjo. I collapsed in helpless laughter. My father had tickled me when I was small, but thank God, it had never occurred to Bubba to try it. I hadn't been tickled in twenty years but it was just as debilitating now as it had been then. I was almost hysterical when he finally stopped. I would murder him when I caught my breath.

"Had enough? Say 'Uncle.'"

"Uncle, uncle," I whispered, my throat dry from forced laughter.

The fool wasn't even breathing hard. I had kicked and heaved, trying to get loose. I was weak from laughter and tired from trying to fight back. He grabbed my hands and pulled me to my feet. His arms went around me and he gave me a very thorough and satisfying kiss. It was the best kiss I had had in months — hell — it was the only kiss I'd had in months.

"Let's finish lunch," he said as he released me.

"Why not?" I said weakly. "I'm much too weak to dance."

I followed him back to the table. After I sat down I shakily lit a cigarette.

"Not hungry?"

"I'm too tired to eat," I said with a groan. I took another puff on my cigarette and waited until he took a bite and had his mouth full.

"I almost had a heart attack back there," I said calmly. "I hope tickling isn't part of your usual foreplay."

He grabbed his napkin to keep from spraying the table with his mouthful of food. I watched his efforts critically until I could see that his face wasn't going to turn from red to blue. I arose and started clearing the lunch ingredients away. He finally got his mouth empty and under control.

He laughed weakly. "We're even now, okay?"

"Not by a long shot," I promised.

He decided it was time to call Fred. I finished clearing the table and rinsed the dishes and silverware. When I joined him in the office, he was just hanging up the phone.

"That was Fred. He has some info I asked him for more than two months ago on another case I have pending. I'd better go see what he's dug up."

"Fine. I have some things to handle here. When you come back, we can hash over what I found out this morning."

"Just tell me one thing — did it clear up any of your questions?"

"Only one," I replied. "It also raises more questions. I have a letter from my father I haven't read yet. It may tell the whole story."

"You want me to stay in case it's bad news? I can see Fred later."

"Nah, I'm a big girl. I can handle it."

He rolled his eyes and left. I went to the bathroom and washed my hands. I picked up the comb and started arranging my curls. I stared at my reflection. Okay, okay, I'm going, I've stalled long enough.

I took a deep breath and marched into the bedroom, sat on the bed and opened the letter. There were two pages, one in a handwritten scrawl I recognized as my father's, but just barely. His handwriting had been so beautifully executed, perfect o's and straight t's and i's. This letter was written with a shaky and barely legible hand. The second page was on the First State Bank's letterhead with the estate trust division's officers listed below along with their titles. I didn't let my eyes fall to the message below. I started reading my father's letter first:

My Dearest Daughter,

Even lying here in this damn bed knowing I'll never be able to walk out of this room and knowing I'm going to meet my Maker very soon now, I can't force myself to tell you everything you should know. Very soon, you'll know all the details.

The most important thing in my mind at this moment is to tell you that your mother and I loved you very much. My actions may have led you to believe differently. I can only plead that I was obsessed, since my teens, with a fierce passion to put paint on canvas. I'm sorry to say that I was so driven and controlled by this desire that I sometimes put it first before you or your mother's needs. I have no excuse, I ask no forgiveness. My guilt led me to lose the past ten years we could have had together. It was easier to avoid facing you than to explain my deficiencies, and the reasons for them.

Simply put, I am a coward and could not face you and see the love in your eyes dim when you heard the truth about me.

Therefore, I have left you a legacy, not of money, or property or securities. I very much doubt there will be much left. Dying slowly can be damned expensive these days, but I have left you something to prove my love.

It wasn't possible to give you this gift while I was alive. It

was forbidden, but it comes to you now, with all my love.
Your father,

Arthur Henry Stonley
November 21, 1991

I gazed out the bedroom window through a blur of tears. I knew what I had been doing in January — three years ago — when my father had visited Carl's law office to sign the will. I had been watching the construction of my kennel and my home. I remembered it had been unseasonably cold that January. The workers would build a fire near the work area and would stop working occasionally to stand with their backs to the flames. I would sometimes stand with them; I arrived early and left late, not wanting to miss a minute of the construction of my dream.

My father had only been about three miles from me the day he signed the will. How I would have loved to have heard some of the words on this paper come from his throat, rather than deciphering his scrawl more than two years later. Heated resentment flowed through my veins. I loved the man, but he was correct — he had been a coward and cheated me out of hearing what I most wanted to hear. I sighed and said to hell with it, I would not let him spoil my image of him. I knew he was obsessed with painting. I was fairly sure he loved me, and that was enough for now. He had left me pictures. I was sure they would be paintings of Cumberland Island. This time I would not be foolish and hold on to them. These paintings would go to auction houses. These paintings would erase my humongous mortgage. I could train my dogs, knowing I had security and would be able to feed them — and myself — for the rest of our days. Nothing else mattered.

I picked up the bank letter. It was short and to the point. The bank had in its possession a wooden box, forty-two by thirty-four by twenty-four inches, until I presented this letter, with proper identification, to claim it. It was signed by Stephen Drew, an executive officer of the estate trust division. I looked at my watch. It was quarter of two and the bank closed at two. I reached across the bed, grabbed the portable phone and dialed the bank's number and his extension. I prayed he was still with the bank. I didn't recognize the name. That proved I didn't know every person in town by name. The phone was answered by a male.

"Stephen Drew's office," a baritone voice stated.

"Mr. Drew?"

"Speaking."

"Mr. Drew, my name is Jo Beth Sidden. I have a letter here that you signed in nineteen ninety. You are holding a box for me in your trust department. I know you close at two, but I hope you will stay a few minutes until I can get there. It shouldn't take me more than twenty minutes. I would like to pick up the box this afternoon. Will that be possible?"

"Please come to the employees' entrance, Ms. Sidden, and ring the bell. I'll wait for you."

"Oh, thank you," I gushed. "I'm on my way!"

"Ms. Sidden, the box has been here three years. You can wait a few minutes more. Please drive safely."

31

The security guard answered the bell at the employees' entrance to the bank and escorted me down the darkened corridor to Stephen Drew's office. I glanced at my watch and saw it was three minutes after two. Caution is not my middle name. Drew rose from behind his desk and walked over to greet me — an old-fashioned courtesy that has almost gone the way of gas station attendants and home milk delivery. I recognized him immediately. I had seen his face in the bank and around town for years, but I had never needed a name attached to it until now.

"Thank you, sir," I said, "for waiting."

"I have admired your father's work for years," he said with a smile. "I've known who you were since you were in pigtails. I think we can dispense with the proof of identity."

I sat in the chair he indicated and waited until he was seated before I spoke.

"I hope you can enlighten me about a puzzling point. Why the wait for me to receive this box? Did you have any special instructions about the delay?"

"Frankly, I was surprised when you didn't arrive in a timely fashion. I waited a reasonable time for the will to be probated and then called the executor of your father's estate, Carl Bennett. Of course, I had to be very vague with my questions since I didn't want to violate your father's trust in the bank, but Carl seemed unaware of any special instructions to this bank in regard to your father's estate. He explained that the bank didn't enter into any phase of your father's probate since he had survived your father. He read the will to me again, which simply stated we were the executors of your father's will, only if Carl Bennett died before Arthur Stonley. I couldn't comment further without violating confidentiality."

"I'm glad the box is here and I can finally take possession." I was impatiently waiting. On the way over, I made a guess, based on the dimensions of the box. I would say four paintings, maybe five, if they were framed, and more if they weren't. Drew had read my mind. He tented his fingers and spoke.

"The security guard has gone to the vault to get your property," he told me. "He was told to bring it in as soon as you were in my office."

"I'm impatient," I said. "Sorry."

"Not at all. I share your feelings," he answered. "I hope you won't be offended if I mention that for three years now I have been hoping the box contained paintings."

"If there are paintings, I would expect you to keep this information confidential. I would hate for it to become general knowledge until I decide to release the information."

"You have my word," he said.

"Then you have my word. If it is possible, I will show them to you."

I was learning to be more careful in making promises. For all I knew, the box could contain a stamp collection or art he had picked up in Europe.

We both turned when the security guard rolled a hand dolly into the room. I rose slowly and approached the box, lightly touching it with my fingers. I knew it had been packed over three years ago; how much longer had whatever was inside been there? I had been wool gathering and didn't hear the start of what Drew was saying.

". . . so I hope you'll let the guard here, Mr. Ashton, escort you home. I can follow and bring him back to his car."

"That isn't necessary. In fact, I would prefer not to draw attention to the box. If Mr. Ashton can load it in the van, I will be all right."

Drew looked doubtful, but I acted confident that my statement had settled the matter and asked the guard to follow me. Drew reminded me that I had to sign a receipt. I walked to his desk and signed my name in two places. He informed me the vault rental had been paid seven years in advance and the difference would be refunded by check and mailed to me. I thanked him and shook his hand.

The guard followed me to the van and looked around nervously at the deserted parking lot. I unlocked the van and he undid the straps and slid the box carefully into the back in the walkway. He asked if I thought it should be strapped down. I put my hand on the box and exerted pressure, but it didn't slide. I told him the box was secure and thanked him for staying late.

I drove home carefully; this wasn't the time to have a fender-bender. Wayne was standing near the doorway to the grooming room. Ever vigilant, he was never lax with our security precautions. He came over quickly when I beckoned. I unlocked the back of the van and explained I wanted the wooden box in the living room and that I would need a small crowbar. He signed and asked what I had bought. I told him the box was from my father. He didn't comment, just wrapped his strong arms around the box and lifted it like it held feathers.

Wayne placed the box on the floor and left to fetch the crowbar. I stood gazing at it until he returned. He handed me the crowbar and I gave him an absent-minded smile of thanks. He left, closing the living-room door behind him. He was sensitive to my mood and knew this was one job I wanted to do alone. I gave him a couple of minutes and locked the door.

I knelt next to the box, placed the crowbar under the edge of the cover near a nail and, using pressure, pushed downward. The nail released its hold and came up slightly. At the next nail I repeated the prying pressure and it released with a small sound, almost like the sound of chalk scraping on a blackboard. I went all around the top, releasing the nails carefully. Finally, I prized one end free and twisted the top loose. I laid the top on the carpet and peered into the box. It was packed tightly with excelsior.

My heart quickened. It wasn't popcorn or bubble plastic or Styrofoam ghost poop. This meant it had been packed for a while. I hadn't seen excelsior used this way since I was a little girl. This also ruled out Europe; in his years abroad, they were using newer packing materials. My father had done his best work from the time of my birth until I was fifteen.

I suddenly grew impatient and began to scoop out the excelsior, not caring that I was making a mess I would have to clean up. It never entered my mind to get a trash bag and do the job neatly. When the excelsior level was down about three inches, I could see yellowed, newspaper-wrapped bundles secured with masking tape. Each bundle was supported by two pieces of unfinished half-inch pine lathing. Using my fingers, I worked the lathing back and forth until I could slide them out. I put my hands around the middle bundle and slowly pulled it up and clear of the box, scattering excelsior all around.

It was a painting, I could feel the curve of the frame through the wrapping. My heart soared. I sat cross-legged on the floor and balanced the wrapped painting in front of me, trying to find a date on the yellowed newspaper, prolonging the suspense. Nothing on the front side, but when I turned it, I saw the masthead of Fred's newspaper and the date, February 5, 1974, six months before my mother died. I took a fingernail and inserted it carefully under the yellowed masking tape and tore off a four-inch strip from the frame.

Tears welled up in my eyes and I had a feeling of lightheadedness. With only a small square of the frame showing, I knew without a doubt it was my mother's work. She had made the frames for these pictures. Mother's frames were used up quickly after her death. When I fell in love with the four paintings I already possessed, I had been twelve years old. I had to wait four years before I could buy good-quality frames with my father's generous allowance. What a wonderful gift. I knew now the paintings had been rendered at least nineteen years ago and during his most productive and, according to the experts, his most talented period.

I finished pulling off the newspaper. The painting was three feet tall and two and a half feet wide. I was holding it with the back toward me. I turned it around and forgot to breathe. It was a portrait of my mother. She was sitting on something low, a stool perhaps, and her dress was spread around her. I remembered the dress well. It was her Easter dress, her best frock. The same dress for Easter for at least three years, that I could remember. The first year it was white, the second year she had dyed it a delicate pink and the third year, a dusty rose. It was a simple dress, light cotton eyelet material with a sweetheart neck and full skirt. I touched the pearls, painted a soft luminous ivory in the painting. She had bought two strands of the cheap gaudy pearls from the dime store, for something like fifty-nine cents each. She had sanded just the smaller ones in both graduated strands and had painted them with my father's tiny edging brush with his oyster-pearl, tinted oil paint, and created a single strand, strung on dental floss, that looked real and expensive. I still had them packed away in her chest.

To me she was very beautiful. A stranger would see a slim woman in her middle forties, sitting erect and graceful in a dusty rose dress and wearing pearls. They would see the small black mole high on her left cheek. I had completely forgotten the mole in trying to reconstruct her features from memory. My father had not painted a glamour portrait, he had painted her so exact that the oils seemed to bring her to life. Her eyes were her best feature — large, dark brown and framed in long lashes. Her hair was darker than mine, worn long in layers of waves around her shoulders.

She always wore her hair up during the day. Only at night did she remove the hairpins and brush it till it gleamed in the lamp light. Then she would brush mine, and we would sit and talk about our day. Lamplight glowed on her skin in the picture. It was coming from her left and in the background I could see just an edge of some furniture. I could recognize the two edges of furniture only because I knew where they were in relation to the lamp. Anyone else would only see a hazy background with two unrecognizable objects. I saw the fine wrinkles under her eyes that time had made my memory erase. Had she ever seen this portrait? I had no one to ask. My mind swirled with the question. Had she or hadn't she? Now I would never know. For a minute, I simmered with hatred for my father. How could he let her die without letting her see this? He must have shown it to her; he couldn't have been so cruel, to deny her a wish he could have fulfilled.

I propped her portrait carefully against the wall. I pulled out the second picture and stripped off the newspaper. It was a portrait of me. I sucked in my breath. I looked so real. It was painted just after Dad and I had moved into the new house, when I was fifteen. So, the pictures were painted at different times. I searched the old newspaper for a date and found May 9, 1979. I focused my eyes back on the painting. I was wearing my junior high school cheerleader outfit, the short pleated wool skirt in gold and the heavy sweater of garnet with the school's initials a foot high in front. I was lying on my stomach in front of the fireplace in the living room, my legs in the air. My head was propped up with my right hand and I was holding a school textbook with my left.

The carpet was olive green and the fire in the fireplace cast a golden glow on my face and the walls of the room. My hair was long then, a mass of medium brown curls cascading down past my shoulders and turning a beautiful titian red reflecting the firelight's glow. Dad had been more father than artist in rendering this work. I looked beautiful and I knew I had never looked that good on the best day of my life. I reluctantly propped it next to Mother's portrait and pulled out the third picture.

It was a painting of me and Herman T. My eyes kept filling with tears and blurring my view. Herman T. was about a year old. We were on the rickety back porch. I was sitting on the edge of the porch, barefoot and in a pair of ragged, cut-off jeans and a dirty white T-shirt. Herman T. was much larger than I was at that age. I was almost ten and small for my age, looking like a waif. Herman T. was gazing at me with a listening stance and had his head cocked in my direction. I reached out and stroked the picture. His coat, his ears and wrinkles looked so real and natural, I could almost feel his warm hide beneath my fingers.

Every detail of the shabbiness in which we lived was revealed. Every crooked rotted board, the warped window casings, and the missing boards in the floor. The porch was so low, one step was sufficient. It was a board across two cinder blocks. The yard had only red clay and a few weeds. You could see my dad's old abandoned Chevy, at least one side of it, in the left corner. Herman T. had a frayed rope for a collar. I remembered wishing a few months later I could buy him a new collar to be buried in, since I never could afford one before he died. We both looked like we would have been right at home on Tobacco Road. I placed the painting against the wall beside the first two.

The fourth picture was of Mama and me sitting in her rocking chair. In this one I was ten and she was forty-five. We were in the shack that was our home and the lamp was again to the left of the chair. This portrait didn't have the masking swirls of gray and white in the background. This painting was true to life and showed the wealth of poverty we had endured. The old gas range was to the right in the background. A huge monster, twenty years old even before my mother started using it. Mother used to say she knew it had been on Noah's Ark. Her three good pieces of furniture didn't show from the angle my father had painted. In this picture he seemed to know this scene was what I remembered most from my childhood.

He had placed every imperfection in this picture so I could remember more clearly. I couldn't make up my mind whether he did it out of love or a sense of guilt. God, I loved the picture. It was so realistic it broke my heart. My mother was wearing one of her faded house dresses. She owned exactly three and she washed one of them daily. She tried to keep me clean and presentable, which at my age was impossible, but she was always neat and clean and smelled of soap. I don't believe she ever wore perfume. My only memories were the smell of soap and the warmth of her hands when she touched me. I was squeezed into the chair by her side wearing shorty pajamas she had made out of feed sacks. Grain for chickens used to come packaged in colorful cotton material. I remembered that print: red strawberries on a white background. I thought they were great. I was barefoot in the painting and the bottoms of my feet were dirty. The shack had bare boards for flooring. Mother had scrubbed them with bleach until they were white; still, my feet would get dirty. Every night, before she put me to bed, which was our couch, she would wash my feet and dry them before I could lie down.

In the fifth picture, I was a cute chubby baby about two years old with a mass of blonde curls, wearing a diaper. I had a wide smile and drool was running down my chin. This picture didn't do much for me, but I could imagine what my mother would have said if she had seen it. Her speech was liberally sprinkled with old Southern sayings, saws from the dark ages, almost. Things she had heard her parents and her parents'

parents repeat. Mother would have said, I am sure, as she looked at the painting, "A jewel beyond price."

I lined up the paintings and laughed with irony. These were not my mortgage payments, or the instruments of my prosperity. I could never part with these, not one, not even the baby picture that didn't move me. This was my family, my mother and me, painted by my father. These, also, were not for sale at any price. Sorry animals, we'll just have to stumble along with the heavy mortgage and hope we can make ends meet and I can save enough to keep us in kibbles and vittles through our old age.

At six, I heard a timid knock on the living-room door. I cracked it and saw George standing in the hall.

"Am I interrupting something?"

"Nope," I replied as I went out into the hall and locked the door behind me. I motioned toward the door.

"Something I can't share right now," I explained.

"No sweat," he said easily. "Hungry?"

"Starved. Let me grab a quick shower and I'll dig something up."

"I have a better idea. Why don't I get some pizza?"

"Great."

I went to the bedroom and took two twenties out of my purse, returned and handed him the money.

"Wayne likes anchovies, and we need lots of salad. I like pepperoni and Rosie will want sausage and extra cheese. Get two biggies, at least."

George arched his brows and held up a finger to silence me. He pulled out his notebook and wrote my detailed instructions down. He also didn't give me a protracted argument about the money, which I know is difficult for a Southern gentleman — even on an employer-employee level. I should have considered his tender male feelings and let him buy, then put it on his expense account. I just acted without thinking. This is what happens when you live alone too long; you often act without thinking about others and what they are feeling. Ah well, if I had hurt his feelings, he was covering it well.

I called Rosie and she protested that she had a pork loin roast and sweet potatoes baking in the oven.

"They are better warmed up the next day. Turn off the oven and come on down. We'll have those goodies tomorrow night."

"Wednesday night is pizza night," she said with a sniff.

"Let's throw caution to the wind and have it twice this week," I told her with gusto.

"Have you been drinking?" She seemed cautious.

"Nah, just high on life," I told her. "Come on down and join the party."

We did party. We drank wine George had bought. Now I knew why he didn't make a fuss about the money. He knew he was going to bring back two bottles of wine to compensate for me paying for the pizza.

We ate, drank, played Scrabble and made up some questionable words that caused loud arguments about their merit. At ten, all my sawdust ran out; I was one limp doll. I begged a highly emotional day, apologized, and went to bed. Rosie and Wayne wanted to stay awhile if George was agreeable. He was, and they stayed.

I brushed my teeth and crawled into bed. I was exhausted from emotional stress and pleasantly tiddly from the wine. I tumbled down the dark tunnel of sleep. Once again, I was young and carefree and running through knee-high grass with Herman T. by my side. Mama was standing under the shade of a huge magnolia tree at the edge of the field, her arms holding wildflowers, and looking beautiful in her Easter dress and pearls. She beckoned and I flew lightly in the sunshine toward her and knew I wanted this moment to last forever.

32

"IT TAKES ONE TO KNOW ONE"
April 17, Saturday, 6 A.M.

The sister on WAAC C93 with her dulcet voice fed me the local news. No one I knew had been arrested for pot, moonshine or blow. No friend had wrapped himself or herself around a pine tree, speeding down a lonesome county hardtop in the early morning hours. Two local public officials had been indicted for fraud. The morning had definite possibilities. I popped out of bed and waltzed through my morning ablutions, then dressed in a sweatshirt and jeans and went to the kitchen to start coffee. I hadn't heard a peep from George. They must have partied late into the night.

I was on my third cigarette and finishing my second cup of coffee when I heard George in the shower. Breakfast this morning was pancakes, bacon and scrambled eggs. He came in as I was ready to flip the pancakes. I made small ones and used a Teflon-coated pan, so I decided to show off, holding the pan in one hand and deftly flipping the pancakes in the air to turn them. I only dropped one on the stove and George said a save of two out of three wasn't bad. He poured coffee and lit a cigarette and then started rummaging in the refrigerator.

"Where's the maple syrup?" His voice was muffled.

"Oh my," I said aghast. "I can't believe my ears. A native Georgian asking for maple syrup when we are fortunate enough to live in Georgia, the state that makes the best cane syrup in the whole wide world."

"Where do you hide it?" He didn't bother to remove his upper body from the fridge. All I could see was his rear end extending upward, the door of the refrigerator braced against his left hip.

"In the back of the vegetable crisper," I told him, "where everyone else who can't stand the taste of cane syrup puts it. Do you solemnly promise you won't tell a soul?"

"Gimme a break," he said, as he plopped the bottle on the table. "You hypocrites really amaze me. Why don't you just say you don't like the taste when it's served to you?"

"And get thrown out of the DAR? Also, I'm a grand dragonette in the Daughters of the Confederacy."

"You belong to the KKK?" He had yelled his outrage.

"Of course not, silly. It was a joke. Lighten up," I told him.

"In very poor taste," he countered.

"Listen, friend," I explained, "the Daughters of the Confederacy is a fine organization and I am a member in good standing. I pay my dues — promptly. We don't condone slavery or bigotry. We just want to preserve our Southern memories of our ancestors and some — and I stress some — of our traditions. I don't believe in the new movement that's underfoot to rewrite history. I'm not a grand dragonette; it's just the first make-believe title that popped into my head. If it reminded you of the KKK, then I apologize, because no hinted connection was meant or intended. I am proud of the Confederate flag and fly it on proper occasions.

"People in Texas are proud of the Alamo, although what the men did there was stupid, senseless and suicidal. Yet no one wants to abolish the Alamo. The Civil War was — for the South — stupid, senseless, and suicidal, so we celebrate and remember their courage, not the cause they died for. Now, some people want to change history and destroy a flag which is a symbol of our ancestors. I don't agree."

"To each his own," he mumbled between bites of food and sips of coffee. He saw we were having a disagreement and he didn't want to argue.

We sat and ate in silence for a while.

"You forgot the people from the North who migrated to the West and the terrible things they did to the Indians. They took away their lands, herded them onto reservations, slaughtering them left and right. Seems like that would be a better allegory than the Alamo," he said between bites.

"Well," I said, "I didn't mention the Indians because there were a lot of Southerners who migrated West along with the Northerners."

"You're saying everyone is guilty?"

"Exactly," I said sweetly. "Let's stop, we've just agreed on something."

"Done," he said. "Listen, Jo Beth, you're not getting your money's worth with me. I've made a few phone calls and talked to a couple of sources. There's nothing more I can do here. There's no investigative leads to run down locally. All the action seems to be in New York. I'm not earning my keep."

"Hey," I said, "let me be the judge of that. There's the funeral at eleven and the pictures. What if we are wrong and Jackson Hanaiker isn't among the mourners and he isn't the one who set me up for Bubba's attack? I wouldn't know what to do next. I need advice."

"To tell the truth, Jo Beth, I wouldn't know what to do either — to find a solution — other than trying the fifty states for a birth certificate, and that could backfire if you had a different name at birth."

"Let's see what happens today, then we can discuss what we do next," I suggested.

"It's your call," he said with a shrug. I poured more coffee for us, lit up and looked at my watch. It was too late to call Hank at home, it was ten to seven and he would just be getting to work. I'd have to wait another hour until he finished roll call, and got his troops dispersed, before he was free to talk.

I went to the office and made coffee for Wayne. I then grabbed a large trash bag, the vacuum and headed for the living room. I emptied the wooden box and vacuumed inside it. I repacked the paintings, without the excelsior and lathing slats, and tapped the lid down with the crowbar, just enough to hold it securely. I opened the living room closet, pulled the box inside and laid the crowbar on top. I crammed the excelsior and torn newspapers into the trash bag and vacuumed the floor.

When I returned to the office, George had finished the dishes and was seated on the new couch balancing an ashtray on his lap and reading the paper. I had to get some end tables, lamps, and a coffee table. I pulled a set of four graduated TV tables out of the hall closet. Susan and I used to eat on these when we watched movies. I wondered if we would ever have another movie, beer and popcorn night. I don't know why I hadn't remembered the tables before now. I set the unit to George's right and he looked up from the paper and smiled his thanks.

Wayne entered and we all exchanged good mornings. He gave George a grin and held up a circled finger to signal his enjoyment of last night.

He signed to me that I had missed the good part of last night and he didn't know how I had slept through George and his mother's duet of "The Rose of Tralee."

"Thank God," I said. "Rosie murders that song." George lowered his paper and gave me a dirty look.

"Did you help or hinder?" Wayne read my lips and grinned as he signed.

"I thought they sounded pretty good."

"You nut," I signed with fondness, "some music critic you are."

"We were great," George said firmly and went back to the paper.

Wayne and I discussed his four sweeps for today. He was going to Rosewood Industries, a mercantile factory that manufactured nylon windbreakers and sports jackets with team emblems. Mostly women were employed. A few mechanics and cutters, but the rest were eighty percent young girls fresh out of high school and young married women. The other twenty percent were older women whose husbands had retired, or were about to. The young girls were the problem. Pot, crack and now we were finding tabs of LSD. They ran sewing machines, snap-applying machines, banders and bailing machines. Dangerous work while high on any substance.

"Wayne, have you ever noticed that foreman who's short, wears sweatshirts with the sleeves rolled up to display his tattoos? He works in the back section."

He nodded and signed he knew who I meant.

"I know he's dirty. I've tried twice and I've never found anything on or near him. I believe he's a pusher. What's your read?"

Wayne shrugged and signed, "If he is, he's smarter than both of us. He looked suspicious the last time I was there. I did everything but vacuum around his desk. The dogs don't react when they get near him."

"Well, be careful when you're around him. He looks the type to carry a five-inch blade to bring his height up to six feet, in his mind. Don't get too close."

"Yes, Mother," he signed.

"Watch your lip." I signed back. He winked and wiggled his fingers as he left.

I should have done this sweep and let him do my Elliston Grade School on Monday. Elliston was where I had served my first six years in school, from first to sixth grade. When I attended, the only contraband found in the lockers were crude photostats of human anatomy — and most were found in the girls' lockers, not the boys'. It was hard to believe we were now finding pot, blow, acid — and the occasional gun.

I called the carpenter brothers. I needed five sliding panels this time. The only wall space where I could display the paintings was in the living room across from the fireplace. They didn't answer. I would have to call them later. It was still too early to call Hank. I loaded the drier, set it in motion, and was vacuuming the bedroom when George tapped me on the shoulder. I hadn't heard him over the noise of the vacuum and went three feet in the air.

"What?" I said with bad grace.

"You're wanted on the phone," he said, really trying to hide his humor about my upward lunge. I didn't thank him as I left to see who was calling so early.

"I have a collect call for Jo Beth Sidden at this number from Fontain, New York. Will you accept the charges?" a nasal voice said in my ear.

"Yes," I answered.

"Hello?" a small tentative voice.

"This is Jo Beth Sidden," I answered. "How may I help you?"

"Miss Sidden, my name is Jonathan Nielson. I'm calling from Fontain, New York. Can you hear me?" The name was not the name George had mentioned yesterday. I could hear him clearly, but he must be having trouble hearing me. I raised my voice.

"I can hear you," I said.

"I do volunteer work for the SPCA here in town. I wanted to check with you to see, if by any chance, you are missing two bloodhounds?"

"No . . . wait, why are you calling and where did you get my number?" Damn, I was getting slow. I knew in the next heartbeat what he was going to say.

"Well, I removed one of the dogs' collars and found your name and phone number stamped into the leather. Can you hear me?" The voice was thin and flutelike.

Oh God. It had to be O'Henry and Sally. SPCA? That bastard Hanaiker had dumped them.

"Mr. Nielson," I pronounced each word carefully and very loudly. "Should I call you back? We seem to have a bad connection. I can hear you. Can you hear me?" George was now standing beside me, listening. I covered the receiver and told him to grab the extension in the bedroom and listen. Two sets of ears were better than one.

"I can hear well enough when I'm facing a person, but I do have trouble understanding phone conversations. I'm eighty-two years old and my sister has been telling me I should get a hearing aid, but I can hear well enough. I don't talk on the phone that often." I mentally groaned and waited. Three very long seconds passed. I began to panic.

"Mr. Nielson?" I yelled.

"That's better," he said. "Those two dogs were dropped here Wednesday, about nightfall. I wasn't here. I saw them in the cages Friday morning. I always come in at seven on Friday. They are beautiful animals and are in excellent shape. I became worried when Clarence — he's a friend of mine and works here on Wednesday evenings and Thursday mornings — told me the dogs slept all his shift Wednesday night and the man who left them here had trouble unloading them from their traveling cases."

The bastard had tranked them — loaded them with tranquilizers — and flown them there. It was the only way they could have arrived in New York on Wednesday evening, unless Hanaiker had someone to spell him at the wheel and had driven straight through — a twenty-eight-hour trip. I missed the first part of his next sentence.

". . . should be worried too, but he wouldn't let me call the vet, said the vet was out of town all day Thursday. By Friday they had perked up a little, but they still won't eat. Are they your dogs?"

"Yes, Mr. Nielson, they are my dogs," I yelled. "I thank you very much for calling. I was very worried about them. Are they all right now?"

"That's why I'm calling. Today is Saturday. They are such beautiful animals, I would love to take them home with me, but on my pension I just couldn't feed such large dogs and take proper care of them. Money just doesn't go too far these days." He sounded sad and wandered off the subject again.

"Mr. Nielson," I yelled. "What happens on Saturday?" He was my hero, but I was getting antsy here.

"Oh, I didn't finish. I'm so sorry. I meant that three days had already passed and no one had wanted them. Well, only two people have been in — wanting dogs — and they wanted puppies." I clenched the phone tighter and waited.

"You see, our policy is very strict: five days only and no exceptions. I was becoming worried about their future. That's why I took a collar off, to see if anyone had bradded a metal or leather tag on. Sometimes they put them on the inside of the collar, but I don't understand the logic of that."

Suddenly my stomach flipped and I knew what he was wondering and worried about. After five days, if the dogs weren't claimed and no one wanted them, they were destroyed. The polite term was "put to sleep."

"Do you drive a car? Do you have your own car?" I thundered at him. I had to take charge. The dear man was taking all day.

"Yes," he answered. "Martha, that's my sister, said I shouldn't drive anymore, that I was menace on the highway, driving only forty miles per hour, but I told her that forty was a respectable speed and I would not be reckless and go faster."

"Mr. Nielson, is there a veterinarian in practice near the SPCA?" I was shouting.

"There's young Harvey, but he's only been here about three years. We use Henry Alsong here at the SPCA because we all know him, and he's been taking care of the animals in this town for more than thirty years. Good man."

"What's the name of Harvey's practice," I yelled. "Can you get me his name and phone number?"

"Just one moment. I'll have to put my glasses on. My eyes aren't what they used to be." I heard the phone clank against an object. I waited. George stuck his head around the hall doorway and winked.

"Want to have a quick one while we wait for him to get back?"

"God, don't knock it. Without him, my dogs would have been killed on Monday."

"Your dogs?" he asked with raised brows.

"They are now," I said with determination.

When Mr. Nielson came back on the line, he gave me the name "Harvey Gusman," the name of the clinic and the phone number.

"Mr. Nielson, do you have a Western Union office in Fontain?"

"Yes, I believe it's now handled out of the bus station. I have seen a sign there to that effect. We used to have a nice Western Union office on Main Street, but that was years ago. Times have changed."

"Do you have a bank open on Saturday in Fontain, until noon maybe?"

"Miss Sidden, we have two banks here and both stay open until two in the afternoon. This is a rural community, but it's the county seat and everyone comes into town on Saturday to shop and take care of business. Years ago, both banks stayed open until six p.m., but again, times have changed."

"Mr. Nielson, would you look in the phone book and give me the names of two local lawyers and their home phone numbers?"

"Are you going to call them today?" he asked me.

"Yes sir."

"Then you'll need their office phone numbers. There is no courtroom activity on Saturday, but the courthouse is open until two and the lawyers are all in their offices until then. People out in the rural areas also need to see a lawyer when they come to town." He made the town sound like it was operating in the early nineteen hundreds. I hoped he knew what he was talking about.

"I'm going to put the phone down now to get the numbers. I know the two you should call. Please wait."

Bless him, he might be eighty-two, but he was still sharp and articulate. He came back on the line, eventually, and gave me the names and numbers.

"Thank you so much, Mr. Nielson. I need you to do something for me and please say you will. The dogs are very dear to me. I am going to wire one thousand dollars to the Western Union in your name. It should be there in a couple of hours. They will give you a check. You can cash it at your local bank. I am going to call the veterinarian, Harvey Gusman, and have him pick up the dogs from your SPCA and ship them back to me. I want you to pay his fee for picking them up and shipping them back, and also the adoption fees to release them from the SPCA. Would you be able to do that?"

"I certainly will, Miss Sidden. I am relieved here at eleven and I will go immediately to the Western Union. After I have paid the adoption fees and the veterinarian's bill, what moneys I have left, I will send back to you as soon as possible, to your kennel address. I have it written down here, from copying it off the dog collar. You can depend on me, Miss Sidden. I'm glad the dogs will find their way home. I was very worried about them."

"Mr. Nielson, I want you to keep whatever money is left and pick out a dog of your choice from your SPCA. The balance of the money will buy dog food and veterinary care for some time to come. Will you do that for me? You have my heartfelt thanks for returning my dogs to me."

"Miss Sidden, I certainly appreciate the offer, but you are too generous. The change could be several hundred dollars. I couldn't possible accept that much from you."

"Mr. Nielson, you have saved two very valuable dogs for me and I insist you spend the money exactly as I instructed. I will be very angry with you if you don't accept my chance to repay you."

"If you insist," he said in a wavering voice. "I've wanted a dog for a long while."

"Bless you, Mr. Nielson, and thank you again."

I hung up, poured a cup of coffee and searched my desk drawer for aspirin. My throat was dry and I had a pounding headache from tension and yelling my responses. George came back into the room.

"Want me to run to the bank for you?" he volunteered.

"Great, I was going to ask you. I have an Excedrin headache this big," I said with my arms extended wide. "I feel like I have been yelling for hours."

"Nice old man," he commented. "A truly dedicated dog lover."

"I sense a 'but' in there somewhere," I said slowly, massaging my temples.

"I like dogs, don't get me wrong. I just don't understand the love and passion a lot of people exhibit toward them. I would just as soon, frankly, see that much love and passion lavished on the starving and homeless children we have in pitiful abundance in the world." He eyed me, sensing I would snap up the challenge. He was correct.

"I support two children under the UNICEF program," I said softly. "In the summer, when school is out, I teach two children to read who are functionally illiterate. When I possibly can, I donate one morning a week at a day care center. I have missed the last two weeks, because extraordinary things have been happening in my life. I donate twenty-five dollars a month to the Salvation Army to feed the homeless. I serve food there on almost all holidays. Tell me, what have you done in the past year for the starving and homeless children of the world?"

"You put me in my place very neatly," he said with embarrassment clearly evident. "I coach a little league softball team, but it's because I love the sport more than the children. I buy gloves and mitts when the kids are needy. I donate to charities when the money is coming in and look the other way on slow months. That's about it."

"You're forgiven," I said with a smile. "Go forth and sin no more."

I pulled my personal checkbook out of my purse and made out a check for one thousand dollars in his name and handed it to him. I would have to check with Sinclair to see if I could charge my gift to Mr. Nielson to my business account.

"I don't know what the transmittal fee will be. You can put it on your expense account."

"Anything else you need while I'm downtown?"

"You like Cuban sandwiches?" I asked.

"Never had one — I don't think."

"You don't know what you've been missing. Stop at Pete's Deli. It's three blocks down from the bank on the right. Tell him you want all the fixings for Cuban sandwiches for four, and don't forget the Cuban bread. It's a tube loaf, about three feet long. And pick up a twelve-pack of Bud. This also goes on the expense account."

"You bet," he said with a grin. "See ya."

I picked up the phone and called the vet, Harvey Gusman. A male answered after six rings.

"Yo."

"Harvey Gusman?"

"You got him."

I gave him all the details about the dogs, my name and address, and the arrangements I had made with Jonathan Nielson.

"Did Mr. Nielson recommend me?" He sounded surprised.

"Nope, I asked for a vet close to the SPCA."

"I thought not," he said cheerfully. "Henry Alsong handles all the SPCA's business along with the rest of the town's."

"Business slow?" I was curious.

"I only get a patient when Alsong's out of town or down with his back," he admitted candidly.

"Why don't you try a different town?"

"I've got expectations. Alsong is seventy-three. He can't last more than another twenty years. I've been helping him along by poisoning his water supply. I pee in his pond when I'm poaching fish from his reservoir."

This guy was a character.

"Will you handle this job for me and ship the dogs? You'll call me as soon as you have the schedule of their flight? I will want to meet the plane."

"Sure, be glad to. I'll put them on a feeder flight to a major city. When I find out when and where, I'll give you a call."

"Thank you," I said, a little doubtful about using him.

"Don't worry, I'm not a nut. Just using humor to explain a lousy situation here in town, for me anyway."

"Good luck," I said. "I'll be waiting for your call."

"Be back at you," he said and hung up.

I called the carpenter brothers and explained what I needed done. I think I was talking to Sven. They both sounded so much alike, it's hard to tell. They would be over Monday to measure and start the carpentry work, but they would have to order the motors for the panels and that might take a few days. I went to the bathroom — I'd had too much coffee this morning. I called Hank. My head was still thumping.

"Hey, Jo Beth, how you doing?" he asked when he recognized my voice.

"Can you talk?"

"Sure, everyone is squared away and working but me. I'm having a cup of coffee."

"Hank, I want you to do something for me, and I can't explain why. You are to know nothing about this, so it can't backfire on you later. I think you would approve of what I'm doing. Later, if it is possible, I'll tell you all about it. Right now, just don't preach to me when I tell you what I want. Okay?"

"Jo Beth, you're making me nervous."

"Don't be, I know what I'm doing. I want you to set up a meet with the sheriff, tentatively for six this afternoon at Johnston's Landing. Just me and him, alone. I'm giving him plenty of notice so he can get his electronics van and a hand-picked crew out there to tape me. Impress on him that you don't know what I want and I only called you to set it up because I was afraid he would hang up on me and not listen. Got it?"

"Don't do this, Jo Beth, I'm begging you. You're gonna get jammed up. He's in a mean mood and he's furious at you. He didn't like getting lectured by the judge in front of an audience. It's added to his hatred of you — if that's possible."

"I can't do it without you, Hank. You'll be messing up something pretty important if you don't help. Please?"

He groaned. "Don't do this, Jo Beth. Whatever it is, don't do it." I switched the phone to my other ear and leaned back in my office chair. I focused on my father's landscapes. I was staring at the one entitled *Spring*.

"I'll do this another way, Hank. I'm gonna do it whether you help me or not. The other way will be a lot more dangerous for me, but what the hey, I've got to try."

"What am I supposed to do?" He sounded down and discouraged.

"Hey," I said softly, "it's gonna be safe, I promise. And, Hank, listen to a word of advice. You've kept your nose very clean, don't confuse loyalty with stupidity. If asked, don't make the same mistake as Pinnochio. *Comprende*?"

"Nope, would you like to explain that remark?"

"Nope, just think on it. Six o'clock at Johnston's Landing and stress he's to come alone. If something happens and I have to change the time, I'll call back. If you leave the station, be sure and leave a number."

"I've got it. Anything else?"

"Yes," I said, "have a nice day, you big lug." I hung up before he could reply.

I studied the names of the two lawyers Mr. Nielson had given me and decided to call the first one. It was eight thirty-five. He might not be in his office before nine, but I dialed his number anyway. I got an answer on the second ring.

"David Sherwood speaking."

"Mr. Sherwood, my name is Jo Beth Sidden and I'm calling from Balsa City, Georgia, and I hope you can handle a legal chore for me today. It should only take a few minutes of your time."

"I'll certainly try, Miss Sidden. What can I do for you?"

"I need to contact a lawyer in Andrel, New York, to draw up a bill of sale for two pedigreed bloodhounds. I want to make sure the document will hold up in court in New York and Georgia, if the need arises. You would give this lawyer the information he needs and it would have to be ready for the seller's signature in this lawyer's office at ten this morning. He must not have any current legal dealings with Jackson Hanaiker in Andrel or ever represented him in the past. The same restrictions would also apply for Benson T. Hanaiker, now deceased. Could you do this for me?"

"I'm not sure I can, Miss Sidden. Benson Hanaiker of Andrel is, or was, a mover and shaker in this county for many years. Andrel has only two attorneys and I'm sure both of them have had extensive dealings with both Hanaikers in the past. Benson Hanaiker loved litigation and all its ramifications, which means he loved to sue people for any and many reasons. He was what we call a 'billing bounty,' an attorney's dream. What you are hearing from me is sour grapes, since I never worked for him or his nephew."

"His nephew? You mean Jackson Hanaiker is the nephew of Benson Hanaiker?"

"Yes, he is. He is the only son of Benson Hanaiker's deceased, and only, younger sister. Does that change anything?"

My mind was trying to take in all the implications. I had assumed he was the child mentioned in the old article Fred found about Hanaiker's wife who committed suicide. This didn't have any bearing on what I was trying to do now, however.

"Not at all. Could you write up this bill of sale, drive to Andrel, wait in a hotel room until he comes to sign it at, say, one this afternoon?"

"Miss Sidden, are you aware that Benson Hanaiker's funeral is at eleven this morning?"

"Yes, sir, I am."

"I don't know what happens in Balsa City, Georgia, when an influential man of the community and rumored-to-be-millionaire dies, but here they get quite a send-off. I doubt if the eulogies will be over by one, much less the ride to the cemetery and the interment. It takes a long time to bury a well-known and controversial man. About half will be there to sing his praises and the other half to see, with their own eyes, that he is really dead and they will not have to fear him any longer."

"What do you think about three, Counselor? I'm running out of time here. Four is the absolute deadline. I have to have them signed and safe, out of his reach, by four."

"You haven't mentioned the sale price and how I should handle the funds."

"Make it one dollar for both of them. In cash."

"I'm afraid that sounds a little shaky, legally."

"Okay, how about ten dollars and other valuable considerations?" I suggested. "Can you do this for me?"

"You intrigue me, Miss Sidden. If I do this for you, do I get the full story? You have aroused my curiosity. My friends say it's insatiable."

"After I receive the signed, witnessed, and legal bill of sale by express mail," I said carefully, "if it is at all possible, I will relate to you the whole story."

"I have the feeling your conditional response will net me zilch."

"I keep my word, Counselor."

"I'll do it for you, Miss Sidden. I can't take the chance of missing an interesting story about Benson Hanaiker, or his nephew."

I pawed through my desk for O'Henry's and Sally's papers. I was so thankful I had only given Jackson Hanaiker a bill of sale with his check. I would have filled out the AKC papers later, transferring ownership and registry. I gave all of O'Henry's and Sally's statistics to David Sherwood, their registration numbers and their registered legal names. I gave him my phone number and address. He was to call immediately when he reached the hotel.

"Miss Sidden, my billing fee is one hundred dollars per hour. Is this satisfactory?"

"It's acceptable, Counselor. I'll mail you a check the same day I receive your statement."

"Until I call back, Miss Sidden."

"Right," I said and hung up.

I massaged my temples. The headache had eased a little, but hadn't disappeared. I went to the kitchen, filled a glass with ice and poured a Diet Coke. Taking it with me, I returned to my desk. Now the hard part. I lit a cigarette and took several deep breaths to give myself added oxygen in my system. I dialed the area code for Andrel, New York, and added the information numbers. The operator gave me Benson Hanaiker's number. The fate of O'Henry and Sally hung on this phone call, legally. I could possess them, but not legally own them without his signature. Nothing ventured, nothing gained. I dialed the number.

"Mr. Jackson Hanaiker's residence." It was a mature-sounding female voice. Ol' Smiling Jack had worked fast. He must know he's the heir apparent, taking over the house and having the servant calling it his. I wondered what had happened to Benson Hanaiker's child. Probably died, or maybe disinherited. The will usually isn't read until the body was planted. Maybe he had no competition.

"Mr. Jackson Hanaiker, please," I said in an officious voice.

"May I say who's calling?"

"Cartier's in New York," I replied in a haughty tone. Who could resist a call from that prestigious store? Someone might want an address in order to send diamonds.

"Please wait," she told me. I took my right hand and rubbed it on my jeans. My palms were sweating.

"Jackson Hanaiker," he answered. It was the same man. I had been afraid someone might have been using his name, but I would recognize that voice anywhere.

"Hello, slimeball. This is Jo Beth Sidden. Don't hang up on me. You need to hear what I have to say if you want to stay out of jail."

"I don't think we have anything to discuss, Ms. Sidden," he said with certainty. I gripped the phone in silence. He hadn't sounded shaken or nervous. I'd have to work on that, if he didn't hang up on me.

"What's this ridiculous statement you're making about staying out of jail? My check to you was honored. In fact, I know it has already cleared my bank."

Gotcha, you bastard! You're hooked, you couldn't resist. You have to know how much I know.

"Bubba," I began conversationally, "is going to live. He's conscious and describing you to a tee. I know you tried to set me up for his attack, but you were careless and let him get a good look at you. I've been cleared of all charges. I'm free."

"By the way, Ms. Sidden, if you are taping this conversation, you do not have my permission. Therefore, you can't use any tape in a court of law."

"I'm not taping you, you pompous ass. I don't need to. I know who you are and where you live, which is more than Bubba and the sheriff know at the present time. Am I making myself clear?"

"One more question, before I commit myself. Were you indicted by the grand jury? Did they get that far, before Bubba woke up?"

"Yes, I was indicted by a grand jury. Does that please you?" This guy was a nut. Why should he care if I was indicted or not?

He sighed audibly in the phone. "Well, at least I got part of it right. Your Bubba was much stronger than I imagined. He almost turned the tables on me. His strength caught me off guard."

"What on earth did you have against him and why try to frame me? I don't know you from Adam."

"You'll be given the answers quite soon, I imagine," he said thoughtfully. "This won't matter to you at all, but I hope you'll remember this later. I am sorry about what I had to do to you. You struck me as someone I would like to know better — at our first and only meeting."

He actually sounded sad. I had better get to the point. He might hang up.

"This is what I want you to do," I told him. "An attorney whose

name is Sherwood is going to be calling you very soon with the name of
a hotel where he will have papers for you to sign, a bill of sale for
O'Henry and Sally. You are to go to that hotel and sign the document
immediately after the funeral. Failure to do so will be detrimental to
your freedom. Do I make myself clear?"

"How do I know you won't call the sheriff, even if I do sign the
papers?"

"You don't, but if I were you I'd sign them, because if you don't, I
sure as hell will notify the sheriff of your identity."

"I'll be glad to sign your papers," he said in a good-natured tone.
"What good will the papers do if you don't have the dogs?"

"I'll worry about that later. Just sign them, okay?"

"Your dogs are at the SPCA in Fontain, my county seat. I knew I
might not be able to take care of them. They are beautiful dogs and I
know someone in Fontain will give them a good home."

I blinked. What was with this guy?

"I know where they are, you bastard. Just sign the papers. We won't
be having any future conversations."

"Oh, I'm sure we'll be talking again, real soon," he said with what
sounded like sadness. I hung up without answering him. I washed the
coffeemaker and tossed the Coke can. I needed some iced tea. I was dry
and nervous. This last phone call made me feel uneasy and hadn't helped
my headache.

George arrived back a little after ten. I told him everything that had
transpired since he left. We mulled over what Hanaiker had said and
what he hadn't said, and could come to no conclusion about what was
going on. George went outside to watch Rosie teach an obedience class.
We had heard people arriving for the last fifteen minutes. I was staring
out the office window when I noticed it was eleven o'clock. I felt cold
and had a smattering of chill bumps on my arms. As we say around here,
"A possum walked over my grave." I checked the setting on the air
conditioner, but it was correct, seventy-two degrees.

Back at the desk waiting for the phone to ring, I wondered again
who in hell was Benson Hanaiker, and how did he and his nephew figure in my life? Why did I have to wait almost a full year after my father's
death to receive my inheritance and the paintings? Why had my father
mentioned in his letter, "It wasn't allowed"? Who could have stopped
him and why? When my father called Hanaiker a "devil," years ago,
what had their business been, and what had made him hate the man?

I realized there was an important question I had failed to ask Carl's
old partner, Andrew Carpenter, when he had finally handed over my

father's letter. How could I have been so dense and not thought of it sooner? Was he instructed to hand over the letter on that particular day, or was it simply because he had the two letters and had been gone the month immediately after Carl's death and didn't have the opportunity?

I looked up Andrew Carpenter's number and called him. A female answered the phone.

"Hello."

"Is Mr. Carpenter in?"

"No, he's playing golf this morning. Would you like to leave a message?" She sounded cheerful and open. It was worth a shot.

"This is Jo Beth Sidden," I said casually. "I just remembered a question I should have asked him yesterday, when he handed over Wade's and my letters from our fathers." I waited.

"You won't remember me, Jo Beth," she said, "but when you were little, we saw quite a bit of you. Carl, Andrew and your father were good friends and fishing buddies. Arthur used to bring you over when you were just two or three years old and I would scold him for wanting to take a baby out on the boat in cold and rainy weather. Then I would get to take care of you while they were fishing. You were such a sweet child."

The sweet child had grown up to be devious. I felt bad about pumping her for information. Andrew would be furious with her if I could get anything out of her.

"I wish I could remember the times with you," I gushed in girlish enthusiasm. "It's silly, but all I wanted to know was when Mr. Carpenter received the instructions to hand over my letter. It's not important. I was just curious." I held my breath.

"Oh, I can answer that for you, dear," she said brightly. "I answered the phone Wednesday afternoon when the call came in. When Andrew finished his conversation, he told me it was too late to get to the bank; he would have to wait until Thursday. Thursday morning he was planning to go straight to the bank when it opened, but he received a phone call just before nine and he became very upset. He rushed out of here like a house was on fire and didn't say a word about when he would be back. He was gone for hours and very agitated and irritable when he finally got home. He practically snapped my head off when I asked him where he had been. Then Friday morning, he remarked that he had to go to the bank for your letter. Does that answer your question, dear?"

She sounded a little miffed that he had kept her in the dark about where he had gone. My guess was Hector had found out their marijuana crop had disappeared with no explanation and called Carpenter in a panic. It would have been unsettling news he couldn't share with his wife, especially this one. She loved to talk. Men have their golf and fishing and hunting and bars in their retirement years. She probably had an empty house most days, a few women to gossip with, and not much else.

"Oh, you answered my question beautifully," I told her. "No need to bother your husband now — it was just an idle question. Let's don't tell him I called and was being nosy, okay? He probably thinks a woman's place is in the home and not to ask unnecessary questions. You won't tell him, will you? I don't want him to think I'm flighty."

"He thinks all women are flighty," she answered with spirit, "especially me. Of course I won't mention your call if you don't want me to."

"Listen, Mrs. Carpenter, I'm very busy right now, but in a couple of weeks, I'd love to call you and make a date to have lunch. We could talk about old times — when you knew my father."

"That will be lovely, dear," she said merrily. "I look forward to your call." I said a protracted goodbye and hung up. At least I had kept her from getting in trouble with her husband, unless she slipped up and told him anyway. My conscience felt a little better.

I sat back and rummaged through my new information, picking at it here and there. Carpenter had received a phone call telling him to deliver my letter. From whom? Who was left to call? Carl was dead, my father was dead, it wasn't the bank — so who called? Why Wednesday? Why not eleven months ago, or ten days ago? I was going in circles. I guess I was too close to the problem to see the solution. I was much better at solving other people's dilemmas. I sat and tried to fit the small pieces of the knowledge I now possessed in the large square void of conjecture and wild assumptions. No divine, remarkable or workable solution appeared.

My analytical mind was chuckling derisively and feeling superior. It had come up with the logical solution on Thursday evening and each resulting bit of data was confirming, not denying its premise, while my silly, impractical heart had been digging in, fighting with animal ferocity and unwilling to concede an inch of lost ground. I left them to it; the battle was too wearying for me. I was the numb survivor on the sidelines waiting for the victor to emerge, not trying to participate in or anticipate the outcome.

33

"ALL THAT GLITTERS IS NOT GOLD"
April 17, Saturday, Noon

A little after twelve, I went into the kitchen and cut the long loaf of Cuban bread into four equal portions. They were about eight inches long. Perfect, I was starved. I unloaded all the makings from the refrigerator and prepared four whopping sandwiches. I placed two on a serving platter, covered them with a cloth napkin and took them upstairs to Rosie. She admired them and said she wouldn't be able to eat more than half of hers, they were so big.

I came downstairs, told Wayne his lunch was upstairs and told George to come in for lunch. I popped the tops of two cans of Bud and set the sandwiches on the table.

"Looks good," he commented. His hair was damp from washing his face. I said the blessing and we both dug in. After his second chomp, he looked at me with bulging eyes, swallowed hastily and grabbed his beer.

"I forgot to mention that besides bell, banana and sweet, I add lots of green chili peppers. Too hot for you?"

"No . . ." he said, sounding hoarse. "If I ever did have a delicate palate, it's history — God!"

"I like a spicy Cuban." We both had sweat on our foreheads and our eyes were tearing.

"That's the understatement of the year," he mumbled between gulps of beer.

The phone rang. Shit. Something had gone wrong somewhere, just my luck. I raced to catch it before the answering machine clicked in.

"Hello."

"Jo Beth, this is Wade. Can you spare a few minutes? I have that personal information I discussed with you yesterday."

"Sure, come over anytime. I'm free till five o'clock."

"I can come over now — if you're not busy."

"Come ahead. Have you eaten?"

"I just finished lunch," he told me before hanging up. Wonder what he had to tell me? I went back to the kitchen.

"That was Wade, my attorney. He's coming over in a few minutes. He has something to tell me." I got us two more beers.

"Is he the current boyfriend?" He took another bite of his sandwich.

"Nope, just a friend."

"Do you have a current fella?" He looked down at his plate and wouldn't meet my eyes.

"Not at the moment. My life has been too complicated since Bubba has been out of prison on parole. I've had to spend all my energy on defense. The way I have to live to exist inhibits a serious romance."

"I can understand the problems," he said in agreement. We finished our sandwiches and lit up.

"It's my turn for the dishes," I said, being gracious.

"Of course," he said dryly. "Two plates, no silverware, glasses, or pots and pans. I guess it will be my turn at supper?"

"You got it," I agreed. "It's really nice to share the chores equally with an intelligent man." I picked up the plates and carried them to the sink. He walked up behind me, placed a hand on the nape of my neck and slowly began to massage my back and shoulders. I leaned back into his touch. The harsh bing-bong of the first gate alarm startled both of us.

"Shit," he muttered, releasing me.

"It's probably Wade," I said in a husky voice and moved reluctantly away from him.

"Great timing," George said with irony. We walked out on the back porch and watched Wade climb out of his car and approach.

I introduced George to Wade as a friend and Wade, as my lawyer. The two shook hands. George spotted Wayne coming down the stairs and turned to me.

"I'll be out in the kennel with Wayne," he told me. George looked at Wade and said, "See you later." Wade nodded.

Wade and I went into the office. He sat on the couch and said no thanks when I asked if he would like a beer or soft drink. I sat in one of the occasional chairs and looked at him expectantly.

"Is he business or pleasure?" He asked the question brusquely. I stared at him with surprise.

"What an odd way to put it," I said thoughtfully. "A friend of four days and a business associate. He's a private detective from Waycross I hired to help me dig out some information."

"I guess you thought I wasn't capable of handling your affairs?"

"Wade, you seem to have forgotten about telling me to find another lawyer when I couldn't tell you where I was last Monday — remember?"

"I was upset. I still don't know why you wouldn't tell me, but that's finished business. Thank God, you don't need an alibi any longer." He sat silently, like he was waiting for me to ask him what he had to tell me. I was going to wait him out, but after lighting a cigarette and inhaling in silence for thirty seconds or so, I spoke.

"Well, my friend of eleven days and lawyer, what did you want to tell me?"

He smiled in victory. "I have good news for you. Last Monday morning, I contacted the DEA and they invited me to their office in the courthouse. I told them all of your suspicions, only I told them they were my suspicions."

"You didn't," I said weakly. "You couldn't have been so stupid."

"I was not stupid," he said with satisfaction. "I put my trust in my father and refused to consider your suspicions and I was correct. They couldn't search until Thursday. It took them two whole days, all of Thursday and all of yesterday. They did the aerial search on Thursday and the buildings and penetration of the woods on Friday. They went into the woods with almost twenty men. They found absolutely nothing. I was elated, but they sure acted surly and disappointed. They never thanked me for coming forth and telling them my suspicions."

"They probably thought you were as stupid as I did," I said and broke into howling laughter. I couldn't help it; the more I thought about it the funnier it got. He sat quietly and eyed me with disfavor. The more he gave me the fisheye, the more I laughed. I wiped tears with the palms of my hands and finally had to fetch tissues, because my nose started leaking. I hiccuped a couple of times and was finally able to straighten my features and try to act normal.

"Are you finished?" He sat quietly, waiting.

"I'm truly sorry, Wade," I said with sincerity. I had no right to make fun of this good man. He had done what he thought was right and I had done what I considered right and, boy, our rights were poles apart.

I didn't want to consider the trouble the four of us would have found ourselves in if the DEA had responded immediately to Wade's announcement. They would have caught us red-handed during their copter search, in the middle of the woods, or in the upstairs apartment vacuuming up marijuana seeds. They would not have believed our story of destroying the pot until we had spent some time in a cell, spent a lot of money on lawyers, and taken lie-detector tests up the kazoo. I grew sober when I realized the jail I would have spent some time in was run by Sheriff Carlson.

Wade seemed to be mollified with my apology. I sat and studied his features. Here was a decent guy who was ready to settle down and have children. I tried to picture him beside me, stretched out on my bed. I couldn't bring his features into clear focus. I couldn't imagine him naked and the two of us making love. If that was the measure of love, I would flunk the course. Maybe I had been without love too long.

Wade told me he had met briefly, yesterday afternoon, with bank officials and, so far, he hadn't found much in my father's accounts or been able to trace any securities. He said when an IRS agent was available, he would make an appointment for the three of us to be present when Dad's safety deposit box was opened. I told him I didn't expect much; Dad had explained in his letter that I would receive next to nothing.

He seemed relieved I was taking the news so calmly about the money situation. He said he wouldn't have a full and exact accounting for several days. I told him I understood. He looked at his watch and said he had to run. I thanked him again for all he had done for me. I apologized again for laughing. I told him my nerves had been on edge for days, that that possibly could explain my actions. I walked him to the car and gave him a hug. He looked as if he had forgiven me for my bad display of manners.

The hours from two to four went by ever so slowly. I received only one phone call: Sherwood, the lawyer, called to report he was in a hotel room, had called Jackson Hanaiker and he had promised to come to the room immediately following the funeral. I sat and fretted. George calmly read a book, the one he had started the night he arrived. Once in a while he would raise his eyes from his book and make a soothing comment. He knew I was almost sick with suspense.

At five after four the phone rang. I jumped in shock and grabbed it. It was Harvey Gusman, the vet. He had the flight schedule for the dogs. A small feeder flight to Albany, New York, and from Albany to Jacksonville, arriving at two in the morning. I asked him how they looked and acted.

"Beautiful animals. Jonathan Nielson explained their condition on arrival Wednesday evening, so I didn't sedate them. I think they will travel well. They act a little lost and bewildered, but that's because of strange surroundings. I believe they will be fine, once they arrive home."

"Did Mr. Nielson pay you?"

"In full and in cash. I gave him a receipt. Thanks for the business.

You wouldn't consider moving your kennel up here, I reckon," he said, imitating my Southern drawl.

"No, I reckon not," I drawled in a slow parody. "You all take care, you heah?" He hung up laughing.

I called Ramon. Carol answered and said Ramon was with a patient and could he call me back. I gave her the time the dogs would arrive and asked if they could pick them up in Jacksonville. She was elated. She said she and Ramon could have dinner out and catch a movie while they were over there. It would be a night out for her. I suddenly realized how young she was and that being the wife of a vet was very confining. Most nights, in a thriving practice, there are animals recovering from accidents, illnesses or operations that need hands-on care. I bet she hadn't been out in weeks. I told her to call Wayne and he would sit with any patients that couldn't be left alone. She said that unless some emergency came in, the clinic would be free of overnight guests. I could tell that she was praying for no last-minute accident victim.

At 4:20, Alicia from Sinclair's office called and said the faxes were coming in from Fontain. I ran to the bedroom and grabbed the very expensive bottle of perfume Hank had given me for Christmas last year. I hadn't even broken the seal around the bottle. I had wrapped it earlier, addressed an envelope in Alicia's name and placed two twenties inside. When I had asked Sinclair if he had anyone to man his office this afternoon, Alicia had volunteered.

She was nineteen and, knowing Saturday afternoons were important at that age, I had paid her accordingly. Sinclair had a water polo game, or was on the water-skiing team or something. He was unwinding from the rigors of the "Ides of March," plus thirty days grace we receive for filing our taxes.

George and I climbed into his car and drove to Sinclair's office. The insurance agent had taken good pictures. He had faxed only twelve. He explained in a note that all the other people had been too old or too young. Jackson Hanaiker gazed out from the fourth fax as he was going up the church steps. He was very handsome in his dark suit with a subdued tie. He looked solemn to fit the occasion, but I bet he was dancing for joy inside. His uncle had finally expired and he was now King of the Hill. It was a close-up shot and very clear. His very white teeth looked large in the crude reproduction of the fax. His eyes looked familiar, like they resembled an old friend. I felt strange, staring into the eyes of the photograph.

Alicia was thrilled with the perfume and protested that forty dollars was too much, but I waved away her protest and she almost beat us out the door in making her escape. The three of us walked down the stairs together.

Back at home, I checked the answering machine. I had a message from David Sherwood. It was brief and to the point. "He arrived, the deed is done. Fed-exing the bill-of-sale and my bill out tonight. Both should arrive Monday. Don't forget your promise. Good luck."

I had no idea that lawyers could talk in shorthand. In all my dealings with them, they tend to draw out simple statements into prolonged lawyerspeak. I breathed a sigh of relief. Today had been very productive so far. I knocked on the nearest wood. Everything was clicking into place. Lady Luck, smile a little longer — the sheriff was next.

I told George I was meeting the sheriff alone for a little conference and he started finding objections. When he saw that wasn't working, he came up with a compromise.

"Let me hide in the van. I won't come out, but I'll be there if you need me. What do you say?"

"I say, no. If I get into trouble, you popping out of the cake is not going to help. It would only get you arrested and charged, along with me.

"Arrested?"

"Look, George, this has nothing to do with the problem I hired you to help me with. I need you here to wait for my one allowed phone call or my return, whichever comes first." I gave him my address book for Wade's and Sinclair's numbers. "If the balloon goes up, do what you can. Sinclair is out on the water somewhere, but if you can get Wade, he will know what to do."

"Why won't you tell me what this is all about?" he said in exasperation. "I'm a big boy, I can keep a secret."

"You could also be an accessory before the fact of a crime. Just what you need in your line of business," I retorted.

"Crime? For God's sake, what are you going to do?" He looked perplexed. I patted his shoulder and mustered up a big smile.

"Just put a light in the window. I'll be home before you miss me."

I called Rosie and told her not to expect me home for dinner and for Wayne to check with Ramon before he left the house if he had a date. He might be needed at the clinic tonight.

George walked with me in silence to the van. He wasn't pouting; he had just said everything that needed to be said. At the van, he put his hands on my shoulders and looked me in the eye.

"When you come back, we'll put on our glad rags and go out to dinner, maybe some dancing."

"Swell," I said with a lump in my throat. "I'll hurry back." He watched from the drive until I rounded the curve out of his sight. As I headed for Johnston's Landing, I pondered why I was always taking risks and trying to sound so in control and nonchalant about it all. I was scared and wanted to call the meeting off and hurry back to George. I felt what I was doing was worth it, however, so I continued to Johnston's Landing and my meeting with a nasty piece of work who was currently sheriff of this county.

I drove into the landing area at seven minutes before six and spotted the surveillance van, parked in the woods about a hundred yards to my right. Everyone over the age of ten recognized the van and knew its function from the second day it had been in possession of the sheriff's department. School kids made jokes about it. Sheriff Carlson had ordered it repainted a sedate blue, with a bakery home delivery name printed on the side. The only ones it fooled were tourists passing through town. It really looked ridiculous nestled among the cypress tree knees and swamp flowers near the edge of the road. The landing was deserted even on Saturday afternoon. The pan and bottom fish weren't biting; with high water they were bedding this time of year.

The sheriff hadn't arrived. He would make his entrance several minutes late, to show me that he didn't come on command. I looked around and spotted a huge sycamore tree that had just reached full leaf, about a hundred yards away. It looked ideal.

I sat quietly rehearsing my lines until his personal patrol car slowly pulled into view. He parked near a picnic table, furnished by the road department or the parks department, I wasn't sure which. I got out of the van and strolled over, leaving my .32 locked in the van's glove compartment. When I was near enough for conversation, I motioned that he should walk to me. He hesitated; he didn't want to leave the table. It was probably wired as a back-up precaution — one of the reasons I wanted him to walk over to me. I was fifty yards from the table, and I hoped I was in the correct spot. It was a grassy field where the boaters and picnickers parked. Other than a couple of discarded beer cans, some Hardee's sandwich wrappers and a few pine cones blown from the trees some distance away, the field was bare of debris. He finally joined me — fuming.

"Make it snappy. I'm a busy man. What do you want?"

"I want to ask a favor of you. I know you don't like me; the feeling is mutual, but I wanted to appeal to your better nature, if you have one."

"Spit it out, prissy. People in hell want ice water. I don't think there's any favor . . ." He checked his speech and his pig eyes narrowed to slits.

He had my right arm behind my back before I sensed his intention. I tried to turn, but the cuff clamped shut on my right wrist and he levered my left to meet it. I tried to struggle, but he had caught me completely unprepared for the move. My heart started hammering in my chest and my mouth dried with fear, making me stutter.

"Wh . . . what are you do . . . doing? Why did you force handcuffs on me. I've done nothing . . . let me go!" He was deceptively fast for a man about forty pounds overweight on a five-foot, five-inch frame.

He spun me around by my right shoulder, almost making me lose my balance. He gave me an evil grin, running his hands roughshod over my body, under my arms, cupping my breasts, feeling my buttocks, running his hands down my thighs, up the inside of my legs and finished off his disgusting performance by giving my pubic mound a vicious squeeze. He grunted and conversed as he stooped to reach my ankles. I gritted my teeth and resisted the strong urge to bring my knee up quickly and ruin his nose and dental work.

"Making sure you ain't wearing a wire, you prissy-pants cunt. I didn't even enjoy feeling you up, you feminist dyke. What was so all-fired important that you wanted to ask me? But I can already tell you that you're wasting your time. I wouldn't give you air if you were in a jug. Speak up, you've got me curious."

"I wanted to beg you to quit treating the women prisoners who are booked into your jail so horribly. You let your female jailers abuse them physically and allow the male deputies to watch. Also, Jasmine Jones hasn't been on the streets for six years. She's a law-abiding citizen and lives in virtual seclusion to keep from being falsely arrested by your deputies. Please, won't you show some milk of human kindness and stop physically and mentally abusing these women? I want to hire Jasmine to work with me . . . please?"

"Please?" he mimicked in a high squeaky voice. "Let me tell you, cunt, my deputies don't just watch, I've got four of my men that get to knock off a piece of black pussy right in the cunt's cell — when I'm feeling generous. As for that nigger whore, Jasmine, you want to hire, I don't think she'll want your job when I get done with her. She'd slipped my mind, since I hadn't had her inside for so long. As soon as I get through here, I think I'll send a couple of deputies over to her place and have her picked up for 'soliciting,'" he said with a chuckle. "I've got a little 'milk of human kindness' right here for her." He grabbed his crotch and pumped the lump several times so I wouldn't miss his point. Through a red haze of anger I tried to speak in a normal tone, as though I was disappointed and defeated.

"Take the cuffs off — you've made your point. I see I can't reason with you."

"Well now, I'm not that hard to get along with," he said in a sneering tone. "If you want to make 'nice,' I might change my mind."

"TAKE THE CUFFS OFF!" My voice was out of control. You feel so helpless when your hands are bound.

He laughed and gave me a push, to turn me. He took the handcuffs off a lot slower than when he had snapped them on. He gave me another shove in the direction of the van.

"Get out of here. I've got other fish to fry. You have a nice evening, you heah? Enjoyed our little chat."

I kicked a discarded beer can out of my path on my march back to the van. I didn't look back. I didn't feel safe even after I reached the van. I cranked up and got out of there. He stood and watched me pull away. Back on the highway, my right knee started jerking nervously and I had trouble controlling the accelerator. I pulled in the driveway at Jiffy Foods, a convenience store just down the road. I hopped out and went inside, purchased a canned Diet Coke, lit a cigarette and went through the wide double doors into the back storage area.

"If you missed one word of that miserable conversation, I'm gonna inflict some serious damage in here!" I was speaking in general to the three men and one woman who were sitting and leaning against the excess stock in the cramped space. One black man, two whites and a plain-looking black woman, about forty. They didn't have happy expressions. Several pieces of expensive-looking electronic equipment shared what little space was available. A tall black man with glasses and a sweet smile inched toward me and clasped both of my hands in his. He was James Carmichel, Chief State Attorney for our local district. One of his twin sons, Rodney, worked at the kennel each summer and helped with training.

"We got every word, clear and pure, Jo Beth," he said quietly, "and you've already inflicted some damage in here. Johnson had on earphones with the audio gain as high as it goes when you kicked the beer can as you left. We had five receiving units scattered around where you were supposed to stand. We had two in the beer cans, two taped to the underside of the pine cones, and one in the sandwich box. We're so sorry that Carlson gave you such a rough time out there."

"Well, I guess it will be worthwhile, if he gets some serious time. He will get prison time, won't he?"

"I doubt it," said the black woman. She leaned forward and shook hands with me. "Let me introduce myself. I'm Lila Green, an investigator for the Governor's Ethics Commission. If he writes his confession to the crimes and signs it, and also writes his resignation — effective immediately — the governor will allow him to resign without scandal and being held responsible for his despicable crimes. We'll be playing the tape for him as soon as we pack up here. I'm sure we'll have his confession and resignation in hand immediately thereafter."

"It sucks!" I said hotly.

"I agree," she said in a firm voice. "If it were my choice, he'd be hung by his balls on the courthouse lawn, but we're three months away from the primaries and we've had a little too much corruption in law enforcement lately. It's politically expedient." She dropped her gaze when I stared at her.

"Good luck with your 'ethics,'" I said softly with contempt.

I turned to Carmichel. "I need a phone. I have to warn Jasmine."

"She's safe. I sent two state patrolmen to her residence as soon as Carlson uttered his threat. They will stick to her like glue until we get the sheriff and his four deputies in custody. Let me introduce you to the rest of the personnel here."

"Don't bother," I said quietly. "I have to hurry home, take a hot shower, brush and gargle. Suddenly, I have a very bad taste in my mouth." I turned around and got out of there.

George was waiting in the courtyard when I drove up. I gave him a wave and drove on past to put the van under cover. When I reached the porch he gave me a relieved grin and a hug.

"How'd it go?" He asked, acting casual and unconcerned.

"Piece of cake," I said. I noticed he had showered and dressed in nice slacks and polished loafers. He smelled wonderful. Either aftershave or cologne, but I knew it was Old Spice. He was wearing just his white undershirt.

"I wanted your opinion on the shirt," he explained. "Should I go with the Italian silk or the Georgia casual?"

"Give me twenty minutes, then put on the Georgia casual," I told him, glancing at my watch. I flew to my bedroom. Imagine me, going out to dinner with an m-a-n. I wanted to call the hospital to make sure Bubba was still a patient, but I knew I was being silly. I took a five-minute shower and put on a white waffle-check piqué dress that was tight enough — I had to suck everything that would move, to get it to zip. I added turquoise teardrop earrings, turquoise high-heeled sandals with thin straps and added the matching bag. Shit, the gun wouldn't fit in with the other necessary items. I reluctantly left it under my pillow. I brushed my hair, used coral lipstick, then dropped the tube in the small bag. I used mascara, blush and a bit of pressed powder. It would be sweated away within the hour, but maybe he would remember how it looked. I eyed the finished product. Some people have it and some don't. I was one of the don'ts.

His eyes widened when I entered the office.

"Man, you look great!" He sounded surprised. Did he think I was gonna appear wearing jeans?

"You look pretty spiffy yourself," I replied. He was wearing a casual white shirt with a tiny stripe of gold. With his cream-colored slacks and his light brown sports coat, he looked cool, comfortable and classy. I was already regretting my tight skirt. I wouldn't be able to eat much.

We went to Attenburg's King Steer Steak House, where I had slaved six nights a week for five years, saving money for my kennel. We sat at the bar and had two beers while we waited for a table. Everyone spoke to me. The women checked out George, while the men checked my boobs. I told him about working in this establishment, about my day job and some hilarious episodes that happened when Georgia rednecks and the Balsa City elite sat down in the same restaurant at the same time.

Patsy, our waitress, took our order and cheerfully held up her hand when I started to tell her how I wanted my steak.

"Butterflied and well-well-well done," she said laughing. "You won't have to worry about sending this one back, Jo Beth. Our chef this evening is death on steaks that are ordered well done. It makes him angry and he cinderizes them."

"Then it should be perfect," I said smiling at her. George looked at me strangely. His order had been rare, normal for rednecks.

"I just want to make sure it's dead," I replied to his look.

He laughed, then looked over my shoulder and remarked, "Your lawyer just walked in with a knock-out date."

"Describe her," I demanded as I raised my beer mug to take a sip.

"Short, beautiful, blonde — no, ash blonde, gorgeous, maybe five-four, a hundred pounds, a knock-out."

"You're repeating your praises," I said in waspish haste. "Are they heading this way?" I had been running through the available women in Balsa City. The description of ash blonde had narrowed the field.

"Is she wearing yellow?" It could be none other than Sheri Dawson, our local librarian, divorced and our only resident beauty queen. Yellow was her favorite color.

"As ever was," George murmured as he pushed back his chair to rise.

Wade and Sheri were standing beside the table when I lifted my eyes and acknowledged their presence. Wade looked embarrassed and Sheri looked smug.

"Hello," I said brightly. I introduced George to Sheri. "The men know each other; they met at my house earlier today," I explained to Sheri.

The smug look vanished and was replaced with a possessive glitter in her eyes. She was clinging to Wade's arm like the lifeboat was sinking and she didn't have a life vest. George invited them to join us but Wade said they were joining friends. Wade was within a foot of me, so I reached out and gently tugged his sleeve. He leaned toward me slightly and I gazed into his eyes.

I spoke softly, so he would have to bend closer.

"Thanks for today, Wade. I've thought about what you said and I totally agree."

"I'm glad," he said with a smile. Sheri's look was now bordering on frantic. I gave her a sweet smile.

"You're looking well, Sheri," I told her. This was like throwing a breath mint to a starving lion. She gave me a stiff smile, but her eyes were declaring open warfare.

When they left to join her friends, I didn't watch their progress. I couldn't care less who they were dining with this evening.

"I can't believe you're jealous of her," George announced. "You have her beat by a country mile."

"Oh no," I said sternly, "you can't weasel out of that glowing description of her that easy — and I'm not jealous of her. She just brought out the cat in me by hanging on to him like she was unable to stand alone. I hate to see weak and clinging females."

"Some men love weak and clinging females," George remarked.

"Is that your type?"

"Not any more," he said softly. I looked at him and ran the same test I had tried on Wade earlier. I narrowed my eyes and tried to imagine him stretched out beside me in my bed. I could see him clearly. Broad chest, tapering waist and strong thighs. I could visualize us making love. I could almost feel the heat of his body against me.

He looked at me, "What are you thinking?"

"I'm fantasizing," I said with a slow smile of contentment.

"Damn, I was really looking forward to my steak and those potatoes you described," he said with great reluctance. "Shall we go?" He started to rise from the chair.

"Don't be silly," I said, laughing. "Sit down. I'm hungry."

"So am I," he admitted with a grin.

412

The steaks came and he looked at the shoe leather masquerading as steak on my plate.

"You can't possibly be serious about eating that," he stated, as he cut into his own steak. When I saw the blood following his knife cut, I looked down at mine, thankful I didn't have barbaric tastes.

"You deliberately goaded her," he said, referring to Sheri. "Why?"

"Her feminine wiles and the fact that she was a beauty contestant just rubs me the wrong way."

"You don't approve of beauty contests?" I knew he was trying to hear some more of my homespun philosophy and I should have shut up, but I was off and running.

"Parading around on display, shaving her pubic area so she can wear a strip as wide as a Band-Aid between her legs? I'm a staunch defender of women's rights, but I also think they have a certain responsibility for having some personal decency and respect for their body. We were doing a drug sweep a few weeks ago in a dive. I'm talking sawdust on the floor and you pee in the alley. Three women came in from out of town, they weren't locals. I swear to God, George, they had on slips. Just a silk slip, an easily recognizable garment, and absolutely nothing on underneath. The colors were white, pink and peach. They stood silhouetted by the jukebox lights and were making crude sexual movements to the music. Tell me something, George, if you had witnessed this scene, and one of our local boys had slung one of these women over his shoulder and headed for the parking lot, what would you have done?"

He thought for a few seconds. "Worried she might trip him and beat him to the floor and I would have to witness their tender mating."

"Great, you just proved my point. Any woman earns respect in direct proportion to how she dresses and handles her body."

"You were worried about these women's virtue?"

"Nope, what I worried about was the sicko standing in the shadows drooling over these bitches and getting primed. He heads out home and runs across a decent wife and mother who had a flat tire driving home from the last shift. You read about it in the morning papers. You wouldn't wear snowshoes picking your way through a mine field, and you wouldn't lean against a lion's cage and feed him raw meat with your fingers in your birthday suit. All women would be safer if they used a little common horse sense, but some women break the rules and others suffer because of it. Damn it, George, why didn't you stop me? I climbed on my soap box again."

"I gather you don't . . . wear a bikini?" He made the remark to lighten the mood.

"Nope," I said shortly, ashamed I had spouted off and changed the mood of the evening.

"It's hard to find a one-piece suit nowadays you can pull down to cover the cheeks of your ass," I said with a smile.

We both went back to our steak. I will not do that again, I chanted to myself, I will not do that again. Talk, talk, talk. I never know when to shut up.

When we were crossing the parking lot to George's car, he asked if I felt like a little music, maybe some dancing. I told him I'd rather go home, it had been a long emotional day, and I was tired. I felt I had ruined the evening, after it had looked like it was perking merrily along. George was quiet on the way home. I racked my brain trying to think of a funny story to lighten the mood, but decided to keep my mouth closed.

When we arrived home, I told George I was going to take a long, hot bath. He said he thought he would call it a night and went to his room. I started filling the tub and dumped in some expensive bubblebath. I opened the dresser to my "saved for special events" drawer. I decided on a pale blue satin gown — the feel of satin is so sensuous against bare skin. I brushed, gargled, flossed and climbed into the tub.

As I soaked, I thought of George. He had left it entirely up to me if anything happened tonight. There was one thing you couldn't accuse good ol' George of, he certainly didn't believe in the hard sell, I thought in irritation. I stayed in the tub twenty minutes then toweled off, dabbed some potent perfume on my wrists and in the bend of my knees and slipped on the gown and brushed my hair. I looked in the mirror and started fussing with my hair. For God's sake, I was acting like a skittish bride. Either set the alarms and go to bed or set the alarms and join George in his bed.

I set the alarms, walked down the hall, continued past my room and stopped in his open darkened doorway. The nightlight in the hall cast just enough light to see the pale blur of the bed, since I knew where to look.

"Do you have room for a guest?" I asked in a tiny voice. He might be asleep.

"I thought you'd never get here," he said.

34

"FORGIVING OTHERS IS MUCH EASIER THAN FORGIVING YOURSELF"
April 18, Sunday, 5:45 A.M.

When I woke up I was on my back and entwined in the sheet. I focused on the time projected on the ceiling from the digital clock in the guest bedroom. The figures were a foot high but it took several seconds before the time-display registered on my mind: 5:45 a.m. I felt a warm heaviness on my thigh and by moving my head sideways a bit, I could see what was causing the pressure. George was on his stomach and had one heavy leg thrown over mine. Lack of circulation had caused a mild numbness the entire length of my right leg.

I eased my leg free and worked it clear of the sheet. My bladder telling me that it was time to get up. I became conscious of a persistent buzzing sound and distant thumps. I first blamed the clock but after listening closely, I could tell the sound was much further away. I mentally groaned. It must be the refrigerator. You're really never immune from household disasters when you're prone to having gremlins in your appliances. I wanted to snuggle close to George and drift back to sleep, but my bladder and the annoying sound conspired to make me rise.

I padded down the hallway toward the bathroom. The noise was louder in the hall and I decided it wasn't the refrigerator. That left the computer in the office and that thought brought me fully awake. As much as that sucker cost, it better not be the culprit. Out in the hallway it suddenly dawned on me: the noise I was hearing was a weak imitation of a sound the backdoor doorbell makes when it is healthy. The thumping sounds had to be the old-fashioned door knocker that used to be on the front door of my grandfather's farmhouse. I ran toward the sound, barefoot and wearing only my satin shorty gown.

I threw open the door and stared wild-eyed at Wayne. If Wayne was standing there, something must be wrong with Rosie. I had startled him. He had a finger on the doorbell and was holding onto the door knocker when I jerked open the door.

"What's wrong with Rosie?" I signed with apprehension.

"Nothing," he assured me. He signed quickly. "Monroe correctional has an escape." He glanced at his watch. "About forty-five minutes ago." He was trying to ignore the fact that I was in a satin gown and was looking studiously over my shoulder.

"Hang on," I said, "I'll be right back." I ran to my room, grabbed a shorty housecoat and raced back while I was pulling it on.

"How many?" I asked, as I tried to get my mind in high gear.

"Three, all heavies. Attempted murder, armed robbery with a firearm, attempted murder with a prior attempted escape."

"And they were at Monroe?" I said with disbelief. I was hastily trying to decide which dog to take. I decided on Bo, not Susie, and I didn't let my mind dwell on the reason for the decision. Bo could handle it.

"They were awaiting transfers to Atlanta. I'm taking Caesar and Mark Anthony. You want Susie and Bo?"

"I'm taking Bo and Mark Anthony for back-up. You're not going," I signed calmly.

"The hell I'm not!" He was angry. "Mother told me you were hinting around that you weren't going to use me in searches anymore, but I thought she had misunderstood. Why not?"

"You know why, Wayne," I signed. "I should have told you earlier, but I never seemed to find the proper time. I've been so caught up in events lately. We can talk when I get back."

"I'll load your van, and then I quit!" he signed and stalked off.

Oh shit. I needed coffee and a cigarette, not a resignation before six o'clock. After I put the coffee on, I dressed in jeans, sweatshirt, and Prowings. Back in the kitchen, I poured coffee and headed for my desk. I lit a cigarette and pulled my address book toward me and looked up Monroe's number and dialed.

"Monroe Correctional Institute," a male voice answered.

"This is Jo Beth Sidden, Bloodhounds, Incorporated. Could you give me your name please?"

"Clive Johnson, Dispatcher," he answered.

"Thank you, Mr. Johnson, I am responding to your request for a search-and-rescue team. Who is in charge from Shelton County?"

"Deputy Sergeant Andrew Caslighter, Shelton County Sheriff's Department," he answered crisply. It was a pleasure doing business with a competent person.

"Is it possible to patch me through to him?"

"Surely. Please hold." I spent my waiting time computing my ETA.

"Deputy Sergeant Caslighter" boomed in my ear. I had never met the sergeant.

"Sergeant, this is Jo Beth Sidden, Bloodhounds, Incorporated. My estimated time of arrival is now seven-thirty. If it changes, I will notify you en route. What direction are they heading?"

"Directly for Okefenokee, from near the west gate." Somehow I knew he was going to say that. For once, I wish the bastards would head for high ground. I had pulled out my map of Shelton County.

"I'll come in on State Road Two-sixteen. You can watch for me. Have you gathered any clothing that has been worn by the three of them?"

"No, ma'am, I'm leaning toward leap-frog tracking at this time. We've had a tentative sighting on a road three miles from the wire. It will save time."

I sighed. Another general. Why was it that small counties produced all generals and no foot soldiers? I decided to try to be pleasant.

"Sergeant, you've never worked with me before. Maybe they didn't inform you that I'm in charge of the scene and make the decisions?"

"No, ma'am. I was informed by my shift commander that I was in charge. How do we settle this issue?" He was being just as pleasant as I was.

"Sergeant, I suggest you call your sheriff and get the decision. I'm sitting here having my first cup of coffee and cigarette and it's too early to argue. I'm not moving my butt out of this chair until you call me back and tell me you are ready to follow my orders. And Sergeant, this conversation is taped, in case you conveniently forget the essentials of our conversation. I'm sure you understand." I hung up.

I pulled over a sheet of stationery and scribbled a note for George:
Dear George,

I've been called out for a search and rescue at Monroe Correctional in Shelton County. Three prisoners think they can outrun my dogs. Fat chance! Food in the fridge. Go back to bed, you may need your strength later! Be home ASAP.
Jo Beth

I sipped coffee and studied the map, planning my route. It was twenty-five minutes before the phone rang. I picked it up on the first ring.

"Yes, Sergeant?"

"Sorry for the mixed-up signals, Miz Sidden. You're in charge. What would you like me to do before you arrive?"

Now, this was a man. He wasn't showing anger or frustration. The search came before petty bickering.

"Please call me Jo Beth. Try to get jeans or socks that each man wore. Do you have their records handy?"

"Yes, ma'am."

"What's their weight?"

"Their weight?" He seemed surprised. "Just a minute." I waited while he checked. "One seventy-two, one fifty-six, and two hundred nine pounds," he recited.

"What's the height of the two hundred pounder?"

"Five foot seven," he said.

"Fine, let's concentrate on this man. Try to get something he wore recently. If you come up empty, take his towel, but only if he was in a one-man cell."

"Anything else?"

"I don't think so. My latest ETA is now eight. I'll call if I'm running late. See you at the west gate about eight."

I went to the kitchen and made five large sandwiches of ham, salami, and bologna on rye with mustard and wrapped them in foil. When I have officers with me on searches, they will eye my food and I have to divide with them. I was taking plenty with me this time. I knew I would be hungry in a couple of hours. I took a six-pack cooler out of the closet and put six Diet Cokes inside and filled it with ice. I grabbed my wallet, cooler, and sandwiches and went to the van. Wayne was not in sight. I checked the dogs in their cages, then checked the extra leads, backpack, both weapons, and the deer jerky in the front seat. I pulled out of the courtyard in the early morning coolness.

Thank God, we would be traveling west and have the sun at our backs. I reached for a Diet Coke and lit another cigarette. My entire route was county blacktop but there are a lot of curves around cypress swamps and creeks, and also, early morning traffic. I visualized the to-pographical map I had studied. We would have about three miles of timber with a few isolated residences before we hit the swamp area.

I approached the west gate of the prison less than a mile after turning off the state road. I saw a Shelton County patrol car under the shade of a Bradford pear tree. It was ten minutes after eight, not bad timing. Two deputies were standing by the car and two were sitting inside with the doors open to catch any breeze.

A deputy with sergeant stripes on his tan uniform shirt walked out to meet me when I pulled to a stop alongside his car. I hopped out to greet him and stuck out my hand.

"Sergeant Caslighter?" I asked, smiling up at him. He was a big dude, a little over six feet. Blonde hair, very short, dark blue eyes and a nervous smile. I had to guess thirty for his age. He was the type that would look like a college student when he was pressing forty. He had a firm grip, but didn't try to crush bones, like some of his kind.

"Call me Andy," he said. "Can I ride with you to the starting point?"

"Sure, hop in," I told him. I climbed back under the wheel and once he was seated and buckled up, I asked him which way.

"Straight ahead. It's about a half mile or more." I accelerated on the hardtop that looked to run parallel with the high, heavy-gauged fencing with razor wire on top. The other deputies were following us.

"How many men do you have here for the search?"

"Eight. The rest are at the scene where they cut the wire."

"What did they use?"

"They are still trying to figure that out. The experts on the wire say no ordinary blade can penetrate it. They were advising us by phone that the equipment used was very expensive and hard to come by. They took whatever it was with them."

"If they had access to a sophisticated piece of equipment, let's hope they didn't have a getaway car waiting on the hardtop."

"Security here at the prison says it's impossible. They know the exact time of the break; an alarm sounded on the security console. One of the links cut had an alarm wire running through it. They have a patrol car moving around the perimeter all night. They swear their roving patrol was only four minutes away when the alarm sounded. They radioed the location and he went there immediately. The wire is floodlighted, so the guard focused his spotlight on the three dirt roads to the right. They are padlocked by the hunting clubs that lease the forest hunting rights. It had rained earlier and none of the three dirt roads had tracks. He speeded up and met another guard coming from the opposite direction. No car could have gotten by either one. They went back and personally checked the locks on the cables across the roads. They were all padlocked."

"Well, that means they have to be in the woods, I guess." Andy was still talking when we arrived at the place where the fence had been cut. We both unbuckled.

"Andy, you can send all but three of your men back to other duty. We'll only take three, you and me. You were planning on going?"

"Oh, yes," he said with enthusiasm, "wouldn't miss it."

I stretched several times and did some mild exercises while Andy was sending his excess deputies on their way. The men standing around watching me acted as if I was doing some strange tribal dance. I was loosening some tight muscles from driving under tension for forty miles. I ignored them.

One deputy opened the trunk of the patrol car and the men started strapping on snake leggings. Another deputy was handing out water bottles. I was packing the sandwiches in my backpack when Andy reappeared. I indicated the men in their summer uniform pants.

"That's all they are going to wear for protection?"

"The men agreed that the heavy twill jumpsuits were too hot to wear. Do you think they need them?" I controlled my impatience and reached for my rescue suit.

"Feel the fabric," I instructed him. It is fairly lightweight material, but he could see that no air penetrated the suit.

"I'm awash with sweat five minutes after I zip up and I also carry a thirty-pound pack. I wouldn't step one foot into the woods or swamp without it and sometimes I go out two or three times a week. It's your decision, but the more protection you have between your skin and snake fangs, the safer you'll be. Before the dew dries and it heats up is the most dangerous time. My fabric is snake-proof — your twill isn't, but it could snag a fang where the snake is helpless to bite or deflect a strike, so the full dose of venom doesn't penetrate so deeply. Have you or any of your deputies had any experience in the swamp?"

"I don't believe so," he said. His face was glowing with color.

"Don't worry, I know what I'm doing. Maybe we won't have any casualties." He thought about it and hurried off. I heard groans and distinct curses. I wasn't going to have happy campers today. I saw that Wayne, even in anger, had been efficient. He had added three long, light chain dog leads. Hopefully we would need all three. I pulled out two gallon-size baggies and laid them on the ledge of the dog box. Bo had his nose against the wire mesh and was happily thumping his tail.

"Andy, would you ask one of the security guards standing over there to come over, so I can tell him how to handle the dog I'm leaving here?"

Andy was now dressed in his dark brown jumpsuit with the large white letters on front and back, telling the world he was the L-A-W.

When the guard arrived, I instructed him on how to care for Mark Anthony.

"The dog boxes are ventilated, but it can still get over one hundred degrees inside. Be sure he has plenty of water. Keep moving the van to keep it in the shade, and turn it where any breeze will pass through the cages. After eleven take him out of the box and tether him with the twenty-five-foot chain so he can crawl under the van." I left a spare van key.

I popped another Coke and drank it while I dressed. We were attracting a crowd, even on this deserted road. Two deputies tried to keep the cars moving and kept warning people to keep off the area we were going to sweep.

I finished dressing and Andy helped me get my pack settled. I opened the dog box, released Bo, attached his lead and knelt beside him. This was the difficult part. This had to be a totally quiet search from the get-go. He would run silent during the chase — but he so loved to celebrate his victory. This chase had to be totally silent. Here is where I would find out if my months of silent training for convict searches could override his joy of celebrating by baying. I had loaded my pockets with jerky. I took out a piece and gave it to him and started by whispering.

"Where's your man, where's your man?" I repeated it over and over. Andy had given me two pairs of prison dungarees and a pair of smelly socks. I was glad I was wearing gloves — these socks were ripe. The dungarees were sealed in two baggies and in my pack.

"Where's your man, where's your man?" Over and over and over. I thrust the smelly socks under his nose and chanted the repetitive refrain, "Where's your man, where's your man?" This was repeated in his ear in a light whisper. I always bent close with these whispers, so I knew my back was going to suffer today. This was his command for total silence. This would have to be repeated in five-minute intervals all through the chase, to remind him he couldn't bay.

Bo went to work. I had him at the hole in the fence and he seemed energized and excited to be on his own. I was praying he wouldn't lose that excitement later. I was working a twenty-foot sweep from the fence. Bo locked on to his smell and crossed the hardtop. Three deputies and Andy followed behind me. I waved them back.

"Wait until I reach the edge of the trees and signal you to come forward. We may have to rework this ground." They returned to their vehicle. We went across a shallow ditch that was dry and up on the verge into some low growth. Bo was working a straight line from the fence opening. When we reached the treeline, he started down an open fire lane. It was clear of growth and the path was covered in straw.

Between the trees was low growth, on the average three to five feet in height. This area had been control-burned within the last two years. At least the first part of our search would be easy going. I hauled Bo back with the lead and gave him the command to rest. He was impatient to travel but finally lay down. I waved to the men. When they arrived I started my instructions.

"This has to be a silent search for our safety. The dog is trained to give us no warning when he is approaching his target. If he performs the exercise correctly, I might have a little advance notice. He will remain silent but will start to wag his tail. If this happens, I will give this signal."

I raised both hands over my head and extended them upward as far as I could reach.

"This means draw your weapons; we could be from five feet to a hundred yards away from one or more prisoners, so watch my hands at all times. If you can't see me, watch the man in front of you. We will be walking in single file most of the search. Each man should duplicate all of my signals for the man behind.

"We have one problem. I have put the dog on one scent only. If a prisoner is left behind for any reason — sprained ankle, snakebite, fatigue, whatever — we could walk up on him without any warning, so be vigilant at all times. Go easy on the water. We may pass isolated homes out there. If we do we can get more water, but we can't depend on this.

"If you see this signal —" I flapped my arms from waist high to my knees several times, "— it means we are stopping to rest. Watch where you step at all times. If you see a snake or hear one, stop dead still and don't move until you can assess the danger. Let the man next to you know with a whisper. Don't brush against any low growth until the dew dries and it gets hotter, at least another two hours.

"We are four hours behind these guys, but one or more could be just ahead in the path from injuries he received at night. Even with a flashlight, I wouldn't like to find my way through these woods, so they may have waited for first light somewhere near. Any questions?" I looked at Andy. He shook his head negatively. "Let's do it."

I gave Bo another piece of jerky and patted and hugged him.

"Get your man, get your man," I told him, letting him smell the socks again. He plunged into the firebreak in an eager trot. Andy and the men were in single file behind me.

I had heard on the way over that the weather was to be slightly cooler today. High in the low eighties, with a fifty-percent chance of thundershowers. It was nice now, about seventy degrees under the trees with shade most of the time, but the humidity was brutal. It would make our pleasant seventy feel like ninety on our sustained search.

Bo was eating up ground. We were going in a straight line with no growth interference. When I calculated we had traveled about a mile and a half, I signaled for a rest. It was now a quarter to ten and getting warmer by the minute. I needed water and a pee. I tied Bo to a tree and we huddled in a rough semi-circle. Andy helped me remove my pack. I retraced our steps for a few yards and did the awkward squatting and disrobing.

We were hot from our exertions, but the men seemed fit and able to handle the exercise. The men were in their thirties, no beer bellies or gray hairs in sight. The search was going smoothly. When I returned, Andy was smoking a cigarette. I hadn't warned them. We were in the open air and Bo was about twelve feet from him and a tiny breeze was blowing east to west, so I thought it would be okay. I sat beside him and dug into my pack for the sandwiches. Two deputies didn't want one, but one deputy, Andy and I ate. When I finished the sandwich, I took several swallows of water and bummed a cigarette from Andy. As I smoked, I softly told him my ban on smoking on a search and how I suffered. He grinned. It was a wonderful cigarette — I enjoyed every puff. I began to reconsider my no-smoking ban on open-air searches.

The stop cost us twenty-five minutes, but was worth it. We were rested and would last longer. We began detouring around small cypress swamps and lower ground, and our feet were dry so far. Bo still moved eagerly and seemed to be following a continuous scent. I could only hope he wouldn't lose the trail.

I had picked the two-hundred-pounder because I decided he was the most likely of the three to fall by the wayside. He would be the slowest mover and have more trouble with the heat. I really should have asked for more information. The felon could be a weight lifter for all I knew and in perfect shape with bulging muscles. I had to pick one. It's too confusing for the dog to be presented with more than one scent to follow.

We were making our way around another small cypress swamp area in fairly open growth, when I felt Andy's hand on my shoulder. I whirled, pulled Bo to a halt, grabbed his face and gave him the silent command to sit. Andy was pointing behind us. I tied Bo to a bush and pulled my .22 from my pack. I eased around Andy. The third and fourth men were frozen into position and staring down at the ground between them.

When I got near enough to see the snake, I felt like laughing. It was a medium-sized water snake and completely harmless. I walked closer to the snake and rubbed my foot back and forth to break the snake out of its trance — it was more frightened than the men. The snake suddenly moved and slithered off the path into the weeds. One deputy had his gun drawn. I glared at him, rolled my eyes and shook my head. He looked sullen at my reaction. Where had these guys been living, on the moon? Couldn't they tell a harmless snake from a dangerous one? We had been shown charts and pictures of snakes in grade school and learned to tell the poisonous from nonpoisonous. I didn't see how anyone could live in southeast Georgia and low country without having knowledge of snakes, especially two deputies. Even housewives killed snakes in their yards.

Andy had moved up behind me and was glaring, but didn't say anything. Someone was going to get his ass chewed later. I started Bo on the search again and had just reached my normal stride and rhythm when more open sky started appearing through the trees. We were approaching a clearing of some sort. We continued on for another ten minutes, but I kept my eyes divided between the path and the blue sky appearing between the treetops. I didn't want a clearing and open spaces to appear when I wasn't prepared.

I slowed Bo to a straining walk and gave the signal to rest to the men behind me. I shortened Bo's lead until he was beside me and I dropped to my knees. Holding on to his harness, I crawled on hands and knees until I could see around the low growth. There was a fairly large clearing directly in front of us with a house in the middle of it. I gave Bo the silent command to retreat and we scooted backward to Andy. I tied Bo to a sapling and told Andy with signals to gather his men for a conference. Andy helped me take off my pack and I pulled out binoculars and handed them to him.

The four men gathered close. I spoke, but kept my voice soft and low.

"Andy, it's your turn in the barrel. This is where Bo and I take a rest. There's a clearing ahead, approximately two acres, with a house in the center. I didn't see any movement or hear anything. There's a lot of open ground. A few trees and shrubs and not much cover. A small shed with a lean-to to the left and a small old-fashioned, high-gabled tobacco barn to the right. I saw no vehicles in the drive, but they could be blocked from view by the house. The bad news is, there's a large ant bed directly in the path ahead and it has been trampled. I got close enough to make out at least two different prints, so they're in there or have been there and left."

Andy told his men to wait, he wanted to take a look first. He crawled out of sight around the bend in the path. I asked the deputies if they had any cigarettes. They both pulled out their packs and offered them to me. I took two from each of them and asked to borrow a lighter while they were gone. I was far enough from Bo, but I put them in my pocket. I would wait until they left to light up.

Andy crawled back and explained the layout again to them and told who was supposed to go right and who was to take the left. After they had crawled away, I left Bo tied and found a clear path about ten feet to the left so I could watch the action from the edge of the woods and avoid the large ant bed. I crawled close enough to be able to see and lit a cigarette. I kept it cupped with my palm and moved it back and forth with a slow motion to dissipate the smoke.

The men approached the house slowly and carefully. They used every object for cover, but the last few feet to the house was completely open ground and I watched with a clenched gut as, one by one, they ran and crouched against the house. Two stayed crouched in back and two separated and disappeared around the left and right sides of the house. I lay there and smoked and hoped no one got shot.

The silence was eerie. No radio, no sound of any kind of equipment. I saw a nightlight on a pole, so I knew they had electricity. That meant they had a well pump. They weren't using water in the house. In this stillness I would be able to hear the well pump motor cut on.

A jet passed, flying so low it was seen and gone before the sound hit. It was a whining boom, so loud you felt as if the ground was shaking underneath you. I bet it scared the shit out of the deputies, it was so sudden. We have Moody Air Force Base a short seventy miles away as the crow flies. They fly their practice missions over our area because it is so sparsely populated. When the puppies in the kennel are young, it terrifies them until they get used to the sudden noise, then they just flinch and look up and around them, as if they think one of these days they'll spot the joker making all the noise.

I watched the two deputies at the rear of the house and listened. I saw both of them straighten and enter the house. They weren't hurrying, so I surmised the house was empty. A minute or so later, one of the deputies hurried out of the house, ran a few feet and started throwing up.

My gut clenched in sympathy. My heart started thumping in my chest. I looked around and prepared to stand. I saw a second deputy exit the back door and wave his arm, in an exaggerated motion, for me to come to the house. For a moment I had a sudden desire to stay hidden in the woods. I knew what they had found in the house was bad. So bad that a deputy had thrown up. I struggled into my pack and untied Bo. He put his nose to the ground without urging and led me first to the back of the tobacco barn, around the side, then bush by bush to the back door. I let Bo lead me this way because the officers would need every scrap of information they could get to prosecute the bastards.

As I approached the house, Andy walked out to meet me.

"A couple in their sixties. Killed in their bed. The bastards stabbed them repeatedly." I closed my eyes and sighed.

"Now they are probably armed and have a car," I said angrily.

"That's my guess. There's no car here. I've called it in. We found the man's wallet on the floor, near some trousers on a chair. He had a driver's license. It will take a while to get a make and description on the car or truck. With some luck, they just might make it out of this area. As soon as some help arrives, I'll have you driven back to your van. I'll be busy when they arrive, so I'll take this opportunity to tell you I enjoyed working with you, Jo Beth." He stuck out his hand and I shook it.

"Same here, Andy. When you come to Balsa City, stop by and have a beer."

"I will," he promised. I continued around to the front of the house, tied Bo to a porch support, and removed my pack. I lit a cigarette and stared absently down the small graded dirt road that entered from the woods about a hundred yards in front of me and then became a small circular drive. I stood up and walked out to the drive. I had to get Bo some water. I looked for a water faucet in the yard and spotted one to my left. I went back, unpacked my pack and got his water dish. I filled it and carried it back to him. I frowned down at him as he was drinking. Something was bothering me. Something wasn't right. I scanned the treeline and swept the front clearing with my eyes. I looked at the drive again.

"Andy!" I yelled, starting toward the drive. I heard the front screen door slam back on its hinges and his running steps across the porch.

"What is it?" He yelled, as he ran toward me. I turned.

"When did it stop raining last night? What did the prison security officer say, about midnight?" My heart was thudding with excitement.

"Yes, about midnight, why?" he asked crossly. It was the reaction to the adrenaline that had started pumping into his veins when I yelled.

"Because there're no tracks in the drive. If it stopped raining by midnight, they couldn't possibly have gotten here until five at the earliest and they would have made tracks going out of the drive. They are still in the woods, Andy, and on foot. We can get the bastards!"

35

"DON'T GET MAD, GET EVEN"
April 18, Sunday, 11 A.M.

Andy ran past me and then started walking parallel with the drive on the grass, just as I had. He stared down at the ground and yelled back to me.

"Circle the other side." I went to the right and followed the drive until it intersected with the road. It was pristine all the way, no tracks at all. We met back at the porch.

"I won't call it in. The homicide team will be here shortly," he said as we both lit up. I walked over, unzipped my suit and peeled it off. The air felt wonderful on my skin; I was wet with sweat. I sat down and propped my back against a porch support and drew my knees up. Two of the deputies walked out on the porch. Andy informed them that when the homicide crew arrived we were going back to tracking. Bo was stretched out in the shade of the porch on the damp ground where water dripped off the eaves and he was taking a nap. I felt like joining him; I hadn't gotten much sleep last night with one thing and another.

Andy had posted one deputy on the back steps. The rest of us sat on the porch and didn't say much. You can't laugh and tell jokes with two murdered people just a few feet away. We heard the sound of vehicles approaching down the road. Andy and the others stood. Two trucks drove into view. The first one was several years old, looked beat-up and well used, with a young man at the wheel. The second one was newer with a woman driving and children sitting beside her. I felt sick. I surmised the son or daughter was coming to spend the day with their parents and have Sunday dinner.

The young man jumped out of the truck and ran toward us.

"What's going on here? What's happening?" He anxiously scanned our faces for some kind of clue. "Where're Dad and Mom?"

Andy walked toward him and I got up and slowly walked around the side of the house out of sight and out of hearing. I didn't want to feel their pain and see their misery when they were given the bad news. I walked back to a water faucet next to the well pump and turned it on, sticking my head under the flow. The water ran warm for about thirty seconds, then turned shockingly cold. It ran down my shirt and cooled my scalp. I shut it off and squeezed most of the water out of my hair with my hands and combed it with my fingers. I took a bandanna out of my pocket and dried my face and hands. I smoked the last cigarette from the four the deputies had left with me in the woods. I stood in the shade of the barn and studied the distant trees.

When I returned to the front porch, the man had the truck door open and was hugging his children, two boys about ten and twelve. The woman had her head down on the steering wheel. Andy walked over to fill me in.

"The son took his dad's truck home last night to change the oil and grease it. They were coming here for Sunday dinner. Christ, I hate this part of my job."

"I know it must be rough, passing on such news. Did you get a chance to ask how many guns were inside?"

"Yeah," he said bitterly. "I said, 'Your parents are dead, but before you mourn, how about telling me how many guns he had.' It sounded like I didn't care."

"No, later on, after the initial shock passes, he'll realize you had to ask quickly; lives might be at stake. He's just hurting, Andy."

"He told me his father had a thirty-thirty rifle, a twelve- and a twenty-gauge shotgun and a twenty-two rifle. He said the twenty-two was kept in the barn for potting large wood rats and snakes."

"Plenty of ammo on hand?" I asked, knowing the answer.

"Oh yes. His father bought it by the case. He hunted quail, squirrel, rabbit, deer and turkey. Always had plenty of game in the freezer."

"Any hand guns?"

"Nope."

"Well, they're armed, all three of them, and we damn well know they are dangerous. Could you tell if they stopped to eat anything? Was the kitchen disturbed?"

"The kitchen is a mess: cabinets standing open, food thrown on the floor, refrigerator door standing open when we entered. They ate. We just don't know if they ate it here or took it with them."

"It consumed some time, even if they were hurrying. I hate this waiting around, Andy. The trail is getting colder every minute we waste here."

"They should be here soon," he assured me. "What if it rains this afternoon? Have you noticed the clouds forming?"

"Yep, I saw them. It feels like enough humidity to rain, but you know how that goes. It's a toss-up. A light rain will help, brings out the scent; a hard driving rain washes the air, pounds the scent into the ground and makes it much harder to track. The prisoners are gaining on us as we speak. We'll have to travel much slower to watch for an ambush. They have killed twice. Five more won't alter their punishment. They can only be executed once."

We heard vehicles approaching and turned to watch two dark sedans with county decals on the sides, two patrol cars, and an ambulance come speeding around the corner. I walked over and began pulling on my suit. Bo was awake. I fed him a handful of jerky and went to fill his water dish again. I kept my eyes averted from the truck and the grieving family.

When I returned, Andy introduced me to the sheriff. I had never met him; this was the first search I had done this far north from my tri-county area. We shook hands and he asked if there was anything I needed to continue the search. He was neatly dressed in a Western-cut shirt and pants, and wearing boots. He looked about fifty. Neat, trim, and looked fit.

"A lot of luck, sir," I told him. He agreed and said he wished us Godspeed. I left them and went to the porch to finish dressing. I tightened on my shoe covers and unfastened my holster for the .32. I unzipped my suit, worked it down off my shoulders and strapped my holster back on, next to my sweatshirt. I was going to wear it inside instead of outside. The bugs weren't too bad in the middle of the day even with the high humidity; we weren't on low ground yet. I could leave the suit unzipped a little so I could reach inside if it became necessary. I was thinking about walking around a corner and facing a twelve-gauge shotgun. Maybe if they didn't see a holster, they might hesitate about blowing me away on sight — it was a thought.

Andy came over and helped me to get my backpack on. I untied Bo and presented the socks. Andy reached for my canteen and said he would fill it when he filled his. I smiled my thanks. I had forgotten the canteen was almost empty. Stupid, purely stupid.

Bo put his head down and started casting back and forth in front of the doorway. He went to the right and around the house. When we reached the back door, he started back on the same scent trail we came in on. I waited until he duplicated all the movements and started back on the firebreak. I hauled him back and repeatedly whispered to him.

"Where's your man, where's your man?" He would jerk his head around and peer off into the distance, like he expected to see his man hiding behind the next bush, then lower his head and start scent trailing again. My sweet ol' Bo. He made a lazy-eight pattern with his nose, going about ten feet in each direction before he turned back. I saw the deputies and Andy standing in a group under a tree watching us.

When Bo had retraced his scent trail to the back door, he went to the right. He angled away from the house and went due east across the grass, picking up speed. My heart started beating faster: he seemed to have found his man's scent. He led me to the edge of the clearing and was ready to plunge directly through some medium-sized growth. I made him respond to "rest" after several tries.

I turned around and waved to the men. They came hurrying across the clearing. Andy was carrying my canteen and a radio. He hooked the canteen to my belt and handed me the radio.

"A backup, just in case," he said. I slid it in a side pocket and zipped. I guessed another two pounds to carry wouldn't topple me. The men were watching me in silence.

"This isn't going to be a stroll like this morning. The brush is thicker. It doesn't look like easy going. All the signals from this morning still apply. Any questions?"

I reached down and petted Bo. "Let's get your man. Where's your man? Where's your man?" I presented the socks. He didn't need any urging. He was panting to go. We plunged into the bushes and weeds and I closed my mind to what could be quietly resting under the comparative coolness of the underbrush. This trajectory we were on began to look like panicky flight. Any reconnoitering in either direction would have found easier passage. I didn't know if they thought they heard a vehicle or maybe distant aircraft, which sounds the same in the forest, or if the killings had rattled them, but this path smelled of panic.

Bo was straining against the lead. He was much faster and more nimble than all of us, but I didn't try to slow him down. The first few hundred yards would be free from ambush. They would want to put as much distance between themselves and the murders in the shortest time. I simply gripped Bo's lead more firmly with my glove and turned up the pressure for the ones behind. A trailing edge of a blackthorn vine caught me on my right cheek. I felt the area with my left glove and saw a bright smear of red. I left it alone; I would treat it when we stopped to rest. The blundering herd behind me brought a small smile to my lips. I knew for certain none of my fellow travelers were light-footed squirrel hunters. I maintained the fast pace for twenty-five minutes. When our journey fed into a reasonably clear firebreak, I signaled a rest. I gave Bo the silent signal and eased down on a small mound of knotted roots and dirt.

I inspected the troops. They were huffing and puffing, gasping for breath, and I sounded the same. Two of the men had thorn scratches, and one of them looked deep. He unwound his handkerchief from the wound. I shrugged off my pack and found my small plastic container of alcohol and several four-by-four gauze pads. I cleaned the cuts, wrapped the sliced hand and put a Band-Aid on his other scratch, as well as my own. When my breathing eased, I walked Bo a few feet away and tied his lead.

Thankfully, the sun had disappeared behind a dirty-looking low cloud and we were all in the shade. I pulled Bo's water dish out and filled it half full from my canteen. He lapped it up gratefully. I walked back to the men and Andy handed me a cigarette and lighter. I smiled my thanks and sat on my hump of roots. We sat, smoked and sweated. Andy and two of the deputies were carrying riot guns from the homicide investigator's and sheriff's vehicles. They didn't want to face shotguns with just thirty-eights. The guns didn't have shoulder straps and they were forced to carry them in their hands, which is awkward when fending off branches and vines.

We rested twenty minutes and then started back to trailing. Bo led us down the firebreak. It was easier going, but we were in the open. We were traveling more silently, which was a plus, and we could also see further ahead, so the good and the bad of traveling in the firebreak sort of evened out. We were in the firebreak for another fifteen minutes, until Bo turned into a small, well-worn game trail which continued in a true easterly direction. I had consulted my compass several times during the last two treks. The sun was directly overhead, so they weren't using the sun to navigate. I began to believe the bastards had a compass and they knew where they were heading. You couldn't stay on a due east course in blind flight, and they were traveling east with no deviations. This conclusion gave me chill bumps. I hoped to hell it wasn't another house occupied by innocents or a prearranged rendezvous with confederates. If it was the latter, we would lose them, as we must be at least two or more hours behind them.

We halted temporarily. We stopped, caught our breaths and sipped some water before entering the game trail. The going was fairly easy. There was some low-hanging foliage but we were still in planted timber, not old growth. These sections had been cleared by controlled burning sometime in the past and the path had pine needles that retarded weeds and shrubs.

I was thinking it was time to slow the pace and get more cautious because the path had turns and blind corners. The convicts probably hadn't slept a minute last night. Any adrenaline surge from the killings would have dissipated by now. They would need rest, the same as we, but we hadn't been operating under tension and fear as long.

I saw Bo's tail wagging back and forth and I threw both hands high in the air above me, then put on the breaks and started to haul Bo backwards. This left me with a nagging question I would ponder for years to come: would things have worked out differently if I had reversed my actions?

An arm shot out from behind a thick palmetto clump, grabbed Bo's harness and jerked him sideways off the path. With both arms in the air and Bo's lead high in my right glove, I didn't have a chance in hell of retaining the lead. It was jerked out of my hands and I folded at the knees and tried to roll behind the near side of the palmetto growth. My pack hindered my roll, stopping me before I was behind cover. I scrambled on hands and knees until I was behind a half-grown pine tree with a twelve-inch circumference to its trunk. I began yelling before I was behind the meager cover.

"Please don't hurt the dog, mister. Please don't hurt him! He's a good dog. He won't bite. He's gentle!" I had been unconsciously aware of the scramble of the men behind me to find cover, but I was totally focused on the clump of palmettos. I couldn't be more than six feet away from the man holding Bo. I pulled off both gloves with my teeth while reaching inside my suit for my .32. I released the safety. I laid it on the ground and released the waist catch of my backpack and carefully started to ease it off my shoulder, trying not to make a sound. I was lying on a bed of pine needles, several inches deep. I slid my pack clear and picked up my gun, my eyes never leaving the thick growth in front of me.

Prone, with the gun extended in front of me with both hands, I strained my eyes, trying to see through the fan-shaped leaves and spiny stems. I had now moved to the right of the tree and caught a glimpse of a tiny patch of Bo's red color. Moving my eyes an inch to the right, I saw a tiny hint of blue.

The convict hadn't answered me. The silence was so complete I could hear a woodpecker's knock echoing through the trees and Bo's panting breath. The sun moved out from cover and with the added light, I had a clearer view into the growth. Suddenly I heard a catch in Bo's breathing and saw a fine red mist appear through the leaves. It stained the sunlight and the leaves and the patch of blue I had been focused on. I was on my feet without thought, my gun extended, walking deliberately to the right of the bush. I took in the scene as I began to fire. The convict had laid down his shotgun to wield the knife he had used to slit Bo's throat. He dropped the knife and was scrambling for his shotgun when I started firing. I got off three rounds before I was hit violently in the back from behind. I pulled the trigger twice more on my way down, but I knew before I hit the ground, the last two had missed. I didn't bother to fire the last round; someone's knee was planted in my back and I couldn't see to aim. A shotgun blast went off over my head, and from almost total deafness, I could hear small tinny pops, which I assumed were more weapons being fired as fast as someone could pull the trigger, but I wasn't that much interested in the outcome and the noise surrounding me.

The pressure came off my back but I didn't move. I was rerunning that three-second film clip I had viewed as I started firing the first three rounds: Bo between the convict's legs, a gaping hole saturated with blood in his throat, his mouth open in a grimace, the fading gleam of life in his eyes, gone now I knew, forever.

I could hear excited cries along the path, crackling noisy branches through the brush, but I couldn't make out what they were saying, it seemed so unimportant, somehow. I crawled wearily over and pulled Bo free from the blue lump and cradled his bloody head in my arms. I whispered to him as I closed his eyes and rubbed his ears.

"I didn't mean it, Bo, when I chose you, instead of my prize-winner-to-be Susie. I know I thought she was more important to me than you, but I was oh, so wrong. Forgive me, Bo."

I was still sitting there holding Bo when Andy returned.

"Are you all right?" he asked.

"Yes," I said. I laid Bo down and went to my backpack. Andy followed me.

"What are you doing?" He asked gently. I had pulled out a black plastic body bag.

"I'm going to put Bo in a body bag, in my rescue sled and take him home," I told him calmly.

"Jo Beth," he said softly, "I've called in a helicopter. I gave them directions as best I could. They will find us, probably within the hour. Leave Bo here; the men will bury him for you."

"Not on your life," I said grim and determined. "He goes home with me."

I marched over to Bo, unzipped the body bag and placed it beside him. Andy squatted on the other side to help me.

"Don't touch him!" I yelled. "I'll do it myself. I got him killed. He's my responsibility." I rolled Bo in the bag, straightened his ears and gave him a gentle, final pat. I zipped the bag closed.

"Okay! Okay, Jo Beth, take it easy," he said soothingly. "Can I do anything to help?"

"Nope," I replied as I went back to my pack for the rescue sled. I unzipped the cover and shook it out. I looked at Andy.

"How many body bags do you need?" I asked casually. I hadn't thought, before now, to wonder who had survived and who had perished.

"Three," he said quietly. "You got the first one, we got the other two. Not one of my men was hurt. We were very lucky, thanks to your warning and diversion. They had been asleep, or it could have been a disaster. They were groggy and just not fast enough."

"I'm glad your men are safe," I said, feeling bitter. "At least we saved the taxpayers the expense of lengthy trials and appeals." I rolled Bo into the rescue sled, rolled up the bottom until it was snug and fastened it. I attached the hauling harness and went back to my pack.

"I only have two body bags left," I told him. "I just brought three." I pulled out the two and handed them to him. He left.

When he returned, I was leaning back against a pine tree drinking from my canteen. He lit a cigarette, handed it to me and lit one for himself. I dragged the nicotine into my lungs and tried to relax. We sat quietly without speaking. I glanced at my watch. It was only one. When I finished my cigarette, I remembered my flares.

"I have two red smoke canisters and two white flares for night work." I dug out the compact signals and handed them to him. He pulled his radio from his belt and called in the information: he had red smoke flares. They would be able to find us more quickly.

It was two in the afternoon before the helicopter dropped us on the prison grounds. They had found us easily with the flares, but the closest open area where they could land was several walking minutes away from us. I had relented and let Andy carry my pack as I pulled Bo in the rescue sled. Andy had looked so concerned and miserable when I told him "no" the first time he asked, I reversed my decision. I knew I didn't have to prove myself to him, so it made it easier to say yes.

It was a nine-passenger helicopter that picked us up. They had brought six men and stretchers for the dead convicts. After receiving instructions on how to find the bodies, the fresh troops left. They flew the five of us and Bo's body back to the prison. The sheriff was there with several of his men.

They led us separately into different cubicles to give our statements. Sheriff Sessions sat beside me as I gave my statement orally to a stenographer seated across a small built-in desk. The only time the sheriff spoke during my recitation of the day's events was when I faltered when describing what I saw when I pumped three bullets into the felon. He laid a hand briefly on my arm and asked if I wanted to wait awhile, maybe have a drink of water. I shook my head, straightened in my chair and finished the statement.

Andy, the three deputies and I sat in a security break room drinking Cokes and smoking while we waited for our statements to be typed. The chief guard came in and offered food, and the three deputies left to see what was being offered. Andy and I just sat quietly and smoked. The sheriff returned with the statements and we signed them. The sheriff informed me my van was in the parking lot and they were keeping the news media outside the gates. I was thankful for not having to face their cameras and questions. Andy insisted on giving me an escort home, and the sheriff agreed with him. Andy drove ahead of me a sedate fifty miles per hour for the trip home. Most natives were swimming, sleeping off a heavy dinner, watching the Braves on the tube or indulging in other lazy Sunday afternoon activities. There was hardly any traffic.

Rosie and Wayne had heard the news on the radio. They were outside in the courtyard when we drove in. I didn't see George's car; he must have gone somewhere. Rosie and Wayne hugged me and shook hands with Andy. Wayne signed that he had dug the grave in the pet cemetery. He picked up Bo and carried him the hundred yards or so behind the kennel to the square outlined with three-year-old Bradford pear trees I had planted. Wayne removed Bo from the rescue sled and lowered him into the grave by the body-bag straps. I picked up the shovel and threw in the first shovelful of dirt and turned the task over to Wayne. I walked back to the patrol car with Andy and asked if he would like a beer. He said he had to get back, but he would keep in touch. He gave me a hug instead of a handshake and got into his vehicle and drove away.

I watched until he was out of sight and went into the house. I was a mess. I had left my rescue suit in the van. My hands and face were crusted with dried blood, both mine and Bo's. I took a robe from my room and threw everything I had on in the washing machine on the way to the bathtub. I soaked in a hot tub with my eyes closed, running my three-second tape of Bo's demise over and over. It always ended the same.

Eventually I climbed out, before I wrinkled like a prune, and dressed in a cool shift and sandals. I wasn't hungry, but a beer sounded good. In fact, I might have a dozen or so. I was very thirsty. I stood in front of the refrigerator and saw that the note I had left for George was gone, but one addressed to me was in its place.

Dear Jo Beth,

I think you have most of the pieces of your puzzle and can find the rest without my help. I'll send you a bill for three days, no expenses. It was nice meeting you and I think last night was very special.

I don't want you to misunderstand what I want to tell you on paper, instead of face-to-face. I'm forty-two years old and lived alone over half of my life. It's time for me to come out of the cold, or as some ladies say, I've been listening to the ticking of my biological clock for the past few months.

I'm looking for something permanent. If this idea doesn't make you fall out of your chair from laughter, give me a ring. I'll come a-courtin' with flowers and candy, and we'll get to know each other.

Call,
George

I read the note twice. I didn't know whether to laugh or cry. I just sighed. A lot of us, here and there, would like to come out of the cold, good buddy. Some can, but I wasn't one of them, until I could some-how, some way, remove the threat of Bubba popping out of prison and back into my life. Even then, I don't think George would be what I wanted. I reached into the refrigerator and grabbed a brew. I sat at the kitchen table, drank the beer, and lit a cigarette.

After the first beer, I was so sleepy another seemed too much trouble. I checked and had no messages on the answering machine. I set the alarms and went to the bedroom. It was only six-thirty in the afternoon, much too early for bed. I kicked off my sandals, stretched out in my shift and closed my eyes.

When I awoke it was after midnight. I was disorientated and for a few seconds I couldn't remember if it was day or night or even what day it was. I stretched while memory and flashes of earlier events flooded my consciousness. I put on shorty pajamas and padded barefoot toward the bathroom, starting the washing machine on my way.

Deciding I was hungry, I went to the kitchen. I scrambled two eggs, made toast, and poured a glass of milk. I felt lousy but the food helped a little. I lit a cigarette and let my eyes roam the room. My hide-a-way castle. A little less than half paid for. It was showing the scars and empty slots of missing objects from Bubba's visit, but I would soon have it back to normal and I had my memory of the lost treasures. I had a healthy bank account, a few nice investments, and enough income from my business that held my head above the waterline of expenses.

I had nine paintings, four very valuable, by a famous artist. The other five were very personal paintings of my family by my father, cash value unknown, but priceless to me. I was doing work I loved, every day a new beginning. My eyes fell on Ruby's dish. I couldn't remember if I had filled it this morning, but it was empty now. I got up and filled her dish with dry food and chopped a slice of bologna into bite-sized pieces, an apology if I had forgotten to feed her. I rinsed the dishes and lit another cigarette.

I had lost almost everyone I loved and cared about. My parents in death, my husband because he was a thinly disguised savage that I was too young and too dumb to recognize. Gone was my best friend Susan for meddling in her love life. Going was my best friend Leroy, because his wife's green-eyed jealousy would eventually override our lifelong friendship. Might be going to lose Wayne and Rosie, with his resignation yesterday because I was trying to defend him against dangers he couldn't handle. Strewn along the wayside were friends and confidants I could have cherished without making them enemies or cool toward the possibility of friendship. There were Charlene, Hank, Wade and others I could have treated more kindly, and then there was George. There was also Bo. A sweet, gentle animal I had sent to his death because he wasn't perfect and championship material.

I laid my head on the table and bawled. I cried for all I had lost through death, deviousness, ignorance and making the wrong moves. I moaned and groaned and sobbed out all my frustrations and grief. The flow finally slowed to a trickle, then ceased. I hiccuped. I felt a warm furry pressure on my right leg. I sat very still with my head on the table. Ruby was rubbing up against me. I slowly lifted my head and gazed down at her.

"Well, hello Ruby," I whispered. "You ignore me for six months, and now you decide you want to be friends?" I liked the idea that she had offered her friendship to comfort me. I trailed my fingers down her back and she arched her spine against my palm. I scratched her gently behind her ears. I sat there for a long time. Finally I found the strength to rise, wash my face and hands and go to bed. I slept soundly the whole night.

36

I awoke from a dream in which I was being smothered by a warm cougar that kept telling me she was just a figment of my imagination. Reality was a large black cat draped across my throat and chest. I moved her to my side, raised up on one elbow and studied the look in her large green eyes as she studied me.

"Boy, when you capitulate, you go whole hog," I told her while I scratched her back. She flopped over and presented her belly to be rubbed. I stared down at the generous male appendages.

"My, my. My mistake, but you run just like a girl cat." I searched my brain for a correct alternative for Ruby and decided on Rudy. It sounded close enough that he wouldn't know the difference. I jumped up and ran to the bathroom. Rudy sat at my feet, gazing up in adoration.

"Listen Rudy, some things are private. Kindly scat." He didn't, of course, jump up and leave. I couldn't pee in front of the dogs, but I managed to function with Rudy gazing at me. Go figure. I started coffee, went into the bathroom, brushed my teeth, entered the shower, and sang — with Rudy watching my every move.

I dressed in jeans and a sweatshirt. I was going to train awhile this morning, then call Jasmine to see if she was free for lunch. This afternoon I would shop for the house. I was tired of seeing the empty slots. And I had to convince Wayne just how much I needed him. I had a busy day ahead and didn't need breakfast this morning after eating so late last night.

The carpenter brothers arrived at seven. I detailed the size of the paintings and the three of us decided the inside wall of the living room next to the kitchen was the only place to hang them. It was long enough to display all five paintings and it was across the room from the fireplace so that the heat wouldn't dry the oils. I showed them the damage on the walls and gave them the list of paint colors and numbers they had used three years ago. I told them to order enough to do all the rooms. That way we wouldn't have to paint again for awhile. I only tripped over Rudy twice in the walk-through while showing them what had to be done.

I heard Wayne arrive and went to sell him on staying. I poured him a cup of coffee.

"Jo Beth," he signed, "I need to let you know something. I was wrong yesterday. I realize that now from what happened to you and Bo. If I had been in your place, I'm sure I couldn't have shot that man. I might have wanted to — badly. I just don't think I'm capable. I don't think this makes me less a man and I know you don't think so, either. So, I take back my silly resignation and will manage the kennel for you. My pride got in the way of good judgment, okay?"

"It's great, not just okay," I signed. "Wayne, we're gonna expand. We're going to start training scent trackers, drug sniffers, and rescue dogs for natural disasters and sell them commercially. There are a lot of police, fire departments, prisons and natural disasters out there. It's a good market for dogs trained with different specialties. We can have the carpenter brothers build us some cottages so the buyers can send handlers here for a week to learn how to work with the dogs they buy. A lot of police departments and rescue workers are getting their trained dogs, mostly German shepherds, from Europe. I read in the paper a small town in Georgia received a hundred-thousand-dollar government grant and purchased three German shepherds from Europe for thirty thousand each. Just think what we could get for dogs trained for different specialties. We'll be able to advertise in the correct trade magazines."

"Your ideas are great! Who are you gonna hire to work with you on rescue, Jeral?"

"Nope, I've decided not to offer him the job — not because of his militant leanings, but because I think he's slated to walk a different path. I know a beautiful black girl who I think will be ideal. She may not accept, but if she does, do you think you can work with her?"

"Of course. It was Jeral's wild beliefs I found hard to accommodate, not his color."

"Good. I'm going to offer her the job today, if she's free for lunch. Guess who's lying on my foot under the desk?"

Wayne walked around the desk and gazed down at Rudy. He silently opened his wallet and handed me a five. I grinned and put it in the desk.

Wayne finished his coffee and took off for the kennel with a lighter step. I would have to talk to the carpenter brothers about attaching an office for Wayne to the kennel, call the sign people, add his name to the main sign at the entrance, and get him some business cards printed with his new title. Thank God I wouldn't lose him and also the best cook in South Georgia.

I picked up the phone and called Jasmine.

"Hi, Jo Beth. I'm so glad you called. I heard about you losing a dog yesterday. I'm so sorry."

"Thanks, Jasmine. He was a lovely dog and I'll miss him. Do you happen to be free for lunch?"

"Sure, I'll get Gloria to work in my place here. Where are we going and how should I dress?"

"Dress to knock their eyes out. You wear white and I'll wear black — we'll confuse the hell out of them. We're going to Chester's."

"No!" she said with excitement. "Really? I've got a knock-'em-dead white dress I've never worn that should do the trick."

"I'll pick you up at twelve," I told her.

I had no sooner replaced the phone when it rang. It was Susan.

"Oh honey," she cried, "I just got to work and read what happened yesterday. I'm so sorry about your dog. It wasn't Susie, was it?"

"No," I said dryly, "I saved Susie from destruction. I took Bo."

"Don't feel that way, sweetie. I know you're hurting. Why don't we have lunch so I can apologize for how I treated you over that miserable dirt bag, Brian."

"You don't owe me an apology, Susan. I owe you one."

"Whatever. We'll figure it out later. Can you have lunch?"

"Sorry, I have a previous engagement. Can you have supper?"

"That's better. It will give us more time. Where and when?"

"How about Porky's? We can dance later."

"You feel that good?" She seemed doubtful. She had expected me to be wallowing in misery and soaking hankies. It was another confirmation in my mind that even your best friend doesn't really know what makes you tick. "What's been happening to you while I was being a shit?"

"I guess I realized I'm not getting any younger and life is passing me by. Isn't that what you preached to me so often in the past?"

"Yes, now you're talking. We'll wear them out! How about me picking you up at seven-thirty?"

"See you then," I told her.

So far, Bo's dying had made Wayne see how valuable he would be to me as a manager and trainer. It had also patched up the rift between Susan and me. Even after Bo's death, he was being helpful. I decided to go see O'Henry and Sally. Wayne said they seemed fine now that they had arrived home and were installed in their own pens. I wanted to see and touch them.

They were so happy to see me. Our love was mutual and it would be a cold day in hell before they left again. Their love and joy at being home was a very good omen. This day was my new beginning, I could feel it in the air. I mentally calculated the expenses accrued in getting possession and legal ownership of them and discovered, with wry humor, I had still made a handsome profit. Hanaiker could whistle for a refund.

The phone began to ring as I walked to the office. The carpenter brothers were leaving. They had their measurements for the bookcases and panels and their list for paints and wallboard. They told me they would be back to start work first thing in the morning. Wade left a message on the answering machine and hung up before I could get to the phone. I called him back.

"Hi, Wade. What's up?"

He expressed condolences for Bo and said he was glad I hadn't been hurt. I thanked him.

"Jo Beth, I know you mentioned the name Hanaiker to me on the phone last week, but I'm afraid I wasn't paying much attention. I was very upset with you. Anyway, this morning before I left home, I received a call from a law firm in New York. This is a very prestigious law firm. I heard about them while I was in Boston. This lawyer, Jason Finch, is in our local Howard Johnson's and wants to meet with you in my office at ten this morning. Can you come in?"

"He passed up 'The Hickory?' What's the world coming to," I said in a mocking voice.

"H. J.'s is rated higher. I checked," he replied with equal good humor. "Only the best for this dude."

I smiled. This guy was loosening up fine. Sheri must be doing something right. He was shedding his stuffy attitude along with his Back Bay speech.

I sang to him, "I'll be there with bells on," in my best Dolly Parton voice.

"Very nice," he said in a wry way. "Maybe you should fill me in on what to expect."

"Better yet, let it come as a surprise, Wade. It's not important, but it will put closure on my mysterious past. I was expecting a lawyer to get in touch, just not this soon. Let's wait and see what he has to say. See you at ten."

I sat and pondered how fast the law firm had moved. I suspected that megabucks were floating around and they had grabbed their butterfly nets and were ready to join the hunt to try and capture their expected share.

Friends had been hesitant to mention that I had killed a man yesterday. They had shown sympathy for Bo, but no one had asked me, as yet, how it felt to know you had killed a man. Before the scum killed Bo, I doubt if I would have fired to kill, except to protect my life. After he killed Bo, I wanted to make sure I didn't just wound him, I wanted to kill the sucker. I now knew that sufficient motivation could make me kill. It was a chilling thought when I had been so sure I would never be able to kill Bubba and didn't think society should thrust that upon me as the only way I could have a safe life. I had sufficient motivation with Bubba; I just didn't want the solution to be by my hand. With Bo I didn't mind being the solution. In fact, I preferred it; that was the difference. Weird maybe, but it was the way I felt.

Once again my training plans were on hold. These puppies would be on Social Security before I could get them trained.

At nine-fifteen I took another shower and, while still wet, rubbed on baby oil. I toweled off and felt sleek and soft. I chose gossamer sheer black hose with a seam in the back and attached them to a black satin garter belt. Black lace bra and panties were next. I slipped on the black broadcloth-lined dress that was very simple, very tight and looked expensive. I slipped into black linen four-inch-heeled pumps and transferred the essentials into a black linen envelope-styled purse, which also included my .32. The tiny bit of black nonsense that sat on the top of my head was laughingly called a hat. It had a wispy clutch of lace and veiling pinned back with a four-inch white feather. I wore my mother's pearls and they looked at home with my expensive pearl-drop earrings. I picked out six very thin bone bracelets, half white, half black, and placed them on my right wrist. I studied my reflection in the hall mirrors. With all this black and white I expected to resemble a zebra, but it all meshed and I looked damn good, if I did say so myself.

Wayne was crossing the courtyard when I reached the drive. He stopped, stared wide-eyed, and then hastened to open the door of the van for me. I offered my hand in a royal gesture and he bent low and air-kissed it, continental style. We were both laughing as I climbed into the van. I moved the seat forward, not having much leeway to navigate wearing the tight dress. I slipped off the pumps and drove in my stocking feet for more comfort.

I swept into Wade's waiting room exactly on time and received a critical appraisal, then an envious look from the temp, which bolstered my ego. When Wade came out to fetch me, he stopped cold for a second in surprise at my appearance, then came forward and complimented me on how nice I looked. I checked my face in the pier glass on his wall to make sure he couldn't see the briar scratch from yesterday. It was invisible. I took his arm, gave him a grin, and strolled with confidence to meet this New York lawyer.

He was as distinguished-looking as his firm's name implied. There were seven names listed. I was glad I didn't answer the phone at their place of business. He was immaculately turned out. It wouldn't have surprised me to hear his suit had cost over twelve hundred dollars. His shirt was spotless, his shoes gleamed, and his expression was as sour as if he had just bitten into a persimmon. I knew at a glance we would never be friends and, in his opinion, not even nodding acquaintances.

His name was Jason Finch. He stood when we entered the room. Wade introduced us. He offered his hand, which I ignored.

I took a step closer to him, into his personal space, and peered into his face.

"Are you related to Simon?" I used my best grand duchess voice, and I can be a very grand, grand duchess when I try.

He confessed he didn't know to whom I was referring. I didn't either. I had pulled the name out of thin air.

"Well, if you don't know him, you can't be related to him," I uttered in a rude tone.

"Really, Wade, you told me he was from a prestigious firm and he doesn't even know Simon." I shook my head and took a seat.

Wade's ears turned pink and he was trying to catch my eye. I was careful not to look his way. It would spoil the whole scene if I laughed.

"Please hurry, Wade," I said impatiently. "I have some shopping to do and a very important luncheon at twelve, precisely. I believe it's gauche to appear late at a luncheon in one's honor, don't you agree?"

Wade saw I was going to be impossible, so he concentrated on Finch.

"Would you care to explain to Miss Sidden what this visit entails?"

Finch pursed his lips and reached into the briefcase by the side of his chair and withdrew a very thick blue-backed document.

"I am here in the legal capacity as executor of the estate of the late Benson T. Hanaiker, and to read his last will and testament. As Miss Sidden is mentioned in the will, I will read it to her, thus fulfilling my legal duty," he said, sounding very churlish indeed.

"Listen, Jason, old buddy, I have no desire to be a captive audience while you drone through a boring document that I already know the salient points of, and understand enough to let you know my decision. I'm going to save all of us some time. I have more important things to do than listen to a lot of herebys and wherefores you must charge at least ten bucks a letter for, the only reasonable explanation as to why you use so many of them."

"Miss Sidden," he rebuked in sonorous tones, "I will not allow you to speak to me in this fashion. Please sit and listen quietly. This could have financial import in your life. You must hear me out."

"Jason, you must not get upset. You might find you have blood in your veins and it might rise and gouge you if you don't remain calm."

Finch glared daggers at me and turned to Wade. "Please inform this woman that I must read this document. Can't you control your client?"

Wade turned to me with a smile. "Can you be controlled, Sidden?" I smiled back at him; he was sounding like a good ol' Georgia boy now, not a Back Bay Boston attorney.

"Wade, tell me," I asked quietly, ignoring the glowering Finch, "if you requested a copy of this document, once it's filed in the state of New York and becomes part of the public record, wouldn't they mail you a copy when you paid the required fee?"

"Absolutely," he answered.

I turned to Finch. "I know that Wade, as an excellent and dutiful attorney, will file for a copy and explain carefully where I stand and what my options are, but I can tell you right now what the will says in common everyday language. Benson T. Hanaiker was my biological father and most probably left his estate to me in its entirety, except for maybe some bequests to faithful retainers, a few charities, maybe even leaving a sop for his nephew, Jackson Hanaiker, whom I shall refer to as 'Smiling Jack' for the rest of this conversation. Later, much later in this man's life, he added a rider or codicil, or whatever it's called, to the will, instructing that I would be disinherited if I turned to a life of crime, or even gave the appearance of being a lawbreaker. I think the key word in the will must be 'indicted' for a crime. Whether I was innocent or not, or even set up for the indictment, must not be important. All I had to do was actually be indicted for some crime and I would lose the inheritance to, guess who, none other than Smiling Jack.

"For some unknown reason, which isn't important for me to know, my father palmed me off on Arthur Henry Stonley, after my biological mother committed suicide before my second birthday. My guess would be that he hated my mother with a pure purple passion for committing suicide and removing herself from his reach. He let his nephew in on the news of the codicil, most probably only weeks ago, and again it's just a guess, but I would say it was to keep Smiling Jack around so he wouldn't die alone."

It was difficult with the tight dress, but I crossed my legs, gave Finch a bland smile and continued.

"Smiling Jack tried to frame me for attempted murder or murder, whichever occurred. He took a ridiculous chance with his freedom for no reason. He's screwed up his life because he made some wrong moves, all for nothing. I wouldn't touch a dime of the old buzzard's money even if he owned all of Andrel and the continent of Australia."

I stared at Finch. "I want you to read my lips. Jackson Hanaiker is a slime ball, but he's my slime ball. I recognize his relationship to me. He's the only blood relative I have left standing. You're not going to make hundreds of thousands of dollars from the estate, like you're anticipating, with me and Smiling Jack battling for years while you run up the bill. I'm going to inform him that a long legal battle is not necessary. I will be glad to sign anything required so he can inherit. I know I have upset your apple cart. This will seriously put a large dent in your future billings, and all I can say is, it tickles the hell out of me."

Both of them stared at me.

"Where did you get this information?" Jason Finch asked in a deadly whisper. He was furious.

"Elementary, my Dear Watson," I told him. "I'm able to cogitate with the best of them. Smiling Jack dropped clues like bread crumbs on a path to lead me to the truth. He really isn't cut out to mastermind a crime. He made too many mistakes."

Finch took a ragged breath and spat out some facts. "Your saintly 'father,' Arthur Henry Stonley, took money from Benson Hanaiker to raise you from the time you were two until you were fifteen! Muriel Hanaiker committed suicide because she was an adulteress and a convicted felon. She was sentenced to prison for trying to kill her husband, Benson Hanaiker!"

"Well, of course my father took money from the bastard. He needed the money for paints when his work wasn't selling. He had to paint; it was his passion and purpose in life. As for my biological mother being an adulteress, she probably fell in love with someone else and the old buzzard wouldn't give her a divorce. My proof of his perfidy is that he took out his hatred of her on his only child."

I stood and spoke to Wade. "Walk me out, Counselor."

Outside in the hallway I turned to Wade before he spoke. "Pay no attention to that nonsense I spouted in there. My natural aversion to lawyers — present company excluded — made me lust for revenge.

That blood-sucking parasite in there will have an upset stomach for days. Also, my cuz, ol' Smiling Jack, will think he's home free for a short time without paying the piper for his crimes. I hope I've given you a few days' grace so you can plan your strategy. 'Unleash the dogs of war,' Counselor; let's give them a run for their money. I've got a mammoth mortgage and many mouths to feed."

"I'll do my very best, Sidden," Wade said with a wide grin.

I felt like skipping down the stairs, but it would have been suicidal with my heels. I had figured out most of the answers with very little help and I was proud of that. I hadn't heard any earth-shattering facts that would alter my life. It happened long ago to people I didn't know, in a faraway place. I had my memories of one set of parents, and since the other set was dead, and I could never know them, they wouldn't cause me any grief.

I shopped for an hour before picking up Jasmine. While I was trying to decide on end tables and occasional pieces for the office, I suddenly remembered the expensive dishes I had left sitting on the loading platform last Tuesday morning. I would have to call the store this afternoon and find out what happened to them.

On the way to pick up Jasmine, I ran my thought process of hiring her through my simple system of making decisions about people. Most everyone, at one time or another, has made snap judgments about someone they have just met. I am guilty of quick positive and negative reactions as well as many others, but I pride myself in taking a second evaluation. I had done so with Jasmine. I clear my mind, place a blank page in front of me and evaluate attributes and attitudes.

Jasmine's beauty was not a consideration. Her basic goodness shined like a beacon of light, cleansing her soul of the repulsive and mind-numbing existence she had endured from twelve to nineteen. She was far from an angel, but her six years of self-exile had started her scars to healing, not festering with disgust and remorse. Her religious belief had helped. She was quick and bright, would be easy to teach, and might desire an education.

That was the good news, the plus side. On the other side of the page were facts and suppositions. She would be a liability with every man who knew her past; Southern males — maybe all males, who knows? — deal in absolutes. Black and white. Once a whore, always a whore. They use them, then abuse them. They forget that it takes two to turn tricks. I would be her protector and, as such, could expect to get caught in the crossfire of hated insults and recriminations. Her religion, a crutch now, could become an obsession. I remembered the old adage, "There's nothing quite so pious as a reformed drunk, or a whore." A dark specter loomed on the horizon: the haunting threat of AIDS. It had been six years, but some strains of the disease take a decade for the symptoms to appear. This was the down side, the minus column. The easiest decision would be to hire someone else, but it seemed I never took the easy way out. If I am ever impregnated, it will probably occur while I'm standing in a hammock, simply because it sounds difficult.

When I drove to Jasmine's front door, she tripped out on extremely high heels like mine and I laughed in delight. We were going to turn some heads and stop traffic in Chester's.

She wore a white silk suit that showed off her gorgeous figure to perfection. The suit had four cut black onyx buttons from the neckline to the waist. Her little white sailor hat had black dots here and there. She was wearing sheer black stockings and when she turned slowly on the walk for my inspection, I saw she also had the black seams up the back. She had white linen pumps and a white linen square purse with a black onyx clasp. Her earrings were white shell drops with an onyx band dividing each drop. She wore a white wide-clasp bracelet with alternating white and black bone squares. We were coordinated, but it didn't look deliberate, just striking.

I was a pale imitation to her gleaming black beauty.

"I don't know if this is wise," I told her. "People will be bumping into me and won't even see me for staring at you!"

"Nonsense!" she declared. "You look sensational!"

I asked her what she weighed. We were within five pounds of each other, but her pounds were distributed much better than mine.

Just inside the door of Chester's, we stopped momentarily to decide if we wanted a drink before lunch. All conversation ceased. Every eye of the male patrons turned our way. So did the eyes of three female attorneys and two female accountants who were having lunch together. A waiter appeared, staring at Jasmine. I told him we would have a drink before we ordered. He didn't even glance in my direction.

I ordered imported beer and Jasmine had white wine. Even before our drinks arrived, male near and dear friends whom I hadn't seen or heard from in months started coming out of the woodwork.

"Hey, Jo Beth," they would yell, patting me on the back and staring at Jasmine, "introduce me to this lovely creature." They would then tell Jasmine what good friends of mine they were. I couldn't remember one's name and had to ask him before I could introduce him. That didn't slow him. He was the one who finally got around to asking for her phone number.

She smiled at him. "Write down your home phone number," she told him. "I'll call you at home later." He suddenly became vague, restless, and darned if he hadn't forgotten to make a phone call and would you pretty ladies please excuse me.

"You have a delicate touch, Jasmine," I told her.

"Thank you," she dimpled at me with her eyes sparkling. She was enjoying herself.

When I saw a waiter approaching, I eased off my stool and, with my back to Jasmine, slipped him a folded ten.

"Put us behind a potted plant or something. This is a business meeting. Try to hold back the stampede," I whispered.

"You got it," he murmured while palming the ten.

"Jasmine, our table is ready," I called.

She got up and joined us. The waiter led the way to a high-backed booth set in an alcove along with three others. We still had a decent view of the restaurant patrons; we just weren't so obvious.

"You're hiding me," she chided.

"I want to talk business. I told the waiter to guard the corral."

She laughed. "Jo Beth, you have no idea how much I needed this. I felt like I couldn't bear to face another barbecued spare rib. I warn you, I'm gonna order something light, frothy and expensive."

I gave her a nod. "The food is so delicious and they serve such generous portions, both our dresses are in danger of split seams before we finish."

"I can't take a deep breath now, for fear of popping a button."

"Since we last met, how are things going for you?" I gave her the opening to bring up what had happened to her Saturday night.

"First, let's savor the wonderful announcement in this morning's paper. Isn't it awesome? Our mutually detested county sheriff — resigning — for reasons of 'ill health!' I truly wish it was his black heart and it was running down like an old-fashioned time bomb with a short fuse. As a hard-shell Baptist, I'm appalled at my un-Christianlike thoughts and the woman in me is bursting for joy. Do you think this puts my chances of attaining the Rapture in jeopardy?" She had an unholy gleam in her eye.

I lifted my beer bottle. "I propose a toast. To ex-Sheriff Carlson's timely demise, and may the good Lord forgive us both!"

We giggled like teenagers.

"Jo Beth, something weird is going on. Wait till I tell you what happened to me Saturday night. I got my wits scared out of me. There I was, sweating away over my grill, about six-thirty. It's my busiest period. They were lined up for take-outs and Shirley was screwing up the orders in her haste to clear the line. My eyes were watering from the smoke and heat, when in walked two Georgia Troopers, in uniform, asking for me! Half of my patrons, the younger half who wear running shoes," she said with a knowing smile, "were immediately poised to put their shoes and sprinting ability to the test. I thought I was being arrested when they walked over to me. Before I could even panic, they had hustled me into my apartment and explained they were sent to protect me!"

"From what?" I asked.

"The exact question I yelled at them. I was really scared. They were pleasant and stated they had been informed of a terrorist threat against me and were on duty to protect me. They sent me back to the grill and one of the men pulled up one of the dining chairs and sat peeking through a small crack they made by leaving my apartment door slightly ajar. I was back working the grill, but now Shirley wasn't the only one who screwed up the orders. I couldn't concentrate. God knows what some of my customers went home with, instead of what they had ordered. I closed at ten. The GSPs sat in my apartment until ten till eleven. They received a phone call, told me everything was peachy-keen, thanked me for my patience and departed, without any further explanation. Needless to say, I didn't rest very well that night."

"Let's order," I said, when I saw the waiter approaching our table. I ordered the trout almondine. She ordered the broiled trout with lemon sauce. After the waiter brought Jasmine another white wine and a beer for me, I started my pitch.

"I have a theory," I offered. I lit a cigarette.

"Good, I need one," she said.

"While I didn't know what was happening to you Saturday evening," — partially true — "I received some additional information yesterday from a quote, reliable source, unquote, confirming Fred's conjectures this morning in the local paper. Sometime this morning, Hank is going to be named interim sheriff until the county holds a special election. My 'source' is sure the county doesn't want the extra expense of a special election with the primaries just three months down the road. I agree with his reasoning. I think Hank will have three months as acting sheriff before we can vote."

That's the best news we could hear," Jasmine exclaimed. "I'm so happy for Hank. He will make the best sheriff this county has ever seen. He's a professional; he's fair and he's kind to us 'fallen women.' What more could you ask for?"

"You don't have to sell me, Jasmine. He has my vote."

She gave an embarrassed shrug. "He's my hero."

"I won't go that far," I said with a smile, "but he'll make a fine sheriff. Here comes the food."

After the waiter had delivered the food and deftly placed the side dishes, between bites we continued the conversation.

"More of my theory. Another hot piece of news that hasn't as yet made the papers — four of the worst-offending deputies were fired by our outgoing chief just minutes before he 'resigned' because of his health. Are you picking up some suspicious vibes?"

Our eyes met and she suddenly smiled.

"It's a cover-up. The powers-that-be have stumbled onto something. Do you think its drugs? Pay-offs?" She took a bite and slowly chewed. I watched her.

"Could it possibly be the conditions that exist in the women's section of the jail?" she wondered.

"Give the little lady a Kewpie doll; she just hit the bull's-eye. I couldn't tell you — my lips are sealed."

"Really? Thank God. It's about time. I'm so glad."

"Mum's the word. Our elective officials are scandal-shy."

"I can live with no retribution for their crimes as long as the abuses are stopped."

"Good for you," I said warmly. "Let's change the subject. You like animals, dogs, bloodhounds?" I asked.

"Never been around them. I've never had a pet."

"Are you afraid of big dogs?"

"Not unless they bite," she replied.

I took the plunge. "How would you like to work with me in search and rescue: tramp the woods, get hot and sweaty, train dogs, give them baths, things like that?"

She stared at me. "Are you offering me a job?"

"Yep, sure am. How about it?"

"Oh, Jo Beth, that's so nice of you, but I couldn't possibly," she said with a brave smile.

"Why not?"

"You know why not," she said, looking me in the eye. "Hank is a friend, but the rest of the deputies would make my life miserable. You know that. They would have me in jail within the week. After six years, I'm a different person. This Jasmine could not stand the treatment or a jail cell."

"You're forgetting that Hank's in charge now. Do you honestly think he would let you be arrested for something you didn't do?"

"No . . . but the city patrolmen are just as bad."

"Jasmine, you can do what you want to do. You don't have to sit home and hide and fear arrest if you go to the mall. You can go back to school at night, maybe take some college courses after you get your GED, and that should be a snap for you."

"You're talking about my daydreams. Do you really think I can start going out at night, live like other free souls?"

"Absolutely. Think on it. I don't need a decision tonight. Tomorrow maybe, but not tonight."

It was four-thirty before I arrived home. It had taken me until two-thirty to convince Jasmine to go to Porky's tonight with Susan and me. We would have to work to make the evening a success.

My ankles and arches were aching from the spikes I had tottered around on and I longed for my Pro-Wings.

As I turned into the courtyard from the drive, I saw a white limo that resembled a battleship parked under one of the pecan trees in the shade. Christ, those babies were long. I hoped they wanted a matched pair of puppies instead of just one. If their transportation was any measure of their affluence, these people would be able to indulge themselves. Maybe I should tell them the puppies were cheaper by the dozen.

Wayne rushed out to meet me as I parked the van.

"Boy am I glad to see you," he signed, looking harried. "I put the father in the office. He's a bit ticked off. The daughter wanted to tour the kennel. My mom is with her. The chauffeur refuses to leave the limo. I've been running back and forth playing host. They have been waiting over two hours. The father is mad and the daughter is on crutches. I don't know the story, but it needs your touch."

"Thanks, Wayne. Why don't you take a folding lawn chair out to the kennel and see if the girl needs to rest. If she's been on crutches for two hours, she may be tired. I think I'll see the father first."

When I entered the office, a distinguished gentleman who looked to be about fifty laid aside some papers he was perusing and rose to his feet from the couch. He was dressed conservatively in a business suit, about my height without heels, and looked tan and fit. He also looked affluent, competent and pissed for having to cool his heels on my couch for the last two hours.

"Miss Sidden?"

"I'm Jo Beth Sidden," I replied. "How may I help you?"

He offered his hand. "I'm Philip Riddel from Jacksonville, Florida." We shook hands and I went to my desk and sat down. If this was to be a discussion, I was gonna conduct it on my butt. My feet were killing me. I was sorely tempted to ease my pumps off behind the cover of the desk, but was afraid I couldn't get them on again when I had to stand, so I suffered. I saw Rudy stroll in from the kitchen and join me, without showing any nervousness, and curl up at my feet.

Riddel moved over to a side chair facing the desk, leaving his papers on the couch beside his briefcase.

"I need your help, Miss Sidden. My daughter has multiple sclerosis. She was diagnosed last year. It is a crippling progressive disease. She needs extensive therapy and to focus all her energies on keeping well. She has this ridiculous desire to emulate you and raise pedigreed bloodhounds. She has a clipping service that sends her everything printed in the newspapers about you and about bloodhounds. It's all I've heard for the past year from her. I want you to help me convince her that she is not physically able to do this and it is not a goal within her reach."

"How old is your daughter?"

"She turned eighteen last week."

"Is she financially dependent on you for bed, board and medical treatment?"

He gave me a strange look. "She came into her inheritance from her deceased mother's estate when she turned eighteen. She has a substantial fortune in her own right."

"Is she retarded, slow or mentally incompetent?"

"Of course not," he answered, showing indignation. "She's very bright. She graduated from high school in January, early, with honors."

"Let's review your options," I told him. "She's eighteen and legally an adult in Florida, where she resides. You can't withhold funds to make her toe the line — she has her own. You can't declare her incompetent — by your own admission she's bright. Mr. Riddel, I can clearly see your problem. Your chick is ready to leave the nest, fly off on her own, and there's not a damn thing you can do about it. If she wants to do this, I would suggest you encourage her and give her your loving support, which she will need very badly when the disease progresses. If not, you stand to lose a chance to be part of her life. I speak from experience in this matter. My father and I were estranged the last ten years of his life. We both bitterly regretted it — when it was too late."

He opened his mouth to answer, then closed it. He seemed to deflate and slumped back in his chair. When he spoke he sounded weary and despondent.

"I've read about your father and also read most of your press clippings, when Mary Catherine wasn't there to see me. I really don't know why I expected help from you."

"You're getting my help, Mr. Riddel, the best advice I can offer. It's just not what you wanted to hear."

"I could be very generous if you could convince her she isn't able to handle, train or supervise the animals."

"Get stuffed," I said calmly. "You don't know me, so I'll let that pass. I'm sure it must work for you most of the time, but not here, and not with me."

"I'm sorry. I'm desperate. I don't think she should be attempting to do this."

"Relax, Mr. Riddel. I'll go talk to her, see what she has in mind. Do you like landscapes?"

He brightened. "You have one of your father's paintings?"

I indicated the south wall of the office. When he turned his head, I reached over and pushed the button and stood. He watched the panels rise and reveal the landscapes.

"Why do you keep them hidden?" He asked as he rose from the chair.

"It's a long story. Enjoy. I'll go talk to your daughter."

He walked toward the paintings and I went outside to the kennel. Wayne was in the grooming room working on some leather leads and signed that the girl said she didn't need the chair and that his mom was talking to her out by the nursery. I picked up two folding lawn chairs from the equipment closet and tottered out to the nursery.

The girl was holding on to the chain-link mesh in front of a pen of puppies, her crutches propped between her and the fence. She was short, maybe five feet and a couple of inches, and looked like she might weigh a hundred pounds, dripping wet. She had long blonde hair and looked fragile. She had color in her face, but it was cosmetic, not good health. Her arms and legs were bone white. She wasn't beautiful but had an aura about her in her expression and stance that made you want to cuddle and comfort her. No wonder her father was so protective. One glance and I was ready to defend her from all harm myself. Rosie was patiently standing near her by the fence. I motioned her over to me.

"Thanks, Rosie," I told her. "I'll take over now. Would you go ask Mr. Riddel if he would like some coffee or something? Also check with the chauffeur. It's a hot day. Sorry I was so long getting back."

"The poor thing is exhausted, but she didn't want to sit down," she whispered.

I walked over to the girl, opened both chairs and slid one over to her.

"Sit," I commanded. "Do you need help getting in the chair?"

"No," she said, then hesitated when she saw my expression. "Maybe, if you would steady the chair from behind, to keep it from sliding," she said reluctantly.

"Good," I said with a smile. "Lesson number one. Never refuse help if you need it just to impress someone or for your silly pride."

I stood in front of her. "Before I lecture you further, I have to get these shoes off, there're murdering my feet." I inched up my tight skirt, unhooked my stockings from the garter belt, sat in the chair, kicked off my pumps and rolled the stockings off carefully and tucked them in the shoes. I gave a loud sigh as my bare feet rested on the warm cement. I saw her startled gaze.

"All the time I was talking with your father, my arches were aching and my toes were numb, but I suffered because I wanted him to like me and I wanted to look nice. Aren't women silly?" She smiled. "I'm Jo Beth. I'm glad to meet you, Mary Catherine."

"My father calls me Mary Catherine," she said with a small frown. "My friends call me Mare."

"I can understand why he calls you Mary Catherine. It rolls off the tongue and sounds dignified and stately. It is poetic. Some names cut it and some don't. Mare doesn't cut it. I think I will call you Mary Catherine."

She thought about it. "Okay, and you're Jo Beth?"

"Always. Your father tells me you're planning on opening a kennel — breeding and showing pedigreed bloodhounds."

"He doesn't want me to even try," she said. "He thinks I'm a child."

"Well, I can understand why he thinks you are because legally you were, until last week. It takes overprotective fathers longer to keep up with their offspring's aging process."

"Do you think I can handle it?" She had hope in her eyes.

"I don't know you, Mary Catherine. I don't know how much you want it, or if you'll cut and run when the going gets tough. If you want it bad enough, you can run a kennel from a wheelchair. Keep that in mind, if you build your kennel. Make sure a wheelchair would have access to every area of your operation. Don't close your eyes to your physical condition and pretend it won't get worse. It will; you just have to plan to meet every change in your life and figure out how to meet the challenge. Stay ahead of the game; plan ahead."

"I'm going to try, whether my father approves or not," she said with determination.

"If you really want it, go for it," I told her. "Be smart. Learn not to waste your strength standing unnecessarily for two hours when you could have been resting. Do only as much as your physical therapists tell you to do. Take expert advice. That's all I have to tell you. To learn about the dogs, read, study and again, take expert advice. I'm just starting really. I've read and studied and know I don't know it all and probably never will. Just do your best."

"I want my first dog to come from your kennel. I have read everything in print about you for over a year. Do you have one you will sell me that I can learn to show in dog shows and start my breeding kennel?"

"I thought you'd never ask," I told her lightly. "Mary Catherine, I have the perfect dog for you!"

It was after six-thirty before Mary Catherine and her father departed. I hugged her and told her to keep in touch. Riddel got a handshake and a wink. He asked me on my return to the office if one of the landscapes was possibly for sale. My laughter answered his question and he had the grace to redden slightly and shrug. He had watched Mary Catherine write out her check for her new breeder without snatching the pen out of her hand, but it looked like a close call. He was unhappy, but I think he realized he had lost control of his pride and joy and loved her too deeply to take the chance of completely destroying their relationship. I hoped so, anyway.

I dressed for the night out with comfort in mind: white off-the-shoulder blouse, full twirly skirt of blue, green and yellow swirled print and low-heeled dancing shoes. I placed my .32 in my white straw purse and put a colorful silk scarf over it before adding my other essentials. When Susan picked me up, I filled her in on Jasmine's past and my future plans to hire her, but didn't mention anything about Sheriff Carlson and my ordeal.

Susan was wearing a pale blue dress with matching belt and full skirt. Jasmine had judged the night out and our destination correctly. She was in a pink shirtwaist dress with pink sandals and matching purse. She looked fabulous. We received more than our share of cheers, whistles and catcalls when we entered Porky's. We ordered cheeseburgers with the works, French fries and beer. Susan and I instructed Jasmine to eat, then dance. We explained if she didn't, it would take her all night to consume her supper. After the three of us waved everyone away every time they approached, they finally let us finish our meal in comparative peace. They only stopped by every thirty seconds to check our plates and to inquire if we planned to have dessert.

Jasmine was trying to relax and have a good time. Susan and I took turns jumping in with a joke every time we saw her falter. I sat out about half of the dances. My feet were sore and tired from wearing the ridiculous spikes for seven hours straight. I listened to the music, joked with the rednecks and ran to pee every ten minutes.

We all received our share of indecent proposals — from a quickie in a truck in the parking lot to one that included marriage and a forty-acre farm between Balsa City and Mercer where our dancing partner grew the best damn vegetables in the state. Jasmine and I both received invitations to share his bed, name and farm work. Susan was hurt.

"All he mentioned to me was the bed in the cab-over camper he uses on hunting and fishing trips he just happened to be driving tonight."

"You're just too old for him," I told her.

She glared at me. "And you're not? I seem to remember, there are only eighty-seven days between our births!"

"It's the state of mind, my dear, not what's on the calendar," I told her in a fair imitation of Mae West.

Porky's always had at least three heavy bouncers patrolling the barnlike structure, so the men behaved themselves. Porky's policy was no touchies, no feelies and no tongue sucking on the dance floor or in the building. It was safe for three well-behaved dames like us, but the parking lot was another story. The bouncer's territory didn't include the parking lot. On weeknights, Porky's closed at midnight. The Dunston County Sheriff's Department usually had a couple of patrol cars on the lot at closing time — whenever possible. It saved them from being called to the site for breaking up fights, separating angry husbands and wives who waited to argue outside, and the occasional assault on a lone woman. I hoped our new sheriff had placed a high priority on lecturing his men on the perils of mistreating women. If not, we might have a sticky situation if a deputy on duty out here recognized Jasmine. I started to worry.

As the bar emptied at midnight, the three of us headed for Susan's car. Susan had the keys in her hand before we left the building. She had parked under a light pole. It was our familiar stomping ground, but we weren't stupid and careless. I heard Jasmine's quick catch of breath as we spotted the same thing — a patrol car between us and Susan's car. As we approached, I watched Jasmine out of the corner of my eye. She took a deep breath and straightened her shoulders, wiping all expression from her face.

"Good evening, ladies," one deputy sang in a high male tenor voice as we drew abreast of their car.

I stopped the others with an outstretched arm and turned toward him.

"I beg your pardon?" My voice rang out loud and clear. "Did you say something about ladies of the evening?"

"Ah, no," he said with haste. "God, no," he said when he realized what I meant. "All I said was good evening, ladies — honest. No offense meant." The other deputy remained silent. When I felt he had sweated long enough, I let him off the hook.

"I must have been mistaken," I said in a softer voice.

"You have a nice night, officer," Jasmine sang in a clear evenly spaced soprano.

"Thank you, ma'am," he uttered in a polite dead voice.

We continued to the car silently and once inside, we collapsed with laughter. Susan gasped and nudged me.

"Jesus, Sidden, he almost wet his pants!"

"You can't let them get away with anything. Give them an inch and they'll take a mile." I turned to Jasmine. "Are you okay?"

"God," she breathed. "I hate to admit it, but I thoroughly enjoyed watching that jerk squirm! If it wasn't for all those pictures I know they carry around in their wallets, I could look them square in the eye and not blink."

I didn't think Hank would mind if I broke my promise to keep his secret of the pictures, if it gave Jasmine the courage she needed.

"Well, you start looking and quit blinking," I told her. "Hank took care of the pictures over the past several years. He bought them back, one by one."

"Dear God. You people," she said almost in tears. "How can I ever pay you back?"

"You can help us harmonize on our school song," I told her. We had discovered earlier that Jasmine had entered the first grade at Elliston Elementary when Susan and I were being propelled through the sixth. We sang imperfect and ragged harmony all the way home.

EPILOGUE

Today is the last day in April and I view its passing with mixed emotions. Most mornings I spend a few minutes with my family portraits. The carpenter brothers did a beautiful job on the panels. They rise and close silently, controlled by a hidden switch across the room. Susan gets a lot more business from me. I'm filling the bookshelves — slowly — with all my favorite books from her stock. I plan on reading them after I retire so I can peruse them in leisure.

Wade and Sheri are together now. I still haven't found a way to let Wade know about his buried fortune. When I'm sure it's permanent with them, I may tell her. She's smart enough to feed the money into their budget without rocking the boat — I think. I'll have to wait and see. After the events of this month, I'm trying to be less hasty with my decisions and slower to interfere in my friends' lives. I know now that I'm hotheaded and impulsive and I'm gonna work hard to change my ways. My gut just clenched. I refuse to consider this as an omen of my chance of success; I'd rather believe I ate too much for lunch.

Jasmine leased her business and is now working for me. She started last Monday. She is living with me, temporarily, while her cottage is being built. It is to the right of the driveway and courtyard entrance.

My father's estate is finally settled. There was much more money than I expected. We found two hundred shares of some plastics stock in the safety deposit box when the IRS, Wade and I were allowed to open it. The sale will net about seventy thousand, after taxes. It will help with the construction and new vehicles. With Jasmine on board, we needed more wheels so I bought another used van. It's being customized like the other two. I bought a new truck for Wayne. It just didn't look right to see the manager of such a successful establishment as Bloodhounds, Inc., tooling around town in a beat-up pile of junk.

Bubba was arraigned last week on charges for the damage he inflicted on my house and possessions, violation of parole, violation of the restraining order and resisting arrest. He waived his right to a trial by jury and was immediately sentenced by Judge McAlbee to serve out his time remaining from the parole violation and two additional years for the rest of the charges.

Hank supplied me with the details. He said all the players who were involved with this travesty of justice were beaming and shaking hands upon hearing the verdict. Hank, with wry humor, said he was surprised that Buford Senior hadn't had the event catered and hired a band. The way the system is releasing felons, I wouldn't be surprised if Bubba is home for Christmas. He still has revenge in mind, my destruction or whatever. He called the night before they sent him back. His only words to me were, "Soon, bitch," but I got the message.

Wade is energetically fighting to break the last will and testament of Benson T. Hanaiker, my biological father, with the help of co-counsel David Sherwood, of Fontain, New York. He is the lawyer I hired a couple of weeks ago to meet with my cuz, Smiling Jack, to secure my legal ownership of O'Henry and Sally. I suffered dutifully through a forty-five minute conference call yesterday as both of them happily outlined their strategy to secure my fortune in the legalese their respective law schools had taught them. After a few minutes, I tuned them out and was mentally sailing the Mediterranean on my sixty-foot yacht, sipping Dom Perignon and admiring the bronzed muscles and tight buns of my all-hunk, all-Italian crew, attired in almost nonexistent white net briefs. Some cautionary words from both David and Wade brought me back to Balsa City and my desk. They've only had ten days and at first blush, it seems I might not become a millionairess after all. David explained that Hanaiker had plunged heavily into futures in recent years, trying to recoup his mega-losses in the stock market several years ago, and the more he plunged, the more he lost. I assured both of them that my expectations were modest. If I received enough to erase my mortgage and a small nest egg for the future, I would be content. It would probably be for the best. I get enough sun and water slogging through the Okefenokee on my searches; there are some good-looking local buns, and I know my dogs would miss me.

Albert Fender, the not-so-gentle giant, was indicted by the grand jury for the second-degree murder of his father-in-law, Ancel Tew. I heard his wife was in the process of divorcing him.

Jackie informed me three days ago, by phone, not to visit Leroy and the girls at her home anymore. I won't appeal her decision to Leroy. I know wives have a much, much higher priority than lifelong friends. I'll miss them.

George called last Saturday morning. We had a pleasant conversation for ten minutes or so. He was charming and I was charming, but nothing was said about the note he left or the contents. There were a few awkward pauses, then one of us would quickly jump in with a remark on the weather, or the current book we were reading. He mentioned the next time he came to Balsa City, maybe we could have a couple of beers. I laughed and said, maybe three or four. He said goodbye, and so did I. I felt a brief pang of regret, but as I said, it was brief, and I knew he wouldn't be stopping by. We had just said our goodbyes.

Hank informed me last week that my cousin, Jackson Hanaiker (Smiling Jack) had been arrested in New York and was fighting extradition to Georgia. Charlene had secured a true bill from the grand jury with Bubba's sworn testimony and identification of the funeral photos, which I had given to Hank. Everyone is pleased with the arrest with the exception of the arrestee. I read somewhere that over seventy percent of all homicides are committed by close relatives, live-in lovers, and exes. I guess I have enough to worry about with Bubba — I don't need a lethal relative in the picture.

I finally sorted out all the details of my father's will and the relationship between him and Benson T. Hanaiker. When you had all the pieces to the puzzle, you wondered why you couldn't see it sooner. Hanaiker, my biological father, had imposed certain restrictions on the man who raised me and who was the only man I would ever refer to as my father. My father couldn't paint me; therefore, he couldn't paint his wife. She would never have understood. If he died before Hanaiker, he couldn't let me inherit his estate until Hanaiker's death. Carl, Wade's father, was the executor of his estate. He died before Hanaiker did, and Carl's executor was his ex-partner, Andrew J. Carpenter. Carpenter was out of town for a month when Carl died. When Carl returned, he planned on going to the bank and getting Wade's and my letters, but he couldn't release my father's codicil to his will, because Hanaiker was still alive. When Hanaiker died, his law firm, who was represented by Jason Finch, the New York lawyer, called Carl to report Hanaiker's death. That was the phone call that Carl had received, enabling him to release my father's will so I could inherit. It wouldn't have been so confusing if Carpenter had been in town when Carl died. I was just glad to get the full story.

Kealon's mother and father donated five thousand dollars to the local SPCA. Their accountant must have told them it was a sound financial ploy, or maybe you can make a yuppie bleed by hinting they can't afford a grand gesture. For whatever the reason, the animals of Dunston County will benefit.

"Sidden's Southern Lady of Sagaces Endeavors," or Susie to her friends, is being carefully schooled and groomed for a dog show in Long Island, New York, next month. Mary Catherine promises to let me know the minute the judging is over. Wayne, Rosie and Susan, the three who knew how much Susie meant to me, could not understand why I sold her to Mary Catherine. Part of my decision was penitence for Bo. The other part was: Mary Catherine's future probably doesn't extend as far as mine. She needs success in a short period of time, so she needed the best to begin with, and Susie is the very best of the breed. My heart tells me I can breed another Susie, that I can get lucky twice in a lifetime, but my mind will only say, maybe.

The phone is ringing and it's Hank.

"Do you have plans for tonight, Jo Beth? I was thinking maybe we could have dinner," he says, hopefully.

I laugh. "Tonight is Friday night, Hank. It's the only night of the week I do have plans."

"Oh . . . well, some other time, maybe."

I suddenly decided that Susan and Jasmine could catch a movie and split a pizza without me.

"Do you have any movie tapes? *Casablanca*? I don't mean the jazzed-up version that's tinted," I asked.

"I have *Casablanca* in black and white."

"Good. Grab a pizza. I want pepperoni on my half. I have plenty of beer. About eight?"

"I'll be there at eight," he promised before he hung up.

I did mention the good-looking local buns, didn't I?